THE

Rats and the Ruling Sea

—◦◦◦—

Robert V. S. Redick

GOLLANCZ

LONDON

Copyright © Robert V. S. Redick 2009

The right of Robert V. S. Redick to be identified as the author
of this work has been asserted by him in accordance with the
Copyright, Designs and Patents Act 1988.

First published in Great Britain in 2009 by Gollancz
An imprint of the Orion Publishing Group
Orion House, 5 Upper St Martin's Lane,
London WC2H 9EA
An Hachette UK Company

1 3 5 7 9 10 8 6 4 2

A CIP catalogue record for this book
is available from the British Library

ISBN 978 0 575 08179 6 (Cased)
ISBN 978 0 575 08180 2 (Trade Paperback)

Typeset by Input Data Services Ltd, Bridgwater, Somerset

Printed and bound in the UK by
CPI Mackays, Chatham ME5 8TD

The Orion Publishing Group's policy is to use papers that
are natural, renewable and recyclable products and made
from wood grown in sustainable forests. The logging and
manufacturing processes are expected to conform to the
environmental regulations of the country of origin.

www.redwolfconspiracy.com

www.orionbooks.co.uk

Para Kiran, de corazon nómada

Editor's Note

The final, disastrous voyage of the IMS *Chathrand* gave rise to many myths. It is my singular honour to be tasked with setting a more truthful account of the journey before the world.

In Book I of these recollections, *The Red Wolf Conspiracy*, I limited my personal comments to the odd footnote. The complexity of this second volume, however, persuaded me to be more generous with my remarks: two hundred pages more generous, to be exact.

I regret to say that the worth of my commentaries has eluded the team of younger scholars on whose goodwill (and laundry services) I most tragically depend. Their cheek is frankly astonishing. Some have gone so far as to suggest that my remarks did not so much illuminate the tale as put one in danger of overlooking its existence.

Of course I fought this sabotage, this so-called 'petition for readability.' But the upstarts held firm. Only a few, *absolutely essential* notes have I guarded from their merciless sheers. The rest has been stripped down to story. An awful deed, of which I hope never to stand accused.

And then the deer and birds were told by the Maker, Modeller, Bearer, Begetter: 'Talk, speak out, don't moan, don't cry out. Please talk, each to each, within each kind, within each group,' – they were told, the deer, birds, puma, jaguar, serpent . . . But it didn't turn out that they spoke like people: they just squawked, they just chattered, they just howled . . .
Popol Vuh, Translated by Dennis Tedlock

The voice of passion is better than the voice of reason.
The passionless cannot change history.

Czesław Miłosz

Prologue: Treaty Day

—⟋⟍⟍—

A cup of milk tainted with blood. Pazel looked down into the steaming chalice and felt trapped, an actor in a part he never wanted, in a play full of violence and rage. They were waiting for him to drink: the priests, the princes, the three hundred guests in the candlelit shrine. His best friends were waiting, and a few men who wished him dead, and one man who wanted everyone dead and just might get his wish. The guests were staring. A red-robed priest gestured firmly: *Drink*. Thasha herself glanced back from where she knelt on the dais, beside the man who thought he would be married in a moment's time.

Thasha was radiant. Sixteen, golden hair bound up impossibly with orchids and lace, grey gown sheer and liquid as mercury, silver necklace dangling innocent at her throat. The lips he had kissed the night before were painted a dark cherry-red. Powder hid the welts on her neck.

He could still stop this. He could break the chalice on the floor. He knew the words for *Lies!* and *Treason!* in twenty languages; he could tell them all how they'd been tricked. But he could not just wish the necklace away. Thasha was still looking over her shoulder, and even though half the blood in the milk was hers, Pazel knew what she was telling him. *It has to happen, you know it does. Every other door is locked.*

He raised the chalice. The hot milk burned his tongue. He clenched his jaw and swallowed and passed the cup on.

The priests resumed chanting: 'We drink to the Great Peace. We drink and become one family. We drink and our fates are mingled, never more to be unbound ...'

Pazel slipped a hand into his pocket. A ribbon lay coiled there, blue silk, with words embroidered in a fine gold thread: YE DEPART FOR A WORLD UNKNOWN, AND LOVE ALONE SHALL KEEP THEE. It was the Blessing-Band, a gift from the crones who ran Thasha's old school back in Etherhorde. He was supposed to tie it to her wrist.

Pazel imagined an old woman – bent, wrinkled, nearly blind – sewing those ornate letters by lamplight. One of thousands who had worked for this day, Treaty Day, the day four centuries of war would end. Outside the shrine, a multitude; beyond the multitude, an island; beyond the island, a world waiting, holding its breath. He looked at the faces around him: great lords and ladies of Alifros, rulers of lands, cities, kingdoms, waifs by candlelight. How had Hercól put it? *Possessed by a dream.* The dream of peace, of a world that could stop shedding its own blood. It was a good dream, but it would kill them. They were chasing it like sleepwalkers towards a cliff.

There was a man at the back of the shrine who was making it all happen. A well-fed merchant with a soft, boyish face. An innocent face, almost amusing. Until he looked at you with a certain intent, and showed you the sorcerer inside: ancient, malicious, mad.

His name was Arunis. Pazel could feel him watching, even now. But when he raised his eyes he found himself looking instead at Thasha's father. The admiral sat stiff and grim, an old soldier who knew what duty meant, but the eyes that swept Pazel were beseeching. *I have trusted you this far. How will you save my child?*

Pazel could not meet his gaze. *You'd never understand, Admiral. And if you did, you'd try to stop us, and no one would be saved.* Kings, peasants, enemies, friends: Arunis was marching them all towards that cliff. And over they'd go, with their dreams and their children, their smiles and songs and memories, their histories, their gods. In short order, a year or two at the most, unless he let Thasha die.

So Pazel stood, motionless, silently screaming, and the cup went from hand to hand. At last it returned to the red-robed priest, standing before Thasha and her groom. The priest cleared his throat and smiled.

'Now, beloved Prince,' he said, 'what would you avow?'

The prince was gentle as he took Thasha's hand. But before he could speak she pulled it roughly away. There were gasps. The prince looked up in shock.

'Your Highness, forgive me,' she stammered. 'I cannot wed you. This marriage is a *tr—*'

The last word had no chance. Under her gown, the silver necklace moved like a snake, and Thasha rose with a little twist of breath, clawing at it, unable even to scream. Her eyes wild, her face the colour of a bruise. Pazel howled her name and leaped to catch her as she fell. Voices exploded around him, her father's and the priests' and three hundred more. *Sorcery get it off her cut it off the girl's going to die.* Hercól was beside

2

him, Arunis was battling forwards; the elder priest was waving a knife and shouting *Betrayed, betrayed, if she dies the peace dies with her.*

Thasha kicked and flailed and arched her back in agony. But death was the answer, Pazel knew; death was the one door left unlocked, and so he held her, in the tightest grip of his life, as the thousands massed outside the shrine caught the rumour and sent a wail up to heaven, held her and absorbed her blows, and told her several things he'd never dared to, and waited for her struggles to cease.

1

Dawn

—∿∿—

7 Teala 941
86th day from Etherhorde
(Treaty Day – six hours earlier)

'Eyes open, Neda.'

The Father had come to her alone. He held his own cup and candle, and he smiled at the girl asleep on the granite slab under the woollen shift, who obeyed him and smiled in kind and yet did not wake or stir. Her eyes when they winked open were blue; he had seen nothing like them in any other living face. A strand of weed in her hair. Dry streaks of saltwater on her neck and forehead. Like his other children she had spent the night in the sea.

She was twenty-two, the man six times her age, unbent, unwearied, his years betrayed only in the whiteness of his beard and in the voice deep and travelled and kindly and mad. The girl knew that he was mad, and knew also that the day she revealed such knowledge by glance or sigh or question would be the day she died.

She knew many secret things. Until the Father woke her she would sleep like the other aspirants, but there was a disobedient flame in her that gleamed on, thought on, insensible to his orders. She wished it out. She tried to snuff it with meditation, inner exorcisms, prayers: it danced on, full of heresies and mirth. And because the Father could peer into her mind as through a frosted window it was but a matter of time before he saw it. Perhaps he saw it now, this very minute. Perhaps he was considering her fate.

She loved him. She had never loved another thus. It was not an earthly or a simple love but he could read its contours in her sleeper's smile as he had on his children's faces for a century.

'You dream, do you not?'

5

'I do,' she replied.

'And yet the dream is unsteady. You are nearer to waking than I've asked you to be.'

It was not a question. The girl lay watching him, asleep and not asleep. The Old Faith she had taken for her own states that life is not a struggle against death, but rather towards that authentic death inscribed at the instant of one's birth. If he had come to kill her it meant fulfilment, the end of her work.

'You must not wake, best beloved. Turn your face to the dream. And when it surrounds you again, describe it.'

The girl's eyes rolled, the lids half-lowered, and watching her the Father trembled as he always did at the immensity of creation. She would see nothing more of the shrine about her – not the dawn light on the huddled sleepers nor the west arch open to the sea nor the quartz knife on his belt nor the pure white milk in his cup – but what endured were the territories within. Outside, fishermen were picking a trail through the sawgrass down to the shore, greeting one another in the happy lilt of Simja, this island unclaimed by any empire. Under the sheer wool the girl's limbs began to twitch. She was not quiet in the place of the dream.

'I am in the hills,' she said.

'Your hills. Your Chereste Highlands.'

'Yes, Father. I am very near my house – my old house, before I became your daughter and was yet simple Neda of Ormael. My city is burning. It is on fire and the smoke trails out to sea.'

'Are you alone?'

'Not yet. In a moment Suthinia my birth-mother will kiss me and run. Then the gate will shatter and the men will arrive.'

'Men of Arqual.'

'Yes, Father. Soldiers of the Cannibal-King. They are outside the gate at the end of the houserow. My mother is weeping. My mother is running away.'

'Did she speak no last word to you?'

The sleeping girl tensed visibly. One hand curled into a fist. '*Survive*, she said. Not how. Not for whom.'

'Neda, Phoenix-Flame, you are there at the rape of Ormael, but also here, safe beside me, among your brothers and sisters in our holy place. Breathe, that's right. Now tell me what happens next.'

'The gate is torn from its hinges. The men with spears and axes are surrounding my house. They're in the garden, stealing fruit from my orange tree. But the oranges are not orange, they're green, green still. They're not ripe enough to eat!'

'Gently, child.'

'The men are angry. They're breaking the lower limbs.'

'Why don't they see you?'

'I'm underground. There is a trapdoor hidden in the grass, over-looking the house.'

'A trapdoor? Leading where?'

'Into a tunnel. My birth-father dug it with his smuggler friends. I don't know where it leads. Under the orchards, maybe, back into the hills. I thought he might be here, my birth-father, after leaving us long ago. But no one's here. I'm in the tunnel alone.'

'And the men are looting your house.'

'All the houses, Father. But ours they chose first— *Aya!*'

The girl's cry was little more than a whimper, but her face creased in misery.

'Tell me, Neda.'

'My brother is there in the street. He's so young. He is staring at the men in the garden.'

'Why do you not call to him?'

'I do. I call Pazel, Pazel – but he can't hear, and if I raise my voice they'll turn and see him. And now he's running to the garden wall.'

The Father let her continue, sipping thoughtfully at his milk. Neda told how her brother pulled himself up by the thrushberry vine, crept in at his bedroom window, emerged moments later with a skipper's knife and a whale statuette. How he fled into the plum orchards. How a mob of soldiers drew near her hiding place and spoke of her mother and the girl herself in terms that made the Father put the cup down, shaking with rage. *As if they were cannibals in truth. As if souls were nothing and bodies mere cuts of meat. These men who would civilise the world.*

The dawn light grew. He pinched his candle out and beckoned the vestment-boy near to keep her face in shadow, and the lad quaked when her blue eyes fixed on him. But Neda was gone – gone to Ormael, possessed by the dream she was speaking. The soldiers' roar at the discovery of the liquor cabinet. Her girlish clothes tossed with laughter from a window, socks in the orange tree, blouses held up to armoured chests. Bottles shattered, windows smashed; a ruined bleat from the neighbour's concertina. Sunset, and endless dark hours in the cave, and frost on the trapdoor at morning.

Then she cried much louder than before and he could not comfort her, for she was watching the soldiers drag her brother down the hillside, hurl him flat and beat him with their fists and a branch of her tree.

'They hate him. They want to kill him. Father. Father. They are screaming in his face.'

'Screaming what?'

'The same words over and over. I did not speak their language, then. Pazel did but he was silent.'

'And you recall those words, don't you?'

She was shaking all over. She spoke in a voice not quite her own. '"*Madhu ideji? Madhu ideji?*"'

The Father closed his eyes, not trusting himself to speak. Even his own slight Arquali was enough. He could hear it, in all its snarled violence, bellowed at a child in pain: *Where are the women?* And the boy had held his tongue.

When he opened his eyes she was gazing right at him. He tried to be stern. 'Tears, Neda? You know that is not our way. And no fury or grief or shame can best a child of the Old Faith. And no Arquali is your equal. Stop crying. You are *sfvantskor*, best beloved.'

'I wasn't then,' she said.

True enough. No *sfvantskor* or anything like. A girl of seventeen at the time. Captured that very night, when thieves skulking deeper inside the tunnel chased her out at knife-point, into the hands of the Arqualis. Unable to speak to them, to plead. Brutalised, as he would not ask her to recall, before the strange Doctor Chadfallow intervened, freeing her in a shouting match with a general that came almost to blows.

The doctor was a favourite of the Arquali Emperor, who had named him Special Envoy to the city before the invasion. A friend to Neda and her family too, it seemed, for he took the girl bleeding as she was to his Mzithrini counterpart, who was to be expelled with his household that same afternoon.

'Save her, Acheleg,' he pleaded. 'Take her with you as a daughter, open your heart.'

But this Acheleg was a beast. He had failed to predict the invasion, and so was returning to the Mzithrin in some disgrace. He saw no reason to help his rival. Both he and Chadfallow had wished to marry Suthinia, Neda's mother, and although she had refused both and vanished none knew where, Acheleg still fancied himself particularly spurned. Now fate had given him Suthinia's child. Not the great beauty her mother was, and left unclean by the enemy, but still a prize for a slouching ex-diplomat whose future conquests would be scarce. He took her to Babqri – but as a concubine, not a daughter. And only because the man was fool enough to bring her to court, when he came beetling through with his lies and flattery for the king, had the Father spotted her.

Blue eyes. He had heard of such things in the East. And when the girl saw him watching and raised those eyes, the Father knew she would be *sfvantskor*. A foreign *sfvantskor*! It was a sign of catastrophe, of the old world's end. But in a hundred years of choosing he had never needed more than a glance.

Such an odd fate, Neda's. Saved from an Arquali by an Arquali, and from one Mzithrini by another. Twice taken as plunder, the third time as a warrior for the gods.

But still not a *sfvantskor*, in point of fact. None of his children (he moved among them, speaking the dawn prayer, breaking their sleep-trance with his fingertips) could claim the title until he gave them up. It had always been so, and always would be: only when they knelt before one of the Five Kings and swore fealty were they *sfvantskor*s, warrior-priests of the Mzithrin. Until that day they were his aspirants, his children. Afterwards he would not even speak their names.

Not a *sfvantskor*, thought the girl, her dream dissolving and the tears quite gone. Not even a normal aspirant, for she was foreign-born. It made a difference. Even the Father could not pretend otherwise, although he forbid the others to mention it. For two thousand years the elders had moulded youth into *sfvantskor*s to serve the Mzithrin Kings, to lead their armies and terrify their foes. Power dwelt in them, power from the Forts of Forever, from the shards of the Black Casket and the vault of the wind. It was more than an honour: it was a life's destiny and a sacred trust. And only native-born Mzithrini youths were called. That was the order of things, until the Father brought Neda to his Citadel.

Neda Pathkendle. A row of old Masters spoke her name in the Greeting Hall that first day, as if the very syllables displeased them.

Neda Ygraël, said the Father. I have renamed her. Watch her; you will understand in time.

Ygraël, Phoenix-Flame. The grandness of his gesture did not help. The other six aspirants (four boys, two perfect girls) were scandalised. A hazel-skinned refugee from Ormael, one of the vassal-states of the enemy? Had they been singled out for shame? Were they such poor candidates that the timeless customs need not apply?

One did not question the Father – he who had sucked a black demon from a wound in King Ahbsan's neck, and spat the thing into a coal stove, where it howled and clattered for a month – but his choice tested faith. There was open hissing at the feast of Winterbane, when the new aspirants marched through Babqri City. There was the dove's carcass, burned black and left on her pillow, with the words *Never to Rise* in ash upon the floor. There was the day she learned about Belligerent Expulsion: an ancient rule by which the other aspirants, if they declared unanimously that one of their brethren had 'sought to make enemies of them all,' could cast that member out.

Neda had done no such thing; she had been obedient to their whims, tolerant of their spite; and yet five of the six had voted for her removal. When the effort failed, Neda had gone quietly to the one who sided with her, a tall proud girl named Suridín. Neda knelt before her and whispered her thanks, but the girl kicked her over with a bitter laugh.

'It wasn't for *you*,' she said. 'I want to serve the navy, like my birth-father, and they bring witches who can smell a lie to the swearing-in. What am I going to say when they ask if I've ever given false testimony?'

Suridín's birth-father was an admiral in the White Fleet. 'I under-stand, sister,' said Neda.

'You don't understand a thing. I wish you *would* start a fight with one of us. You don't belong here, and I'd vote against you in a heartbeat if I could.'

All this was horrid and prolonged. But five years later it was over, and it had ended just as the Father said it would: with Neda trained and deadly and strong in the Faith, and her six brethren embracing her (some loving, others merely obedient), and the Mzithrini common folk no longer quite sure why they had objected.

Neda, however, suffered no such confusion. They were right, her enemies. They saw what the Father did not: that she would fail, dis-gracing her title, if it were ever bestowed. She had fired an arrow over the River Bhosfal and struck a moving target. She had walked a rope stretched over the Devil's Gorge, and carried her own weight in water up the three hundred steps of the Citadel. But the way of the *sfvantskor* was perfection, and in one matter she was gravely imperfect. She could not forget.

For an aspirant nothing could be worse. Besides martial and religious training, a great part of the making of a warrior-priest occurred in trance. Only with those in trance could the Father share the holy mysteries; only those souls could he cleanse of fear. Neda drifted easily into the first layers of trance – sleeping and waking at his command, obeying without question, focusing her mind on whatever thought he named. But never *only* on what he named. The deepest and most sacred mode of trance was achieved when all other distractions melted away: in other words, when one forgot. *Remove the dust of Now and Before*, went the proverb, *and things eternal are yours.*

This Neda could never do. Year upon year she tried, stretched out on granite, listening to his voice. While the others shed memories like old clothes, she lay still and pretended. *Forget yesterday and today. Forget the breath before this breath.* She remembered. And when the Father told them to forget certain lessons, certain books suddenly gone from the library, certain Masters lecturing one day and the next quite vanished, Neda recalled them too. Every word, every face. And other weaknesses of the Father, shameful for an aspirant to know.

But what damned her beyond redemption were her lies. They were skilful – flawless even – for it was never an effort to recall exactly what she should pretend *not* to know. But how long could she hide this loathing for herself?

Alone at prayer, she beat her head on the floor. In bed she cursed herself, *sfvantskor* battle-curses and sea-oaths in her father's Ormali and sibilant Highland witch-curses from her mother, whose dabbling with spells had almost killed Neda and her brother before the invasion.

And should have. For her brother Pazel had been carried away unconscious, to be buried with the day's thousand dead, or nursed back to health and enslaved. And Neda, spared such a fate by the Father, could not stop her mind from betraying him.

'Rise, my seven.'

Quick as cats, they obeyed. All were dressed, none armed: the Simjans allowed visitors many privileges, but weaponry was not among them. The Father led them in silence through the east arch and along the marble wall, to the foot of a narrow unrailed staircase. At its top stood the Declarion: a high pedestal, topped with four pillars and a jade-green dome, on the inside of which was inscribed the Covenant of Truth in a script of flowing silver. The Father climbed, and they waited to be called.

The sun had not yet risen: its light touched only the peaks of the distant mountains of Simja, leaving the land below in darkness. Around the shrine a flock of goats had settled for the night and lingered yet, barely stirring, and not a window gleamed in the city of Simjalla across the fields. Neda listened to the waves' cotton roaring, felt the pull of them still. *I was all night in the sea. I walked from here to the surf in trance. The creatures swarmed round me, the anglerfish and skates. A witch sang spells over the water. A murth-girl was crying for a boy she loves. I'm not supposed to remember.*

She tried to empty her mind for prayer. But on the last step below the Declarion the Father abruptly turned to face them. His disciples jumped: the morning rites were not casually altered. The Father gazed at them fiercely.

'You know how long they have sought our destruction,' he said. 'You know the price in blood we have paid to survive. Now much is changed. Our Five Kings of the Holy Mzithrin have laboured long for peace with the enemy, and when today in this very shrine our prince weds Thasha Isiq, they say the time of pain and death will be over. But I see something darker, my children. A new war: brief but terrible, as if these several centuries of war were compressed to a single year, with all the ruin but no rebirth. I see the spectre of annihilation. Would you know where it resides? Look behind you, then.'

As one his disciples turned. There lay Simja Harbour, thick with ships: their own white warships and Arquali dreadnoughts, the island's tiny fighting fleet, scores of vessels bearing rulers and mystics of the lesser faiths, all gathered for the wedding that would seal the peace.

Yet dwarfing them all was the Great Ship. The *Chathrand*, ancient of ancients, seemingly immortal in her sea-worthiness, made by forgotten artisans in a lost age of miracles. They said six hundred men were needed just to sail her, and that twice as many could ride with ease, and still leave room for grain enough to see a city through the winter, or arms enough to gird whole legions for war. She belonged to the enemy, though not to the enemy crown. By some mad twist of Arquali thinking her ownership was private: the Emperor had had to *pay* some merchant-baroness for the right to convey the Treaty Bride in such style.

'The *Chathrand*,' said the Father. 'Like the Plague Ships of old, she comes flying the colours of peace, but in her hold the air is rife with evil. When first she weighed anchor in Etherhorde, half a world away in the bosom of the enemy, I knew she bore a threat. Each league closer I felt it grow. Wide across the Nelu Peren she sailed, and there far from land the danger grew. Then six days she lay in Ormaelport, Neda's old home, and took on some monstrous new power. And yesterday – yesterday the sun dimmed at noon, and the spell-weave of the world was stretched, almost to tearing. Then nearly I saw her true intent. But the power hid itself away, and now she lies like a great docile cow, awaiting our summons.

'And we must summon her – summon the bride's party and our own Prince Falmurqat, summon all the visiting lords and nobles to this our shrine. For that is the will of the Five Kings. Who can blame them? Who does not want peace? And perhaps yesterday's burst of magic saw the evil in *Chathrand* destroyed. But my heart says otherwise. This Thasha of Etherhorde will not marry our prince, and her Empire seeks no end to war – unless our end as a people be part of it.'

The Father's jaw tightened. 'The Five Kings would not hear me out. "You live in the past, Father," they chided. "All your long life the war has raged, and now in your waning years you can imagine only more of the same. The world has changed; the Empire of Arqual has changed, and so must we. Train your *sfvantskors* a little longer, if you are not content to rest, but leave off statecraft." But when have I been wrong?'

He paused deliberately. Neda dared not breathe: she alone knew when.

'They are blind,' said the Father. 'They see only the riches to be had through trade with the East. I see further. But I am no king, and have no spies or soldiers to command. Yet I have the friendship of certain officers in the White Fleet. And I have you, children: *sfvantskors* in all but final vows. You are here because of *Chathrand*; you are here to save us from the evil she brings. More than this I have told you in trance, but it is not right that you should remember yet. When the time comes the memory will return of itself. Now we must be quick: take my blessing, and confess your fears.'

He stepped beneath the dome, and the first aspirant ran up the staircase and knelt. The Father spoke only briefly to each, for the sun would not hide much longer. But when Neda's turn came he set his hand upon her head, and she felt him tremble.

'Would you speak?' he asked her.

Her nails bit into her palm. 'I have no fears to confess,' she said.

'You will have,' he said. 'Your brother is aboard that ship.'

In shock Neda raised her eyes. The Father's own grew wide: aspirants were forbidden any glimpse of the dome's interior. Quickly she looked down again.

'Forgive me,' she said.

'He is a servant,' said the Father. 'What they call a *tarboy*, I think. And he is the special friend of Doctor Chadfallow, who is also aboard.'

'Pazel,' she whispered. *He was alive, alive—*

'You must not speak to him, Neda.'

She swallowed, fighting for calm.

'Not until the wedding ends. Indeed he must not see your face. His presence here cannot be an accident. You and Ultri shall stand behind me, masked, until it is over.'

'Yes, Father. But when it's over?'

He sighed. 'Dear one, even I do not know what will happen then.'

The Father blessed her, and she groped shaking for the stairs. The last disciple knelt before him briefly. Then the lip of the sun rose over the sea and the Father raised his arms and cried out in a voice like a roll of thunder, sending the goats bolting for their lives and larks and sparrows rising in terror across the fields. It was the *Annuncet*, the Summons, heightened by the magic of the dome, louder than Neda had ever heard it. The Father sang the ritual words again and again, seeming to need no breath at all, and he did not cease until the lamps were burning across the city, in hall and tower and anchored ship.

2

Manhood

―⟡―

In his twenty-one minutes of unbroken song the Father woke tens of thousands, and sang the holy word *karishin* ('purest good') exactly forty-nine times. But his first utterance of the word – the most auspicious, though few Simjans knew or cared – reached the ears of fewer than one hundred: sixty lobstermen wrestling traps from the seabed; eighteen Templar monks, already rowing for the Great Ship and their rendezvous with Thasha Isiq; five deathsmoke addicts; two lovers outside the West Gate and the callous guard who refused to let them steal back to their marriage beds; the warrior Hercól Stanapeth, who had not slept at all; a murderer hiding in the mouth of a silver mine; Lady Oggosk, plugging her ears with greasy thumbs as she sang an enchantment-song of her own; a moon falcon standing restless on a windowsill; a poet whose twelve years without a poem had led him to a clifftop but who was now, as he listened, considering conversion; a child locked in an attic – and three men on the *Chathrand's* quarterdeck.

One of these was Old Gangrüne, the purser, who had the dawn watch. He slouched across the lightless deck, in a temper even before he was fully awake.

'That'll be your Black Rags now,' he said aloud. 'Call that a prayer, d'ye, Sizzy? You're just howlin' like an animal, and some of us ain't surprised. Oh, yes, yes, there's no need to tell *me*. You're decent folk now, ain't ye? Gentlemen, honest coves. Until you whip out the knife when our back's turned and *errrrgh!*'

He mimed a murder, perhaps his own, then shuffled off towards the jiggermast, oaths still leaking from his lips.

He did not see the man in the shadow of the wheelhouse, on hands and knees, shuddering, naked but for a pair of ornate gold spectacles in danger of slipping from his nose. This man's eyes were pinched shut, and a cascade of expressions played over his mouth – now a smile, now a grimace of fear, now a thought so striking that the mouth froze altogether. A pale man in the prime of life, though perhaps a little thin and austere.

'Dawn is come,' said a voice beside him. 'Stand up before it's too late.'

A hand appeared at his shoulder, offering help. The naked man seemed to battle with himself harder than ever. He took a deep breath and opened his eyes.

For a heartbeat he stayed perfectly still. Then in one motion he rose, astonished, his back straightening was like rebirth after illness, his gaze above the rail like the view from a watchtower.

Beside him stood a man in a black seafarer's jacket, black leggings and a white scarf that might have stood out distinctly in a stronger light. He was tall and thickset, and his eyes had the sharp ravenous look of a spider's. He gestured at a pair of trousers and a shirt folded over the rail.

The shirt was a lustrous green. The thin man reached out and stroked it.

'That is silk,' said the other. 'And there are calfskin shoes at your feet.'

Fumbling, the man in spectacles put on the clothes. He touched them reverently. 'They warm you,' he said.

'Of course.' The man in black knelt and tied the other's shoes. 'And what is more, they distinguish you. Green is the colour of the learned, the natural leaders of men. You may walk about, now – walk, and look, and be free.'

Slow and astonished, the thin man circled the quarterdeck. Old Gangrüne stood blinking by the mast, one finger digging half-heartedly in his ear. The bespectacled man stared at him, open-mouthed, three inches from his face. Gangrüne neither saw nor heard him.

'Eye to eye, we call that,' said the man in black. 'It is how you will look at all men. Did I not say you would like it?'

'Like it!' The man in spectacles seemed overcome with joy. But all at once his smile disappeared. He glanced darkly at his companion and scuttled away, as if he preferred a little distance between them.

On the ladder his shoes gave him trouble and he almost fell. The man in black chuckled and followed him down to the deck. They glided forwards along the starboard rail, past the captain's skylight through which a lamp shone already, the mizzen shrouds, the stone-faced Turach soldiers with their heavy crossbows and their scars.

Then the thin man gave a squeal of terror, recoiling. A red cat had climbed from the No. 4 hatch and stood stretching its hindquarters. While the animal was undeniably huge for a housecat, the man's reaction more befitted one facing a tiger with gore-stained jaws. Before he could run the man in black seized his arm.

'She cannot touch you. Have you forgotten yourself already?'

The cat walked primly towards them. The thin man positively writhed with fear. When the animal passed them, it paused and crouched, and the fur rose along its back. The thin man squealed again. But the cat heard nothing, and though it looked about suspiciously, its eyes passed over them unseeing.

'One kick,' said the man in black. 'Your left foot, or your right.'

'I won't do it!'

The man in black took a step forward and seized the cat by the scruff of the neck. It yowled and twisted, but before it could scratch him the man flung it with all his strength over the rail. Two seconds sprawled, noiseless; then came a faint splash.

He turned on the man in glasses.

'Imbecile. Where is the intelligence you're so proud of? Any such creature you may now drive off, or kill, or punish as it deserves. Savour the fact. Taste that new joy. We have a word for it, incidentally.'

'Wh-what word is that?'

'Safety.'

They went below. Even one deck down it was still very dark. Soldiers groped for boots and helmets. A pair of tarboys brought their ration of water; they gargled and spat. The man in spectacles knew they could not see him, and in truth felt his fear of the soldiers melting away. But one of the boys, tall for his age with a finger-sized hole in one ear, gave him such a fright that he ducked behind the shot garlands. His bright eyes peeped timidly between the rows of cannonballs. The man in black shook his head.

'Why can't you act like a man?'

'That boy tried to kill me!' squeaked the other.

'If he touched you now he'd get a dozen lashes.'

The thin man raised his head and gave a tentative smile. 'Oh yes, lashes. He deserves lashes. A dozen lashes, boy!'

'That's better,' said the man in black.

He took the thin man's arm. 'Notice, my friend, how great ships resemble great houses: each deck with its open central compartment, its courtyard. Each with its brighter rooms and its darker. Grand airy spaces for the masters, cupboards for those who serve. Most beings in this world cling to the place where fate has dropped them, even if that place is a stinking hold, where they scrabble about on hairy bellies, cursing and cursed. You must be strong indeed to change your fate.'

The thin man looked to his right. Beside the shot garlands lay a row of corpses, wrapped in shreds of canvas and tied up with twine. Another row lay between the cannon on the starboard quarter.

'Killed yesterday,' said the thin man. 'Killed by your fleshanc ghouls. I didn't realise there were so many.'

The man in black turned him away. 'The dead are none of your concern. Look here! A man after your own heart.'

A sailor had found a patch of light beside an open gunport. He had a sheet of tattered paper and a pencil stub. With the sheet spread flat on a 24-pounder, he was writing in a quick, clumsy hand. Now and then he glanced up at his shipmates, but few of them met his eye.

'He's writing a letter, you see? Touch it, take it from him!'

'Is it a love letter?' asked the man in spectacles, drawing near despite himself.

The man in black laughed aloud. 'What else? Go on, read it to me. I know full well you can read.'

He snatched the page from the sailor's hand, and gave it to the thin man. The sailor appeared to forget the letter the moment it was taken from him: he merely crossed his arms and looked out of the gunport. On the back of his hand was a tattooed **K**.

'It may make you blush,' said the man in black.

The other adjusted his spectacles. *Dear Kalli*, the letter began. He could not make himself read it aloud. There was something wrong about the letter, anyway, for although it began as one thing it soon became something else.

Dear Kalli how are you how's my one true love? Are there peaches in Etherhorde are you canning some for me? Have you fattened up a bit Kalli sure enough the men are courtin' you now I'm away. Kalli you had best choose one and marry. Write me off won't you sweetheart as I can't see surviving, tell your dad tell your uncles tell the whole blary world what a great crew of monsters is Chathrand's they seem like men but they'll kill us like insects the Swarm's to be set free Rin help us the SWARM—

The man in black grabbed the page and crushed it, then tossed it with a snarl through the open gunport. He looked accusingly at the thin man.

'Satisfied?' he said.

In the galley, the morning chill was replaced by smoky warmth. The smells were intoxicating. All sailors dined like kings – the thin man had known that for years. The man in black made him lift the ladle and taste the breakfast gruel. It was glutinous and barely salted. It was manna from the gods.

'And this,' said the man in black, 'is the worst you shall ever taste again.'

The thin man emptied the ladle with a slurp. Gruel on his lips, tears in his eyes.

'It's not fair,' he said.

'But it is,' said his guide. 'You help me, I help you.'

They did not knock at the captain's door: they pushed it open and stepped right in. Captain Rose stood before a dressing mirror, fastening his cufflinks. He had combed out his great red beard, and a new dress coat hung on a stand beside him. His steward was in the after-cabin, polishing his shoes by the window.

'So much room!' cried the thin man, spreading his arms and turning in a circle.

The man in black looked contemptuously at Rose. 'The fool. He's loathed in these islands. He won't be allowed anywhere near the wedding ceremony.'

They looked on as Rose took something from his watch pocket. It was not a watch but the head of a woman, carved from a pale white stone. The captain put the head in his mouth, where it bulged between his cheek and gum.

'A twisted man,' said the visitor in black.

The thin man suddenly found his courage. He bolted across the cabin to the dining table and snatched at Rose's breakfast with both hands. Orange slices. Kidney pie. Three round raw eggs the size of cherries. A boiled radish. A wedge of soda bread with butter, still warm from the stove.

He ate everything before him, then sucked his fingers, and finally lifted the platter and swabbed it spotless with his tongue. Neither the captain nor the steward turned him a glance. He looked at the man in black with amazement.

'I have just eaten Rose's breakfast!'

'Next time leave the eggshells. Go on – see what a captain's bed feels like, while you're at it.'

The sheets were newly laundered; the pillow beneath his head brought back dim memories of fluff and mother's warmth. There were books in a shelf built into the headboard. The man in spectacles reached behind his head and took one. He caressed the leather, then drew the volume reverently to his chest.

I cannot give this up, he thought.

'Nor need you,' said the other, as if he had spoken aloud. 'Well, then, do we have an agreement?'

'I – You see, sir, there are obligations—'

The man in black crossed the room in four strides.

'Obligations?' he said venomously. 'Only to me, henceforth. What obligations can your kind feel, save bestial urges?'

'Please,' rasped the thin man, clutching the book even tighter. 'Don't misunderstand me. That is the horror of my life, being misunderstood.'

'The horror of your life is what you are,' said the other. 'You're a freak, an abomination. I alone can change that. And all I ask in return is that you tell me what goes on in that stateroom. Thasha Isiq's stateroom, the place I cannot see.'

The thin man pinched his eyes shut and rubbed his hands quickly together, a spastic gesture of nerves. 'But I am only dreaming this, dreaming you and these people and that lovely food. None of it is *real*.'

'You talk like a simpleton,' said the other, 'but that is not your fault. Most beings see consciousness as no more than a coin: heads you're awake and busy, tails you sleep and dream. But reality is not so flat. It is more like a die of many sides. You toss it, and live with whatever it reveals. A mage, however, can read all sides of the die at once. I have shown you this day's beginning as the men of *Chathrand* are living it. As you will live it, when you become a man.'

'But in plain fact? Am I not there in Thasha's chambers, safely asleep?'

The other's patience was fraying again. 'A body lies there. A maimed and vile organism. Your mind is with me – and what is a body without a mind? Which part is really you? And if your very soul longs for a human life, and I offer it to you forever – have I not *understood* you, Felthrup? Have I not grasped the very dream you live for?'

'Yes, you have,' said the thin man, avoiding his eye.

'Good!' said the man in black. 'Then let us shake on it, like men. I will give you this body forever. And you will be my eyes and ears.'

The thin man felt his sweat on Rose's pillow. Slowly, fearfully, he shook his head. 'They are my friends,' he said.

'They are nothing of the sort. They have toyed with you from curiosity, and for their own gain. Men befriend other men, not craven things like you.'

'They have been so kind.'

'What of it? What are their little kindnesses, beside the world I have opened to you?'

'Not *opened*, sir.' The thin man's voice shook. '*Expanded* is perhaps the better word. The world opened to me just once, in a house in Noonfirth, when the dumb brute in me died and I became a woken being, reasoning and aware.'

The man in black stared at him a moment. Then his face contorted with such pure hatred that the other scrambled away from him across the bed.

'Reasoning and aware!' he shouted. 'You cesspool filth. Go, then, return to what you were. Run and hide and eat dead things, and be hunted by all creatures. Oh, see!'

He pointed, feigning shock. The thin man looked at his own left arm and gave a wail. From the elbow down it was lifeless, withered, crushed. The man in black reached forward and tore the glasses from the other's head.

'Gold spectacles,' he hissed derisively. 'A scholar, Felthrup, is that how you picture yourself? How fine, how truly noble – but *what is this?*'

A tail! The thin man had grown a tail, leathery and short and ending in a stump, as if long ago bitten in two.

'Arunis,' he said, 'please, I beg—'

The sorcerer struck him across the face, and when the thin man raised his right hand to his aching cheekbone, the hand was a long pink paw.

'Down, vermin!' bellowed the sorcerer. 'Crawl and whimper and weep! And pray that Arunis is merciful when he comes again – for I will come, and you will do my bidding, or by the Beast in the Pit I'll see you broken and mad.'

He was gone. Rose's cabin was gone. The thin man lay on gritty planks in the bowels of the ship. And when he tried to stand he toppled over onto his three good feet, and was himself again, the black rat with the soul of a scholar, caged in the nightmare that was his body. There were eyes in the darkness – his rat-brethren come to kill him, under orders from their lunatic chief – and he leaped up and ran.

'Wicked Felthrup!' they hissed, giving chase. 'Unnatural rat! Friend to men and crawlies, slave to thought! Let us eat you and end it!'

Such temptation. The deck was endless and foul. Ixchel voices laughed on his right, *He only thinks he thinks*, and he turned and barely saw the little figures in the shadows before their arrows began to pierce him like needles of glass. He ran on, bleeding. Walls and stores and stanchions flashed by, and there was nowhere safe from his persecutors, and from the crates above him the red cat (deathless like all his demons) purred for his blood, and ahead loomed the shapes of men deadliest of all, and he ran and dodged and prayed but there was no salvation for those cursed by the gods.

3

Procession

⁕

7 Teala 941

'You will allow, sir, that the *Annuncet* is more than noise: it is music, after a fashion. No two Mzithrini elders sing it quite the same, although I'm told the words are simple: *This house is open to men and gods; none need fear it save devils and the devilish; come, and find the good you seek.* All very pleasant. Still our *sfvantskor* guests were loath to part with their blades.'

King Oshiram II, Lord of Simja, chuckled at his own remark. Walking at the royal elbow, at the centre of a vast, ecstatic throng, Eberzam Isiq returned a smile: the most false in his long public life. His heart was pounding, as from battle. He was hot in his wedding regalia – antique woollens, leather epaulettes, otterskin cap with the admiralty star – and the king's chatter grated in his ears. Still the old admiral walked with lowered eyes, measured step. He was an ambassador, now, and an ambassador must show the greatest deference to a king, even the petty king of an upstart island.

'Enlightened policy, Sire,' he heard himself say. 'Simja has nothing to gain by allowing armed and violent men to walk her streets.'

'Nothing,' laughed Oshiram. 'But by that token who can we afford to exclude, hmmm?'

The sun was high over Simja: it was approaching noon. The mob of well-wishers assaulted the king's retinue with their cheers, their spark-flinging firecrackers, their piercing fishbone whistles. Onlookers filled every window, the young men dangling perilous from the balconies. Flightless messenger birds nine feet tall skirted the crowds, grimy boys clinging to their necks. Monks of the Rinfaith droned in harmony with their bells.

They passed under an arch between the port district and the Street of the Coppersmiths. The king pointed out the workshop from which he'd ordered lamps for the ambassadorial residence. Isiq nodded, in agony. *The blary fool. Does he think I wish to speak of lamps?*

Before the two men walked a vision. His daughter, Thasha, had been at war with lavish clothing since she was old enough to ruin it. She was not a good Arquali girl but a bruising fighter, with a conscript's temper and a grip to make a wrestler wince. And yet here she was: grey-gowned, satin-shoed, cheeks dabbed with powdered amethyst, golden hair twisted up in a braid they called a Babqri love-knot. *Exquisite, beautiful, an angel in the flesh:* the mob breathed the words after her in a sigh no effort could contain.

Thasha looked straight ahead, back rigid, face quiet and resolved. Isiq's pride in her stabbed him at every glance. *You did this. You brought her here. You dared not fight for your child.*

A small entourage surrounded Thasha: the personal friends custom allowed her to name. The swordsman, Hercól Stanapeth, her friend and tutor of many years, tall and careworn and matchless in a fight. Mr Fiffengurt, the *Chathrand's* good-hearted quartermaster, whose stiff walk and one-eyed way of looking at the world ('the other just points where it pleases') reminded the admiral of a fighting cock. And of course the tarboys, Pazel and Neeps.

The two youths, despite vests and silk trousers hastily provided by the king, looked terrible. Ragged, red-eyed, bruised about the face. Pazel Pathkendle, child of vanquished Ormael, gazed out through his straight nut-brown locks with an expression more like a soldier's than that of a boy of sixteen. A searching look, and a sceptical eye. He had turned that sort of look on Isiq at their first meeting, when the admiral found him with Thasha in her cabin, and Pathkendle declared, in so many words, that her father was a war criminal.

At the time the charge had felt outrageous. By tonight it could well be an understatement.

The other tarboy, Neeps Undrabust, fidgeted as he walked. A head shorter than Pathkendle, he glared at the crowds on both sides of the street, as if searching for a hidden enemy. *They fear the worst,* thought Isiq, *but have they lived long enough to withstand it when it comes? For that matter, have I?*

They had argued the night away – the tarboys, the admiral, Hercól and Thasha – and yet they'd failed to find a way to save her. Not from a loveless marriage; she would suffer that but briefly. Days, weeks, a fortnight or two. The Mzithrin Kings would need no longer to discover how they had been deceived, and to murder the girl at the deception's heart.

His cravat was too tight. He had dressed without a mirror, repelled by the thought of the face awaiting him there: the face of an imbecile patriot, a blind blunt tool in the kit of Magad V, Emperor of Arqual, and his spymaster Sandor Ott. *By the fiends below, I hate myself more than Ott.*

The king touched his elbow. 'Are you quite well, Ambassador?'

Isiq drew himself up straight. 'Perfectly, Sire. Forgive me, I confess I was lost in thought.'

'As a father must be at such a time. And I know the matter of your musings.'

'Do you?'

'Of course,' said the king. 'You're pondering what last words of wisdom to bestow upon the child of your flesh. Before another man takes your place, as it were. Do not fear: Simjan custom shall be observed today as well as Mzithrini. On this island fathers and daughters enjoy a private leave-taking. I trust you've understood? It is of course why we make for the Cactus Gardens.'

'I'm aware of your tradition, Majesty, and glad of it.'

'Splendid, splendid. You'll have eleven minutes alone with her. But do wave to my people, won't you, Isiq? They've had no small bother about all this, and see! They've laid down flowers for the Treaty Bride.'

A whole street of flowers, in fact: the last approach to the gardens was buried in blossoms, a thousand yards of yellow scallop-shell blossoms with a honeyed scent, poured two inches deep and bordered with rosewood. Children from the mob had been allowed past the guards and stood with eager handfuls, presumably to toss at the Bride. It seemed a crime to walk on the flowers, but that was clearly the idea.

'Isporelli blossoms, Excellency,' said the king's chamberlain from behind them.

'Are they? Pitfire!'

His little outburst turned heads. Isiq had not seen isporelli in fifteen years, nor wanted to. They were his late wife's favourite.

'You may thank Pacu Lapadolma for this intelligence,' said the king, as they trampled beauty flat. 'She has exchanged letters with our Mistress of Ceremonies for the better part of a year, now, and helped out in many particulars.'

The girl in question walked just behind Thasha's entourage, on the arm of Dr Ignus Chadfallow. Isiq could hardly bear to look at

Chadfallow, a favourite of the Emperor and, until yesterday, Isiq's best friend. Better to look at Pacu, lovely Pacu, daughter of a general and niece of the *Chathrand*'s owner. She was sixteen, like Thasha and the tarboys, and already a widow. She was also Thasha's Maid-in-Waiting. Thasha had once remarked that the girl could as easily have done her 'waiting' back in Etherhorde and spared them months of misery: she and Pacu did not get along.

'She has generosity of spirit,' Isiq had retorted. 'She loves Arqual as passionately as any man in uniform. And she believes in the Great Peace. I heard her say as much to her aunt.'

The Great Peace. He had believed in it too. Desperately, although in secret, for a soldier of Arqual was not expected to waste his energies imagining peace with the enemy he had been trained to destroy. Isiq had been born into a world of chaos and fear. He could not remember a time when the spectre of war, and annihilation should the war go badly, had not hung over his family. Defending Arqual against the Mzithrin, and the numberless small foes and revolutionaries that boiled up from the marshy edges of the Empire, was the noblest life he could have chosen. *The* only *life, by damn. The only choice you could have lived with, once you knew you had it in you.* He was a soldier of Arqual, and even if he sat out the rest of his days in the court of this foppish King Oshiram he would never truly be anything else.

Half a century in the service. Half a century of struggle and blood-shed, maimed friends, fatherless children: he saw now that they had all built to this moment. Treaty Day. The Great Peace. Millions were waiting for it to begin.

And it was all a monstrous sham. Peace was the furthest thing from the mind of his Emperor, as Thasha and her friends had grasped before anyone. For chained in the bowels of the *Chathrand* was a deposed king of the Mzithrin, the Shaggat Ness, a madman who thought himself a god. His twisted version of the Old Faith had seduced a quarter of the Mzithrini people, and inspired a doomed but hideously bloody uprising. When the Mzithrin Kings at last crushed the rebellion, the Shaggat had fled in a ship called the *Lythra* – right into the jaws of Arqual's own navy.

The *Lythra* had been blown to matchsticks. But the Shaggat, and his two boys, and his sorcerer: they had been plucked from the waves alive, and whisked off to a secret prison in the heart of Arqual.

He was the most dangerous lunatic in history, east or west. For forty years now the world had thought him safely drowned. And for forty years Arqual's guild of assassins, the Secret Fist, had been infiltrating the Shaggat's worshippers. On Gurishal, the fanatics' war-blighted island of exile, the Secret Fist had stoked their faith, encouraged their martyrdom, assassinated the moderates among them. And above all, it had spread a false prophecy of the Shaggat's return. *Those gods-forsaken wretches! They might have abandoned their cult and rejoined the Mzithrin by now, if only we'd let them be!*

Instead, the spymaster Sandor Ott had prepared them for a second uprising, even as Arqual and the Mzithrin prepared, with the greatest sincerity, for peace.

If you want a lie to fool your enemy, test it on a friend. The proverb was surely Ott's cardinal rule. Even the highest circles of the Arquali military (of which Isiq was indisputably a part) had been kept ignorant. And the blood-drinking Mzithrinis: they had taken the bait in both hands, as King Oshiram's prattle made clear.

'They've loaded three ships full of presents, Isiq. Sculpture, tapestries, fiddles and flutes, a whole spire from a ruined shrine. A petrified egg. A miraculous talking crow. All for Arqual – the ships as well, mind you. And they're sending artists to paint your Emperor Magad. I gather they're dying to know what he looks like.'

'The world changes swiftly, your Highness,' mumbled Isiq.

'It does not seem very swift to me – one day I will show you the City of Widows – yet I understand you, Isiq, I declare I do. Peace is our destiny, and we who have lived to see these days must rejoice. The future! How welcome it is!'

A few decades without a bloodbath, and he thinks it's for ever. But how could anyone have guessed the sheer, foul audacity of the plan? For the prophecy Ott had spread among the Shaggat's faithful came down to this: that their God-King would return *when a Mzithrin prince took the hand of an enemy soldier's daughter.* Isiq was that soldier, and Thasha the incendiary bride.

Horror and betrayal: and that was before the sorcerer entered the game.

Isiq waved to the mob, despair gnawing his heart like some ghastly parasite. Who among them would believe, even if he screamed it, that as soon as his daughter took Prince Falmurqat's hand the Great Ship would set sail – not for Etherhorde, as they'd pretend, but for the depths of the Nelluroq, the Ruling Sea, where no other ship left afloat could follow her? That by crossing that chartless monstrosity of ocean, resupplying in the all-but-forgotten lands of the southern hemisphere, and returning far to the west of Gurishal, they would do the impossible – sail *around* the White Fleet, that impenetrable naval wall, sweep down on Gurishal from the Mzithrinis' blind side, and return the Shaggat to his horde? Preposterous! Unthinkable!

So unthinkable that it could just come to pass.

No, King. Do not welcome the future, do not hasten it. A cracked mirror, that is all it will prove: a desert where we maroon our children, a broken image of the past.

The Cactus Gardens were the pride of Simja. Tended by a guild of botanical fanatics, they stretched over four dry acres in the heart of the city, a patch of earth that had never been built upon. There were cacti tall as trees and small as acorns, cacti that climbed and cacti that wriggled along the ground, cacti disguised as stones, or heavy with armoured fruit, or bristling with six-inch spikes.

At the heart of the garden rose the Old Sentinels: two rows of ugly, blistered, thousand-year-old plants that groped like tortured fingers at the sky. Between them walked Isiq and his daughter, hand in hand, alone. The procession had swept on without them, into the Royal Rose Gardens next door. Their eleven minutes had begun.

'Failed,' said Isiq.

'Stop saying that,' said Thasha, pulling a wayward spike from her gown. 'And pick your feet up when you walk! You never used to shuffle along like a clown.'

'I won't waste these last moments bickering,' he said. 'Nor will I ask you to forgive me. Only to remember, to think of me now and again, should you somehow—'

Thasha put a hand to his lips. 'What a silly ass you are. Why won't you trust me? You know I have a tactical mind.'

Isiq's brow furrowed. Despite his best efforts he had dozed off briefly in the night. One moment he had been seated on a bench in his cabin, his great blue mastiffs snoring at his feet. The next she was kissing him awake, saying that the Templar monks had drawn their boat alongside the *Chathrand*, waiting for her. A new steadiness had shown in her face, a resolve. It had frightened him.

Now between the monstrous cacti he pressed her hand to his chest.

'If you have devised some plan, you and Hercól and those mad-dog tarboys, it is for you to trust *me*. Reveal it now. We'll have no other chance to speak.'

Thasha hesitated, then shook her head. 'We tried, last night. You started shouting, remember? You forbade us to speak.'

'Only of madness. Only of running, or fighting our enemies head-on, or other forms of suicide.'

'What if suicide's the answer?' she said, looking at him fiercely. 'No marriage, no prophecy come true. It's better than anything you've come up with.'

'Do not rave at me, Thasha Isiq. You know His Supremacy left me no choice.'

'I'm tired of that excuse,' said Thasha sharply. 'Even today you're saying "no choice," when the most dangerous thing would be to take no risks at all.'

'That is juvenile idiocy. I know what risk is, girl. I have been a soldier three times as long as you've been alive. You have courage, that's something no one denies. But courage is just one of the virtues.'

Thasha heaved a sigh. 'Daddy, this is the *last* thing—'

'Another is wisdom, rarer and more costly to earn than skill with a blade. And dearer than either of these is honour, which is a sacred trust, and once lost not easily—'

Something changed in Thasha's face. She snatched her hand away and boxed him in the ribs. The blow made a dull *clink*.

'Ouch! Damn! What's that blary thing in your coat?'

Isiq looked embarrassed. 'Westfirth brandy,' he said.

'Give me some.'

'Out of the question. Listen, girl, we have just—'

'GIVE ME SOME!'

He surrendered the little bronze flask. And the Treaty Bride, head to toe the image of a virgin priestess of old, tilted back her head and drank. After the fourth swallow, quite deliberately, she spat brandy in his face.

'Don't even say the word *trust*. You sent me away to a school run by hags. Offered me to your Emperor when he snapped his fingers. You brought me halfway round the world to marry a coffin-worshipping blood-drinking Black Rag—'

'For Rin's *sake* lower your voice!'

'You denied what I told you about Syrarys.'

Isiq closed his eyes. Syrarys, the beautiful consort who had shared his bed for a decade, had been exposed two days ago as Ott's lover and spy. She had made a deathsmoke addict of him. She would have killed him as soon as Thasha wed.

'You laughed when I said the Shaggat Ness was aboard,' said Thasha, 'and that Arunis planned to use him against us. You've watched every-thing I warned you about come true – and you *still* think I'm a child.'

With slow dignity, Isiq dried his face with a sleeve.

'I also watched your mother fall through a rotten balustrade. Four stories, onto marble. She'd been waving to me. She reached out as she fell. She was twenty-six, with child again, although we'd told no one. That child would be twelve, now, Thasha. Your little brother or sister.'

He could tell she was shaken. Thasha knew, of course, how her mother had died, that horrid fall from a theatre balcony. But Isiq had never told her he'd witnessed the accident, or that Clorisuela had been pregnant at the time.

'You're all I have left,' he said. 'I can't watch you die before me as she did.'

Thasha looked up at him, tears glistening in her eyes. 'Don't watch,' she said.

Then she raised her gown and swept away down the path. 'Thasha!' he cried, knowing she would not turn around. He huffed after her, cursing his stiff joints, the throbbing in his head that had only worsened since the removal of Syrarys' poison, the red silk shoes he'd consented to wear.

Silk. It was like going out in one's socks – in women's socks. How was it that no one had laughed?

'Come back here, damn it!'

In a heartbeat she would be gone for ever. There were things yet to say. Humility to recover, love somehow to confess.

'Where are you?'

He would confess, too. Before the Mzithrin prince, that irritating king, the whole distinguished mob. Stand before them and declare that the Shaggat lived, that the wedding was a trap, and Arqual ruled by a beast of an Emperor. *I am guilty. She is not. Exempt her from this infamy; let it be me whom you punish.*

But of course he would do no such thing. For beneath his daughter's gown hung the necklace – his late wife's gorgeous silver necklace. Arunis had put a curse on that silver chain, and had sworn to strangle her there on the marriage dais should anyone interfere with the ceremony. He had demonstrated that power yesterday, though Isiq would never have doubted it. This was, after all, a man who had come back from the dead.

He had been hanged. Everyone agreed on that point: Arunis had been hanged, nine days on the gibbet, and his body chopped into pieces and tossed into the sea. Chadfallow had described the execution in detail; he had been there. Yet through some black magic Arunis had cheated death. For twenty years there had been no hint of him, no rumour. Like Sandor Ott, he had astonishing patience. And only when the spymaster was at last ready to deploy the Shaggat, his master weapon – only then did Arunis suddenly return, and strike.

'Do you hear the horn, Thasha? We have five minutes! Come back!'

What fools the sorcerer had made of them all. Under their very noses he had left the *Chathrand* in Ormael, rendezvoused with Volpek mercenaries, and raided the sunken *Lythra*. With Pazel's forced assistance, he had retrieved an iron statue known as the Red Wolf. The statue itself was no use to him, but within its enchanted metal was the one thing he needed to make his Shaggat invincible: the Nilstone, scorge of all Alifros, a cursed rock from the world of the dead.

Yesterday, in an unnatural calm, the mage had demonstrated his power to kill Thasha with a word. His advantage proved, he had forced the crew to raise the iron forge to the *Chathrand*'s topdeck, and to stoke a great fire under the Red Wolf. Bit by bit the Wolf had succumbed to the flames. At last, before their eyes, it had melted to bubbling iron.

There had followed an hallucinatory succession of shocks. The Nilstone, revealed. Captain Rose flying like a madman at Arunis; Sergeant Drellarek clubbing him down. The molten iron spilled, men in agony leaping into the sea. The Shaggat bellowing triumph as he grasped the artefact – and death running like a grey flame up his arm: for the Nilstone (as they all learned presently) killed at a touch any with fear in their hearts.

Finally, strangest of all, that instant silence, like the deafness after cannon-fire, and a brief but ghastly dimming of the sun. When Isiq recovered his senses, he saw Pazel with his hand on the Shaggat – on a stone Shaggat, one withered hand still clutching his prize.

It seemed this dusty tarboy was himself steeped in magic: he had a language gift (the little bastard spoke some twenty tongues; Isiq had heard him; he was a walking Carnival of Nations) as well as three powerful spell-words, Master-Words he called them, each of which could be spoken only once. He had used the first yesterday: a word that turned flesh to stone. And in a burst of genius for which Isiq would thank him forever, Pazel had foreseen that if the mad king died, Arunis would slay Thasha the next instant. Before the Nilstone could kill the Shaggat, Pazel had leaped forward and petrified him. Arunis believed he could reverse the spell – and as long as he dreamed of doing so, he had a reason to let Sandor Ott's game of betrayal go forwards.

But the necklace – every scheme for saving Thasha foundered on that necklace. Arunis would kill her if they talked, if he overheard the least rumour of a conspiracy, passing among the guests. And the necklace tightened of its own accord if any hand sought to remove it. *I cannot even sacrifice myself for her. I have the courage. And no cause left to live for, witless servant that I have been. I would humble them ere they slew me, if I could but strike—*

'Confound it all!' he thundered. 'Where are you, girl?'

'This way, Daddy.'

He turned a corner and there she was, sipping from his flask again, beside an odd little reflecting pool. No, it was a birdbath. No—

'Is that . . . a *plant?*'

Thasha pointed to a sign at their feet.

Bird-Eating Bramian Cactus
DO NOT TOUCH!

What seems a multicoloured pool is in fact a highly toxic jelly above a vegetal maw. Birds as large as vultures spot this cactus from the air, stoop to drink, and die. Those falling forward pass through the jelly over the course of several weeks and are dissolved. The body of a single desert finch can sustain the cactus for a month.

Isiq put an uncertain hand on her shoulder. 'A strange, cruel world,' he said.

'Yes,' said Thasha, leaning against him, 'it is.'

'They're fighting again,' said Neeps.

Pazel held still, listening. '"A coffin-worshipping, blood-drinking" – Rin's teeth! She shouldn't say that.'

The two ex-tarboys stood near the garden wall, Hercól and Fiffengurt at their sides. Unlike Thasha they kept their voices low. These rose gardens were smaller than their cactus counterparts, and the wedding entourage quite filled them. The flowers were scarlet, white, yolk-orange; their perfume hung like a sweet steam in the air. Caterers in royal Simjan livery were dashing among them with with trays of clinking glasses. Servants fanned the elder statesmen, who grumbled in their chairs. Beside a fountain in the shape of the Tree of Heaven the king was promising the wilting dignitaries 'a feast for the ages' when the ceremony ended. Pacu Lapadolma, true to her Maid-in-Waiting role, hovered by the gate to the Cactus Gardens.

Fiffengurt trained his good eye on her. 'Perhaps we should confide in Mistress Pacu.'

'No!' snapped Neeps.

'No,' Pazel agreed. 'She's fond of Thasha in her way, but her only real passions are horses and the glory of Arqual. Who knows what she'd do if we told her the plan?'

'The boys are right,' said Hercól. 'The Lapadolmas have fought and bled for the Magad Emperors for two hundred years, and Pacu embraces that history with measureless pride. We must assume, moreover, that Sandor Ott's spies remain active, no matter what has happened to their master.'

'I hope a ton of bricks happened to him,' said Pazel. 'Maybe one of those half-ruined buildings in Ormael.'

'He may have fled Ormael by now,' said Hercól, 'whether or not the Imperial governor has had the courage to order him brought to justice. But his agents are still in place, and they will be watching us. We shall be in danger by land and sea. Yet I cannot forget Ramachni's warning. At some point we must risk confidences again.'

Pazel felt a stab of worry. Ramachni was *their* mage, a good wizard in the body of a coal-black mink, who for reasons he would not discuss had taken an interest in Thasha for years. His home was not Alifros but a distant world. Pazel had glimpsed that world once, through a magic portal, the thought of which thrilled and frightened him to this day.

But last night Ramachni had left them. The battle with Arunis had taken all his strength, and forced him to crawl back through the portal to his own world, to recuperate. *Find new allies*, he had told them as he left: *find them at all costs, or you can't hope to prevail.* And when would he return? *Look for me*, he had said, *when a darkness falls beyond today's imagining.*

To Pazel that sounded like a very long time. He wondered if the others felt the same vague terror as he did. Without Ramachni's wisdom they were fumbling, blind – lost in the darkness already.

'You took one risk this morning, didn't you?' said Fiffengurt. 'You trusted me.'

Hercól laughed. 'That was not difficult. Pazel, Neeps and Thasha all vouched for you. Agreement among them is too rare a thing to ignore.'

'Yet I'm fond of Arqual myself,' said Fiffengurt. 'Not the Empire, mind you: I mean the old notions we sang about in nursery-days – *Arqual, Arqual, just and true, land of hope forever new* – before all this lust for territory and hugeness. They stole that Arqual out from under our noses a long time ago, in my granddad's day, maybe. If it ever existed, that is. By the Blessed Tree, I always thought it *once* had. But after what I've seen aboard *Chathrand* I don't know what to think.'

Hercól gave a rueful smile. 'It existed,' he said. 'But not in your grandfather's time. Perhaps *his* grandfather saw its twilight, as a young man. Such talk must wait, however. We must concentrate on Thasha if we are to save her.'

'I just wish we could tell the admiral,' said Pazel, looking sombrely through the gate.

'Not a chance,' said Fiffengurt. 'Thasha said it herself: old Isiq would never have agreed.'

'Master Hercól,' said a voice behind them.

The friends fell quickly silent. A young man with a bright smile and handsome, chisel-jawed features was standing a few paces away, hands folded. He was dressed smartly, dark vest over white shirt, billowed sleeves held snug at the wrists with cufflinks of polished brass: the uniform of a page or errand-runner for the well-to-do. He gave them a slight, ironic bow.

'What do you want, lad?' said Hercól. 'I don't know you.'

'Not know me?' said the youth, his voice amused. 'Does the leaf forget the tree that made it, or the tree the wooded mountain?'

Hercól froze at the words. Then he slowly turned to face the young man. The youth gave him a barely perceptible nod.

'Keep an eye out for Thasha,' said Hercól to the others. Then he took the young man by the elbow and moved swiftly away through the crowd. Pazel watched them cross a pebble-strewn path, around a trellis of scarlet flowers, and disappear towards a far corner of the garden.

To his surprise, Pazel felt a sudden, irrepressible desire to know what they were up to. Leaving Neeps protesting by the gate, he darted after Hercól and the youth. The rose bushes were tall and thick, and the guests were many, and it was several minutes before he spotted the pair – through the sun-dappled spray of the fountain, as it chanced.

Hercól was standing beside a pair of tall, fair women, wearing sky-blue gowns and circlets of silver in their hair. They were twin duchesses from Hercól's country; he had pointed them out to the tarboys just an hour before. The three were chatting quietly, sipping cups of hyacinth nectar. The Simjan youth was nowhere to be seen.

Pazel felt rather a fool – Hercól was making pleasantries, like everyone else. But when the sisters took their leave Hercól did not start back to the gate. Instead he turned very casually to face the juniper bushes. Pazel followed his gaze. And to his great surprise, he saw a face.

The junipers, he realised now, were arranged to hide a section of the iron fence around the gardens. The gaps were few and narrow. But framed in the largest, just beyond the fence, were the head and shoulders of an old but striking woman. She was tall and stern, grey eyes under a grey mane of hair, a face not so much wrinkled as creased with long thought. A royal face, Pazel thought, for he had been looking at royalty all morning; and yet there was something about this face that was like no other he had ever seen.

Her eyes met the Tholjassan's. Hercól kept very still, but it was like the stillness of a hunting hound tensed to spring. Then the woman drew a hood over her face and turned away. Pazel saw a pair of large, hard-faced men beside her, gripping her arms in the manner of bodyguards. An instant later she was gone.

'What in the Pits?' muttered Pazel.

A hand touched his elbow. It was Neeps, looking rather flustered. 'Where've you been?' he demanded. 'Thasha will be here any minute, and Pacu's throwing a first-class fit.'

'You won't believe what I just saw.'

'Try me,' said Neeps.

Before Pazel could say more, a voice cried shrilly: 'Here she comes now! Boys! Boys!'

Neeps sighed. 'Come on, before she calls out the marines.'

They hurried back to the gate. The fact that they were Thasha's best friends did not matter a fig to Pacu Lapadolma. To her they were just tarboys, born to serve their betters, and nothing short of marrying royalty themselves could change that.

She snapped her fingers at them. 'Get in position! You' – she pointed at Pazel – 'must straighten your coat, and your hat, and keep your hair out of sight if possible. And there is a rose petal stuck to your shoe.'

Pazel raked uselessly at his hair. They had already thought of a dozen choice insults for the general's daughter. Neeps for his part was only awaiting the end of the crisis to deliver them.

'Do you have the Blessing-Band?'

Pazel tapped his vest pocket, where the silk ribbon lay coiled. 'Nothing's happened to it since the last time you asked.'

The young woman might have snapped a retort had Thasha not appeared just then at the gate.

'Darling!' said Pacu, seizing her arm.

Thasha firmly detached the hand. 'The last person who called me 'darling' was poisoning my father, Pacu.'

'What a dreadful comparison, you heartless thing! Syrarys never meant the word, and I love you like a sister. But you're simply gorgeous, Thasha Isiq! Yes, a sister, that's the exact sensation in my heart!'

'You're an only child.'

Pacu rescued an orchid that was sliding free of Thasha's love-knot. She gave an inquisitive sniff, and her eyes widened. 'Have you put on some new perfume? Or is it your father's cologne?'

'Never mind that,' said Thasha quickly. 'Be an angel, Pacu. Fetch me a glass of water.'

When she had gone Thasha turned and looked at the tarboys. 'Darlings!' she said.

'Thasha,' said Pazel. 'You're swaying.'

'You'd be swaying too if you tipped left and right.'

Neeps' jaw dropped. 'Lord Rin,' he whispered. 'She's drunk.'

Pazel leaned closer, sniffing. 'Brandy! Oh Thasha, that was a bad idea.'

'Yes,' she said. 'It took me about half a minute to realise that. But I'm all right.'

Hercól returned, with Mr Fiffengurt at his side. 'The girl's been drinking,' Neeps informed them. 'Eat something, Thasha. Anything. Rose petals. Grass. Make yourself sick before—'

'Neeps,' said Pazel. 'She's not exactly falling down.'

'Ha!' said Thasha. 'Not yet.'

'Don't joke about *that*,' hissed Fiffengurt. 'You shouldn't have drunk a blary thing! Foolish, foolish, mistress!'

'That it certainly was,' said Hercól. 'More than any of us, you need your wits about you. But we must make the best of it now. Perhaps the drink will steady you for the ordeal to come. Hello, Admiral.'

Eberzam Isiq had arrived at the gate, quite winded. He waved at Thasha in distress. 'She has – I objected fiercely – but the fact is—'

'We noticed, Excellency,' said Pazel. 'Don't worry. Neeps and I will stay close to her.'

'He will worry,' said Thasha. 'And just wait – he's going to try once more to tell us all what to do, even though he has no idea and will have to make up some useless flimflam on the spot. He's an old buffoon.'

'No he's not,' said Pazel, startling everyone. 'Leave off baiting him, won't you? Think of what Ramachni said: we're a clan, like Diadrelu's clan, and we have to work together.'

'Dri's clan took her title away,' said Thasha.

'And we are humans, not ixchel,' said Hercól. 'There are worthier comparisons. But Pazel speaks a vital truth. Our enemies bicker; we must not, for whatever advantage we may have can be lost in a heartbeat.'

At that moment King Oshiram spotted Thasha and her father. He gestured to his guard captain, who sounded a note on a boar's-tusk hunting-horn: the signal for the march to the shrine. The dignitaries rose and hurried to their places. Thasha looked Pazel swiftly in the eye. It was an involuntary look, a reflex. It was the first time since daybreak that he had glimpsed her fear.

The road to the Mzithrini shrine stretched for a gentle mile, but some of the older dukes and bishwas had not walked so far in years (or their whole lives, in some cases); and the Templar monks at the head of the procession were much given to their gongs, and stopped dead for their ritual beatings; and the Boy Prince of Fuln was stung by a wasp; and goats defiled the road, leading to an ablutionary summit of all the attendant holy men. So it was that a walk the young people might have finished in half an hour stretched to thrice that time and more.

Treaty Day was a holiday, naturally. From all over Simja the common folk had come, and from neighbouring islands, and well beyond. At first light they had rushed to the city square to watch the Rite of the Firelords, in which masked figures representing the Night Gods were driven back to their dark kingdom by dancers with torches, who then proclaimed Simjalla ready to receive the bride. Later when Thasha approached the Cactus Gardens, the crowd stretched far ahead of her, and so again when she left the city by the North Gate.

Everyone who had entered the city seemed to have raced out of it again, eager for another glimpse of the procession. Beyond the wall the land was mostly field and heath, but wherever a barn or goat-shed or granary abutted the road it was covered with well-wishers, crammed in the windows and on the rooftops. Others had scaled the stormbreak pines that rose in a thin stand halfway between the city and the shrine.

But most simply swarmed alongside. They could draw only so near: the king had caused a chain to be stretched waist-high on either side of the road, and the palace guard saw to it that the crowd stayed on the outside. But there were exceptions. Those especially favoured by King Oshiram had the freedom of the road. So did certain musicians, city elders, the rich and their voluminous families, children in school uniform, and a few dozen others whose form of distinction no one could recall.

In the last category was the same pale young man who had conducted Hercól to his meeting with the woman behind the fence. He was alone as before, although he greeted certain of the wealthier citizens with a bow. He trotted along quite close to Thasha's inner circle, hands in pockets, and now and then glanced at them sharply with a bright, knowing smile. His expression suggested a great desire to please. But he unsettled the wedding party, for none of them knew why he was there.

'If he smiles at me again I'll throw a rock at him,' growled Neeps.

'You do that,' said Pazel.

'Don't you dare, Undrabust!' said Fiffengurt. 'You stand for your birth country, and must do proud by her. But what do you suppose that hoppity-smiley fellow wants? It's blary plain he wants something. Each time I think he's about to speak he runs off again. And now there's a dog!'

For there was a dog: a little white creature with a corkscrew tail, dashing through the legs of the guard (to the king's great amusement), darting ahead of the monks, spinning on its hind legs before them all, yipping once, and vanishing into the throng.

The guests roared. 'Jolly old Simja! What next?' cried an Ipulian count.

Thasha and her friends did not laugh. They all knew the dog. It belonged to the sorcerer, Arunis.

'That cur's woken, I'd bet my beard,' hissed Fiffengurt. 'I reckon Arunis sent it to remind us that he's watching our every move.'

'It never speaks, though,' said Pazel. 'Arunis said it hadn't woken *yet* – as if he expected it to, one day. But it's a nasty little brute, woken or not. We'd never have been taken prisoner back in the Crab Fens if it weren't for that dog.'

'There are woken beasts cropping up everywhere,' said Neeps. 'Do you know what the tailors who dressed us this morning were gossiping about, Mr Fiffengurt? A rabbit. A little brown hare who screamed "Mercy! Mama! Mercy!" as it ran, until the hounds caught up and killed it. And I swear I heard one of those messenger birds talking back to his rider.'

'And two woken rats on the *Chathrand*,' said Pazel. 'And Ott's falcon, Niriviel. Five animals in three months. Five more than I'd met in my lifetime to this point.'

'Or I in mine,' said Hercól, 'except for Ott's bird. That poor creature I have known for years.'

'Something's happening to the world,' said Thasha with conviction, 'and all these wakings are a part of it. And so is Arunis.'

Pazel looked at Hercól with alarm. 'Could he literally be *causing* it all?'

'No,' said Hercól. 'He is mighty, but not so mighty that he can light the flame of reason in creatures from one end of Alifros to another. If that were the case he should hardly need such servants as a prancing dog, or a washed-up smuggler like Mr Druffle. Besides, why should he wish for beasts to wake? Arunis dreams of enslaving this world, and nothing is so inimical to slavery as a thinking mind.'

'I'm a part of it too,' said Thasha, 'and the Nilstone is a part of me.'

'You're drunk,' said Neeps.

Thasha shook her head, then turned and glanced over her shoulder. 'He's close, you know.'

The others were startled. Neeps, feigning a stone in his shoe, stepped to one side of the procession and bent down. A moment later he caught up with them. 'She's right,' he said. 'Arunis is *very* close. Uskins is with him, looking scared out of his mind. And Dr Chadfallow's between them, talking.'

'Damn him,' whispered Pazel.

The remark did not escape Hercól. 'The doctor did not choose his walking companions,' he said. 'Rose provided a list to the Mistress of Ceremonies, and she decided who should stand with whom.'

'That doesn't mean he has to talk.'

'Nor does talk mean he is betraying us.'

'Let's not argue about the doctor,' said Fiffengurt. 'He's lost your trust, and that's the end of that. You've got a mighty task before you as well today, Pathkendle.'

'One you ought to let me help with,' said Neeps sulkily.

'Those debates are behind us,' said Hercól. 'Look: we are almost to the shrine.'

Indeed they were climbing the last little rise. The broad, whitewashed structure loomed before them, and the jade-green dome of the Declarion shone brilliant in the sun. On the broad stairs hundreds of figures, in robes of white and black, waited in silence.

'Thasha,' whispered Pazel with sudden urgency. 'Let me hear your vows.'

She looked at him blankly.

'You know,' said Pazel. 'Your *vows*.'

'Oh. My vows.' She pushed a drooping orchid from her face. Then, leaning close, she rasped out a string of wet Mzithrini words. The smell of brandy notwithstanding, Pazel was relieved.

'Almost,' he said. 'But for the love of Rin don't leave out the *r* in *uspris*. You want to call Falmurqat "my prince," not "my little duckling."'

'Hercól Stanapeth,' said a sudden voice behind them.

It was the pale young man from the gardens again. Hercól turned and looked at him.

'Well, lad?'

Again, that shallow, ironic bow. Then the young man fell in beside them and pulled a small envelope from his pocket. 'A gentleman stopped me at the gate, sir, and bade me deliver this to your hand.'

The young man was looking at Thasha, who returned his gaze warily. Hercól snatched the envelope. It was sealed with oxblood wax, and bore no writing. Hercól made no move to open it.

'What is your name, lad, and who is this gentleman?'

'I am Greysan Fulbreech, sir. King's clerk, though my term of employment is coming to an end. As for the gentleman, I did not ask his name. He was well dressed, and he gave me a coin.' He was still looking at Thasha. 'This message, however, I would have delivered free of charge.'

Pazel was finding it hard not to dislike this clerk. 'I'm sure King Oshiram's keeping you *very* busy,' he said.

'I don't get a moment's rest,' said Fulbreech, not sparing him a glance.

'Then be on your way,' growled Fiffengurt, 'unless you've more to tell us?'

The young man looked at Fiffengurt, and for a moment his smooth demeanour failed him, as though he were struggling to reach some decision. At last he took a deep breath and nodded. 'I bear another message,' he said. 'Master Hercól, she on whose answer you wait has decided. This winter there shall be fire in the hearth.'

Fulbreech stole a last glance at Thasha, and left without another word.

Only Thasha, who had known Hercól all her life, saw the shock he disguised so well. *A code*, she thought, *but who could be sending coded messages to Hercól?* She did not bother to ask for an explanation, and was glad to see the tarboys keeping silent as well. Hercól would explain nothing until he judged the moment right.

But Fiffengurt could not restrain himself. 'What in the bower of the Blessed Tree was *that* all about?'

'Very little, maybe,' said Hercól. 'Or perhaps the whole fate of your Empire. How does the rhyme, go, Quartermaster? *Arqual, Arqual, just and true?* We shall see.'

He would say no more, but in his voice was a happiness Thasha had not heard in years. Then he opened the little envelope, glanced at the single line of writing it contained, and the joy vanished like a snuffed match.

He put the envelope in his pocket. 'Greetings from the Secret Fist,' he said. 'They are watching us. As if there could be any doubt.'

The Father stood atop a staircase of great stone ovals, before the central arch of the shrine. His arms were spread as if in welcome, or perhaps to hold back the procession. Here in the sunshine his great age was more apparent, and so was his unnatural vigour. His raiment was black, and the white beard against it was like a snowdrift on a hill of coal. In his right hand he clasped a sceptre: pure gold but for a crystal set at the top, within which some dark object glittered.

His aspirants stood below him, three to a side (*Look at them*, people whispered, *they're sfvantskors, they can kill you with their eyes shut*). Like their master they wore black, but their faces were young: faces of men and women barely out of their teens. Symbols for birthplace and tribe gleamed in red tattoos upon their necks. Those nearest the Father wore white masks – ghostly against the sable robes. A seventh knelt just before the Father with a silver knife across his lap.

On the steps below the aspirants stood rows of women – a hundred or more, old and young, light and dark. Below these stood as many men, holding strange glass pipes of many colours, each one dangling from a braided thong.

Like a wave about a sandcastle the crowd engulfed the shrine, blanketing the low hills on either side of the road. A hush had fallen over them: the old man's stillness had erased all sense of a carnival from the proceedings. Toil and wind, hard stone, cold seas: these were what they saw in his unblinking eyes.

'I am nameless,' he said, and his voice carried a surprising distance. 'My holy office is my fate: there is nothing more. I am Father-Resident of Babqri City, Master of the Citadel of Hing, Confessor to His Serene

Majesty King Somolar. I am the sworn foe of things evil, for ever.

'Two thousand years ago the shrines of the Old Faith stood on every isle of this archipelago, and the Gátri-Mangol, the White Kings of Mangland, presided over an age of wealth and order. Here where we are gathered rose one of the most beautiful shrines of all, destroyed by the rising sea in the Worldstorm. Twenty-six years ago I sent a letter to a monarch, new to his throne but wise beyond his years, and begged a great favour, and he granted it. We of the Faith bow before thee, Oshiram of Simja, first king of these isles to allow the rebuilding of a Mzithrin house of prayer.'

And with that the Father descended to his knees, placed the sceptre with infinite care before him, and bent his forehead to the ground.

The king fidgeted, cleared his throat. 'You're welcome, Father, very welcome. Now do rise.'

Slowly the Father took his feet.

'This house is young, but its founding-stones were recovered from the old shrine, and they are sacred. Therefore will I take my place beneath the great arch and bar the path to those whom devils claim. They may not enter here. Let them fear the attempt.'

He raised the sceptre high, and the sun gleamed on the crystal at its tip, but the dark heart was not illuminated. Then with a last fierce look he turned and marched into the shadows.

'Oh happy day,' muttered Neeps.

Thasha elbowed him. 'His sceptre,' she whispered. 'There's a drawing of it in the *Polylex*, or of one just like it. Something blary special, it was. Oh, what was its name?'

Pazel sighed. Thasha owned a copy of the most dangerous book ever written: the forbidden thirteenth edition of *The Merchant's Polylex*, the mere possession of which was punishable by death. Earlier editions, and later ones, were to be found in every ship's library and seamen's club; they were simply huge (and untrustworthy) one-volume encyclopedias. The thirteenth, however, was crammed with the darkest secrets of the Arquali Empire. But the book was more frustrating than useful, for the author had hidden those secrets in over five thousand pages of rumour and hearsay and outright myth. It was a wonder that Thasha found *anything* within its pages. The priest's sceptre, now—

A terrible thought came to him suddenly. He gripped Thasha's arm.

'What if he's a mage?' he said, looking from one face to another. 'What if he *can* keep evil from entering the shrine? *All* evil?'

Neeps and Fiffengurt paled. Even Hercól looked alarmed. Thasha seemed to have trouble catching her breath.

'In that case . . .' she stammered. 'Well. In that case—'

She was interrupted by a burst of song from the Mzithrini women. It was a frightful sound, nearly a shriek. At the same moment the men raised their glass pipes and began to whirl them overhead by the straps, faster and faster, until they became mere blurs of colour in the sunlight. Astonishingly, although their orbits criss-crossed endlessly, the pipes never collided. And from them came a hundred eerie notes, high otherworldly howls, like wolves in caves of ice. It was the summons to the bride.

Thasha turned and looked back at her father. Isiq raised a trembling hand, but she was too far ahead of him to touch. She looked at each friend in turn, and longest at Pazel, who was fighting an impulse to shout, *Don't go in there*. Then she left her entourage and walked quickly to the steps.

The men fell back, still whirling their pipes, and so did the chorus of wailing women. And as Thasha climbed the stair a new figure emerged from the shrine. He looked to be in his thirties, nimble and straight, with a martial air about him: indeed he wore a kind of dark dress uniform, with a red sun pendant on his chest.

'Prince Falmurqat the Younger,' said Hercól.

'He's not young enough if you ask me,' growled Fiffengurt.

'A capable officer, according to Chadfallow's informants,' Hercól continued, 'but a reluctant one. Above all things his father desired a soldier-son, but until the Treaty raised the prospect of ending the long war, the son refused to have anything to do with the military. I gather he paints quite beautifully.'

'You're a lucky girl, Thasha,' said Pazel.

'And you're an idiot,' she said.

Behind the man came his parents, Falmurqat the Elder and his grey princess, and with them another Mzithrini holy man. This one was old, but not as old as the Father, and dressed not in black but a deep blood red.

Thasha and the prince met exactly as planned, on the step below the boy with the silver knife. The singing ceased; the men stopped their whirling display. Thasha looked utterly serene, now: she might have just climbed the steps of her own house on Maj Hill in Etherhorde. Without a word she lifted the knife from the boy's knees, turned and raised it to the watching thousands, and replaced it. Then she curtseyed before her prince, and he bowed in turn.

Thasha held out her hand, palm upwards and the prince studied it for a moment, smiling curiously. He spoke a few words in a voice meant for Thasha alone. Then he took up the knife and pricked her thumb.

Instantly the red-robed cleric held out a small clay cup. Thasha let seven drops of blood fall into the milk it contained. The cleric swished it seven times. And laughed – a deep, almost manic laugh. He raised the cup high.

'Mzithrin!' he boomed. 'The Grand Family! Brothers and sisters of Alifros, learn but this one word in our tongue and you learn the essence of the Old Faith. None stand alone! None are worthless, none sacrificed or surrendered, every soul has a destiny and every destiny is a note in the music of the several worlds. Before us stands Thasha Isiq, daughter of Eberzam and Clorisuela. What is to be the destiny of the Treaty Bride? I look into this milk and cannot see the gift of her blood. Has it ceased to exist? Only a simpleton could think so – only a heretic or a fool! So I ask you: can it be the fate of Thasha Isiq to vanish, dissolved in our gigantic land?

'We of the Old Faith do not believe it. The blessed milk in my cup has not destroyed her blood. No, her blood has changed the milk, irreversibly and for ever. The milk we tint red is a bond and a vow. Drinking it, *we* are changed: a part of this daughter of Arqual enters us, and remains. Blessings on your courage, Thasha Isiq! Blessings on our prince! Blessings on Mighty Arqual and the Holy Mzithrin, and all lands between! Blessings on the Great Peace to come!'

The crowd erupted. All that had been said until this moment left them confused, but they knew what peace was, and their cry was a surging roar of hope and excitement and remembered loss. Beaming, King Oshiram looked at his new ambassador. *Smile, Isiq! One would think you were at an execution, you queer old fellow.*

'But the time to drink is still a moment off,' shouted the red-robed cleric, over the lasting cheers. 'Enter now, Thasha of Arqual, and be wed.'

4

A Sacrifice

—◦◦◦—

Seven thousand candles lit the shrine's interior: green candles with a sharp camphor scent. The place was smaller than Pazel had imagined. When the king's retinue, the foreign royals and dignitaries and Templar monks were all seated on the little stools brought in for the occasion, and the Mzithrinis (who considered chairs unnecessary, but not unholy) were seated cross-legged on the floor, there was scarcely room for the wedding party itself.

But squeeze in they did. Thasha and the prince stood on a granite dais; their families and closest friends stood below them in a semicircle. All save Pazel: as the holder of the Blessing-Band he merited a place on the dais, where he could tie the ribbon to Thasha's arm at the required moment.

One way or another, of course, that moment would never arrive.

The last of the invited guests were still filing in past the Father, who glared like a fury, now and then making threatening bobs with his sceptre. The guests, all cultured and important people, were not so awed by the man as the great throng outside. Some hurried past him with a shudder. A few rolled their eyes.

Last of all came Arunis. Pazel held his breath. The sorcerer looked exactly like what they had all taken him for – a thickset merchant, rich and rather tasteless, dressed in dark robes as expensive as they were neglected. He wore a little self-mocking smile, and kept his pudgy hands folded before him like a schoolboy. Less than a day had passed since those hands had worked spells of murder aboard the *Chathrand*.

'*Kela-we ghöthal! Stop!*'

The Father brought his sceptre down like a nightstick, square against the mage's chest. Arunis halted, blinking at him. Pazel saw Thasha glance up in fear. The Father was chanting in a rage: Pazel heard something about a devil's chain and a Pit of Woe. *Aya Rin*, he thought helplessly, *this can't be happening.*

Every eye in the shrine focused on the two men. Arunis smiled timidly, like an obliging citizen at a military checkpoint. He made a wobble with his head, as folk of Opalt do when they wish to show either goodwill or confusion, or both. The Father answered with a growl.

Arunis dropped his head. He shrugged, his lower lip trembling, and even those who knew better saw him for an instant as a good soul, one used to being last in line, one who had never dreamed he would be lucky enough to witness history in the making but who even now would give it up rather than cause any trouble. He turned to go. But as he did so he glanced once more at the Father.

Their gazes locked. Arunis' cold eyes glittered. Then quite suddenly the Father's ferocious glare went dull. Like an automaton he took the sceptre from Arunis' chest and stepped back, waving him through the arch. Smiling, the mage scurried inside.

Pazel closed his eyes. *If he had been turned away! Oh, Thasha! We thought of everything but that!*

He was so relieved that he barely noticed the ceremony itself – the monks' recitation of the Ninety Rules, the song of the Tree of Heaven, some baffling Simjan custom involving an exchange of horsehair dolls. But he noticed other things. Prince Falmurqat was smiling genuinely at Thasha – the poor dupe. And the Father, who had come forward into the shrine, seemed to have recovered both his hawklike gaze and his wrath. But he never directed these at Arunis – indeed, he seemed to have forgotten the man altogether.

Stranger still, one of the aspirants beside the Father kept turning to look at Pazel himself. It was one of the mask-wearers – man or woman Pazel could not tell. And of course he did not know if the gaze was kindly or cruel, or merely curious. But why should a young *sfvantskor* be curious about him?

Then he caught Thasha's eye, and saw her courage and clarity, and even a hint of the mischief that was hers alone in all the wide world. And suddenly his fear for her leaped out, like a predator from the grass, and he could think of nothing else. *Stop it, stop the ceremony, get her out of here!*

It was time: Thasha and her groom were kneeling down on the stone. Once more the cleric raised the knife and cup. Falmurqat held out his thumb, and seven drops of his blood were added to the milk already tinted with Thasha's own.

'Drink now,' said the cleric, 'that our fates be mingled, nevermore to be unbound.'

He sipped, and handed the cup to Falmurqat the Elder. The cup made its way around the dais, everyone taking a tiny sip. But when Pazel's turn came, he froze – furious, horrified, his brain on fire. The cleric prodded him, whispering: '*Drink, you must drink.*' The Mzithrinis stared with the beginnings of outrage. Thasha flashed him a last look, impossibly fearless. He drank.

The guests breathed a collective sigh, and the cup moved on. Pazel took the Blessing-Band from his pocket and held it in plain view. Thasha and her betrothed drank last. The cleric took the cup again.

'Now, beloved Prince. What would you avow?'

Prince Falmurqat took Thasha's hand, and stroked it ever so gently with his thumb. He was about to speak when Thasha wrenched her hand away.

'Your Highness, forgive me. I cannot wed you. This marriage is a *tr—*'

She got no further. At the back of the congregation Arunis made a furtive gesture. The lethal necklace tightened. Thasha reeled, clutching at her throat.

Pazel dropped the ribbon and lunged to catch her. Pacu Lapadolma screamed. Eberzam Isiq leaped onto the dais, shouting his daughter's name. The cleric dropped the sacred milk.

Pazel held her to his chest, hating himself, hating the world. *No answer but this one. No other door to try.* He whispered to her, kissed her ear. Falmurqat watched in speechless horror. Thasha writhed and twisted, her face darkening with every beat of her heart.

'Away! Give her air!' Dr Chadfallow was battling forwards. Behind him, wrathful and suspicious, came the sorcerer.

Thasha's struggles grew so violent that Pazel almost lost hold of her. He was flat on his back, arms locked desperately around her chest, face buried in her shoulder. Then all at once her struggles ended. Her eyes widened in amazement, then dimmed, and her head fell back with an audible thump against the stone.

Pazel surged upright, raising her, choking on his tears. 'You Pit-damned devil!' he shouted. 'You killed her this time!'

None knew who he was accusing – the boy was clearly hysterical – but from the gaping crowd Arunis babbled in protest.

'Not I! Not with that little squeeze! Look for yourselves! The chain is loose!'

Few heeded the raving merchant from Opalt (by now everyone was shouting something), but to Thasha's friends his words meant just what they had prayed for: an instant when the very power that had laid the curse was consciously holding it at bay. Pazel's hand shot out, caught the necklace and snapped it with one brutal wrench. The silver sea-creatures Isiq had had fashioned for Thasha's mother – naiads and anemones, starfish, eels – flew in all directions. The necklace was destroyed.

But Thasha lay perfectly still.

Pazel spoke her name again and again. Dr Chadfallow felt her bloodied neck, then bent an ear swiftly to her chest. A look of pain creased the surgeon's face, and he closed his eyes.

Utter pandemonium broke out.

'No heartbeat! No heartbeat!' The cry swept the shrine. Already guests were spilling out through the arches, taking news of the disaster with them. A vast howl rose from the mob outside.

'Annulled!' shouted the Father, raising both his sceptre and the ceremonial knife. 'Without a marriage the Treaty of Simja is annulled! There is no peace between the Mzithrin and cannibal Arqual! I saw death, did I not tell you, children?'

'There *must* be peace, there must!'

'There won't be!'

'We'll be killed! They'll punish Simja for sure!'

'Death! Death!' screamed the Father.

'Get that blade out of his hands!' shouted King Oshiram.

'Where is the monster?' bellowed Isiq. 'Where is he, where's the fiend who slew my Thasha?'

But Arunis was nowhere to be seen.

Falmurqat the Elder took his son by the arm. 'Let us away!' he said bitterly. 'This is all a deception, and an old one at that. To marry off a convulsive, one not long for the world, and thus to shame the enemy when she expires.'

'Hush, Illoch, what nonsense!' cried his wife.

But the old prince paid no heed. 'Some of us read history,' he said. 'Huspal of Nohirin married a girl from the Rhizans. She died of seizures in a month, and the Mzithrin took the blame. This pig admiral must have counted on his girl lasting a bit longer, that's all.'

Pazel thought the worst had come. Isiq would fly at the man; the insults would reverberate beyond the shrine, beyond Simja; in hours or days there would be sea-battles, by week's end a war. But Isiq did not react at all, and with immense relief Pazel realised that the older prince had used his native tongue. But what if that changed?

Switching to Tholjassan, he looked up at Hercól.

'We've got to get her out of here *now*.'

Hercól nodded. 'Come, Eberzam! We must do as Thasha would wish, and bear her to the *Chathrand*. A proper burial at home in Etherhorde must be hers.'

'But it's months, months away,' Isiq wept. 'Her body will not last.'

'There are remedies,' said Chadfallow quietly.

Isiq turned on him savagely. 'Want to pickle my daughter like a herring, do you? False friend that you are! Never again shall *you* touch one of mine!'

'Steady, Isiq, he's a doctor,' said the king.

'What do you know of him?' roared Isiq, making the crowd gasp anew. 'Fatuous fool! What do you know of *any of this*? Puppets on strings, that is all I see around me! Little helpless dolls, twitching, dancing to the hurdy-gurdy.'

New gasps from the onlookers. 'Do not touch him!' shouted Oshiram, for the guards were already starting for Isiq. No tragedy could excuse such words to a sovereign, in his own realm and before his peers; men had been executed for less. Only the king himself could pardon Isiq, as everyone present knew.

'But she *must* go to Etherhorde,' wept Pacu Lapadolma.

'Indeed she must, your Excellency,' said one of the Templar monks. 'Only this morning she put it in writing, when we inscribed her name in the city register: "Though my body rot in transit, let me be buried at my mother's side on Maj Hill." She was *quite* insistent on that point.'

To this Isiq made no rebuttal. Someone spread a cloak upon the floor. Gaping, the admiral watched Hercól lift Thasha's body and place her on the cloth.

Pazel felt a hand on his elbow. He turned, and to his amazement found himself face to face with the *sfvantskor* he had caught stealing glances at him during the ceremony. Below the white mask the lips trembled slightly.

'The Father was right. There's evil on your ship. Are you part of it?'

It was the voice of a young woman, speaking broken Arquali, and whispering oddly as though trying to disguise her voice. Nonetheless Pazel felt certain he had heard it before.

'Who are you?' he demanded.

'Turn away before it's too late. You'll never belong among those who belong.'

'*What did you say?*'

She made no answer, only turned her back and fled, and then Neeps was tugging at his arm.

'Wake up, mate! It's time to go!'

Pazel's mind was in a whirl, but he knew Neeps was right. Bending, he seized a corner of the cloak on which Thasha lay. Hercól, Neeps and Fiffengurt already had their corners. Together they lifted her body, and amidst fresh wails from the onlookers bore her down the aisle and out through the arch.

The sun blinded them. Isiq followed on their heels, weeping: 'For naught, for naught! My morning star—'

Before they reached the bottom step they heard King Oshiram above them, ordering his guards to form a phalanx before the corpse-bearers. 'To the ship! Drive a wedge if necessary! Let no one hinder them in their grief!'

The palace guard did as they were told, and the stricken mob fell back as the men and tarboys rushed Thasha back towards the city. Most were too shocked even to give pursuit. Pazel knew their paralysis would not last, however. And what then? *The crowd may go mad*, Hercól had warned them. *It can happen, when the world seems poised to collapse.* Would there be a revolt? Would they try to seize her body, steal a piece of her garment or a fistful of hair, bury her with the martyrs of Simja?

The others might have had similar thoughts, for all four ran as quickly as they could. When Pazel glanced back he saw that the admiral was falling behind.

'Do not wait!' Isiq shouted, waving him on. 'All speed, Pathkendle! Protect her!'

Affection as well as grief in the old warrior's voice. Pazel raised a hand to him – he meant it as a promise, though it looked like a farewell – and staggered on.

When he was six years old, Pazel's mother disappeared. It was his first taste of terror, of the possibility of wounding loss, and he never forgot it, although his mother returned in just a week.

A sentry on the city wall had watched her departure – men were always watching Suthinia Pathkendle – all the way to Black Stag Road, where she turned east towards the valley of the Cinderling. The neighbours relayed this news to Captain Gregory Pathkendle with their usual blend of sympathy and scorn. The Cinderling was an old battlefield, left for dead after the Second Sea War, and still a place of bandits and beggars and unmarked graves. The neighbours had sighed and clicked their tongues. Only Suthinia, they said.

Pazel's sister had taken the news with a shrug and a laugh; she was determined not to care. Captain Gregory had just rolled his eyes. 'She'll be back,' he said. 'This isn't the first time, but we can hope it's the last.' Pazel had waited for his mother in silence, too frightened for tears.

As it happened Gregory was right on both counts. Suthinia came back, sunburned and road-filthy but otherwise unharmed. Nor did she ever vanish again — until the Arquali invasion, when every beautiful woman in Ormael vanished, mostly into Imperial hands. No, Suthinia stayed put, because a few months after that mysterious week Gregory himself sailed out of Ormaelport, never to return. To make matters worse, Captain Gregory's sister, who had helped out often with the children, picked that spring to elope to Étrej with a fallen monk. Suthinia, never the most attentive mother, was suddenly on her own.

Pazel liked to think he'd not added to her worries. His father had declared him bright. Dr Chadfallow, their illustrious family friend, had challenged him to become trilingual before his ninth birthday, and he was well on his way. Pazel wanted to sail like Gregory, but once he opened the grammar books Ignus provided, he somehow had a hard time putting them down.

Neda was eleven and at war with everything. She hated her father for abandoning them, Suthinia for giving him reasons to, Chadfallow for not talking him out of it and Pazel for not hating the others with her own intensity. To top it all, her mother and Chadfallow were becoming close. This, she told a mystified Pazel, was a betrayal of the father who had betrayed them.

Pazel just wished everyone would shut up. He loved them, despite a growing fear that they were all insane. Or rather all but Chadfallow — he was a gift from the Good Lord Rin. He had travelled the world; he could speak of medicine and history, wars and animals and earthquakes and ghosts. And in those days he still laughed, once in a long while, and the sound always surprised Pazel with its unguarded joy.

Years went by, and their mother's peculiarities deepened. She locked herself away with books, scaled the roof in thunderstorms, gave Pazel syrups designed to loosen his bowels and then studied the results with a long-handled spoon.

Then came the day of the custard apples. From dawn to dusk, Suthinia had forced a gruel made of the strange fruit on her children, although one sip told them that the drink was dangerous: In fact it proved both poisonous and enchanted. After a month-long coma, Pazel had awoken with his Gift, Neda with her anger at Suthinia redoubled.

Their mother had become a witch. Or stopped hiding the fact. Either way it made her odder and more dangerous. She stopped bathing, and neglected to cook. When Neda moved out it took Suthinia three days to notice that she was gone.

Later that year Mzithrini warships had begun raiding the Chereste coast. The mayor of Ormael turned to Chadfallow, Arqual's Special Envoy, and begged for Imperial protection. Pazel learned another reason to adore Chadfallow: he was the Man With the Emperor's Ear.

One day Captain Gregory's ship was spotted near Ormael, with Gregory himself at her wheel: but now the ship was flying the colours of the Mzithrin. Gregory was at once renamed Pathkendle the Traitor, and Pazel's family shared in his disgrace. The neighbours looked through them; Pazel's friends discovered that they had never really liked him at all. Neda, who had taken work on a goat farm, paid them brief, resentful visits, leaving gifts of sour cheese, but she never again spent a night under Suthinia's roof.

Only Chadfallow was unchanged. He still came to dinner – brought dinner, usually, for Suthinia was all but destitute – and drilled Pazel in Arquali for an hour. He was the best thing that could have happened to a traitor's son. Until he became the worst.

The night before the invasion – about which Chadfallow had breathed not a word – Pazel had found himself seated beside the doctor, under Neda's orange tree, assembling a kite. Pazel could not recall much of what they talked about (his mind was on the doctor's present more than his words) but the last part of the conversation he would never forget.

'Ignus, where did my mother go? That time she ran away.'

'You should ask her, my boy.'

Pazel said nothing; they both knew he had asked a thousand times.

'Well,' said the doctor reluctantly, 'let us say that she went to be with her own people awhile.'

'My father never came back. What if she hadn't either?'

'She came back. You're her son and she loves you.'

'What if she hadn't?'

Pazel's question was a plea. As if he could already sense them, somehow: the fire and the death shrieks, the enslavements, the notion of rape, the battle axe history was about to take to his world.

Chadfallow looked at him squarely. Lowering his voice, he said, 'If she had not returned I would have taken you to Etherhorde, and made a proper Arquali of you, and sent you to a proper school. One of the three High Academies, to be sure. And when you graduated, you would not have received a pat on the head, but a line of your own in the Endless Scroll, which the Young Scholars of the Imperium have signed for eight centuries. And you should have had friends who loved you for your cleverness instead of being jealous of it. And though you may not believe me, in a few years you would have forgotten these dullards and jackanapes, and been at home as never before.'

Pazel was dumbstruck. He couldn't possibly deserve all that. Chadfallow looked at him, almost smirking – until Suthinia appeared from nowhere, pushed the doctor back in his chair, and smacked him hard.

'You'll take him when they *bury* me, Ignus,' she said. Then she grabbed Pazel by the arm and marched him into the house.

'Mother, Mother,' Pazel said as they rushed up the stairs. 'He meant if I was *alone*, if something happened to you. Let go. You don't understand.'

'I understand more than you think,' she snapped.

She was hurting his arm. 'You're an animal,' he shouted, inspired. 'I wish you *had* stayed away. I want to go with him to Etherhorde.'

She dragged him into the washroom, thrust him before the mirror. 'Look at your skin. In Etherhorde they'd take you for a tarboy, or a slave.'

He bellowed right back at her: *'I'm not the colour of Ormalis either!'* Which was true, if just barely: he had a bit too much caramel in his complexion, and his hair was too brown.

Suthinia shrugged. 'You're close enough.'

'I look like you,' he sobbed. At that moment it was the worst insult that occurred to him. His mother began to laugh, which enraged him all the more. 'Etherhorde's a proper city,' he shouted. 'Ignus belongs there, and so could I, if you'd just leave me alone.'

She would leave him the very next day, and possibly for ever, but at that moment his words had a curious effect. Her laughter and her fury vanished, and she looked at him with a kind of sad wonder, as if she had only just understood what they were talking about.

'You couldn't belong there,' she said. 'We will never belong among those who belong. The best thing to do is to cobble together some tribe of outcasts, when you're old enough to find them.'

'But Ignus—'

'Ignus is a dreamer. He's thinking of some other boy, some life that might have been, if the world were very different. I don't care if you believe what I say. Just remember it, love, and decide for yourself who told the truth.'

Pazel stumbled, bashing Thasha with his shins. Her body was growing heavy. Fiffengurt was hobbling, favouring a knee.

'This blary guard's right on top of us,' he said in a low voice, glancing nervously at Pazel. 'You'll never be able to – you know.'

'Sure he will,' said Neeps. 'You didn't see us in the Crab Fens, with the Volpeks behind us. My mate here can run like a whiplash hound.'

Pazel smiled grimly. He had a stitch in his side. 'I'll lose them, don't worry,' he said.

'They may not even try to stop you,' said Hercól. But his voice was reluctant, as though something else entirely was worrying his thoughts.

Fiffengurt took no notice. 'I'll miss you, Pathkendle,' he said gruffly, 'damned troublemaker though you are.'

Pazel dropped his eyes. He would miss them too. For somewhere in the heart of the city he was going to slip away. He had to do it; even Hercól had agreed. There was a fight to be waged on the *Chathrand*, but there was another, just as vital, ashore: the fight to expose the conspiracy. No better chance would come than this one, with delegations from every land packed into Simjalla. And no better person existed for the job than Pazel. He had learned something from his Gift: when you spoke to people in their own language, they tended to listen. Pazel would speak the truth to everyone he met – servants, sailors, kings – until it was the talk of Simja, and no power on earth could suppress it.

'You won't be missing him long,' said Neeps vehemently. 'Just watch, he'll be aboard the *Chathrand* by nightfall.'

No one said anything to that. There was no telling what would become of Pazel, once he started speaking the truth. It was more likely that sunset would find him in some kitchen, cowering under the sink, or at the bottom of a laundry hamper, or in a temple belfry, hiding from the Secret Fist. And then only if he managed to win someone's trust. If he sounded not just clever, but sane.

They had carried Thasha as far as the stormbreak pines when the

Fulbreech youth reappeared. The palace guard warded him off at spear-point, until Hercól told them to let him approach.

'The lady Thasha is dead,' he said to Fulbreech. 'Send a carriage for her father – that is him on the road behind us – and find us at the docks, straight away. You and I must must speak again, Fulbreech.'

The youth stared at Thasha, wide-eyed. 'I shall fetch that carriage,' he said at last, and dashed ahead of them towards the city.

Pazel was burning to ask Hercól about Fulbreech. Who was he, why did he keep popping up? But the Tholjassan's face made it plain that he would breathe no word of explanation, at least not here in the presence of the guard.

Some minutes later they reached the city gate. Poor folk were busy here, filling sacks with isporelli petals to render into perfume. Thasha's body gave them a terrible shock. Old monks, too feeble for the march to the shrine, burst into shouts of *Aya Rin!* Children screamed; old women raised their arms to heaven and wept.

Straight through Simjalla they ran, a morbid reversal of the procession, and with every block the wails grew louder. Pazel was tensed, now, waiting for his chance to break away. But the chance did not come. The captain of the guard was following the king's instructions to the letter: his men ran ahead and behind the foursome and let no one approach. Pazel glanced beseechingly at Neeps, who frowned and shook his head.

As they neared the port the streets were lined with men and women, moaning in disbelief, flags of Arqual and the Mzithrin slipping forgotten from their hands. Pazel was growing desperate. Once they put him in a boat it would be too late.

They turned another corner. At the end of the block, Pazel could see masts and rigging and wooden hulls crowding the quay. 'Listen,' he whispered urgently to the others, 'I'm going, it's time.'

'Pazel, no!' hissed Neeps. 'Everybody and his brother's watching us!'

'So what? It's Thasha they're worried about.'

'This mob's crazy with grief,' said Fiffengurt. 'You run off now and someone's likely to chase you down and break your teeth with a brick.'

'They don't care about me,' Pazel insisted. 'I'm just a tarboy who happened to know her.'

Hercól too shook his head. 'You cannot go now, lad. We must find another way.'

Pazel looked from friend to friend. They were protecting him, even at the cost of disaster. Just as old Isiq would have done, if they'd tried to reason with him, explain the path Thasha had chosen.

Pazel did not look at her, fearing he would choke if he saw her pale, cold face. How had her last minutes been with Isiq? *You knew, didn't you, Thasha? A time comes when you just stop arguing.*

Seconds later he was leaping and shoving his way through startled onlookers, making for a sidestreet, running for all he was worth. The other three cried out, but they were still supporting Thasha and could not let her fall. Members of the guard hooted and jeered – 'Run, you bastard! Fair-weather friend!' – but as he'd expected, none gave chase. The sidestreet had been roped off during the procession, and it was not hard to see why. It was narrow and steep, twisting up a hill by way of many crumbling staircases. After the first bend he saw only a handful of people; after the second, none at all. Still he kept running, as though speed were the only way to make sure he went through with the plan. He thought: *Lose yourself. That life's finished. A new one has to begin.* True, Ramachni had said that their greatest strength lay in the family they'd built on the voyage to Simja. But families splintered, and Ramachni was gone – he had been, Pazel suddenly reflected, the very first one to leave.

He turned left into an even narrower street. Here at last he allowed himself to catch his breath. He was well away from the port and the mob of mourners. It was time to think about where he should be going.

Unconsciously he put his hand in his pocket. Something sheer and light met his fingers, and he drew it out. It was the Blessing-Band, the blue silk ribbon from Thasha's Lorg School. YE DEPART FOR A WORLD UNKNOWN, AND LOVE ALONE SHALL KEEP THEE. How had it gotten there? He could distinctly remember dropping it in the shrine.

Pazel looked down the street. Decrepit balconies, bright streamers of hanging laundry. Then he lowered his eyes and saw that someone had entered the street from the far end. It was a rider, seated on one of Simja's giant messenger birds. He stopped the bird with a sharp tug on its wing harness some thirty feet from Pazel, and stared openly at the boy.

A soft sound behind him. Pazel whirled and saw another man, afoot, leaning in a doorway that had been empty a moment before. He was dressed in humble Simjan work clothes, a street sweeper or a mason perhaps. But he looked at Pazel with the same intensity as the rider.

Pazel felt the danger in them at once. Impulsively he began to walk down the alley towards the rider, as though merely continuing on his way. The bird pranced and croaked, and then the rider moved into his path. He held up his hand for Pazel to stop.

'The grain in the fields is yellow, but?' he said.

'I b-beg your – ?'

'That is the wrong answer.'

The man spurred his mount towards Pazel, and the bird lowered its head and struck him a blow like a blunt axe to the chest. Pazel staggered, his breath knocked out of him. The man in work clothes was strolling towards him, grinning. The rider turned the messenger bird again, and Pazel saw a long steel nail protruding from the toe of his boot. Pazel leaped sidelong as the man lashed out. The nail missed by inches. Cursing, the man began to dismount.

Then his head shot up. Pazel turned and saw Hercól leap into the air like a dancer, feint with his right leg, and deliver a lightning strike with the left that felled the man in work clothes like a puppet whose strings have snapped.

The moment he touched the ground Hercól was sprinting for Pazel. The rider hauled his bird about, kicking savagely with his heels. With a deep croak the bird bore him away.

Hercól seized Pazel by the chin. 'All right?' he said.

'I think so. *Ouch!*' He put a hand to his chest.

'You'll be sore for a fortnight, if it was that *fenneg* bird that struck you.' He shook his head. 'Why didn't you listen, Pazel? I told you not to go through with it.'

'I thought you were just trying to protect me,' said Pazel.

'So I was! I saw the Secret Fist watching us from every third corner, the moment we entered the gates. Come quickly! When that rider sounds the alarm they'll fall on us in force.'

They ran back the way Pazel had come. The man Hercól had kicked lay still, his neck twisted at an unnatural angle. Pazel shut his eyes a moment, but he never forgot the man's look of shock, the gape of the bloodied mouth, the wide-open eyes. Like the faces of so many dead, he would glimpse it in dreams for years to come.

When they reached the port they had to fight their way through the crowd. Even in the short time he had been gone it had swollen, and its anxiety had increased. Some were literally weeping with fear. There would be war, another eternity of war; how had they ever let themselves hope it could end? Others vented their anguish on Pazel: '*Caught the little deserter! Good work! Always whip a ship-jumper, I say!*'

Hercól led him to a fishing pier, at the foot of which King Oshiram's men were holding back the crowd. They were let through, and Pazel saw Fiffengurt and Neeps standing beside Thasha's body at the end of the pier. Both were looking in the direction of the *Chathrand*, which loomed like a sea fortress three miles offshore.

Their faces lit up at the sight of Pazel. 'Welcome back, fool,' said Neeps.

Pazel didn't argue the point. 'What are we going to do now?' he said.

'First, get Thasha back to the *Chathrand*,' said Hercól. 'When that is done, we shall seek another way to reveal Arqual's plot to the world. A way that doesn't require tarboys to play cat and mouse with assassins.'

'That'll be a pleasant change,' said Neeps, watching the bay. 'Dancing devils! Why are those rowers so slow?'

'Because you're watching 'em,' said Fiffengurt.

Pazel paced the dock, trying not to look at the bundle at Hercól's feet. After an interminable wait the skiff reached the pier. The men at oars saw Thasha and began shouting at once: 'Who did it, Mr Fiffengurt? Who would lay a finger on her? Can we kill him, sir?'

Lowering Thasha into the boat was an undignified affair. The Babqri love-knot slipped, and her golden hair spilled onto the slimy floor. They could not stretch her out, and at last placed her feet on the bench between the rowers. Neeps tried to clean her hair on his trousers.

The sailors wept. Like most of the crew they had not cared much for the Treaty Bride at first. Noble-born passengers came and went, often greeting sailors, if at all, with a barely disguised sneer. The men returned the favour, and accounts of first-class ignorance, seasickness, fear of rats and fleas and bedbugs and general uselessness were traded like hard candies on the lower decks.

But they had not sneered long at Thasha Isiq. Rather than fine food or bleached petticoats she had wished for a chance to climb the masts or explore the black cavern of the hold. She was also a virtuoso swearer: a lifetime of eavesdropping on captains, commodores and other guests at her father's table had made her a walking scrapbook of naval curses. By the *Chathrand*'s first landfall men were boasting of her beauty, and when a rumour spread that she had flattened a pair of thuggish tarboys in a brawl, they had added ferocity to her list of virtues. She was 'a good 'un,' they decided, and there was no higher praise.

A sudden voice from the *Chathrand*: 'What is this, Quartermaster?'

It was Captain Rose. The red-bearded man was studying them with intense suspicion, his enormous hands gripping the rail. Beside him stood Lady Oggosk, his witch-seer, old eyes gleaming from beneath a faded shawl.

Before Fiffengurt could reply, Hercól shouted: 'This, Rose, is the end of your conspiracy – and what will concern you far less, the end of one nobler than certain minds can grasp.'

'I've seen enough of corpses. Bury that one in Simja, whoever he is.'

Hercól reached out and uncovered Thasha's face, now deathly grey.

'You would do well not to impede the return of Thasha to Etherhorde. His Supremacy will wish to pay his respects.'

'What, what?' cried Oggosk. 'The girl is dead?'

'I believe I just said that, Duchess.'

Rose did not stand in their way. Indeed he helped by clearing the deck of all but essential hands. Nonetheless as the lifeboat drew alongside the towering vessel, Pazel heard cries of anguish and disbelief. Oggosk's voice had carried: the news was already loose on the ship.

The davit-lines were made fast, and heave by heave the men of the watch hauled the lifeboat up the ship's flank.

'Line a casket with paraffin,' said Rose when they reached the topdeck. 'We'll send ashore for an embalmer.'

'Dr Chadfallow will do,' said Hercól.

Rose nodded. 'She was brave. I am saddened by this.'

Pazel looked at him with fury. *Liar.*

Across the deck men stood gaping, holding their caps. Lady Oggosk muttered a prayer. As they lifted Thasha from the boat, the witch suddenly put a hand on the girl's cold, colourless forehead. Oggosk's milk-blue eyes opened wide. She turned her gaze on Pazel, and for a moment he was transfixed. It was as if she could see right through him.

'What have you done?' she whispered.

With a great effort Pazel wrenched his gaze away. Oggosk stepped back, but Pazel seemed to feel her eyes drilling at a point between his shoulders as they crossed the endless topdeck, silent but for creaks of the rigging and the sighs of stricken men.

Demons of cruelty had sewn his wedding shoes.

Half a mile behind the bearers of Thasha's corpse, Admiral Isiq kicked the silk things into the roadside brush. At once he felt better. He had been no poor runner once – ages ago, before his first command – and the feel of dry, dung-laced earth on his bare feet summoned memories of Túram, the old Isiq homestead in the Westfirth, where his father had killed a marauding bear with just a hunting knife. He loosened his cravat. He was gaining on them.

Behind him, the mob wailed in their thousands. Soon the youngest would catch up, shout their sympathies, get in his way. He broke into a cautious run. Misery it seemed, like fury, could give one strength.

I've lost my girl. Lost her mother twelve years before. Lost Syrarys – she was ever my foe but I possessed her body, her hands, possessed a lovely illusion. Even that they have taken from me. But not this body, you bastards, you filth. Not this mind pitted against you for ever.

He was thinking of his Emperor, and Rose, and above all Sandor Ott. Arunis might have killed Thasha, but Ott had spun the web in which the sorcerer found her, hopelessly tangled. Arunis had come out of nowhere; Ott had shadowed Isiq for years, disguised as an honour guardsman.

By the Gods, it felt good to run again. The road burned the soles of his feet and each slap said, *You live, you can act, you have nothing left to fear.*

He saw now what he had to do. Thasha's sacrifice meant the prophecy was annulled: no stirrings of revolution would begin on Gurishal, no preparations for the return of their god. But the Shaggat remained. So did the will to make him flesh again. Above all, so did the Nilstone.

Which meant that some other vessel would have to bear his daughter home: the *Chathrand* must never leave this port. And there was only one power in the Bay of Simja that could stop it. For all their show of guns, the Mzithrini ships would never dare to act against an Arquali vessel. Not here anyway, before the eyes of the world. But King Oshiram would have every right. Simja's navy might be a pitiful thing, but ten or twelve warships were surely enough to hold the *Chathrand*, immense as she was. *You never dreamed I would go this far. You have counted on my blind love of Arqual, my soldier's oath. You will regret it.*

Thasha's body passed through the North Gate, and Isiq was but minutes behind. The flower-collectors pointed the way. He would be mortally sick with fatigue when this task was done. But done it would be, and let the night come after.

'Your Excellency!'

He raised his eyes: a dark two-horse carriage was pulling up to the corner. The driver reined the animals in, but it was not he who had called to Isiq. On the seat beside the man sat the same well-dressed youth who had approached Hercól in the procession.

'Your valet bid me fetch you a carriage, sir.'

'Kind ... not necessary ...' Isiq found he could barely speak.

'Bless me, sir, you're unshod!'

The young man leaped down, ran to Isiq and took his arm. By the time they reached the corner the driver had opened the door and placed the footstool. The inside of the carriage was plush and empty. Isiq paused and stared at the boy.

'Who—?'

'Greysan Fulbreech, Ambassador. King's clerk, and your humble servant. Come, we shall reach the port in no time.'

He whipped a fresh handkerchief from his pocket and offered it to Isiq. The admiral mopped the sweat from his bald head and entered the carriage. A moment later the driver cracked his whip and they were off, and at startling speed.

But why were they turning? He was quite sure the port lay dead ahead. Isiq groped at the door and found no handle to open. He reached for the window: barred. Then he felt the handkerchief, still clutched in his fingers, yanked roughly through the bars. As the horses charged ahead he saw the Fulbreech boy on the streetcorner, waving goodbye.

The joyful whines of the mastiffs turned to whimpers: their mistress had not stirred to greet them. Jorl nudged Thasha's chin with his muzzle. Suzyt padded in breathless circles as the party crossed the stateroom.

'Quickly, now,' said Hercól.

They laid her on the bench under the tall gallery windows. Hercól opened the cabinet beneath the bench and reached inside, and when his hand emerged it held a naked sword. Pazel had seen Hercól's sword before – seen it dark with blood, and awhirl in fights – but he had never beheld it this closely. The blade was dark and cruel, and nicked in two places. A flowing script ran up the steel, but the years had worn the engraving almost to nothing.

Hercól noticed his look. 'Ildraquin,' he said. "Earthblood. That is its name. One day I shall tell you its story.'

He turned and swiftly inspected the chamber, then moved on to the sleeping cabins and the Isiqs' private washroom. When he returned Ildraquin was sheathed.

'No one has entered in our absence,' he said. 'We are as safe here as one can be on this ship.'

'Then I'd best see to my duties, if you don't need me,' said Fiffengurt.

'We need you,' said Hercól. 'But we need you most as quartermaster. Who else will keep us informed of Rose's schemes?'

Fiffengurt shook his head. 'Rose trusts me like I trust a rattlesnake.

Still I overhear things, now and again. What I learn, I'll share. And I'll send Thasha's father to you the instant he boards.'

'You're a good plum, Mr Fiffengurt,' said Pazel.

'Seeing as you're an Ormali, lad, I'll take that as a compliment.'

They locked the door behind him. For a moment no one moved or spoke.

Then Hercól said, 'Are you here, Diadrelu?'

'Of course.'

The voice came from overhead. There she was, atop the book cabinet: a woman with copper skin, short hair, black clothes, gleaming eyes. An ixchel woman, a queen until she cast her lot with humans. Crouched on the edge of the cabinet she looked no larger than a dormouse. Standing, she might have been eight inches tall.

'I know you trust the quartermaster,' she said, looking down at them intently, 'but I must tell you that we consider him one of the most dangerous humans aboard. He is inquisitive, and he knows more about the crawlways and secret spaces of the *Chathrand* than anyone save Rose himself. And when he speaks of my people they are *crawlies*, and a note of disgust enters his voice.'

'Fiffengurt hates ixchel?' said Neeps. 'I don't believe it! He's the most soft-hearted old sailor I've ever met.'

'But a sailor nonetheless,' said Diadrelu, 'and schooled in the vices of sailing folk. I do not know if his feelings stem from his past experience or general fear. But I will not soon reveal our presence to this ally of yours.'

'We wouldn't ask you to,' said Pazel.

Dri gestured at the stateroom door. 'Someone tried to pick the lock while you were on the island,' she said. 'Twice. I jammed the mechanism with my sword.'

'Well done,' said Neeps.

But Hercól shook his head. 'What if they had forced the door? You would have been caught in plain sight.'

'Hercól Stanapeth,' said the ixchel woman, 'I have lived my whole life within yards of human beings, men who would have killed me without a second thought. You have little to teach me about stealth.'

Hercól smiled, not quite conceding the point. 'Are you ready, my lady?' he asked.

For an answer the woman descended – three shelves in the blink of an eye, a spring to the back of Isiq's divan, another to Hercól's shoulder, and a last jump to the bench under the window, a few inches from

Thasha's neck. When their eyes caught up with her they saw that she was holding something sharp and translucent. It was an ixchel arrow, two inches long – fashioned, as she had told them earlier, from the quill of a porcupine.

'Who will say what must be said?' she asked.

'That had better be Hercól,' said Pazel.

'No,' said Hercól. 'You were there when she fell, Pazel, and yours was the last face she saw as her eyes dimmed. The task is yours.'

Pazel took a deep breath. 'All right,' he said. 'But I'd feel better if a doctor were here. I'd even settle for crazy old Rain.'

'Kneel,' said Diadrelu.

Reluctantly, Pazel obeyed. He put his face close to Thasha's own. It was only then that he realised how truly frightened he was. Thasha's eyes looked withered. The lips he had kissed the night before were flecked with dirt.

Diadrelu reversed her grip on the arrow – and with the whole force of her arm plunged it into a vein in Thasha's neck.

Her eyes flew open. And Pazel began to talk as fast as he could. *Don't shout don't shout Thasha you're safe you're with us you're with me Thasha trust me don't shout.*

She did not shout. She leaped away from him in terror, nearly crushing Diadrelu beneath her and striking the window so hard that a crack appeared in the nearest pane. When Pazel tried to steady her she kicked him savagely away.

'Peace!' hissed Hercól. 'By the Night Gods, Thasha Isiq, I may have trained you too well! Your pardon, Lady Diadrelu, and you too, Pazel! Enough, lass, take a breath.'

Pazel picked himself up, relief breaking over him in waves. She was awake, alive–and free of Arunis' trap. It had all gone according to plan.

Or had it? Thasha's eyes were strange, savage. At last she appeared to recognise their faces, but would let no one comfort her. She shivered as though from deadly cold.

'It worked,' said Neeps softly. 'You were perfect, Thasha.'

Thasha raised a hand to her throat. Her voice was a dry, pained whisper.

'We fooled Arunis?'

'We fooled them all,' said Hercól. 'You did not marry, and Ott's false prophecy cannot come true.'

He spread a blanket over her legs. Thasha looked out at the sunny bay. Looking at her, Pazel thought suddenly of a group of sailors he had glimpsed long ago: hurricane survivors, coaxing a ruined ship into Ormaelport, their faces ravaged by memories of wild fear.

'I touched ice,' Thasha whispered. 'I was in a dark place all crowded with people, but there was no light, and then I began to see without light and the people were hideous, they didn't have faces, and that old priest was there waving his sceptre, and there was ice under my wedding shoes, and black trees with little fingerbone-branches that grabbed at me, and there were eyes in the slits of the trees and voices from holes in the ground. I was freezing. I could feel you holding me, Pazel; I could even feel the scar on your hand. But then the feeling stopped. And then everything began to vanish in the dark – the monster-people went out like candles, one by one. And the voices faded, until there was just one strange voice calling my name, over and over, like something that would never stop, like water dripping in a cave forever. But there was no water, no walls, there was nothing but ice, ice under my skin, ice in my stomach and my brain.'

She hugged herself, looking slowly from one face to another.

'Was I dead?'

'No,' said Diadrelu, 'but you were as close to death as a human can be, and return unharmed. *Blanë* means *foolsdeath*, but not because it deceives only fools. The name means rather that the spectre of death himself should not know the difference, if he came upon one in the grip of the drug.'

'And brandy on top of that,' Neeps sighed.

'Did old Druffle go through something like this, when you and Taliktrum drugged him?' Pazel asked.

The ixchel woman shook her head. 'There are several forms of *blanë*, for various uses. We only needed Druffle to sleep. But when Thasha drove that quill into her palm on the marriage dais, she had to appear dead beyond all suspicion. That called for *blanë* of the purest kind – and the most dangerous. Without the antidote, Thasha never would have woken from its grip. She would have slept until she starved.'

'I'm still cold,' said Thasha.

'You will not cast off the chill for days, perhaps,' said Diadrelu. 'My father once pricked his thumb with pure *blanë*. A week later he still suffered nightmares, and felt the drug's cold grip. Sunlight helped, he said.'

'Alas, she will have little of that for a time,' said Hercól. 'This cabin must be your cage, Thasha, until King Oshiram learns the truth of our mission. If I can find a way to contact him at all, that is.'

'And what then?' asked Diadrelu. 'Has he the stomach to quarantine the Great Ship, and fight his way aboard against a hundred Turachs?'

'We must hope so,' said Hercól. 'But there is another question: what if he succeeds? No doubt he will destroy the Shaggat, lest by some guile of Arunis the madman be returned to life. But the Nilstone he cannot destroy: no power in Alifros can. Will he consent to guard it until some better resting place is found? It could break his dynasty – for although its merest touch slays the fearful, someone will always dream of using it, and perhaps succeed. Arunis for one believes that is possible.'

He looked gravely at each of them in turn. 'We must never forget that our fates are tied to the Stone. By our oath, first – to place it beyond the grasp of anyone vile enough to seek to use it – and by the mere fact that we are children of this world. Alifros is great, but the power of the Nilstone is limitless. There will be nowhere to hide if its power is unleashed.' Hercól turned to Thasha with a sigh. 'I had counted on your father's help in persuading Oshiram. But now—'

Thasha gasped. 'Oh, the fool! What happened? He hit the king, didn't he?'

The others smiled at each other but did not laugh. It would not do to be overheard; they were in mourning after all. Before anyone could explain, however, they were interrupted by a shrill cry.

'Hark the voice!'

They jumped. By the door to the washroom stood Felthrup Stargraven, the woken rat, terribly injured in yesterday's battle. They crowded around him, overjoyed. He seemed remarkably steady on his three good feet (the fourth had been crushed by a drainpipe lid) and he twitched his short tail impatiently (another rat had long ago bitten it in two). Jorl and Suzyt barrelled forwards and licked him, an act of love in which Felthrup might soon have drowned. But the rat shook them off and squeaked again:

'Hark the voice, the voice in the distance! Can't you *hear*?'

They held still. And hear it they did: a man's voice from an impossible distance, rising and falling gravely.

'It's that priest again,' said Pazel. 'The one they call the Father. But I can't make out what he's saying.'

'He is saying we shall die!' cried that rat.

'What?'

'Die, die! Not literally, of course Not even metaphorically. Nor by inference intended – but how, pray, does a speaker know what his listener infers? And in the strictest sense what he is saying is not the point so much as the indisputable fact that *it is being said*. Bellowed, blasted, harrooed—'

'Felthrup,' said Diadrelu. 'You are healed. Your chatter proves it. But whatever are you talking about?'

'There's a bell ringing now,' said Pazel.

Felthrup spun in a circle, too upset too hold still. 'Not one bell – two! Disaster, disaster!'

They opened more windows: indeed there were two bells, one high, one low, sounding precisely together so that the notes seemed to fuse as one. And now from the shore came voices, incredulous voices, crying out in delight.

'But that's the wedding signal,' Thasha said. 'Simjans ring two bells at once to show that a couple is married. But we're not! We never spoke any vows!'

'Besides, they all think you're dead,' said Neeps.

'So what's happening?' Thasha demanded.

'Oh, woe, woe, woe!' cried Felthrup.

Like the rat himself, Pazel found he could be still no longer. Despite shouts from the others he dashed across the stateroom, slipped through the door, and ran along the short passage to the upper gun deck. Men were hastening to the ladderways (really the ship's staircases; but so steep that handholds were carved into the steps), leaving swabs and buckets and half-spliced ropes where they lay. Pazel climbed with them. When they reached the topdeck the crowd was already enormous. All stood to portside, gazing at the shore.

Among them Pazel was glad to find Dastu, his favourite among the senior tarboys. He was a broad-shouldered twenty-year-old from the rough Etherhorde district of Smelter's Den. Like nearly everyone, Dastu was a bit afraid of Pazel – at his touch a man had turned to stone, after all. But Dastu had never once called him *muketch* (mud-crab) as almost all the other boys did when they realised he was Ormali. Dastu still looked him in the eye. And Dastu shared his knowledge of the *Chathrand*, its hidden corners, legends, slang. The No. 5 ladderway, close to the stateroom: that was the Silver Stair, because rich passengers used it, and sometimes sealed the Money-Gate to keep the riffraff away from their cabins. Ladderway No. 1 (at the starboard bow) was the Holy Stair, because it was there that old Captain Kurlstaf had heard the voice of Rin. In a sense these little details hardly mattered. But Dastu's efforts did, immensely.

The older boy made room along the rail. 'No one knows what's

66

happening,' he said. 'Those cheers sound blary happy, though, don't they? Strange way to show respect for the dead.'

'Any sign of Admiral Isiq?' asked Pazel.

Dastu shook his head. 'Nobody's come aboard since you did. And the rest of us are trapped out here, blast it.'

Trapped. Dastu was not exaggerating. Captain Rose and the marine commander, Sergeant Drellarek, had authorised no shore leave: only the wedding party had touched land. Sickness had provided a handy excuse: two days earlier the talking fever had broken out in Ormael, where the *Chathrand* had lain at anchor for a week. Dr Chadfallow had pronounced Thasha and her family in perfect health, but cautioned that the rest of the crew would have to be examined one by one – a process that might take days.

The truth, of course, was that anyone who did go ashore would surely speak of the violent madness they had witnessed on the Great Ship. That was a risk the conspirators could not take.

'The men must be angry,' whispered Pazel.

'Fit to be hog-tied,' said Dastu. 'And the passengers! Do you realise we're holding forty passengers hostage? Just for appearances, mate! There's a big Atamyric family – parents, children, old aunts and uncles – trying to get home via Etherhorde. Some Simjans too. How do you think *that* would play ashore?'

'Where are they? Locked down in steerage?'

Dastu nodded. 'Except for Latzlo and Bolutu. Uskins boarded them up in their cabins 'til we get underway. You can bet your breakfast those two are wishing they'd disembarked in Tressik.'

Pazel shook his head. Latzlo was a dealer in exotic animals. He had been with them all the way from Etherhorde, selling walrus ivory in one port, buying sapphire doves in another, trading six-legged bats for fox pelts in a third. But trade alone had not kept him aboard. He wanted to marry Pacu Lapadolma.

No one could deny that he was an optimist. In three months Pazel had heard the girl speak just four words to her suitor: 'You reek of dung.' If she mentioned him to others it was not by name but as 'the imbecile' or 'that wrinkled ape'. Latzlo did not seem to mind: indeed he went on discussing names for their children with anyone who cared to hear.

Bolutu was an even stranger case. A veterinarian much favoured by the Imperial family, he was also a student of the Rinfaith and had taken the vows of a journeyman monk. He was a black man, and there was even a rumour that he was a Slevran, one of the savage nomads of the northern steppe – but yesterday Pazel had heard him speak Mzithrini. Surely, then, he was an enemy spy? But what good was a spy whose looks, acts and voice drew so much attention?

Pazel winced. Not his voice, not anymore. Yesterday, enraged at the man's interference, Arunis had magically forced Bolutu's mouth open and set a live coal upon his tongue. Ramachni had stopped the burning with a counter-spell, no doubt saving the veterinarian's life. But nothing could be done about the tongue. Already Pazel had noticed Bolutu communicating through scribbles in a notebook.

Another happy roar from the city. Pazel looked towards the port and saw men dashing, leaping from one tethered boat to another, making for the city centre. 'It's too weird,' he said to Dastu. 'What've they got to cheer about?'

'See that boat!' cried a sailor on their left. 'Ain't that Dr Chadfallow in the stern?'

And so it was. The doctor was seated in a long skiff, helping out with the oars. Pulling away on his right was Arunis. Uskins, the first mate, was also aboard. They were nearing the *Jistrolloq*, the White Reaper, fiercest warship of the Mzithrinis' White Fleet. She was anchored less than half a mile from the *Chathrand:* close enough for Pazel to see the enemy sailors gathering at her bows.

'They look like old shipmates,' growled Dastu. 'He's as much a villain as Arunis himself, that doctor is.'

Pazel's hands tightened on the rail. *We won the first round*, he thought. *We smashed Ott's prophecy to pieces*. So what was Felthrup afraid of? And what on earth was keeping Eberzam Isiq?

Now the little boat drew alongside the *Jistrolloq*, and Pazel saw Chadfallow stand to speak with a Mzithrini officer, possibly the captain himself. What the doctor said he could not hear, but the sailors clustered at the warship's rail greeted his words with astonished cries. After a moment the doctor sat again, and the skiff turned towards the *Chathrand.*

'By the Tree,' said Dastu. 'The Sizzies are running a new flag up their mainmast! Not their Imperial banner, either. What is it?'

All the Mzithrini ships were doing the same. There were cheers as the pennants rose.

'It's a coat of arms,' said Pazel softly. 'It's *Falmurqat's* coat of arms.'

'Falmurqat?' said Dastu. 'The prince who was supposed to marry Thasha? Why?'

At that very moment the fireworks began to pop. Whistlers and crackers, bomblets and boomers, followed by the neighs of frightened horses and the barks of hysterical dogs.

Pazel watched the skiff approach. Dr Chadfallow was grim, his face hardened against the rancour virtually everyone on the *Chathrand* felt for him. But Arunis was smiling: a smile of triumph, or so Pazel imagined. Mr Uskins just looked afraid.

Neeps appeared beside them. He looked at Pazel, ashen-faced.

'Felthrup has this horrible idea—'

'*Chathrand! Urloh-leh-li! Ahoy ship Chathrand!*'

It was a shout from the *Jistrolloq:* a Mzithrini officer on her foremast was hailing them through a voice-trumpet. On the *Chathrand*'s own maintop the officer of the watch put a hand to his ear.

'Felthrup's right,' said Pazel.

Dastu looked from one to the other. 'What are you talking about? Who's Felthrup?'

'*Admiral Kuminzat begs the honour of serving Captain Rose, Admiral Isiq and such officers as you choose,*' boomed the Mzithrini. '*An hour past sunset, aboard this his flagship. Seven dishes and a puff pastry, with Mangali cordials to follow.*'

On the skiff, Arunis put back his head and laughed.

'I think I'm going to be sick,' said Neeps.

'A soldier's daughter.' Pazel ground his fists against his forehead. 'Damn him. Gods damn that man.'

Dastu was at a loss. 'Who, damn who?'

'They're chanting her name,' said Neeps.

'Whose name, blast it?' said Dastu. 'Thasha's?'

'No,' said Pazel. 'The *other* soldier's daughter. The one Sandor Ott had in his pocket all this time. The girl Prince Falmurqat just married. Pacu Lapadolma.'

Without another word he and Neeps turned and headed aft. All night the circle of friends huddled in the stateroom, conspiring anew but feeling checkmated. All night the fireworks exploded over Simjalla, gold and green and silver, and when the wind blew right they heard the chanting, even to the hour of dawn: *Pacu, Pacu, Queen of Peace!*

5

From the Editor: A Word of Explanation

I will ask you very plainly: has anything, ever, been more absurd, more whimsical, more devoid of probability and good sense? That I should be given to witness these events and record them, here in my palace of books and meditation and cold unsalted soup? That with an iron stylus I should scribble away the fair days and the foul, write past the stroke of midnight under a lamp burning the ooze of a giant beetle, gaze like a bird hypnotised by the sway of the cobra's hood at the events that shaped my life – their lives – all lives in unlucky Alifros?

Do I deserve this honour? By no means. I invite the reader to observe that I have never stated otherwise. So many deaths on the *Chathrand*, so many days of agony and despair, so many forms courage took, the sword through the fangs of the flame-troll, the gangrenous leg under the saw, the war in the brine-reeking darkness of the hold. But there are more fundamental questions. Who killed? Who refrained from killing? Who shielded reason, frailest blossom ever to open in the soul of man, from the hailstorms of violence and revenge?

Not me. Not this poor editor to whom the angels lend their vision for a time. I read, I write, I drink my cave-shrimp soup and pour my energies into a task for which I know I am unfit. No more can I offer history. No more do I covet for myself.

It seemed essential to me to clear this matter up. Now we may proceed.

6

Conversation by Candlelight

—⟶⟲⟳⟵—

The horses were strong, and the driver whipped them without mercy, so that the carriage flew heaving and rattling down the cobbled streets. Eberzam Isiq set his back against the wall and kicked until his bare feet bled. The door held. He shouted, but no one answered his cries.

Soon the voices in the street began to fade, as if they were leaving the city centre behind. Stone became wood under the horse's hooves: they were crossing a bridge. He tried to recall the king's chatter, where the river lay, how many crossing-points. Isiq could not even recall its name. Then blackness fell. A tunnel, the driver's shout echoing along its length, the crash of an iron gate closing behind them.

The carriage door opened. Isiq looked out into a large stone chamber. The light was dim; the clammy air was like depths of a hold. Before him stood a trio of young men. They were neatly but not elegantly clothed, and apparently unarmed. Bowing, they apologised for the rough ride. But Isiq knew military manners when he saw them, and military eyes. These men watched his hands as he climbed stiffly to the ground.

'You're Arqualis,' he said.

It was not a question, and they made no denials, but merely turned and led him across the hay-strewn chamber. He passed an open doorway, heard the flutter of some large bird in the shadows. He wondered vaguely if he could ask for shoes.

'Mind the step, Admiral.'

'Am I to be killed?'

The men looked at him, and one of them shrugged. 'We're not given to waste,' he said.

Then something caught his eye. Quick as a snake, he plunged a hand into Isiq's waistcoat vest and removed the bronze flask.

'Not much of a weapon, that,' said Isiq.

The man smiled slightly, opening the flask. 'The Westfirth,' he said, sniffing. 'Fine brandy, that.'

'Stay in the service long enough and you'll be able to afford it. Ah, no. Your kind don't live that long, do you?'

A change came over the young man's face. It was Isiq's last memory, for a time.

'Wake up, Admiral.'

'Kill you . . . damn and blast.'

He was slouched against a grimy wall. Searing pain, like the worst moments of brain fever induced by Syrays' poisons. His hair stank of spirits and blood. The lad had clubbed him down with his own flask.

'There is shaved ice in the bucket beside you, and a rag.'

His mind was clearing. He knew that voice, and loathed it like no other. He raised his eyes.

Sandor Ott stood before him. The spymaster's arms were crossed; his gaze was calm, but he looked even worse than Isiq felt. The tapestry of old scars that was his face was overlaid by fresh ones: the raking claw-cuts of Sniraga, Lady Oggosk's cat, who had mauled Ott two days before in Ormael. There were other gashes, made perhaps by the stained-glass window through which he had hurled himself to escape arrest. The wounds were field-dressed, but ugly all the same.

'When you became a spy,' said Isiq, fumbling at the bucket, 'did you seduce many powerful women? For I'd say those days are through.'

'When I became a spy I found I could murder any number of people who displeased me a tenth as much as you have over the years.'

'What I mean is that you're an ugly dog.'

Ott shook his head. 'Displeasure and anger are not the same thing, Isiq. You cannot anger me. I hope, however, that you will not waste my time.'

'I was tortured during the Sugar War,' said Isiq. 'I revealed nothing. And I have less reason to fear you than I did those rebels with their whips and scorpions.'

Ott sighed. 'More reason, in fact. You simply haven't been briefed.'

He sat down beside the admiral, hands on knees. Only then did Isiq realise that they were completely alone. A few yards away stood a mean little table, two chairs and a candle, the only source of light. Beyond the table he saw a vague metallic gleam, possibly a hinge or doornob. He could not see the other walls.

'Before the Oshirams came to power in Simja,' said Ott suddenly, 'there were eight King Ombroths, who were in turn preceded by a century of rule by the Trothe of Chereste. And before the Trothe this island was ruled by a demonic queen, a madwoman with a crab's claw where her left hand should have been. She had congress with spirits, and unnatural long life: one hundred and twenty years she sat on the throne. An age the Simjans would rather forget.'

Isiq looked at the man on his right. He was close enough to touch. One of his eyes was grotesquely bloodshot: the cat must have sunk a claw there. He had no visible weapon. Not that it mattered. Sandor Ott was the most notorious killer in the Empire. He could kill Isiq in seconds, any number of ways.

'She outlawed funerals, this queen.'

'Did she.'

The spymaster nodded. 'When a citizen died she sent men for the bodies at once. She injected them with preservatives, bandaged them, soaked them in sesame oil, and lastly encased them in clay. Before the clay dried she would arrange the corpse in some lifelike position – the farmer with his hoe, the smith at his anvil, the child bent to tie a shoe – in a specially built dungeon beneath her chambers. Quite creative: the dungeon was constructed around a coal furnace, so that it might be heated like a kiln. In this way she baked the corpses hard as stone. Not as quickly as young Pathkendle dispatched the Shaggat, but effective nonetheless.'

He knows what happened yesterday, thought Isiq. *He still has spies aboard!*

'The queen had the idea that the ghosts of the dead made her powerful, and that they would linger so long as the bodies themselves did not perish. She became known as Queen Mirkitj of the Statues. She was hated and feared beyond description – even before she modified the practice for use on the living.'

'You will be remembered as her soul's kindred,' said Isiq.

'I will not be remembered at all. Oh, there will be rumours – for a generation at the most – rumours of an old spy who was behind Arqual's triumph. But no histories shall name or describe him. My own disciples will see to that. Your memoirs, for instance, will not be published, or archived, or even left in private hands. Your letters will be retrieved and burned.'

'Why have you kidnapped me, Ott?'

The spymaster ignored the question. 'When Queen Mirkitj died at last, the palace was razed, and the upper levels of the dungeon with it. But the queen had made thousands of these statues, and the dungeon ran nine levels deep – one for each Pit of the Underworld. In any case, only the first three levels were discovered, until rather recently. We are in the seventh.'

'Now I see,' said the admiral. 'You will subject me to this ancient torture unless I do your bidding. What can be left for you to want, though? What but your bidding have I done these many years, although I knew it not?'

'Not the least thing,' agreed Ott, smiling. 'But you're wrong again. I will inflict no pain on you if I can avoid it. For many years it was necessary to poison you – necessary, not especially pleasant – but that time is done. I merely intend to prepare you for the next phase in your service to the Emperor.

'Your daughter is dead. My cause is defeated. Gloat if you will. You are retired, and need not show a soldier's dignity any longer.'

'You lie. You haven't given up at all.'

'I never give up – that is true. But my great plan is thwarted. The Shaggat Ness is a block of stone, and the wedding cancelled, and the prophecy I spread in Gurishal among his worshippers cannot come true.

'Gloat then, but listen: you have some years of service left in you, Isiq. But they cannot be spent here. You have insulted the king of Simja. It is unthinkable that you should serve as ambassador.'

Isiq pressed ice to his temple. He studied Ott. A corner of the iris of the man's wounded eye was clouded by blood. Opaque, as of yesterday. Blind.

'In the drawer of that table,' Ott was saying, 'is a letter of writ from the lord admiral, countersigned by the Emperor himself. It appoints you to a lectureship in the naval academy at two hundred cockles a year.'

Isiq snorted. 'Does it come with directions to the almshouse?'

'What nonsense. That mansion on Maj Hill should fetch you enough to live out your days in comfort, albeit in tighter quarters.'

'I still own, it then? Free and clear?'

Ott was silent a moment. 'There may be certain duties owing, taxes—'

'Ha!' said Isiq. 'Who have you promised it to, Ott? Have you plucked another girl out of the slave school on Nurth? One who just happens to have reason, like Syrarys, to take a dried-up old murderer like you to bed now and then – as part of her service to the Emperor, of course.'

To Isiq's infinite satisfaction he saw Ott's mouth betray a certain tightening. He was getting through to the man.

'We should trade stories, don't you think?' Isiq pressed. 'Did she give you the same sort of massage I was used to, starting at the nape of the neck? Did she whisper the same words to both of us, in the same intimate moments?'

'You are reckless,' said Ott quietly.

Blary right I am.

'Which of your men was she grooming to kill you?' he pressed. 'You must have some idea. Why should she stay with you? A broken-down, gap-toothed butcher with rhinoceros skin and nothing to live for but conspiracies and lies. You must have guessed she'd try to dispose of you soon. Did you kill her yourself yesterday, before she could admit that she hated you?'

'I would dodge it,' said Ott.

'What?'

'Your fist. When you think me entirely distracted by rage, you are, I suspect, planning to strike out with your right fist as hard as possible, hoping to smash my head back against the wall, leaving me stunned. Then you would lift me by the shirt and slam me down over and over, perhaps pausing first to stuff that rag into my throat. You noticed my eye. But I have never let that arm of yours slide into my blind spot, Admiral, and I should merely have dodged it, and dealt with you.'

Isiq felt naked. Ott had described his intentions almost perfectly.

'Anger, like fear, hones the senses to a razor's edge,' the spymaster went on. 'You'd have done better to raise some intellectual point. Abstract thought slows our defences. Even I am not entirely immune.'

He arched his back against the wall, at his ease once more. 'Shall I tell you what fascinates me at present? The Nilstone. I did not believe it existed, and I laughed at Dr Chadfallow, who did. But as we both know, the Stone is terribly real. And it seems that long before Arunis took the Red Wolf from the depths, and melted it to reveal the artefact, someone else aboard the *Chathrand* knew as well.'

Ott took a scrap of parchment from his vest pocket, unrolled it, and passed it casually to Isiq. 'That came from the ship's hold. My man took it from the jaws of a rat, if you can believe it. Probably getting set to make it his dinner.'

Isiq tilted the parchment towards the candlelight. The scrap was crumbling, and burned on two sides, but he could still make out a spidery hand.

'—call't it DROTH'S EYE, or en Arqual fe NILSTONE, a cursed fing t'be sure, es it slays whoms'ever shel touch it, with a swiftnef hideous to bihold, all save fe littlest vermin, who furst suffer grotesqueries of change.

'Tis stone yur Wizardess hath entombed in fe WOLF OF SCARLET IRON, lately taken by fe arch-heretic NESS, and lost in fe havoc of his fall.

'The language is a mystery,' said Ott. 'Almost Arquali, but not quite. One might think it simply an antique variant, except that it speaks plainly of the Shaggat's theft of the Red Wolf, just forty years ago. It is not Arunis' hand: we have samples of that in the purchase-orders he wrote out as Mr Ket; nor is it like the sorcerer to commit any of his secrets to writing.

'Here we have the strangest of circumstances, no? Someone aboard the *Chathrand* knew what was to come – not only that we were bound to find such a thing as the Red Wolf, but also that said Wolf contained a horror called the Nilstone.' Ott gave him a sudden direct look. 'You wouldn't have any thoughts as to who such a person might be, would you?'

Isiq returned the parchment. 'Now you wish me to bargain for the liberty you will never grant.'

'Ah, but can you be certain?' said Ott. 'I discard nothing that is of use to our Emperor. Help me see you again in that light, as I have these several decades, and anything is possible.'

'Really?' said Isiq. 'Can you bring my daughter back to life?'

Ott gave a noncommittal shrug. 'Close your mind to nothing, Admiral. But for today let us speak no more of women. What of Ramachni? Who or what is he?'

There it is, thought Isiq. *Your real blind spot, the one that scares you.*

'A woken mink, wouldn't you say?'

Ott just looked at him. The question clearly did not merit a reply.

'Well,' said Isiq after a moment, 'perhaps he's a mage at that. The wizard who served the Becturian Viceroys could turn himself into a golden eagle, if you believe the—'

'Is he comatose, or just deeply asleep? Can he be relied upon to kill the sorcerer?'

Isiq felt his heart sink. Ramachni had answered that question clearly enough. Arunis was the stronger, at least in this world; Ramachni was a visitor, forced to crawl back to his own world in exhaustion. Isiq thought of the mage's departure, of the melancholy that had settled over them all. Ramachni had trusted them to find a way to keep Thasha alive, and they had failed. And now Ott was trying to play him again.

'Ramachni is an angel,' he heard himself say, 'one of Rin's golden angels, like my Thasha and her mother. Go ahead, recruit him if you can. But he may prove harder to deceive than I was.'

Ott shrugged again, then rose lightly to his feet. 'As you will. But don't look so morose, Admiral. You *did* anger me, and that is not easily done. You're not one to give up – in that sense we're very much alike. Perhaps that is why we are among the last men of our generation left fighting for His Supremacy's cause.'

'What cause? Dominion over the whole of Alifros? That is no cause of mine.'

Ott's eyes grew cold; he turned and walked to the table, where his face glowed ghastly in the candlelight. Then he opened the drawer and removed a pen, an inkstand and a sheet of linen paper.

'Speak no words of treason in my hearing,' he said. 'Tell me, does anyone have a cause you believe in? The group who meet in your stateroom, for example?'

Isiq looked up at the spymaster. In his mind's eye he saw the scars etched on the skin of his daughter and her friends: the mark of the Wolf that had safely hidden the Nilstone for a millennium.

'Yes,' he said, 'they do.'

'Then come here and write them a letter. It will be delivered, I assure you.'

He slid the blank page across the table. For a moment Isiq did not move. Then, slowly, he got to his feet and approached the table.

'Anything I want?'

'Once you've explained that you will not be returning to Etherhorde on the *Chathrand* – yes, anything you want. You may give such reasons as occur to you. But if you tell them that you are being held, you should expect a rescue attempt. Of course they could not find this tomb with a thousand men, but how are they to know? They will try to leave the ship, and will die with arrows in their backs. There will be no one to watch over Thasha's body on the journey home, or to see that she is buried honourably beside her mother.'

'If I'm really to go to Etherhorde, why not let me return on the Great Ship?'

Ott smiled. 'There is no hurry to assume your new post. Besides, I can't guarantee that you're ready to shape the minds of future officers, just yet.'

'You never mean to let me go, do you?'

Ott tapped the paper. 'Come, sir. If you wish to write, you must do so now. I am to meet Drellarek within the hour.'

He sat back, waiting. After another pause Isiq lowered himself in the opposite chair. He stared at Ott, his body rigid with hate. Then he took up the pen and began to write very quickly. He wrote in a kind of fever, filling the page in minutes, and signed his name with a last earnest stroke.

Ott lifted the sheet and waved it gently, drying the ink. Then he gave a sharp whistle. Light from a doorway gleamed suddenly, fifty feet or so away, and the same men who had taken Isiq from the carriage walked into the room.

This time they did not hide their contempt. They took hold of Isiq and roughly pulled him to his feet. Ott looked at the page again.

'"Comrades fall, but the mission endures,"' he read, and nodded. 'I couldn't agree with you more. Indeed your letter is quite satisfactory' – he looked up at Isiq and smiled – 'except that you neglected the star.'

Isiq grew very still.

'The star,' Ott repeated. 'That tiny, seemingly accidental ink blot that you always, without fail, let fall on the third line of your letters, and tease vaguely into a star with the tip of your pen. A sign that you are safe, and not being forced to write against your will. Leave out the star, however, and Hercól Stanapeth will know at a glance that you're a prisoner.'

Isiq felt the hope that had supported him dissolve. He was falling into darkness, and who could say where the fall would end? Ott pressed the nib of the pen to the letter, leaving a droplet, and with great care scratched it into a star. Then he looked up at Isiq and smiled.

'Years ago the Emperor commanded all his high officers to take such precautions. At my insistence. Syrarys made it a point to learn your method, of course.

'Now then: the eighth and ninth levels of Queen Mirkitj's prison are intact, along with their statues. I wish you to spend some time there, among the dead. You will have water and food but no light. Get to know them by feel; I assure you they are fascinating. Only, if you find a broken limb, move quickly away. The rats nibble at them, you see. The dry marrow, the powdery flesh. They are quite territorial, and vicious in the dark.

'When the time is right, we will return and present you with a choice. You can die at once, painlessly. Or you can return to public service, doing the Emperor's work. But know that you will forever be observed. And should you dream of mentioning what you like to call a conspiracy, then Hercól and those two tarboys and Nama your cook and any other you esteem will die by the queen's technique. And I will see you obtain souvenirs that prove it.'

His smile was gone. He nodded to his men, and they began to drag Isiq away. But then with a quick gesture Ott detained them again.

'I did not kill Syrarys, nor would I ever harm her. The years she spent with you were a misery, but she endured them out of love.'

'Love – for you?'

'And duty, Isiq.' The edge of rage was back in Ott's voice. 'To Arqual, our mother- and fatherland, the one hope of order left to this world. But this is useless talk. Some, like you, can never be enlightened. For them the darkness is best.'

'You're not enlightened, Ott,' said Isiq. 'You're enthralled. It's not remotely the same.'

'Syrarys understood,' said Ott through his teeth. 'Every kiss she gave you was necessary. Like Thasha's death. Like the death of your wife – I sawed through that balcony rail myself, Isiq – which allowed Syrarys to take her place at your side.

'I leave nothing to chance, you see. That is a way in which we are not alike.'

7
The Incubus

—⦿—

8 Teala 941
87th day from Etherhorde

Uthrol, Sarabin, Elegortak, Ingod-Ire of the Killing Dream. Nelu in the lightless depths, and Droth the Master of Masters, Despoiler of Worlds. From a circle of ash within a circle of salt within a circle of tomb earth I call thee, old powers never equalled, ye Lords of the Houses of Night.'

The sorcerer's chant was sibilant and low. He sat on the floor of his cabin; the room was closed, airless; musky smells of bile and camphor and cured meat hung about it. Midnight had come and gone; a blustery wind rattled the glass on the porthole. The white dog slept beneath the bed. From a shelf, a walrus-oil lamp cast its failing light on Arunis, hunched inside the three circles like a dark, thick-bellied spider at the centre of a web.

'Shamid, Woedenon, dread Varag in the Ice . . .'

Now and then, from a crack in the wall over the mage's shoulder, the light also illuminated a tiny, copper-coloured spark: the gleam of an ixchel eye.

'A demon,' said Ludunte. 'He is a demon in human form.'

'Perhaps,' said Diadrelu. 'And perhaps he is something worse.'

They were inside the wall, supporting themselves with their legs, feet pressed to the planks of Arunis' cabin and backs against those of the adjoining room. They looked down on the sorcerer through a gap in the planking no wider than a needle. They had made the gap themselves, with a spyjack: a mechanical wedge that could be hammered between two boards and widened with a crank. For the ixchel it was a survival tool.

'Is he summoning those beings?' whispered Ludunte fearfully.

Diadrelu shook her head. 'If he could bring the Night Gods among us to do his will he would have little need of the Shaggat Ness, or perhaps even the Nilstone. Yet no doubt he seeks their aid. Those circles are a magic quietus: through them he seeks to cleanse himself of any spells placed on this cabin that might prove distasteful to the gods he flatters. And possibly to protect himself. From what I cannot say.'

'You are very learned, Mistress.'

'Call me Dri.'

'As you will, m'lady. Did you not say he must be weakened, after all his black sorcery of recent days?'

'So Ramachni believed,' said Diadrelu. 'And if nothing else we have learned one thing tonight: he still fears Ramachni, unless there is another mage aboard to cast the spells he is fighting.'

'Where did Ramachni go? When will he return?'

'Far off – and not for a long time,' said Dri gravely. 'We must stand alone through many dangers, I fear. And speaking of which, why were you alone? Did my brother's order of two men per watch expire with his death?'

Ludunte dropped his eyes, suddenly uneasy.

'Ah,' said Diadrelu, in a changed voice. 'Taliktrum has ordered you not to discuss matters of the clan with me. Am I right?'

Ludunte gazed at her, in plain distress, but he said not a word.

'This was to be expected,' said Diadrelu, turning away. 'Well, well. Keep your silence, of course.'

She spoke as if of something trivial, but could not quite hide her displeasure. Ludunte was Diadrelu's *sophister*, her apprentice. Ixchel swore seven-year vows of obedience to their mentors, with only one chance – on the day they completed their second year – to rescind the vow without disgrace. Ludunte's second-year confirmation had come and gone as they lay in port at Ormael. Dri had missed it, and the ceremony she conducted on her return was perhaps less than Ludunte had hoped for: she had simply gathered his friends and the clan elders, described his progress without exaggeration, and passed the House Cup full of spiced wine from hand to hand. That was her way: she did not fuss and flatter. To be one of just five *sophisters* she had accepted in thirty years should be honour enough.

Of those five, two had completed their studies and moved on. Another, Nytikyn, had been killed before the start of the voyage, by a tarboy on the pier in Sorrophran. Nytikyn had been engaged to marry Ensyl, the youngest of Dri's *sophisters*. Dri had refused Ensyl at first, fearing that her sympathy for the grieving girl might cloud her judgement. But Ensyl had proven herself brave and thoughtful on the voyage to Simja, and shortly before their arrival Dri had accepted her vow.

Now Ensyl and Ludunte alone were left to her. By immutable law they must obey her every command, yet if she ordered them to disobey Taliktrum, the clan leader, she would be condemning them to join her in disgrace.

She looked at Ludunte, and thought for the first time what a terrible burden she had placed on the two of them. *Mother Sky*, she thought, *I've ruined everything.*

Since the arrival of Pazel, the tarboy who could speak their language and hear their natural voices – and Dri's terribly unpopular decision not to kill him – her reputation for wisdom had been thrown into doubt. Over the course of the summer, as the *Chathrand* ploughed west towards Simja, she had fought for the life of the boy with her brother, Lord Talag, with whom she had shared the rule of Ixphir House for decades. It was an ancient house and a proud family. Their direct ancestors had founded it, abandoning the nomad practice of living in ships for the first time since her race was stolen, in cages and specimen jars, from across the Ruling Sea.

The whole of that House was now aboard the *Chathrand*: six hundred ixchel men, women and children, following a dream of escape that had come to Talag in childhood and pursued him to his death.

There, again: the blunt blow to the heart. A vision of her brother in the mouth of Sniraga, as the huge cat leaped away down a passage. His limbs were scarlet; he flopped like a dead thing in her jaws. They had never recovered his body.

'Feel that thunder,' said Ludunte, pressing a hand to the wall. 'A storm will be here by morning.'

Diadrelu had had no time to grieve for Talag; with his death she had become sole leader of the clan. Talag had been about to recognise his son, Taliktrum, as a full Lord of Ixphir. That task had fallen to Diadrelu – but she had not done so. Taliktrum was of age, and had passed every test of strength and courage. But what of judgement? Dri could not see herself standing before the clan. *Here is your liege, your shield and protector, trust him with your lives.* Ritual words, some would say. But for Diadrelu they contained a promise she could not give lightly.

For with Talag dead, his son would have joined her as co-commander the instant his title was conferred. And he was not ready. Talag had been a genius, if angry and vain. Taliktrum was merely ambitious. Like his father he distrusted the very air humans breathed, but never realised that Talag's anger, however blinding, was born of a careful study of history. If Taliktrum actually believed in the same dream as his father – to lead their people to safety on Sanctuary-Beyond-the-Sea, the island from whence they'd come – he did so without the least curiosity as to what they might find when they got there.

When Taliktrum was a child Dri had loved him as best she could. But she doubted that he had ever looked at her and seen a loving aunt. For his tenth birthday she took him on a daring expedition: an ice-skate by moonlight on the frozen River Ool. He had been cross to learn that skates could be worn and used by anyone, not just ruling elites. 'Why do we bother with them, then?' he asked, bewildered.

'There's the rain now,' said Ludunte.

No, Taliktrum had seen only the Lady, the office, the power in her hands. It had taught her a lesson, that cold appraisal. It had made her distrustful of titles for ever.

Now this boy of twenty had the power he had always wanted, and she had none. To a people used to being slaughtered by humans, sparing Pazel's life had been bad enough. Revealing their presence to a cabin full of humans was simply unthinkable. The clan assembled; a Council of Witness was elected to hear the case, and three hours later her people stripped her of command. Dri knew it might have been worse: Taliktrum had wanted her guarded day and night, and barred from all further contact with those he mockingly called 'her tame ones'. What would he do if he learned that she had sworn to stand beside those humans, even before her own kin, until Arunis fell and the Nilstone was somehow put beyond use?

'Mistress,' said Ludunte. 'He is on his feet.'

She took his place at the spyhole. Arunis was standing in the centre of the three rings, watched by his motionless dog. Taking care not to brush the circles with his cloak, he reached onto the shelf and took down the lamp, a ceramic water jug and a small wooden box. The first two items he placed on the floor just outside the circles. Then he opened the box and took out several handfuls of downy weed of the sort used for packing breakables. Tossing these aside, he at last removed a black kerchief bound carefully with string. Gingerly he untied the string and unfolded the cloth.

'Rin's blood,' said Diadrelu.

On the kerchief lay a handful of human bones. There were three teeth, what might have been a fragment of rib, and an entire, articulated finger. All were yellow-brown and clearly old, perhaps even ancient. The mage looked at them warily, like things that might jump from his hand. Then he returned the box to the shelf and took down a small brass bowl.

'What is that devil up to now?' asked Ludunte.

'More than prayer, I think,' said Diadrelu.

Arunis sat again upon the floor. The kerchief he spread before him, within the innermost circle. The bowl he placed between the rings of ash and salt, and Dri saw now that it contained a few teaspoons of a pale, lumpy substance like crumbled cake. From the folds of his cloak he produced a match. Lighting it by the oil lamp, he held it above the black kerchief.

'Lords of Night,' he whispered, 'unbar your ways, unlock your gates and posterns, withdraw your jealous guard. Let the one who dwells with you gaze on these relics of himself.'

He dropped the match into the bowl. The yellow substance blazed ferociously, crackling and spitting. The air filled with a reek so sharp and bitter it even passed through the ixchels' tiny spyhole, and Dri reared back for a moment, fearful she would cough. The dog whined. Ludunte was almost gagging.

'What is it? A drug, a poison?'

Dri could make no answer. When she looked again the walrus-oil lamp was out, and the fire in the bowl was reduced to a low, sputtering flame. Arunis had not moved a muscle.

And then the flame spoke.

'*Hideth venostralhan, Wytter.*'

Ludunte stifled a gasp. Dri seized his arm in warning, though she herself felt stabbed with horror. The voice was cold and dry and powerful, but what made it truly ghastly was its indifference. She had no idea what the words meant, but they were said with the drawling unconcern of one who would cut off another's limb out of boredom, or perhaps his own. It was appalling even to know that such a voice could exist.

'He has brought it, Sathek,' said Arunis. 'He has brought it to this island, not three miles from here, and I must have it for my king.'

The voice from the flame spoke again, with the same lazy savagery.

'Your time in this world has passed,' said Arunis. 'But through the Shaggat I can complete your work.'

A flat, slow sigh: a death sigh, or the ghost of a laugh.

'Yet I must have it,' said Arunis. 'With or without your help. Only if you help me our victory will be more swift. Imagine him when the Swarm returns. The Nilstone in one fist, your sceptre in the other! Armies shall wilt before him, like petals in the frost.'

'*Saukre ne Shaggat prelichin.*'

'He will be flesh again. Mark my word. Not even Ramachni of Nemmoc can prevent it.'

They spoke on. The sorcerer was angry and pleading by turns, but the voice of the other never changed. The fire dimmed in the bowl. Whatever it was consuming was almost gone.

'M'lady, the fumes—'

'Hush, Ludunte!'

'I ask nothing for myself,' hissed Arunis, leaning over the dwindling flame. 'Near death have I been, and wrung dry of magic, yet I seek no help on that score. But can you not stir yourself for the sake of what you built? Can you truly wish it left for ever with that old Babqri fool? Do this for yourself, Sathek. Let me be your instrument of revenge!'

The sorcerer spread his palm an inch above the jumbled bones.

'Do this, and when I regain the Nilstone I shall build a tomb for your relics the size of a castle, upon a peak in Olisurn. Deny me, and I shall toss them into the bay.'

The fire winked out.

'Sathek!'

The sorcerer froze, listening intently. The cabin was black. With their exceptional night vision the ixchel could still see well enough, but Dri could not tell if his expression was one of triumph or defeat. She kept her hand on Ludunte's arm, warning him not to make a sound.

For several minutes Arunis did not seem to breathe. Then suddenly he rose to his feet and leaped out of the circles. Rushing to the porthole, he tore frantically at the bolt and threw open the round glass window. The sound of rain filled the cabin; Dri could hear it lancing against the floor. Arunis bent and peered through the opening, then gave a laugh that must have carried through several decks.

The dog yipped from beneath the bed. At the sound Arunis looked at it for the first time, and an alarming thought seemed to strike him. Rushing to the bed, he snatched up the dog and leaped back within the three circles, holding the squirming animal tight against his chest.

A thump. Something had alighted in the porthole. It was about the size of a gull, but it was not bird-shaped. It was so black Dri found she could not make out its features. Did it have two legs, or four? Was that a tail or a lanky braid?

'Go,' Arunis told it, and the fear was naked in his voice. 'Go and get it, creature, and bring it to me.'

The thing made an animal yowl and leaped at the mage. But at the edge of the first circle it stopped short, groping at the air as if entangled in a web. It spat and clawed, but could not break through. In a fury the creature circled the cabin, smashing cups and flasks and inkwells, overturning the table, emptying the shelves, as Arunis shouted *Go, go!* and the dog barked murder. But the thing would not cross the lines on the cabin floor.

'Your master set you a task, incubus! You dare not return to your sphere without seeing it done, and the night is half-spent already. Obey him!'

The creature hurled itself once more at Arunis, and once more the circles proved impossible to cross. Hissing with rage it returned to the porthole, then seemed to twist and look back. Lightning crackled over the bay, and in its glow Dri saw a face out of nightmare, a baby fused with a rabid dog, and then the thing was gone.

Arunis leaped to the porthole and slammed it fast. Dropping his pet, he staggered back to his bed and threw himself down. Gasping, he covered his face with his hands.

Dri motioned to Ludunte: *We climb.* In a few seconds they were up the wall and crawling away across the ceiling of the adjacent cabin. When a good distance separated them from the mage, Dri sat down and began to work the cramps out of her legs.

Ludunte spoke in a hoarse whisper. 'He summoned a fiend, m'lady. Right before our eyes.'

She looked up at him sharply. The boy was in shock.

'Even now,' she asked, 'will Taliktrum deny the peril this mage represents? Does he think Arunis will suffer a nest of crawlies to divert this mission for ends of their own?'

Ludunte swallowed. His mouth twisted in frustration.

'I begin to understand,' said Diadrelu. 'He placed you here alone *because* you are loyal to me, didn't he? So that whatever you might observe should be tainted and unconvincing to the clan. After all, you're just the sworn servant of a madwoman.'

'No, no—'

'And then of course there were the fumes. Perhaps we hallucinated. Who wouldn't prefer to think so? Especially if believing meant turning away from that old story, ixchel against all humans everywhere, and admitting that *we must find some to put our faith in*, or die with them all alike?'

'M'lady, do you order me to speak?'

'No!' said Dri quickly. '*Héridom*, I order you *not* to. You must be able to stand before Taliktrum and declare in all truth that you never told me anything. If he intends to spy on me I'd rather he use you than anyone else. I depend on you now more than ever.'

Ludunte gazed at his feet for a moment. Then he raised his head and asked, 'Where did Arunis send that creature, do you know? To attack your friends in the stateroom?'

Dri shook her head. 'His ultimate goal is to recover the Nilstone, but he sent the incubus ashore. *Not three miles from here*, he said. Whatever he wants is on the island, and in the hands of the one he called *that Babqri fool*. A Mzithrini, in other words. Well, it is time we left. Go and close the hole.'

'M'lady, I do not have the spyjack crank.'

Dri thought she had misheard. She got to her feet, and there was cold fury in her voice.

'They left you tending a spyjack with no means to close it behind you?'

Ludunte nodded reluctantly.

Dri took a deep breath. 'Listen to me, *sophister*. You will never again consent to watch a spyjack you cannot close – not if the ghost of Yalídryn the Founder himself should rise and demand it. Go to Night Village and fetch a crank. There is no shortage of them. Report what we have seen to Taliktrum, then come back and close the hole. Those are my express commands.'

'Yes, Mistress.'

Night Village was the mercy deck; the nearly lightless floor just above the hold, where the ixchel dwelt in a fortress of cargo-crates, ten yards from the bow.

'Report all that we have seen to Taliktrum,' Dri continued. 'It may be some time before I return.'

Ludunte looked at her fearfully. 'Where are you going, mistress?'

She hesitated, then smiled and laid a gentle hand on his arm. 'Where the clan must not follow,' she said.

She did not go directly where she had planned, however. There was one other matter to attend to first.

Hercól Stanapeth still slept in his valet's cabin on the berth deck. Diadrelu had no means to enter the stifling little chamber, but as she wriggled between the ceiling and the floor above she heard him move. A rustling in the darkness, then a slight scrape. A pale shaft of light sprang up through a crack she would never otherwise have seen. Hercól was lighting a candle. Dri crawled forward to the crack and looked down.

He was seated cross-legged on the floor, shirtless, back straight and eyes half-closed. A posture of meditation. His arms and chest were muscled like an ixchel's: no weak spots, no inch of flesh allowed to luxuriate in softness. His blackened sword lay before him like a talisman. This was good luck, Dri decided: it was hard to catch Hercól by himself.

He raised his hands in a seated stretch. How serene he was, how purposeful. She had come to tell him of the incubus – *only the incubus, keep that clear.* But doubts assailed her as she watched his steady breathing. What would they say, her people, if they saw her now? There were scores of men in this compartment. The walls were thin, and the air was still and noiseless. It would be reckless to make contact here.

He twisted his upper body, and she saw the wolf-scar on his ribcage, glistening with sweat. She should have gone to the stateroom, she told herself, to the tarboys and Thasha. What need did she have to approach this man directly?

Dri felt her heart begin to hammer. She rehearsed her words. *I must talk with you, stand up, let me in. I will trust you with knowledge that could kill me. Not of the incubus, but of—*

She caught herself up short. Mother Sky, what was she thinking? To speak . . . of *that*? Could she tell a human about *that*, and still call herself a member of the clan? She closed her eyes and pressed a clenched fist against her mouth, as though it might speak without her consent. Impossible. Impossible. You are losing your mind.

One level below, in the gloom of the orlop deck, the Shaggat Ness, God-King of Gurishal and Fifth Monarch of the Mzithrin Pentarchy, stood with his stone ankles buried in straw. Dri studied him with equal parts fascination and disgust. His lifeless face wore a look of outrage, and the beginnings of fear. His left hand, held high but shrunken and withered, grasped the deadliest object on earth.

The Nilstone. It was small and round and pitch black. *Too black*, like the body of the incubus: Dri's eyes seemed to stop working when she tried to focus on its surface.

The large compartment was known as the manger; it was a fodder room for the ship's cattle. Half the straw bales had been removed, the rest stacked against the aftermost wall to within a few feet of the ceiling. Atop these crouched Diadrelu, studying the men below.

Two of the group, dressed in yellow robes, were chained to the aft bulkhead. One sprawled on the floor, asleep; the other paced the length of his chains, scratching and arguing with himself. These were the Shaggat's sons. They looked to be in their twenties, but were in fact more than twice that age. On the prison isle of Licherog the men's chatter had so annoyed Arunis that he had cast sleeping-spells on them both. The spell had never quite worn off: to this day they were given to fits of narcolepsy.

They had aged more slowly in their sleep. But the long captivity, and perhaps the oddness of passing so much of their lives unconscious, had eroded a good deal of their sanity.

The others were all Turach soldiers. Three guarded the room's single door (left open in the vain hope of a breeze), and three more stood in precise formation around the stone king. They were gigantic and terrible men: elite commandos, rated worthy to guard the Emperor himself. They drank fire storax at dawn to shock themselves awake, gulped pills made from the bones of Slevran panthers to increase their strength (though Dri had heard Bolutu begging them to give up the 'vicious habit'), plunged their fists into buckets of gravel and scarlet chilis to deaden them to pain.

But yesterday, facing Arunis and his corpse-warriors, some of the Turachs had hesitated, seemingly afraid, and in those few seconds lives had been lost. Punishment had come this morning. Sergeant Drellarek, their commander, had stood all those who had retreated in a line on the main deck. He then told his lieutenant to recite the seventh of the Ninety Rules of the Rinfaith.

'Rule Seven,' the young man had shouted. 'Fear rots the soul and gives back nothing, but wisdom can save me from all harm. I shall cast off the first for the second, and guard the sanctity of the mind.'

Then Drellarek had drawn his knife and slit the throat of every seventh man in the lineup. Those who escaped bound their comrades' bodies in sailcloth and twine. *Monstrous*, thought Diadrelu. *And very effective. From now on they'll fear nothing but him.*

But was there nothing else to be afraid of? Yesterday they had all learned that to touch the Nilstone brought instant death to any with fear in their hearts. What about standing near it, though, for hours on end? The men looked well enough – just itchy and uncomfortable in the heat. For the moment that was all Dri needed to know. She did not think Arunis would soon come for the Nilstone or his king. By his own admission he was weak – and after Drellarek's measures, she had no doubt that these men and their eighty fellow Turachs would fight him to the death.

She tried again to see the Nilstone. *How can it be there and* not *there at the same time? What is that damned thing?* Ramachni had said it was 'death given form', and had indeed come to Alifros from the world of the dead. He had also assured them it could never be destroyed. And yet she and her human comrades had sworn to get rid of it somehow, before Arunis found a way to use it against them all.

'I want wine!'

It was the Shaggat's son. He was glaring at his captors, stamping his feet.

'Is that a fact,' muttered a sleepy Turach.

'My father is a god! His hour is come! Surely you don't want to die?'

'He's not a god, you wretch. Why don't you blary sleep?'

Diadrelu crawled back from the edge of the straw bale. Nothing more to be learned here. With a sigh she decided to return to the ixchel compound. She did not relish the abuse and ridicule that would await her there. But she was hungry – and like any member of the clan she had communal duties to perform: cooking, maintenance, care of the sick and wounded. Taliktrum had let her know that he had taken a personal interest in her chores.

'Give that bottle here!' said the Shaggat's son.

'It ain't wine, it's water. And it's ours. You threw yours up in the hay like a naughty baby, didn't you?'

Dri smiled: the remains of a shattered bottle lay a few feet to her left.

The son was actually starting to cry. 'You despise me.'

'Now you're catchin' on.'

'Very soon you'll be sorry. When he is flesh again, and the Swarm explodes from the grey kingdom, you shall answer to my father. I will tell him and you will be crushed. You worms, you tiny insects, you – bullies.'

'What's this *swarm* you're always on about?'

But the Shaggat's son had lost the thread of his rant. 'Is it so much to ask, Warden? A good bottle and a bit of cheese? Even local cheese would do.'

Dri rose, stretched – and a flash of movement overhead sent her leaping, spinning, drawing her sword in midair, and the quickness of thirty years' training saved her life.

A hideous insect crouched before her. It was as large as Dri herself, double-winged like a dragonfly, with barbed limbs, green composite eyes and a long stinger like a wasp's curled under its body. That stinger had just stabbed the spot where Dri had lain a moment before.

She drew her knife as well. The creature made a sudden deep buzz, like a crosscut saw biting into a tree. It swivelled its black hairy head, fixed an eye on her, and launched itself into the air. *Skies, it's fast.* She couldn't see it: then it attacked again. This time she felt the brush of a leg. She struck, but her sword cut only air.

'Wine and cheese! Wine and cheese!'

'Shut up! Shut up!'

The thing was faster than Sniraga the cat. It dived a third time, vanished, dived again and missed her neck by a finger's width. Dri spun into battle dance, into the desperate pinwheeling that can hold off four humans at once. *If I stop, I die. If I leap from the hay it will sting me before I land.*

The room was a blur. In ecstatic dance she moved backwards through the shards of glass. There was a higher bale there; she could back against it like a wall, burrow into it if need be. *If I have time. How many are there?* Then the insect was on her and the stinger pierced her cloak beside her ribs, and knowing she had won before she struck Dri snapped the stinger in two with a twist of her body and plunged her knife-hand to the wrist into the insect's eye.

It was minutes in dying. Its gore and spittle burned her, head to foot, and a barb on its leg pierced her thigh. But at last its convulsions ceased. She threw the carcass down, bleeding, dumbfounded. What in the black Pits of woe had just attacked her?

'Will you fetch my bottle, please?' sniffed the Shaggat's son.

A Turach groaned. 'Fetch it yourself – the chain's long enough. Only I think you broke it, your daftness.'

Dri took a few staggering steps. The insect's bile stank beyond description. No one in Night Village was going to believe her. She should take back its head, or what was left of it. Then the hay bales moved.

She whirled. Pithor Ness was gaping at her, chin on the edge of the straw bale, not two feet away. One hand hung frozen above the broken glass. He was terrified.

'Guards,' he croaked.

'Careful! Careful, you blary—'

His hand withdrew. She saw his lips curl, forming another word, and then she flew at him, sunk her knife through his cheek, and using it for leverage stabbed down through his jugular with her sword. Blood struck her in a torrent: she was practically inside the wound. He made a sound that was not the word she feared, groped at the crimson straw, and watched her in disbelief as he died.

She leaped once more. He took four bales down with him, glass and all.

It was four in the morning when Diadrelu reached the ixchel stronghold. Men and women who had known her all their lives fell back in astonishment. Blood soaked her from head to foot; even her hair was stiff with it; yet her only wound was a minor cut on the thigh.

Taliktrum appeared, surrounded by his Dawn Soldiers, the shaved-headed fanatics he had inherited from his father. He questioned her in a sharp, peremptory voice. Was it the rat-king again? Or Sniraga? Was there danger to the clan?

'Yes,' she said.

'Of what kind, Aunt?'

She looked at him, the nervous young leader of Ixphir House. She did not know where to start.

'You must answer my questions the same as anyone,' said Taliktrum, almost shouting. 'We survive through clan cohesion. We are not threads but a woven fabric, and discipline makes the weaving strong. Let it fray in one corner and the whole cloth unravels.'

'You don't need to recite children's lessons to me,' said Dri softly. 'I taught them to you, by Rin.'

The soldiers tensed. Taliktrum looked from one to another. 'My aunt is very fond of invoking Rin,' he said with a nervous sneer. 'As often as she does Mother Sky, or the Wanderer, or any other ixchel figure.'

Dri shrugged. A part of her was screaming at his weakness, this ugly groping for standing and respect. 'The tradition's old,' she mumbled.

'And taken from the giants, like certain drugs and diseases. Tell me, Aunt: is Rin a god or a devil for you?'

She sensed the aggression in his words and was appalled. He was displaying her to his fanatics: 'Here is one unlike myself, one I have risen above, despite our kinship.' It chilled her to the core to imagine what such tactics implied for the future of the clan.

Suddenly her other *sophister*, Ensyl, rushed into the chamber. A thin reed of a girl with a prominent forehead, widowed before she could marry, Ensyl was quiet to the point of invisibility much of the time; but Diadrelu knew the iron at the heart of the reed. The girl elbowed her way through the Dawn Soldiers, shot one furious glance at Taliktrum, and led her mistress out.

In her own chamber, Dri let the girl tear off her ruined clothes, then sat as ordered in the herring tin that served as her bathtub. She did not speak as her *sophister* poured bucket after bucket of cold water over her, scrubbing fiercely at the blood and insect substances. The girl had to hack some of it from her hair with a knife.

After several minutes Dri wet her lips. 'Ludunte,' she murmered. 'Didn't he make a report?'

'He tried, mistress. Lord Taliktrum was in the High Loft and would not see him. Skies above, lady, there's glass in your hair!'

That broken bottle had been a godsend. As she crept away the guards were already debating whether the death was an accident or suicide.

'But it was neither,' Dri said aloud.

'What was neither, mistress?'

She looked up at her *sophister*. 'I killed a human,' she said.

The girl was quiet a moment, then nodded. 'I thought so.'

'He was afraid. I don't think he'd ever seen one of us.'

'If you did it, mistress, I know it was the right thing.'

Ensyl's faith stung worse than scorn. Dri hugged herself. Surely the word on his lips had been *crawlies*. What else did humans say at the sight of ixchel? Surely his death was unavoidable.

Given that she had let herself be seen.

She thought of Talag. His brilliance, the mad strength of his quest. *Reveal our presence and you condemn us all. If you can't kill to silence a giant's tongue you're not fit to leave the shelter of a House. Stay in Etherhorde and be hunted. Do not follow us aboard.*

The man she killed had spent nearly his whole life in chains.

'Mistress,' said Ensyl, wondering. 'You're ... branded. There's a wolf burned into your skin.'

Dri nodded, covering her breast. Why was this happening, what was she doing here? How could she possibly keep faith with them all?

8

Faith and Fire

—◦◦◦—

The incubus hurled itself landwards through the storm. Every minute spent in this world was a torture, a pricking and burning as of a thousand acid-tipped needles in its flesh. Nothing existed here but hate: for the pale and wriggling humans, the rain that scalded, the black wind, the reeking sea.

The city loomed closer, its gas lamps hazy in the downpour. The celebrations had moved indoors, now: every tavern, temple, flophouse and cut-rate bordello had been swamped by revellers, still drunk on bad wine and universal brotherhood. The incubus lifted a ragged wing and veered north, over a corner of the wall. A figure appeared at the parapet: a sentry in helmet and ring mail, looking down on the sodden fields. The incubus did not stop to think: it let itself plummet onto the wall a few yards from the man, gasping, burning, freezing all at once, and when the man turned with a shout its bloodlust rose and it flew at him.

The sentry raised his spear, but the demon struck like a frenzied cat. It dodged the weapon, gripped the mail in its claws, shredded the hand that groped for it, then rose to do the same to the detested face. The man was still alive when he fell from the wall, but he died before his body struck the ground.

The incubus lifted away from the falling corpse. Blood soothed it. Like many creatures whose souls extended beyond a single world it suffered immense change when dragged from one to another. In its homeworld it was a passive domesticated animal rather like a sheep, though its keepers sometimes fancied they saw mischief in its eyes.

The rain stripped the blood from its body. Long before the creature reached the shrine the needles of acid were back.

A sceptre. A sceptre. A gold thing with a black crystal surmounting. The incubus could sense it ahead of him.

The Mzithrinis were feasting that night, for their visiting princes would depart in the morning, along with most of the official retinue. They had erected a great tent in the fields beside the shrine, along with brick ovens for the roasting of poultry, venison and shark. The crowd had overflowed the tent, filling the nearby pastures. At the height of the revelry the Mzithrinis were vastly outnumbered by other guests: the meat was excellent, and they were all friends now.

The tent was open-sided and the rain gusted in. Some of the guests were giving up, running for carriages back to the city. The incubus landed on the shrine's gabled roof, and scuttled crablike towards the edge, mewing and snarling with pain.

The artefact it had been summoned to steal lay beneath its feet. But to enter the holy shrine, the creature knew, would be to increase its torments beyond measure. Of course the sceptre was guarded, too. *A mage*, thought the incubus, feeling the throb of magic through the roof, *the thing is in the hand of a mage.* And for all its pain and bloodlust the little demon was afraid. *I will not enter. I will not fight him in his lair.* It stood shivering, moaning, gnawing its wrists until they bled.

Sandor Ott found the rain pleasant against his scars. He was rarely cold. He sat on a low bluff overlooking the shrine, beyond the glow of the sputtering fengas lamps in the tent, feeding scraps of venison to the falcon beside him, watching the cream-coloured bird swallow each piece before giving him another. Now and then he paused to stroke the animal's neck.

'The Sizzy sailors have all gone, then? The officers, I mean?'

'Every one,' said the falcon, his voice like a high cello chord.

'And Kuminzat – the admiral – he left his daughter with that elder priest?'

'She walked a while at her birth-father's side, Master. But she is a *sfvantskor*. There are three young *sfvantskor* women, four young men. The Father keeps all of them close.'

'And he never left the shrine, this old Father?'

'Not since the procession yesterday. And then only to the top of the stairs.'

'Where he knelt to King Oshiram,' said Ott, and a grin passed briefly across his face. He looked approvingly at the falcon. 'Your report is precise, as always. I shall reward you one day, Niriviel.'

'Arqual's glory and gain,' said the bird at once, as if the phrase were something it had learned to say at such moments. 'That is my reward. That is the only true reward for those who love the Empire.'

Childlike pleasure in the raptor's voice. Ott fed him the last bloody morsel. 'Are you ready for the journey, finest falcon?'

'I am, Master,' said Niriviel.

Then the spymaster took a ring from his finger. It was a simple thing of brass, much like a tarboy's citizenship ring, though the numbers engraved upon it were subtly different. He took out a leather cord and tied the ring to the bird's outstretched leg. 'Be careful with this; it is the one thing I have kept from childhood.' he said. 'You know whom I wish to receive it, I think.'

A moment later the bird was winging north towards Ormael, and Sandor Ott was circling the tent, silent as an old panther, well hidden in the dark. He could pick out his agents among the guests in the tent, one arm-wrestling a Sizzy, feigning drunkenness; another seducing a young Locostrin priestess with his eyes. Ott was especially careful to stay hidden from these men. Spying on his own agents was a part of the game.

His inspection complete, Ott walked north around the shrine and started down the narrow goat-path to the sea. Niriviel had reported a single figure there, wading in the surf, with the distracted air of a sleepwalker. A fool in love, probably. But tonight it merited a look. The Mzithrinis' own spy network, the Zithmoloch, had thus far been conspicuous by its silence. Ott almost hoped for some encounter with his rivals before their departure. It was a matter of professional courtesy.

The storm was ending, and the moon thrashed about in the thunder-heads, seeking open sky. Ott crouched where the pasture crumbled into sand. He could see no one on the beach in either direction. Not a structure or a stone. He waited for the moonlight, his thoughts on the days ahead, the war he was brewing among these Sizzy savages, the dire importance of timing and tact. He had placed the fate of the Empire on a single ship, and the twitching madman who captained her. *Rose! If there were anyone else but that delusional Quezan swindler and his witch!*

Ott loathed magic, a province from which he knew he was barred. There was altogether too much of it on the Great Ship. Lady Oggosk, Ramachni, Arunis. The Nilstone, a weapon he had never believed in, and could not use – yet. And Pazel thrice-damned Pathkendle, who had saved the Shaggat's life, but only by turning him to stone.

'Why don't we just knock the blary thing out of his hand?' Drellarek the Throatcutter had demanded yesterday. 'You could put a spear through the belly of that Ormali runt tomorrow. You could kill the lot of 'em. They're no more use, are they, with the wedding behind us?'

So very tempting. But a close inspection of the Shaggat proved the notion impossible. The Shaggat's hand was tight about the Nilstone: that hand at least would shatter if they sought to loosen it by force. And hairline cracks radiated down his arm as far as the shoulder – many cracks, and branching. The whole arm might go, and the madman bleed to death in seconds, when he became a man of flesh once more.

Ott shut his eyes. He was feeling his age tonight. Arqual's triumph would come, sure as that yellow orb would clear the clouds. And Rose would play his part. Whatever else he was, the old bull was always ambitious.

He stood and walked down to the beach. Someone *had* come this way; he could see the footprints even by the fitful moonlight. One person, barefoot, about his height. A night swim? Ott peered at the dark water; there was nothing to see but the waves.

Then the moon broke free and drenched the beach in silver. Ott looked right, left – and there, as if the moon itself had spawned her, he saw a young woman stepping naked from the sea.

She was about twenty yards from him, climbing quickly out of the surf, eyes straight ahead. Ott held his breath. The girl's hair was cut short as a naval cadet's; her limbs were pale and well-muscled. She could not have been much more than twenty but she moved with the gliding step of a warrior.

She reached the top of the beach where the grass began. Crouching beside one of the denser clumps, she pulled out a bundle of clothes. Ott watched her dress: black blouse and leggings, loose-fitting but tight at wrists and ankles. Then she bent down again and lifted a knife.

Gods of death, she was a *sfvantskor*! For the knife was unmistakable: the glint of quartz, the hawksbill curve at the tip. It was the ritual blade from the wedding ceremony – the only weapon King Oshiram had permitted the Mzithrinis to bring ashore. Only the *vadhi*, the Blessed Defenders, could carry such knives. And the only *vadhi* as young as that girl were the newly-trained *sfvantskor*s. There'd been a report. Girls among them. *Yes, three of the seven were girls.*

What in Rin's name was she up to? The way she held the knife – as though it were burning her, but impossible to drop – told him she had blood to draw. But whose? The girl was walking back to the waves, with resolve and something like fury in her movements. Someone else in the sea? There was light aplenty now, and Ott saw no one at all.

Then the wind gusted from her direction and it carried a sob and he knew at once what was happening.

We will never belong among those who belong.

Neda set the knife to her throat. The waves striking her knees made it hard to stand still. One swift cut, long but shallow, not over the vein. She had to be strong enough to swim beyond the breakers, where the sharks would find her before she sank.

Bad blood in her. Sooner or later it had to come out.

They were out there, hungry, circling. They would come like flies to a feast. She had moved among them in another form, with her brothers—

No, no, they were not brothers or sisters. They hated her, the Ormali intruder, the walking shame. They had always known she would fail, and yesterday she had. What had the Father forbidden her? To speak to Pazel, and that she had done. Someone at the wedding had noticed, and word had come to Cayer Vispek, the great *sfvantskor* hero who served on the *Jistrolloq*. Cayer Vispek had whispered to the Father. The old priest had jerked his head upright, looked at her quizzically across the shrine, and some pride or hope for her had fled his eyes. It had not returned at sunset, when the *sfvantskors* performed feats of strength and acrobatics for the awestruck crowd. Nor at predawn prayers, when he touched her forehead with the sceptre and pointed at the sea. *Go and swim, and forget this pain. Above all forget the one named Pazel Pathkendle.* She swam, she changed, she became herself again, but she did not forget. She would never forget, and the Father's look of love would never return.

The other aspirants knew she had fallen into disgrace. Malabron, big pious Malabron of Surahk, had started the gloating. *Bad blood. It's not her fault, really. The faith burns right through weaker souls. Like fire through a thin-bottomed pan.*

Little Phoenix-Flame, another had whispered, his voice dripping scorn. And Suridín, Admiral Kuminzat's daughter, had simply watched her with knowing eyes. She was the best of them, Neda thought, and her silent judgement hurt more than all the insults combined.

Bad blood. She had known it even as a child. Blood of Captain Gregory the Traitor. Blood of Suthinia Pathkendle, who had tried to poison her children. Look what had become of Pazel. He was no slave. He loved those Arqualis, the people who had burned their city, stabbed children in Darli Square, rutted inside her one after another for a day and a night. There were words for women like her in every tongue. Unclean. Unchaste. Damaged goods.

She knew now that the Father had only wanted to spare her pain. He had forbidden her to speak to Pazel, or even to remember him, because Pazel like their other enemies had forsaken his soul.

Tasmut. Stained. That was how you said it in Ormali. She was a stained rag, fouled, reeking, and no power in Alifros could—

'Lower that blade, lass.'

She whirled. An old man in a dark shirt and leggings stood behind her with his feet in the surf. Not armed, not moving. A scarred and battered face, bright with savagery and thought. He had spoken Mzithrini, but he was not one.

'Get away,' she said, in a warning tone.

The old man shook his head. 'You don't want to fight me. I can see you'd be a blary hellcat, but odds are I'd kill you. I've had more practice in the art, you see. More practice than a man ever should.'

Neda rushed him. Astonishingly he did not move. As she raised the knife for a killing stab he looked casually aside, and something in his very calm made her freeze, shocked and terrified. He turned and glanced up at the blade.

'You wouldn't mind me killing you,' he said, matter-of-fact. 'You were about to do it yourself, after all. But you're a *sfvantskor*, a true believer. And if I do manage to kill you, I'll carry your body back to the shrine and tell your priests the simple truth – that I'd interrupted a suicide. And I know you don't want that.'

Neda gaped at the ugly old man. Suicide was an unforgivable sin.

'Or maybe,' he said, 'you're *not* a believer any more? Is that what's brought you to this pass?'

'I will kill you,' she stammered. 'Monster. Who are you?'

'A spy,' he said. 'And you, lass, are a brilliant young novice with much to live for, though obviously you cannot see it. What's the matter, then? Lost your faith in the Faith?'

'No!'

'It's strange,' he mused. 'When the thing we most fear comes to pass – the thing all our will is bent on avoiding – it sometimes proves exactly what we need.'

She lowered the knife halfway to his throat. The old man watched her arm. 'Bastard!' she hissed. 'You're an Arquali!'

'Like the shedding of a skin,' he continued. 'One we'd die inside, if we didn't cast it off. Ah, but once we let it fall – new worlds, lass. New worlds await us.'

Suddenly Neda leaped back and away. 'You don't know a gods-damned thing! A spy, an Arquali spy!' She was weeping, outraged and disbelieving that he should be here, poisoning her last thoughts, coming between her and death.

For the first time he took a step, in her direction. Stiff, old, slow! He was mad, or lying. He would be easy to kill.

'I don't know why you want to die,' he said, 'but I know the *sfavntskor* way – better than you, perhaps. I've watched your kind for years. Go on, lass, give it up. You don't want *soul-traitor* for an epitaph. You don't want to be buried with the waste from the slaughterhouse.'

Such was the fate of suicides in the Mzithrin. The man knew. Perhaps he was exactly what he claimed.

'I'll kill you,' she said again, without conviction.

The man grinned – wolfish, hideous. 'Don't make threats,' he said. 'Not when I can tell your masters exactly what I saw tonight. And I saw quite a lot, lass. A privilege: I suppose no other man ever shall, until the day they strip you for the tomb. Unless the old Father's more corrupt than I know?'

Neda lunged. No man alive would slander the Father to her face. As she drove forward she tossed the blade expertly from right hand to left. Her eyes did not betray the move, nor did her right hand fall away. It was a feint she'd practised ten thousand times.

But her left hand closed empty. The man had moved like a cobra and plucked the knife from the air, and in the split-second that followed Neda learned the astonishing limits of her skills. She was face-down, choking on sand and seawater, helpless with the pain of blows she'd never seen coming.

He spoke from off to her right. 'You're the foreign-born *sfvantskor*,' he said. 'I've heard rumours about you. Tell me, where did the father dig you up? Where is home?'

With a gasp Neda rolled on her side. The man was holding the blade by two fingers as he studied her face. 'Do you know,' he said in a changed voice, 'I've just had the strangest – Rin's blood, the *strangest* – idea about you.' He squatted close to her. 'How's your Ormali, girl?'

She spat out a mouthful of sand. The old man laughed and shook his head. Then he rose and walked around her, not too close, and started up the beach.

'If you are his sister, consider this: he was smitten with the Treaty

Bride. The daughter of the man who sent the marines into Ormael. He'd have died in her place, I'll warrant.'

Neda managed hands and knees. She crawled after him, feeling her strength return. The man called over his shoulder:

'They told you no Arquali could outfight you, didn't they? Well, girl, I've stolen your death tonight: a shameful death it would have been. Go back, and wonder what other lies your masters are peddling.'

He was gone. Neda put her forehead down on the sand. Wishing her heart would stop, knowing it wouldn't. Even at death she was a failure.

Pazel, in love with that butchering admiral's daughter? That couldn't be. She'd seen what they did to him. She'd watched the blows, felt them. The old man was a liar and a fiend.

Then she saw the glint of the knife. He'd left it blade-down in the sand. She rose and went to it and pulled it free, and as she did so she felt exactly what he had described, a rupture of her certainties, a skin tearing away. What was beneath it? Was there anything she would recognise as herself?

A flash of red light. Brilliant, almost blinding. Neda froze: it had come from the direction of the shrine. Then, faint above the noise of the waves, she heard the screams begin.

'Father!'

She ran as she had never run before. The Father was using Sathek's Sceptre: he was facing some terrible threat. She clawed her way up the beach, passed the horrible old man (transfixed, staring), and flew straight at the shrine. There was fire in the courtyard: fire among the pillars, fire spinning overhead like a great ignited bird.

She could hear war-cries from Cayer Vispek and Suridín, and then came the Father's roar and another flash of light. Neda ran blind, smashing through the underbrush. When her eyes cleared she saw an impossibly hideous shape – burning, fanged, dog-like, child-like – dive from the air over the courtyard.

The Father waited beneath it, his beard half scorched away, and he caught the incubus with a blow from the sceptre that hurled it shrieking into the night.

Howls from the windswept pasture. The last of the revellers were fleeing for their lives.

Suridín chased after the thing, wielding an iron skewer from the feast. Cayer Vispek held the Father in his arms: the old man had nearly collapsed. Then Neda's feet touched marble and she was in the courtyard, shouting to them, raising the blade she had stolen to end her life. The Father whirled to face her, his eyes brightening with what looked like joy. And then the demon screamed back through the pillars and struck him in the chest.

Both men were felled by the blow. Cayer Vispek grabbed at the creature, though it was still wreathed in flames. The Father, his chest spouting blood, cried out in a strange language, and the black crystal in the sceptre glowed. A sudden change came over the incubus: the deformed creature vanished, and some milder, weaker shape flickered where it had been. Only for an instant; then the incubus resumed its monstrous form and closed its jaws on the Father's neck.

Neda closed the distance and pounced. Down she stabbed, burying the knife in the creature's spine. The incubus twisted, slashing at her arm, spitting fire. The knife shattered. The incubus released the Father and rose on its burning wings. It flew wild about the courtyard, howling with the voices of the damned, spilling gouts of blood that vanished in flames before they touched the ground.

A hand closed on Neda's arm: Suridín was hauling her to her feet. The girl shoved Neda to the left of the Father while she took his right, and Cayer Vispek tried to staunch his gushing wounds.

Again the incubus pounced – this time on the sceptre, tearing it from the Father's weakening grasp. The Father cried out. The demon leaped, beating its wings with effort, rising—

Suridín grabbed its leg. Neda could smell her hands burning – it was like taking hold of a log in the fire. The demon dragged her across the courtyard as Neda tried desperately to strike the creature herself. Then the incubus dropped the sceptre, twisted in mid-air, and tore into the arm that held it earthbound.

Suridín screamed in agony. With no forethought at all Neda snatched up the sceptre and struck. The incubus wailed and its flame sank low. Neda felt the power in the black crystal, shard of the Casket that was the bane of demonkind. Suridín fell; the incubus crashed beside her on the marble, and with a cry Neda brought the sceptre down again.

The fire went out. The demon fought on, a black smoking shape. Neda struck again and its howling ceased, but still its claws tore at Suridín. Once more Neda struck, with a cry of '*Rashta helid!*'

And suddenly it was gone. No corpse lay beneath the sceptre. Not a whiff of its demon-smoke lingered in the air. The incubus left nothing in its wake but wounds.

*

Cayer Vispek brought the other aspirants back from the sea. The Father lived two hours more: long enough for Neda to summon the courage to tell him where and how she wished to begin her life as a *sfvantskor*, and for the old priest to give his consent. It was long enough too for old Cayerad Hael to be woken and rushed ashore from the *Jistrolloq*, for the sceptre belonged in the hands of the eldest *sfvantskor*. And it was long enough for the Father to point in the direction of the harbour, and wheeze into Neda's ear:

'The demonetta ... it came from that ship ... from *Chathrand*. I knew. I knew from the start.'

Neda did not leave the Father's side. His life was slipping away, and so was the aspirants' self-control. They bickered and shouted and stood apart to hide their tears. He could not leave them, the world could not be meant to turn out this way. But the Father looked at Neda and his smile was proud, as if to say, *Remember, daughter. They despaired; you did not. You were stronger than any of them.*

Could he see through her, even now? Would he learn how wrong he was?

When he died at last their grief spilled over. Malabron was the worst. He spoke blasphemies about the death of the Faith, and glared at Cayer Vispek as if he would fight him, and said that the whole tragedy was Neda's fault.

At that the others shouted him down. The Father had clung to Neda in his last moments, after all, and it was she who had dealt the creature its death blow. And Suridin, the admiral's daughter, who perished just minutes after the incubus, had put three fingers on Neda's cheek in an old Mzithrini gesture, one reserved for closest kin. 'Sister,' she'd said.

9

Stand-off in Simja Bay

—⟞∘∘⟝—

8 *Teala 941*
87th day from Etherhorde

Esteemed and Cherished Friends,

If you are reading this, you will know that I have not returned to the Great Ship. With great regret I must declare that I do not intend to.

My daughter is dead. My heart has sustained a blow from which it will not recover: not in a century, let alone in the few years that remain to me. Like all of you I hoped we might somehow triumph over sorcerer and spy. We did not triumph. The enemy was stronger, better prepared. It is my shame to have misidentified the enemy – and to have been slow to identify my friends.

But the fight does not end with this parting. I have begun to mend ties with King Oshiram. Already I have persuaded him to ask a few key delegations, including the Mzithrinis, to linger after the other guests depart. To them I shall reveal all I know of our Emperor's conspiracy, the plottings of Arunis and the threat of the Nilstone. From this base of believers I will set out to convince the world, and to build a sea-wall against these twin evils. At the very least the Mzithrinis will be warned to guard every approach to Gurishal, even from the western Nelluroq, from whence they have assumed no approach could ever come. The Shaggat, stone or flesh, will never reach his worshippers.

I told Thasha once that I had set aside my admiral's stripes for good, and I meant it. Now more than ever I believe in my duty as a diplomat – but not Magad's diplomat. Arqual must be represented by a voice and a face besides the Emperor's: a voice men will learn to trust; a face associated with honour and goodwill. Our future – and never again shall I believe that there is any future but that which we build together –

depends on these things, even more than on tactics and the sword.

When you have taken a moment to reflect, as I have, you will realise that this task is mine alone.

You five swore an oath, and to that oath you must hold true. A mighty spirit chose you for the task, no doubt because it sensed in you the strength to see it done. Thasha's sacrifice will not be the last. But you must never falter. Let an old soldier tell you: comrades fall, but the mission endures.

Farewell, friends. We shall never see each other more, unless as some believe there is peace hereafter in the shade of the Tree.

Unvanquished,

E. Isiq

Thasha put down the letter, stunned. 'He's not coming with us,' she said.

'Don't tell me you believe that thing,' said Neeps.

'Don't you?' said Pazel.

It was midmorning, the day after the wedding fiasco: another glorious, gusty day at summer's end, but in Thasha's cabin there was barely light enough to read. A dark cloth hung over the porthole: she was still in hiding, still dead as far as anyone knew beyond her circle of friends. She parted the cloth an inch and looked out. Pilot boats were skimming across the Bay of Simja, directing larger vessels out into the Straits. In a few hours *Chathrand* herself would be setting sail.

'Of course I don't believe it,' said Neeps, picking up the sheet of wrinkled paper again. 'The letter's obviously a fake. Thasha, if your father had really decided to stay here, don't you think he'd sail three miles to tell you goodbye?'

'He would if he knew I was alive.'

'Even if he *didn't*,' said Neeps, 'he'd want to, you know, take his leave of your body. And to see the rest of us off.'

'He'd want to,' said Pazel. 'But if he's watching us through a telescope he'll have noticed the archers along the rail. Not to mention the fact that no one's been allowed on or off the ship besides the wedding party, and that Fulbreech fellow. We're prisoners here. He's too smart to get caught as well.'

'He could take a boat out to hailing range, and shout us a farewell,' said Neeps.

Thasha laughed bitterly. 'And tell everyone on the *Chathrand* the sort of things he's just written down? Not likely.'

'You've both lost your minds,' said Neeps. 'This is Admiral Isiq we're talking about. The man who never lost a naval battle. The man who tells kings to get stuffed.'

They were interrupted by a whimper. Beneath Thasha's writing desk sat a low basket, and in it upon a folded blanket lay Felthrup the rat. He had returned to the basket shortly after his outburst the day before, and had not woken since. Now he twitched, mumbling and moaning in his high-pitched, nasal voice.

Suddenly, without waking, he cried out: 'Don't ask me! Don't ask!'

Thasha went to his side and stroked the little creature. 'He has awful dreams,' she said. 'I wake him up sometimes, poor thing, but then he's afraid to go back to sleep. And he needs some sleep, Rin knows.'

'That kick from Jervik would have killed him, without Ramachni's help,' said Neeps.

'Nerves may kill him yet,' said Pazel.

Thasha pointed at the letter in his hand. 'Look at it again, will you? Do you see anything odd – *see* anything, I mean, outside the meaning of the words?'

The boys studied the letter again. Both shook their heads.

'Exactly.' Thasha took the sheet and pointed to a tiny, vaguely star-shaped fleck on the third line. 'You took it for an ink blot, and you were *looking* for something strange. But it's his mark, his code. And the only thing it means is, "Nobody's holding a knife to my throat." He never told anyone about it except for me and Hercól.'

'Well it didn't work,' said Neeps stubbornly. 'Thasha, I have a nose for lies, and that letter stinks like a fisherman's boot. Tell her, Pazel.'

'He's usually right,' Pazel admitted.

'*Usually?*'

'Well it's not as if you're perfect, mate.'

'I see,' said Neeps crisply. 'Not as if I've got a magic gift, is that it?'

'Come off it,' said Pazel.

'That's what you're thinking. "Why trust him? It's just his natural brain at work."'

'You *are* making me worry about your brain, that's a fact,' said Pazel.

'At least mine doesn't turn me into a dry-heaving rooster every month or—'

'Stop it!' said Thasha. 'You're driving me mad!'

The boys clammed up at once. Thasha turned back furiously to the window. The last of the supply boats had drawn alongside; stevedores were piling goods onto cargo lifts. They had taken on more food and water – and scandalously, more passengers, five or six poor souls bound for Etherhorde – the better to sustain the illusion that they were making for the Arquali capital. Who were those people? How much had they paid? When would they find out that they were never going to arrive?

She heard again her father's words in the Cactus Gardens. *You're all I have left, Thasha. I can't watch you die before me as she did.*

'Find Hercól,' she said. 'Bring him quickly. Please.'

'Do you think the letter's real?' Pazel asked.

'Daddy wrote it, if that's what you mean,' she said. 'And those tactics, and the way he blames himself, and that bit about completing the mission no matter the cost – it's exactly what I'd expect from him. And there's the star.'

She touched it with a finger, drew a deep breath. 'There's only one thing I'm sure of: Daddy *has* to be told that I'm alive. Maybe he's right – maybe he shouldn't come with us. But it would be heartless to sail off and leave him in the dark.'

When the tarboys were gone, Thasha pulled a trunk from beneath her bed and removed her training gloves. They were ugly things, iron gauntlets with wool padding over the knuckles and rusted chain looped tight about the wrists. Hercól had wanted them tight, and heavy. A hundred shadow-punches in those gloves usually left her gasping. But she wanted more than that today.

She stepped into the outer stateroom, locked the door, ordered her dogs to lie still. The ship was in some sort of commotion; men's voices, and their pounding feet, echoed through the floor and ceiling. Perfect, she thought, and launched into a battle drill.

Thasha was a fine fighter, exceptional in a few respects. But she also had a wilful streak. It did not express itself as anger – Hercól had taught her never to rely on rage – but as impulsiveness. Hercól had detected the flaw at once. *Inspiration is a fine ally, but a fatal master,* he would say. *Be warned, Thasha: I shall make you feel the folly of your impulses, until you learn to know the good ones from the bad. It will sting and you will hate me, but at least you'll be alive.*

Even bare-handed the drill was exhausting, full of leaps and blocks and whirling jabs. With the heavy gloves it became so taxing that Thasha could think of nothing else. The world emptied of everything but sweat, poise, balance, the duel with her unseen foes. She fought in circles. *Thump thump!* went her fists against her father's reading chair. Each glove like a stone mallet in her hand.

When she completed the routine she began it again. *Faster, girl!* scolded Hercól's voice in her head. *It's your blood they want to spill!* Her heartbeat as sharp and urgent as the blows. At last, almost delirious, she ran to the wall and pulled down one of the crossed swords issued to her father decades ago when he became an admiral. It was a thin blade, but in her gauntleted hands it felt like a six-foot Becturian sabre. In a perfect fury of concentration she fought her way once more about the chamber, slashing, thrusting, Hercól's voice goading her, pitiless when she missed the mark. *Someone's trying to cut off your head!* he'd shout. *Do you see him or don't you? It's not a game, you spoiled bitch, you're striking to kill, you're striking to kill.*

She came out of the trance with the sword half-buried in an imaginary chest. Sickened by what she saw in her mind, as her tutor insisted she must always be. Elated by her own strength. And so tired she could barely stand.

Her father had thought she might take up painting. A gentle suggestion, he'd said. The day he and Syrarys delivered her to the fanged gate of the Lorg School.

She staggered to the washroom, opened the tap on the cast-iron tub. *Painting. Had he ever known her at all?* She stripped off her clothes, stepped into the cold saltwater and scrubbed herself clean, then rinsed off the salt with a few precious cups of fresh water. She looked at her body in the mirror on the door. Sun-darkened arms, breasts no longer quite a girl's, muscles quivering with cold. Men had started to notice that body. Falmurqat certainly had. The prince would have lain with her by now, in his own stateroom aboard his long white ship. Instead Pacu Lapadolma was there across the bay, faithful daughter of Arqual, naked in the arms of her Mzithrini husband. For a time.

Hercól was not in his cabin, nor any of the common rooms. The boys made next for the upper decks. Before they reached the midship guns, however, they found that a great commotion was brewing somewhere above. Men were dashing forward, flowing around both sides of the tonnage hatch and up the ladderways. From above came the sound of voices raised in anger.

'What is it?' Pazel cried. 'A fight?'

'Fight?' someone echoed, not looking back. 'That's just what I said!'

'Fight! Fight!'

Too late, Pazel realised that none of the men knew what they were running towards. But his offhand word seemed to be what everyone wanted, and as they ran it spread around them like an oil fire. Men seized knives and bottles and boarding-pikes, off-duty marines snatched up their spears.

'A damned riot, that's what!'

'Plapps versus Burnscovers!'

'Can't be! Rose would skin 'em alive!'

There was a stampede on the ladderway. Pazel and Neeps were carried upwards past the main deck, where still more sailors jammed the stair, and were spat with the rest into the dazzling sunlight near the foremast. The jeers and shouts grew louder. Pazel leaped up on the fife rail and shielded his eyes.

'Oh Pitfire,' he said.

The *Jistrolloq* was lying alongside *Chathrand*, barely a yardarm between them, and an even larger crowd of Mzithrinis – all bearing weapons – had thronged to her rail, bellowing and chanting.

'*Waspodin! Waspodin!*'

'What are they saying, Pazel?' Neeps shouted.

Pazel jumped down again, foreboding like a sickness in his belly. 'Don't repeat it, whatever you do,' he whispered. 'They're chanting "*murderers*".'

Neeps' mouth fell open. At the bow, the taunts were growing louder.

'All hail the Great Peace,' said a voice from behind them, acidly.

It was Lady Oggosk. The boys drew instinctively away. They had long counted the old witch among their enemies. True, she had turned on Syrarys and Sandor Ott just a few days ago, and Thasha had some murky idea about her being in a secret order connected to the Lorg. But Pazel didn't much care. Oggosk was the lifetime servant of Captain Rose, and he wanted nothing to do with her.

'Do you know what's happening, Duchess?' he asked cautiously.

'Treachery, that's what,' said Oggosk. 'Base scheming, and not our own sort. Last night the Father was assaulted.'

'Whose father?' cried Pazel.

She looked at him, and seemed to comprehend a great deal. 'Not Isiq. Forget Isiq. He was doomed from the start.'

The shouts were growing dangerous. Pazel stared at the old woman, trying to grasp what her words could possibly mean. At last, sensing that she would tell him no more, he turned to go. But before he had taken a step her clawlike hand seized his arm.

'Where is her body?' she demanded.

Pazel pulled his arm out of her grasp. 'With friends,' he said, 'where it's going to stay.'

The boys pushed forwards. At the spot where the two ships were nearest the shouts became deafening. The White Reaper was nearly motionless, lying to on a single topsail beside the anchored *Chathrand*. She was over half their length, which made her the biggest vessel Pazel had ever seen after the Great Ship herself. And while the *Chathrand's* cannon were formidable enough, the *Jistrolloq's* were awe-inspiring: row upon row of massive forty-eight-pounders; longer weapons for distant targets, thick-bodied 'smasher' carronades, gleaming bronze culverins at the stern. Platforms across her topdeck sported giant crossbow-like ballistas, and grappling-guns that could hook another vessel and tear out its rigging. There was no mistaking the *Jistrolloq* for anything but a weapon of war.

Fortunately no one was manning those guns: at present the Mzithrinis were content to threaten their old enemies with swords, spears and curses. The *Jistrolloq's* deck stood twenty feet lower than the *Chathrand's*, so the furious mob had crowded onto the forecastle, and up the masts and shrouds. From all points her men launched the accusation: *Waspodin!*

At the *Chathrand's* starboard rail some twenty tarboys were squeezing and shoving for a view. Dastu stood among them, calmer than the rest. 'Pazel, over here!' he called, making room. 'What are they blary saying, mate? What's that word?'

Pazel scanned the Mzithrini faces, trying to think how he might get out of answering. At the back of the *Jistrolloq's* forecastle stood three black-cloaked *sfvantskors*. They did not shout, but their eyes had depths of rage beyond any of their countrymen. One was older, a man of thirty or thirty-five. The others were in their twenties, their faces hard and menacing.

'You're lookin' at them sfanksters, ain't ye?' said another tarboy, whose nickname was Fishhook. 'There was more of 'em a minute ago – and one was a girl.'

'A girl?' said Pazel sharply.

'Fishhook's right,' said Dastu. 'But the girl didn't stay on deck very long. Just took one good look at us and ran for the ladderway. I thought she was going to cry.'

Pazel thought of the masked girl at the wedding, whose voice still echoed in his mind. Could that have been her? Had she been looking for him again?

The Mzithrinis grew louder. Nor were the Arqualis content to be out-screamed: some accused the Mzithrinis of killing Thasha – hadn't they pricked her with a knife, just before she collapsed? Others demanded that they hand over Pacu Lapadolma.

'Blood-drinkers!' they howled, red-faced. 'Black rags! Want to get whipped like forty years ago?'

Pazel could scarcely recognise his shipmates. Were these the same people who had witnessed Arunis' black magic two days ago? The men who had run in terror from the fleshancs? Where had they found this courage, and this crazy pride? They didn't know what they were being accused of, but they were damned well going to deny it. And though they hated and feared Arunis, the sight of their old enemies brought out a deeper loathing, almost a mania. *Arqual, Arqual, just and true.*

He looked around wildly for an officer. At last he caught site of Mr Uskins, pressed bodily against the rail. But to his horror he saw that the first mate was egging the sailors on. 'Told you, didn't I?' Uskins screamed. 'Never trust a Sizzy!'

Suddenly a man on the *Jistrolloq* pulled himself up into the foremast shrouds. He was a strong, lean man of middle years, and he climbed nimbly, reaching the shielded archery platform called the fighting top in less than a minute. From his bearing and his gold epaulettes, and the way Mzithrini faces began to turn in his direction, Pazel knew he was their commander.

'That's Admiral Kuminzat,' said Dastu. 'Scary looking bloke.'

The officer stretched out his hand above the crowd. At once the Mzithrinis fell silent. Startled, the Arqualis too broke off shouting for an instant. Before they could resume the man pointed his finger and spoke.

'Deceiver. You have killed the Babqri Father.'

Kuminzat spoke in his own tongue, and no sign of understanding passed over the Arquali crowd. But all eyes looked where he pointed. There at the back of the mob, silent and until this moment unnoticed, stood Captain Rose. Lady Oggosk had hobbled to his side; Rose leaned down and let her whisper in his ear.

And suddenly the captain was looking right at Pazel. 'Not a word from anyone,' he said aloud, and there was a threatening rumble in his voice. 'Get over here, Pathkendle.'

The crew parted in silence. Pazel took a deep breath and crossed the deck, Neeps at his side.

As Pazel had already guessed, Rose wanted him to translate the

Mzithrini's words. Pazel did so, and Rose nodded grimly.

'Tell him we know nothing of any deaths but our own,' he said, loud enough for all to hear. 'Tell him only a fool throws accusations like that around – or one with a guilty conscience of his own.'

'Tell him nothing of the kind!'

The voice rang out from the *Chathrand*'s bowsprit. It was Ignus Chadfallow. Despite a stinging distrust of his old benefactor, Pazel was relieved: Chadfallow at least was no hothead – and he too spoke Mzithrini.

Chadfallow seized the jib stay, and pulled himself onto the planksheer above the crowded forecastle. His voice rang out sharp and clear in Mzithrini:

'Admiral Kuminzat. Sailors of the Pentarchy. No one aboard this ship has attacked you.'

Cries of scorn and disbelief from the *Jistrolloq*. The doctor pressed on: 'We mourn with you, for our beloved Treaty Bride lies dead as well. And no sane man among us blames—'

'Chadfallow,' cut in Rose. 'You'll speak for this ship when I say so, and not a moment before.'

The doctor bowed to Rose. But at the same time he shot Pazel a look full of desperate supplication.

All at once a voice rang out from the *Jistrolloq* – in broken Arquali. 'Great Peace you are promising! Not real! Not a real thing!' It was one of the *sfvantskor*s, an enormous young man with a hard, pinched face. 'You are the liars, the old way, the old world that is finished! Bad faith, false doctrines! These will die out everywhere, and better men—'

'Malabron, it is not your place to speak!' snapped the older *sfvantskor*. The younger man fell silent, abashed. Then Admiral Kuminzat spoke again.

'In the darkest hour of the night a beast attacked our Father when he stepped from the shrine. An unnatural creature, an abomination with wings. There was a terrible battle, with fire and spells. In the end the Father slew the thing with the help of his aspirants, but it killed one of them—'

Kuminzat choked on the last words. He drew a sharp breath and continued.

'—and gave the Father his death-wound. His disciples could not save him. But before he died, he pointed across the water – at your ship.'

At his last words the Mzithrinis erupted again, and the Arqualis followed suit. It was all Pazel could do to shout a rough translation into Rose's ear.

'Tell him—' boomed Rose, in a voice used to carrying over gales. 'Tell him that even we expected the Mzithrin to keep the treaty longer than a day. And then tell him to take his ship off our bows, before we take offence. And to the Pits with his crackpot stories!'

The Arqualis roared approval: '*Tell 'im, tell 'im, tarry!*' Pazel winced. He could not imagine something he'd less like to say. Inadvertently he glanced at Chadfallow: the doctor was urgently shaking his head.

'Do it!' snapped Rose.

Pazel felt suddenly nauseous. All around him sailors and marines were bellowing encouragement.

'The captain says,' he began, instantly silencing the crowd, 'he says, ah, that he expected the treaty to last longer than a single day—'

'The boy's Mzithrini is rusty!' Chadfallow cried. 'Allow me to take over, sir—'

'Is lie,' said the young *sfvantskor* called Malabron. 'Boy speaking fine. Less fine is this doctor.'

'Carry on, Pathkendle,' said Rose. 'Chadfallow, interrupt again and I'll have you in chains.'

Suddenly an idea came to Pazel with the force of revelation. He had to tell the Mzithrinis everything, in their language, before they sailed away. Thasha's father might not succeed, and if he didn't there would be no one else. It had to be Pazel, and it had to be now. But why was he so dizzy?

'That Ormali runt,' sneered Uskins. 'He's stalling!'

Neeps put a hand on his arm, steadying him. Pazel bent over, hands on his knees. The noise, the heat, the stink of angry men: was it making him ill?

And then all at once he knew better. He looked up at Neeps. 'Oh gods above, mate,' he whispered, covering his ears.

Neeps understood in a flash. 'It can't be! It's just been three days!'

'I feel it,' said Pazel. 'Oh *credek*, not here, not with so many people—'

'Captain!' shouted Neeps. 'My mate's sick! Let Chadfallow translate, Pazel can't—'

'Sergeant,' said Rose.

Drellarek barked an order. Suddenly Turachs were dragging Neeps and Chadfallow away. Rose took Pazel by the shirt with both hands and hoisted him bodily atop the *Chathrand*'s inverted longboat.

His huge hand closed like a vice on the back of Pazel's neck.

'Speak!' he thundered.

'Lie!' shouted Neeps in Sollochi, as he vanished down the ladderway.

Rose was no fool, Pazel thought. He would know Pazel was twisting the message, just by the Sizzies' reaction to it. *I'll have to get away from him first. Otherwise he'll choke me before I can explain a thing.*

But how long would his own mind obey him?

Pazel cleared his throat, and shouted: 'Captain Rose says there's a treaty in place, and no reason to feel offended, because after all, one of you married one of us, and we're happy and glad and expect the most honourable – babies.'

Kuminzat stared at Pazel in disbelief. Some of the *sfvantskor*s were shaking their heads.

'Tell him we didn't kill his bleedin' Father,' said Rose.

'He's very sorry the Father bled. To death.'

'And we can settle this with cannon if he doubts my word.'

'My word, those are unsettling cannon.'

'And there's no demonology practised on the *Chathrand*.'

'There is no demonology practised on – *SQUAAAGH! CHATHWA! GRAFMEZPRAUGHAAAAA!*'

Rose leaped away from him, aghast. Pazel fell writhing from the longboat, his voice an inhuman wail. The mind-fit was on him, and he was trapped in the centre of a furious mob, and the noise tore at his brain like a thousand shrieking, stabbing birds. There were stomping feet, flying bottles, blood. Uskins and Drellarek closed in, bellowing in Pazel's face. They seemed to think he was faking – or that faking or not, they could beat him into silence.

Suddenly a figure interposed itself between Pazel and Drellarek. It was Hercól, grave and terrible. Pazel saw him standing eyeball to eyeball with the Throatcutter, both of them poised to draw swords.

More Turachs fell in on either side of Drellarek, but Hercól stood his ground. Pazel rose to hands and knees – just in time for Uskins to kick him hard in the stomach. If the first mate had kept his balance a little better, the kick would have finished him. As it was Pazel fell gasping, and Uskins, spitting with hate, drew his foot back for another.

The blow never fell. Uskins spun sidelong, as though struck by a hammer. Mr Fiffengurt was there, brandishing his fists at the first mate and clearly challenging him to come back for more.

Uskins took no persuading. Larger and younger than Fiffengurt, he picked himself up and lunged. Pazel groped to his feet as the two men collided. Hands at each other's throats, they strained against one another. Then Uskins' greater height prevailed, and he threw Fiffengurt down against the carronade. The quartermaster gasped as his head struck the potbellied cannon. Uskins raised his fist to strike again.

Without a thought Pazel dove at him. Uskins swung with all his might, but the force of Pazel's collision brought his fist down just left of Fiffengurt's cheek – where it struck the cannon dead-on.

Uskins howled with pain, and the sheer ugliness of his distorted voice snapped Pazel's last vestige of control. As the first mate lurched away cradling his fist, Pazel ran, fingers in his ears, biting his lips against the scream inside him. The mob fell back, as if from a rabid dog. Pazel hurled himself down the ladderway to the main deck, where to his indescribable horror he found three real geese pursued by Frowsy the tarboy, all of whom ran before him down the length of the ship trailing noises so painful they seemed to leave red welts in the air, and then through an open hatch he saw Arunis and Jervik, huddled like two men at dice, gazing at him with crafty smiles from the deck below.

10

Thasha's Choice

—◦◦◦—

Q. How long have you worked for the Trading Family?
A. Thirty-six years, my lords.
Q. And in that time, how many inspections of the Chathrand *have you conducted?*
A. None, my lords. Inspections are the duty of the Yard Manager.
Q. The Yard Manager answers directly to the Fleet Superintendant, does he not?
A. Not directly, sir. The Superintendant's office is located on Nickel Street.
Q. You are being evasive. How many reports have you reviewed in that time?
A. Nineteen or twenty.
Q. And in any of those reports was there mention of . . . irregularities, shall we say, in the lower decks?
A. Does my lord refer to something beyond regular damage and restoration—
Q. Of course he does. Answer the question.
A. There is a tradition of rumour and yarn-spinning among the crew that no effort by the managers can extinguish.
Q. Did those rumours include mention of compartments that only certain members of the crew could find, or areas of the ship where men were wont to vanish, nevermore to be seen? [Extended Pause] Let the record note the witness' disinclination to cooperate with this inquiry—
A. I answer, my lords, I answer. Yes, I have heard both rumours, and seen them in draft reports. But the Trading Family has never considered it fitting to place such rubbish before the Ametrine Throne.
Q. Drafts, you say? Do you mean that these rumours were later omitted?
A. They were struck from the final reports.

Q. Superintendant, have you any comment on the high incidence of madness in commanders of the Great Ship?

A. My lords, I think I shall not be accused of evasion if I declare myself unfit to speculate on matters medical.

Q. Agreed, agreed.

Lord Admiral's Inquest, Fort Ghan, Etherhorde, 2 Nurn 953.

8 Teala 941

'Tea is served,' said Thasha. 'Syrarys may have been a backstabbing traitor, but she did squirrel away some fine Virabalm red. Don't worry, it's not poisoned: she brewed her own cups from this tin.'

It was an odd tea party. Pazel was sequestered in the reading room, moaning softly with his head between pillows. Neeps sat on the great, tawny bearskin rug, cross-legged and furious, sewing a patch on one of the ninety-two sailors' shirts he had been ordered to repair as punishment for his interference on the topdeck. Jorl and Suzyt sprawled beside him, watching adoringly as Felthrup hobbled back and forth, shaking his head in ceaseless worry. At the table, Hercól sharpened a knife with a small black stone.

'This isn't my job,' Neeps grumbled. 'Pazel and I aren't tarboys any more.'

'You're not anything, matter of fact,' said Fiffengurt, smiling. 'Legally speaking Rose could cast you ashore without a coin or a crumb. If I were you I'd stitch those rags like my life depended on 'em.'

The quartermaster had a cut lip and a dark-purple bruise on his forehead, but somehow his face was the brightest in the room: Thasha might even have said it was aglow with happiness.

The Third Sea War had not broken out quite yet: after a few minutes of bluster and bent bows, Admiral Kuminzat had abruptly called for silence. At once his crew stopped their riotous behaviour and formed ranks along the gunwale. The *Chathrand* mob raged on, but the men of the *Jistrolloq* were oddly serene, and withstood the insults and flung garbage without blinking or uttering a sound.

Three or four minutes had passed. Then, in perfect unison, all five hundred men had raised their left hands and pointed at the Great Ship. Once again the Arqualis were startled into silence. Their enemies' faces were set, and their eyes were cold. From the deck of the *Jistrolloq* a drum sounded: five sharp, well-spaced beats. On the last the Mzithrinis turned and walked to their stations, and in unnerving silence the *Jistrolloq* wore away, on a rendezvous course with her departing squadron.

'Eerie,' said Fiffengurt. 'It was like they were marking us, if you know what I mean. I was glad to see the back of 'em.'

Indeed he seemed glad of almost everything, despite his account of the standoff. Felthrup, however, was squirming with unease. 'A bad sign, an omen,' he said. 'And the mad priest slain by devilry! We are not safe, friends. The dangers gather round us like beasts in a forest, and thus far we perceive only their eyes.'

Hercól drew his knife across his palm, testing the sharpness. 'Thasha,' he said. 'You cannot put off a decision much longer.'

Thasha's hands trembled on the samovar. 'This clerk, this Fulbreech,' she said. 'He told you he would deliver the message personally?'

'To no one but your father.'

'When did Fulbreech promise this?'

Hercól sighed. 'As I said before: after he delivered the Imperial mail. Drellarek did not let him stray five feet from the ladder, or stay longer than it took him to sign a receipt. And of course there was no question of Fulbreech taking mail *off* the ship. But Drellarek made one mistake. The ladder was deployed close to a porthole, looking into a cabin that has stood vacant since Ormael. I saw it and ran below, and caught Fulbreech on the descent. *"If there's good in your soul, boy, find Eberzam Isiq. Tell him his Morning Star was only dimmed, not extinguished. Tell Isiq alone, and by the one we serve, do not fail me."* Fulbreech was stunned, of course. But he dared not speak: Drellarek was watching him from three decks above. The lad gave me a look, and a tiny nod. He could do no more.'

Thasha stared into her tea. Her father had called her 'Morning Star' since her birth on a winter dawn sixteen years ago. He would understand the message, if he ever received it.

'I'm guessing *the one we serve* means that woman in the garden,' said Neeps. 'The one you slipped away to meet, but won't talk about.'

'When I am free to talk, you will understand,' said Hercól. 'But I swore not to breathe her name within a hundred leagues of Simja, and I will keep that pledge. For now I can only promise you that she is good, and that I trust her as I do all of you: with my life and the cause I live for. Indeed she *is* that cause, as much as anyone in Alifros.'

'And the errand boy?' asked Thasha. 'Do you trust him too?'

Hercól shook his head. 'I know nothing of Greysan Fulbreech, and that is certainly not to my liking.'

'Then he could be an enemy!' cried Felthrup. 'Perhaps he never even saw Admiral Isiq! How can we know anything for certain, trapped here three miles from shore?'

'Gently, my boy,' said Hercól. 'Not long ago you stood at death's door.'

'You've been crying out in your sleep,' said Thasha. 'You're having nightmares, aren't you?'

The rat looked startled, and abruptly shy. 'I – I don't remember my dreams, Mistress; they shatter as I wake. But you mustn't worry about me. What are we going to do about your father? What *can* we do?'

'Only one thing,' said Hercól. 'We can swim ashore – or rather, I can. Three miles is no difficulty; I swam twenty in my youth, in the glacier-lakes of Itholoj. But you must understand: whoever goes ashore will remain there. I can dive from these windows, or a gunport, and swim deep enough to escape the arrows that will surely rain down on me. But I cannot reboard this vessel in secret.'

'Even if we wait for nightfall?'

'Perhaps, then. But nightfall may well be too late. The moment Rose finishes his recruiting we shall weigh anchor and depart.'

'Recruiting men, is he?' asked Thasha.

'That's right, lass,' said Fiffengurt. 'The fleshancs killed twenty sailors, along with eight Turachs, the surgeon's mate – and old Swellows, the bosun.'

'Who's on this recruiting job?' Neeps asked.

For the first time that hour Mr Fiffengurt's aspect darkened. 'That would be Darius Plapp and Kruno Burnscove,' he said. 'And their thugs, of course.'

Neeps all but choked on his tea. Felthrup rubbed his face with his paws. 'Oh misery, misery,' he said.

'Should those names mean something to me?' Thasha asked.

Neeps looked at her in amazement. 'Thasha! You've lived all your life in Etherhorde, and don't know about Plapp's Pier and the Burnscove Boys?'

'Why should she?' said Fiffengurt. 'Nice girls don't muck around with that sort.'

Thasha's eyes flashed. Despite six years of *thojmélé* battle-training with Hercól, she had lived a sheltered life; and when at last she was old enough to slip out and explore the city, her father had locked her away in the Lorg Academy. With the other nice girls. She reddened. A foreign tarboy – and a rat, apparently – knew her city better than she did.

'They're the gangs that run the waterfront,' said Neeps. 'You want your ship loaded or unloaded quickly, you've got to bribe the Plapp's Pier gang in the north end, or the Burnscove Boys in the south, where the Ool meets the sea.'

'The same goes if you're looking for hands,' said Neeps. 'You can see them hawking sailors like regular Flikkermen, in taverns all through the port district.'

'They compete for business?' she asked.

'Compete!' said Fiffengurt. 'They blary well go to war over it, every few years. It's no joke, mistress: Plapps and Burnscovers hate each other with a consuming fire, and not a few of the murders in the back-streets of Ormael have to do with that hate. I call it an absurdity that Rose brought *any* Plapps aboard. The Great Ship's been Burnscove territory for generations. Until this voyage, that is.' He shook his head. 'A full crew is six hundred strong, as you know – not counting Turachs, officers, passengers or tarboys. Well of those six hundred, about two hundred are Burnscovers, and nearly two hundred more are with the Plapps. That leaves a final two hundred up for grabs. Why, I should like to know? What good's a powder-keg crew like that?'

'Rose has a reason for everything – a vile reason, usually,' said Hercól. 'But I cannot decipher the game he is playing now.'

Fiffengurt was shaking his head. 'Those gang bosses will have to talk fast, and pour liquor faster, if they want men to sign with the ship that brought Thasha Isiq here to die.'

'Except that I didn't,' said Thasha.

'Yes – no – the point is, mistress, everyone believes in your death. A distinguished and a tragic death. And that makes *Chathrand* unlucky, don't you see? Rarer than rooster eggs are the men who can laugh off that superstition.'

'We are all Ott's fools,' said Hercól. 'Not only have we failed to nullify his sham prophecy, but we have made it easier for men to believe in the *Chathrand*'s sinking, when the time comes.'

'Hark!' said Fiffengurt suddenly. 'Do you hear that?'

'I hear Pazel making sick-cow noises,' said Neeps.

'No, no. Listen!'

They all fell silent. Over Pazel's moans and the general hubbub of the ship, they heard a deep, rumbling roar, such as a bull elephant might make after a nap. It came from somewhere far below. Moments later a second roar blended with the first.

'They've woken the augrongs,' said Fiffengurt. 'The captain's ready to weigh anchor.' He rose and stepped to the window, nodding. 'The tide's not with us, so it may take a few hours. But make no mistake: we sail tonight.'

At once Hercól got to his feet.

'I will watch the docks,' he said. 'Thasha, the choice is yours. If it is your wish I will quit this ship in search of Eberzam, though he will be the last to thank me for abandoning you.'

He sheathed his knife, and left the cabin without another word.

'You mustn't send him away,' said the quartermaster. Felthrup squeaked his agreement.

'But she's *got* to,' said Neeps.

'No, mate,' said a groggy voice from across the room. 'They're right.'

It was Pazel, leaning against the doorframe. He looked like someone arising from a three-day whisky binge. Neeps rose and went to steady him.

'Back to normal?'

Pazel nodded, shakily. 'But I'd give my eyeteeth to know why I had two fits in one week. If this keeps up I'll jump over the rail myself. Listen, Neeps, they're right. I had two chances to get the truth out, and I botched 'em both. If old Isiq fails too, then we have to stop this ship ourselves.'

'And we shall need Master Hercól for that,' put in Felthrup. 'Without his wisdom we should be lost.'

'Without his sword, too,' said Fiffengurt. 'Make no mistake: we're in deadly danger. And there will be no kings or nobles to witness what is done aboard *Chathrand* once we leave Simja behind.'

He reached into his pocket and took out an old, well-seasoned blackjack, its leather grip worn to the shape of his hand. 'I've had to crack some skulls with this ugly thing,' he said. 'And I'll do so again if I must, by the Night Gods. But I'm not the brawler I used to be. We need some deadly, cold-blooded swordsmen beside us, and that right soon.'

'Arunis can't kill us,' said Pazel hotly. 'None of them can go around killing. Ramachni said it in front of them all: if they kill the spell-keeper, whoever he turns out to be, their precious Shaggat's dead – for ever dead, not just turned to stone.'

'You and I understand that, Pathkendle,' said Fiffengurt, 'but we've got eight hundred men on this ship. And they're in mortal terror of Arunis, and the Nilstone – to say nothing of the Ruling Sea. Terror begets desperation, and desperate men strike out blindly. That's what frightens me.'

'Besides,' said Thasha. 'Arunis may be afraid to start killing people, but that doesn't mean he won't cast a spell to turn our hands into stumps, or blind us, or something worse. And it won't stop Captain Rose from locking us up in the brig.'

'Exactly right,' said Pazel. 'He was insistent about that – he all but *promised* we'd fail, if we didn't recruit some allies. That's our top job, along with figuring out what in Pitfire it means to "put the Nilstone beyond the reach of evil."'

'Allies,' said Neep sombrely. 'That's a tall order on this boat. Where do we start?'

'Where indeed!,' said Felthrup. 'Who can we trust with our lives – with the fate of Alifros itself?'

The silence was unnerving. After a moment Thasha rose and went to her cabin. She returned with her notebook and a pencil. 'What about it?' she said.

They debated the question for some minutes. Names were added, only to be scratched out again. 'Too bad Marila left us,' said Neeps. 'She was an odd girl, cold as a catfish. But you could trust her. Amazing diver, too.'

Thasha drew a sharp line across the page.

'Let's try again,' she said. 'Who do we *hope* we can trust? Who *might* turn into an ally, if we're careful?'

This time the names came as fast as she could write them down. 'Dastu,' said Pazel. 'And Bolutu. I've always felt he was on our side, though he's never said anything.'

Fiffengurt snapped his fingers. 'Big Skip Sunderling! A hefty son-of-an-Arquali-brown-bear, is Skip, and fists like pile drivers. He's just signed on – went up to Burnscove and *volunteered*, can you beat that? He had a Simjan sweetheart, but I guess that's ended. And he knows the *Chathrand* too; he was my midshipman a few years back. Right, who else?'

The names came even faster. 'Coote, the old bloke from the *Swan*.'

'Tarsel the blacksmith.'

'And that half-deaf gunner – Byrd.'

'And Mr Druffle,' said Thasha.

The naming stopped. Four pairs of eyes snapped to Thasha.

'What's the matter?' she demanded. 'I know he was under Arunis' spell – that's why I thought of him. Druffle hates Arunis more than anyone aboard.'

'It's not just the spell he was under,' said Pazel uncomfortably. 'Druffle is . . . strange.'

'So are you,' said Thasha. 'We can't rule people out just because they give you a funny feeling.'

'We can't?' said Felthrup, dismayed.

Thasha slapped the notebook down on the table. 'This is *hopeless*. They're going to beat us like a blary rug.'

Neeps glanced at her cautiously. 'Listen to me, that letter—'

Thasha lunged at him. Neeps smiled, but only for an instant. Thasha was on him before he could stand, and when he raised an arm to shield his face she grabbed it and threw him over her outstretched leg. Jorl and Suzyt exploded in barks. When Neeps hit the floor Thasha dropped on top of him, pinning his throat to the ground with the point of her elbow.

'Thasha! Thasha!' said Pazel, struggling not to shout. 'What in Pitfire's wrong with you?'

'Bakru's Beard, mistress!' hissed Fiffengurt. He and Pazel leaped to their feet, but the mastiffs' growls froze them where they stood. Felthrup ran under Isiq's reading chair, whimpering *rabies, fever, musth*.

Thasha let go of Neeps and rolled smoothly to her feet. The tarboy seemed to spring up by the force of his embarrassment. 'Come on, nutter girl, face to face!' he growled as softly as he could.

Now Pazel was struggling not to laugh. 'Don't make it worse, mate.'

'But what in the Great South Sea was *that* about?' said Fiffengurt.

Thasha dropped into her father's chair with a sigh. 'I wasn't about to hurt you, Neeps. But it's true what Mr Fiffengurt says. We're in danger, and we don't have many fighters on our side. Without Hercól we'd be nearly helpless.'

'I've been fighting since I could walk!' Neeps snarled. 'You bring a damn Volpek in here and I'll take him on!'

'That's the problem,' said Thasha. 'You would. And I already know how Pazel fights.'

Pazel reddened in turn: he had never quite gotten around to telling Neeps about their first encounter, when Thasha had flattened him even more quickly. 'Don't like fighting,' he muttered.

'I do!' said Neeps.

'Hush, you donkey!' said Thasha. 'Can't either of you think? If we have to fight I want you to blary *win*. For that you need training and practice. Swordplay, knifeplay, bare-knuckle, staves. Archery. Trickery. Everything.'

The boys looked at her, finally starting to understand. 'And if Hercól leaves now,' she went on, 'there'll be no one to teach you but me.'

'You're good enough,' said Pazel.

'Good enough!' said Fiffengurt. 'You're a right monster, you are, Thasha!'

She turned him a curious look. 'I declare, Mr Fiffengurt, no matter how bad this conversation gets, a smile keeps creeping back onto your face. Do you know something we don't?'

Fiffengurt glanced vaguely around the room – more vaguely than most people were capable of, given his wandering eye. He looked for a moment as though he might deny the charge of happiness.

'You wouldn't be the sort to talk, or think ill of me?' he said.

Never, they assured him.

With that the struggle ceased. He leaned forward and whispered: 'I'm going to be a father!'

The boys and Thasha muffled whoops of surprise. Felthrup hopped and squeaked. 'Hooray, hooray! A new litter of Fiffengurts!'

The quartermaster pulled a folded sheet from his jacket and kissed it. 'Just got the letter, dated the twenty-first of Vaqrin – that's nine days after we left! The wee thing'll be born before the new year!'

'I didn't even know you were married,' said Pazel.

'Well now,' said Fiffengurt, blushing, 'that's the "don't think ill of me" bit.'

Felthrup ceased hopping.

'Now don't jump to conclusions!' said Fiffengurt hotly. 'My Annabel and I have been pledged to each other for ten years. But her parents want no more seafarers in the family. Two of her uncles died on a frigate in the Sugar War, and her grandfather drowned hunting seals. Arrigus Rodd, Anni's father, brews beer. They're good folk but strict as schoolmarms. Old Arrigus is fond of quoting Rule Fifty-Three of the sacred Ninety.'

The boys glanced at Thasha expectantly. The Sisters of the Lorg School had made her recite the Ninety Rules every morning before breakfast.

'"Love must sometimes bow to elder wisdom, patron and keeper of her honour,"' said Thasha.

'Aye, m'lady, but Arrigus leaves out the *sometimes*. He'll not consent to our marriage without my pledge to sail no more for ever. He's fond of me, though. I've apprenticed myself to that old man at every shore leave, learning his trade. This past spring I was set to give that pledge, and take over as Master Brewer. Want to know why I didn't? Thugs from the Mangel Beerworks came in the night, that's why, and torched his little brewery.'

'Oh no,' said Thasha.

'Anni and her folks barely got out alive,' said the quartermaster, staring fixedly at nothing. 'Her mother spent the winter in bandages. Those Mangels already sell nine of every ten pints of ale in the city, you know, but it seems that wasn't, wasn't—'

He got to his feet, shaking all over, and raised both fists in the air. 'The bastards! The bastards!'

They implored him to lower his voice, but it was some time before he could continue.

'Well, then,' he huffed. 'No family business to join, and no money for me and Annabel to set up a household with. And so it's back to sea for Fiffengurt. But what now? A little baby? How could I do this, how could I get her with child?'

'Same way as anybody else,' said Neeps.

'That's enough out of you, Undrabust!' Fiffengurt snapped. Then he dropped back into the chair with a moan.

'Sounds like you're the one who should abandon ship,' said Thasha.

'Can't swim half that far,' said Fiffengurt, with a glance towards Simja. 'They'd find me washed up on the jetty. No, there's only one thing to do – and I'm going to do it, by damn, I've made up my mind.'

Looking rather proud of himself, Fiffengurt took out another letter, fresh and unwrinkled, and waved it significantly.

'I'm telling her to marry my brother, Gellin. He's a bachelor and plannin' to stay that way – never could settle on just one girl, he said. But he worships the ground I walk on, and he has a snug little watch-mending business. And here's the best part.'

He leaned closer, eyes twinkling again. 'My first name's Graff. And we both sign our names *G. Fiffengurt*, see?'

Pazel glanced at the others. 'Uh – not quite, sir.'

'Well now, the neighbours don't much know what those *G*'s stand for. And you can be sure the monk who marries 'em won't. So Gellin will just sign my name to the marriage deed, in place of his! On the sly! When I get back I'll be Anni's husband already, and that babe's legal father!'

He could scarcely contain himself. 'Gellin won't refuse, I know it! He loves Anni, calls her sister already! Hey now, what's the matter?'

All of them, even Felthrup, were looking at him with pity. But no one met his eye.

'They won't let you send the letter,' said Pazel at last.

The quartermaster's face froze. He had been so obsessed with matters in Etherhorde that he had completely forgotten his inability to affect them. Now the plain truth crashed down all at once. His chest heaved, the muscles in his throat constricted. Suddenly he leaped up again and tore the letter once, twice, thrice before their eyes. Then he ran for the stateroom door.

'Wait, wait!' they cried, as Thasha dashed for cover.

But it was too late. Fiffengurt threw the door wide. And there at the cross-passage, some twenty feet away, stood Dr Chadfallow.

The surgeon's jaw dropped. Realizing what he had done, Fiffengurt slammed the door anew. Then he beat his head against it until it shook.

'Fool, fool, fool!'

'Stop that!' hissed Thasha. 'Pazel, Chadfallow knows – he looked me right in the face. Go after him! Hurry!'

'I don't trust him,' said Pazel bitterly.

Thasha dragged him to the door. 'We have to tell him *something* – he's supposed to be embalming me! Oh, catch him, Pazel, quickly, before he talks! And get back in here as fast as you can.'

She opened the door just wide enough to shove him out. Chadfallow had not moved from his spot at the intersection of the passages. His face was bewildered, and he seemed unable to catch his breath.

'*What have you been doing, boy?*' he stammered.

'It was the only way to save her,' Pazel said. 'We had to make Arunis believe she was dead.'

'You fooled someone far more difficult than that sorcerer. You fooled me. How did you do it?'

Pazel shook his head. They had made a promise to Diadrelu: no other humans would learn that ixchel were aboard without permission from the clan.

Chadfallow stared at him fixedly. 'What would Ramachni make of this showing off?' he demanded.

'Showing off?' said Pazel. 'Ignus, what are you talking about? Anyway, Ramachni's gone.'

The doctor looked as though he'd been struck in the face. 'Gone, now? He leaves us *now*?'

'He had to,' said Pazel. 'He was so worn out he could barely walk. Look, if you won't come in—'

'I am no mage,' Chadfallow interrupted, 'but I know more about these arts than you ever shall, boy. I know their dangers, their limits. Above all I know what they do to those who dabble in them untrained.'

'So naturally,' snapped Pazel before he could stop himself, 'you helped Mother experiment on me and Neda.'

Chadfallow was furious. '*Helped?* You wretch, I opposed it with all my heart!'

'After providing everything she needed,' said Pazel. 'The books, the strange little jars and potions – the custard apples.'

Chadfallow appeared to bite back a retort, and Pazel nodded, satisfied. It had been a guess, but a safe one. The night before his mother tried her hand at spellcraft, the doctor had come to their house in Ormael with a bundle wrapped in heavy cloth. Long after the children were in bed he had argued bitterly with Pazel's mother, and finally left in a rage. The next morning she had greeted Pazel and Neda with frothing mugs of custard-apple juice.

'I had no idea what use she had in mind for those apples,' said Chadfallow. 'I was thrown out that night, if you care to know. Such apparently is the fate of those who would befriend your family – to stand like fools on the threshold.'

He reached into his vest and withdrew a pale white cylinder. It was a parchment case, made of some fine wood. 'Is Ramachni truly gone?' he asked.

Pazel nodded again. '*I* haven't been lying,' he said pointedly.

It was the last straw for Chadfallow. Grimacing, he tore open the case and pulled out a sheet of parchment. He held it up to Pazel, displaying an elegant, formal script. Then (much in the same manner as Fiffengurt) he tore the sheet to pieces, flinging the bits in the air as he did so. When the deed was done he turned on his heel and left.

All this Pazel watched with folded arms. He barely noticed when the door behind him opened and Neeps stepped close.

'I guess he didn't care to come in, eh mate?'

'I guess not.'

Neeps went forward and picked up a few bits of parchment. He turned them this way and that, fitting them together. Then he grew still.

'Pazel,' he said. 'Come here.'

Pazel didn't much care what the parchment said. Anything from Chadfallow's hand was a lie. But there was something odd in Neeps' voice. He moved behind Neeps and read over his shoulder.

– ay, 26 Halar 941

– der the auspices of His Royal Highness King Oshiram of Simja:

Negotiant:

Dr Espl. Ignus CHADFALLOW
Envoy Extraordinaire to His Supremacy Magad V,
Emperor of Arqual

and

The Honourable Acheleg EHRAL
Vocal, Court of His Celestial Highness King Somolar of the Holy
Mzithrin

LET THESE BE THE NAMES PUT FORWARD BY ARQUAL: LORD FALSTAM II OF ETHERHORDE, COMMODORE GILES JASBREA OF ETHERHORDE [HIS LIVING PERSON OR UNDESECRATED REMAINS], TARTISHEN OF OPALT [SON OF LADY TARTISHEN], SUTHINIA PATHKENDLE OF ORMAEL (NON-NEGOT.), NEDA PATHKENDLE OF ORMAEL (NON-NEGOT.), AREN MORDALE OF SORHN—

Pazel snatched at the bits of parchment. Suddenly nothing else mattered. 'This was written in Halar – last spring.' Pazel's mind was racing. 'That was two months before we sailed. *He's been carrying this blary thing all along!*'

Neeps picked up the last of the pieces. 'There's another list here,' he said, 'with Mzithrini names, or I'm a dog! Pazel, do you realise what this is?'

Pazel looked at him blankly. Then all at once he went sprinting after Chadfallow.

'Ignus! Ignus!'

He raced across the upper gun deck, past a group of Turachs betting excitedly on an arm-wrestling match. They'd watched the doctor march through the compartment 'steaming like a fumerole,' they said. But when Pazel left by the forward door he was nowhere to be seen.

He tried the surgery, the sickbay, and the doctor's own cabin. He climbed back to the topdeck and walked the length of the ship. No one had seen Chadfallow. Defeated, Pazel started back to the stateroom.

All around him the ship was in a frenzy. The anchors were rising, and yard by yard the green, slippery, thirty-inch thick cables attached to them were spooling in through the hawse holes, where teams of sailors wrestled them into coils that rose like battlements above their heads.

The agitation in Pazel's own heart was even greater, however. Chadfallow had been at work on a prisoner exchange with the Mzithrinis – *and his mother and Neda were on the list*. Clearly the doctor still loved Pazel's mother. And for the first time since the invasion of Ormael Pazel felt he undestood the man. In one respect at least they shared the same loss.

Neeps, to Pazel's great surprise, was still standing at the centre of the crossed passageways, twenty feet from Thasha's door. He turned to face Pazel, wide-eyed.

'You're not going to believe this, mate.'

He raised both fists over his head and brought them down, hard. At the precise centre of the passage they stopped dead, and soundlessly. He spread and tensed his fingers, as though trying to push a heavy crate. He looked for all the world like a mime.

'It's Arunis,' he whispered. 'He's found a way to pay us back already.'

Pazel felt his breath grow short. He drew up beside Neeps and cautiously put out his hand.

Nothing. His fingers met no resistance at all. He stepped forwards, then looked back accusingly at Neeps. 'Will you stop mucking around?' he snapped.

'*Mucking around*, is it?' Neeps leaned again – but this time at an impossibly steep angle. He pressed his face forwards and squashed a cheek against thin air. It was true: they stood on opposite sides of an invisible wall.

'It runs the whole length of the passage,' said Neeps. 'Port to starboard, hull to hull. The whole stateroom's closed off behind it. So is Pacu's old cabin, and that cupboard where she stuffed the wedding gifts, and two more cabins at the end of the hall.'

'No wonder Ignus was so angry,' said Pazel. 'But why can I pass through?'

Behind Pazel the stateroom door opened a crack, and Thasha peeped out. 'What's wrong with you two clowns?' she hissed. 'Get *in* here!'

The instant she spoke Neeps fell to the deck with a crash and a florid

Sollochi curse. But when he rose and stretched out a hand there could be no doubt: the wall had disappeared for him as well.

They locked the stateroom door behind them (though to do so suddenly felt unnecessary). Fiffengurt was gone; Felthrup was reading the bits of his letter on the dining table. When the boys told them about the invisible wall, Thasha paled. After a long silence, she said, 'I made it possible for you to come in, didn't I? Just by telling you to.'

'It sure looks that way,' grumbled Neeps, rubbing his kneecaps.

'I *felt* it,' said Thasha. 'I mean, I didn't know the wall existed. But just as I said *Get in here*, I felt something on my palm, right here—,' she pointed at the wolf-scar '—like the scratch of a little nail. I also felt it when you left, both of you.'

'Why didn't the wall stop me, though?' asked Pazel. 'You hadn't said anything when I stepped back through it.'

'But she had,' said Felthrup, sitting up on his haunches. 'Don't you remember, Pazel? Before you ran after the doctor, Lady Thasha said, *"Get back in here as fast as you can."*'

Pazel looked at the rat, amazed. 'I'll be blowed, you're right.' He stood thinking for a moment, then turned back to Thasha excitedly. 'What if it's not a curse? What if something's *protecting* you, by letting you decide who can enter the stateroom?'

Thasha sank slowly into a chair. 'Ramachni,' she said. 'Who else could it be? But he was so tired, so drained. Where did he find the strength for this sort of magic? And why me?'

'That last bit's an easy one,' said Neeps. 'These are your rooms, Thasha. And *only* yours, now that the admiral—'

'Neeps!' said Pazel.

Thasha looked at them vacantly. 'Now that he's gone. And Syrarys too. At least we'll have plenty of space. We can move the furniture and have your fighting-classes right here.'

'There's still time for him to get here,' said Pazel.

Her face made Pazel wish he hadn't spoken. Thasha wanted to believe her father was coming back: she must have thought of little else since waking from the *blanë*-sleep. But Pazel knew she didn't believe it. His letter was on the table, his intentions plain. And even if Fulbreech spoke to him in time, did they really know that Eberzam Isiq would discard all those grand duties and manoeuvres for her?

'Maybe it's for the best,' he heard himself say. 'He's an important man. People will listen to him, and we have to get the truth out somehow. Maybe he's right to stay.'

Thasha rose and walked into her cabin. Felthrup watched her go, then looked back at the tarboys and shook his head.

Pazel felt vile. He thought of his own father, Captain Gregory, sailing away when he was six, with never a word or letter sent back to Ormael. Nothing at all, until the previous week. Then Gregory and his freebooter friends had suddenly joined the battle against Arunis: for the sorcerer had raided their territory on the Haunted Coast. Pazel had nearly drowned in that battle; his mind-fit had struck at its peak. Thasha had met his father, spoken to him. But she had failed to convince him to scribble so much as a note to Pazel, let alone wait for him to recover. Urgent smuggling duties, no doubt.

Get used to it, girl, he thought with sudden bitterness. *Fathers don't give us time to grow up and leave. They leave us. Some of them can hardly wait.*

The main anchors weighed eighteen tons apiece. Legend held that *Chathrand*'s first launch, six centuries ago, was delayed because no horses could be found strong enough to haul the iron monsters from the foundry to the docks. Tonight, after a four-hour struggle, one was lashed up on the cathead. The second was rising like a black leviathan from the bay.

Mr Uskins felt he was making it happen. Every two seconds precisely, standing before the mighty capstan, he bellowed, '*Heave!*' Fifty men answered, '*On!*' and threw their bodies at the capstan bars, making the device turn a reluctant few inches. One deck below another thirty men heaved in synchrony, and with them laboured the augrongs, Refeg and Rer. They were survivors of an ancient race: hunched-over giants with yellowish hide, enormous chipped fangs, eyes like bloodshot goose eggs, and limbs heaped with muscle almost to deformity. They mumbled words in their own strange tongue, a noise like grinding stones.

The new recruits had almost wept with fear when Uskins placed them beside the creatures (the first mate himself kept a safe distance). But long before the miserable work ended they were thanking the gods for Refeg and Rer. Tarboys mopped the sweat from their faces and threw sawdust at their feet, but the augrongs did the work of a hundred men. By the time Uskins at last yelled '*Stand down!*' they loved the beasts like brothers, dropped beside them on the deck, gasping, moaning, dizzy, united in exhaustion.

The *Chathrand* floated free. It was nearing midnight: a cool, cloudless night of many stars: the great Tree looming west, the Wild Dogs chasing Paldreth the Nomad, and in the distant south the Lost Mariner shining blue and forlorn. Beneath the stars another net of light was spread: the farewell lamps on the docks and temples and towers of Simjalla, and the red and green running-lamps of the departing ships.

A stiff west wind, nearly perfect for getting under way. Mr Elkstem, the *Chathrand*'s austere sailmaster, pulled hard on the wheel, and beneath his feet great chains and counterweights rattled in their shafts. Lieutenants shouted, watch-captains roared, men swarmed like ants up the rigging. The vast ship turned; the huge triangular staysails filled; the prayer to Bakru the Wind-God flowed through the decks in hundreds of earnest whispers. Rose watched the winking lighthouse on Nautilus Point and moved the carving of the woman's head back and forth in his mouth.

'Fore and aft topsails, Mr Frix,' he said softly.

The second mate howled out the order, and the lieutenants flung it forwards like a ball. When the cry reached Hercól it snapped him out of his fixation on the shore. Thasha had told him to remain aboard, and he thought her decision wise. Still the urge to leap was powerful: Eberzam Isiq was dear to him, although the old man served an Emperor Hercól was sworn to depose. For hours he had stared at the wharf, hoping more than believing that Isiq might yet appear. Now at last that hope was gone.

Behind him a man cleared his throat. He turned. There by the hatch combing stood Arunis, his little white dog beside him. The sorcerer grinned and made a mocking bow, spreading his arms as if to say, *Look, we depart, the wheels are turning and you cannot stop them.*

He brushed past the mage and descended. In the stateroom he found no lamps burning: Thasha had asked the boys to blow them out. She was seated by the gallery windows with Felthrup beside her on the bench. Hercól touched her chin; she glanced up, eyes bright, but said not a word. They sat a long time in the dark, listening to the wind grow into the first true squall of autumn and thinking of her father, his imperious moods and strange choices, until the lights of Simja could no longer be seen.

11

Perils of a Perambulator

—◦◦◦—

RATS. One of creation's great failures. The term encompasses a variety of deplorable rodents, unwelcome colonisers of the basements and back-alleys of mankind, ranging in size from the four-ounce abalour 'pocket-rat' to the hulking twenty-pound ghastlies of GRIIB. Science tasks us to suspend our instinctive judgements, but on this point the merchant traveller may take our word: the creatures have nothing to recommend them. Rats are vectors of disease; the WAX-EYE BLINDNESS itself is now known to have spread with the aid of these unclean detritivores *(Chadfallow, Annals of Imperial Physic 2: 936)*. Rats kill infants and newborn animals, destroy food stocks, rampage in the henhouse, foul the common well.

But it is the rat's mind, not his habits, that reveals nature's condemnation. Alone of beasts, the rat lives trapped in a state of pseudo-intelligence: too smart to be excused of his wrongdoing, too dull to resist the filthy orders of his gut. If (as the best minds in Arqual assure us) the WAKING PHENOMENON is an expression of the gods' great scheme for Alifros, what must we make of the fact that *not one* of the teeming millions of rats has ever woken? Only one conclusion may rationally be drawn ...

... Dr Belesar Bolutu has championed an odd alternative, namely that rats (and human beings, for good measure!) are in fact transplants from another world, grafted like exotic fruits onto Alifros' tree of life. This alone, he argues, can explain why the minds of both are so unlike those of any other creatures of our world. We hardly need add that the good doctor has this conviction all to himself.

— The Merchant's Polylex, 18th Edition (959), p. 4186.

133

The man with the gold spectacles touched the eyelids of Thasha Isiq. The girl's sleep was restless, busy. He could feel the eyes dart this way and that under his fingertips, mice beneath muslin. Her bed resembled something tossed about in a cyclone. She slept curled on her side in a jumble of sheets, shawls, blankets, pillows, notebooks, discarded clothes. A nest, as it were. The man with the spectacles couldn't have been more pleased.

Thasha's brow furrowed; her lips made sudden twists and contractions. She is reading, he mused: reading a dream text, one that requires all her attention.

In the outer stateroom he found the lamps extinguished. On the bearskin rug, beside the cobalt mastiffs, Pazel slept in a pose quite similar to Thasha's. For that matter, so did the dogs themselves: spines curved, limbs folded, heads drawn down to their chests. *And below us*, thought the man, *rats by the hundred are curled up almost the same. How our differences diminish, once we are still.*

As he watched, Pazel's hand rose and gently pinched the skin at his collarbone. A curious, barely audible sigh escaped his lips. Neeps lay under the gallery windows, snoring.

The boy made an unusually feral grunt and woke Suzyt, the female mastiff. She raised her groggy head and looked around. Her eyes settled uncertainly on the man in spectacles.

'Go back to sleep, friend,' he said aloud. 'It's only your Felthrup. Going out for a midnight stroll, a meandering, is that the word I'm looking for?'

The dog made no response whatsoever. Felthrup's voice grew anxious.

'Don't look at me with those accusing eyes. A dozen lashes! Men stroll about when the mood takes them. They perambulate. Go to sleep!'

Suzyt growled low. Felthrup turned quickly and slipped out of the stateroom.

He felt a faint electric shock as he stepped through the invisible spell-wall. *The mage will notice that. He will not be long in coming.*

On these dream excursions, Felthrup sometimes inhabited a *Chathrand* as gritty and material as the waking ship. On other nights he turned corners and found himself transported, felt himself rise suddenly on a gust of wind into the high rigging (ghastly, wonderful) or felt the boards melt beneath his feet so that he sank abruptly to the deck below.

This was one of the latter nights. He should have been on the upper gun deck after passing through the spell-wall. Instead he was back in his old netherworld, the hold. He felt an immediate desire to flee, to wriggle into the shadows, out of sight. But that was his rat-self thinking.

I am a man. All things fear me here. I am six feet tall.

He was on a catwalk, a narrow path of planks that jutted from the sloping hull. Beneath him yawned a canyon of shelving and stanchions, wooden crates, grain sacks, lead ballast, sand ballast, tar drums, timbers, barrels of potted meat. He should not have been able to see the hand before his face, but somehow on his dream-walks the dim shapes of things were always visible.

In that time of terror and loneliness before Ramachni (bless him now and for ever) brought him half-drowned to Thasha's cabin, Felthrup had feared the hold most of all. The darkness was often total, and never fully dispelled. Enemies lurked in even more hiding places than on the mercy deck above, where the ixchel had nearly murdered him – and where prisoners in the brig were sometimes given rats to eat, out of malice or pity. Most of these rats were caught in the hold, in razor-toothed iron traps. Others, succumbing to temptation, nibbled at the plates of savoury mush that Old Gangrüne the purser set out, telling themselves that perhaps this one, just this plate, would fail to be poisoned . . . .

Felthrup stepped out onto a flying catwalk, one of the flimsy bridges that spanned the depths of the hold. Traps and poison were no use, of course: day by day the rats multiplied, and any fool could see why. *Chathrand* was provisioned for a voyage across the Ruling Sea. She lacked vegetables, maybe, and certainly limes and pap-root against the scurvy. But she was literally bursting with dry foods, and the rats took their share. More importantly, they were led by a woken rat. Not a cowering, emotional creature like Felthrup: Master Mugstur was fearless and obscenely strong, and ruled his warren in the forward hold with savage efficiency. Mugstur was also a true believer. He claimed to take orders directly from the Angel of Rin, but Felthrup had difficulty believing that the 'Benevolent Bright Spirit' really wanted him to slaughter humans and eat the captain's tongue. *I should like to find Mugstur tonight,* he thought. *To dig him from his nest and fling him to Jorl and Suzyt, if only in my dreams.*

Where was he going? He never knew until he arrived. The marvellous thing, though, was that the more he walked, the longer it took Arunis to find him. *But I must never run. If he thinks I'm avoiding him his wrath will be hideous. Everything in balance, Felthrup my dear.*

'Fall back! Fall back! Mission aborted! Kalyn, Sada, Ludunte!'

The voices were sweet and faint, like the piping of swallows from somewhere deep in a barn. But they were not birds, they were ixchel, and suddenly they were flowing past him, sprinting for their lives, more than he had ever seen in one place. There were archers and swordsmen, spear-carriers, and some with tool cases lashed to their backs. They ran in diamond formation, over and around his calfskin shoes, oblivious to his presence. Some were bleeding; one young woman ran with a groaning man slung over her shoulders.

Where was Diadrelu? It would have been a comfort to see her, even though they could not speak. But of the dozens of ixchel Felthrup saw just one face he recognised – that of her nephew Taliktrum, who paused at the bridge's centre and urged his people to greater speed.

The others shouted as they passed him. 'Ambushed, m'lord! They knew we were coming! What shall we do?'

'Kill them, but not today,' said Taliktrum. 'Get to safety, run!'

Soon all the little people were gone into the shadows – all save Taliktrum. He stood foursquare in the centre of the bridge, sword in hand, looking through Felthrup, waiting for something. It was not normal ixchel behaviour, to stand still in the open. Nor did Taliktrum look certain that he should be there, although he had struck a courageous pose for his kinsmen. Felthrup bent down: the young man's brightpenny eyes were full of rage, and some fear, but most of all agonizing doubt. He gritted his teeth, cut the air before him with his sword. What had led him to this pass? Felthrup wondered. And where in Alifros was Diadrelu?

Rat! Where are you?

Arunis' voice burst like a thunderclap in his skull. Felthrup shot to his feet – too quickly. His head spun. He fell, his flailing hand missed the rail, and he only just managed to seize the catwalk itself as he tumbled. And dangling there over the depths, two feet from the grimeyed Taliktrum, Felthrup realised that he was about to betray the little people to the sorcerer. The ixchel were geniuses at avoiding detection – but how could you hide from a dream figure you couldn't see? And while Arunis prevented Felthrup's waking self from remembering any of what occurred in the dream-time, the sorcerer had made it clear that he remembered everything.

Rat! Answer me!

The mage would be here in seconds. And in the morning he would tell Rose of the 'infestation.' They would seal the lower decks, smoke the ixchel out. And murder them all.

A scraping noise made Taliktrum raise his head. And then the last thing Felthrup ever thought he would see took place. Master Mugstur himself slouched from the darkness and onto the bridge.

'Ay! Help! Help!' squealed Felthrup, utterly forgetting himself.

Stay where you are! boomed Arunis' voice in his head.

The great bone-white rat dragged his thick belly along the catwalk, his purple eyes locked on the young ixchel lord. His hairless head and chest gave him a strange resemblance to a shaved monk.

'The One who planted the Tree of Heaven frowns on you, Talag's son,' said Mugstur, his voice rasping and low. 'Do you pray for your soul's deliverance, or make haste for the Pits?'

Taliktrum fingered his sword hilt, but made no answer. Mugstur waddled closer. A rust-coloured stain surrounded his mouth.

'I am the instrument of Rin's Angel,' he said. 'You will know this to be true, if you but look into your soul.'

Felthrup tried to swing a leg onto the bridge, and failed. A rat would have pulled himself up in half a heartbeat. But he was no longer a rat.

Mugstur took a step closer, and Taliktrum raised his sword. 'You live in doubt,' said the white rat. 'Your life is an endless torment. But if you call to Rin, He will answer you. He will make you whole again. You have but to ask.'

'If he were to alter one drop of my blood to resemble yours, I should slit my own throat,' said Taliktrum, breaking his silence at last. 'But instead I have a mind to slit yours. I possess the skill. Has your Angel promised to keep me from doing so, this very moment?'

'Yes,' said Mugstur, his confidence absolute. 'For she has given unto me the one thing you cherish above yourself, little lord. Steldak has seen the proof – he will tell you. But you blaspheme when you talk of suicide. To harm the body is a sin.'

He belched, and spat some chewed and bloody flesh onto the planks.

Felthrup squirmed and struggled, fearing his arms were about to break. *I must go, I must flee, I will doom them.*

'What do you want from us, you foul sack of grease?' demanded Taliktrum.

'Peppermint oil,' said Master Mugstur.

'What?'

'Or brysorwood oil, or red lilac. We are tortured by fleas. They have always been vicious on *Chathrand*. But lately they have become unspeakable.'

'It's true!' croaked Felthrup.

What is true, rodent? The sorcerer was in the hold, his footfalls ringing on the catwalk, seconds away.

'They gnaw us like termites,' said Mugstur. 'They will drive us mad. Do this, and with the Angel's consent I shall give you what is in my keeping. Fail and my people shall devour it.'

'But where in the black Pits am I to get peppermint oil?' demanded Taliktrum.

Felthrup saw Arunis across the hold, a few steps from the bridge. With a wrenching final effort he shot out a hand and grabbed Taliktrum about the waist. The ixchel's eye's went wild, Mugstur leaped snarling into the air, Arunis shouted, '*There you are!*' And Felthrup dropped like a stone into the darkness.

He was flat on his back, his hand empty. No longer in the hold – the dream had moved him again. He blinked. A crystal chandelier. Scent of leather and ladies' perfume. He was in the first-class lounge.

He sat up, straightening his glasses. Taliktrum and Mugstur were gone. He had done it; he had saved the ixchel for another day.

'Witless oaf,' said Arunis.

Felthrup jumped violently. The mage was seated in an elegant chair, eyes fixed on him. His pale hands issued from the black sleeves of his jacket like two cave creatures, unused to the light. His tattered white scarf was knotted at the throat. A second chair stood near him, and between the two was a little table supporting a round silver box.

'How did you manage to fall like that?' Arunis demanded.

Felthrup scrambled to his feet. 'I saw – a rat! A number of rats! They startled me.'

'So naturally you leaped into the hold.'

'I—'

'What did you mean by shouting *It's true?*'

Felthrup chuckled nervously, brushing himself off. 'It's true that they're loathsome – that we are loathsome, we rats. Once you're used to human form.'

'Do not get used to it,' said Arunis. 'You will not get to play at being a man much longer, unless you give me what I seek. But I shall not threaten you tonight, Felthrup. I think we both understand the situation. Come and sit beside me.'

His eyes indicated the empty chair. Felthrup did indeed understand the situation. He could refuse, he could turn and walk away, but Arunis had found him now and would not lose him until he woke from the dream. Better to keep the mage from anger, if he could. He went to the chair and sat down.

'Try these candies, won't you? Men call them pralines.' Arunis raised the lid of the silver box and chose one of the multicoloured sweets within. Felthrup hesitated, but only for a moment. He chose a large square candy and bit it in half. Despite himself he gave a whimper of delight.

'Raspberries above, hazelnuts below! It is two delicacies in one!'

'And you are two beings in one, Felthrup. A rat who collaborates with fools, plagued by dreams he cannot remember. And a man who remembers everything, what the rat sees and what Arunis teaches, the shame of being a filth-creature and the nobility of human form. A man who could spare the rat much agony, and make him the loved and lauded scholar he was meant to be.'

'Please don't, Arunis,' said Felthrup softly.

'And all so simply, what is more. No one need ever know what he'd done. Why, the rat himself would never know. Do you realise that, Felthrup? Your dream-self can do everything. Your rat-self will not even be aware that it has happened, and none of his friends will suspect a thing!'

'I am one being, not two. You have interfered with my dreams.'

The mage shook his head. 'I have but listened to them. We want our dreams heard, after all. It's the deepest wish of every woken creature, to be heard by those with power to make dreams come true. I alone have paid attention to the longings of your heart.'

Felthrup smiled oddly. 'That's not true, not true in the least.'

'But of course it's true. Felthrup, you give your loyalty too cheaply. What has it brought you? Ramachni saved your life – but only because you knew about the Shaggat Ness, and could inform him. What I ask is no different, except that I put our relations on a more honest footing.'

'Honest?' Felthrup wrung his hands, still smiling. 'You say you will make me a man for ever, but you never say how you would accomplish this miracle. You cannot even make your Shaggat *back* into a man.' He looked up, suddenly fearful. 'Pardon my bluntness, sir, I didn't—'

Arunis lifted a reassuring hand. 'No need to apologise; it's a business-like question. And I'm happy to answer, since you have no means of passing on what I say to your waking self. I shall make you a man by the power of the Nilstone. I am destined to wield it, Felthrup, and by its might I shall remake the world. Your friends have not the least inkling of my purpose. They are the rodents, truth be told. They are ground-hugging mice; they see but inches through the grass. You have chosen to stand up, to comprehend a larger world. You see further, Felthrup – but I see for ever. I see the grim truths, the choices, the destiny of Alifros. With the Nilstone I can guide that destiny as surely as the gods themselves.'

'Do the gods require such assistance?'

Arunis' smile disappeared. After a pause, he said, 'Isiq's stateroom. It is the one place on the *Chathrand* that I cannot see, cannot enter. Give me this simple gift, won't you? Tell me what happens in that stateroom, and the world is yours.'

'I suppose,' said Felthrup, averting his gaze, 'that you want to know if they speak of when Ramachni might return, and how they shall fight you in the meanwhile – that sort of thing.'

The sorcerer's soft jowls broke once more into a smile. 'Exactly so – and you have just answered the first question I would have put to you, without my even asking. You have told me that he is not back *yet.*'

He appeared immensely relieved. He laughed, gazing almost fondly at the other man. Felthrup laughed too, but only to disguise his horror at what he had just said.

'Not back,' said Arunis, 'and perhaps never to return at all. I knew it. Deep inside, I always knew he was not so great a mage as they claim. Now then, my good rat, there is one thing, one very essential thing, that I am certain is never discussed outside that room. Who is Ramachni's spell-keeper? Whose death will turn the Shaggat back into a living man?'

Felthrup snatched another candy and popped it into his mouth. He didn't know; as far as he was aware it was a secret kept even from the spell-keeper himself. Felthrup swallowed the candy and smacked his lips.

'You're very clever, Arunis,' he said.

'I am three thousand years old,' said the sorcerer amiably.

'And what would you do if I couldn't help you? If I couldn't bring myself to say another blessed word about the stateroom, or my true and only friends?'

Arunis considered his nails for a moment. Then he too reached for the candy box, and lifted the lid.

White froth erupted from the container. Felthrup tried to leap up, but found his arms and legs bound to the chair by iron shackles. The mage rose and stepped away as the cascade poured from the little table to the floor. Not froth, but worms: slick, ravenous white worms, gushing into the room through the silver box like the sea through a hull breach. Felthrup was screaming, he could see their faces, their barbed and distended mouthparts, their intelligent eyes. They reached his right ankle first, punctured the skin there like nails through dough, he pleaded, howled, they were tunnelling deep into his human flesh, scaling him by the hundreds, thousands, he was being devoured and he felt every point of mutilation, he was vanishing, vanishing into the bodies of the worms.

Thasha was wrenched from her own troubled sleep, in which she was puzzling over the entry 'Fulbreech' in the *Merchant's Polylex*, by a sudden jolt she couldn't identify. It was still night. The dogs were barking. Her hand closed on her knife hilt before her feet touched the floor.

But in the outer stateroom she found the tarboys stumbling and swearing, and Jorl and Suzyt desperately licking Felthrup, who had exploded from his basket moments before with a bloodcurdling squeal.

'Another nightmare,' groaned Pazel, who had bashed his knee on the samovar. 'At this rate we're going to have to take him to Chadfallow.'

'Or Bolutu,' said Neeps. 'Maybe a horse pill would keep that rat asleep.'

They were trying not to look at Thasha – or trying to seem as though they weren't. She was wearing lace underthings and no more. Irritated at everyone, she fell back into her room, laid down the knife and pulled a dressing robe over her shoulders. Then she crossed the stateroom and gathered Felthrup into her arms.

He was shaking uncontrollably, drenched in cold sweat. 'The w-wor . . . ' he stammered.

'The worst one yet?' she asked, stroking the lame little creature. 'You poor thing. Tell me about it; that always helps with nightmares.'

'Don't remember. Never can remember. My legs hurt. Oh Thasha!'

'Hush now. It's over.'

'All over. All finished, done.'

'Felthrup,' she said gently, 'can't you remember anything? It really might do some good, you know – like coughing up a poison, rather than keeping it inside.'

The rat squirmed in her arms. His stump-tail twitched. He made an obvious effort to still himself, to bring something, anything back with him from the darkness.

'Where are my spectacles?' he said.

12

Lady Oggosk's Warning

—⁓—

10 Teala 941
89th day from Etherhorde

'You are Alifros,' shouted Captain Rose.

He stood at the quarterdeck rail, red beard tossing in the wind. As he spoke, he swept a hand over the sailors and tarboys, the hundred Turachs, the forty passengers let out on deck for the first time since Ormael: literally the whole ship's company, swelling away from him across the gigantic topdeck, or watching from their stations on the masts.

No one looked impressed by his remark. At the wheel behind Rose, Elkstem shook his head slightly, as if to say *Any old tosh* – though neither he nor any member of the crew would have risked such facial dissent in Rose's sight.

They had sailed thirty-nine hours, east by south-east: a fast, flawless running. The waters east of Simja were deep and well-charted; there would be no hazards sooner than Talturi, another day's journey at the least. No rain, nor any hint of it. Still it was odd to summon all hands just to talk philosophy.

But then everything was odd. The sailors gazed up at Rose, fear and anger mingled in their eyes. Most had not set foot on land since Tressek Tarn, eight long weeks ago. None had gone ashore in Simja. And their noble mission had been reduced to one of plotting and deceit. Thasha was dead; none knew why. Pacu Lapadolma had married the Sizzy in her place; then the Sizzies had come and called them murderers.

That particular notion was becoming more likely by the day. The men were filthy and stiff and tired of each other's smells. The new hands (including five new tarboys) were still in shock: the night before Rose had called them to his cabin and, surrounded by Turachs, revealed that they were not, in fact, bound home to Etherhorde. By the time he had explained their true mission the boys were shaking, and the men pale as death.

Some of the old crew had yet to move beyond such terror. Most, however, had turned it into a sort of doomsday rage. Their ultimate fate was beyond their control: they were little people caught in the affairs of kings. But they bitterly resented the loss of the earthly joys of shore leave.

Fear might nonetheless have kept these longings buried had not the *Lily of Locostri*, a floating brothel famous throughout the Crownless Lands, made an appearance in Simja. For two nights she had worked her way quietly about the bay, passing close enough for the breeze to carry hints of jasmine and mysorwood perfume to the *Chathrand*. Such teases were bad enough, but the sound of young women's laughter had sparked fights and fits of weeping, self-inflicted wounds with rusty knives, the drinking of walrus oil and other acts of pure hysterical frustration. Mr Teggatz, the mildest-mannered cook in fleet history, had thrown back four pints of basting wine, insulted the gods, chased his tarboy assistant with a meat cleaver and vomited into a dumpling stew. And then the orders had come: *Stations! Weigh anchor! All hands make ready to sail!*

'If we're Alifros, Rin save this blary world,' muttered Neeps.

Rose had yet to speak again. He gaze swept fore and aft, and his hand was still raised above the crowd.

'He's up to something,' said Pazel. 'He's got that gleam in his eye.'

Jervik Lank, standing right in front of them, glared over a burly shoulder. 'And you've got bilge for brains, Muketch. Shut your gob.'

There were sniggers from several tarboys. Pazel looked at Jervik's broad back with contempt. The older boy's hatred of Ormalis was as strong as ever, but his superstitious fear of them had lately diminished. That could be remedied: a few Flikkerman-hisses or Augronga roars would set him straight. Pazel was far more worried by Jervik's new ties to Arunis. He had spotted them together again just that morning.

'What's the matter, then, Undrabust?' said Jervik, seeing Neeps' look of rage. 'Ah, I know. You're missin' that village girly, ain't you? I've been hearin' about the two of you.'

Pazel struggled to hide his fury. Jervik could only mean Marila, the Tholjassan girl they had met among Arunis' captives, and left behind with her little brother in Ormael. Neeps turned scarlet, and Pazel wondered if he *had* taken taken a shine to Marila.

'Let it go, Neeps,' he said softly.

'Tha's right,' laughed Jervik. 'Listen to your mate, Undrabust. After all, his girly's dead.'

His laughter carried to Mr Uskins, who turned and froze the boys with a stare. Pazel clenched his fists until the nails bit into his palms. Jervik was goading them, as he had done from the start of the voyage, as he had done to Pazel for years on an earlier ship. But knowing that his abuse was tactical did not make it any easier to bear, and neither did the fact that Thasha was actually safe and sound. Pazel felt a loathing for Jervik so tangible he could almost chew it.

'You are Alifros,' Rose repeated at last. 'Few among you will under-stand me, and the time has not yet come for me to explain. But there is one matter about which you should have no doubt. *Everything has changed*. The known world lies behind us. The lives you have lived, the comforts you grew fond of, the very people you have been until this moment – *gone!*'

He bellowed the last word, snapping more than a few wandering eyes back to his face. When he continued his voice was lower.

'We've said our goodbyes, men. Not just to the Imperium, but to the world of law itself – any law, save that of nature and her occulted guardians. You're amused, I know. You think, "We're not even out of the Peren, who does he think he's fooling?" But you're wrong. Every-thing has changed. Very soon you will discover this for yourselves.'

He leaned towards them, daring eight hundred souls to give so much as a giggle. No one obliged. Then Rose straightened, nodded to Uskins, and went to stand beside Elkstem at the wheel.

Mr Uskins leaped up the quarterdeck ladder and faced the crowd. He raised a sheet of parchment above his head. The first mate's teeth were set in a grimace. He crushed one end of the parchment in a fist.

'New crewmembers will fall in on my left and be recognised!' he screamed, in a voice that suggested he would fall on them with beak and talons. 'Face forward, order of rank! And by the lions of the sea, if you waste our time I'll have you lick every man's heel on the *Chathrand*, beginning with those sporting boils or open sores, Rin drown me if I lie! Mr Kiprin Pondrakeri, seaman!'

A muscular sailor with a shaved head and tattooed arms leaped forward through the crowd, knocking aside men and boys in his haste.

'Mr Vadel Methrek, seaman!'

A turbaned man followed the first. As they scrambled for the ladder the crew struck at them – not gently at all – and hissed, and growled

Rotter or *Lousehead* or *Bottom o' the barrel!* The soldiers joined in; even the tarboys struggled to land a few blows.

The mystified passengers looked on, appalled. But the crew were relieved: now at last they knew why they had been called on deck. No one, not even Uskins, was truly angry. This was a procedural passion, and one more way of seeking good luck on the voyage. From time out of mind it had been the practice of the Merchant Service (and the Arquali navy) to induct crew members with threats and insults – the better to protect them from the ghosts of dead sailors, who might feel jealous if they received smiles and friendly applause. Every recruit knew of these rights. They would, in fact, have taken grave offence if treated kindly.

Pazel and Neeps jostled with the rest, looking for someone to abuse. By the weird logic of the service, to hang back now was the only true form of contempt. Rounding the starboard windscoop, Pazel saw a wiry Simjan sailor rushing forward, arms wrapped protectively about his head. '*Scum!*' he cried, and pulled back his fist.

A rough hand caught his arm. He was yanked backwards, off balance. Jervik's fist came down like a club against the side of his head. The next moment he was on the deck. Moisture struck his chin: Jervik's spit.

'You ain't crew no more,' he said. 'Don't you forget it.'

Then Jervik was gone into the melee. Pazel felt as though a horse had kicked him in the face. In a blind rage he forced himself to stand – and just as quickly fell, dizzied and weak. *I'll get you, Jervik, I'll get you, damn your dumb soul.*

Neeps found him as the free-for-all came to an end: Pazel had crawled to the back of the crowd and laid his face against a cool iron breastplate. Neeps helped him stand up. The look the small boy wore might have given a Turach commando pause.

'That's it. Jervik's dead. He's blary dead, is all.'

Pazel probed the already-welling bruise at his cheekbone. He knew his immediate problem was no longer Jervik but Neeps, who might just be capable of attacking Jervik in front of eight hundred witnesses. But before Pazel could speak a new hush fell over the ship. Rose was stepping forwards. Once more all eyes were on the captain.

'Our new bosun, Mr Alyash, will be making some changes to the rotations—'

'Alyash looks like he just got sick on himself,' snarled Neeps, who hated everything at the moment.

Pazel looked at the short, broad, powerful man on the quarterdeck. His skin was very dark, but on his chin and at the corners of his mouth there were pale pink blotches. A few ran in streaks halfway down his neck.

Pazel squinted. 'There's nothing on him, you dolt. That's his skin. If he got that way by a wound it must have been a long time ago.'

'A *wound?*'

'Don't ask me,' said Pazel. 'And for Rin's sake don't ask him either! I'll bet you he's an improvement on Swellows anyway.'

'Captains of the watch will report to Mr Alyash when we adjourn,' Rose was saying. 'Now then: as we set sail, Dr Rain was struck down by gout. I have relieved him of his duties. Henceforth Dr Chadfallow will be our chief medical officer.'

There were hisses, but not too many. Chadfallow stood accused of many things – even of collaboration with Arunis – but poor medicine was not among them. Rain on the other hand was a fumbling menace. Better to be cured by a traitor than killed by a quack.

'Admission to sickbay requires his signature,' Rose continued, 'but for minor concerns you may apply to our new surgeon's mate, Mr Greysan Fulbreech.'

The boys could scarcely believe their ears. During the ceremonial violence neither had heard Uskins shout out his name (it must have come after Jervik laid Pazel on the deck). But there Fulbreech stood among the new recruits: the same glamorous young man who had accosted Hercól during the wedding procession, making the same shallow, almost condescending bow.

'Say, we can ask him about Thasha's father!' said Neeps.

Pazel nodded. 'And we can ask him what in the Nine Pits he's doing aboard.'

'There is one further matter,' said Rose, silencing the crowd again. He nodded to someone below, and the tarboy Peytr Bourjon started up the ladder to the quarterdeck. Peytr was a tall, lean whip of a youth. He and Dastu were the ship's senior tarboys, just one voyage away from making full sailors. Peytr was climbing awkwardly. As he stepped onto the quarterdeck, Pazel saw why: he had a large red object tucked under one arm.

'I'll be blowed, that's a gumfruit,' said Neeps.

So it was: a scarlet gumfruit. The lumpy, bright-red fruit was about the size of a pineapple. The flesh was said to be spongy and bitter; they were no one's favourite, as far as Pazel knew. Pazel had never seen one aboard a ship: they spoiled quickly and attracted flies.

'Gumfruits come from Ibithraéd,' said Neeps. 'My grandmother used to buy 'em for Fifthmoon dinner.'

'Peytr's from Ibithraéd too,' said Pazel thoughtfully.

'Is he? Pitfire, that's why he hates me! He thinks my granddad pissed on his granddad.'*

Peytr handed the gumfruit to Rose, and took a few steps back. Clearly someone had explained what was wanted of him.

'The worst is behind us,' shouted Rose unexpectedly. 'Do you know why that is, men? Because we've left something heavy, something suffocating, behind us in the Empire. That something is hope. I see your faces! You would laugh at me if you dared. But look at the old men among you. They are not laughing. They know what you will come to know. Hope was never something to cling to. Not for us, lads. Not for you, or for me.'

He lifted the great scarlet fruit above his head. 'Look at this gorgeous thing,' he said. 'Brighter than the red lanterns on the *Lily of Locostri*. Brighter than the girls' painted nails. Who wants a bite? First come, first served! Come on, no tricks – who wants a great, juicy bellyful of red?'

The eight hundred before him stood silent, for everyone knew that gumfruit rind was toxic.

Rose nodded, satisfied. Then he lowered the fruit and squeezed hard with his left hand, digging in with his fingers. With wrenching motions he tore the rind away in inch-thick chunks, letting them fall carelessly about the deck. Ten seconds, and it was done. Now his hands cradled the inner fruit, cream-white and slippery as a newborn.

'Hope is the rind,' he said. 'Beautiful, and poisoned. *This* is life, naked life, and it's all we've ever really had. Do you hear me, lads? You've got to *strip that rind away*.' His eyes were blazing now as they had not done once since Etherhorde. 'I couldn't do you that service until now – Ott would have stabbed me, if Sergeant Throatcutter over there didn't do it first. But I'm doing it today – I'm handing you the blary respect you deserve.

'Hope is back there in Simja, back in Ormael and Opalt and Etherhorde and Besq. Hope belongs to somebody else. We're done with it. And that means I don't have to lie to you any more. Fact: we do the Emperor's

* Sollochstol and Ibithraéd went to war in 828, after four drunken Sollochi teens climbed and desecrated an Ibithraen burial mound. Sollochstol contends that the youths were in fact Arquali provacateurs, sent to stir up a conflict that would weaken both nations, making them easier to conquer. Given the events this book relates it is perhaps time to take their claim more seriously. – EDITOR.

bidding or he kills us, and kills our kin. Fact: we're to cross the Ruling Sea with no trial run, and in the time of the Vortex. Fact: what awaits us in Gurishal is worse, if we're ever lucky enough to get there.'

Moans began escaping from the onlookers, but Rose spoke over them. 'Keep looking at this fruit. Look hard. It's not a choice of this or something better. We don't even have the choice of tossing it and going hungry – not unless we want our families nailed up for the birds to pick. Now get over here, Mr Bourjon, and tell me what you think of gumfruit.'

Peytr jumped; he had been gazing at Rose in blank confusion. 'The ... the truth, Captain?'

'Gods of Death, boy, the truth!'

'I ... I like 'em, sir. Always did. Since I was small.'

Rose looked hard at him, then nodded. Very carefully, the captain passed the wet pulpy fruit into the tarboy's hands. Turning to face the mob again, he raised his sticky fist before his face and sniffed appraisingly.

'Gumfruit kept his people from starving, through nine known famines,' he said, pointing at the tarboy. 'He likes it, d'you hear? When it's what you've got, you learn to like it. *And that is how you stay alive!* Eat it, Peytr! Show us how it's done on Ibithraéd!'

By the way the youth ate he might have spent days in preparatory fasting. He anchored his fingers deep in the fruit and tunnelled with his mouth, biting, tearing, swallowing, now and then pausing to sop his chin with his shirtsleeve. It was amazing how quickly he diminished the fruit.

'Eat it! Eat it!' The chant began somewhere among the tarboys, and was quickly taken up by all the crew. Peytr rose to the occasion, gobbling even faster, barely seeming to breathe.

'The koyfruits we grow on Sollochstol are tastier,' said Neeps.

'Oh shut up,' said Pazel.

In less than five minutes a pulp-smeared Peytr had completed his mission, and nearly every voice on the *Chathrand* was roaring approval. He gave them a woozy grin. Rose held out his hand for the gumfruit pit, then raised the other for silence once again.

The thumb-sized pit was the same bright scarlet as the rind. Rose held it aloft. His face showed neither mirth nor anger, but his eyes blazed still.

'That's hope, too, lads,' he said, extending his hand towards them. 'Hope when the bitter meal's finally over, hope at the end of everything. The kind of hope you plant in fair soil and pour sweet water on, year after year. Let an island man tell you: gumfruit trees are kindly things – good shade, sweet spring blossoms. We just might have that kind of hope to look forward to, if we're as strong and smart as I think we are, which is stronger and smarter than any crew in the history of this grandest of ships. But if you weaken yourselves by *dreaming* about that hope – never, never.'

He closed his fist around the seed. 'We're off to the Nelluroq, on a voyage of ruin and death,' he said quietly. 'Some of us will perish. All of us certainly may. But so long as you count yourself among the living, guard this thought: no one can give you this little red seed but me. Some will lie and claim otherwise, but you know who tells you the truth. Dismissed.'

Six sharp notes from the bell: it was eleven o'clock in the morning. Down on the berth deck, Pazel and Neeps were lending the other boys a hand caulking seams – driving tar-coated bits of old rope, called oakum, into tiny crevices between planks, then painting on hot resin to seal the crack against moisture and decay. The crevices were so tight one needed a mallet and chisel to force the oakum into place. But without such tender care the planks would soon leak; Pazel could touch his tongue to an old seam and taste the salt of the ocean, fighting to get in. The work was never completed: hammer in the oakum, slap on the hot resin, chalk off the plank, trade with your mate when your arm grew tired or the resin-fumes made you too dizzy to aim. Up and down ladders. Up and down the endless curve of the hull. Four times a year for six hundred years, and counting.

'That crafty, cunning, sneaky old *beast*,' said Pazel, hammering. 'He's got the crew back in his pocket, doesn't he?'

'He's a good liar,' Neeps conceded, slapping hot resin over the seam Pazel had just filled.

'He's a monster,' said Pazel. 'He kept an ixchel man locked in his desk, and only brought him out to check his food for poison. He probably made Swellows kill Reyast, too, come to think of it.'

'Poor Reyast,' said Neeps, remembering the gentle tarboy with the stutter. 'He would have stood with us for sure. He *did* stand with us, for a little while. But let me tell you something about lies, Pazel. The best kind, the kind hardest to see through, are the ones that mix a little truth into the recipe. Take Captain Rose, now: he says he's the only one who can give us hope. Well that's nothing but a dog-dainty. But it is true that he's the only one aboard who's commanded a boat on the

Ruling Sea. No, he didn't cross her, but he flirted with her and lived to tell the tale.'

'So what?' said Pazel. 'I'll bet a lot of ships have made little darts into the Nelluroq in good weather. How do we know Rose did more than that?'

'The Emperor must think so,' said Neeps, 'otherwise he'd have put someone else in charge. Your arm tired yet?'

'No.'

Pazel liked striking the chisel: he could pretend it was Jervik's skull. And the scent of resin made him think of pine trees in the Chereste Highlands, on summer days long ago. Beside him the wall sizzled like bacon with each stroke of Neeps' brush.

Pazel shot Neeps a cautious smile. 'You did like her, eh?'

Neeps blinked at him. 'Who, Marila?' he said, flushing. 'Don't be a clod, mate, I barely spoke to her. I just think she might have come in handy, that's all. She sure did on the Haunted Coast.'

'She seemed blary smart,' Pazel ventured.

Neeps shrugged. 'She was just a village girl. She probably had even less schooling than I did.'

A note of bitterness had crept into Neeps' voice. Pazel stared at the wall to hide his unease. You could be both smart and unschooled, of course, and he wanted to say so. But how would that sound coming from someone who'd gone to city schools, and been tutored by Ignus Chadfallow?

No, he couldn't say anything of the kind. And before he could find another way to break the silence it was broken for him by a pair of tarboys approaching from portside. Swift and Saroo were nicknamed 'the Jockeys,' for the brothers claimed to be great riders. They were nimble, quiet boys with sharp glances. Rumour held that their father had been a horse thief in Uturphe, and was shot dead in the saddle on a stolen mare.

'Give us them tools,' said Swift. 'We're to relieve you, Uskins' orders. You're wanted topside, double quick.'

'Wanted by Uskins?' said Pazel with a groan.

'Not exactly,' said Saroo.

Neeps lathered boiling resin on a final seam. 'Who wants us, then?'

Saroo leaned close. 'It's Oggosk,' he said. 'Lady Oggosk. She wants to see you in her cabin. Uskins was just passing the word.'

Pazel and Neeps traded startled glances. 'Oggosk?' said Pazel. 'What can she want with us?'

The Jockeys shrugged, in a way that made it clear they would rather not know. 'Just don't keep her waiting,' Swift advised. 'One dirty look from that witch could kill a buffalo.'

Pazel and Neeps handed over their tools. But even as they turned to leave cries broke out in the next compartment.

'You give that blary thing back to me, Coxilrane!'

'Can't, sir, can't!'

'Blast you to Bodendel! It's mine!'

All down the passage boys were turning from their work. The voices drew nearer. Suddenly Firecracker Frix galloped into the compartment in a kind of terror, his long beard flapping and a notebook of some sort tucked under his arm. Behind him came Fiffengurt, barefoot and red with fury, shaking his fists above his head.

'Thief, thief!' he roared. 'I'll tear out your damned beard by the roots!'

Frix apparently believed him: he was running for his life. But as he drew even with Pazel he took a bad step. Groping for balance, his palm slapped the last spot on the wall Neeps had painted with resin. There was an audible sizzle. Frix screamed; the notebook flew from his hands, slid across the deck – and stopped at the feet of Mr Uskins, who had just entered the passage from the opposite side.

'What's all this, Second Mate?' he snapped.

'My h-hand—'

Uskins scooped up the book and examined it suspiciously.

'Now, Uskins, don't involve yourself,' shouted Fiffengurt, closing the distance.

Uskins put his back to the quartermaster. 'Mr Frix?' he demanded.

'It's his p-private journal, sir,' said Frix, still shuddering on the deck. 'Captain Rose knew about it, somehow. He sent me to take it from his quarters – it wasn't my idea, Mr Fiffengurt! See here, he gave me the master key and all! Whoopsy!'

Frix dropped the key and scrambled after it. Fiffengurt kicked his prominently displayed backside, then reached out to Uskins for the book. Uskins ignored the gesture. He had opened the journal and was flipping through the sheets of neat blue handwriting.

'There must be two hundred pages,' he said. 'You've kept yourself busy, Quartermaster.'

'It's none of your business,' said Fiffengurt. 'Hand it over.'

'"*I doubt I have ever missed her more*,"' Uskins read aloud with mock reverence. '"*All the beauties of this world are dust without my Annabel.*"'

'Devil!'

Fiffengurt lunged for the journal, but Uskins kept his body between the quartermaster and his notebook. He was very nearly laughing. 'Carry on, Frix,' he said. 'I'll see that this reaches the captain.'

'But it's my blary property!' shouted Fiffengurt.

Uskins looked at him with naked malice. 'I am glad to hear you say so. First, because you will be held to account for whatever libel or mutinous matter I find in these pages.'

'*You* find?' said Neeps.

'And second,' Uskins continued, 'because to keep such a journal is a crime in itself.' He backed in a circle, holding off the quartermaster with one hand and waving the open book above his head with the other. 'Except for letters home, an officer's every written word is the property of the Chathrand Trading Company. Imperial law, Fiffengurt. We'll see how Captain Rose decides to punish— *Ach!*'

Pazel had crept around behind him and grabbed the journal. Uskins was caught off guard and stumbled over the resin-can, which oozed bubbling across the deck. But he kept his grip on the book. Furious, he slammed Pazel against the wall with his shoulder, even as Neeps and Fiffengurt grabbed at the book themselves.

'The lamp! The lamp!' cried the other boys.

Fiffengurt looked up: Uskins must have struck the oil lamp with a wild swing of the notebook. The peg on which it hung had cracked, and looked set to break at any moment. Walrus-oil lamps were sturdy but not indestructible, and fire in a passage awash with flammable resin was too grim a thought to contemplate. Fiffengurt let go of his journal and grabbed the lamp with both hands.

Uskins gave a vicious, whole-bodied tug. Pazel and Neeps held fast – and the journal ripped at the spine. Man and boys fell apart, each side gripping half the ruined book.

The first mate looked at what he held. With an approving snicker he jumped to his feet and ran off along the corridor, leaving sticky resin bootprints.

'That pig got almost everything,' said Neeps, riffling the mangled pages. 'This is the empty half of the book.'

'Are you hurt, lads?'

They assured him they weren't. Fiffengurt inspected them to be sure, moving slowly, as if in a daze. At last he turned to his beloved journal. Out of two hundred pages he was left with three.

'I'm so sorry, Mr Fiffengurt,' said Pazel.

The quartermaster stared at the crumpled sheets, as if expecting them to multiply. Slowly his jaw tightened, his teeth clenched and his hands began to shake. The tarboys shuffled backwards. Fiffengurt turned on his heel and bellowed:

'Uskins! Son of a leprous limp-teated dog-spurned side-alley whore!'

The Oggosk, Eighteenth Duchess of Tiroshi, had for reasons never well explained made her quarters in a little room inside the forecastle house, between the smithy and the chicken coops.

The cabin had been hers for a quarter century, since her first voyage with Captain Rose. When Rose was stripped of his captaincy in 929, Oggosk departed as well, but her last deed was to mark her cabin door with a strange symbol in chalk. According to tarboy legend, anyone who set foot in Oggosk's cabin from that day forward broke out in chills, boils, warts or mortifyingly confessional song, depending on who was telling the story. There was no proof of these claims. What was certain was that her little cabin had stood untouched for twelve years, until she and Rose returned in triumph to the *Chathrand*.

The door was painted robin's-egg blue: a strange choice for a woman nearly everyone on the ship was afraid of. Pazel had had time to reflect on this curiosity for some minutes now. Oggosk was making them wait.

'We don't have to be here,' said Neeps. 'We're not in the service; we don't have to hop when Uskins says so.'

'Don't be a fool, mate,' said Pazel. 'We may not be tarboys, but we're sure as Pitfire not Rose's guests. We'd be better off if they gave us *more* work to do. If Rose ever gets it into his head that we're useless, why, he'll toss us down to steerage with the rest of those poor louts, and only let us out to use the heads.'

Neeps grunted. 'I'm blary starved. When we're done here we *have* to make Teggatz slip us something to eat. It's our meal shift right now, you know.'

Pazel smiled. 'Your stomach's growling like a street dog.'

'I want to be strong for our fighting lesson, that's all,' said Neeps.

'There's one thing we have to do before we eat,' said Pazel, his mood darkening. 'Track down Greysan Fulbreech.' He glanced about nervously, then whispered: 'You know that the minute we're past Talturi, Thasha's coming out of hiding.'

'So?'

'Neeps, if Fulbreech has anything – well, *shocking* – to say about her father, I want us to know first, so we can break it to her gently.'

'Right you are,' said Neeps. Then the ship's bell began to ring, and he stamped his foot. 'That's eight bells, by damn! What in the Nine Pits can that old crone be—'

The latch clicked. The blue door swung wide, and a pungent odour met their nostrils: incense, ginger, old sweat, dead flowers. 'Come in, monkeys,' said Lady Oggosk from the shadows.

They entered, warily lifting aside an old batik curtain, and saw the duchess seated on a black cushioned chair against the far wall, with her enormous cat Sniraga pacing before her, its red tail twitching like a snake. The light was dim: no lamp burned, but a six-inch-square bit of glass planking was set into the ceiling, allowing a little pale, diffuse sunlight to enter from the deck above. 'Close the door behind you,' said Oggosk, 'and sit down.'

But where? The cabin was small and preposterously cluttered. The boys' shoulders bumped together as they took in the shelves, footstools, scroll cases, stoppered flasks, ancient sun parasols, bead boxes, cigar boxes, dangling bunches of dried herbs, weird animal statuettes. It was not clear where Oggosk slept: the furniture was buried under shawls and sea-cloaks and massive age-darkened books.

There was literally no space free of clutter except for the thin path between Oggosk's chair and the door. So when Oggosk indicated with an impatient gesture that she really did mean for them to sit, that is where they did so.

'Did you hear that messenger bird on Simja?' she asked without preamble.

'The woken bird?' asked Pazel.

'Of course.'

'I did,' said Neeps, 'what of it?'

'Do you know the story of the Garden of Happiness?'

Pazel sighed. 'You can't grow up in Arqual, or anywhere near it, without hearing that stupid tale.'*

---

* In the late Becturian era, Prince Axmal of Dremland persuaded four minor lords, who had taken up arms against one another and Axmal himself, to drop their feuds and attend his son's tenth birthday party. Each lord had a son or daughter of about the same age, and Axmal hoped to pacify the lords with the sight of their children at blissful play in his courtyard, over which he had hung a sign reading, 'The Garden of Happiness.' The plan worked: the lords were entranced by the children's innate goodness, and toasted one another, and declared themselves brothers for all time.

But the children of the minor lords had heard their fathers curse Axmal night after night, and were jealous of the gifts lavished on his son, which were finer than what they

'There was a peacock, too,' said Oggosk, 'in the governor's palace at Ormael, who fawned on his brainless wife. "O saintly lady," it called her. And one of Mr Latzlo's beasts, a climbing anteater, has the look in its eye right now: the look of terror that comes before a waking. The animal should have been given to the Simjans – where is it to find ants, on the Ruling Sea? – but Sandor Ott's order that no one be allowed off the ship extends even to animals, it seems. And perhaps he was right, at that.'

The boys exchanged a look of impatience.

'That odious man spoke of *selling* his anteater,' she went on, 'with no more concern for its well-being than if it were a piece of taxidermy – bloodless, soulless, stuffed.'

'Like Arqualis do with slaves,' Pazel couldn't resist adding.

'Just so,' agreed Oggosk. 'Though the ban on slavery that has taken root in Etherhorde may be extended to the outer territories, soon enough.'

'*Soon enough?*' Neeps said, laughing under his breath.

Suddenly the old woman's glance was sharp. 'We were discussing the waking phenomenon,' she said. 'Consider, boys: it has been going on for some eleven centuries. But in the first ten, only a few hundred animals awoke. There have been that many in the last forty years alone, and the rate is still increasing.'

'We can see that,' said Pazel. 'But what does it have to do with us?'

'Try thinking before you ask,' she said. 'What happened forty years ago?'

'The great war ended,' said Neeps at once.

'And?'

'The Mzithrin drove the Shaggat's followers back to Gurishal,' said Pazel, 'and Arqual took the Shaggat prisoner, in secret.'

'Yes, yes, *and?*'

'The Red Wolf,' said Pazel. 'The Red Wolf fell into the sea.'

'With the Nilstone inside it,' said Oggosk. 'Precisely. The Shaggat Ness, with Arunis goading him on, squandered the last of his military strength on a suicidal raid on Babqri City. He took the Wolf from the Citadel of Hing, though the Mzithrinis blasted most of his ships to matchwood as he did so. But the Shaggat escaped with the Wolf, and

received on their own birthdays. When the adults went in to table, they stripped and gagged the boy, tied him to his birthday pony, set the beast's tail on fire and whipped him around the courtyard. Two days later the domains were at war. – EDITOR.

made it as far as the Haunted Coast before we sank his ship. And from that day the Nilstone itself began to wake.

'The Citadel, you see, was a containment vessel for the Stone – a protection against its evil, like the Red Wolf itself. Half our protection, then, was stripped away forty years ago when the Shaggat raided the Citadel. The rest melted away with the Wolf.'

'So the Nilstone *is* behind all these wakings!' said Neeps.

'The Nilstone's power, yes,' said Oggosk, 'but the spell was cast by a living person.'

Her lips formed a tight line, and she studied them as though reluctant to share anything more. But after a moment she continued: 'Beyond this world and its heavens, in the Court of Rin if you like, there is a debate about the worth of consciousness. What good is intelligence? What's it *for*? Shouldn't Alifros be better off without it? And if not, which creatures should possess the sort of minds we call *woken*? It is an ancient debate, and a hard one, even for eternal beings. It is not settled yet.

'But centuries ago, an upstart mage decided to take matters into her own hands. Every other wizard and seer in Alifros opposed her – but she held the Nilstone, and did not listen. Ramachni may have told you about this mage; I am certain he told Thasha. Her name was Erithusmé.'

'He told us,' said Pazel. 'He said she was the greatest mage since the Worldstorm.'

'Undeniably,' said Oggosk. 'She healed many a country devastated by the Storm, and drove the Nelluroq Vortex away from land, and put the demon lords in chains. But Erithusmé laboured under a curse, for her power had been sparked by the Nilstone. She was the first being capable of using it in twelve hundred years, and no one has succeeded since. Courage made it possible: Erithusmé was born with an almost total lack of fear, and as you know it is through fear that the Nilstone kills. Without the Stone, her magical powers would have been unre-markable. With it, she changed the course of the world – and not for the better, mind.'

'Are you saying she was evil?' Pazel asked.

'I am merely saying that she relied on the Stone,' said Oggosk, 'and the stone is evil perfected: a coagulate lump of infernal malice, spat into Alifros from the world of the dead. She never let it master her, as the Fell Princes did of old. She was that strong. But no mage is strong enough to stop the *side effects* of using the Stone. Every miracle she worked came with a cost. She chained the demon lords, only to learn that it was in their nature when free to devour lesser demons, who began to flourish like weeds. She banished the Vortex to the depths of the Ruling Sea, but the spell-energy that pushed it there also doubled its size.'

'And the wakings—'

'The wakings, yes. They were Erithusmé's last great effort. She looked at the world's suffering, its violence and greed, its long history of self-inflicted harm, and decided that it all began with thoughtlessness. And so she decided that the cure must be more thought, and more thinkers. She prepared a long time in secret, for what would be the mightiest deed of her life. And when she was ready she took the Stone in hand and cast the Waking Spell.

'It swept over Alifros like a flame. Everywhere, animals began erupting into consciousness. Soon they were learning languages, demanding rights, fighting for their lives and territories. But the spell did not stop with animals. There were stirrings even among the lowest things, a hum of thought in certain mountains, awareness in the flow of rivers, contemplation in boulders and ancient oaks. Her idea was to let *all the world* talk back to man, to help him see his mistakes, end his plunder, live at last in balance with the rest of Alifros. Paradise would be achieved, she thought, when all creation found a voice.

'The Nilstone, of course, had other ideas. Rather than create a Garden of Happiness, the Waking Spell plunged Alifros into a nightmare. The side effects! The monsters unleashed into Alifros, the diseases! The talking fever is but one example, and far from the worst. What does a mountain think, when a wizard shakes it from peaceful slumber? Not thoughts of gratitude, I can assure you.'

Pazel fidgeted; Oggosk's gaze always seemed to unsettle him. 'Couldn't Erithusmé just cancel the spell?'

'Obviously not,' snapped Oggosk. 'Her mastery of the Stone was not total — otherwise she would hardly have devoted the rest of her life to getting rid of it, would she? No, she is gone, but the Waking Spell continues. And will continue, in all its glory and perversion, so long as the Nilstone remains to give it power. With the Red Wolf destroyed, that spell is returned to its full force, and we are all in danger.'

Her cat hissed suddenly, from just behind Pazel's back. Neeps cried out, clutching his arm. There was a bright red scratch on his elbow.

'Damn that beast!' Neeps shouted. 'Why'd she attack me? I didn't even look at her!'

'You were not paying sufficient attention,' said Oggosk. 'But my tale is finished now – and here, for your easier digestion, is the moral. The universe has a texture, a weave. It cannot be improved by meddling, by tugging at one thread or another, especially when the hand that tugs is an ignorant one. Disaster alone follows from such interference.'

Blood oozed through Neeps' fingers. Pazel was enraged. 'Is this why you brought us here?' he demanded. 'So you could lecture us about interfering, and attack us with your blary pet?'

Oggosk studied them with the disdain of a jeweller handed some trinket of rhinestone and glass. 'Neither of you is a fool,' she said. 'Not a hopeless and abandoned dullard, I mean.'

'Thanks very much,' said Pazel.

'Unfortunately your antics make it hard to remember.'

'Antics?' said Neeps. 'What would those be, I wonder?'

Pazel saw that the witch's eyes had come to rest on his hand – his left hand, the one burned with the medallion-hard mark of the Red Wolf. At once he closed his hand around the scar. Her eyes moved to Neeps, with keen interest. The smaller boy carried the same wolf-shaped scar at the wrist.

Pazel felt his anger deepen. 'Antics, Neeps,' he said. 'You know, like getting burned with hot iron. And stopping Syrarys from poisoning Thasha's father.'

'Ah, right,' said Neeps. 'I was forgetting. And getting Hercól out of that poorhouse before his leg rotted off. And exposing Sandor Ott.'

'And keeping Arunis and his Shaggat from using the Nilstone.'

'And harbouring ixchel,' said Lady Oggosk.

Pazel knew in a split-second that his face had betrayed him. He had given a guilty jump, and that was all Oggosk needed. She cackled, but the laugh had none of her usual acid glee: it was a savage, embittered sound. She raised a claw-like finger and pointed at the boys.

'All your high-minded dreams of stopping Arunis, stopping this final war between Arqual and the Mzithrin abomination, taking the Nilstone beyond reach of evil for ever – where will they be when the crawlies do as they have *always* done, for centuries without a single exception? What will you say when your Diadrelu turns and spits in your face, and laughs as the sea claims the Great Ship through a thousand secret bore-holes?'

Now Pazel was frightened as well as angry. *How the blazes did she learn Dri's name?*

'I don't know what you're—' he began, but Oggosk cut him off angrily.

'My time is precious, in a way almost impossible to understand at sixteen. Don't waste it. I know about Ixphir House and the crawly fortress on the mercy deck. I know about Diadrelu and her jealous nephew Taliktrum, son of the late Lord Talag. Stop shaking your heads! Look at this, you fibbing urchins.'

Twisting, she reached back over her shoulder to a little shelf. From the clutter of vials and bent spoons and bangles she extracted a tiny wooden box. She tossed it to Pazel with a flick of her wrist.

Inside the box something rattled softly. Pazel glanced warily at Oggosk, then freed the clasp and opened the lid. Inside lay two shoes, well-worn, soft-soled, each less than an inch in length.

'Those are Talag's,' said the old woman. 'Sniraga brought him to me, slain by her own fangs, I think. Another crawly came to me later, to plead for the body. I gave it to him, but in exchange I made him talk.'

'Why didn't you tell the captain, if you're so afraid of ixchel?' Pazel asked.

Oggosk looked at him severely. 'I reveal what I choose, at the time of my choosing.'

'That's right,' said Neeps, sounding even angrier than Pazel felt. 'We take the chances. You just croak and complain about how badly we're doing, and pile up your stories, and shoes, and things to chuckle over. Your cat goes out stealing and murdering, and you sit there like a plum duff—'

'Have a care,' said Oggosk. 'I've killed smaller fry than you.'

'We risk our lives fighting Arunis and Ott and your mad old butcher of a captain—'

'Silence!' snapped Oggosk. For the first time she looked truly furious. 'Insult Nilus Rose again and you'll learn just how much these old bones are capable of!'

Pazel laid a restraining hand on his arm, but Neeps shrugged it off. He got to his feet, a move that scarcely made him more imposing.

'I'm not afraid, you blathering old hag.'

Pazel leaped up, throwing himself in front of Neeps. Oggosk rose stiffly from her chair. Her milk-blue eyes were pitiless and bright. 'You should fear me, Neeparvasi Undrabust,' she said. 'What I may do, and even more, what I may choose to neglect.'

'Get out of here, Neeps,' Pazel pleaded, shoving his friend towards the door. 'I'll handle this, go on!' Neeps protested, but Pazel was unyielding. At last Neeps stormed out, slamming the door behind him with a noise that set all the chickens squawking.

'It's a wonder that boy has made it through sixteen years,' said Oggosk, settling back into her chair. 'You choose odd friends, Mr Pathkendle.'

'Neeps is my *best* friend,' said Pazel coldly.

'"Odd" is not a term of disparagement, boy,' said the old woman. 'I rather like him, if you care to know. We Lorg Sisters admire purity among other virtues, and your Neeps has a glimmer of purity about him − at least where pride is concerned. That doesn't mean he won't get himself killed, of course. The Lorg also teaches respect for the *sebrothin*, the self-doomed. He certainly qualifies.'

She bent down and picked up Sniraga, groaning a little as she straightened. The cat quite filled her arms.

'He isn't doomed,' said Pazel, thinking that he would soon be as angry as Neeps if she kept on in this vein. 'He loses his head sometimes, but that's what friends are for − to step in and catch you. Isn't that what you're always doing for the captain?'

Oggosk stroked her cat, watching him steadily. 'Arunis has a *Polylex*,' she said at last.

'So what?' said Pazel. 'Everyone has a *Polylex*.'

'Arunis,' said the witch with growing irritation, 'has a *thirteenth edition Polylex*.'

Pazel started. The forbidden book! The same magic volume Thasha kept hidden in her cabin. 'How − how did he get it?' he whispered.

'Like any merchant, he bought it,' said Oggosk. 'Between the things that are bought and sold and the things that cannot be had for any price, there is a third category: things that appear to be beyond anyone's reach, but which may sometimes be acquired for a *phenomenal* price. The thirteenth *Polylex* is one of those. Arunis must have hired someone to search for it on his behalf − search the world over, for only a handful survived the bonfires of Magad the Third. It's a pity you take so little stock of your surroundings. Whoever found the book for Arunis must have passed it to him right there in Simja, under your noses.'

Pazel felt his anger rise again, and tried to suppress it. 'What is he doing with the thing?'

'What Thasha should be,' said Oggosk with a little sneer. 'He's reading it – night after night, at a fever pitch. Do I really need to tell you what he's searching for?'

Pazel was silent for a moment, then shook his head. 'The Nilstone,' he said. 'He wants to learn how to use the Nilstone.'

'Of course. And the knowledge is there, Mr Pathkendle. Hidden in that sea of printed flotsom, and – we may hope – by evasion and metaphor and double-meaning, but there nonetheless. The book's mad editor, your namesake Pazel Doldur, considered no field of knowledge too dangerous to include. And when Arunis learns the truth he will have no more need of us. He will go to the Shaggat and touch the Stone, and in that instant we shall be overwhelmed. Ramachni will hold no terror for him, and the wall about your stateroom will pop like a bubble of foam. The Shaggat will breathe again, and Arunis will take his king home to Gurishal by wind-steed or murth-chariot. There, thanks to Sandor Ott, he will find his worshippers in a fever of expectation, ready for vengeance. And with the Nilstone for a servant they will be all but unstoppable. The Mzithrin will fall, and so, in time, will Arqual and the East. Twenty years from now, boys your age in Ormael and Etherhorde could be praying to little statues of that lunatic, and marching in his batallions.'

'We'll get the book,' said Pazel, his voice low and earnest. 'We'll take it from him, before he finds out how to use the Stone.'

Oggosk's eyes widened, amusement and contempt struggling for control of her features. '*You'll* get the book? The mighty Ormali and his suicidal friend? That's a capital idea. Knock on his door and ask to borrow it for the evening. No, monkey, I didn't call you here for that. I want something altogether simpler.'

'And what might that be?'

'I want you to stop caring for Thasha Isiq.'

This time Pazel gave the old woman just the right sort of look: baffled and offended, but with nothing to hide.

'I am not being spiteful,' said Oggosk. 'This is a grave matter, as important in every way as Arunis and his *Polylex*. Indeed the two issues are one and the same.'

'We're *not* handing over her body, if that's what you—'

'Thasha is alive and restless in her stateroom,' said the witch with finality. 'And you'll do exactly as I say. Dine with her, conspire with her, let her and the Tholjassan teach you to handle a sword. Flirt with her, if you like. I know better than to expect young men to do otherwise, even when to do so is to risk everything. *Glah*, that's a permanent flaw in humanity, and there's no cure under Heaven's Tree.

'But let your kisses be cold ones, boy. Do not love her. Do not let her love you. Enjoy yourself, but if she looks at you with tenderness you must laugh in her face, or walk away, or show her some other form of contempt. Do you understand me?'

'I understand you to be out of your nasty mind.'

'We should have brought other girls aboard,' said Oggosk, vexed. 'Girls your age, I mean. There are a number of women in steerage, however, and some have a look of experience about them. One or two are even attractive.'

'Goodbye,' Pazel sang out, for that was all he could do short of cursing her aloud. He made quickly for the door. He was appalled; he felt as though she had torn open a secret part of him and defiled it.

Oggosk's voice froze him in mid-stride. 'This is the only warning you will receive. Where Thasha is concerned I shall not be in the least forgiving. If that girl begins to love you I will send Sniraga into the *Chathrand*'s depths, and have her bring back an ixchel body to lay at Rose's feet. When he learns of the infestation he will slay the whole clan in a matter of hours – and believe me, the captain knows how it is done.'

Pazel spoke over his shoulder. 'You'd kill them all, just to punish me.'

'I would,' said Oggosk. 'I do not shrink from the obligations of history. But they need not die. You may advise them to disembark at our next landfall – provided you do as I say with Thasha. Give her no reason to love you, and your ixchel friends may survive to raid another ship.'

'As if anyone would trust you to keep a bargain like that,' said Pazel.

'You have no choice but to trust me,' said Oggosk simply. 'But listen: why not tell Thasha about the murth-girl? Say that you're still fond of her, that she fascinates you, haunts your dreams. You wouldn't even be lying, would you? But never let Thasha set a finger on you here!' – Lady Oggosk indicated her collarbone – 'Rin save you if you break the heart of a murth.'

He was dreaming. Not even Oggosk could be so senselessly cruel. But when she spoke again her voice was in deadly earnest.

'Removing the admiral from the scene was no pleasure,' she said.

'Don't share his fate, Mr Pathkendle. What Thasha is to do, she must do alone. You can only get in her way.'

Once more Pazel met the old woman's eyes. There was no gloating in them, and no hesitation either.

'I hate you,' he said. 'I hate all of you, with my soul.'

'Souls are exactly what concern me,' said Oggosk. 'Get out.'

13

Illusions at Talturi

—∽∾∽—

29 Teala 941
108th day from Etherhorde

The Honourable Captain Theimat Rose
Northbeck Abbey, Mereldin Isle, South Quezans

Dear Sir,
Fond greetings from your only son.* We are making no less than fourteen knots as I write these words, for the gale that carried us from Simja still blows favourably, east by south-east, and the warm Bramian Current works to our advantage as well. Today we passed the islet called Death's Cap: that lone round rock with its forest of poles, on which for countless years the Arquali Navy has displayed the skulls of pirates and mercenaries, and others who dare to live untamed by Magad's fleets. Our last glimpse of Imperial civilization.

We are yet some days from the Ruling Sea; by my reckoning the ship is currently due west of the Quezans. I shall ~~drink your health~~ *raise a glass in your direction at supper tonight.*

In fact I should like a bit more of a storm. Not only to speed us on our way, but also to keep lesser boats in port. Now that the deed at Talturi is done we must, above all things, remain unseen. And while we have kept to the loneliest stretch of the Nelu Peren, there is always the chance of an encounter. Last Thursday a ship appeared on the northern horizon, but she was too far even to count our masts, let alone identify us.

---

* Rose began this letter several times. A draft recovered from his personal effects contains a variety of first sentences, all discarded: 'I trust this finds you well', 'Rest assured that [unfinished]', and most curious of all, 'Ghosts and sorcerers lie, but from you, Father, I expect no less than perfect truth.' – EDITOR.

We kept our distance until nightfall, and when the dawn came there was fog to the north, and we saw her no more.

Rougher seas would have made the great charade at Talturi more convincing as well. You know the island: brave mariners along the western coast, especially those from the city-state of Manturl Cove. But the north-east is another world: the men there are witless clam-diggers and reef fishermen, all under the sway of a daft Bishwa who has them forever building seawalls against a tidal wave that never appears. This is where we chose to sink.

The fog might have ruined everything – for on this one occasion we had to be noticed. Fortunately it did not reach Talturi until well past dusk, and in the end it even worked to our advantage. Just before nightfall we paraded, close and clumsy, along the north shore and the Village of Three Rivers. I made certain they saw us; I even saluted their mean little wharf with one of the forecastle guns. The storm was chasing their fishing-fleet home with tucked tails, though of course we barely felt it on the Great Ship. We ran before the wind with excessive canvas. If any true sailors watched, they must have noted our fouled mizzentop, our wagging rudder, our overall carelessness (it cost me much to force the men to work poorly; it appalled my every instinct, and theirs). Worst of all, we ran due east: straight at Talturi Reef, as though we knew nothing of it and could not hear the clang-clang-clang of the warning buoy. The fisherfolk leaped and gestured, and one or two signalled danger with a scarlet flag. We ignored them and ran on.

But as soon as night closed in we tacked three points to windward, circumnavigated the reef, and crept back under shortened sail to Octurl Point, the eastern extreme of Talturi Island. The Bishwa keeps a lighthouse there, but its lamp is weak and could not pierce the fog: only the buoy told us our distance from the coral. I need not explain to you that the danger was real: dropping anchor was out of the question, and yet we were not half a league from a submerged wall that would tear the bottom out of Chathrand as surely as any other ship.

We turned Chathrand into the wind, striking all but the fore topsail in order to keep us pointed true, and to hold our shoreward drift to a minimum. Then I set six hundred men to work.

All that vital and expensive wreckage had been raised from the hold already: broken spars, shattered mastwood and gunwales, cabin doors with brass nameplates, boxes of engraved cutlery, footlockers, water casks, wine bottles, life preservers, a perfect replica of the Goose-Girl, a fine Arquali cello, first-class children's toys, a ruined longboat with IMS

Chathrand *emblazoned on her stern. All was genuine; even the tar on the tattered rigging matched our own. At my orders men pried open the crates, slit the burlap, severed the ropes that had secured all this flotsam, and dragged it to the gunwales, port and starboard, bow to stern. It was a weird sight, Father: our untouched* Chathrand, *draped in artifacts of her own demise.*

Then we distributed the bodies of our slain. Rarely have I seen men look more mutinous, sir. Even that trader in pelts and carcasses Mr Latzlo (still mooning for the Lapadolma girl, who despised him) roused himself to grumble about the wrongness of tossing our own sailors and soldiers out with the garbage, especially as they had died fighting for the ship. Probably Sandor Ott intended to use the bodies of criminals: the governor of Ormael had some twenty waiting to be executed. But after the violence in which Ott was driven from the palace, the governor (too great a fool to be trusted with details of the Plan) was no longer cooperative. In a sense we are indebted to Arunis for killing as many of us as he did: shipwrecks must have bodies. Old Swellows, who served you as a tarboy on the Indomitable, *lay among them: bloated and red-faced, a drunkard even in death.*

Brother Bolutu prayed beside each corpse, and sent their spirits to final rest with the sign of the Tree. His gesture calmed the men. It was the first time he has proved useful since the start of the voyage.

For two hours I stared into perfect darkness. The clanging buoy grew louder, nearer; all over the ship men listened, barely breathing. We were surely no more than a quarter-mile off the reef.

In another minute I would have given the order to abort and run. Then a dim glow swept over the Chathrand. *It was the lighthouse: the fog was thinning at last. 'Over the side!' I declared. 'Over the side with everything, the whole confabulation! They can see our lights too, make haste, make haste!' I did not shout, for the wind was behind us and my voice might have carried to the lighthouse keepers. But the lieutenants took up the command, and at once the men began to heave and hurl the wreckage into the sea. Ott's attention to detail was flawless, not to say maniacal: he had lain away bags of straw, silage, chicken feathers and other debris that would toss on the wave-tops, and casks of walrus oil and turpentine to stain the Talturi shore.*

The corpses proved most difficult: even after Bolutu's blessing we had to tear some of them from the arms of their shipmates, who sobbed like children. I let them. If those voices reached Talturi, so much the better.

Next we extinguished every light aboard, save the running lights

167

facing the island, and a few handheld lamps. There are five of these running lights: big fengas contraptions designed to self-extinguish if their glass hoods so much as crack. With great care my men detached them from the rigging and lowered them, still burning, towards the sea. Those of us holding lamps rushed and staggered, dipped and bobbed: I think Mr Uskins was quite enjoying himself.

By now I could hear voices hailing us from Octurl Point. We answered with screams, distress-whistles, frantic peals of the ship's bell. Teggatz beat a cauldron with an iron spoon. Alyash, the new bosun, lit a flare and hurled it in a blazing arc into the sea. Of the officers, Fiffengurt alone stood silent, arms crossed, as if the scene was highly offensive to him. I know what you will say, Father: that I have not punished him sufficiently, taught him to fear my every glance, my least displeasure. Better a dead man than a disobedient one, etc. But I cannot do without Fiffengurt yet. Although he suspects nothing, he is going to betray his friends to me. He is a man with too much to lose.

The storm had us rolling, and one of the running lights smashed against our hull. But the others we managed to drown in the waves – one after another, as though our keel had shattered on the reef and we were flooding fast. I sent the men with the deck lamps a short way up the masts: they were the lone survivors, now, trying to keep their heads above water. One by one we snuffed the lamps. I dangled the last one from the quarterdeck, waved it fitfully and blew it out. And in deep darkness the men set mainsails, and we tacked sharp into the wind and bore away.

'Congratulations, Nilus,' said Lady Oggosk, who had come out into the rain to watch the show. 'Once more you prove that you were born to deceive. By mid-autumn all Etherhorde will know that the Great Ship went down off Talturi. Lady Lapadolma will die of heartache. Come to think of it, she'll learn of her niece's death at about the same time.'

'She took the Chathrand from me once,' I said. 'Now I have taken the ship from her and her damnable Company, for ever.'

It was then that the ghost intervened. Oggosk's lips kept moving, she was cackling and delighted, but instead of her voice I heard another, cold as a tomb, and saw the walking shadow approaching me from the jiggermast. 'For ever!' it hissed. 'That is but one of the black immensities! You know nothing of them, but I do. I know them, Nilus Rose. They gape at me like cavern mouths. One of them shall claim and devour me.'

The wind tore at its burial wraps. The rain passed through it, however: a sign of one whose years of death do not yet outnumber those of his life, if you believe the Polylex.

'Captain Levirac,' I guessed aloud, pretending I did not feel its icy hand on my heart.

'No more!' hissed the faceless thing. 'I am forbidden that name, any name, they took my names from me as they shall take yours from you.'

All the same it was Levirac. His wheezing voice had not changed in forty years: from the time when he commanded the Chathrand, and I the young purser waited on his orders. I fancied I could still smell his rotten teeth: in life he chewed sugar cane day and night.

'Go to your rest, and pay me no further visits,' I said (one must never show weakness before a ghost).

The thing slipped behind me. I heard its voice at my shoulder. 'Beware. You insult the dead. When all else is robbed of a man in death, he has yet dignity. This you stripped from your fallen sailors, using their bodies to gild your lie.'

'The Emperor's lie,' I protested, but the spirit clawed at me, annoyed by the contradiction. 'This false wreck you have authored, Rose: it is a prelude. A rehearsal for the death awaiting Chathrand, a ship that was mine and many others', in a proud fellowship over centuries. Never once was that fellowship broken except by death or honourable retirement, until you in disgrace were relieved of command.'

'Damn your crooked tongue! I was reinstated!'

'For a little while,' said the ghost. 'Her next pilot is already aboard.'

His insolence astonished me. 'Her next pilot? Get hence, you old vapour, or I'll have my witch root you out of these boards with a cleansing spell!'

That frightened Levirac: I felt him withdraw a step or two behind me. His voice was softer now: 'One other will stand at Chathrand's helm – and that one briefly, briefly. You are this vessel's doom.'

'And you're a lying, man-shaped stench. Prove you know something, Levirac. Give me a name.'

The spirit only tittered behind me. I started away, and then under his breath I heard him slander you and Mother, sir, with a lie too noxious to repeat. I turned on him in wrath.

What a shock! In his place stood Thasha Isiq, alive, solid as the hand that writes these words. Her mastiffs were beside her; they held me in their gaze and growled. I said nothing; I was waiting for her to thin and vanish like any ghost. But those blue-black dogs were real – and so, I knew in a moment, was the girl.

Pathkendle and Undrabust came up the ladderway and stood beside her, and all three glared at me with hatred. Then I knew who the real deceivers were.

'You sent Pacu Lapadolma to her grave,' I told them.

'We didn't,' said Pathkendle. 'You did. You and Ott and your Emperor and your whole bloody gang.'

Then Firecracker Frix saw the girl and squealed like a pig. The commotion was immense: first terror, then wonder, at last elated cheers. 'Thasha Isiq! Thasha Isiq! The longest of lives to Thasha Isiq!'

If I had been quicker I might have moved against them: killed the mastiffs, tossed the girl overboard, declared her a risen corpse and an abomination. I know this is what you would have done in my place, Father, and you need not chastise me for the missed opportunity. I am not perfect. This we both know, and I humbly suggest we cease pretending otherwise.

Now in any case it is too late: the men are quite aware that she is flesh and blood. They were only too happy to learn that the former Treaty Bride had been hiding from them, behind the spell-wall that keeps us from the stateroom. The only gloomy faces were those of the youths themselves. They saw how well our 'sinking' went, and knew that for all their tricks, the Plan marched forward, unstoppable, with war and ruin (and riches, for some) its only conclusion.

Fiffengurt meanwhile has gone from bad to worse. He is often red-eyed, as if from crying, and goes on about a 'wife' back in Etherhorde who will soon be reading of our deaths at sea. He may have a sweetheart or two, but I know for a fact that he has no wife. Man's capacity for self-deception is a wonder, is it not?

This morning we found ourselves in a pod of Cazencian whales. I had thought the great toothed things all but extinct, for the folk of Urnsfich like nothing so much as the taste of 'sweet whale,' as they name them. On another voyage I should have put down a boat or two and given chase. But Cazencians are fierce fighters, though small for whales, and I should have trusted no one but myself to take them on. Above all our time is short. Each day we linger the Vortex grows, and with it the danger of the crossing.

Once again we have spotted a ship to the north: the same vessel, I think, and a little closer than before. There is still no danger of being recognised, but I must end this letter and adjust our course.

Enclosed is a diamond wristlet. Mr Druffle the freebooter gave it to me in exchange for a midshipman's berth. How Druffle, threadbare slave of the sorcerer that he was, came by such a priceless thing I cannot guess. But maybe it will bring a smile to Mother's eye.

As ever I remain your obedient son,
Nilus R. Rose

P.S. If you are, in fact, dead, may I trouble you to state as much in your next communication?

14

Among the Statues

Lightless. The cage was lightless, and his mind was already succumbing. Not a cage; why had he called it a cage? That was for animals. This was a dungeon made for ordinary people. Bakers, shopkeepers, farmers on the fertile slopes above Simjalla. A carpenter. A schoolboy or -girl with her books still under her arm. His arm? What did it matter, when arm and books and heart were locked in clay?

He walked carefully, heel to toe, from the carpenter to the dancer, arms outstretched in the blackness. He was far from the door, which smelled vaguely of food and was therefore a place of danger. Rested his hand on a gritty clay elbow. *They are safer than I. The beasts will attack me first, each other second. Last of all these bodies in their stony sheaths.*

He had done as Ott knew he would. He had touched them, explored their features, wondered at the attention to detail. Noses, eyebrows, lips. He would not give them names, though: that was a game for madmen, and Admiral Eberzam Isiq was not yet mad.

Ott himself came no more. The spymaster had stood outside the door on two occasions, issuing hushed, clipped commands to someone who called him 'Master.' Had he hoped Isiq would cry out, beg for deliverance or deathsmoke, weep? The admiral would not give him that satisfaction. *When you lose your sword you have your hands. When your hands are tied there remain your teeth. When you are gagged and bound you may still fight them with your gaze.* Isiq clung to the litany, an old War College saw from forty years ago, and tried to keep his mind from mocking it.

The want of deathsmoke. He huddled often with his back to the door, sweat-drenched in the hollow cold, heart racing, mind prey to ghoulish fixations. The eyes of the statues. The last thoughts baked into their brains.

Syrarys had kept him from feeling these pangs, by mixing an extract from the deathsmoke vine with the other poisons she passed him in sweet teas and brandies. Just enough to ease him along, believing himself sick but not envenomed, slowly forgetting what it meant to be well.

The detail, the *ludicrous* detail. Nearest the door stood a woman (do not recall how you learned it was a woman) clutching her throat with her left hand and reaching down it with her right. Choked on a shard of bone, a bit of gristle or hard bread. She was his height. He would not name her. She seemed to be aware of the door. As if dreaming that some bright angel would yet appear there, melt her agonies with a waking touch, lead her by the arm into paradise.

They slid his dinner plate halfway to this woman at every meal, with an insolent shove that left part of the contents behind on the floor. Isiq had to pounce on it, kicking at the rats that hurled themselves on the food the instant it appeared, stumbling quickly behind the choking woman with his prize. A metal plate with three sections; he had licked it clean after every squalid meal, saying 'fourteen', 'fifteen'; struggling thus to keep count of the days he had lain in Queen Mirkitj's private hell. But what if they did not come at regular times? What if they fed him twice in one day and skipped the next altogether? He had only the cycles of his body to judge by, and they were becoming erratic. To breathe on one's hand and be unable to see it. To rest one's chin on a stone shoulder and have no idea of the face.

Someone's name engraved on the back of the plate. Isiq had caught himself licking the signature, over and over, for his tongue was more sensitive than his fingertips, though not sensitive enough to feel out the tiny letters. Had an earlier prisoner used this plate, etched his name in it somehow, declaring, *I still exist, you have not reduced me to perfect nothingness for I remember myself, you have not erased me, you have not won.*

More likely it was the name of the manufacturer. *Do not believe it.* Believe it was defiance, stubborn will, blazing on like a mad candle in the dark.

Such were the orders he gave himself. He who had commanded fleets, abolished nations with a word, shaped the lives of thousands with a sharp decision, was now reduced to praying for obedience from an army of one.

He succeeded for a time. With the edge of the plate he was able to scrape a thin groove in the floor, a barely perceptible scratch, from the doorway to the choking woman, from the woman to the room's central pillar, from the pillar to the pit. When Isiq got lost, when the smothered feeling rose in his chest and threatened obliteration, he dropped to hands and knees and sought out the groove, and followed it like an ant from one marker to the next, until he returned to the door. And with his forehead pressed to the crack between door and frame he could actually detect a light, the palest imaginable gloaming, a microscopic flaw in this perfection of darkness, this black stomach in which he was being digested.

That is why they wear stone. It makes them harder to digest.

Madness. He took deep breaths, forcing the air from his lungs over and over, as if pumping bilge from a hold. What if the light is imaginary? The light is not imaginary. And he did not need a speck of light, a name on a food plate, a companion in agony. *I am a soldier, I solve problems, I will go about my tasks.*

Leaving the plate near the door he had set off on a tour of hell, groping left along the wall. It was a slow and frightful business. He had not gone forty squatting, creeping paces when he nearly died. A pit, yawning beneath his outstretched foot. He had teetered, then let himself fall sidelong, landing on the edge of the pit and just managing to twist back onto the floor. He had lain there, petrified. Cold air flowed from the pit like some fiend's long and rapturous sigh. At last he had risen to hands and knees and groped on.

The pit was shaped like a tongue. At the point where it curved furthest from the wall his fingers had brushed a knobby protrusion. A foothold. He had extended his arm and found another below. One could climb down, deeper into hell. He had lain on his side and reached farther. And then screamed with pain and rage.

The rat's bite was deep; its jaws had locked onto his flesh with a starved thing's ferocity. '*Damn you! Damn you!*' Isiq had rolled away from the pit with the creature still attached to his hand, swung it writhing and squealing over his head, slammed it down on the stone floor beside him. Again. And again. Only on the fourth blow had it released his finger, slashed to the bone by the rodent's teeth. Even then it had refused to die, but had leaped on his stomach and thence back into the pit, splattering him with his own blood.

For two days he had urinated on the wound: Dr Chadfallow's field trick for avoiding infection. Miraculously it had worked; the cut was painful but clean. Gangrene in this festering hole would be certain death.

That night as he pawed at his food, a flaky substance met his fingers. Ashes? Not quite. A herb, sprinkled on his half-raw potato? He touched it with his tongue. And dropped the plate in a panic. And squatted, and scraped together what food he could. And flung it down again, howling in rage and hunger. *They* were the beasts, his jailkeepers. They had dusted his meal with deathsmoke.

A time came when he knew he must enter the pit. He realised that Ott could not have left such an obvious means of escape; he knew also that the rats came from the pit, and that he risked being gnawed alive. Somehow none of that mattered. A sense of the physical space around him was one of his few holds on sanity, and the pit was a blank spot on the map.

He swept each foothold with his boot. There was a great smell of dung. He eased himself down and felt the air grow fouler; a mould-heavy dampness bathed the walls. Far-off noises, drips and splashes. After twenty footholds his boot met the ground.

An ovoid pit; a low-roofed passage; a shattered door. And then rubble. He knelt and groped. Big rocks, sand, masonry, utterly filling the corridor. A large part of the ceiling must have collapsed.

He felt every inch of the rubble-mound before him, and met with no rats at all. Near the top of the mound, however, he located the fist-sized tunnel by which they surely came and went. He plugged the hole with the largest stone he could lift, but the earth was soft around it, and he knew it would not slow even a single animal very long.

But for many days the rats did not come.

He flexed his finger: it was almost healed. He had an idea that this was his twentieth day among the statues. He had a pair of weapons, now: an iron bar and a vaguely axe-shaped stone, both of which he had pulled from the detritus at the bottom of the pit. The bar had not been worth the trouble: it was too heavy to swing, too thick to pry into cracks. Since heaving it up from the pit he had found no use for it at all.

But the stone was another matter. He swung it experimentally, thinking again of the blow he had not landed on Ott's face, when the arrogant old killer sat beside him. Maybe what Ott said was true, and the attack could only have failed. Or maybe that was pride: perhaps there had been a window between his inspiration and Ott's awareness of the danger, when he might have struck. *Why do we wait?* thought the admiral, suddenly on the point of tears. For his daughter's face had risen before his eyes.

What had they done with *her* body? They were not going to Etherhorde, so Thasha would never lie beside her mother in the family plot on Maj Hill. The best he could hope for was that she had been buried at sea, with honours, like the soldier another world might have let her become.

Sudden noise from the middle of the chamber. Clanging, rasping – the same horrid mix. Isiq left the dancer and shuffled towards the central pillar, taking his time. He did not much want to see what awaited him there.

The pillar was six or eight feet in diameter. It was made of heavy brick, not soft stone like the rest of the chamber. Gaps the size of half-bricks had been left intentionally, and from them crept a smell of ancient coal. The pillar also had a great iron door.

It was unmistakably a fire-door, of the kind installed on furnaces. It had a small square window that must once have been glazed. The door was rusted shut, the heavy bolt and staple fused with age into a solid thing, but there was no lock his fingers could detect. For several days he had struggled to open the door, to no avail. Then, on the third day after the rat bite, the noises had begun.

Isiq bent his ear to the window. Crashing, hissing, scraping. All from below – the pillar must have contained a shaft of some kind – and blurred by echoes and distance, but soul-chilling nonetheless. He was hearing the rage-stoked violence of living creatures, battering and biting whatever they could find. *And speaking.* That was the true horror of it. Most of the voices (he had noted at least a dozen) spoke only gibberish, a snarling, whining, moaning, murderous barrage of nonsense sounds. They suggested some horrible perversion of babies trying out their vocal cords for the first time – but the throats that made those sounds must have been larger than a grown man's.

And some were using words. Simjan words; he caught no more than the odd interjection. *Mine! Stop! Egg!* Isiq was cross with himself for not following the meaning – he was ambassador to Simja; he had been tutored in the tongue – until he realised that the words were not arranged in sentences. At most, two or three were strung together and repeated endlessly, with a kind of agonised inflection. *Hagan reb. Hagan reb. Hagan hagan hagan REB! Reb reb reb reb reb—'* The words broke off in screeches of lunacy.

All save one. A nattering, sorrowful, sharp-edged voice. *Penny for a colonel's widow?* Just those words, gabbled and blurted and wept. *Penny for a colonel's widow?* The voice appeared never to tire.

'Rin's mercy, what do you *mean*?' groaned Isiq.

At once he clapped a hand over his mouth, silently cursing. He had never uttered a sound near the pillar. The creatures fell absolutely silent. Then they all began screaming at once.

'Hraaaar!'

'Egg!'

'Penny for a—'

'Mine!'

Sounds of spittle and claws. The thrashing grew so crazed that the pillar actually shook. Then, beneath the pandemonium, his ears detected a tiny squeak. Putting out his hand, he found that the great bolt had at last broken free of the rust. It would move. With a bit of a struggle he could slide it free.

But why open the door? What if they could climb? Nothing but this slab of iron would stand between him and them. Fortunately the door was mighty, the bolt despite its rust still massive and intact. *This was where they stoked the fires*, Isiq realised suddenly, *this is what turned the prison into a kiln.*

Futile to fight on. Damn it, that was the truth. Already the things were scratching open the little tunnel at the base of the pit.

He was sweating again. *Those things must have devoured the rats. How is it that they speak? What will they do when they find me? Where is my suit of stone?*

He stumbled away from the pillar, holding his forehead, trying not to moan aloud. Almost at once he collided with a statue, his faithful sentry, the woman choking on the dark. She toppled; he tried to catch her but her weight defeated him; she struck the floor with a muffled boom.

'Oh my dear madam, forgive me—'

He found pieces of her in the blackness. Various digits. Her forehead, shattered on the stone. He felt the sting of other eyes, the focused hate of all the statues, that frozen family, that congregation of the damned.

He would have to watch himself.

15

The Voice of a Friend

—◦◦◦—

4 Freala 941
113th day from Etherhorde

In a way unimagined by even the most superstitious crewmembers, the Great Ship had become a ghost ship, living but presumed deceased. The effect this had on those aboard her is difficult to pinpoint. At first there was bravado, and much talk of the cleverness of Rose and their Emperor. The gang leaders, Darius Plapp and Kruno Burnscove, led the cheering: they were competitors in patriotism (or what passed for it) as in every other sphere. 'We've a right to be proud,' Burnscove declared. 'Arqual's going to remake the world. A world without the Black Rags, a world of straight talk, straight deeds, and Rin's Ninety Rules taught to every wee baby with his mother's milk. And don't we know that means a better world?'

Darius Plapp had less to say on the matter, trusting his sonorous voice and deep-set eyes to carry the message. 'We're sailing into history,' he would announce, with a grave, portentous nod.

Sergeant Drellarek played his part as well. Amazingly, he had managed to portray the execution of one-seventh of his men as a victory for the rest. The price of greatness, he said, had always been far higher than ordinary men could understand. But Turachs were different: they were Magad's warrior-angels, they were the fine edge of the knife with which the Emperor was pruning the tree called Alifros. 'In the end this world will be a fair reflection of the Tree above us,' he told them. 'Most men would shrink from such a challenge. But not us. When Turachs pass through fire they emerge with the hardness of steel.'

These three men – Burnscove, Plapp and Drellarek – also began to talk about the enemy. This was done rather quietly, and often late at night, after one or more of them appeared unexpectedly to pitch in with a bit of labour, or to top off the men's grog with a flask produced from none-knew-where. Talk of the Mzithrinis invariably meant talk of war crimes, atrocities committed by whole legions or a bloodthirsty few.

'Little Orin Isle, now,' said Drellarek with a sigh, at one such gathering. 'That little speck of a place off the side of Fuln, with no more than three thousand men. You wouldn't think it would be worth much bloodshed to take her, now would you? Ah, but you're not thinking like a Black Rag! Orin had a fortified jetty, and strong memories of what them butchers did to their grandfathers. So they fought like tigers, and kept the Sizzies from landing for a week. The Sizzies took 'em at last, of course. And when the brave men of Orin knew they were beat, they lay down their weapons, and their leaders came forward and gave their word of honour that they'd fight no more, and asked for mercy.

'Do you know what sort of mercy they got? The Sizzies marched every man who could still walk out to a lead mine in the hills. They sent 'em underground, all chained together. And then they knocked out the roofing timbers and the tunnel collapsed.'

Drellarek paused, looking grimly at the shadow-etched faces about him.

'Their women and children dug with picks and spades, with their blary fingernails. For days on end. They could hear the tap-tap-tapping, the cries from under the earth, the calls for water. But each day the voices were fainter, until one by one they stopped. Can you imagine what that silence was like, gentlemen? For the little children? For the wives?

'That's the Black Rags' idea of honour. And that's why His Supremacy launched this ship. Not for some make-believe Peace. Oh we played along with their charade, all right. But just like those brave men on Orin, some of us *remember*. The Black Rags kill, mates. And if the Shaggat Ness gets them killing each other again – so be it. We can watch them kill each other, or wait for them to kill us. Which do you prefer?'

Soldiers and sailors alike did their best to look satisfied with this reasoning, and to a certain extent they were. None had ever dreamed of being part of such a grand effort – the triumph of Arqual, the remaking of the very order of the world! Part of the crew breathed easier, thinking of Mzithrini atrocities. Most at least felt they understood what the journey was all about.

But not all were comforted. Many recalled what Captain Rose had said the day Peytr Bourjon ate his gumfruit. *Strip that rind away,* he'd said. Go on without dreaming of hope. On slow watches, over breakfast biscuit, or high on the topgallant yards, they began to murmur, to frown. In their hammocks, blind to one another in the dark, they whispered: We don't exist, boys. We wiped the slate clean at Talturi. Our girls will cry, but not too long. Don't kid yourselves. They'll dry their eyes and paint 'em pretty, women are faithless useless calculating gossipy gone-with-a-sob-and-a-hankie. And what about us, eh, what about us on this ship? Memories. Names mumbled by an old aunt, a quick prayer in the Temple, a list on page ten of the *Mariner*, used to wrap someone's pound of halibut. That's all we are, by Rin.

For the three youths it was a time of anxiety. Thasha could tell that Pazel was struggling with some new fear: he walked about as though under a stormcloud, waiting for lightning to strike. But she never could find a chance to ask him about it, for he seemed to go out of his way not to be caught with her alone.

Their allies were troubled as well. Fiffengurt raged and sulked; he had not forgiven himself for getting his Annabel with child ('like a common rascal on shore leave'), and he was half out of his mind at the thought of Rose, or worse yet Uskins, going through his private journal. Felthrup still cried out in his sleep.

Hercól, for his part, expected an attack: some midnight assault by one of Ott's men, or a siege by Rose and Drellarek, or worst of all an attack by the sorcerer. 'Why Rose allows us to come and go from these chambers is a mystery,' he said. 'But of this I am certain: nothing could be more dangerous than coming to depend on that magic wall.'

He abandoned his valet's cabin in favour of a small chamber that Pacu Lapadolma and several other first-class passengers had used for storage. The room was still crammed with footlockers and crates and swinging garment bags, but it had the advantage of being just outside the stateroom door. He refused to sleep in the stateroom itself, saying that if some enemy should find a way through the wall he intended to be the first one they met. His own door he never closed.

He strongly embraced the idea of training the tarboys, and quickly carved two blunt-edged practice swords. But he was dismayed at the anger in the youths.

'Anger is a fire,' he told them. 'And that fire is your servant – *potentially*. But right now all I see is two fools trying to grab it barehanded. That may get you burned, but it won't get you through a swordfight.' When this warning failed to cure the boys of recklessness, he made them recite the first apothem of Tholjassan battle-dance at the start of every lesson – not just in Arquali, but also in their individual birth-tongues:

A fight is won or lost in the mind, not the body. The mind is present in the fingertips, the eyelash, the leaping forward and the holding back, the side-spring, the death-blow, the choice not to fight at all. The mind discerns the needle-narrow path to victory among the thickets of defeat.

His melees with Thasha were bruising affairs, which Pazel and Neeps watched in awe. Thasha had a good sword of her own, but Hercól had Ildraquin, and decades of skill and cunning. He was merciless and calculating. He mocked and insulted her, trying to break her con-centration. He hurled bricks and staves and chairs at her, shouldered over the crates they'd stacked up as obstacles. He drove her in circles around the stateroom, kicked and beat and even cut her if she gave him a clumsy opening. After watching the first such lesson the boys realised they had been treated like children.

Pazel and Neeps found her breathtaking, but Thasha felt slow and awkward in her lessons. She had no idea why it was happening: Hercól had not actually injured her, and the chill of the *blanë* was a fading memory. But though she held her own the fights were more taxing than they should have been, and her mind felt clouded with vague fears and phantoms. A similar feeling had lately come at night, just after she blew out the candle by her bedside – a sudden rush of doubts about her choices, the tasks before them, herself. Then she would fall asleep and dream of whirlpools, as she had been doing for months.

She knew Hercól was aware of her distraction – you could not hide that sort of thing from your martial tutor, not when he was coming at you with a blade – and knew as well that he was holding back out of concern. It was only a slight handicap, but it flew in the face of his code as a teacher. He had sternly forbidden her ever to ask for lenience, and to do so had never crossed her mind. Now she was deeply shamed. Hercól was not even reprimanding her when the lessons ended. He didn't think she could take it.

Her agitation reached a new pitch some three weeks after the Talturi affair, when she awoke with an irrepressible desire to eat an onion. She had never felt such a weird craving – an onion, for Rin's sake – but it swept over her like the onset of fever, and before she knew it, she was back in the main cabin, poking about in the food cupboards, popping open tins.

It was past midnight; the sounds of the ship were at their lowest ebb.

Felthrup, who had yet to lose his battle against sleep, poked his weary nose out from her cabin door. Neeps groaned from his spot under the windows. 'Dogs,' he said.

Pazel sat up. 'No, it's Thasha. What in the Nine Pits are you up to?'

'I want an onion.'

'Well you're as loud as a pig in a pantry – did you say *onion*?'

Thasha turned to look at him. The sharpness in his tone caught her quite off guard.

'Well?' he demanded.

'Yes,' she said, 'onion. Didn't we have one? A big red thing.'

'What do you think we could do with a big red onion? Eat it raw?'

That was exactly what she had in mind. 'I know how crazy this sounds, Pazel, but—'

'No you don't,' he said. 'Go away and let me sleep.'

Thasha returned to her cabin without a word. But moments later she was back, fully dressed, and making for the stateroom door. 'Oh, stop, *stop*,' Pazel groaned. 'Wake up, Neeps, Thasha's gone mad.'

They pleaded with her to forget the onion. Thasha began to scratch nervously at her arms.

'I can't stop thinking about it. I don't know what's happening.'

'Sounds like Arunis' handiwork to me,' said Neeps, rubbing his eyes.

'Maybe,' said Thasha. 'I've been feeling a little strange for days. Not sick. Just … strange. But this is a different feeling. How late does Mr Teggatz work in the galley?'

'Depends on what's for breakfast tomorrow,' said Neeps, who'd often worked the galley shift.

'I will fetch my lady an onion,' Felthrup volunteered.

'That's blary good of you, Felthrup,' said Neeps. 'We accept.'

'No we don't,' said Pazel. 'Rin's chin, mate, you want him killed? Teggatz brags he can skewer a rat with a cleaver at thirty feet.'

The boys pulled on their clothes, surly as gravediggers at dawn. Outside the cabin door they found Hercól in a chair, sleeping with his back to the door and his hand on the pommel of Ildraquin. As Thasha opened the door he surged to his feet, unsheathing the great sword even as he leaped sidelong into fighting stance.

'What's the matter?' he said. 'Where are you going at this time of night?'

'Onions,' grumbled Neeps.

'Just one,' Thasha protested, still scratching at her arms.

Hercól also failed to turn Thasha from her goal, and so he sheathed

Ildraquin and joined the march to the galley. The heat of the day was gone, and Thasha wished she had brought a coat. She wished even more that she had slipped out of the cabin without waking the boys. Neeps might groan and fuss, but then he was always groaning and fussing. There was nothing mean about it, ultimately. Pazel, on the other hand, had sounded furious, and his anger stung all the worse for being so unexpected.

But as they neared the galley she could think of little but her thirst for the vegetable. *Let it be open, let it be open*—

'Closed,' said Mr Teggatz, rounding the corner, wiping his water-pruned hands on his apron. His soft mouth gave its usual smile, one that apologised for the incoherent words that usually came from it. 'All closed, cleaned, locked. How terrible, Master Hercól. Hello.'

'We don't need food, exactly,' said Pazel.

'Of course you don't,' said Teggatz. 'So be it. Good night.'

'Mr Teggatz,' sad Hercól. 'The lady requires an onion.'

Teggatz looked mortified. 'Impossible. There's a directive. Punishments, too! If I lie Rin can squash me like a *roach*.' He stomped in violent demonstration, eliciting groans from the berth deck.

Neeps sighed. 'He's right, you know. Rose is a monster when it comes to galley privileges. No badgering the cook, no requests to be honoured once the galley's closed, no arguments, on pain of who-knows-what.'

Thasha scratched as if her arms were covered with biting ants. Teggatz balled up his apron in a knot. Four enemies of the crown were trying to get an onion out of him at midnight. It was more than he could bear. He bolted for the passage.

'Five bells,' he said over his shoulder. 'That's when we light the stove. Not before. Captain's rules.'

They stood staring at the locked galley door. 'Five bells is *hours* from now,' said Thasha, her voice desperate.

'You'll just have to survive until then,' said Neeps.

'Maybe we should tie her up,' said Pazel.

The others looked at him, stunned. Pazel shoved his hands into his pockets. 'To keep her from scratching herself raw, that's all I meant.'

Hercól struck a match, then whisked a candle from his pocket and held the wick to the flame. 'Pazel,' he said quietly, 'go to the next compartment and keep watch. Neeps, be so good as to do the same at the ladderway.'

'What are you going to do?' asked Pazel.

'Get Thasha her onion, what do you think?'

Astonished, the tarboys did as they were told. When they were alone Hercól took Thasha's hand.

'This is an unnatural hunger,' he said. 'You must not give in to it as soon as your hands close on an onion. It could very well be a trap.'

Thasha nodded. 'I know. But Hercól, you can't break down that door. You'll bring people running from all over the ship.'

Hercól smiled at her. With a quick glance along the passage, he put a hand through the neck of his shirt and drew out a leather strap. On it hung a tarnished brass key.

'This is one of the ship's master keys,' he said. 'Diadrelu found it on the berth deck.'

'You've seen Dri!' whispered Thasha.

'Alas, no. One of her *sophisters* appeared two nights ago in my cabin. I gather Mr Frix used the key to confiscate Fiffengurt's journal, and lost it in the scuffle that followed. As for Dri, I begin to worry. The ix-girl who brought that key looked troubled when I asked after her mistress, though she would tell me nothing. But hurry, now—' He lifted the key around his shoulders and gave it to Thasha. 'Get your onion, and get back out here, and whatever you do, *don't take a bite.*'

Thasha put the key in the lock. The door protested, and Thasha had to shake it up and down in its frame, but at last the key turned and the door sprang open.

Hercól passed her the candle, and when she was safely inside he pulled the door shut behind her. The galley was long and narrow, and stank of coal and scrubbing lye. Its centerpiece was the *Chathrand*'s great stove, an iron behemoth about the size of a cottage, with twelve burners, four baking ovens (one large enough for a whole boar), a firebox for coal and another for fuelwood, various warming, smoking and steaming chambers, and a hot-water boiler. Heat throbbed from it still, although the fire had been snuffed; Thasha couldn't imagine what the galley was like when the stove was roaring. Down the starboard wall ran a long cooking counter, with drawers, cabinets, and storm-safe racks of cooking implements above and below. Along the opposite wall ran the sinks and the racks of plates, bowls and cutlery.

Onion. Thasha tiptoed forward, squinting. The counters were spotless, the dishracks empty, the towels knotted on their hangers. There were garlands of dry chilis like spiny red snakes nailed up on the beams, and hanging baskets of garlic, and (Thasha caught her breath) a skinless, salt-cured deer dangling from its antlers and dotted with flies. But no onions.

Thasha rounded the stove. There had to be another storage area. Where was the flour, the rice, the biscuit soaking for tomorrow's meals? She scratched at her arms, thinking *I can smell the damn thing*.

Turn around.

Thasha froze. Had someone spoken? No, no: she was talking to herself. She turned around, raising the candle as she did so.

Between the third and fourth sink, which she had passed just moments ago, stood a little waist-high door. Amazed that she had failed to notice it the first time, Thasha approached. The door was cracked and pitted, its green paint flaking away; it was clearly very old. Could that be the pantry? What an odd piece of junk, she thought, in a place that was otherwise as neat Chadfallow's surgery.

She took hold of the iron knob – corroded, rough against her palm – and hesitated. For some reason she was apprehensive about the door, and what might lie beyond it. Absurd, she told herself. What could possibly threaten her in an empty galley? *But this is the* Chathrand, *and that door's blary strange. No, it's not quite absurd to be—*

Twang. Thump. She whirled about, drawing her knife from her belt in a flash. Dangling into the passage was a wicker basket. It was strung beneath the first and second sinks, on short cords, but one of the cords had just snapped, tipping the basket on its side. Potatoes and cabbages rolled across the floor – and yes, there was an an onion, huge and red and perfect, the very specimen she had been craving for an hour.

She pounced on it, and the smell made her moan. Hercól's warning stood no chance. Setting the candle on the counter, she dug her nails into the dry outer skin, found purchase, ripped.

Instantly her craving vanished. The skin of the onion came off in a single sheet, and beneath the crackling outer layer it was strong and supple as leather. Thasha turned it over in her hand. The onion itself meant nothing to her now. It was the skin she needed, the skin that had called out to her in her sleep.

She spread it flat beside the candle, with the slick inner surface facing up. She brought her face close. And where her breath touched the onion skin, words appeared: words written in fire.

She had seen their like once before, on her bedroom ceiling in Etherhorde. Pale blue fire in a handwritten script – Ramachni's script. The mage was speaking to her at last.

Forgive me, Thasha: I am weak, and fall back on what tricks and small powers I can to send word to you. Worse still, Arunis has painted your ship in spells of warding and interference. I had a long search for a means of reaching you that he would be unlikely to detect – if only because a craving for onions should strike him as too foolish to investigate.

The sorcerer taxed me more than he knows in our last battle – and far more than I wish him to know. But return I shall at the promised time, and fight again at your side. Before that day I may be able to send another message, or messenger – and then again, I may not.

For today, three warnings: first, YOU MUST READ THE POLYLEX. Knowledge cannot spare you pain, indeed it may increase your suffering, but what is that compared to the doom on the world? If you have left off reading it, as I suspect, my advice is to start at the bitter end and work back to where you stand.

Second, keep an eye on anyone who spends time with Arunis. Like me he is hiding his battle-wounds, but whatever the extent of his powers, his cunning remains. I am worried also by the way he controlled Mr Druffle: the human mind is easily swayed, but rarely seized by force. What is certain is that he will do the same to others, given the chance.

Third, beware your own great heart. Our enemies will try to use it against you, having failed to kill you or make you afraid.

You, Pazel, Neeps, Hercól and Diadrelu were singled out by the spirit in the Red Wolf. That spirit, be it Erithusmé's or some other's, believed you could defend your world from the Nilstone. But this much I have learned from afar: your guess was right. There were seven, not five, burned by the molten iron of the Wolf. You must find the other two and enlist them, no matter who they are.

I will not lie to you, my champion: you stand over a precipice, upon a bridge so frail that it will crumble at the slightest misstep. And yet you must gain the other side. We all must, or perish together in the fall.

Ramachni

P.S. Here is a fourth warning: do not open that green door behind you. Keep your loved ones from it too.

Thasha blinked: the mage's scrawled signature was fading, fading – gone. And when she raised her eyes, she saw that the entire letter was gone as well. Just as before, the act of reading had erased them; the only place where they remained was in her mind.

Three warnings ... anyone who spends time with Arunis ... two more bearing the wolf scar ... How could he possibly expect her to remember everything? She wasn't a mage; she wasn't even a particularly good student, as Pazel had reminded her over their Mzithrini lessons. But after a moment of panic, Thasha found herself growing calmer. The message was frightening, but not so complicated. And if Ramachni believed she could remember it, then she would do so. She would hurry back to her cabin and write it down.

Her eyes fell once more on the ancient door between the sinks. *Keep your loved ones from it too.*

As she emerged from the galley, Hercól called softly to Pazel and Neeps. The tarboys came running. 'What happened?' asked Neeps breathlessly. 'Did you find your onion?'

'Please tell me you got what you wanted,' said Pazel.

'Not exactly,' said Thasha, relocking the door. 'But don't ask me any questions. I'll tell you everything in the morning.'

'Then there's something to tell?' said Neeps.

'Lots. But tomorrow, please! Let's get some rest while we can.'

Hercól reached for the key, and paused a moment, feeling the tremor in her hand. 'Yes,' he said softly, 'I think we shall need it.'

16

Dhola's Rib

———————

5 Freala 941
114th day from Etherhorde

A sharp rap of wood on wood. Jorl and Suzyt erupted in howls. On the bench under the gallery windows Pazel jerked awake, hit his head on the window casement, tangled his feet in the blanket and fell to the floor.

It was pitch dark. Outside the stateroom Hercól was shouting 'Madam! Madam!' The dogs bayed; Neeps flopped over with a groan. Pazel heard Thasha sweep from her cabin. They collided; she cursed, pushed a dog to one side, and threw open the stateroom door.

Yellow light flooded the room. There in the doorway stood Lady Oggosk, dressed in a sea-cloak, holding a lamp and a walking stick of pale, gnarled wood. Hercól stood beside her, distressed by the old woman's intrusion but unclear whether to prevent it by force. Oggosk pointed at the youths with her stick.

'Get dressed,' she said. 'We're going ashore. The captain has need of your services, Pathkendle.'

Hercól loomed over her, furious. 'I do not know how you passed through the barrier, old woman. But you give no orders here.'

'Shut up,' said Oggosk. 'You're coming too, girl. Bring a weapon. And bring this valet of yours; he's useful in a fight. The Sollochi runt I will not allow.'

Thasha looked at her coldly. 'We're not going anywhere with you. Are we, Pazel?'

Pazel was distracted by the hope that he was dreaming, and by the memory of Oggosk's threats, and above all by his collision with Thasha's soft, invisible, bed-warmed body moments ago. 'Of course,' he blurted. 'That is – no, absolutely. What?'

Lady Oggosk turned him a scalding look.

'We are at Dhola's Rib. The sorcerer is already halfway to the beach, with his *Polylex* in hand. If we sit back and wait he is going to learn the secret of the Nilstone's use – today, right under our noses. You won't be bickering with me then. You'll be dead, and so will I, and so will the dream of Alifros. I will see you on deck in five minutes.'

It must have been too small, or too unimportant, to appear on the chart in her father's cabin. As she dressed, Thasha snatched a look at her own *Polylex*, tearing through the pages by candlelight. *Daggerfish. Death's Head Coin. Deer's tongue. Dhol of Enfatha. Dhola's Rib.*

In the outer stateroom Hercól was shouting her name. Thasha read only: *a thin, curved islet between Nurth and Opalt, abandoned by man.* Then she slammed her *Polylex*, hid it in a place not even Hercól was aware of, and sprinted for the topdeck, still carrying her boots.

The island was invisible as they pulled for shore: Thasha could see only a dark silhouette blocking the stars of the Milk Tree. They were in the twenty-foot skiff, rowing hard but freezing nonetheless, for the wind was carving spindrift from the wave-tops and flinging it in their faces. It was frightening work, making for a shore you couldn't see. Rose held a lantern at the bow; Oggosk sat curled in her sea-cloak. Four hulking Turachs sat behind the duchess, armour clinking as they rowed. Hercól and Drellarek took an oar apiece.

Thasha's rowing-partner was Dr Chadfallow. The man's nearness made her bristle: he lied, he conspired; he had brought the Nilstone aboard in the first place! And despite his help in exposing Syrarys' treachery, Thasha could not bring herself to believe that he'd known nothing of the Shaggat.

On the other hand, Dastu was along. That was a stroke of luck, even though his orders (he'd confided in a whisper) were to keep an eye on her and Pazel. There had been a slight hint of mischief in his voice: enough to let Thasha know that he might not follow those orders to the letter.

A blast of spray caught Drellarek in the face. He growled with fury. 'How did this happen? What fool let Arunis put a boat in the water?'

'No one authorised it,' Rose shouted back. 'The sorcerer launched the dory with the aid of one tarboy – Peytr Bourjon.'

'So Jervik's not the only tarboy he's got his claws into,' said Pazel quietly.

'They are not so far ahead,' Rose was saying, 'and it is always possible that they have struck a rock in this darkness. In that case we will try to rescue Bourjon, and let Arunis drown, as he should have forty years ago.'

'He will not drown,' said Hercól.

'But what does he *want* out there?' demanded the Turach commander.

Oggosk pulled back the hood of her cloak. 'I told you he has the forbidden *Polylex*. That book holds more than knowledge embarrasing to kings. Priests and mages feared it too, for what it revealed of their own arts – the *worst* of their arts, the black charms and curses they would rather keep from the minds of men. Arunis may have stumbled on one he thinks he can use against the power that resides on Dhola's Rib.'

'I hear music!' said Dastu suddenly. Thasha heard it too: a strange, rich, hollow sound, as of many notes played together by a crowd blowing horns. The sound came from the darkness ahead.

As they rowed on the sky began to glow in the east, and the shape of the island emerged. Thasha did not like what she saw. It was a giant rock, nothing more: high and jagged at one end, smooth and low at the other. The ridgetop looked sheer and lifeless.

The landing, however, was not as bad as she feared. The beach was narrow but sheltered and gently sloped, and a sandbar broke the force of the waves. Everyone leaped into the cold surf except Oggosk, who waited until the others had dragged the skiff well ashore before allowing the captain to lift her down.

The mysterious noises blended eerily with the moan of the wind. Soaked and shivering, Thasha glanced up again and saw patches of sun on the ridgetop. A great building loomed there, carved from the native stone. It might once have been a mighty keep or temple, but time and countless storms had melted its edges to a waxy smoothness. The domed roof bulged out over the walls, then tapered swiftly to a weathered peak.

Higher up, where the sand gave way to rock, they found the dory beached on its side, oars tucked under the hull. Rose bent and placed a hand on the gunnel. 'Still dripping,' he said. 'Arunis is just minutes ahead of us. You—' He pointed at a pair of Drellarek's soldiers. '—will remain here and guard the shore. The rest of you will climb with me.'

'Captain Rose,' said Drellarek earnestly. 'Why go any farther? Maroon him here! Tow the dory back to *Chathrand* and set sail! He's made no progress turning the Shaggat back into a man, and he nearly got us into a shooting war in the Bay of Simja. Let Arunis plague us no more, Captain. With any luck he will starve!'

'On Dhola's Rib men die of thirst before hunger,' said Chadfallow, 'and there are quicker ways than thirst.'

'Thirst, hunger! What do we care?'

'One of my crew is with him, Sergeant Drellarek,' said Rose.

'That Bourjon imbecile?' scoffed Drellarek. 'Good riddance! If he's taken up with the sorcerer then he's long since broken faith with the ship.'

'So did you,' said Rose, 'when you raised your hand against the captain appointed by your Emperor. Listen to me, Turach: I alone will decide who is to be disposed of, and when.'

One side of Drellarek's mouth curled upwards, as though Rose's words amused him, but he said no more. Again Thasha felt her suspicions rise. Whatever Rose was up to, it wasn't about saving Peytr. She had her doubts that he meant to confront Arunis at all. *But Oggosk means to, that's for certain.*

Oggosk was already hobbling up the slope, leaning heavily on her stick. The others followed, hugging their soggy coats more tightly about them. Soon they were exposed once more to the wind, which was fierce and cold.

Once Pazel stumbled, and began to roll perilously towards a cliff. Thasha, Hercól and Dastu all leaped after him, but swifter than any of them was Dr Chadfallow. With a scramble and a tremendous lurch he reached Pazel and caught his arm, stopping him just feet from the cliff. Breathless, Pazel looked the doctor in the eye. Neither he nor Chadfallow said a word.

Minutes later they gained the ridgetop, not far from its crowning temple, and stepped into the full morning sun. A spectacular sight opened before them. Dhola's Rib was much larger than Thasha had supposed. It was shaped much like its namesake bone. They had landed on the only west-facing beach. The eastern side of the island, however, curved away for nine or ten miles, before sharpening to a wave-swept point. The long beaches there were ablaze with sunlight.

And covering those beaches were thousands upon thousands of animals. They were seals, enormous, rust-coloured seals. They lolled and flopped and surged in and out of the waves, one huge congregation after another, merging into a solid carpet of bodies in the distance. From every pod came the booming, wailing, rippling song they had heard in the darkness. It rose and fell with the gusting wind, now soft, now suddenly high and drowning out all speech.

'Pipe-organ seals!' grunted Rose with a vigorous nod. 'It fits. Yes, it fits.'

'Well I'll be a candy-arsed cadet,' said Drellarek. 'Pipers? Them beasts that come ashore just once every nine years?'

'And on just nine beaches in Alifros,' said Hercól.

'Eight,' said Chadfallow. 'The ninth beach was on Gurishal, where the Shaggat's worshippers have known generations of hunger. One night a few decades ago they heard the singing, and rushed the beach, and killed thousands for their meat. The seals that escaped never returned to Gurishal.'

He shielded his eyes, marvelling at the sight before them. 'To the old tribes of the Crownless Lands these animals were sacred, and to hear their song was a mighty omen. What a stroke of luck to arrive today! Look there, the pups are learning to swim!'

For a moment they all watched in silence. Then Drellarek pointed and gave a belly laugh. 'And the sharks are helping out with the lesson! D'ye see 'em, boys?'

Thasha saw them: the churning dorsal fins, the pups vanishing one after another beneath the darkening foam. Those ashore kept coming, unaware of the carnage farther out. Thasha repressed a shudder, irritated by her response (Hercól would not flinch, her father would not flinch). But laughter? That was worse, abominable. She saw Pazel looking at Drellarek with unguarded hate. Was he thinking of Ormael – the men gutted and thrown from the fishing pier, while her father, in command of the attacking fleet, sat at anchor offshore?

'Ouch! Pitfire!' cried Drellarek happily, still watching the sharks. 'You're right, Chadfallow, you don't see *that* kind of show every day! Don't look, Lady Oggosk – Lady Oggosk?'

The witch had left them behind again. They hurried after her, climbing straight for the temple. Thasha could now see a curious feature of the building: its windows. They were small, irregular ovals, scattered apparently at random across the domed roof, gaping like toothless mouths.

'That is Dhola's Manse,' said Chadfallow as they climbed. 'It is only a ruin, now, but centuries before the Rinfaith was born it was a mighty cloister, built over the island's only spring. I do not know if anyone in Alifros knows the full story of its builders. They vanished, leaving only a name – *Bracek Dhola*, Dhola's Rib – and a handful of legends among the shore folk of the western isles.'

'So we don't even know how they died?' asked Thasha.

'It may have been the spring,' said Chadfallow. 'At some point in history the water changed, arising from the depths tainted with oils and harsh minerals. It is deadly, now — and in some chambers, boiling hot. One of those legends holds that outsiders came and seized the temple for a war-base, and killed the priests who lived here. In some stories those outsiders are Arqualis, in others men of the Pentarchy, or Noonfirth, or even some realm south of the Ruling Sea. But all the tales end the same way: with the last priest uttering a curse, and the poisons appearing in the spring.'

They hurried up the trail. The wind grew even stronger, as though trying to blow them sideways off the ridge. Soon Pazel's teeth were chattering. Thasha looked at him and tried to smile.

'Hot water,' she said. 'That sounds blary wonderful.'

Pazel grinned at her, and at all once Thasha felt more hopeful than she had in days. Then Pazel glanced up to where Rose and Oggosk waited in the temple doorway. His face darkened with confusion, and he turned from Thasha with a scowl.

The doorway was a square black hole. The party huddled just inside, out of the wind, as Hercól and the soldiers lit torches. The air inside was warm and moist. Thasha sniffed: there was a strange odour, too, a biting smell, like a harsh drug or mineral spirits. Before them ran a rough stone corridor, strewn with the bones of birds and the leavings of other visitors: a broken sandal, a ring of fire-scorched stones, an obscene rhyme scratched in charcoal on the wall.

Rose beckoned Pazel near. He clapped a hand on the tarboy's shoulder.

'What's on Dhola's Rib?' he said, in the manner of someone asking a riddle.

Pazel looked him up and down. 'I don't know, Captain,' he said at last. 'Seals?'

'Seals, and a sibyl,' said Rose. 'A sibyl, a creature with the second-sight. She could tell you the very hour of your death if she wished. But don't fear her. You're with me, and the sibyl is fond of Nilus Rose. You might say she's an old friend of the family.'

He put two fingers in his mouth, and withdrew something about the size of a peach pit. He held it up for all to see. It was a white stone, carved on one side in the form of a woman's face.

'I've kept this in my mouth since Simja. She likes that sort of thing. Likes her presents to have felt the warmth of human flesh.'

Thasha fought the urge to back away from the captain. He was mad; and his eye had a crafty gleam.

'I have a little question for her,' Rose went on. 'A private matter between me and my kin. But she's tricky, this sibyl. When she comes you have to think fast, and talk sweet. And even if you persuade her you're a friend, she may answer in some language you don't understand. That's where you come in, Pathkendle.'

He put the stone back in his mouth, and placed his hand on Pazel's shoulder.

'Arunis wants her to answer *his* questions,' he rumbled. 'But he's never bothered to come here before. I have the sibyl's favour, and a present, and a wise witch to help me. And you, lad – you're of great worth to me, this day.'

'Don't forget the girl, Nilus,' said Oggosk. 'She too is here to help you.'

Rose glanced doubtfully at Thasha. 'I'll not forget any aid I receive today. Nor any hindrance.'

He took a torch from one of the soldiers and led them down the corridor. After about twenty yards it ended in two narrow staircases, rising to left and right, and a third, wider, that descended straight ahead. The steps were worn until they seemed half-melted, like steps carved from soap. The middle staircase divided into two some thirty feet below.

'The maze begins,' said Rose.

Thasha saw Hercól and Drellarek exchange a look. The Turach's lips shaped a silent question: *Maze?*

Oggosk pointed to the left-hand stair, and up they climbed, single file, with Rose leading the way and the Turachs bringing up the rear. It was a stumbling, awkward climb: the corroded steps had no truly level surfaces any longer, and their feet tended to slide. They passed a tiny corridor exiting the stairs, and then another identical. At the third such hallway Oggosk pointed with her stick. Rose left the stairs and crept into the hall, crouching low. Embers fell from his torch as it knocked against the ceiling.

Even in this black, cramped corridor they could hear the wind outside, and the endless song of the seals. They passed many other halls, and took several turns, all chosen by the witch. Once they passed through a little chamber with an iron grate set in the floor. Steam issued from it, and a stronger whiff of that druglike smell Thasha had caught in the doorway.

Then Rose turned a sharp corner, and they were descending again: this time down a spiral staircase, even more corroded and hazardous than the previous steps. The air grew warm and heavy with moisture. Around and around they went, shuffling, choking on torch smoke, until Thasha was certain they had descended much farther than they had climbed.

Finally the staircase ended, and Rose led them down a hallway tighter than any of the others, the Turach's armoured shoulders scraping the walls with every step. The narcotic smell was all but overpowering here. Thasha tensed, aware that some deep part of her was shouting an alarm: *You could get drunk on that smell – drunk, or worse.* Then they turned a corner, and Lady Oggosk cried, 'Ah! Here we are!'

A great chamber opened before them. It was round, and composed of many stone rings, one within another, descending like the levels of an amphitheatre. The edges of the room were dark: Thasha could just make out a number of stone balconies, some with crumbling rails, and many black corridors leading away.

But the centre of the room was lit by fire. It was a breathtaking sight: a polished stone circle twenty paces wide or more, orange like the sun before it sets. The stone was cracked into a dozen pieces; it resembled a dinner plate smashed with a rock. The spaces between these shards were filled with water, to within a few inches of the top of the stone. And the surface of the water was burning: low blue flames that raced and died and puffed to life again, as though fed by some vapour bubbling up through the water itself.

At the centre of the cracked orange stone sat Arunis, cross-legged, his tattered white scarf knotted at the neck. His back was to the newcomers, and his *Polylex* lay open before him.

Peytr crouched a few paces away, hugging his knees. When the big tarboy saw the newcomers he rose with a cry: 'Captain Rose! I didn't want to help him, sir! He said he'd kill me in my sleep if I didn't!'

The newcomers filed into the room. Rose, Hercól and the Turachs descended the stone rings towards the room's fiery centre. 'You're a coward and a fool,' Drellarek shouted at Peytr.

'Or a liar,' muttered Pazel.

'Get over here, Bourjon,' snapped Rose.

The big tarboy was panic-stricken. He looked from the captain to the sorcerer and back again. Then Arunis turned his head, showing them his profile.

'Go,' he said.

Peytr ran to the captain, hopping over the cracks with their whispering flames. Rose stepped forward and intercepted him, seizing a fistful of hair. 'Drellarek here thinks I should have left you to die,' he said.

Peytr's eyes pleaded for clemency. Thasha looked at him with a kind of disgusted fascination. There was nothing false about his fear.

'The sorcerer can kill no one, Mr Bourjon,' said Chadfallow. 'Have you forgotten that to do so would risk the death of his own king?' But Arunis, still watching them from the corner of his eye, smiled at the doctor's words.

The captain raised a fist high over his head. Then, gradually, he relaxed his grip on Peytr's hair. He pointed at the doorway they had come by. 'Stand there. Don't move and don't speak.' Peytr leaped to obey, shoving between Pazel and Thasha in his haste.

Arunis turned away once more. He placed one hand on the open *Polylex*, on a page with a large circular diagram. Drellarek looked sharply at Rose, drew his fingers across his neck. The mage was as vulnerable now as he would ever be. Hercól raised a cautioning hand, and Oggosk shook her head. Rose hesitated, eyes full of wrath and distance. Then he glanced up at Drellarek and nodded.

Drellarek moved with brutal swiftness. He glided softly down to the orange stone, unsheathing his Turach greatsword as he went. Nearing Arunis, he raised it for a single, killing blow.

'Can your witch detect a lie?' said Arunis, without moving.

Drellarek hesitated, looking back over his shoulder.

'She can,' said Rose, 'if her captain requires it.'

'Then ask her the truth of this, you spawn of a toad-faced polygamist: I, Arunis Wytterscorm, have the power to sink your ship whenever I choose, and will do so if you harm me.'

For a moment no one breathed. Oggosk put out her withered hand and took hold of Rose's coat, made him bend to her ear and whispered urgently. Rose's face hardened with repressed fury. He pulled irritably away from the old woman, and waved Drellarek off.

Arunis laughed, closing the *Polylex*. He tossed the end of his white scarf over his shoulder and rose slowly to his feet. Thasha saw that he had concealed a weapon beneath his cloak: a black mace, studded with cruel iron spikes. She had never seen it before.

'I told you in the Straits,' said the mage, looking them over, 'that I was the sole master of the *Chathrand*. What you did to my king only delayed the last reckoning. You are my instruments. You are small flutes and horns in the symphony of my triumph. What do I care if you manage the occasional squeak?'

'You monster,' said Pazel suddenly. 'We'll see who plays with whom when Ramachni comes back.'

'Ramachni?' said Arunis, as though trying to remember. 'Ah yes. The mage who enlists you to a deluded cause, then scurries away to safety like the rodent he is, leaving you to fight alone. The trickster who hides under the skirts of a girl, only to cast her off when it seems her life is forfeit. Would he return if you were writhing in pain again, girl? Not sure, hmm? Never fear, you will be.'

Pazel started forward, seething, and Thasha barely had time to grab his arm. Then she saw that Hercól too was moving towards Arunis. His sword was sheathed and his hands were empty; still Arunis took a hasty step backwards, raising his mace. Hercól drew a step closer, well within the weapon's reach. But now it was Arunis who looked uncertain.

'Do *you* know when a man speaks the truth?' Hercól said.

Arunis gave a nervous laugh. 'Better than the man himself.'

'I thought as much,' said Hercól, and turned away. But when he had taken two steps he moved with a speed not even Thasha had ever witnessed, and suddenly Ildraquin was in his hands, and its tip rested on the soft flesh beneath the mage's ear.

'This is Ildraquin, the Curse-Cleaver, the Tongue of the Hound of Fire,' he said. 'And this is my promise: Ildraquin will end your cursed life if you should ever again touch a hair on the head of Thasha Isiq.'

Arunis sneered, and pushed the tip of the blade away – but gingerly, as if he hated to touch it even with his fingertips. 'Only a fool makes promises he cannot keep,' he said.

'Quite so,' said Hercól.

'We are not here to kill one another,' said Drellarek awkwardly – it was an unusual statement from the Throatcutter. 'Captain, you have your tarboy back. Now let's say we forget that silly sibyl, and be on our way.'

'Save your breath,' said Oggosk. Then suddenly she raised her scrawny arms, so that her gold bangles clattered, and her milk-blue eyes were wide. 'Be still, Nilus! Be still, all of you! We have come in the right year, and the right season for divination. This, now, is the right hour – the only hour, for another nine years. Put out your torches! Quickly!'

'Do it!' snapped Rose.

With some difficulty Drellarek and Dastu extinguished the torches. The room was now lit only by the blue flames dancing in the cracks of the stone. Arunis turned in circles, like a wary cat. Oggosk groped for Rose's arm.

Then she pointed, high across the chamber. There, upon one of the ruined balconies, shone a tiny pool of light. It was daylight, a single focused beam. Tracing it with her eyes, Thasha saw that it had entered by a tiny hole in the domed ceiling. She realised that there were scores of such holes. All at once she remembered the odd little windows in the temple roof. *They're not just windows, they're light-shafts.* Just like those on the *Chathrand* that brought light to the lower decks, except that these must have run through immense tunnels of stone, and were so narrow that only a pencil-thin beam of light could pass through.

Suddenly both Oggosk and Arunis began to chant. The old woman's voice was loud and strong, but somehow humble, almost pleading:

Sélu kandari, Sélu majïd, pandireth Dhola le kasparan mïd.

But Arunis, though he chanted similar words, cried out in a harsh and threatening voice:

Sathek kandari, Sathek majïd, ulberrik Dhola le mangroten mïd!

At the same time he drew a grey powder from his sleeve and tossed a handful of it into one of the flaming cracks. It burned in a flash of blue sparks.

Witch and sorcerer were both watching the light on the balcony. The sounds of wind and seals blended into a weird, throbbing moan. Rose looked anxiously up and down the beam of light, from balcony to window and back again. His fists opened and closed; he looked like a man whose time was running out. *Of course!* Thasha realised. *It can't last more than a few minutes. Once the sun moves at all it will be gone.*

She felt Pazel's hand in her own – but no, it was Dastu's; the older boy thought she was frightened. She wasn't, or not severely; in fact her strongest feeling was curiosity. Was there a different light-shaft for every holy day in the old monks' religion? Was there a soul alive who knew what they had believed? She looked again at the light on the balcony – and cried aloud, and so did everyone else.

Later, no one could agree as to what had happened on that balcony. They all said that the light had changed, growing less like daylight and more like that of the moon, or fireflies, or something spectral. They agreed as well that *someone* had appeared. But no two of them saw the same figure.

Thasha saw her mother, waving to her (or to her husband?) with a smile of recognition; then the banister parting, and horror replacing joy as Clorisuela Isiq fell to her death. Sergeant Drellarek saw the woman he had killed six years ago while drunk on grebel, after she insulted his manhood in a brothel in Uturphe. Dastu saw the Etherhorde nurse who had saved him from consumption.

Dr Chadfallow saw Pazel's mother Suthinia, driving him from her door. Hercól saw a grey woman in a silver crown, with two dead boys at her feet, pointing an accusing finger. Lady Oggosk saw an enraged woman sixty years her junior, who nonetheless resembled her greatly, except for the sleek red tail that twitched behind her. Captain Rose saw almost the same figure, but tailless, and with larger, more heartbroken eyes.

Pazel saw his sister, Neda, struggling in the hands of Arquali soldiers who tore at her clothes. But as she fought and whirled, the figure changed. One turn, and she was his mother, shaking her head and mouthing those heartless words: *We will never belong among those who belong*. Another turn, and she was a woman in the prime of life: a woman of great beauty and seriousness and strength, holding up her arms in a roaring wind. He had never seen her before, and yet he felt, strangely, that he knew her as well as his mother or sister.

Arunis too must have seen a figure, but his reaction was not one of awe, like that of the others. He tossed another handful of dust into the flames, and shouted at the balcony.

'Dhola! Come down! I am Sathek's heir! I am the new steward of Alifros, the hand that moves the Shaggat, the will that bends Empires to my purpose! I shall wield the Nilstone, and loose the Swarm of Night, and scour this world for its new dispensation! Come, sibyl! Come kneel before me!'

On his last words, the light vanished: the figure disappeared. Captain Rose gave a howl of frustration, but Oggosk silenced him with an urgent wave. No one moved. Then Arunis whirled to face the righthand wall.

A new pool of light, small and blue and restless, hovered on the wall above a dark doorway. This time it took no human form. But a voice came from it all the same: a woman's voice, distant as thunder's echo, yet somehow clear as temple bells.

'Arunis Wytterscorm,' it said. 'Great mage, death-deceiver, Elder of Idharin. You whose gifts were given that you might seal the wounds of Alifros, the torn flesh, where the black blood of the underworld seeps in. You who preferred the commerce of devils and wraiths, theft from neighbouring worlds, a shameless auction of your own. Why should I kneel? You are not *my* elder. And this is my house. No, I do not kneel, but I challenge you: catch me, blood mage! Catch me and drink of my wisdom, or go with my curse!'

And with that the light made a furtive, teasing dart into the doorway.

But Arunis scowled and stood his ground. 'I will not follow where you lead,' he said.

The voice laughed softly. 'And I will not suffer your evil touch. I see what is in your book. You would draw the six-sided prison and trap me inside. But that will never be.'

'Ah!' cackled Lady Oggosk. 'That's your game, is it, mage?'

The blue light emerged from the doorway, slid down the stone rings one by one, and vanished into the flames. A moment later Dastu pointed: there it was again, sliding from the burning water on the opposite side, pausing on a broken step.

'Hercól of Tholjassa,' said the woman's voice. 'Have you come to ask for knowledge, or forgiveness? I think you have great need of both.'

'As do all who walk the earth,' said Hercól, gruff and startled. 'But I do not seek them here.'

'You were always wise,' said the voice, soothingly. 'Love, then – love, which is where knowledge and forgiveness meet; love, which alone is balm to broken souls. You have lived too long without it, warrior. You have fought in its name, but the love was always for others to enjoy. Come and take it, before you grow old, before it is too late forever. For you too carry an open wound.'

Thasha looked with distress at her friend and tutor. Hercól told her so little about his past – nothing of the Secret Fist, next to nothing of what came before it, or after. Was the sibyl speaking the truth? What kind of wound could he be suffering from, and why hadn't she seen it herself?

Again the light began to slide towards an archway. Hercól watched in silence. But when it reached the threshold, his eyes changed. A shocked and naked look stole over him, and he reached out helplessly towards the light. He took a step forward, and Thasha moved to stop him. To her surprise, Dastu's hand tightened on hers.

'Let him go,' he whispered. 'Poor man, let him find her, whoever she is.'

Thasha hesitated, then shook her head. She pulled away from Dastu and rushed to Hercól. At the touch of her hand the swordsman jumped, 'Thasha!' he breathed, like a man waking from a dream.

Thasha glanced up at the doorway, and her breath caught in her throat. Just beyond the threshhold, where the dancing light hovered still, the floor ended in a steaming pit. Hercól had been walking towards his death.

Now the light pulled away from the door, and came to rest at Thasha's feet.

'For you,' it said softly, and almost in a tone of respect, 'I have nothing to offer. For what good is a lighted lamp, or a book lain open on the table, until the reader takes her hands from her eyes?'

Thasha felt her skin grow cold. The sibyl had to be speaking of the *Polylex*. It was ghastly, however, to realise that a creature that had just tried to kill her oldest friend seemed to be giving the same advice as Ramachni.

The blue light vanished into the flames once more, and when it emerged it began to circle Pazel. Three times it swept around him, and several times Pazel reached out, only to drop his hands swiftly, as if fighting some impulse he knew to be dangerous. When the light spoke at last, it used a strange, inhuman language that made Pazel cover his ears in sudden distress. Thasha had heard it before: it was the unforgettably strange tongue of the sea-murths, who had nearly killed Pazel and Neeps along the Haunted Coast, before helping them to raise the Red Wolf from the depths. Then the light abandoned Pazel and raced to yet another doorway.

'Well, Captain,' said the woman's voice, suddenly bright and airy. 'Twelve years ago you fled my Manse with unsightly haste, and I doubted you would ever return. Yet here you are. Curiosity was ever the death of cats and pleasure-seekers, isn't that so?'

Oggosk glared in sudden anger. Rose bowed his head and said nothing.

'And what can I do for the commander of the Wind Palace,' the voice continued, 'that I could not do when last we met?'

'Accept a gift, lady,' said Rose. 'A small token of my esteem, and an apology for the noise and violence of our last encounter.'

'It is not to *me* that you should tender your regrets,' said the voice. 'But if you have brought me something, some warm and pretty *megigandatra*—'

She said several more strange words, and slowly the light descended towards the broken stone once more. Thasha was amazed: despite her coy words, the voice was suddenly childlike, hungry for the captain's gift, trying and failing to hide its eagerness. Thasha reeled at the wonder of it all: they were haggling with a strange and mighty being, spiteful and even murderous, and yet no more immune to loneliness and want than the very beings she was trying to entrap.

'*Falindrath,*' said the sibyl, as the light crept nearer. '*Apendli, margote, bri?*'

Rose turned and lunged for Pazel, dragging him forward. 'Answer her, Pathkendle!' he cried, breathless with excitement.

Pazel waved his hands in protest. 'Captain! I don't speak – I've never heard—'

'You'll do fine! She always talks in riddles! Say whatever you like, but say it sweetly! Here, that's a good lad, take the present, give it to her!'

'When she asks!' hissed Oggosk.

'When she asks!' cried Rose, shaking Pazel violently by the arm. 'Only when she asks, damn it, don't be so eager, she's a lady!'

Hands trembling, he took the carved stone from his mouth and held it out to Pazel. Flabbergasted, Pazel reached for the stone—

—and squeezed too hard. The wet stone popped like a grape from between his thumb and forefinger. Rose made a wild grab, and only managed to send it flying like a shuttlecock across the room. In the darkness they heard it strike the wall – and then a soft splash.

Oggosk shrieked. Rose dealt Pazel a blow that sent him flying. The sibyl gave a wail of regret, and the enchanted light swept across the floor in the direction of the stone. But as it passed Arunis, the sorcerer's hand shot out and seemed to close on something invisible. The voice gave a cry of pain.

Arunis pulled hard, like a fisherman setting a hook, and grimaced as the light throbbed in his fist. There was no doubt: he had her. And with the *Polylex* in one hand and the sibyl trapped in the other, he leaped headlong over the flames, up the stones rings, and vanished through a lightless arch.

'After him! After him!' shrieked Oggosk. 'Didn't you hear the sibyl? His book has a drawing of a spirit cell! If he copies it out and imprisons her inside, she'll be forced to tell him anything he wants. Do you understand? *Anything!* Run, run, you jackdaws!'

The next minutes were mad. The men and tarboys (except Peytr, who crouched in the doorway where Rose had left him) marauded into the darkness after the sorcerer. Thasha started to go as well, but Oggosk grabbed at her arm.

'Not you, girl. You stay here at my side.'

Thasha was incensed. 'Let go! I have to help them!'

'You will be. By staying put.'

'I can fight as well as they can! And Pazel's barefoot, and hurt, thanks to your favourite thug. Why does it have to be *me*?'

Oggosk slapped her.

'Because I wish it, you arrogant girl! Because I'm your elder five times over! Because you'd still be flouncing about in your nightdress on the *Chathrand* if I hadn't brought you along!'

Thasha was bleeding; the witch's rings had cut her face. 'Why did you bother?' she asked.

Oggosk leaned close to Thasha, blue eyes shining in the blue firelight. 'Listen to me, you fool. If he succeeds – if Arunis wrests a means of controlling the Nilstone from that creature – you and I just *might* be able to stop him. It would kill me, and damage your mind forever. But no one else in this world would have a chance. Now shut your mouth and draw your sword. I'd damned well prefer to get out of this alive.'

For Pazel the hour that followed was one of the most desperate, frightened and confused times he had ever known. There was no light, except in chambers where the blue fire gleamed. There were pits and caved-in hallways, and others on the point of caving in. Worse still, a great deal of the level to which they had descended was full of water. Some of it was cool, but most of it was hot – very hot, even scalding. When they neared such waters they were forced to turn back and seek another way.

They could hear the sibyl wailing, her strange voice echoing in the dark. But the depths of the temple were as tangled as the rooms above, and there was no telling into what distant chamber Arunis had fled, bearing his enchanted book and supernatural captive. They split into pairs, groping along the walls, feeling for stairs and holes and drop-offs. Pazel was with Chadfallow, whose hand on his arm felt like a surgical clamp. The darkness was horribly complete; they groped, swore, cracked their heads on unseen walls. Sometimes the passage dwindled to a crawlway; at other times they wriggled through gaps only to find themselves in tiny, tomblike spaces that seemed to shrink as they patted the stones. At every moment Pazel expected an ambush. Chadfallow carried a sword strapped to his back, but Pazel had only his skipper's knife, small and sweaty in his hand. Yet what scared him most was the thought of the unseen, scalding water. He could hear it in side-passages, bubbling and hissing. He thought suddenly of a crab he'd watched Teggatz drop into a boiling kettle. It had died with one twitch of its claws.

Chadfallow whispered constantly, mostly warning Pazel of dangers as they groped down those hideous halls. But at one point he said: 'Find the book. That's all that matters. Until he copies out the design of that spirit-cell he cannot make the sibyl tell him anything. Take the book before he finishes, lad, and then run, run for your life.'

There came a flash of blinding light from the room ahead, and Chadfallow whipped out his sword. But it was only Drellarek and Dastu. They had relit their torches, somehow. Both man and tarboy looked deranged, their faces bright with soot and steam, their eyes wild and twitchy.

'Not a sign of him,' said the Turach, spitting. 'And Rose scalded his blary leg halfway to bacon, stumbling into a pool. I had half a mind to knock him over the head and carry him out of here. But your friend Hercól had other ideas. It almost came to blows.'

'We must stop Arunis,' wheezed Chadfallow.

'We can stop him by sailing away!' Drellarek poked the doctor in the chest. 'You're supposed to be bright. Tell me: is this madness or isn't it?'

'It will be over soon,' said Chadfallow.

Pazel and Dastu exchanged a look. 'Aye,' whispered the older tarboy, 'one way or another. Here, take this.' He handed Pazel his torch.

'Thank you,' said Pazel, gripping his arm with feeling.

Dastu managed a feeble smile. 'Watch them bare feet of yours,' he said.

They parted and went on. It should have been better with a torch, but it was not. There was too little air, and too much of the cloying scent, and the shadows seemed to leap out threateningly at every turn. And now that they could see the walls, they found that many bore hideous murals: sinking canoes, slaughtered animals, men maimed and fleeing through palm forests, warriors lifting severed heads.

Pazel was sweating and breathing hard. Time and again he had to crouch low, out of the worst of the steam, just to catch his breath. Chadfallow fared even worse. He discarded his coat, wrenched his shirt open at the collar. Soon he began to stop, crouching low, gasping as though about to faint. Pazel would creep a few paces ahead, considering the choices, longing for daylight as much as any glimpse of the sorcerer.

Then Chadfallow disappeared. Pazel felt a stab of panic. How could he have missed him? How far had he crept alone? He rushed back down the corridor, around their last two turns. He raised his voice to shout, but the steam burned his lungs so badly that he staggered and clutched at his chest.

The torch spilled all its embers. They lay at his feet, hissing and dying, the only light left in the world. Pazel began to crawl forward, croaking, 'Ignus, Ignus.' After a few yards his hand came down in hot water. He jerked back with a cry of pain. Trapped, blinded, burned. He closed his eyes in despair.

And then something startling occurred. Pazel thought once more of his mother. It was not the same vision as that on the balcony. This time Suthinia was looking at him as she so often had: sternly, but with love. *Your Gift, our sacrifices, all these years you've survived on your own. Is this what they were for?*

Pazel was shaken. Almost six years since he had heard that voice, but how vividly it came back to him now! He turned and crawled back to the torch, shook the wetness from his hands. Then, using embers that had already died, he coaxed the few live coals back into the mantle. He lifted the torch and blew gently, and soon a meagre flame sprang to life.

Just then a loud wail echoed down the corridor. It was the sibyl, nearer than he had yet heard her – dead ahead, unless the echo deceived him. He went forward on hands and knees, until he entered a taller chamber, where the steam was not as thick. Here he rose, swaying a little. It was an unusual room: painted with images of a rice harvest and grazing animals along a palm-lined river, not slaughter and war. And right across the floor ran a deep, gushing stream in a tiled sluice. The water when he touched it was clean and cool.

There were several exits from the room. Pazel listened for the sibyl again, but no sound came. Then on a sudden impulse, he bent and splashed the water against his face. The feeling was blissful. He cupped more water and soaked his chest, holding the torch at arm's length. He closed his eyes and sighed with pleasure.

The third time he put his hand in the water, something took it and held tight.

He should have been terrified. But recognition came too soon for fear. Gold, a wondrous rush of gold through mind and heart, and joy like sudden deliverance from pain. He opened his eyes and there she was, rising from the water, her face aglow.

'Land-boy,' she said.

It was Klyst, the sea murth who had tried to kill him on the Haunted Coast, only to fall magically in love with her intended victim. Klyst, who had begged him to stay with her, to live enchanted in her people's kingdom in the Gulf of Thól.

She looked strange and unhealthy. Her impossibly thick hair hung like a great mat of seaweed on her head, the hundreds of braided kulri shells merely a limp bead curtain tangled up in the mess. Her gown, which had once seemed a net of lights, was now a threadbare rag that clung like soggy tissue to her body.

But her eyes were unchanged. The love-spell had not broken, though she had never meant to cast it on herself.

'It's really you, isn't it?' he said. 'You're not a phantom, not a trick.'

The murth-girl nodded. She took an uncertain step in his direction. As though he might be the phantom, an apparition that could vanish with a word.

'Klyst, look at you,' he said. 'You're not well. What's happened to you?'

'Nothing,' she said, recoiling slightly. 'It's the waters of this place. They're unhappy. I'll be ... pretty again, once I'm back in the sea.'

'You followed me in here,' he said, aghast. 'You've been following us all along, haven't you?'

She nodded again, and flashed him the briefest smile – just long enough to show her glistening, razor-sharp teeth. She put her arms around his neck. 'I followed,' she said, 'because you called.'

Pazel was sure he had done no such thing. He struggled to think – there was no time for this, no time to talk gently, as he'd have to if she was ever going to understand. No time to remember how he'd made her cry.

'You don't come aboard the *Chathrand*,' he said.

Klyst shook her head. 'Not allowed. Not on the Wind Palace. I'd be trapped there, forever.'

Then she opened her mouth against his shivering chest. For a moment he feared she was about to use those teeth. But no, it was a kiss, right on his collar bone, and he felt the tiny rose-coloured shell – her heart, she'd called it, when she placed it beneath his skin – begin to warm.

You're *still* pretty, he thought.

Suddenly the sibyl cried out again – in rage or pain, and very near. The wail came from a waist-high tunnel on his left.

Klyst turned and looked down the tunnel. Suddenly she clutched him tight. 'You'll die if you stay here,' she said.

'That occurred to me already,' he said. 'But there's something I have to do first. Can you come with me?'

He led her, crouching, down the low tunnel, in the direction of the scream. It was very hot; and once more the steam thickened around them. He could hear a waterfall, of all things, growing louder as they went. He tried to explain, in whispers, what Arunis was seeking, and why they had to stop him. Klyst listened, anger flashing in her enormous eyes. It was Arunis who had brought evil to her country to begin with.

The tunnel curved. Suddenly a pale blue light glimmered ahead of them. Pazel put a finger to his lips, and set the torch carefully against the wall. They crept nearer. There was the waterfall: steaming, boiling, a lethal curtain of water capping the tunnel. And through it Pazel saw Arunis, distorted but unmistakable. Beside him lay a book that could only be the *Polylex*.

The sorcerer was in a large cave. It was lit by the same blue flame as the main temple chamber, but here the burning oil ran in rivulets across the floor. Arunis had placed the book on a flat, table-like rock, some ten feet from the waterfall. It lay open. He was studying a page.

As they watched, Arunis suddenly left the *Polylex* and ran to a spot across the cave, skipping over the little streams of fire. Pazel nearly gasped: there at the far side of the cave stood the glowing figure of a woman. She twisted and struggled, as though trying to free herself from invisible bonds. Arunis was circling her. He held a lump of charcoal, and was drawing an elaborate pattern of words and symbols on the floor.

'A cage,' said Klyst, with hatred in her voice. 'He is drawing a cage for Dhola. A cage of twisted *ripestry* – what an ugly, ugly, thing!'

'We're too late, aren't we?'

'No,' said Klyst. 'But almost. He hasn't finished the drawing; she can still break free. And he has to draw carefully. One little mistake and the cage will break.'

Arunis returned to the book, placed his finger on the open page. Then once more he left it on the rock, hurried back to the captured sibyl, and started to draw.

Pazel struck the wall with a fist. 'Pitfire! It's right *there*!' He put out his hand, cautiously, until a fingertip just grazed the waterfall, then jerked it back with a silent curse. The water was scalding.

'I'm going to have to find another entrance,' he said. 'The one he used. Somehow.'

'Leave him,' said Klyst. 'Leave with me. I can make you like you were in the Nelu Peren, when we met.'

Her voice was miserable with longing. Pazel took a deep breath, remembering what it felt like to breathe water, to hear her laughter echoing in the deeps. 'Listen, Klyst, I've never lied to you, do you hear? Not once.'

'You couldn't. You don't know how.'

'You only love me because your *ripestry* went wrong.'

She stared at him, bewildered. 'What do you mean? Bad *ripestry* goes wrong. Good *ripestry* goes right.'

'I'm not a murth!' he said desperately. 'And I don't know what to do about *this*.' He touched the shell, and she shivered as though he'd just caressed her.

'You know,' she said. 'Cut it out, destroy it. Then I'll be gone.'

'Is that what you want?'

But Klyst just looked at him. That was one question she would never answer. In the cave beyond the waterfall Arunis was again bent over the book. Pazel saw him from the corner of his eye; he could not turn his gaze from the murth-girl. His heart was hammering; she was smiling again, and her eyes seemed to have grown. *Damn you, are you weaving another spell?*

He forced himself to speak, forming each word with slow concentration. 'Arunis took a stone from the Red Wolf your people used to guard. An evil stone, made of the worst *ripestry* in the world. If he makes that sibyl tell him how to use it, he's going to become so powerful that no one will be able to stop him. He wants to kill *all of us* – Rin knows why – and when he's through with humans, you can bet he'll move on to murths.'

Before he had finished Klyst had put her head on his shoulder and started to cry – soft little *Hoo*'s, as if she had already known what he would say, and hoped unreasonably that she was mistaken. He tried to raise her head, but she looked away.

'Go get your book,' she said.

Arunis at that moment was rushing back to the sibyl. And Klyst, releasing Pazel, jumped into the scalding waterfall and disappeared.

It was all Pazel could do not to scream. He lunged forward, reaching out with both hands as close as he dared. She was simply gone. And then a tingling of his palms told him that something had changed. The waterfall had cooled. The edges steamed hot as ever, but there was a band of tepid water directly ahead.

He touched it. *She was there, she was standing disembodied in the water.* He seemed to hear her voice, shouting *Go go it hurts me!* And then he plunged through her, and emerged into the cave.

Arunis' back was still turned; he was drawing feverishly. In three bounds Pazel crossed to the flat rock, leaping over the flames. He swept up the book and rushed back, dived again through the waterfall, and for a strange thrilling moment he felt Klyst's body surround him once more. Then he was back in the tunnel. The *Polylex* was sopping, ruined. He turned to look at the waterfall and spoke her name. But the water was scalding again, and the murth-girl was gone.

Arunis had never lain eyes on him. But as Pazel emerged from the tunnel the sorcerer began to howl. The cries grew quickly fainter, however: Arunis was searching in the wrong direction. Either he had overlooked the dark tunnel, or could not believe that anyone had passed through the waterfall alive.

'Tell him nothing,' Oggosk had commanded. 'Nothing with your voice, nothing with your eyes or your movements or your hands. Do you understand me, girl? Any slip could bring disaster. Let me match wits with Arunis, this time: you'll have your own chance, maybe, after I'm gone. Right now you have nothing to say to him that's not best said with a sword.'

Thasha had sensed the candour in Oggosk, the rare absence of ridicule. So she had held fast to the witch's order, despite the maddening vapours and the heat, and the hypnotic dance of the blue flames in the shattered floor. She was thinking of it still when the sorcerer burst in.

Arunis lifted the mace above his head. 'Where is it, hag?' he raged. 'Which of these bastards took it? Speak!'

Oggosk and Thasha stood flanking the doorway that led up to the temple exit. Beside them, looking rather feeble, stood Dr Chadfallow. He had crawled into the chamber minutes before, drenched and gasping. Peytr crouched a few yards away, silent and fearful.

The old woman leaned heavily on her stick, frowning, studying the mage's face. Then she glanced at Thasha and nodded. Thasha drew her sword.

Arunis descended the stone rings, snarling: 'Do you think I will hesitate to kill her, hag? Do you think me that afraid of Ramachni's spell?'

Still Oggosk said nothing. Thasha's hands were slick on the hilt of her sword. She felt terror surge in her heart – and buried it, as Hercól had taught her to do, under focused observation. The length of the mage's stride. The set of his shoulders. The bulge at the hip beneath his coat, in all likelihood a dagger.

'I knew before I landed that I would kill today,' said Arunis, still approaching.

Chadfallow gave a throaty cry: 'Pazel!'

Oggosk smacked him with her walking stick. Arunis laughed, but Thasha could tell that the laugh was forced. 'The book!' raged Arunis. 'Return it now!'

The witch placed a hand on Thasha's elbow. Arunis began to climb towards them. A look of desperation filled his eyes.

'The agony you risk by defying me exceeds the limits of language, Duchess,' he said. 'Did you not hear the sibyl? I am death's master, not its slave. I will live on when the very dust of this world disperses in the void. You prove yourself capable of some three-for-a-penny spell, the hiding or moving of a book, and you imagine this prepares you to challenge Arunis?'

Thasha risked a glance at the old woman. There was a gleam of satisfaction in the milk-blue eyes.

'Oh no,' said Oggosk. 'I imagine nothing of the kind. No, Arunis, you have nothing at all to fear from *me.*'

The sorcerer froze. His eyes shifted to Thasha, and narrowed suspiciously. Thasha felt a sudden prickling along her spine. *He's examining me!* She felt Oggosk's hand tighten in warning: *Not a look, not a whisper.* Unblinking, Thasha stared Arunis down. The prickling subsided. Arunis went pale.

'You,' he said.

Lady Oggosk cackled, her voice echoing loud across the chamber. Arunis retreated a step, his eyes still locked on Thasha.

'Duchess! Duchess!'

Rose's bellow filled the room. Thasha looked up with a start as the captain and Drellarek staggered into the chamber. A moment later Hercól and the two Turachs appeared as well.

In that distracted split-second, Arunis pounced. Thasha instinctively threw her arms around Lady Oggosk, knocking the old woman backwards just as Arunis swung his mace. Thasha felt a spike on the weapon flick her hair above the ear. She whirled and drew her sword, dragging Oggosk by the arm lest the next blow find the old woman prone. But there was no second blow: Arunis barrelled headlong into the exit corridor, and disappeared. Thasha heard him scrabbling up the spiral staircase as though afraid for his life.

'Let him go,' croaked Oggosk, who had fallen on her back.

Thasha bent to help her. 'Are you hurt?' she asked.

'Pah. I'm not made of crystal, girl.'

The witch was soon on her feet, though she leaned heavily on Thasha's arm. She cackled, delighted with herself. Then she pulled Thasha close and whispered, 'Don't ask what I let him believe about you, Thasha Isiq: you'll get no more out of me than he did.'

Thasha was barely listening. 'Pazel!' she shouted, pulling away from the witch. 'What happened to him, Captain? Don't any of you know where he is?'

Pazel was a long time in returning to the chamber, although he could hear the others shouting his name. He was in pitch darkness again, but the fear was mostly gone. He had crept back to the chamber where Klyst had first appeared, and put his feet in the cool water. He called her name, but neither heard nor expected a reply. Eventually he placed Arunis' *Polylex* in the stream and let the current bear it away.

17

A Name and a Cause

—∾∾—

11 Freala 941
120th day from Etherhorde

Four days after the madness at Dhola's Rib the wind swung round to the south, and a white fog came with it. Denser and lower than the fog at Talturi, it soaked the men of the First Watch right through their woolens, and brought curses from the few passengers who still participated in Smoke Hour: their pipes were wet even before the midshipman handed them out.

On the fourth day Rose shortened sail, for they were approaching the eastern Ulluprids, where charts conflicted, and there was no certainty that a rock or barren islet would not loom suddenly out of the mist. The watch-men were on edge, straining their eyes for a lee shore, their ears for breaking surf. But the featureless world gave no clues. Men on the lower spars were as blind as the deckhands, while those in the crow's nests stood just above the mist, looking out over a cotton moonscape with no visible end.

Hatches were sealed against the creeping damp: a foe more stealthy than rain but just as likely to rot the wheat in the hold. That night was chilly, and men awoke with a cough. For the better part of the fifth day they held the same slow, nervous course. Mr Elkstem sailed by the binnacle, and memory.

As night fell Captain Rose asked Fiffengurt what he could smell on the wind. Startled to be asked his opinion after months of disdain, Fiffengurt drew a deep breath and held it, considering.

'Smoke, sir,' he said at last. 'No doubt about it. But not from a land fire, I think.'

Rose nodded. 'Nor from a burning ship. That's blubber and oil, cooking down over coal. There's a whaler nearby.'

Dawn proved the captain right. The fog rose with the suddenness of a dustcloth whipped from a table; and there, broad on the port beam, rode a two-masted vessel belching dark smoke from its furnace as it crept along.

Thasha had been on deck since first light: days of fog had made her hungry for the sun. She leaned on the mizzen rail, studying the whaler through her father's telescope.

'The *Sanguine*,' she read aloud.

'Out of Ballytween, m'lady,' offered a sailor, swinging up to the shrouds. 'See the pennant with the wee gold harp, under His Supremacy's own? That's the Opalt flag.'

'How far off is she, do you think?'

The sailor twisted for a second glance as he climbed. 'Four leagues at the outside, m'lady.'

Not far enough, Thasha knew: if she could read that whaler's nameplate, the men aboard her could read their own. Rose had ordered black paint spread over the three-foot gold letters that spelled out CHATHRAND, but that would not prevent the men of the *Sanguine* from recognizing the largest ship in the known world.

Good luck at last, she thought. For it was exactly what the conspirators had been afraid of. Whaling was a cruel business – Pazel had told her ghastly stories of his days on the *Anju* – but for the moment she looked fondly on the smoke-spewing vessel. *I hope you sail straight to Opalt and tell the world we lied.*

Rose emerged from his cabin, accompanied by his steward and Mr Alyash. With dire faces they stalked to the port rail. The captain's telescope snapped up and open. Rose gave a quick order to his steward, who bolted away.

'Thasha.'

She turned. Pazel had come up behind her, alone. Thasha glared a little. He had been so odd recently: one minute watching her with strange intensity, as if brooding on some great dilemma, the next downright rude. It had started before Dhola's Rib, but grown ever so much worse since their return from the island. What had happened to him there in the dark?

He had only said that he happened on Arunis, saw a chance to steal the *Polylex*, and took it. "Arunis never knew I was there. I got lucky, that's all." Thasha knew quite well that that was *not* all. The sibyl had shown something disturbing to each of them. What if Pazel's vision had been the worst? Yet what could be so much worse than watching your mother fall to her death? Besides, after several days, she had seen Pazel smiling, even laughing a bit, with Neeps and Marila. He had even wrestled with her dogs. It was only when Thasha herself drew near that he groused and snapped.

Thasha was angry, but she had made a firm decision to bear it with grace a while longer. She had told Pazel before anyone else about Ramachni's message in the onion-skin, hoping he'd see the gesture for what it was: a sign of her trust. Pazel had listened intently, hanging on every word, and gazing rather pathetically into her eyes. When she finished he shook himself, and his gaze hardened.

'You're still not reading the *Polylex*? What's the matter with you?'

'I don't know,' she'd answered, humbly enough. 'Something about that book makes my flesh crawl. Pazel, if you and I sat down together—'

'He didn't ask *me* to read it.'

'No, but I don't think he'd mind if you helped me.'

'So now you're second-guessing Ramachni, are you?'

That last remark had stung. For two days now they had barely spoken. That was the worst of it, she thought: how his sharpness always came when she tried to be open to him. And yet somehow he couldn't leave her alone.

'Well?' she demanded.

Pazel looked at her uncertainly. 'Heard you get up, that's all.'

He was a light sleeper; the slightest sound brought him wide awake. Then he would shift and toss or pace the outer stateroom for an hour or more. But lack of sleep alone could not explain his moods.

'You know,' she said, 'we're all proud of you for getting the *Polylex* away from Arunis. Oggosk talked about it all the way back to the ship. She said that Arunis would have found other ways to use the Nilstone, hidden in its pages, and that we'd never have found where he keeps it on the *Chathrand*. She says she underestimated you.'

'I'm ... overjoyed,' said Pazel.

'When are you going to tell me how you really did it?'

Pazel raised a hand to his collarbone. He looked at Thasha warily. 'Never,' he said.

'What's the matter with your chest? Sore from our fighting lessons?'

He nodded. 'Yes, rather.'

'That's the problem, isn't it?' she said. 'You're tired of the bruises. You want me and Hercól to quit knocking you around.'

Pazel looked surprised. 'I don't give a damn about that,' he said, 'and neither does Neeps. We've got to learn somehow.'

But Thasha knew she'd gotten close to the truth. Clearly unsettled, Pazel looked across the choppy sea. The whaling vessel had tacked in their direction, and even as Thasha watched her topgallants sheeted home. She was coming to greet them.

'Of course,' said Pazel, 'I'm not exactly a *quick learner.*'

Thasha hid her smile. Jealous idiot! He was comparing himself to Greysan Fulbreech. Thasha had told the older Simjan youth he *must* be a quick learner, just the day before, as he rattled off the medical topics he was studying under Chadfallow: salves, smelling salts, bone pins, leeches. Pazel had stood by, looking like he was being bled with leeches himself. But why should he compare himself to Fulbreech?

'Have you seen him?' asked Pazel suddenly.

'Greysan?' She shook her head. 'Not yet. Is he looking for me?'

Pazel nodded reluctantly. 'I told him I hadn't seen you anywhere, and – oh, here he comes now.'

Fulbreech was near the mainmast, a long stone's throw away, but she could already see his smile. Thasha couldn't help but smile in return – at times it seemed Fulbreech had been put on the ship just to beam in her direction. She did not feel guilty in the least for her friendliness towards him. It felt good to be smiled at, and she had some hope that Fulbreech might be recruited to their side. He had already mentioned quietly that the Sailing Code declared that men recruited through 'bald lies and distortions' were to be treated as kidnap victims, and that 'a kidnapped man cannot mutiny.' It was a brave statement, even if Fulbreech had said it mostly to impress her.

Pazel turned away. 'I'd better go wake up Neeps,' he murmered. 'You don't need me here.'

Thasha could have kicked him. As if he had a rival in Fulbreech! She had never kissed anyone but Pazel – and she had done it *twice*, for Rin's sake. True, that first kiss had been more to fool Arunis than to win his heart. But there had been nothing false about the second, later that night in the washroom. And both times his reaction had been to twitch and jump away, as if someone had just slapped him with a fish.

'Stay a minute,' she said. 'It won't kill you.'

Pazel sulked, but he stayed. Fulbreech waved to her, and she returned the gesture, seething inside. *What do you expect me to do? Hate him?*

Fulbreech had, after all, done just as Hercól had asked, and informed Eberzam Isiq that Thasha was alive. It was very nearly his last act in Simja, before Kruno Burnscove signed him onto the *Chathrand*. Fulbreech had told her the story in detail: how the old admiral had received him in the parlour of his new ambassadorial residence, still grateful that Fulbreech had arranged for his carriage after the ill-fated wedding ceremony. How he'd listened to Hercól's message, then begun to tremble until he spilled his tea. How he'd made Fulbreech repeat the words, tears of joy flowing down his cheeks: *Your morning star has not set. Her light is hidden, not extinguished.*

Then Fulbreech had paused in his storytelling and looked up at Thasha. 'As all stars hide at daybreak, no? Although a few make us wish the morning would never come.'

Probably that was when Pazel had begun to hate him. But Thasha had laughed and rolled her eyes. Fulbreech was out of line, of course – but he had said it so lightly, almost self-mockingly, that she hadn't even bothered to reprimand him.

'Lady Thasha,' he called out now, reaching them at last. 'I've made a tour of the ship, seeking you out – Mr Pathkendle had the idea you might be somewhere about the forecastle.'

Thasha threw Pazel a murderous glance. 'What can I do for you?' she asked Fulbreech.

'You have done it already,' he said, gazing into her eyes.

'Mr Fullbreech,' said Thasha, regarding him with Lorg School severity, 'I must forbid you to address me in that way.'

She was embarrassed, knowing Pazel would think she had asked him to stay in order to make him suffer, listening to Fulbreech's gallantries. The Simjan, for his part, realised that he had overstepped. 'I do ask your pardon, m'lady,' he said. 'I confess I am easily carried away.'

'That's a dangerous trait,' said Pazel. 'Had it all your life, have you?'

Fulbreech kept his eyes on Thasha. 'No,' he said. 'These past weeks, only.'

Thasha's smile threatened to resurface, so she trained the telescope on the whaler again. The ship had closed more than half the distance.

'Is that all you wanted to say, Mr Fulbreech?' she asked.

'Not quite, m'lady,' he replied. 'I woke this morning and recalled something else that happened on Treaty Day – a minor matter, perhaps. I worked straight through that night, running errands for King Oshiram. I had pledged to stay in the Royal Service through the day of your wedding, for His Highness was quite overwhelmed. And of course when Pacu Lapadolma took your place, the business of the crown was doubled: receptions, gifts, letters of congratulation—'

'I don't see why you're telling me all this,' said Thasha, disturbed by the mention of Pacu.

'Lady Thasha, the carriage that took your father to his residence that day was later used by others, and it was but one of many I kept track of. These carriages worked the streets until dawn. At that point, an honest driver brought me something left behind in his coach. I was never able to determine the owner, and the truth is that I forgot I carried the thing, when Mr Burnscove invited me to join your crew.' His voice grew animated. 'Such a thrill I had at the thought of it! To see mighty Etherhorde, and to earn my passage in the service of Ignus Chadfallow! But Burnscove lied to me. We will not see Etherhorde. We will not see any familiar place again.'

'We were all lied to,' said Thasha. 'But we're going to stop them, you know, we—'

She checked herself. It was too soon to offer Fulbreech confidences of that sort. 'What was this thing you carried?' she demanded.

'See for yourself,' said Fulbreech.

Thasha and Pazel both turned to look. There in his hand lay Eberzam Isiq's little bronze flask. Thasha's breath caught in her throat.

'You recognise it,' said Fullbreech, satisfied. 'Then my guess was correct. This was the admiral's property.'

Pazel's eyes narrowed. '*Was?*' he said.

Fulbreech started, as if taken aback by the question. Then he bowed slightly in Pazel's direction. 'I stand corrected, *is*. And now, m'lady, you can look forward to the day you return it to him personally.'

Thasha took the flask. She blinked at the handsome Simjan face before her. 'Fulbreech − Greysan − thank you ever so much. For all you've done for us.'

Fulbreech shook his head. 'You owe me no thanks.'

Pazel's mouth twitched, as if he agreed wholeheartedly. Fulbreech noted the expression with a raised eyebrow, then turned a brief, sly smile on Thasha, who had reddened, although she was not sure why.

'I must be off,' said Fulbreech. 'The doctor wants a report on the reading he assigned me last night, on the subject of brain deformities. Lady Thasha, Pathkendle.'

Another bow, and he was gone. Thasha whirled on Pazel.

'You prat. How could you make that face at him?'

Pazel managed to look sheepish and angry at once. 'I'm surprised you looked away from *Greysan* long enough to notice.'

'I'll look where I blary please. And you can dine on dung.'

Pazel's retort was interrupted by Uskins' deafening howl: 'All hands! Bracing stations. Watch captains forward. Topmen aloft. Stand by the fore topgallants. Handsomely, you lard-arsed layabouts!'

'Pitfire!' said Pazel, as the lieutenants' shrill pipes began to sound. 'What's he need all hands for? We're laying alongside that ship, not racing her.'

'How do you know what we're doing?'

Pazel looked at her with unconcealed scorn. Then he turned his eyes up to the tip of the mainmast. Thasha followed his gaze: a streaming pennant had been loosed there: two green stripes with a yellow between.

'"Draw Along and Confer,"' Pazel told her. 'Surprised you don't know that, given whose daughter you are.'

She could have slapped him. *Wait till our next lesson, you dog.*

Mr Elkstem put the helm to port, and the *Chathrand*'s bow swung towards the whaler. Just then they heard Neeps shouting their names. A moment later he arrived, entirely winded. 'Looking everywhere for you,' he gasped. 'Hercól's doing the same. Come on, we've got to get to the orlop – *now.*'

'All the way down there? What for?'

'Just come on.'

He took off running again, and they followed, mystified. 'We're going to have to use the gunner's pole,' Neeps shouted. 'Ladderways are blary jammed – everyone's coming up!'

Between the port ladderway and the capstan was a four-foot-square hatch that stood up several feet above the deck. Its cover had not yet been removed since the lifting of the fog, but Neeps knocked out the pins without hesitation and pushed the cover aside. The next moment he was over the lip of the hatch and gone.

Pazel followed, tucking his elbows close to his body and vanishing down the square black hole. Thasha did not hesitate for an instant. She had wanted to do this since the day she came aboard. Climbing onto the rim of the hatch, she looked down and saw the top of the greased iron pole just a foot beneath her, bolted firmly to the deck beams.

'Upa! Get down from there!'

It was Alyash, the new bosun with the frightening scars. 'You've no right to open that hatch! You could hurt someone! What are you playin' at, missy?'

He darted forward with startling speed. Thasha jumped feet-first through the opening, felt the man's blunt fingers graze her cheek, and then she was gone, flying down the pole with the cool slick grease flowing through her fingers and spattering her face, laughing as the decks flew by – main, upper gun, lower gun—

'*How do I blary stop?*'

Even as she cried out, she understood: the grease turned to thick tallow, her hands began to rasp, and beneath her the boys shouted *Squeeze! Use your legs!* and she did so, and stopped almost elegantly a foot above the berth deck.

'. . . see those men in the gun compartments?' Pazel was saying. 'What are they up to? What's Uskins doing with them?'

'Not a clue,' said Neeps, cleaning his hands on a rag hung for that purpose beside the gunner's pole. 'And there's no time to find out. Come on, we have to take the ladderway from here.'

There were no crowds at this level, and they descended the ladderway at a run. In the main compartment of the orlop deck, however, they met a troop of some dozen tarboys preparing to ascend. They were carrying cannonballs, plungers, and buckets of gunpowder.

'Saroo!' Pazel cried as the tarboy struggled past. 'What in Rin's privy are you doing?'

'Gun duty,' Saroo called over his shoulder. 'Just for show, mate. Rose don't like the looks of that whaler, somehow. Wants 'em to see we're armed.'

Thasha watched the tarboys lumber up the stairwell. The explanation did not satisfy her, but Neeps was tugging impatiently at her sleeve. 'I didn't mean *tomorrow*, Thasha.'

They ran diagonally across large and shadowy compartment and into the starboard passage. There they met Hercól, pacing nervously in the shadows. 'We are too late,' he said. 'She has gone.'

'Who's gone?' Pazel demanded.

'Diadrelu,' said Neeps in a furious whisper. 'Oh, hang it all! She warned me she couldn't stay!'

He led them on, past the starboard sail locker and the midshipmen's cabinettes. Stepping through a bulkhead door, they came suddenly into a passage strewn with crockery, much of it broken, and a number of dirty spoons.

'Teggatz sent me down here to collect the steerage dishes,' said Neeps. 'I had a perfect stack in my hands and was making for the ladderway when something pricked my foot.'

'You mean you stepped on a nail,' said Pazel.

'Hardly, mate.' Neeps glanced up and down the hallway, then knelt and began to probe the dusty boards with his fingertips. After a moment he seemed to find what he was looking for, and struck a board with the heel of his hand. There was no click, no creak of a hinge. But where the blow landed a tiny trapdoor sprang open. Within they could see only darkness.

'Pitfire, Neeps,' whispered Thasha. 'You've found an ixchel door.'

'I didn't exactly *find* it, to tell you the truth,' said Neeps. 'She caught my attention with the tip of her sword. Oh blast it, if only you hadn't been so hard to find! Dri had something terribly important to tell us.'

'Close the door, Neeps,' said Hercól.

'Just a minute,' said Thasha, startling them. She knelt and put her hand through the trapdoor. It led onto a narrow rectangular tunnel between the upper and lower floorboards. In one direction the way was blocked by a joist, but in the other the tunnel was open. Twisting, Thasha crammed her arm farther inside.

'Be careful!' said Pazel.

Thasha gave him an exasperated glance. 'How?'

But even as she spoke her fingers met with a tiny scrap of paper, wedged into a crack in the floor. With great care she pinched it between two fingers, plucked it free and extracted her arm from the tunnel. Between her fingers lay a sheet of parchment no larger than a postage stamp.

She raised the little sheet before her eyes. 'There's writing,' she said. 'Can you read it, Pazel?'

The writing was finer than the veins on a fern. Pazel brought her hand close to his eye. 'It's in Ix,' he said. "*Destroy this note. Close door. Return at five bells exactly. D.T. ap I.*" Those are her initials, all right.'

Hercól peered at the note in amazement. 'Never in my life have I heard of ixchel deliberately leaving proof of their presence for a human to find,' he said.

'She must be in danger,' said Thasha.

'Or in great fear,' said Hercól. 'In any case it will be five bells in some thirty minutes. Let us scatter: the less we are seen together, the less we have to explain. But return to this spot promptly, I beg you. We must not make her wait again.'

'Right,' said Pazel. 'Let's see what's brewing with that whaler.'

He and Neeps set off for the topdeck like a pair of racing hounds, and Hercól departed forward, leaving Thasha quite alone. She swore. It had seemed the perfect moment to catch Pazel alone, drag him to some empty corner and straighten him out about Fulbreech. *Blast the fool!* Time was short, life slipped away. Wasn't it obvious that every hour they spent fighting was a gift to their enemies?

She sighed: if they were really to scatter she would have to walk the length of the orlop deck, to the No. 5 ladderway in the stern.

The passage led her back to the main compartment, where to her consternation Dr Chadfallow and Fulbreech himself were the first persons she saw. They were making for the surgery; Chadfallow was describing the proper placement of tourniquets above a severed limb. He barely glanced at Thasha, but Fulbreech gave her another of his dashing smiles. This time Thasha found it unsettling. Did some teasing knowledge reside in that face? Or was it simply the most handsome she had ever seen?

She stormed across the compartment, barely conscious of where her feet were taking her. Men and boys, fibs and violence, games played with ships, hearts, weapons, worlds. *To the Pits with all of them. To the Pits with you, Pazel, if you think I'm some rock for you to lean on one day, and piss against the next.*

'Help me!'

Thasha drew her knife in a flash. The voice seemed that of a young woman's. It had come from the passage ahead. 'Who's there?' she shouted, dashing forwards.

Two sailors in an adjoining hall came at a run, brandishing sail-cutting shears. But they had heard no voice save Thasha's, and looked at her dumbfounded when she claimed to have heard another girl crying for help. Thasha could scarcely blame them. She knew quite well that she was the only female anywhere near her age on the Great Ship.

'That's live animals, up ahead, mistress,' said one of the men, pointing with his sheers. 'Like as not you heard one of Mr Latzlo's birds. Them golden parrots chatter up a storm, come feeding time.'

Thasha believed she could tell the difference between a woman's voice and that of a bird, but rather than argue she simply hurried on her way. The passage darkened. She had no lamp, of course, and the orlop deck was submerged and windowless. The light-shafts were all but useless at this early hour; until high noon they produced little more than a twilight glow. But the ladderway ahead should have been easy enough to spot. Where had it gone?

Far off to her left a familiar voice was chattering. It was Mr Druffle, the freebooter. He was terribly excited about something, but the walls between them prevented Thasha from catching a word. Then, just ahead of her, came a soft, bovine grunt.

She had reached the live animal compartment. Thasha had visited this place before, and hated it. Groping forwards, breath held against the reek, she saw the black rumps of cows in their stalls, the gleam of padlocks on Mr Latzlo's crates of exotics. She heard the sudden beat of caged wings, the furious snorts of the Red River hog bashing tusks against its wooden cage, the whimpers and squeals of countless smaller creatures. The planks were sticky underfoot. The thirty feet or so seemed endless.

As she stepped through the raised lip of the door at the compartment's end, something very shocking happened. The ship rolled. Instinctively, Thasha reached for the wall. Of course the *Chathrand* was always rolling gently, but this was different: a huge slow heaving, worse by far than the stormiest moments since the voyage began. The wind had exploded too: even here in the depths of the ship she could hear it, a monstrous moaning. *Tree of Heaven, shelter me*, she thought, involuntarily quoting a Lorg School prayer. *How could the sea change so quickly?* A moment later the ship rolled again.

'Mr Druffle?' she called aloud. Her voice sounded small and weak. The enormous motions of the ship continued.

Then the girl cried out again: farther ahead, and fainter. '*Don't touch me! Stay away!*'

At once Thasha broke into a run. She was certain now: whatever else was happening, that voice belonged to a girl her age, and it was sharp with terror. Someone was trying to do her harm.

But now Thasha was truly lost. The passage stirred no memory in her whatsoever. It elbowed left where she expected a right. Doors she had never noticed stood closed, some bolted, others locked. The moan of a high wind reached her ears. Strangest of all, the air grew colder with every compartment she entered. It was more than the night chill that lingered in the *Chathrand*'s depths: this was a biting cold, like stepping into winter darkness from the warmth of one's home.

'*Vadul-lar! Corl habeth loden!*'

The shouts came from her left: big men, shouting encouragement to one another. A moment later Thasha caught sight of their lamps. There were a great many of them, broad-shouldered men with stern faces, running parallel to Thasha down another corridor. *But what on earth was the language they were speaking?*

She sprinted ahead of them, losing her balance as the great swells heaved the *Chathrand* left and right, smashing heedless against the walls. Her training had taken over, her mind was awhirl. *I'm in darkness, they can't see me, they have axes, they are chasing a girl.*

The mass of men had dropped fifty or sixty feet behind her when suddenly the girl appeared dashing across a wide-open chamber: a round-faced, dark-skinned girl of Thasha's height, dressed in clothes four sizes too large for her, the cuffs hacked off at wrists and ankles. On her heels were two of the strange men who had somehow out-distanced their companions. Still screaming for help, the girl weaved and darted, putting crates and stanchions between her and the men. But her exhaustion was glaringly plain: in another minute they would have her.

Thasha flew at them, an attack plan crystalizing in her mind without the benefit of conscious thought. As she crossed the chamber one of the men caught a fistful of the girl's dark hair and wrenched her head back. So it was that Thasha saw her face even as she reached them, and shouted her name instead of a battle cry:

'Marila!'

The first man snapped to face her, and his own turning magnified the force of her fist. Even without such an advantage Thasha could land blows that would be the envy of many a fighting man: she felt teeth give way to her knuckles, and checked the weak jerk of his axe-hand with her elbow, and thought no more of him as he fell.

The other man fared better. He was broad-shouldered and strong. Astonished as he was, he had the presence of mind to haul the screaming girl to his chest, a move that kept Thasha from striking him instantly. She feinted; he lurched to block her, thrusting with his axe, both of them staggering with the roll of the ship. Then Marila wrenched her head around and sank her teeth into the soft flesh of his forearm. The man howled and flung her forwards. Thasha leaped at him, twisting to let Marila fall past her. She had resolved to have his axe, nothing else mattered. The man was drawing back for a killing swipe when she closed on him.

Thasha was no master fighter – that was the attainment of decades, not years – but she knew as they connected again that her opponent was not trained at all. Her left hand rose to meet the axe. Her eyes never left it. And his eyes followed hers, unthinking, so that he never saw the knife that ripped across his belly, parting shirt and flesh in a foot-long gash. Thasha spun beneath his still-upraised arm, twisting the forgotten axe out of his hand. As the man doubled over she clubbed him down with the weapon's heel. He crumpled, beaten but still conscious, holding his gut and screaming for aid.

Now Thasha leaped to Marila's side, her mind surfacing from its trancelike concentration – but only just. *Marila, aboard. The others are coming. Why is it so cold?*

For it was freezing now: her breath plumed white before her eyes. And wasn't that a skin of frost upon a barrel-top?

'Thasha,' gasped Marila, looking up at her in terror. 'Am I dead?'

'What are you talking about? Get up, hurry!'

'Where will you take me? Can you help me?'

'I'm trying, Marila. Get up!'

But it was clear that Marila wanted something more than protection from the men. Whatever that something was had to wait, however. Thasha pulled her to her feet, turned, groped for the lantern the first man had dropped—

—and watched oil gush from its broken side as she lifted it. Oil suddenly blinding as the flame jumped from the mantle to the leak, and then spread with a terrifying *whump* across the racing slick on the deck.

'*No!*' cried Thasha.

The oil forked and slithered, and the flame moved with it. Suddenly the whole pack of men burst into the chamber. They stopped dead at the sight before them: two girls ringed in flames, above two wounded men. Then they all began shouting the same word:

'*Surl! Surl! Surl!*'

Thasha didn't have to ask what *surl* meant. She pulled Marila away as they attacked the blaze, stumbling into the darkness of the passage behind.

'Are you bleeding?' she demanded.

'No,' said the Tholjassan girl. 'Thasha, who are they?'

'I don't know. Stowaways, thieves. The Turachs will slaughter them. Blast it, dropped my knife—'

'Thasha, you're not – I heard them shouting that you were—'

'Dead? Not quite, Marila. Hurry up, now, before they find a way around.'

'That man will bleed to death, won't he?'

Thasha's breath caught in her throat. She hauled Marila by the arm. 'No more questions. Not until we're out of this blary mess. Rin's teeth, that's *ice* on the deck!'

They stumbled on, feeling their way through a *Chathrand* both familiar and intensely strange. The very air had a different smell, and the wood itself felt smoother, less cracked and pitted with age. Thasha had a vague hope that they were still making for the stern, where they could not possibly fail to come across a ladderway. But in darkness the ship felt larger than ever, and in truth she had no idea where they were.

Suddenly she caught the scent of animals again. Impossible! But there it was, dead ahead: the dim shape of the compartment door, the screeching birds, the cattle. Somehow she had turned about completely and run back to the bow.

They dashed through the straw-littered compartment. Instantly the air warmed, and the far-off howl of the wind died away. Thasha pulled Marila to a halt. She touched a beam: the chill was gone. And now she realised that the violent rolling of the ship had ended too. Thasha cast a wild eye back over her shoulder. *What in the Nine Pits is happening?*

Marila gazed at her, perfectly expressionless and still. Then she threw her arms around Thasha and hugged her, shaking from head to foot. Thasha patted her back. The girl smelled rather worse than the cows.

They walked on in silence. Daylight streamed down from the tonnage hatch. As they passed the surgery Thasha heard Chadfallow lecturing Fulbreech on the miracle of blood coagulants.

'There's Thasha now,' said an approving voice, farther ahead. 'Right on time.'

It was Hercól. The Tholjassan stood with the tarboys at the spot where Neeps had opened the ixchel door. But when the boys caught sight of Marila they ran forwards, muffling shouts of astonishment.

'You mad cat!' said a delighted Neeps. 'I thought we'd seen the last of you in Ormael! Where's your little brother? What on earth are you *doing* here?'

'Stowing away,' said Marila, in the flat tone she used so often.

'But what on earth for?' Neeps pressed.

Marila hesitated, looking at him. 'I didn't want to go home,' she said at last.

The boys looked at her awkwardly. 'Home must be blary rotten,' said Pazel.

Marila shrugged. 'There's always work in Etherhorde.'

It was never easy to read emotion on Marila's face, but when they told her that the ship was not bound for Etherhorde the corners of her mouth drooped visibly. And when they told her they were bound for the Ruling Sea her mouth fell open and her breath caught in her throat. She looked at them each in turn.

'You're crazy,' she said. 'We're all going to die.'

No one was prepared to argue the point. Then Thasha shook herself, as if trying to cast off a sudden drowsiness. 'The fire,' she said.

'Fire, fire?' cried the others.

Only Marila looked at her with comprehension. 'The fire! The men with axes! Where did they go?'

She and Thasha struggled to make themselves understood. Everything that had happened in the darkness – the freezing cold, the violent pitching of the ship, the quick, bloody battle – had very nearly disappeared from their minds. Only when Marila had said the word *die* had the memory rushed back, whole, like a dream recovered by them both. Now Marila was terrified. She had crept out of the sack where she'd been hiding because of the cold, she explained. But the ship she had found herself in was almost unrecognisable.

'I didn't know the men, or their clothes, or the language they spoke. They were horrible, like pirates or Volpeks.'

'They're gone,' said Thasha, looking restlessly up and down the passage. 'Can't you tell, Marila? They're not hiding. They're ... somewhere else entirely. And the fire's gone too, and the storm.'

'It wasn't a dream,' said Marila firmly. "One of them tore out my hair. It still hurts.'

Thasha winced: a man had torn Marila's hair, and Thasa had slashed his belly open. If one was real, surely so was the other? She crossed her arms over her own belly, revolted.

Pazel noticed her distress. 'What's the matter with you?'

Thasha shook her head. 'Nothing. Dropped my knife, I think.' She groped at her belt as if making sure. The others were looking at her closely. She had not mentioned what she had done with that knife, and didn't much want to. 'I think I'm going to be sick,' she said.

'I *am* sick,' said Marila. 'And thirsty. I drank the last of my water yesterday.'

'Thasha,' said Hercól, 'take Marila to the stateroom and see to her needs, and your own. One of you boys put your coat over her head and shoulders. Let her pass for one of you if she can.'

'Right,' said Neeps, shrugging off his coat. 'Get some rest, Marila. You're looking green.'

Thasha took Marila to the ladderway, and they climbed out of sight. Hercól watched them go, then turned with sudden vehemence to face the boys.

'Do either of you have a guess as to what just occurred?'

'Yes,' said Pazel.

226

Neeps turned to him in surprise. 'You do?'

Pazel nodded. 'I think Marila stumbled into a disappearing compartment. Remember the rumours, Neeps, when we first came aboard? Places that just vanish, ghosts trapped in timbers, the names of everyone who ever died on *Chathrand* etched on some hidden beam? What if some of those rumours are true?'

'Ignus has always contended that mages played a part in the making of this ship,' said Hercól.

'He said there were old charms on her, too,' said Pazel, 'and that some of them slept until triggered, one way or another.'

'I don't put much store in Chadfallow,' said Neeps, 'but didn't Ramachni say almost the same thing? That the *Chathrand* was chockfull of old magic – "spells and shreds of spells," as he put it?'

'That she is,' said a voice at their feet. 'No one who dwells in her shadows could think otherwise.'

To their great joy Diadrelu stood before them, in the now-open trapdoor. Pazel and Neeps crouched down to welcome her, but the ixchel woman silenced them with a hand.

'Why is the deck so empty, at this time of day? Are you certain you're alone?'

When they told her of the whaler, and that Rose had called all hands to duty stations, Dri seemed to breathe a little easier. She did not look particularly well. Her face was weary and sad, and her copper skin was paler than Pazel remembered.

'My *sophister* Ensyl is watching the compartment door. If she calls a warning I will be gone before you can wish me goodbye.'

'We've been worried sick about you, Dri,' he said. 'It's been over a month! Where have you been?'

'Under arrest,' she replied. 'House arrest, merely: no fear, I'm quite comfortable. But I am forbidden to leave my quarters except when accompanied by Taliktrum's personal guard.'

'Your nephew gives *you* orders now?'

'Lord Taliktrum rules over us all,' said Dri stiffly. 'But certain orders I find impossible to obey.'

'Hear, hear,' said Neeps approvingly.

But the ixchel woman shook her head. 'This is a grave matter for the ixchel. Our survival has always depended on strong clans, and the very bone and sinew of a clan is obedience. I have come to understand, however, that there are higher allegiances even than clan.'

'You speak the truth,' said Hercól. 'The carnage Arunis will unleash if he finds a way to use the Nilstone – through his Shaggat, or by some other means – will sweep aside the little people and the large. Does Taliktrum know of the oath we took together, then?'

'Rin forbid!' said Dri. 'If any part of him believes in me still, it will die when he learns of that oath! No, the story is far simpler. When Taliktrum discovered my use of *blanë* and its antidote on your wedding day, he chose to call it theft. When I told him that I had killed the Shaggat's son, he thanked me for my "decades of service to the clan" and imprisoned me.'

'It was you who killed him, then,' said Hercól. 'I did wonder about that curious accident.'

'It was I,' said Diadrelu, 'though I had no joy in the act. Those two were children when the Shaggat began his crusade. They are as much the victims of his evil as anyone. First they paid with their sanity; now Pithor Ness has paid with his life!'

Dri suddenly pricked up her ears, and so did Pazel: his Gift had tuned his ears permanently to the ixchel register no normal human could hear. A young ixchel woman was announcing Thasha's return. A moment later Thasha entered the passage, breathless, her dreamy look quite gone.

'We're tied up beside the whaler,' she said, 'and their captain's aboard, talking with Rose in his day cabin.' But it's strange: Rose is keeping the whole crew on alert. They're all at their stations, waiting. Oh, Dri!'

Thasha's troubled face lit up. She bent down, and the ixchel woman reached out to touch her hand.

'It is good to be back among you! said Dri. 'But I fear the chance will not come often. Taliktrum's fanatics lurk outside my door, as if expecting some wickedness to issue from it. They do not yet know of this secret passage – my *sophister*s and I built it alone, some months ago – but how long before they begin to enter my quarters without knocking? Some call me a traitor already.'

'How dare they!' hissed Thasha.

Dri smiled sadly. 'They dare more every hour,' she said. 'The time may soon come when I flee this way not to return, and then you shall have yet another lodger at your inn, Thasha Isiq. Now hear me: I have come with both pleas and warnings. You know, first of all, of the accusation hurled by the Mzithrinis, back in Simja.'

'Know of it!' said Pazel. 'I *translated* it. They accused someone on the *Chathrand* of sending a murth or demon or some such creature to attack their old priest – the one they call the Father. And they say he died fighting the beast.'

Dri nodded. 'We had our spies on the topdeck that day, as every day. Some of my people found that standoff between your giant-clans amusing.' She shook her head. 'They might have felt otherwise if Taliktrum had shared the report I gave him.'

Then she told them of the night Arunis had communed with Sathek, the dead spirit with the terrifying voice; and of the arrival of the incubus out of the storm, of its rage, and how Arunis at last had commanded it to go and retrieve a sceptre of some sort from the mainland.

'Sathek's Sceptre!' cried Thasha. 'That was it! I saw a drawing of it in the *Polylex* months ago! That was the sceptre in the Father's hand!'

'Well this is splendid,' said Neeps. 'Add summoning demons to the list of foul things Arunis can do. Who is this Sathek? Or who *was* he, when he lived?'

'I hoped you could tell me,' said Diadrelu.

'I can,' said Hercól.

The others turned to him in surprise. Hercól's face was very grave. 'Sathek was the father of the Mzithrin Empire,' he said. 'Mind you, he is not a father they care to speak of today, much less embrace. Some say he was part demon himself. What is certain is that he was the first warlord to conquer all the Mzithrin lands, from the Mang-Mzn to the Nohr Plateau. He did not rule long – the Worldstorm was already raging by the time he built his palace on Mount Olisurn. And his cruelty inspired rebellion. His own people called him 'the soulless one.' Nonetheless he created them, in a sense: the five city-states that rebelled most fiercely grew into the five kingdoms of the Mzithrin Empire.'

'And the sceptre?' asked Pazel.

'He is always depicted with a sceptre,' said Hercól. 'But I know nothing of its purpose. Consult that book of yours, Thasha.'

'Arunis was not capable of summoning the incubus himself,' said Dri thoughtfully. 'If he could have, why beg for Sathek's help? In fact he seemed to fear for his life, until the creature left his cabin.'

She sighed. 'I must proceed to my other warning. Something is amiss with the insects aboard the *Chathrand*. The night I killed the Shaggat's son I very nearly died as well, on the stinger of a wasplike beast as large as myself. It was deadly, but also tormented and deformed. In a strange way it reminded me of a boar I saw once in the Emperor's own piggery on Mol Etheg. The creature had been bred too aggressively, and fed too much. It was as if Magad had set his heart on having the world's largest, meanest swine. What he got was a beast heaped with more muscle than its own frame could endure. It was in constant pain, and attacked even those who came to feed it, and had to be slaughtered before it was full grown. This insect was misshapen too, and for all its speed it flew somewhat drunkenly. I thought later that it would soon have died even if I had not slain it.'

'And you fear there could be more of these things?' Pazel asked.

'I do,' she said. 'The clan has not met with any – I have a few loyal aides of my own, who bring me news. But a scout in the afterhold reported a moth as large as a human dinner plate, writhing in the air as if in agony. Yesterday, moreover, I heard my earnest caretakers speaking of *the biggest, ugliest horsefly ever to wing out of the Pits*. And there is one more thing: the rats in the hold and lower decks are miserable with fleas, of a kind more bloodthirsty than any known to rat-kind.'

'Felthrup was complaining of fleas,' said Thasha. 'I'd forgotten all about it. He drowned them in a saltwater bath.'

'Since my arrest I have begged for the right to share this warning with you,' said Dri. 'My nephew has always refused. "When humans pay attention to insects, they pay attention to rats, and we shall all perish if Rose decides to cleanse the ship of rats." Such is Taliktrum's argument, and on this point I cannot disagree. But you have proven your good faith. And why not seek out the source of these deformed insects ourselves?' Dri sighed. 'He will not spare one ixchel for the task.'

'Fleas.' Neeps sat back on his heels, squeezing his eyes shut with the effort of memory. 'I'll be damned if someone *else* wasn't talking about them. Who was it? Pitfire.'

'There is another matter,' said Dri. 'Too strange for coincidence, I think. Both the Shaggat's son and Arunis mentioned something called *the Swarm*. The mage said that "armies would wilt before it" like flowers in winter. Can he mean that a horde of such insects is breeding somewhere? Or is it another kind of threat altogether? Whatever the truth, this Swarm has something to do with the Nilstone, and that sceptre. I know no more than this – but be on your guard, and learn all that you can.'

'Lady Dri,' said Pazel with a certain reluctance, 'there's something I have to tell *you*. We're not the only ones who know about your people any more.'

The ixchel woman turned to face him. A look of pure dread appeared on her face.

'What are you saying?'

Pazel told her of their summons by Oggosk, and how the witch spoke of Diadrelu and Taliktrum by name, and how she claimed Sniraga had brought Lord Talag's body to her in her jaws. He left out only her final threat, concerning Thasha and himself. Dri listened, mute as a stone. Something close to disbelief shone in her eyes.

When she spoke at last her voice was changed. 'The witch told you one of us came for my brother's body?'

Pazel nodded.

'And she gave it to him?'

'That's right, Dri. I'm sorry.'

Suddenly Diadrelu began striking violently at her own head and face. The humans cried out. Thasha raised her hand – and dropped it just as quickly. There could be no graver insult than to use force, even loving force, against this tiny queen. 'Stop, stop!' they begged her. A moment later she did, and stood with moist and furious eyes, looking at nothing.

'He will have been parcelled,' she said. 'I was not told. I should have been there, done him that last service, or shared it with his son at least.'

'Parcelled?' asked Neeps quietly.

'Drained of blood, then cut into twenty-seven pieces and incinerated. There is never any delay, no time of mourning such as you have. The pieces are bound in clean cloth, with private messages from the twenty-seven closest to the dead one tucked within. If a clan is at sea, where burning is difficult, the pieces are tied with stones or bits of lead ballast, and sunk in the dead of night. It is always done thus, so that the body may not be found by your people, and our loved one's souls may depart without fear for the clan.'

She dried her eyes with a sleeve. 'You must find it a grisly custom. But it is how we say goodbye.'

'No people should have to face the choices yours have,' said Hercól. 'It is not for us to judge you, ever.'

Dri looked up at the swordsman with affection. Just a month ago he had been struggling with a deep distrust, perhaps a hatred, of ixchel, born of some long-ago tragedy of which he never spoke. Ramachni had chastised him: who among them took the greatest risk in giving trust? The mage's reprimand had shaken Hercól. Solemnly he had asked Dri's pardon, not denying the anger that dwelt in him but swearing to defeat it, and he had proved better than his word. *Give me one flawed but honest man*, she thought, *and keep your legions of hypocrites.*

She took a deep breath. 'Now for my plea,' she said, looking at the three youths. 'It is a bloody thing I ask, but you are the only ones who might accomplish it.'

'Tell us,' said Thasha.

'My nephew has made many errors in his first weeks as commander,' said Dri. 'I did not want to admit the extent of them. I told myself they were flaws of inexperience, that he would grow into wisdom as he faced the daily urgencies of leadership. I believed this despite my own arrest, despite his denial of the menace of the Nilstone, despite misgivings about his every action since the death of his father.

'Until today. With my breakfast Ensyl slipped me a note, revealing that Taliktrum has been meeting in secret with the rat-king, Master Mugstur. The same animal who has murdered twelve of our people since we boarded in Sorrophran, and left their nibbled corpses outside our dwellings. The same creature who ambushed and nearly killed his father, to say nothing of his aunt. The same Rin-obsessed lunatic who has sworn to kill Captain Rose for his "heresy", and to eat his tongue. And Taliktrum calls *me* a traitor!

'He has tried kept these meetings secret, of course, and Ensyl could not get close enough to hear what he and the rat discussed. But Mugstur will keep no promises, except possibly those he makes to the Angel of Rin.'

'What do you want us to do about all this?' asked Pazel.

'I want you to lure Master Mugstur into the open,' said Diadrelu, 'before some terrible harm is done to us all. Use blasphemy, use bribery – use your Gift, Pazel, if it gives you rat-speech, although Mugstur speaks a passable Arquali. Say whatever you must to coax that murderous beast out of his warren and into the cabin of your choice. And be sure he does not leave that cabin alive.'

'You're asking us to kill a woken animal?' said Thasha, frowning. 'The only woken rat on the ship besides Felthrup himself?'

'Mugstur's fate is sealed already,' said Diadrelu. 'He thinks himself the instrument of divine retribution. When he attacks Rose he will die, but what harm might he do with my nephew's help before then?'

'Incalculable harm,' said Hercól.

Dri nodded. 'Together they might even deal the *Chathrand* her fatal blow. Yes, I am asking you to commit a murder, if by that act you prevent many hundreds more. Have no illusions, my friends. We shall all of us be murderers before this voyage ends.'

'You sound like my father,' said Thasha, 'telling Pazel why he had to destroy Ormael before someone else did. Well, I don't believe anyone's fate is sealed.'

'Mugstur's is,' Dri insisted. 'He has sealed it himself, and tightens the screws every waking hour.'

'But that's the point, he's *woken*. You know what Ramachni told us, that when these creatures suddenly—' Thasha waved her hands '—*erupt into consciousness, after years as simple animals, they're so frightened it's a wonder they don't all run mad. It must be horrifying! Like your mind-fits, Pazel, but with no escape.'*

Pazel shuddered. 'What would you have us do?' he said to Thasha. 'Go down into the hold and reason with him? Tell him this Angel business is all in his head?'

Thasha looked wounded by his spiteful tone. 'We could trap him,' she said. 'In a box, or something.'

'We're talking about a *rat*,' said Neeps.

'Oh, just a rat!' said Thasha furiously. 'Just another vermin. Not worth the air he breathes. Where have I heard that before?'

'Everywhere,' said Hercól. 'It is the false, cursed verdict of our times. Somewhere in Alifros one resentful soul inflicts it on another, every minute of every day. Thasha, the moral point is yours, but the tactical goes to Diadrelu. Mugstur threatens the very survival of this ship – and intentionally so. He must therefore be stopped.'

'Mugstur's too smart to crawl into a box,' said Pazel.

'Oh, can't you blary *concentrate*,' snapped Thasha. But in fact she was finding it difficult to concentrate herself: the axe-man's cries of agony still rang in her mind. 'Listen, Hercól. I can kill if I have to. You've been teaching me how to do it for years. But I'm not a *murderer*.'

'I am,' said Diadrelu. 'And I dare say so is your tutor.'

'I will speak for myself, Lady Diadrelu,' said Hercól quietly.

Dri gave him a startled glance. 'I mean no insult. You come from a warrior people, and have lived a warrior's life. This is not a secret, I think?'

'There is more to the Tholjassan Dominion than warcraft,' said Hercól, 'and more to me as well. I must agree with Thasha in this matter: our fates are what we make of them.'

Dri shook her head. 'That is not what we ixchel believe. We say it is our slumbering hearts that choose for us, and that in them resides the will of a thousand years of ancestors who cannot be denied. And it has always seemed to me that this philosophy is borne out even more by your history than our own. How many wars might have been avoided but for ancient grievances, long-dead matters of honour and revenge? We at least admit this part of ourselves.'

'If that is so,' said Hercól, 'why not tell us what honour or ancestry requires of *your* clan, such that it risks annihilation by boarding the Great Ship on this voyage?'

'You go too far,' said Diadrelu. 'You know that I am not free to speak of such things.'

'We know that much,' said Hercól, 'and not a word more.'

For a moment Diadrelu was speechless. Neither she nor Hercól seemed to trust themselves to continue. At last the ixchel woman turned to look at Thasha.

'If you do not believe that fates can be sealed,' she said, 'I suggest you look to the mark all five of us carry on our skin. A wolf can mean different things to different people, but all wolves are predators.'

'We got these scars to help us save the world from the Nilstone,' Thasha countered, 'not to let us kill anyone who gets in our way.'

'Mugstur is not just anyone. He is a lethal zealot, a depraved and dangerous rat.'

'Felthrup's a rat, too,' said Thasha. 'What if he somehow threatened our safety? Would you kill him, just like that?'

'Yes,' said Dri. 'As I killed the son of the Shaggat Ness – just like that. No ixchel would be alive today if our people had not answered such questions in their hearts long ago.'

'But you spared me,' said Pazel.

The others looked at him in surprise.

'You fought your whole clan the night we met,' he went on. 'They wanted to stab me dead in my hammock, but you wouldn't let them. And come to think of it, you spared Felthrup too – didn't Talag want to kill him after he blocked your escape down that storm-pipe?'

For the first time in many days Thasha looked at him fondly. Pazel dropped his eyes. 'I think I know how the Red Wolf chose us,' he said. 'I think it wanted people like you, Dri. People who can do whatever it takes – even kill – but who hated the idea of killing so much that they'd even fight their friends to avoid it. Because we all do hate it, don't we?'

A long silence. Diadrelu would not look at Hercól. The swordsman, for his part, sat back against the wall. His eyes took on a distant look, as though he were quite alone in the passage, or in some other place altogether.

'Shall I tell you how I broke with Sandor Ott?' he said suddenly. 'It is a dark story, and too long to tell in full, but at the heart of it was my refusal to kill a mother and her sons. They were the lever that has moved my life: had I not faced that choice, to murder innocents or join them in exile, I would today perhaps be serving Ott rather than fighting him. I do not know if you are right about the Red Wolf and its choices, Pazel, but you are surely right about us.'

'What happened?' asked Thasha in a whisper. In all her life Hercól had never spoken so openly of his past.

'We fled together,' said Hercól simply, 'from the Mindrei Vale in Tholjassa over cold Lake Ikren, and thence by the Pilgrims' Road into the icewalled maze of the central Tsördons. And Ott's men pursued us, village by village, peak by peak. For eleven years I gave myself to their protection, and used all I knew of the spymaster's methods against him. It was not enough to save the children. Ott tracked them down and killed them, and took their bodies back to Etherhorde on slabs of ice.'

'And the mother?' asked Diadrelu.

'The mother survives. And with her survives the hope of a better world. She is old, now, but her hand is steady, and her mind is tempered steel. Have you not guessed, Pazel? She was the woman you saw in the garden, and we are far enough from that garden now for me to speak without breaking my oath. Her name is Maisa, Empress Maisa, Daughter of Magad the Third, aunt and stepmother to the current usurper, and sole rightful ruler of Arqual.'

The agitation his words caused can barely be described. Pazel alone knew of Maisa from his school days – Neeps' village had had no history teacher, and Thasha's own had never breathed a single word about such a woman – but they all understood that Hercól was denouncing the Emperor, and even speaking of his overthrow.

'Hercól,' whispered Neeps, 'you sly old dog!'

'My mother used to talk about her,' said Pazel. 'As if she *knew* her, almost.

'Just a minute,' said Thasha. 'If Maisa's the daughter of Magad the Third, who's that woman they call the Queen Mother? The one who hardly ever leaves Castle Maag?'

'That one?' said Hercól. 'A blameless impostor. An old royal cousin, who somehow survived the Twelve Days' Massacre in Jenetra, and who Magad the Third brought to court as a widow. She has lived there ever since, half-mad but peaceful. I believe she really thinks herself a queen. His Supremacy has made good use of her. When foreign princes call on Etherhorde, that woman's mere presence casts doubt on the rumour that someone named Maisa once existed.'

'What about Maisa herself?' said Pazel. 'What in the nine nasty Pits was she doing on Simja – on *Treaty Day*? She couldn't have found a more dangerous place if she tried.'

'That is true,' said Hercól, 'and I said as much to her myself. She replied that the world and its assembled rulers had begun to doubt that she still drew breath. "They will doubt no longer," she said. "Neither will the Secret Fist," I countered, but Her Highness told me that Ott would not catch her unprepared, and would risk no open assault on her in Simja, eager as he was to robe Magad in the garb of peacemaker. I can only pray that she was right.'

He smiled. 'At last I am free to speak her name aloud – and my listeners do not know of whom I speak! Listen; I will tell you of her briefly.

'Maisa was the daughter of Magad the Third – a vain and violent prince in his youth, but one who found wisdom in his declining years. She was his second child. Maisa's older brother was Magad the Fourth, also known as Magad the Rake. This youth had all his father's defects of character, and none of his strengths. His worst fault was to see the world's ills and conflicts with brute simplicity. Enemies were to be crushed. Arqual was to be loved. Arquali customs, poetry, history, gods – they were the best under the sun, obviously. This he knew, without bothering to learn a poem, study a history, or meditate upon the teachings of the faith he claimed as his own. He did not, for instance, obey the Twenty-Second of the Ninety Rules.'

Thasha thought for a moment, then recited: '*To lie with a woman is to pledge oneself to her wellbeing, and that of the child that may follow. I shall seek no pleasure there but in the knowledge that part of my life shall be the payment. Nor shall I . . .*" Blast it, I'm forgetting—'

'"*Nor shall I deny the wages of love, which are the soul,*"' finished Diadrelu.

Hercól looked at her, startled, and appeared to lose his train of thought for a moment. Then he nodded and went on. 'Magad the Rake did just that,' he said. 'At twenty-six, the prince seduced a blacksmith's daughter and got her with child. When she could no longer hide her pregnancy, he paid the Burnscove Boys to whisk her offshore and drown her. But his father caught wind of the scheme in time and brought the girl back unharmed. The old Emperor was livid: word had leaked of the attempted murder, and across Etherhorde thousands were taking portraits of the royal family from their walls and tossing them in shame upon the streets.

'The Emperor hobbled out into the Plaza of the Palmeries and swore that his son would raise the child as his own – or else forfeit the crown of Arqual. But the young prince rode up on a charger, leaped to the ground with a snarl, and spat at his father's feet. What other son could replace him? he asked. And the old man struck his son across the mouth.

'Magad the Rake was driven from Arqual. He fled east, to the Isle of Bodendel, under the flag of the Noonfirth Kings. His father disowned him, and the Abbot of Etherhorde cast him from the Rinfaith. In Castle Maag some months later, the blacksmith's daughter bore a son: Magad the Fifth.'

'His Supremacy,' said Thasha.

'A title invented by his father the Rake,' said Hercól. 'Alas, the blacksmith's girl was still in love with her foul seducer, and blamed herself for tearing the royal household apart. It seems the royal servants blamed her too. One day, for spite, they told her how the Rake had kept other women scattered about the city, and had often declared that the mother of his son meant less to him than the hunting-bitches in the kennels. The girl left Castle Maag, went straight to her father's smithy and drank hot lead.'

Diadrelu closed her eyes.

'The Emperor had no other son, it is true. But he did have his beloved daughter, Maisa. She took the orphaned princeling, Magad the Fifth, as her own child, and vowed to care for him always. And her father, in the finest deed of his life, named Maisa his heir.

'The old man lived another six years, and in that time Maisa wed a baronet, and bore two sons of her own. They were never jealous of their cousin, who would rule when Maisa's time on earth was over; they did not hunger for more blessings than those life had already showered upon them. But jealousy there was: somewhere in East Arqual, Magad the Rake was plotting his return. And the Secret Fist took his side, for Sandor Ott feared to serve under a woman. He knew also that Empress Maisa would not let him run the occult affairs of Arqual as he saw fit – a practice he had grown used to under her father. This was, after all, when Ott first began dreaming of the use he might make of a certain heretic king in the Mzithrin lands.'

'The Shaggat,' said Pazel.

Hercól nodded. 'Ott's agents provoked the skirmishes that grew into the Second Sea War, and the old Emperor, weakened by tales of the ghastly bloodshed engulfing the west, died halfway through the campaign. Maisa was crowned Empress, and at once sent emissaries of peace to the Mzithrin capital. Among them was a young genius of a surgeon by the name of Chadfallow.'

'Ignus?' said Pazel in disbelief. 'But that was forty years ago! He can't be *that* old.'

'He does not look it,' Hercól agreed, 'but he is past sixty without a doubt. Years ago I asked his age. "Old enough to be your father," he told me shortly, "and to be spared such idle questions." In any case, he went to Babqri as Maisa's standard-bearer. It is to the Empress that Chadfallow owes his career as special envoy, although at times I think he forgets this.

'The war was by now quite out of control, raging throughout Ipulia and the Crownless Lands. Still the last, worst years of it might have been prevented, but for what happened next. In great secrecy Ott brought Magad the Rake back to Etherhorde, and with the aid of certain generals who had always loathed taking orders from a woman, drove Maisa from the city. Her baronet was killed, her birth-sons driven into exile beside her. Magad the Fifth, the Rake's child, was torn from her arms and taken to the father who had tried to drown him before his birth.

'To make the people accept such treachery, Ott spread rumours about Maisa: rumours of corruption and graft, and uglier sins. A pack of lies, of course; but by the time the people saw through them it was far too late.

'Having seized the throne, the Rake set out to seize his son's heart by equally brutal tactics. Magad the Fifth was a boy of nine, and loved his stepmother dearly, but his father and a thousand sycophants filled his head with tales of Maisa's wickedness, and kept at them so relentlessly that the boy at last started to believe the lies. They called her embezzler, deathsmoker, torturer of children, unnatural lover of animals and Flikkermen, practicer of dark Western rites. By the time young Magad's half-brothers were found and slain in the Tsördons, the boy was denouncing Maisa himself. And to this day our Emperor repeats these lies, whenever he forgets that his stepmother does not officially exist.'

'But can he *truly* believe them,' Pazel asked, 'after Maisa raised him as one of her own?'

'A fine question,' said Hercól. 'All I can say with certainty is that when it mattered most he permitted Ott to go on hunting Maisa and her children. I do not know if he has ever repented. Still, there was a rumour in the Secret Fist that the death of Magad the Rake was no hunting accident, as the world was told: that he was not tossed from his horse but pulled from it, by his son. The man who is now our Emperor then took a stone and crushed his father's skull – and the word on his lips as he did so was, "Mother!"'

'And yet he sits upon her stolen throne,' said Dri, 'and pretends that she never existed.'

Hercól nodded. 'Worse, he has never pardoned her. If a foreign king or bounty hunter laid hands on Maisa, he could claim to be holding an enemy of the crown. Ott, after all, only let Maisa and her sons flee Etherhorde to save appearances. He always meant to kill them, at a prudent distance from the capital. And as I have already told you, he succeeded with her sons.'

'How has the mother survived so long?' asked Diadrelu.

'Good luck, in part,' said Hercól. 'Even a spymaster has but so many men at his command, and for decades now they have been occupied with their Shaggat deception. And the Mzithrinis have certain brilliant agents of their own, both within the territories of Arqual and in the Crownless Lands, and much of the Secret Fist's efforts go to fighting them. But Ott scorns the very notion of luck. His edict was always *Leave nothing to chance.* And so I think it was with Maisa. He must have decided that an ex-Empress living out her declining years among poor mountain folk was better than a slain Empress who could become a martyr.'

'But she's not in decline, is she?' said Pazel. 'I mean, I saw her, and—'

Hercól looked at him, and a bright ferocity shone in his face, and the memories seemed to dance once more before his eyes. 'They slew her children,' he said. 'And they took her hopes for peace, and her faith in goodwill and honour among nations, and dragged them through sewers of treachery. No, she is not in decline. There is an avenging fire in her that could yet change the fate of this world, and sweep away the lesser men who bleed and abuse it.'

Dri was watching him intently. 'Is that your dream as well?' she asked.

'Yes,' said Hercól. 'And I am far from alone, although I have some-times felt so. And with the approach of Treaty Day I feared I would lose her at last. I wrote letter upon letter, begging her not to gamble with her life on a visit to Simja. No answering letters came. Only once – days before boarding the *Chathrand* – did I receive a scrap of paper, slipped into my pocket by a stranger in a crowd. The words were in Maisa's hand: *Have you forgotten our toast, Asprodel? I assure you, I have not.*'

'What's that name she called you?' asked Pazel.

Hercól smiled again. 'In her service we all bear false names. Her Majesty chose mine.'

'Asprodel,' said Dri, looking up at Hercól. 'The mountain-apple, whose flowers open before all others, even in the melting snow. I would not call that name a false one.'

'But what did she mean?' pressed Thasha. 'What toast?'

Hercól remained silent for a moment, as if struggling to fit words to memory. 'Before Simja,' he said at last, 'I had not laid eyes on Empress Maisa in ten years. Not since the day we learned for certain that her sons were dead. On that day she called me to her cold chambers, in that forgotten colony of timber men, and sent her one servant from the room, and poured us each a cup of steaming wine. "Today I turn, Asprodel," she told me. "Henceforth I shall face the wind, and cease to live as a hunted thing. My own hunt begins, and by the souls of my children, I swear it shall only end with my death."

'"What do you hunt, Your Majesty?" I asked her.

'"Why, my throne," she said, as if surprised by the question. And yet anyone would have forgiven me if I had laughed. She had been a stateless monarch for thirty years. I had been with her for the last twelve, and had watched her entourage dwindle from seven hundred to sixty, half of them old, less than a dozen true warriors. Nine-tenths of her gold was spent, and her sons were in ice-coffins sailing back to Magad the Fifth. How could she even begin?

'I learned soon enough. "Open that chest by the window, Asprodel, and bring me what lies therein," she said. I obeyed her, and this what I found.'

Hercól seized the hilt of his sword, and in a swift, quiet motion pulled the weapon from its sheath. In the dim light the blade was little more than a shadow, and yet somehow they could all sense its nearness, as though it were radiating heat, though they felt none.

'"That is Ildraquin," Maisa told me. "*Earthblood*, in the tongue of the Selk, who made it from the steel of the Gates of Idharin, when that city was no more. Six miles beneath the earth they forged it, under Wrath Mountain. It was their gift to Bectur, last of the Amber Kings."'

'"I have heard of that sword," I told her, "but under a different name: *Curse-Cleaver*, men call it, do they not?"'

'"They do," she said, "for in the deep heart of Alifros all curses die, and something of that heart's molten power was caught, they say, in the tempering of the blade. And Ildraquin did break the curse that had wrapped the Amber Kings in misery and sloth, they say, for Bectur's reign was like a last ray of sun beneath the thunderheads, before a long night of storm. It was far too late to prevent the storm. Let us hope we are not too late again."

'With that she sheathed the sword and passed it to me. I began to object, but she silenced me with an impatient gesture. "Whom do you imagine I am guarding it for? A son?" I found no words to answer, so she continued: "Gather your things, Asprodel. You ride today upon the river, with the timber-men to Itholoj, and thence to the coast, and by the first ship bound for Etherhorde. A great ally awaits us there: probably the greatest we shall have in this campaign, although he shall never wield a sword. He is a mage, Ramachni Fremken, and he has stepped already into the life of the daughter of my admiral, Eberzam Isiq."

'Ha!' cried Pazel, turning to Thasha. 'And you thought Ramachni had befriended you just so that he could find me, and teach me those Master-Words. But he's always been part of something larger.'

'Well I knew *that* much,' said Thasha. 'In fact I always thought he was part of something *enormous* – bigger than who rules Arqual, or whether it fights another war with the Mzithrin. I suppose that something was the Nilstone. But to this day I feel like there's more to the story than he's telling me.'

Hercól was studiously avoiding her eye. 'Ott had chosen you already to play a part in the Shaggat's return,' he said stiffly. 'The prophecy with which he had infected the Nessarim required a military daughter. Ramachni knew of his interest in you almost from the moment of your birth, and bid me watch over you, and befriend your father. Alas, I never came close to guessing the nature of that interest.'

'So the admiral's on Maisa's side as well!' said Neeps excitedly. 'Right, Hercól?'

The Tholjassan shook his head. 'Eberzam suspects that Maisa lives, and even that I am pledged to her cause. But he has always had the tact not to pose the question to me directly, lest he force me into an admission that would inconvenience us both. The admiral long ago swore an oath to Magad the Fifth, and it has cost him terribly to break it. Only knowledge of the Shaggat conspiracy proved strong enough.'

'The loyalties of a lifetime are hard to part with, even for the finest reasons,' said Dri, still gazing at Hercól.

'I wish he were aboard,' whispered Thasha.

Pazel heard the stifled misery in her voice. He had to fight the urge to take her hand, right there before them all.

Suddenly the shell embedded in his skin began to burn. Pazel clenched his teeth. Klyst knew, Klyst always knew, when his heart went out to Thasha. And if the murth-girl – wherever she was, whatever she had become – could read his feelings so plainly, couldn't Oggosk do the same?

Where Thasha is concerned I shall not be in the least forgiving.

He looked at Diadrelu. He could kill this woman and all her people, just by caring too much for the girl at his side.

Sealed fates, he thought. *All of us murderers before the end.* He could almost have laughed at the absurdity of it all.

And then the cannon fire began.

18

—⟋⟋⟍—

Wednesday, 11 Freala 941. Little lad or lass, in Etherhorde or wherever Anni has gone to bring you safe into the world: say a prayer for your father & his shipmates.

What perfect nonsense; the babe is not yet even born. Nor do I see the point in begging those above, whose wisdom after all is perfect, to act according to my reckoning of what is right. Nor do I know what is right. All gone, those certainties. Should I scuttle this ship? Light a flame in the powder room, blow Miss Thasha & Pathkendle & Undrabust & that wee babe's foolish father to smithereens, along with Rose, Arunis, Alyash, Drellarek & the rest of these rabid hyenas?

Should I kill eight hundred men?

Rin help you, Fiffengurt, you're lost.

Early this morning the whaleship *Sanguine* raised a cheerful flag—

[*water damage: four lines illegible*]

—comed their captain aboard, & with us officers in attendance took him to the wardroom for honey-cakes & beer. Rose had Mr Thyne of the Chathrand Trading Family pulled out of mothballs for the charade, and Latzlo too; the old hide-hustler could talk whaling better than most of us, and soon had the *Sanguine*'s skipper [one Cpt. Magritte of Ballytween] rattling on about those Cazencian whales we chanced among twelve days ago.

---

* Admiral Eberzam Isiq had the intention more than the habit of journal-keeping. Among the personal effects he left behind on the *Chathrand* was a fine calfskinned volume of unprinted pages. The first eight sheets are filled with writing in his own hand; thereafter the writing is exclusively that of Mr Fiffengurt. – EDITOR.

Was that Cazencian blubber he had boiling in his try-pots? Latzlo asked, his face aglow with excitement. No, no, said Magritte: they had spotted marblebacks just yesterday, and caught one with ease. But one Cazencian was worth fifty common marblebacks, he reminded us, 'for you just don't meet with 'em no more.' The *Sanguine* had chased the pod from Rukmast without taking a single animal, & Magritte was overjoyed to hear that we had spotted them again.

'I'll catch 'em yet!' he declared with a twinkle. 'Lost two of my lads to those tricky fish. My best harpooner sank his shaft in the largest, and the creature dived, and the line played out a half-league or more – and then a snag! Tragedy, gents! Don't know if it was someone's leg wrapped in the line, a shorn timber, an oarlock – but away that little boat flew, east towards Perdition-knows-where, and by the time the other boats were shipped and we tacked to chase 'em the fog was on us. We've been hunting for 'em ever since.'

I kept on munching cakes. When he hailed us this morning, were his first words, *Have ye seen our lost boys?* No: he asked after the whales, even though that harpoon crew must have cut themselves free in the first half-hour. And didn't they stop to skewer that marbleback? It's profits he was dreaming of, not the rescue of his men.

He had news of his own, this whaler. Volpeks to our east in great numbers. Nine warships at a glance, he claims to have seen, & suspects a raid on the Ulluprids is in the works. Captain Rose thanked him for the warning & poured more beer.

'I am glad the fog lifted, and allowed this happy rendezvous,' he said. But his voice was as cold as a judge preparing to send a man to the gallows.

'And shall I tell you a preposterous rumour?' said Magritte. 'They say the isle of the lunatics is up in arms. I mean Gurishal. That's right, sirs, the stronghold of that murdering madman, the one our fathers killed for the Sizzies. His cult isn't dead; and the strangest part is that those crazies think their old Shaggat's coming *back* from the dead. That's why they're all stirred up.'

'How does a rumour like that make it out of the Mzithrin?' asked Latzlo incautiously.

For once the whaler stopped eating. 'That's a blary fine question,' he said. 'You'd think they'd hush that sort of thing up. Not a bit of it. Everyone's talking about Gurishal, and how the crazies there are all on the lookout for their God-King. Hmph! Give it two weeks, says I.

When he don't come rising up ghostly from the Ninth Pit, they'll all be talking about something else.'

'Everyone but the Nessarim,' said Rose. 'They have waited forty years, and can wait a little longer.'

'Your health, sirs!' said Magritte, oblivious. 'Gentlemen, you are blessed to inhabit a ship that does not reek of whale blood, and whose ovens produced these golden cakes, not slabs of blubber-lard. But tell me: why have you painted over your gilding? I heard tell how the *Chathrand* was decked out in fresh gold from bow to stern for the peace ceremonies.'

'The ceremonies lie far behind us now,' said Rose, 'and one rarely encounters a friendly ship this far from the Nelu Peren.'

'That's the gods' truth, Captain!' laughed Magritte. 'We were frightened, I'll confess here and now, when we spotted you the first time.'

Rose's hands grew sudden still. *The first time.* You could almost hear the glances we shot at each other. Uskins' mouth worked, as if he were trying to swallow a sponge. Mr Thync steepled his fingers.

'You, ah, spotted us before, sir?' he said lightly. 'Days ago, was it?'

'More than a week,' Magritte told him, 'coming on dusk, it was, though, and you were much farther away – and stern-on, too, so we couldn't see your colours. But it could only have been your *Chathrand*, boys, great blary ship that it was.'

'You could not count our masts, then,' said Rose, 'or see our spread of sail?'

'Neither, neither, sir. But do fill us up, Captain! You've no idea the venomous grog my steward serves.'

Rose took hold of Magritte's tankard & poured it half full.

'I hope you will indulge my curiosity,' he rumbled. 'I have been unsure of our heading for some time.'

'I knew that,' said Magritte with a twinkle. '"The Great Ship don't mean to be heading *that* way," I told my men, "unless she's been seized by rogues. Look where her bow's aimed, my ducks! Not the way home to Etherhorde, is it, now?" What's your trouble, Rose? Binnacle out of true?'

'Perhaps,' said Rose.

'Well there's nothing wrong with ours,' said Magritte. 'We're making west-by-ten-south-west, and from the look of it your heading's some forty or forty-five degrees more southerly. You'll sight Bramian on that tack, sir. Just a matter of time.'

'Time is what I wish to ask you about,' said Rose. 'The day you spotted us – the first time, near dusk – was that before or after you put out boats for the Cazencians?'

Magritte blinked at him. 'It was – before,' he said slowly. 'Two days before, as I recall.'

'Then the crew of your lost boat would have known as well.'

'That we'd spotted you?' asked Magritte, his voice increasingly confused. 'Aye, Captain, all the men were aware. *Sanguine*'s not a big ship.'

With an abruptness that turned every head, Rose sat back in his chair. Magritte started, gaping at him. Rose drew a deep breath. Then he raised his own tankard & drained it at a gulp. He pressed an embroidered napkin to his lips.

'Very well, Mr Uskins,' he said.

Uskins shot out of his chair like a bulldog unleashed. He bolted straight for the cabin door, shouting already: 'Mr Byrd! Mr Tanner! Your ports! Matches, matches!'

'Great gods!' cried Magritte, spilling beer on his trousers. 'What is he doing? Who are those men he's screeching for?'

'Our gun captains,' said Rose. Then he swung the tankard with the full strength of his arm, shattering it just above Magritte's left eye.

The first volley was Byrd's, ten shots from the portside forty-pounders, & they all but ripped the *Sanguine*'s rudder-stem from her hull. The force of the blow drove her ruined stern away from us & brought her prow about, so that Tanner's men had an almost dead-on shot at her cutwater, which they promptly blew to pieces. It was evident that Rose meant to kill the ship rather than the men, but he didn't manage a clean distinction. One ball shattered against her starboard anchor, catted up snug on her bow. Iron shards screamed past our heads like bats from the Pits; a Burnscove lad took one in the throat & dropped dead on the forecastle. Men on *Sanguine*'s topdeck were screaming in agony. At her stern, the ship belched whale oil from a holding tank. The oozing yellow stuff on the surface made her resemble some maimed creature herself, bleeding to death in a trap.

Uskins was on the quarterdeck, now, with a voice-trumpet in his hand. He raised it & bellowed at the whaler: '*Sanguine!* Your vessel is destroyed! You will surrender or go down with her! Assemble on the topdeck with your hands empty and your minds resolved to obey your new sovereign commander, Nilus R – Ro—'

He gagged on the cannon-smoke, rising from beneath him. But the poor terrified *sutskas** didn't need to be told a second time. 'Cease fire! Cease fire!' they wept, rushing about with raised hands. We were five times her length, & Uskins had every portside gun aimed at the whaler: enough firepower to blast her into kindling thrice over.

Aboard the *Chathrand* men looked on in perfect horror. At the wheel, Mr Elkstem's mouth hung open like a sack. Frix stood by the mainmast, quivering & shaking his head. On my left, Bolutu the veterinarian stood like a statue, clutching his notebook to his chest. His face was composed; he did not even seem particularly surprised, but tears ran down his cheeks.

I myself felt as though I'd just watched my brother murder a child. Nor was I alone: there was rage, a truly dangerous look, in the eyes of some of the men about me. *More honour to them*, I thought. But that was recklessness: Sgt. Drellarek had clearly been apprised of the attack, & his men stood by with weapons drawn.

All this time Rose stood in his cabin doorway, wordless, leaning on that gnarled cane. From time to time Uskins shot him a nervous glance, rather like a dog seeking to reassure himself of his master's intentions. Rose did not give him so much as a nod.

They brought themselves across the sixty feet of sea, aboard their own whale-boats, & we hoisted them on our lifts. All told they were just thirty two men: sixteen whale-hunters, including a number of deadly-looking Quezan tribals, & an equal number of crew. Five men, they informed us hatefully, lay dead on the *Sanguine*.

For a butchering crime it went very smoothly. I must hand it to Uskins: he has a flair for managing violence. He kept one hand on the speaking-tubes running down to the gun deck & lieutenants along the topdeck & Turachs on the fighting top with their arrows trained at the boats. I almost wish Rose had given him some word of approval: it might have spared us the disaster that followed.

Here is what happened. One of the *Sanguine*'s topmen, a crooked old guttersnipe with three teeth & a face etched with scurvy, was standing passive as a mule while the Turachs bound his wrists. Uskins had come down from the quarterdeck, & was marching swiftly by, hurrying the soldiers along. The whaler had a good look at him, & made a pleased kind of hoot.

---

* Etherhorde slang: a *sutska* is a speckled dove found in parks and gardens and empty lots. A favourite dinner of tramps and vagabonds, it is easily lured into snares with a handful of grain. – EDITOR.

'Stukey!'

Uskins jumped three feet in the air. 'What's that? What's that?' he shouted.

'Stukey – tha's whad! Pidetor Stukey, ain't ye? Of course ye are! Don'd ye know me? I'm old Frunc, old Frunc from the Brillbox, Stukey! Yer pappy's mate!'

Uskins stared at the down-and-out figure before him. The Brillbox (as I learned through the gossip-gale that swept the *Chathrand* within the hour) is a speck of a village east of Ulsprit, nestled down beneath tall sea-cliffs that block the sun. A wet, frigid place that survives by scooping guano off the rocks – a gift from the half-million gulls & terns & razorbills who nest overhead – & selling the muck for fertiliser. Not the kind of settlement that had spawned many officers in the Merchant Service.

For a moment Uskins looked like a man stripped naked. Then he screamed at the Turachs to get 'that demented slagman' off the topdeck. Frunc went on shouting even as the marines thumped him down the ladderway: 'Stukey! Ouch! Stukey!' His voice floated up to the shocked & silent topdeck longer than you'd expect, & each cry brought a wince from Uskins. It also brought certain men who hated Uskins closer to helpless mirth. Uskins had made a career of mocking the so-called lowborn.

'Who's laughing? Who's blary laughing?' Uskins was now racing this way & that, charging at one stone-faced sailor after another, making things infinitely worse for himself. Even some of the prisoners looked morbidly amused. Then Rose's crashing voice silenced everyone:

'DOWN!'

The word was scarce out of his mouth when the cannon boomed. We threw ourselves flat, as a ball screamed from the *Sanguine*, bashed a hole in the midship rail, carried off part of the mainmast shrouds & continued right over the deck, to drop into the waves on our starboard flank. There were men on the whaler yet! Uskins snapped out of his madness & yelled for Byrd & Tanner, who let loose with the most cacophonous broadside I have ever heard or hope to, & from my place by the mizzen I saw the little Opaltine craft slashed open, like a fish by a gutting knife, right along her middle deck. And still Uskins was shouting: 'Reload! Haul in and reload! Tanner, are ye blary deaf?'

We were all half-deaf, of course – & then our own smoke billowed up & draped the topdeck like a shroud. Rose sent his clerk running into it, & I followed on the man's heels. Gasping & retching I saw the man at Uskins' elbow, making cease-and-desist gestures. The first mate understood & somehow croaked out a *Stand down.*

The smoke lifted & I turned to the rail. All over: there was no deck on the *Sanguine* from which to fire at us, no man in one piece to attempt it. She was toppling our way, bubbling, sinking; inside of five minutes her mainmast lowered at us like an accusing finger; in another five she was no more than trash & splinters & a smell of burning whale.

I set about getting the gawkers off the deck. Drellarek watched me with a hand on his sword-hilt. As if he expected some trouble from me, broken old coward that I am. Captain Magritte had regained consciousness & stood weeping between his guards. Chadfallow & Fulbreech staunched wounds. Pazel Pathkendle looked at me & said simply, 'Why?'

'Clear off, lads, clear off.' I made my way along the rail, now & then persuading a Turach to put his blade away. Ahead of me Bolutu was scribbling in his notebook. When I drew near he looked up suddenly & held it out for my inspection. I read: *Every outrage plays into his hands.*

Our eyes met. 'Rose's hands, you mean? Or Arunis'?'

Bolutu shook his head. A quick scrawl. *Sandor Ott's.*

'The spymaster? He's still hiding in the gutters of Ormael, ain't he?'

Bolutu just looked at me.

'Anyway,' I went on uneasily, 'how does a crime like this work to his favour? Weren't you paying attention? Our men were fit to mutiny!'

More scribbling. *But they didn't.*

'Well that's just fear,' I said. 'But it can't last forever. We'll see how things stand when they're more afraid of the Nelluroq than they are of Rose or Arunis.'

Bolutu considered me a moment, his eyes perplexed. Then he tore out a page, wrote until his pencil snapped, whipped out another & finished the message off. He gave the page to me.

They should fear Ott. First he made them lie. Then he made them seem to perish. Today he makes them murderers. Tomorrow he will make them believe. And they will do so. They will have no other purpose in living but the cause.

Rose is Ott's tool, sir. And Arunis you must leave to us. We will fight him when the time comes. To fight him now would be to fight with shadows merely.

'Us?' I said.

Before I could answer Mr Latzlo blundered up & pawed at my elbow. He looked deeply affronted. 'The oil!' he cried, 'All that precious oil!

It's a humiliation! Why didn't we pump her dry first, Quartermaster?'

I barked him off the deck in a voice I hardly knew was in me. Then I came back to Bolutu, still wanting an answer to my question. But the black man was finished with me. The horror of what we had done was back in his eyes, which looked skyward & past me. I turned around & saw the great plume of our cannon-smoke, rising higher & higher as the wind swept it south. The cloud's heart was ink-thick, & seemed like it would go on rising forever, a dark balloon bearing word of our crime to the heavens. But the tail of the cloud was stretching, paling, dwindling to near invisibility. Even as I watched it was gone, & with it a dozen-odd living souls, hope & memory & will & love & struggle, all ended in a moment, so that the heedlessly alive might forget them & rage on.

Need it be so? I ask myself (it is late, I am wretched, the day's blood stains these final thoughts). Need I wait for the next such outrage? I'm the quartermaster. Rose doesn't trust me, but he's not yet stripped me of rank & privileges. They'll admit me to the powder room with no questions asked. Should I bring the era of the *Chathrand* to an end?

Saturday, 14 Freala 941. Well into the Rekere Current. Orange heat lightning all night: the Bramian Beacon, as it's known. Thursday dawn picked up the autumn westerlies & doubled our speed.

Midmorning today (warm, mild, cloudless yet) I let Miss Thasha and her tarboy friends persuade me to inspect a part of the orlop deck, just astern of the live animal compartment. 'Bring a bright lamp, Mr Fiffengurt,' they pleaded, & I did so. Lady Thasha in particular was spooked by the darkness: strange, that, for she is as far from cowardly as any soul on this vessel. I should like to know what they were after. We found very little of note: just a deep axe-mark on a stanchion, a souvenir from the ancient days. The mark fascinated Lady Thasha, somehow. Could I explain it? she asked.

I could, in fact. I knew what legend made of that mark. It came from a dark time in *Chathrand*'s history, when the Yeligs leased her out to Jenetran slave traders. They were in the Nelu Vebre in the far north-east, & it was winter, & the slaves were dying of cold. Well, one girl grew so thin she slipped her irons, & hid away for weeks. And when they found her she ran, cursing them & crying out for help. And just as they seized her another girl appeared, her mirror image, pale where the slave-girl was dark. A spirit-girl, if you please. She fought like a devil, though, & cut one man's gut wide open, & set fire to the deck.

When the men quelled the fire they searched high & low, but they never saw that girl or her protector again. They'd vanished as if they never were.

'And this mark was made by one of those Jenetrans, who took a swing at the devil-girl with his axe. That's the story. And there's hundreds more, if you like that sort of thing.'

They were staring at me as if I'd grown three heads & a tail. And then Miss Thasha took my hand in both of hers & asked if the crew-member had died. 'Well the story ain't that specific,' I said with a laugh. At that she turned right around and faced the wall.

No, I cannot kill them yet. Not those boys, & not dear Thasha, who has given me this new journal & a safe place to keep it here in her chambers, beyond the reach of Uskins, or Stukey, or whatever the fool's real name is. There is some new hope in the faces of those three youths: I see it when they look at Hercól, as if at a man they had never before seen clearly. And the Tholjassan too has the look of one girding himself for battle. Imitate them, Fiffengurt. You may save your honour yet.

19

On the Bowsprit

—⟋⟍⟋—

19 Freala 941
128th day from Etherhorde

Less than a week after the sinking of the *Sanguine*, her captain's prediction came true. At first the only sign was a pea-green cast to the waves. 'The mark of the true tropics,' Mr Druffle informed a small audience of tarboys. 'We're crossing the warm belly of Alifros, my dears.'

Other signs followed: a pod of sea turtles, a lonely frigate bird, a sharp eastward bent to the current. Then, just as Fiffengurt completed the noon measurements of speed and compass heading, it appeared: a dark line on the southern horizon, stretching away east and west as far as the eye could see. Mainland, thought a few with wonder, but it was nothing of the kind.

Mr Elkstem advised the captain, and received a quick reply: a scrap of paper on which was scrawled *ESE.128°30', tgs – w.w.* Such were Rose's abbreviated orders: a new east-by-south-east heading, and a spread of sail up to and including topgallants, 'as weather warrants.'

Elkstem, concluding that the weather did warrant, promptly gave the signal for general quarters. The drums sounded, the lower decks roared to life, and four hundred men poured up through the hatches and took their positions at spar, brace and halyard. Frix and Alyash ran the rails, lieutenant to lieutenant. 'Free that downhaul. Where's the clearance, Bindhammer? Compose your team, sir, for the love of Rin!'

Elkstem put his weight on the wheel. 'Heave!' went the simultaneous orders along the five masts, and hundreds of men complied, and the wheel spun, and the vast mainsails turned into the wind. The *Chathrand* swung east, degree by hard-won degree, until she ran parallel to the dark Bramian shore.

All day they kept their distance. Rose wanted them no closer until they rounded Bramian, knowing (better than most captains in Alifros) how her cliffs gave way here and there to tiny beaches, hidden footholds on her jungles, boundless and wet. An oreship, a pirate sloop, a slaver exchanging pots and trinkets for human lives: any one of these might be anchored off such a landing. Rose did not intend to be spotted again.

They beat a weary path around the giant. For three days they held the same course, until finally the lookout perceived the island's south-ward curve. Even then Rose kept them east, all that day and night, as if making for Kushal or Pulduraj. Only on the fifth morning, with Bramian nearly out of sight behind them, did the order come. *Ware away! West by south-west!* – a hairpin turn, and such an agony of effort that the men recalled previous course changes almost fondly. The topgallants had to be furled, the mainsails double-reefed, the fore-and-aft sails braced to the fine work of running close-hauled to the wind, which now battered their faces and begrudged them every westward mile. No trim would serve for more than three hours; no sailor could long be spared for rest.

Dusk on 19 Freala found the crew limp with exhaustion. The wind had shifted in their favour, but by now they were too tired to rejoice. It was a strange, quiet evening: the sun was still above the horizon, but a sickle moon hung already in the east. The sky between them was convulsed with racing clouds.

Pazel stood on the footropes beneath the bowsprit, that great spear thrust out in front of *Chathrand*. He was in a dark mood, and had hoped being here might dispel it. Every few seconds the bow leaped skywards, then plummeted again towards the waves, whose cold spray just managed to graze Pazel's feet as they shattered on the keel. In normal times Pazel was in his glory here. Only high on the masts could one be flung about as thrillingly by the motions of the ship.

Of course in a storm both mast and bowsprit were living nightmares. Pazel had never experienced those particular miseries. But his spider-monkey confidence on the ropes had been hard-won, and he didn't mean to lose it just because he was no longer a tarboy. When Neeps suggested they crawl out and lend a hand with the jibsails he had quickly agreed.

The sailors, however, had brushed them off: 'No thank you, lads, we'll manage somehow. Mind you, there's always cable to scrape.' The men were afraid, of course: afraid of getting mixed up with 'them two crazy monkeys.' But it had stung to have their offer of help thrown back at them, and Neeps had left in a huff.

Pazel gazed off to portside. The Nelluroq. He was seeing it at last. Even at this distance he thought he could detect a change in the waves: grander swells, a deeper and more sombre blue. Maybe that was just his fancy. What was certain was that a ship could sail twice the width of Arqual in that direction and find no land.

Or rather, the *Chathrand* could.

Or rather, she could try.

The sailors had finished setting the jibs. Pazel climbed up beside the Goose-Girl's figurehead to let them slip by. Some glanced at him with fear. The last, Mr Coote, just looked embarrassed. He had known Pazel longer than any sailor aboard, having served on the IMS *Swan*, where Pazel's life as a tarboy had begun.

'They mean no harm,' he muttered, pausing at Pazel's side. 'Just not sure of their footing, if you follow me.'

'I do, Mr Coote.'

Coote pointed with his big East Arquali nose. 'We'll be headin' in among the Black Shoulder Isles tonight. At least that's my supprazichun.'

Dead ahead, six or eight miles off Bramian, ran a string of uninhabited islets: the Black Shoulders. They were small and jungle-clad, built of dark volcanic stone that still shook and grumbled, troubling the waves and dropping great shelves of rock into the depths on occasion. What slim fondness sailors had for them was due to the harbour they could give, in a pinch, from the battering ram of a northbound Nelluroq storm.

'Do you know why, Mr Coote?' Pazel asked. 'I mean, what have the Black Shoulders got that we need?'

Coote glanced up at him for the first time, and almost smiled. 'Thought maybe you'd know, with all your tricks.'

'I don't have many tricks, Mr Coote. I wish I did, believe me.'

Coote shrugged. 'Well, water, maybe – can't never have too much sweet water in your casks. That one to our north is Sandplume – what some call the Isle of Birds. She might have a pond worth pumping. Come on in, Pathkendle; there's no more work to be done out here.'

'Oppo, sir. I'm right behind you.'

Coote lumbered off, but Pazel didn't leave the bowsprit. He faced the sea again, his arm draped over the Goose-Girl. She was a pretty lump of wood, although her grip on the necks of her two geese always struck him as savagely tight. He had stood here that first day on the *Chathrand*, when Fiffengurt told him to pry the limpets off her, and Dr

Chadfallow raced along Sorrophran Head on horseback, crying across the water to Pazel: *Jump ship! Jump ship in Etherhorde!*

He could have done it, probably. Where would he be now, *who* would he be, if he had obeyed?

The thought left Pazel strangely chilled. For more than five years his only dream had been to find his parents and sister, rebuild his shattered family. Just how that miracle was supposed to happen he had never quite worked out. Not even Chadfallow, personal friend of the Emperor and one of the only men in Arqual with connections inside the Mzithrin, had been able to carry off a prisoner exchange – he wasn't even sure Pazel's mother and sister *were* prisoners, only that they had both been in Simja on Treaty Day. And his father – well, Captain Gregory had found *him*, all right, after the battle on the Haunted Coast. He simply hadn't cared.

Pazel closed his eyes. There was a great black oak in Ormael, in a stand of such trees between the plum orchards and the path to the Highlands. It was not the tallest in the stand, but it was a mighty tree. Passing beneath it one day on a walk with his father, Pazel had declared with confidence that no one could climb it. Captain Gregory had laughed and shimmied up the oak like a topman scaling the shrouds. At eighty feet, he'd pulled out the knife Pazel carried today and begun to carve, slowly and carefully, at the joint of a limb.

When he had returned to the ground, Pazel had asked, 'What did you carve there, Papa?'

Gregory had just ruffled his hair. 'Go and have a look yourself,' he'd teased, making Pazel laugh aloud. It would be years before he could reach the lowest branch.

Gregory never told Pazel what he'd carved, and after his desertion Pazel had decided that he didn't care. He could climb as well as his father, now. But even if he one day saw Ormael again, why should he go looking for that tree? For years he'd tried to convince himself that his father had some heroic reason for abandoning them. But the Haunted Coast had provided a simpler, uglier truth. Captain Gregory didn't give a damn.

All at once Pazel realised that he was quite cold. He'd lingered too long, grown too still, and his pants were soaked with chilly spray. It was time to get out of the wind. Carefully reversing his grip on the Goose-Girl, Pazel negotiated an about-face. He looked down at the forecastle – and saw Arunis gliding towards him with a smile.

The mage had not harmed a soul since the day of Thasha's wedding, but the few sailors in his path leaped away as if from a marauding tiger. Pazel suddenly realised how very vulnerable he was. Everyone but the lookouts had fled the forecastle, and even the latter two sailors stood uneasily by the ladder, as though weighing the danger of abandoning their posts against the threat of that figure in black.

Pazel scrambled down the bowsprit. But Arunis, with startling quickness for such a heavyset man, leaped up to the marines' walk – that narrow platform that was the only way on or off the bowsprit. He raised an open hand, as if warning Pazel to remain where he was.

Pazel stopped. He was some eight feet from the sorcerer, and had no doubt that he could keep out of the mage's grip long enough to shout for aid. But the marines' walk had only two knotted ropes for rails. If he tried to squeeze by onto the deck Arunis could attack him, perhaps even push him into the sea.

'What do you want?' he said.

Arunis' white scarf flapped in the wind. He placed a hand on each rope. 'A little of your time,' he said. 'You have more to spare than other boys on this ship, after all.'

'I don't have anything to say to you. Murderer.'

Arunis gazed at him, unperturbed. 'Even as enemies we have rather a lot to learn from each other,' he said, 'or hasn't Hercól taught you that first maxim of the fighting man? "In single combat, your foe is the only one who can help you defeat your foe." But that, I hope, shall prove beside the point. For there is no reason why we should remain enemies, Mr Pathkendle.'

Pazel laughed. 'No, none at all. Except that you fed me powdered glass, and nearly strangled Thasha. To say nothing of what you told the sibyl on Dhola's Rib. Something about "scouring the world for its new dispensation," wasn't it? Care to explain *that* one to me?'

'I would like nothing better,' said Arunis. 'It is the horror of my life, being misunderstood. What you heard on Dhola's Rib, for instance: of course it sounded vile. And so must all my actions, since we were introduced as enemies. But you do not truly know me, yet – and you do not know the burden I carry.

'I am the greatest mage in Alifros. I am thrice the age of the Empire of Arqual. The Old Faith was but a collection of prayers and mumbles when I first walked the paths of Ullum, and the name of Rin had yet to be spoken by human lips. I have served this world as seer and counsellor for thirty centuries, lad. Her destiny is my destiny; her life is what I live for.'

Pazel snorted. 'Funny how much joy you take in *ending* lives, in that case.'

Arunis shook his head. 'No more than the gardener who pinches cutworms between his fingers to save the crop. You have closed your mind for sentimental reasons, Pazel. Did not Ramachni himself warn you to seek allies in unlikely places?'

Pazel was shocked. How Arunis could have come by such knowledge he could not begin to imagine. *He's spying on us somehow. I've got to warn them.*

'You are convinced you wish my defeat,' Arunis went on. 'You are persuaded that the breaking of two corrupt empires – for that is what the Shaggat's victory will mean, the end of both Arqual and the Mzithrin – will be a bad thing for this world.'

'I'm persuaded that a world ruled by you would be a thousand times worse.'

Arunis stepped towards him, impatience flashing in his eyes. 'And why is that? What do you know of my true intentions? Nothing. But I know a great deal about yours. I know you dream of finding your mother and sister. Would you like my help? I could locate them within the hour, by my arts, and tell you how they fare.'

For a moment Pazel could not speak. The faces of his mother and sister, their smiles, their laughs—

'No,' he said. 'I don't want your help. You wouldn't, anyway.'

Arunis drew closer still. 'I know that you hate Arqual for its crimes. How could you not, when you've seen it destroy your family, your home, your very nation? When you know it is ruled by those who seduce their enemies with talk of peace, all the while hiding a knife called the Shaggat behind their backs? A knife with which they plan to reopen their enemies' deepest wound?

'Think, Pazel, of what will happen if I step aside. Either Sandor Ott's plan will succeed, and the Shaggat will rise and cripple the Mzithrin, and within a decade the Pentarchy will collapse, routed by the armies of Arqual. Or the plan will fail, and provide an immaculate excuse for a new global war – a war of equals, a war of blackest hatred, a war without end.

'In either case the innocent will die in countless numbers, and the survivors inherit a ruined world. If Ott triumphs, you may imagine the future as a bloody rag in the fist of the Magad dynasty, a fist that tightens forever, even when there is no blood left to wring out.

And should he fail – two fists contending for the rag, Arquali and Mzithrini, tearing, pulling, shredding it ever finer.'

'And in your future?'

'In mine, quite simply, the Shaggat's triumph will be so swift that Alifros will be spared the worst part of war. Fleets will burn, but not cities. Armies will be destroyed, but not the countries they hail from. There will be death, but how much less so than otherwise! My future is the least of the evils arrayed before us – surely you see that now?'

Pazel said nothing. Arunis rested a foot on the bowsprit.

'Listen to me, boy. Your morals are a good thing. But they are simple hand-tools, and the world, like this ship, is a vast machine. You cannot expect your notion of the good to serve all purposes, any more than you could cut new lumber for this ship with a pocketknife.'

Pazel averted his eyes. The late sun was blazing behind Arunis, yet he felt colder than ever – almost numb with cold, and his mind was dull and doubtful.

'I don't believe you,' he said.

The mage smiled again. 'But at least you hear me – that is enough. Pazel, there are moments in history when what appears to be an evil is the only path to the good. Humans are a flawed creation. Gather them in any numbers, and they kill. Dreamers like Hercól will never admit this truth – and in the end it is they who must be blamed when their pretty fantasies collapse. Arqual and the Mzithrin are the twin banes of Alifros. How would *you* choose, in your youthful clarity of heart? Destroy two wicked empires – or stand back and watch them destroy the world?'

Pazel clung there, six feet from Arunis, shaking his head. 'Neither,' he managed at last.

'That too is a choice – to do nothing, shrug off the burdens fate gives us, pray that others will lead in our stead. But I do not think you are that kind of man. You're a captain's son, after all.'

Pazel looked up sharply. The mention of his father brought all his anger back in a flash.

'I'll give you one more chance to tell me what you want,' he said, 'before I shout for the guards.'

The mage looked at him steadily. 'You are shivering,' he said. 'Are you coming down with a cold?'

'I've been out here a long time.'

'Quite true,' said Arunis. 'You have been alone in more ways than most men experience in a lifetime, and you have known no rest. Your life has been marked by one terrible change after another. And I can only offer you another – a frightful change, I know, but I promise it will be the last. For you are a *Smythídor*, a being changed by spellcraft for ever, and because of that you will never belong with any but your own kind. You belong with me, boy, at my side as student and disciple, heir to my wisdom and arts. This is what I offer you. Will you not consider?'

Pazel found himself trapped by the mage's eyes, which had taken on a cold, bright sheen. The heat of his rage was no match for that glow, that spider's hunger. He could not look away.

'At . . . your side?'

'Yes, said Arunis, 'for ever. Shall I tell you something? You may be aware that I called a spirit to my cabin, before we left the Bay of Simja. It was the ghost of Sathek, a mage-king of the ancient world, and a wise and terrible king he was. Sathek told me that I should meet a child of Alifros aboard this ship who would grow into as mighty a spell-weaver as I am myself. Of course I knew at once that he meant you.'

'I'm not a mage,' said Pazel.

'But you will be,' said Arunis, extending his hand. 'Come, Pazel Pathkendle. I am the home you've been looking for. I am your natural ally. Not a coarse island boy like Mr Undrabust. Not the doctor who lusts after your mother. Not the vixen child of the man who laid waste to Ormael.'

'Who – who do you . . . ?'

'Thasha, you simpleton, the girl who laughs when she beats you with sticks.'

'Don't you try—' Pazel's shook his head with tremendous effort. '—don't you *dream* of turning me against her, damn you, I—'

He broke off. Why were they even talking? Why wasn't he shouting for help?

Arunis looked at him thoughtfully. When he spoke again his voice was quite changed. 'I would never try to turn you against Thasha,' he said. 'Oh no! You misunderstand me entirely. Do you think that we mages plumb the secrets of the several worlds, yet remain ignorant of the noblest of all human feelings? Do you think us so stupid and cold?'

'C-cold—'

'No matter. Tell me of your feelings for Thasha Isiq. It will do you good to speak of them.'

But Pazel shook his head again.

'I understand,' said the mage. 'You are protecting what is new to your heart, and I shall ask no further. But you *must* let me help you.'

His tone was sharply aggrieved. Pazel felt a sense of guilt creep over him, stealthy and quick. He felt suddenly as though he had spat on the efforts of a kindly uncle.

'Tomorrow we shall make landfall on Bramian,' said Arunis, 'and there – surely you know this already, deep inside? – the two of you must depart. For not a soul on this ship, myself included, will ever see the placid eastern world again, once we enter the Ruling Sea. It is a mission of death, my boy. Why sacrifice yourselves? Why betray Thasha, and the bliss of a life together, before it has truly begun? Tell me, as one man to another: have you not sensed the *possibility* of such bliss?'

Pazel was lost, in a cold, enveloping fog; and Thasha was the only point of warmth. 'Yes,' he said quietly, 'I have.'

'Then you must hold true to that feeling, Pazel Pathkendle, no matter what you are told. Run off with your Thasha! Hide from the savages until your Gift begins to work again. Then approach those forest men and address them in their tongue. They will not only spare your lives, but worship you, and lead you to their river strongholds, and serve you like slaves. Become Lord and Lady of Bramian! There are wonders in her interior mete for a clever lad like you to discover. And you could find no safer place in Alifros to sit out the coming war.'

Pazel gazed at him in wonder. After a moment, he said, 'Leave. With Thasha.'

'Just so,' said Arunis. 'And who could blame you? Both of you have been cruelly exploited by the Empire. But instead of seeking revenge you actually helped them, risked your lives for them, over and over. They cannot ask you for more.'

'How would we get ashore?'

Arunis smiled. 'That will be my gift to you – a small gesture of amends for the feud we've overcome. Merely give me your hand, and think your promise to depart. Give it to me now; I shall hold your promise in my fist, and tend it like a seed, and before we reach the island my spell will be ready. Then bring Thasha to my cabin, between midnight and dawn. Ask her to trust you – as she will all her life, when she is yours alone – and when we three join hands I shall send you to Bramian in an instant.'

The sorcerer extended his hand. 'This should be an easy choice – between death and a strange rebirth, between loneliness and ecstasy. If you have the courage to change, that is.'

He made as if to withdraw his hand, and Pazel's heart leaped. He extended his own, desperately – then pulled back at the last instant, torn with doubt. How could this be true? How could they have got so much wrong about Arunis?

A spasm crossed the sorcerer's face, but he mastered it. 'You realise,' he said, 'that she's going anyway.'

'*What?*'

Arunis nodded gravely. 'Rose means to be rid of her, but he dares not kill her because of Ramachni's spell. How to be sure she lives, and yet tells no one of the conspiracy? Why, by giving her to the savages, people who fear and detest the outside world. They will bear her away to the heart of that gigantic island, and keep her, and make her one of them. Rose has decided already. He knows the trouble a lovely girl may cause on a ship full of desperate men.'

Pazel clutched at the ropes. The cold had reached his fingertips, the roots of his hair, his brain. And as he gazed at Arunis a vision rose before his eyes. He saw himself and Thasha, dressed in a strange finery of wool and parrot feathers and animal skins, standing before a great wooden lodge on a high hill over the jungle. Birds teemed in the treetops, and the sea glittered far away, and purple, snowcapped mountains rose at their backs. Strange men in the clearing below the lodge glanced up with fearful reverence, but kept their distance as befit the servants of a Lord. He and Thasha were older, taller, and she was more beautiful than ever, a woman full grown and splendid, and his arm was about her waist.

Arunis was leaning close to him. 'If she is not yours, and soon, she will be another's. She will give her love to a man of real courage, be it a sailor or some beast of the Bramian jungle. Is that what you want?'

Pazel clung to the knotted ropes. He was a coward, a fool. Thasha was escaping him, slipping through his fingers. She was almost a woman; he was just a tarboy from a conquered race. This was his one chance to have her, his one chance to know love. And it seemed as he extended his hand that it was not Arunis he was reaching for but Thasha herself.

Then something extraordinary happened. Under the skin beside his collarbone an ember of warmth sprang to life. It was distant, but real. And somewhere far away in the hollows of his mind a voice was calling, echoing, like a strange girl's voice from the depths of a cave.

Land-boy, do you forsake me?

'Klyst!'

Arunis straightened, dumbfounded. 'What's that? Klyst?'

The voice was already gone, and the heat from the murth-girl's shell was very faint. But that touch of pure longing from Klyst − still with him, still following the *Chathrand*! − gave Pazel the strength to tear his eyes away from Arunis' own.

The dream of Bramian vanished. The cold retreated, and strength returned to his limbs. Then Pazel saw the strain in Arunis' face, and the sweat on his brow. The spell had cost him great effort, but it had failed.

And now Pazel was angry − angry as he'd never been before in his life. He glared at the sorcerer, who stood swaying across his path, doubled over, drawing laboured breaths.

'What's it all for, Arunis?' he demanded. 'You want to rule the world − *why*? You'd still be a rotten beast full of hate and lies and ugliness. You'd still be you.'

Arunis sagged against the ropes, but there was an odd gleam to his exhausted eyes. 'No I wouldn't,' he said.

But Pazel was no longer listening. 'You're the one who should get off at Bramian. The greatest mage in Alifros! Go on, get out of my way.'

Swaying feebly, Arunis shook his head. Pazel could stand it no longer: he leaned forwards and grabbed Arunis' fingers, prying them easily from the rope.

'*Nauldrok!*'

The mage's voice whiplashed through Pazel's mind and limbs. He felt himself driven backwards. He seized desperately at the ropes, stumbled, caught himself on the bowsprit proper − and there he froze. His fingers went numb, his body weak and lifeless. The heat from Klyst's shell was gone.

Arunis looked even worse than Pazel felt. He might have been a man afflicted by a wasting disease, too weak to do more than prop himself up on the ropes, yet triumph shone in his eyes. After a few more gasping breaths, he found his voice.

'You are about to die, maggot. I would prefer to strangle you, but that would be noticed, and you have caused me difficulties enough.'

He forced himself upright. 'I am what I claimed,' he said. 'Who is greater than Arunis? Your mother, who turned you into a convulsive? The mighty Ramachni? But they show no signs of coming to your aid. And where, for that matter, are Neeps and your lovely Thasha? It appears no one is thinking of you at all.'

Pazel knew where Thasha was − in her cabin, reading the *Polylex* and comforting the still-frightened Marila. She would not be looking for him, true enough – he had been rude to her again, unable to forget Oggosk's threat. Neeps would not come either: he was too irritated with the sailors who had spurned their aid. And if those lookouts or the men on the spars were watching, as surely they must be, what would they notice? Arunis had not laid a hand on him.

'Ah!' said the sorcerer. 'Take heart, Pathkendle. You are not friendless after all.'

Pazel just managed to raise his eyes. Up the forecastle ladder was climbing the last person on earth he wished to see: Jervik. The older tarboy stopped to speak to the lookouts, and glanced warily at Arunis.

'You will soon lose your grip,' said the mage, 'and plummet into the sea. By then I shall be in my quarters. But I have a few thoughts for you to ponder ere you fall.

'It was your own pride that doomed you, of course. Did you feel protected by Ramachni's spell? Idiot. You *were* safe, until you touched me of your own volition. By doing so you let me see through you like a glass. Now I know that you are not the spell-keeper, and I risk no harm to the Shaggat by killing you.

'Consider this as well: your friends will know agony. What Thasha suffered by that necklace is but a foretaste. She will become the plaything of the Gurishal lunatics, or of the Shaggat himself if he wants her. She will bear children who will be taken from her and raised in the knowledge that their mother was a whore. Neeps Undrabust will be lowered into tanner's acid, gradually, until his screaming stops. Fiffengurt will be blinded and abandoned to the lepers of Ursyl. Hercól's queen will be devoured by wolfhounds before his eyes.

'And then there is your city. When I rule this world through the Shaggat, I shall finish the job Arqual began five years ago. Ormael will be razed, the adults taken into the Straits of Simja and drowned, the children scattered to other lands and made to forget their language. All this I shall see to personally – in memory of you, Pazel Pathkendle. Goodbye.'

The mage departed without a backward glance. As he passed Jervik he made a sharp gesture in Pazel's direction. Jervik nodded and hurried to the bowsprit.

'Muketch,' he said, in a low, gleeful voice. 'What've you got yer brown arse into now?'

The lookouts were back at their designated spots on the port and starboard rails. Pazel tried to speak, but only managed a feeble moan. With each pitch of the ship he felt his fingers loosening.

'Quiet, eh?' said Jervik. 'He said you might be. Tha's all right. I can sit here as long as you like. But if you try somethin' I'll deck you proper, s'help me Rin.'

With immense effort, Pazel shook his head. Jervik grinned, his face like a wide-mouthed frog. Then, with a glance over his shoulder, he pulled something from his shirt and held it up for Pazel to admire.

On a leather cord beside his brass Citizenship Ring hung a thick gold bead. It might have weighed as much as eight or nine Arquali cockles, and been worth ten times that, if the metal was as pure as it looked.

'I'm rich,' he said. 'I'll have one o' these every week I do his biddun.'

Pazel was finding it difficult to blink. A few more pitches of the bow and he would drop like a stone.

'What're you doin' out there, you daft pig?' said the older boy after a moment. 'Get in here. I'm s'posed to watch you, is all. I'm not gonna hurt you.'

He stepped forwards. He was getting annoyed at Pazel's silence. And all at once Pazel understood the part Arunis had in mind for Jervik.

You poor imbecile.

There was no way to warn him. When Pazel's head lolled down to his chest he could not raise it again.

'I said, get in 'ere!'

Jervik cuffed the back of his head – signing his own death warrant (for murderers at sea were hanged from the yardarm, no exceptions) if he only knew. Pazel barely felt the blow, but with the next pitch of the *Chathrand* his arm slipped from the Goose-Girl. Jervik gave a sort of woof of surprise. Pazel was looking head-down at the churning sea. Then, as the bowsprit rose again, he fell.

Onto an outstretched arm.

Belesar Bolutu was there, shirtless, wrenching Pazel out of his fall and against his black chest. The man had leaped past Jervik and straddled the bowsprit, clinging for dear life with his legs. An incoherent howl escaped his tongueless mouth.

For a hideous moment Pazel felt them both sliding into a fall – he lifeless as a sack, Bolutu with his arms locked around his chest. Then the lookouts dived on Bolutu with cries of *By the board! By the board!* and hauled the two of them to safety.

Dimly, he felt hands stretch him out on the deck. The forecastle was suddenly crowded: others must have flung themselves down from the rigging the moment his fall began. The voices were far away.

'Another fit! The boy's a menace to himself!'

'He was pushed! Jervik Lank did it, the dirty bastard!'

'Are ye sure it was Lank? What about that damned Arunis?'

Sudden silence. Pazel wheezed, and they all looked down at him thoughtfully. Somewhere in the depths of the ship the white dog began to bark.

'Arunis didn't lay a finger on him,' said one of the lookouts. 'He just talked and went his way.'

'Why don't the *muketch* say nothin'?'

'He jumped! He jumped! Didn't he, Brother Bolutu, sir?'

A pail of seawater struck his face. Pazel gasped, and found he could move again. Even as he struggled to sit up, Neeps and Thasha pushed their way through the crowd.

'Pazel!' cried Neeps. 'Burning devils, what's happened to you *now*?'

'I'm all right,' he said, letting them pull him to his feet.

He was very dizzy. Scores of off-duty men surrounded them, but only Neeps and Thasha held his arms. 'What did you want die for, Pathkendle?' asked one of the lookouts.

'Oh shut up!' said Thasha. 'Pazel, it was Jervik, wasn't it? That vicious thug, I'll—'

'No,' said Pazel. 'Not this time.' He took a stumbling step, and the crowd parted before him. 'Where's Bolutu gone?' he said. 'That man just saved my life.'

'Brother Bolutu took off near as fast as he got here,' said the watch captain, hitching his thumb at the ladder. 'Didn't say a word. Oh, but then he can't, can he?'

They left the gaping men behind. Pazel's hands shook on the ladder, and when he had descended to the topdeck he found himself short of breath. He steadied himself against the wall of the forecastle house, blinking gratefully at his friends.

'Arunis ... is spying on us,' he gasped. Despite his exhaustion he knew the spell was fading; already the warm tropical evening had driven the cold from his limbs. He told them of the mage's attack and the part Jervik had played. But he could not bring himself to confess how Arunis had exploited his feelings for Thasha.

'At least we know he's still weak, still recovering from Dhola's Rib, or even before. He can still cast spells, obviously – but it cost him something terrible. I doubt he could have managed the second one if I hadn't touched him.'

'Not likely he was shamming, either, since he thought you'd be dead,' said Thasha.

'He's afraid of you, Thasha. He wants to get you off this ship. Maybe he really is weak, right now. He didn't want anyone to know that *he* had killed me, so he left Jervik to take the blame. That fool doesn't know how close he came to earning a jump from the mizzenmast.'

'With a noose for a necktie,' said Neeps. 'And I for one wouldn't have shed a – Thasha, what's wrong?'

Thasha's eyes were gleaming with sudden realisation. 'Chadfallow was right,' she said.

Neeps looked at her, then started. 'Blow me down. So he was.'

Pazel looked from one to the other. 'What do you mean? Right about what?'

'There was a fight on the berth deck,' said Thasha. 'Half the crew ran to see it. The crowd was so thick you could hardly move.'

'What sort of a fight?'

Neeps shrugged. 'Plapps versus Burnscoves, that's all we ever heard. It started in the mess hall. Dastu took a few nasty hits – seems he tried to keep the peace, and nobody thanked him. Marila's with him right now in sickbay.'

'By the time we arrived the fight was getting ugly,' said Thasha. 'Hercól was tossing men left and right, shouting at both gangs to come to their senses. I could have helped, but Marila grabbed me around the waist and wouldn't let go. Then Neeps got knocked over and she had to let go of me and grab *him* before he jumped in and got himself killed.'

'Stubborn little devil, that one,' muttered Neeps.

'The next thing we knew Chadfallow was shouting at us from the edge of the mob: "On your guard! This is not a coincidence!" That's when we asked ourselves what had happened to you.'

'A diversion,' said Neeps, 'the whole blary fight. Arunis didn't want anyone watching the forecastle.' He looked at Pazel sharply. 'And you're a daft one, aren't you?'

'Daft?' said Pazel.

'As a dicky-bird!' said Thasha. 'How could you just *sit* out there with your back to the ship? Do you have *any* idea how foolish that was?'

'And it's not even the worst part,' said Neeps. 'He grabbed Arunis by the hand! Rin's chin, mate! Why didn't you just hand over your old man's knife and say, *Stab me?*'

They began a lively quarrel over the signature moment of Pazel's stupidity. Pazel, who thought of both friends as outrageously devoid of fear, was alarmed to realise how badly he'd shocked them. What he'd done *was* idiotic, to be sure. For some reason he recalled a question Chadfallow had thrown at him as a challenge, years ago, at their dinner table in Ormael: *What's the real tragedy, lad? To fall from a cliff and perish – or to be the sort of man who cares so little for his life that he risks it?*

He watched his friends argue: exasperating, irreplaceably dear. He wanted to live for any number of reasons. But first among them was to stop Arunis from carrying out the threats he'd made on the forecastle.

He sighed; there was worse to confess. 'He saw through me when I touched him,' he said, as Neeps and Thasha turned to stare. 'At least that's what he claimed. He said that Ramachni didn't make me the spell-keeper, when I used the Master-Word. So the Shaggat won't be made flesh again if I'm killed.'

A moment's silence. Then Thasha grabbed him by the collar, her hands literally vibrating with rage. 'You *imbecile.*'

'Just go straight back to the stateroom,' said Neeps, 'and get comfortable. You can make the tea from now on.'

Pazel was livid, but he knew his friends were right. Arunis had nothing to lose by killing him now. And why wouldn't he? Pazel had come closer to stopping him than anyone aboard.

'Listen,' he said. 'I'm sorry. But if you want me to spend the rest of this float in the blary stateroom you'll have to tie me up.'

'That's an idea,' said Thasha.

Pazel glared at her. 'In any case, you're the one who's in danger.' And he told them about Arunis' claim that Rose intended to sell her to the Bramian natives.

'What rubbish!' said Thasha when he had finished.

But Neeps looked worried. 'Maybe it's not,' he said. 'Rose is just crooked enough. And the tribals on Bramian wouldn't get much out of killing you, would they? Not as if you're a threat, once they've whisked you off into those jungles. More likely they'd make you a slave or a servant. That way if you turned out to be the spell-keeper the Shaggat would still be in the clear.'

'Think about it,' said Pazel. 'How else could Rose get you off the ship, keep you from dying, and prevent you from warning the outside world?'

'Thasha,' said Neeps, 'just keep to the stateroom for a while. Until we're away from Bramian.'

She looked from one to the other, exasperated. 'What's got into you two? *Hide?* Is that all we're going to do, until Rose decides to starve us out, or Ott starts cutting off our fingers? We need to fight back. We need to get back to the list.'

'The list?' said Neeps.

'The list of allies, you donkey – potential allies, I mean. And we need to do it soon. We can't beat them without more people on our side.'

'You're right about that,' said Neeps. 'But we'll have to be so damned careful.' He leaned closer, whispering, 'I have no idea why Rose has been so easy on us, but one thing's for sure: he *won't* go easy on mutineers.'

Pazel sighed. 'All right, genius. You come up with a plan.'

'We start with one person each,' said Thasha instantly, as though she'd only been waiting for someone to ask. 'Just one. Surely we can each find one person to trust on this ship? If Hercól and Marila do the same thing, we'll have ten people on our side.'

Neeps looked at her eagerly. 'And once we've all met, and decided the best way to fight these cretins—'

'We go out and find ten more,' Thasha finished. 'And if we can just keep doing that, we'll have half the crew on our side before we know it. Of course the trick will be to find them before anyone *else* knows it.'

Neeps was shaking his head in wonder. 'Thasha, you're as clever as my old Granny Undrabust! You really do have a head for – what's the word?'

'Tactics,' said Pazel.

'Tactics, that's it. All right then: we've got our plan, don't we?'

Pazel didn't answer. The others looked at him in surprise. At last he said, 'How can you possibly think this will work? If we guess wrong about just one person, we're dead as slag. Everything hinges on trust.'

Neeps and Thasha exchanged a glance. 'Trust, yeah,' said Neeps. 'Well, that's something we have, and they don't.'

Pazel shrugged. Once again Thasha was seeing it, that sudden darkening of his spirits, that drawing away. It was agony for her to watch, and she fought back an impulse to reach for him, right in front of Neeps. *You're afraid of feeling something. Why?*

Then, to her amazement, Pazel clutched her arm – tightly, a warning. He pointed up at the main yard, the giant horizontal timber that secured the *Chathrand's* largest sail. The yard was still bathed in orange sunlight, although the deck beneath it lay dark. And at the end of the yard sat a bird of prey.

It was a falcon, small and exquisite, black above, cream-yellow below. It was examining them with one bright eye.

Almost as soon as Thasha saw it the bird was in flight, dropping casually from the main yard to vanish below the rail. The three youths raced across the deck. But here at its midsection the ship was over two hundred feet wide, and by the time they reached the rail and leaned out over the sea the bird was gone.

'Damnation!'

'It had to be—'

'Of course it was!'

They dropped back onto the deck, once again earning stares from the crew. Pazel groaned aloud. 'That's *all* we need! Pitfire, why did Ramachni have to let him go?'

But Thasha felt oddly tense, as if tremors had suddenly shaken the boards at her feet. 'He's circling,' she said.

'What?' said Neeps. "How can you know that? What's *wrong* with you?'

Thasha turned in place, her gaze flung wide, as if trying to catch up with something in a hurtling orbit around the ship. 'I don't know how I know,' she said, 'but he's above the deck again, teasing us – he's slowing – *there!*'

A blur of wings, a shrill cry, and there it was, landing neatly on a brace-line seven feet above their heads. Men shouted, pointing: a few of them remembered the falcon. None better than Thasha, however, who had watched the bird for years – loved it, she imagined, though it never paused in its flight – from the gardens of the Lorg Academy.

'Welcome back, Niriviel,' she said.

'You should not welcome me,' said the falcon, in that fierce, high voice she recalled so well: the voice that somehow belonged to both a predator and a homeless child. 'I bring you no good tidings, Thasha Death-Cheater. No comfort to the betrayers of Arqual.'

Thasha shook her head. 'We haven't betrayed anyone, Niriviel. We tried to explain that to you in Simja.'

'After you stabbed my master in the leg. Do you deny this?'

Thasha winced. 'I – no, Niriviel, I don't.'

'Oh come off it, Thasha,' said Pazel. 'It was only a dinner fork.'

Niriviel's wings were aflutter. 'You raised your hand against Sandor Ott, first defender of His Supremacy! If you are not a traitor then the word means nothing at all!'

'Fine,' said Thasha, in what she hoped was a soothing voice. 'You can call me what you like. But even if we're on different sides, I want you to know something. I'm happy to see you again.'

The bird gave an agitated hop.

'It's strange,' said Thasha, 'but I feel you're part of my life, and always will be. I can't watch you fly and not feel, I don't know – joy, I suppose.'

'Twaddle,' said the falcon.

Neeps had had enough. 'What do you want, bird?' he demanded.

Thasha motioned desperately for silence. 'I'm not lying to you,' she told the falcon. 'But why have you come back to us, anyway?'

The bird paused. His head cocked, dipped, darted. Then Thasha had a terrible thought. 'Oh, Niriviel. You didn't ... lose him, did you? Sandor Ott, I mean?'

Niriviel peered at her with great intensity. Thasha arched her neck back.

'You can tell me,' she said. 'I know he was like your father. Is that why you're back? Because you have nowhere left to go?'

'What nonsense!' cried the falcon suddenly. 'And what a fool you take me for! It is not *I* who has lost someone. Where is your own father, girl?'

'He stayed behind. In Simja.'

'And beyond that you cannot say. Beyond that you dare not imagine.'

'What do you mean?' cried Thasha. 'Do you know something about my father? Tell me!'

'Nothing for traitors.'

Pazel tried to take her arm, but Thasha shook him off. 'I'm no traitor, you stupid bigoted bird! I'm an Arquali, do you hear? What else could I be?'

'An orphan?' said Niriviel.

Thasha was almost sobbing. 'Tell me! Tell me what you know!'

But Niriviel only cried aloud – a mocking cry, perhaps – and leaped once more into flight. Seconds later he had vanished westwards, towards the black wall of Bramian.

20

A Sleepless Night

—◦◦◦—

17 Freala 941

Mr Coote had guessed correctly: within the hour the *Chathrand* was among the Black Shoulder Isles. They were dark and stone-shored and choked with greenery, miniature copies of their great mother to the west. Plenty of sea-room, thought Mr Elkstem: two or three leagues between one Black Shoulder and the next, and Bramian itself no closer than five. Still he took no chances.

'Topgallants and courses down, Mr Frix, if you please. We'll stand in on fore and spanker topsails, double-reefed.'

In the moonlight the watch furled sail after sail, and the bow wave sank to nothing. When the log was cast they were all but stationary, rocking forwards at a quarter knot. Shore birds, night jars and kestrels, spun hopefully above the deck, their shrill cries blending with the distant, mortal booming of the Bramian surf.

The three youths were still on the topdeck. Thasha had led the boys on a meandering march, port to starboard, bow to quarterdeck and back. She had barely spoken since Niriviel's departure, but she was glad of their company, and they seemed to understand her silence. The falcon's insinuations about Eberzam Isiq might have been pure spite, but Thasha could scarcely breathe for fear that something real lay behind them.

Eventually their random tour of the topdeck ceased to distract her, and began to make her think of animals in cages. She chose a quiet spot near the No. 3 hatch, folded her legs and sat.

'I don't want dinner tonight,' she said. 'You two had better go ahead.'

She leaned back against a coiled hawser. The boys looked at each other, and she imagined stomachs and solidarity at war. Then Neeps sat down on her left and Pazel, after a bit of awkward foot-shuffling, did the same on her right. She tried to catch his eye, but he avoided it, staring up at the gently billowing mainsail. Sailors of the third watch moved around them, chattering, while off to portside someone attempted (perhaps for the first time in his life, for the sound was painful) to tune a fiddle.

She sat between them, watching them fidget, wondering which of them would break the silence first, and with what kind, doltish attempt to ease her fears. Just when she had decided it could only be Pazel, Neeps began to talk.

'They ought to send us ashore to gather eggs,' he said. 'On the Black Shoulders, I mean. There was a Sollochi fisherman wrecked on one of 'em fifty years ago. He lived for three whole years on seabird eggs. For nine months he ate 'em raw; then he found a big clamshell and boiled his eggs inside it, but after three more months it cracked on the fire. Then the volcano came to life and there were steam vents everywhere, and he found he could cook his eggs by putting 'em in an old piece of fish-net, tying the net to a pole, and dangling it over one of the vents. And when the steam stopped coming he climbed to the lip of the volcano and fried the eggs on hot rocks, but he ended up burning his tongue so badly he couldn't taste 'em any more. But they rescued him soon after, and he lived a good long life back on Sollochstol. I guess there's a lesson in that, isn't there?'

'Sure,' said Pazel. 'Don't be a blary ass and lick hot rocks.'

Neeps leaned over and gave him a good-natured whack on the head. 'You're the ass, remember? I hate to think what you'd have done on that island. Turned your back on the volcano, for starters.'

Thasha smiled despite herself. Neeps had knocked her against Pazel's side, and she had not quite straightened up again. She did want some kind of comfort. Not an arm around her, not a voice telling her that all would be well. She'd been given those sorts of comforts her whole life, and they had usually failed. What she wanted was Pazel's hand locked in her own, fingers laced tight: a promise that *he* at least would not disappear. She wanted his touch, his attention, his eyes, the startled brightness of them before they'd kissed in the washroom. This is first love, she thought, slightly revolted by the banality. I love him. How absurd.

All the same she was glad of the dark. Neeps was saying something about Bramian, about Leopard People and shaggy rhinoceroses and other, stranger things said to dwell in its forests. The fiddle player attempted a song, gave up, tried again in a higher key. Thasha moved her shoulder against Pazel's arm and felt him draw a startled breath.

He was shivering a little, although the night was warm. Thasha felt her own breath quicken. And then he hugged his knees to his chest and edged away.

She was angry, aroused, confused. *Yes*, she thought, looking at the side of his face, *you would turn your back on a volcano.*

For a few minutes no one spoke. Mr Thyne and Latzlo the animal-seller sauntered by, debating the long-term value of crocodile skins. Latzlo at first appeared to have an enormous growth on one shoulder, but as they drew nearer she saw that it was only his pet sloth, the one beast in his collection that the merchant treated with warmth. Thyne nodded to them uneasily, but the animal dealer frowned, and cleared his throat as if preparing to spit.

'Same to you, dung beetle,' muttered Neeps.

Thasha gave the others an awkward look. 'So,' she said, 'I guess it's time we went over that list.'

'Right,' said Pazel glumly.

Neeps glanced inquiringly at Pazel, as though to ask why *his* mood was so black. The fiddle fell silent once more. Then suddenly it burst into song: a wild, bereft, racing melody, a song of flight or exile, and longing for someone or something lost beyond all hope of recovery. The three youths got to their feet to see what was happening.

The musician was none other than Dollywilliams Druffle. The wiry smuggler had taken the fiddle away from its hapless owner, a wan-faced young man who stood gaping at him, holding the empty fiddle-case. Druffle sawed like a man on fire, his spine twisted and his head sharply cocked, as if he were not playing the fiddle but impaled on it − an impression magnified by his grimace of concentration. Every sailor who could legitimately leave his station (and some who could not) pressed towards him, and a rhythmic clapping began. When fifty men or more had gathered Druffle suddenly broke off playing and sang:

> *Hey! Out upon the Nelluroq they took my Nell*
> *To the tower-tall waves and the typhoons fell*
> *Oh get along ye dark mare and bear me straight*
> *To the bottom of the Pits or to the ivory gate*
> *To the shades that gibber by the ghostly wall*
> *To the river-maids that whisper from the waterfall*
> *Oh get along ye dark mare and don't ye rest*
> *'Till I'm once-a-more asleep upon my lady's breast!*
> *Hey!*

With the final '*Hey!*' Druffle applied himself to the fiddle anew, and the song became even faster and madder. The tune was infectious; men who had laboured at the ropes for hours were capering like children, dancing and whirling, arm in arm. Mr Frix appeared from nowhere, and added to the bedlam with a goatskin drum. The deck reverberated with the sound of stomping feet.

'I like Druffle a lot more with a fiddle in his hand than a cutlass,' said Neeps.

Thasha laughed aloud. 'He's *brilliant!*'

Pazel looked up at the quarterdeck. 'Uskins will put a stop to this any minute.'

Thasha turned him a look almost of loathing. But before she could find words to flay him for his dullness a voice called her name.

Dastu was on the edge of the crowd, beckoning to her. Thasha hesitated for only an instant. Then she tied back her hair and ran to him, without another glance at her friends.

The two boys watched her impressive leaps and whirls, hand in hand with a delighted Dastu. 'Hercól really did teach her more than fighting, didn't he?'

'I don't think he's *that* sort of dance instructor,' said Pazel. 'Dastu's trying to dance a Gold Hills ramble, but she keeps messing him up.'

'She's messing with the lot of 'em, if you ask me,' laughed Neeps.

Pazel gave him a surly look. He knew what Neeps meant: Dastu glowed with the pleasure of being close to Thasha Isiq, of having cause to touch her hand and her back. Envy shone in the eyes of the other men, combined with sheer adoration for Thasha. She was a girl (most exotic of creatures to men trapped on a ship), and a lovely one at that, and noble-born as she was, she was dancing with them. Leef the main-top-man cut in on Dastu, and moments later Coote swept her away from Leef. From man to man she went, her hair shaken loose of its hasty knot and her face flushed with joy. The crowd stomped and roared.

'Don't you want to dance?' said Neeps.

Pazel looked startled. 'With her?'

'No, you dolt, with Lady Oggosk. Hurry up, before Druffle collapses.'

Pazel shook his head. 'Why don't you dance with her yourself?'

'Because I'm not the one who's turning pea-green with jealousy.'

At that Pazel guffawed. 'You've lost your mind. Someone just tried to drown me, remember? People want us dead, and there's a statue on the orlop with the most deadly damned thing in Alifros in its hand.

What makes you think I'd give birdsquat for this dancing rubbish?'

Closing his eyes, Neeps lifted his nose and sniffed. 'Mmm, smell that? Fresh from the oven. A big, buttery Ormael plum duff of a lie.'

Pazel jumped on him, not sure if he was furious or amused, but Neeps just laughed and said, 'Don't hit me! Have a look at Thasha now.'

The crowd had fallen back to give her room, for Thasha was at last dancing in perfect unison with a partner: Greysan Fulbreech. He wore the white shirt and close-fitting pants of his new office of surgeon's assistant: clothes so clean they might have just come from the tailor. Fulbreech danced even better than Druffle played. He took Thasha expertly by the waist and guided her through the left-back-double-right-spin of the ramble so swiftly that she never had time to make a contrary step. When they came together at the end of each cycle their faces were inches apart.

Pazel had seen enough. Without a word to Neeps he turned and marched away aft. He had a vague idea of storming into Lady Oggosk's cabin and telling her what she could do with her threats. Of course part of him realised that he could do no such thing – but how long could he keep up this charade? How long before Thasha asked him a question he couldn't lie about?

As he passed under the mizzenmast shrouds Neeps caught up with him, breathless from running.

'You're a first-class rotter,' he said. 'She's gone off somewhere with Fulbreech, and it's your fault.'

'How do you figure that?' Pazel asked without slowing his pace.

'Don't play simple,' said Neeps. 'Thasha's moody and headstrong, but you don't have to act like she's got some sort of plague. Can't you be blary decent? Nobody's asking you to marry her.'

Pazel gave a spiteful laugh. 'That's a damned good thing. She's not exactly good luck where marriage is concerned.'

Neeps leaped in front of him, stopping him dead. The smaller boy's patience was clearly exhausted. 'Are we mates, or not?' he demanded. 'When are you going to tell me what's the matter with you?'

Pazel averted his eyes, afraid of giving himself away. Oggosk had not forbidden him to talk to Neeps, but he would never forget how his friend had raged at the old witch, or her casual threat to murder him. He shuddered to think what Neeps would do if he learned what Oggosk had said after he stormed out.

But there was another reason he was keeping away from Thasha – one he could tell Neeps about, if only he could find the words to explain it.

'You . . . remember Klyst, don't you?' he said warily.

Neeps' jaw fell open so wide that Pazel could see his tonsils by lamplight. 'You're still thinking about that – thing. You're still under its spell.'

'Don't call her a thing, mate. She's a girl, and she's not so bad.'

'She eats people.'

'Well,' said Pazel relucantly, 'yes.'

'Why didn't you tell me the murth-spell was still affecting you? Come on, we're going to Chadfallow right this minute.'

'No!' said Pazel. 'By the Nine Pits, Neeps, the *last* thing I want is another "cure" from Ignus! Besides, I don't need curing. I'm not under her spell.'

'Pazel, her sister tied me up and left me to drown. And she would have done the same to you if your Gift hadn't turned the tables and made her love you. You're lucky she's thousands of miles away.'

'Maybe she's not,' said Pazel. 'She . . . well, she showed up on Dhola's Rib. And I heard her voice tonight on the bowsprit.'

Neeps' face contorted helplessly. 'When were you going to *say* something, you witless prat?'

'When I thought I could trust you not to screw things up.'

'Trust *me?* Oh, that's priceless, that's just—' Neeps was apoplectic. He bit his lips, clawing at the air in front of Pazel's face. 'You make me *angrier* than just about anyone I know.'

'Anyone but your brother, eh? Your older brother.'

For a moment he thought Neeps would hit him. The small boy's face turned dark red, and his mouth tightened to a choleric scowl. 'I told you,' he said, 'never, ever to talk to me about brothers.'

'And I told you I'm not under any spell.'

'Really? What's this, then?' Neeps flicked away Pazel's hand, which he had raised unconsciously to his collarbone, found Klyst's shell beneath the skin – and pinched it, hard.

A searing pain flooded Pazel's chest. He cried out, as somewhere inside him a girl's voice wailed in anguish. He shoved Neeps with all his might; the smaller boy crashed against the block and tackle at the mizzenmast, and struck his head on the rail.

Pazel doubled over, hands on his collarbone. Neeps had not broken the shell, but the pain throbbed on. *Klyst is terrified*, he thought. *She thinks I'm getting ready to cut out her heart*. The sound of her voice was so real he found himself looking about for its source, though he knew the murth-girl would never appear on the *Chathrand*. Her words in the temple came back to him: *Not allowed. I'd be trapped there, forever.*

Neeps got shakily to his feet, rubbing his head. When Pazel reached out to steady him he knocked his hand away.

'I'm finished here,' he said. 'Your cannibal girl's welcome to you.'

He stalked off, and Pazel heard his feet clattering down the ladderway.

The pain took a long time to ebb. Pazel leaned against the mizzen-mast, wondering who was more revolted at his behaviour, Neeps or Klyst herself. He had not been at it long when a shadow crossed his face.

It was Druffle. The pale spike of a man was drenched in sweat and smiling. His breath smelled distinctly of rum. 'Pathkendle!' he barked. 'What's this? You've been in a fight, haven't you?'

Pazel looked away; he had talked enough for one night. 'Not ... a fight, Mr Druffle. Not exactly.'

'If it tastes like a duck, it's a duck, lad.'

Pazel could think of no fitting rejoinder, so he said, 'That sure was some music you played.'

'Somebody had to make that Burnscove halfwit stop torturing his fiddle. And a Plapp's Pier boy was baiting him, calling him a tuneless hack. Of course he *was* a tuneless hack, but many's the brawl that began when one man stabbed another with a painful truth. We're not built to put up with much truth, my Chereste heart.'

'Oppo, sir.'

'The girl's not worth it, you know.'

'I beg your pardon?'

'I saw you and Undrabust watchin' Miss Thasha. No girl's worth losin' a friend over – not even a sweet puff-pastry like her. Take it from an old lady's man: play the game calm and collected. Let Undrabust make a fool of himself. He's got a knack for it, and when he does you'll look all the better in her eyes.'

'Mr Druffle,' Pazel broke in. 'I appreciate your – guidance, really. But you're digging for clams in an oyster bed.'

Druffle laughed. 'By the sweet Tree, you make me miss Ormael! Haven't heard *that* one in years.' Then he looked sharply at Pazel, and a twinkle came to his eye. '"Digging for clams in an oyster bed." D'ye know who used to say that? Captain Gregory Pathkendle, that's who.'

Pazel jumped upright. 'You did know my father! You weren't just spinning yarns back on the *Prince Rupin!* Mr Druffle, tell me about him, please! When did you see him last?'

Druffle's face darkened. 'On the Haunted Coast, lad. When he and Mr Hercól led the charge against the Volpeks. 'Course I wasn't free to speak with him – that adder-tongued mage had me in thrall. But I saw Gregory fight his way onto that Volpek cruiser, side-by-side with Mr Hercól. A truly fearless man, Gregory. He took down the *Hemeddrin*'s captain with one thrust.'

'He seems to be afraid of me,' said Pazel.

Druffle looked at him quizzically. 'Afraid? That's not what I'd call it.'

Before Pazel could ask what Druffle *would* call it, a hand fell heavily on his shoulder. Ignus Chadfallow was there, frowning.

'Pazel,' he said, 'come with me. I need to speak with you right now.'

Pazel shrugged off his hand and stepped away. 'What do you want? Mr Druffle and I—'

'You can trade stories with this rum-runner on your own time.'

'This *is* my own time.'

'Rum-runner, is it?' Druffle assumed an air of dignity. 'As a man of business, I'll have you know I take abjectness to that remark.'

Chadfallow turned Druffle a withering look. 'When I have need of your areas of expertise, such as the best means of passing off muskrat pelts as mink, I shall send for you. Come along, Pazel.'

Suddenly Druffle reached out and seized Chadfallow by the arm. 'You can't talk to me that way no more, Doctor sir,' he snarled. 'We're outside the Empire, and from what I hear you're no more right with the law than Dollywilliams Druffle, maybe less so.'

'This ship *is* the Empire, you fool,' said Chadfallow, 'and its laws apply here as they would in Etherhorde. Now unhand me before I have you caged like a beast.'

Druffle released him, but his eyes sparked with malice. 'Such *good* stock, the Chadfallows. Judges and ministers, doctors and dukes. Such a noble pedicure. But you're not above nicking another man's pastry now and then, are you?'

Chadfallow froze. Druffle eyed him with wicked delight. He turned back to Pazel.

'Aye, lad. Here's a question what's preyed on *your* mind: why did Gregory run off and leave you? Was he afraid of the Arqualis, afraid to fight for his country? No sir, not a bit of it. Fear never got the better of good Captain G. Why, he didn't even know the invasion was coming, because his *dear friend* Chadfallow didn't tell him.'

'What are you talking about?' said Pazel, as Chadfallow tried once more to draw him away.

'I heard it from his own mouth,' said Druffle, 'late one night, by a fire in the Fens. Your dad left Ormael when he learned that his beloved wife had taken up with his fine Arquali *friend*. That they'd been lovers for years. Because Gregory knew that if he didn't get away for a while he'd put a knife through the doctor's treacherous heart – or hers. You want to know why you grew up without a father, Pathkendle? The answer's standing right next to you.'

Pazel turned slowly to face Chadfallow.

'He's . . . lying, right? Tell me he's lying.'

Chadfallow managed a laugh. 'When is he not? If lies were wine, they'd name vineyards after this man.'

At that Druffle's face turned red as a tuna steak, and his hands clenched in fists. 'I was brought up to respect men of letters,' he growled, 'but you're no gentleman. You're a dressed-up Bilsburra ape, and you'd die of shame if you had any.'

Pazel stared at the freebooter, then looked at Chadfallow again.

'I used to compare my father to you,' he said slowly. 'I used to wish he was as fine and cultured as you.'

Chadfallow seemed to grope for a reply. 'This cur makes it sound—'

'You were already aboard, after the battle with the Volpeks. That was why he didn't wait to talk to me, isn't it? Because he couldn't stand being near you.'

'Pazel—'

'I'd started to hate him,' said Pazel, cutting him off. 'To hate him, for not caring more about us. But he left *because* he cared, didn't he?'

'Let me explain.'

'I don't want you to explain any more, Ignus. I want you to say it isn't true.'

Chadfallow stood still, gazing at him, and a terrible struggle raged in his eyes. He looked like an animal caught in a trap, waiting for the hunter to return and take his life. But he made no denial. Instead he took two steps towards Druffle, struck the man across the face, and fled the deck.

Later that evening Neeps sat across the table from Hercól and Marila, fuming, while Jorl and Suzyt watched the stateroom door with melancholy eyes and Felthrup ran worriedly around the tabletop, urging them to eat. Neeps picked at his food. He could not bring himself to tell the others what had happened between him and his friends. He had called Pazel a pig, but he was the one plagued by an embarrassing, swinish sort of question: what if Thasha did not come back tonight?

He felt rotten to the core, even to be visited by the thought. And when Thasha did at last appear, just as the watch-captain struck two bells past midnight, he exploded from his chair.

'There you are! Rin's blood, Thasha, you can't just storm off at night! I say, have you had anything to—'

Her cabin door slammed behind her. They heard her kicked-off boots strike the wall.

'I don't think she's hungry,' said Marila, expressionless as ever.

Hercól rose and walked swiftly to her cabin. When his knock received no answer, he sighed. 'I am glad she is back,' he said. 'Remember what Arunis told Pazel, concerning Rose's desire to be rid of her. It may well be a lie, but we must take no chances. Try to keep her in the stateroom; if she insists on venturing out, say I order her to carry a sword. I have my own appointment to keep with Diadrelu. Afterwards I think I shall try to learn who else may be awake and busy on the *Chathrand* in the dead of night. Besides, of course, Mr Pathkendle.'

'He'll be along,' grunted Neeps.

But an hour later there was still no sign of Pazel, and a newly irritated Neeps set off in search of him. By this time Marila was asleep on the bearskin rug, and the dogs were snoring in a call-and-refrain. Felthrup stood on the edge of the dining table, gazing at the strip of lamplight shining under Thasha's door, and leaning out in such a way that he would lose his balance if he began to doze. It was a cheerless game: each time he began to drift off, the near-fall would wake him. Then he would drag himself once around the table and return to his spot. He had done this for two nights already, unnoticed by anyone. He was terrified of sleep.

A time came when his trick failed: he was so exhausted that he slept through the vertigo, experienced an instant of weightless bliss, and landed with a thump and a whimper upon the floor. Suzyt yipped without quite waking; Marila sighed and turned over on the rug. A moment later Thasha opened her door an inch.

She was still in her deck clothes. Her face wore a distracted look. He was not sure her eyes really saw him.

'What's the matter with you?' she said.

'Not sleepy,' mumbled Felthrup.

Thasha paused, staring at him like a ghost. 'What did you do back in Noonfirth, when you couldn't sleep?' she asked.

Felthrup's ears pricked up instantly. 'In the good times, when I wasn't starving? Read, m'lady, always. Learning to read was the first task I set myself after the miracle of tears – after my waking, you understand. I lived above a bakery, a choice spot for a scavenger, and the baker's daughter was learning to read, and I would listen from the top of the stair. And one day the girl read aloud to her mother from a storybook. It was a profound tale, about a jackal captured on the Samopol Veld. The hunters planned to skin him – he was just the right size to make four jackal-fur hats – but he talked his way to freedom. He told the hunters that he was a murth in disguise, and would plague them with four years of warts and spots and piles and shingles if they harmed him. A year for each hat, you see? And they didn't dare! It was a brilliant story, m'lady. And when the girl finished I told myself that by reading I might learn almost anything, and even answer the riddle of my own existence. I've failed in that last endeavour, so far. Still I became an addict, and read everything I could. Old books, newsbills stuffed in crates, soap wrappers, lists for the greengrocer, orders of execution, ledgers forgotten in city warehouses – anything.'

'You'd read.'

'In a word, yes.'

Slowly Thasha's eyes found him, and focused. 'Why don't you come in?' she said. 'I think you can help me.'

Glad to be wanted, Felthrup went to her. But in the doorway, by long and almost involuntary habit, he stopped and sniffed. Her cabin smelled of dust, sweat, a dozen kinds of food crumbs, and very slightly of blood. He looked at her with concern. 'Are you wounded, m'lady?'

Thasha did not answer him. She shut and locked her cabin door, bent down and gently raised the lame rat onto her desk. There was something in her expression that Felthrup had never seen before. One could almost mistake it for fear; but no, she was not afraid, at least not for herself. Thasha moved around her bed to a spot by the wall, reached high, and ran her fingers along a plank. After eight or ten inches her fingers stopped. The rat found nothing special about the spot, but he could tell her fingers had. Thasha pushed, and Felthrup gave a chirp of surprise, for he could suddenly see the outline of a small door, less than two feet square. Thasha clawed it open; old hinges squeaked.

'Mr Fiffengurt showed this to me,' she said. 'The stateroom used to be the fleet admiral's cabin, when *Chathrand* was a navy flagship.

The admiral hid the code-books in here, and his secret orders.'

In the hidden cabinet lay a book bound in fine leather. 'That's Fiffengurt's new journal; I'm hiding it for him,' Thasha explained. 'And have a look at this.'

She removed the book, and the rat saw a thick metal plate mounted on the wall, and within the plate the outline of a drawer. The latter was about five inches tall and ten wide, with a small handle at the centre. 'Solid iron, and locked fast,' said Thasha. 'And there's no proper keyhole, just a tiny round hole behind the handle. Fiffengurt has no idea what might be in there. He couldn't remember there *being* any inner drawer. But that's not what I wanted to show you.'

There were, Felthrup saw now, two books in her hand. The second book was much older and heftier than the quartermaster's journal. Thasha looked at him. 'I think you know what this one is.'

'Of course,' said Felthrup. 'Your special *Polylex*.'

'I haven't been able to make myself open it for weeks,' she said, laying the book beside him on the desk. 'It's not that the book's cursed or poisoned or anything vile like that. But ever since the Nilstone came aboard something's been happening when I sit down to read.'

'What happens?'

Thasha paused. 'Ramachni didn't want me to talk about it. But he also told me I'd have to decide when to give my trust. And I'd trust you with my life, Felthrup dear.'

The black rat looked suddenly nervous. 'If Ramachni told you to keep it secret, then you must,' he said.

But Thasha went on. 'I don't understand it myself. Sometimes I barely notice it happening; at other times it feels as if I'll never be the same, as if I'm burning inside, or dying.'

At once Felthrup leaped onto the book and raised his paws. 'Then read it no more!' he cried. 'Ramachni cannot see down every path. Surely he was wrong in this case – or perhaps Arunis has flung a curse on the book after all. Let it be, Thasha!'

'I don't understand what happens,' Thasha said again, 'but I have felt it before – or something like it. Just after my mother died, it was. Her family took care of my father, since his own family lived far off in the Westfirth. One day my father and uncle sat smoking for hours in the garden, and I got curious and crept through the bushes to listen. *"No,"* I heard Daddy say, *"we didn't have the heart to go through it again. She lost two children before Thasha, you know."* They were talking about my mother, Felthrup. My uncle said, *"Thasha's was an easy birth, wasn't it?"*

And my father answered, *"It was when the time came. But we almost lost her too, Carlan – early on, just like the others. It was the damndest thing. Clorisuela began to bleed, and weep, and I thought the worst had come again. And then – nothing. The blood stopped, her pain vanished. And she never suffered any but the expected pains from that moment on."*

'You see? I almost died before I was born. And when I understood what I'd heard – that's when I felt it. The ache. Like being tied with ropes that are shrinking, cutting me. I never felt it again until I started reading that book.'

'No more,' said Felthrup. 'We have seen enough black magic, and some of the worst has been hurled at you.'

Thasha went to her porthole window and freed the latch. The lamplight flickered as a cool wind passed through the room. She looked out over the now-moonless sea, and the haunted expression stole over her again.

'I let Fulbreech kiss me tonight,' she said. 'He wanted to do more than that. And I was tempted to let him. What if I die on this ship?'

'Lady Thasha,' said Felthrup, 'I hope you will not soon mate with anyone. It would complicate matters indescribably. And it is most, most unpleasant.'

For a long time she gazed from the window in silence. Then at last she said, 'It's not evil, what happens when I read that book. Maybe it's even good, or at least necessary, unavoidable.' She looked at Felthrup again, and added with a note of pleading, 'I just don't want it to happen yet.'

'You frighten me,' said Felthrup, beginning to quake. 'You have been so kind, Thasha, so generous, and I have nothing to offer in return. I wish I knew what threatened you, but despite my habit of reading I'm a fool. A failure as a rat, of course; and what I know of human life feels like something snatched from a dream. I wish I were learned. I'm not. My knowledge is paltry, puny, slight, a negligible froth of wisdom, a detritus.'

His earnestness brought her back to the room. She laughed, a small frightened sound, then bent and kissed the rat on the forehead. 'Do you know something, Felthrup? I think we were meant for each other. Will you help me face this thing that's coming, whatever it is? Will you read to me from the *Polylex*?'

21

Queen Mirkitj's Revenge

—⁓—

19 Freala 941

The day Simjans would come to regard as the Day of Terror began with a gentle autumn rain, not strong enough to bother the street dogs, nor to wake the island's citizens from the last peaceful sleep they would know for a very long time.

By dawn, however, the rain had strengthened; and by midmorning it was clear that the Nelu Gila had sent a tempest. The four-month drought was ended, and King Oshiram sent invitations to all the clerics in the city (except the Sisters of the Snake, his favourite courtesan being a severe herpetophobe) to the castle for an interfaith prayer of thanksgiving.

In the poorest district of the capital, which even after five centuries had not quite dispelled the infamy stamped on it by Queen Mirkitj of the Statues, the rain found its way indoors by a million paths. Broken roof-tiles gave it entry to rotting beams; crumbled mortar let it seep into bloated plasterwork. Gutters (those still clinging to the row houses) spat torrents onto the streetcorners, and the streets themselves became rushing culverts. The old sewers were soon clogged and overflowing with filth.

Thunder rolled in from the sea and reverberated on the abandoned heap of stone that was the mad queen's palace of execution. At its height the thunder even penetrated to the undiscovered levels of her prison-kiln, where the Secret Fist of Arqual went about its daily intelligence work; and where, at a still deeper level, Admiral Eberzam Isiq stood in the blackness, holding a metal plate against his chest, counting drops of water as they struck some unseen pool.

Thunder, rain. How cruel, the reminder that such things existed. That above the crimes and atrocities of men there arched a heavens, where the Milk Tree shaded the gods, and angels gathered souls like fallen acorns. *What do they do with them?* he had asked his mother once. *Some they send off on Heaven's wind, to realms we cannot know,* she had answered, stroking his hair. *Some become the food of the gods, and dwell within them for ever. And a few they rock in their arms, and shelter beneath their wings at night, until they grow into angels themselves.* That was all young Isiq had known of death, until his father departed for the Tsördon Campaign, and fell there in the snow – bludgeoned flat by a Sizzy mace, as he learned twelve years later in the Officers' Club. The death certificate had merely read, 'Fallen in defence of his comrades.' The commandant had thought it best to spare his mother the details.

He reached behind him and felt the chamber door. He had fallen in love with it. The door was on his side, while all else conspired in his annihilation.

The statues, for example: they were not the friends he'd hoped for. The farmer, the schoolboy, the blacksmith, the monk: perhaps they had never forgiven him for toppling his woman, shattering her against the stone. And how could he blame them, when he had never forgiven himself? She had been waving to him, before the banister split and she dropped four stories onto marble, her theatre gown rippling like a flare. He had idly considered keeping her home that night, of leaving their infant girl with Nama and pulling her into bed.

The statues would not obey him; their silence made that perfectly clear. Indeed they only spoke now when they didn't think he was listening. But was that malice? Couldn't one reasonably presume that they were as frightened as he was by the sounds from the pit?

For they were back, and getting nearer. High, half-strangled voices, snarls and snapping teeth, and always the digging, scrabbling, scraping of claws. From the moment Isiq had shouted they had been trying to reach him. First they had climbed the shaft beneath the pillar-shaped kiln. He had listened at the tiny window in the kiln's iron door. The beasts had climbed almost to his level, and stopped, thwarted. Some brick iron grillework sealed the shaft. The creatures tore at it, screeching like harpies, and then leaped back into the darkness to seek another way.

That other way was the pit, of course. Just a matter of time. Even now he could hear them, digging wildly at the fallen earth and stone. They would have reached him that first day, Isiq knew, had their eagerness not caused a second cave-in, larger than whatever calamity had first sealed the tunnel at the base of the pit. Not a shriek had followed that thunder of falling rock: only blessed silence. Had the beasts all been crushed? After a time Isiq let himself believe it. They were gone, entombed in the hell-holes that spawned them. Even the statues had breathed a little easier.

Then the digging had resumed, and the maniacal chatter. *Snaa! Eat! Egg!* None of it comprehensible in the least, except for the perpetual whimper of the beast that called itself a widow and begged for alms. Long hours Isiq sat by the chamber door, a hand on his axe-shaped stone, hardly daring to breathe. His slightest sound raised the beasts to a frenzy.

> *Sweet isporelli, so yellow and fair*
> *Buy one, ye sailor, for your love's hair,*
> *My love she died, ma'am, died in the spring,*
> *Bless the new angel, bright on the wing.*

Isiq's eyes snapped open. The statues were tormenting him again. Cowards, they waited until he slept to hurl their accusations. But there was another sound, no dream but the sound he had prayed for: swift boots in the hall outside. It was Ott's man, come to deliver his meal.

Isiq put down his empty plate and stood. He faced the door, dragging fingers through his matted hair, trying to compose himself (the statues found it hysterical) after months of darkness and grime.

This would be only his second meal since the noises resumed. The first time he had been irrational, kneeling and begging to be released, abject in his fear of the things behind him. No wonder the man had laughed. This time Isiq resolved to stay calm.

He heard the clank of iron keys. 'There are creatures in here,' he said loudly, not waiting for the door to open, for it was never open longer than it took the guard to shove a plate into the chamber and snatch the empty one away. 'Talking creatures, monsters. They're digging a tunnel from the floor below. You can't want that. Aren't your orders to keep me alive?'

When the door opened the light was searing, although it was no more than a dim walrus-oil flame. Isiq recoiled, a cave-creature himself. Holding the light was the same quick, wiry Arquali youth who had clubbed him down with the flask months ago; Isiq recognised the small wart at the corner of his mouth, only visible when he parted his lips to speak. For once the man looked him in the eye.

'Talking monsters!' he laughed. 'That would be you this past week, Admiral. You're chatting with the statues, aren't you?'

Isiq was unsettled. 'Never mind them,' he said.

The guard shook his head. 'That deathsmoke powder's turned your brains to dairy curd.'

'If you'll but listen—'

'Go to the Pits.'

He slid Isiq's dinner into the room with his toe. But before he could slam the door Isiq lunged forwards and caught his wrist.

'Please,' he said, 'they'll kill me.'

The man cursed and wrenched his hand away, then wiped it on his pants as if he had touched something noxious. 'It's rats, you filthy sod, just rats! Calm down and eat if you want to live. And if you ever touch me again I'll see you get nothing but weevils on your plate from here to springtime.'

The door slammed, and for an instant the statues guffawed. Isiq whirled, furious, daring them to continue. Of course they didn't: he had shown them what he was capable of. He bent and found his dinner, wolfed the old bread, drank the sour and mysterious soup, glaring at his unseen foes. He was not sure whether or not they could see *him*. But he was certain they wanted his food.

He was sucking his fingers when he heard a new and desperate wriggling sound from the pit. At the same time a thought struck him, like a blow from a club. The rats. What had Ott's bit of parchment said? The Nilstone killed all who touched it, save the littlest vermin, *who first suffer grotesqueries of change.*

Little vermin, he thought. Like fleas, maybe? And hadn't he been chewed alive by fleas, even on the wedding day? They *were* strangely large, and vicious: he had dug one out of his hair, and the thing had bloodied his thumb. Could the fleas he bore from the *Chathrand* have bred in the hay-strewn compartment where the Shaggat resided, holding the Stone?

From the pit, the wriggling sound grew louder.

And where had they gone from him, those unlucky fleas? Where else could they go, if they tired of his old thin blood, but to the rats? Hadn't he scrabbled among the rats, right here, day after day, fighting over the littlest crumbs?

What if those creatures were *not* what had devoured the rats, but rather what the rats had become?

It was then that the wriggling stopped, and he heard a creature scrabbling in the pit.

His hand groped first for the axe-shaped stone. But where had he left it? By the kiln, Rin spare him, he'd dropped his stone by the kiln!

The creature was at the rim of the pit, snuffling. '*Penny for a colonel's widow?*' it said.

Isiq dropped to his hands and knees, sweeping the floor with his fingers. After a moment he found the shallow groove he had scratched with the edge of the plate, and began a slow, creeping shuffle towards the kiln.

The creature loped into the room, yowling its eternal question. From the sound of its breath Isiq pictured an animal roughly the size of a sheepdog. Every few yards it would stop talking and take a sharp, deliberate sniff. Isiq raised the metal plate and held his breath.

From the pit came a sudden crescendo of digging, and a muted sound, as of many voices shouting behind an earthen wall. Then Isiq heard the creature paw at the door of the chamber.

'Penny for—'

The creature broke off, snuffling again. Then it gave an ear-splitting caterwaul and lunged straight at him across the chamber. Isiq flung the plate against the far wall. At the clattering noise the beast wheeled around, confused, and in that moment Isiq plunged towards the kiln. As soon as he did so the thing heard him and pounced. But Isiq's hand had found the stone, and he swung into the monster's leap with all the force of the blow he had intended, months ago, for Sandor Ott.

The stone connected with a fur-covered skull. A heavy, short-legged animal smashed into his chest; a drooling mouthful of flat incisors rasped against his head, tore through his right ear and fell sideways. Isiq raised the stone and struck a second time, only grazing the creature, and then it was on him again with tooth and claw, and he was fighting to keep it from his throat. It snarled its question between snaps of its jaws. Finally he threw it down, but this time Isiq kept his left hand locked in the fur, somewhere near the thing's mangy shoulder. Now he had a target. He brought the stone down, a crushing blow on the other side of the animal's head.

'*There's* your penny! And *there's* another!'

It fought on. He struck it again and again. Only when the voice at last fell silent did he realise that someone was talking to him.

'Look out, Isiq! They're coming! They're here!'

The statue spoke the truth: the creatures were erupting from the pit, howling and braying as though maddened by pain. There was no hope whatsoever in fighting. He could not survive an attack by two of them together, let alone more.

Like a spreading stain the creatures fanned out from the pit. He backed against the wall of the kiln. He heard their claws on the legs of statues, their teeth grinding fragments of the fallen woman. A great boil of misery burst inside him – time to go, time to join her – and then his hand fell upon the iron bar, propped against the kiln and forgotten for days.

Something like an electric shock passed from the bar to his mind. He thought at once of the door of the kiln, the iron fire-door with the bolt he had wrenched free. Isiq groped for it, dragging the bar. Instantly the creatures heard him and rushed towards the sound.

Here was the door. Isiq clawed at it, wrenched. It was hinged so as to swing up and inward. What lay within he could not begin to guess. Beside him a creature leaped, a statue fell with a crash, a schoolboy's voice wailed once and vanished like a candleflame, and then Isiq had the door open and was rolling into the kiln.

There was a cast-iron grate for a floor. Isiq was dragging the pole in after him when the creatures pounced. Flat on his back, he held the door down with one foot while the other stomped at the teeth and claws thrusting in at him. The pole at last slid into the kiln, and he pushed the door shut with both feet. But an untold number of the creatures were pushing back, and more were joining them by the second, and Isiq knew that if the pole was too short he would die.

It was not too short. He had it in place now, one end against the door and the other, higher, propped on the opposite wall of the kiln.

'Now you're in for it, you Pit-spawned scum!'

He stood, gripped the upper end of the pole and brought it down with all his might. The creatures shrieked in agony. Those who could wrenched free; others felt their bones crushed. The iron door was closed, and His Supremacy's ambassador to Simja fell back beside it and wept for Clorisuela, his shattered bride; and for Thasha, his darkened star; two angels who might have redeemed the world if he had loved them better, if he had not felled them with his addiction to Arqual, torn the wings from their bodies, if he had forgotten the Empire and lived in their light.

Children were forbidden to play in the rubble of Queen Mirkitj's palace, but older youths were often seen to skulk there at twilight, throwing dice and swallowing a few vile, illicit gulps of grebel, just enough to feel careless and warm. There were a number of such boys about on the evening of 19 Freala, the rainclouds having blown offshore, and they were the first in the city to hear the screams. Appropriately horrified – the voices seemed to come from under the earth – they spat out the liquor and groped for iron knuckles and pocketknives.

Suddenly the ruins were full of maimed and bleeding men. A few were Simjans; most were foreigners (*Arqualis*, someone shouted) and all were running for their lives. The youths asked no questions, for nothing about the men's torn bodies was open to doubt. They ran, howling, beside the strangers, and the swiftest of them lived.

The battle raged through the night, as the plague of creatures spread from the hillside slums to the wealthier districts. The forces of King Oshiram were twice overwhelmed. After the second rout, just blocks from the palace, his commanding general emptied the barracks. *Siege!* went the cry. *War inside the walls! Rise now to save the city!* And every last spear-bearer, conscript and cavalryman joined the fray, along with a good many farmhands, stevedores, stonemasons and virile monks. The last of the beasts fell at midnight on the Street of the Coppersmiths, almost exactly where the king had stood when he described the fine lamps he'd ordered for the ambassadorial household.

Of the eighteen men who had served the Secret Fist, just three were captured alive. One had taken a wound to the throat and could not speak. The other two were brought before the king that very night. Oshiram, who had joined the fighting himself and lost considerable blood (not to mention hundreds of subjects), lifted the chin of the first man with the tip of his yet-to-be-cleaned sword.

'Talk, you monster.'

But the man was already talking, very softly to himself: 'The rats, the rats, the rats,' he said.

'We know they're rats!' exploded the king, 'in the same way that a godsforsaken whale-eating behemoth shark is a fish! Tell me what you know of them!'

'They can t-t-talk—'

'That's more than I can say for you, you slobbering dog! Who are you? What were you doing on that hillside? What sort of black sorcery turns rats into hog-sized killing machines?'

Suddenly the other man raised his head and looked directly at the king. His face was so white with chalky dust that he might have been a thespian painted for the stage – except for the blood that had dried in streaks.

'It's the queen's revenge,' he said.

'What's that? Who are you? What queen?'

The man moistened his dry lips. A small wart in the corner of his mouth began to bleed anew.

'Mirkitj,' he said, 'the crab-handed queen. We jailed a living man among her statues. We violated her unholy tomb.'

Oshiram had outlawed torture, very publicly, on the first day of his reign. Whether as a consequence of this decree or because their minds were broken, he learned little more from either captive. But armed with the mention of 'a living man' he sent eighty of his least wounded footsoldiers into the ruins of Mirkitj's palace. Following a trampled and bloody path they found a door – once well hidden, now torn from its hinges – and descended by stages through the remains of the palace, the basements, sub-basements, and at last to the kiln.

Months of shock and revulsion would follow, as the statues were brought one by one into the daylight and their possible lineages debated. But nothing was so strange as the discovery of a pale old man, barricaded in the cylindrical oven and emaciated, but very much alive. He could not tell them his name, or who had imprisoned him, or for what crime. Indeed none of the soldiers recognised him, and it was only the king who saw the Arquali ambassador and father of the first Treaty Bride beneath the blood and matted hair and months of filth.

He almost shouted, *Isiq! It's you!* But something made Oshiram hold his tongue. He stood a little apart from the delirious man and waved his scribe and chamberlain to silence. He thought of all that had happened in his city that year. A murdered girl. A Mzithrini elder slain in his shrine. A curious silence from Arqual. And no word whatsoever from the west regarding the happiness of Falmurqat and Pacu Lapadolma. He felt the stirrings of fear for his little country, ever between the hammer and the anvil, ever dreaming of the day it would cease to bleed. Then he beckoned to the chamberlain and had him take Isiq to a guest room in the palace, a snug but out-of-the-way place not far from the king's private library.

'Send a doctor – No, send *my* doctor, and have him report to me the minute he leaves this man's bedside. And see that neither he nor the guards nor you yourself ever mention this fellow to a soul.'

22

Bad Medicine

——◦∿◦——

20 Freala 941
129th day from Etherhorde

At dawn the *Chathrand* was no longer alone.

They had heard nothing, and seen no vessel approach for as long as there was moonlight to see by. Yet somehow before dawn a small, single-masted cutter had swept down upon them, around the curve of one of the Black Shoulders, or else out of some hidden mooring on Bramian itself.

She had drawn up under their lee and was closing still. The lookout bellowed; the watch-captain gave a blast on his pipe. Archers raced to the *Chathrand*'s fighting tops.

The cutter was some forty feet long. There was grace to her lines, her tight-fitted timbers, and her silent crew worked the headsails with confidence, riding her gently on the swells. Little by little she edged closer to the Great Ship.

Mr Alyash came on deck and ordered the archers to stand down. 'Let us have the ladder, gentlemen. Helmsman, nothing sudden if you please.'

The accordion ladder snaked down the hull. On the cutter the men were rigidly alert: if they drifted too near they would founder in the *Chathrand*'s underswell: a fatal accident beyond any doubt. The helmsman of the smaller craft fought the waves, shouting orders to the men at the staysail. The gap narrowed: twelve feet, ten—

Suddenly a man was airborne: he had taken a flying leap from the smaller craft. He cleared the gap and caught the ladder in both hands, smacking against the *Chathrand*'s hull. For an instant he vanished completely in a wave; then the Great Ship rolled and his body punched upward through the water. Alyash, watching his progress from above, heard him laugh aloud.

The cutter veered hastily away. The man on the ladder climbed with easy assurance. Water streamed from his loose grey hair and the tip of the scabbard lashed sidelong on his back. Some thirty feet below the topdeck he raised his eyes to Alyash and barked:

'You're the new bosun – Swellows' replacement?'

'Aye, sir,' came the startled reply.

'You'll reopen the midship portal. This is no way to board.'

'We sealed it against the Nelluroq, Mr—'

'Open it. And let Elkstem know he must bear north around Sandplume Isle – tight in, there's a cove.'

'The cove at Sandplume?' Alyash sputtered. 'But sir, the reef blocks the mouth of that cove, it's unapproachable.'

'There *is* no reef, you fool. We tore it out six months ago. Where's the captain? What mischief has that cursed mage been up to? And what the devil happened to the Shaggat's son?'

'He . . . that is—'

'Never mind, give me a hand. By the Night Gods, your face is ugly!'

Alyash glared, but bent over and clasped the outstretched hand – a scar-covered hand that closed on his own like a trap. The bosun grunted and heaved backwards, and the newcomer sprang over the rail and landed four-square on the deck. They stood there, eye to eye. Then Alyash wrenched his hand free.

'You're one to talk, you old spittin' viper.'

A moment's silence. Then Alyash guffawed, and Sandor Ott cackled, and the two men locked arms in what was almost an embrace.

'Bastard!' said Ott. 'We needed you in Simja! I said we wanted you aboard *eventually*. I didn't tell you to ship out as part of the crew!'

'You left it to my discretion.'

Ott shoved the bosun away. 'That was before the Isiq girl's trick in the shrine! You've no idea how close we came to ruin, that day. Pacu Lapadolma's credentials were mistranslated! What good is "a *general* daughter," damn your eyes, when we need the daughter of a general? We had to enlist our reserve man from the shrine to argue on her behalf, keep them all talking and considering, while we dug out old letters from her family.'

Alyash shrugged. 'What could I have done?'

'Examined her credentials before we passed them to that raving Babqri Father, of course. Not that he's raving any longer. That incubus tore him open like a pomegranate; I watched it all from the shadows.'

He lowered his voice, leaned close to Alyash. 'Tell, me, has Fulbreech been exposed?'

'Not a bit of it,' murmured Alyash with a smile. 'He has even claimed a little territory in the heart of Thasha Isiq.'

'Has he, now? Fine work; but let him understand that I will tolerate no scandal. Young fathers make useless spies; if he gets her with child I will toss him from the quarterdeck myself. Here, have a look at this.'

Ott freed the top button of his coat, and from an inner pocket drew out a strange device of wood, bronze and iron. On one end was a handle, somewhat like that of a saw; on the other a dark metal tube.

'What is it?' said Alyash. 'It looks like a toy cannon, except for the handle.'

'That is no toy,' said Sandor Ott. 'It is a pistol. All the mechanics of a ship's gun are right there in miniature.'

Alyash's jaw gradually slid open. 'By the iron kiss of the Arch-Devil,' he said, turning the instrument gingerly in his hands.

'You heretics amaze me,' said Ott, his tone a blend of scorn and affection. 'You're obsessed with purity, yet you invoke only the corruptors – the Pit fiends, the devils you detest. Where do you hide your god?'

Alyash shook his head. 'We've been over this ground for years, Ott – like two old nags. We of the Old Faith do not speak of that which you call "god." We do not cage the infinite in the small mind of man; that vanity we leave to others. Tell me, what is this lever for?'

'That is the serpentine; it lowers a burning match onto the powder charge. The explosion tends to ruin the serpentine, and sometimes the pistol itself. In truth it is not yet a practical tool. An arrow is swifter to fire, and much more accurate; a *vasctha* is deadlier if it strikes. But there can be only so much power in bent wood and stretched sinew, while the potential latent in *this*—' He gazed rapturously at the weapon '—is infinite. You are looking at the invention of our age. In time it will bring an end to all wars, for the alternative – can you imagine it, Alyash? A world equipped with these, and *using* them? – would simply be too ruinous for everyone.'

Alyash shook his head grimly. 'No, I can't imagine such a world.'

'When that day comes, the world will have no more need of us,' said Ott, sliding the pistol back into his coat. 'Enough, where's the captain? We must bear north immediately.'

Alyash led the spymaster forward, past rows of gaping sailors. When he caught their whispers ('Nagan, it's Commander Nagan!') Ott chuckled softly. They knew him – or rather, they knew the captain of Eberzam Isiq's honour guard. That costume, that papier-mâché man, one of the myriad counterfeit selves he had lived within.

Sandor Ott had lately come up with an image for his life. A solitary man on a desert road, the sun at perpetual noon, the road vanishing straight as an arrow behind him, and littered with bodies to the edge of sight. Usually he thought of these bodies as his aliases, the soldiers and merchants and monks he had not just impersonated but become, so completely that he suffered confusion when his fellow spies addressed him by his real name. *Sandor Ott:* what was that, anyway, but an earlier invention? Not a talisman, not a family name, for he had known no family but the Arquali Children's Militia, outlawed now, and slowly being rubbed out of the Empire's official histories. He did not know who in the militia had named him. He did not even know the name of his first language, or where in the Empire it was spoken, or quite when Arquali had replaced it for ever as the language of his thought.

At other times the bodies on the road were simply those who had stood in his way.

He and Alyash walked the length of the topdeck. Ott's eyes darted everywhere, studying the ship he had departed six weeks ago in Ormael. He asked questions in a sharp military style: 'How many tons of grain have you left? When did the men last eat vegetables? Has anyone been murdered? How in the Nine Pits did you damage your shrouds?'

At the mizzen they went below, and continued forward along the upper gun deck. Halfway down the portside battery, Alyash paused and looked the spymaster in the face.

'They sent me, Ott. They *ordered* me to seek a position.'

'Aboard an Arquali ship?'

The bosun shook his head. 'Aboard *Chathrand*. Specifically.'

Sandor Ott held very still. His eyes slid away from Alyash, darting again – but this time they were studying abstractions, facts arrayed before him, words and signs and evidence.

'They suspect us,' he said at last.

'Yes,' said Alyash.

'They cannot know of what. But they do suspect us. That's interesting.'

The bosun turned and spat. 'I suppose that's one word for it. Another would be "disastrous."'

Still Ott did not move. He might have been blind to the ship about him.

'The Babqri Father,' he said. 'Your orders came from him, didn't they?'

Alyash nodded. 'We answered to him, you realise: the Zithmoloch put their spies under his command for the duration of the wedding. And do you know who that girl was – the one the demon killed alongside the old priest?'

'A *sfvantskor* trainee – fully trained, almost, by the way she fought.'

'Ott, she was also the daughter of the Mzithrini admiral, Kuminzat.'

Sandor Ott's eyes refocused on the bosun, and a fascinated smile took possession of his face. Alyash squirmed at the sight of it. He had known Ott for decades, and that smile came to him only when the spymaster sensed an assault or an ambush, violence approaching like a predator from the woods. *No, not like a predator. Not in your case, Ott.* More like a loved one, his cherished intimate, whose absence he could bear only so long.

By midday they had rounded the little isle of Sandplume. On the north shore, two headlands like swollen knuckles bulged northwards, forming a dark, cliff-mantled cove. The reef, as Ott had promised, had been reduced to scattered rubble on the sea-bed, and the *Chathrand* glided easily into the sheltered waters. Inside, she was hidden from any possibility of view from south, east or west; and unless a ship was running between the isles, the next Black Shoulder to the north would hide them from that direction as well. The spymaster's cutter had arrived before them; her anchor was already down.

Captain Rose had not emerged that morning. He had Uskins greet Sandor Ott, to both men's displeasure. But once the Great Ship lay at ease beside the cutter he sat at his desk, uncapped a speaking-tube that rose like a beheaded snake from the corner, and began to issue commands.

Thirty minutes later Ott and Alyash arrived at his door, and the steward waved them in. Rose's cabin was bright, the air close and steamy: hot midday sun poured through the skylight and glittered on the silver service. Rose stood at the head of the table, carving a slab of salt-cured ham on a platter garnished with potatoes and turnips and slices of withered orange. There was also a cold crab stew in a gyroscopic cauldron, its feet screwed into the tabletop, the bowl itself on ball-bearings that kept it level against the rolling of the ship. Lady Oggosk and Drellarek were seated. Uskins was at the sideboard, pouring snifters of brandy.

Drellarek rose and gave Ott a precise military bow.

'Sergeant,' said Ott amiably.

'A great pleasure to have you back, sir,' said Drellarek.

Something hissed. Captain Rose gave a violent start. Ten feet away on his desktop, Sniraga stood with bristled fur, baring her fangs at the spymaster.

Ott's eyes travelled to the far end of the cabin. There, looking out through the gallery windows, stood Dr Chadfallow. He was drawn and dour, and clearly did not mean to offer any greetings of his own.

'He will not kill you, Doctor,' said Rose, whose eyes had not left the ham. 'You may join us at table.'

'I am not hungry,' said Chadfallow.

'Well I certainly am,' said Ott. 'Your hospitality arrives at a crawl, Captain.'

'This is not a social occasion,' said Rose.

'Indeed not,' said the spymaster. 'Come, Doctor, the captain speaks the truth. We all know of how you've broken faith with His Supremacy, and while it might be enough to condemn you in a court of law – well, we are a long way from the nearest courtroom, aren't we? Nor shall I seek vengeance for what passed between us in Ormael, any more than I shall against the duchess here. You were not to know why Syrarys and I were poisoning your old friend Isiq. A case could even be made that you acted out of loyalty to the crown.'

Chadfallow turned from the window and looked across the wide cabin at Ott.

'A false case,' he said.

Ott shrugged. 'This ship requires a doctor, and no one disputes that you are the finest. Indeed, we'll have need of your special skills within the hour. Where is our guest of honour, Sergeant?'

'The Shaggat's son?' said Drellarek. 'He is not fit company, Master Ott. Since his brother died, Erthalon Ness raves like never before. I thought you would prefer to deal with him later.'

'Quite right,' said Ott, 'but that is not who I meant.'

'The other will be delivered as soon as we lay hands on him,' said Drellarek. 'My men face a new complication in that regard.'

'So Alyash tells me,' said Ott. 'A magical wall about the stateroom, astonishing! Your arts are no match for it, then, Lady Oggosk?'

Lady Oggosk was sucking an orange wedge. 'My arts,' she said wetly, 'are at the service of the captain, not the Imperial butcher-boy.'

Ott smiled, but no one imagined he was pleased.

Rose was looking sharply at Alyash. 'Why have you brought him to this meeting, Ott?'

'I'm glad you ask,' said the spymaster, taking Alyash by the arm. 'Gentlemen, Lady Oggosk. You've met your new bosun, but I dare say you were not properly introduced. As well as being a first-class sailor, he happens to be an agent of my western rivals in the field of clandestine security.'

Silence. Drellarek studied the bosun inscrutably. Uskins, bewildered, looked from face to face. At last Ott's meaning dawned on him.

'A spy? A spy for the Black Rags?'

'You watch your mouth,' growled Alyash. 'I'm a son of the Holy Mzithrin, no matter what I'd like to see happen to her five criminal kings.' He surveyed the room. 'You Arqualis mean to conquer and cannibalise the Pentarchy. I know that; I'm not a blary fool. I help you because I realised long ago that domination by Arqual, however great an evil, was the only way to save my homeland from gory suicide. The Shaggat Ness was the worst of the Mzithrin's open sores, but he would not have been the last. I am not a traitor. I am simply a man who faces the truth.'

'Facing the truth is easier with twelve thousand gold a year,' muttered Oggosk.

'Yes, Mr Uskins, a spy,' said Ott quickly. 'What is more, the first spy ever to penetrate the ranks of the Shaggat's faithful on Gurishal. Which is to say, the first man placed on that island who was not quickly discovered, and shipped in pieces back to Babqri. His four predecessors lasted an average of a week before the Shaggat's worshippers found them out. Alyash lasted thirteen years. And even when the doubts began he managed to escape.'

'With a few souvenirs,' said Oggosk, picking at her teeth.

Alyash regarded her coldly. 'The Lady Oggosk makes reference to my scars,' he said at last. 'Would you like to know how I earned them, Duchess?'

'Not if it delays our meal.'

'When the Nessarim suspect a man of treason they hand him a knife and a mug of seawater. In the water floats a sarcophagus jellyfish – a creature so deadly that merely to touch one's lips after handling it means certain death. The suspect is given a choice: to open his veins then and there with the knife, or to swallow the whole mug of water at a gulp, jellyfish and all, and pray that the divine Shaggat neutralises the poison. They believe him capable of such miracles, even before he returns from the dead. They believe he waits in heaven, watching everything they do.

'I was accused of being a *sfvantskor* informant. I struck my chest three times, swore allegiance to the Shaggat, and demanded the mug. As they filled it I went to a corner to pray, and swallowed all the antitoxins I kept on my person. The fanatics knew quite well that no Mzithrini drug could protect against a sarcophagus jelly. But I had drugs from Arqual. That was my sixteenth year in Ott's service.'

'In the service of the Emperor,' Ott corrected.

'To swallow a sarcophagus jelly is to die in seconds,' said Alyash. 'I lay writhing for six minutes, burning inside. Then the believers decided I was one of them, and shoved a goad into my mouth, and I vomited onto my chin and chest, where the dissolved jellyfish burned deep into my skin. I lost consciousness, and they were afraid even to wash me clean. That, Lady Oggosk, is how I earned my *souvenirs*.'

Lady Oggosk's eyes were downcast. Then all at once she glanced up, realised he had finished, and waved at Rose impatiently. 'Serve the ham, Nilus, the ham!'

Ott and Alyash took their seats. Chadfallow walked to the threshold of Rose's day cabin, and leaned on the doorframe, watching the others attack their meal.

Rose pointed at Ott with his serving fork. 'You have robbed me of a bosun, Spymaster.'

'Not at all,' said the spymaster. 'Alyash has always worked from the deck of a ship – albeit a Mzithrini ship. There's more of worth in this officer than you realised, that's all.'

Chadfallow asked a clipped question in Mzithrini. Alyash glanced up at him, then lifted his bowl of crab stew and slurped.

'The doctor wishes to know how I came to be in Simja,' he said as he finished.

'That is the best part of it,' said Ott. 'The madmen on Gurishal were close to the truth, of course: Mr Alyash was not the Shaggat-worshipper he claimed. But they guessed that he was a *sfvantskor*, rather than what he was: a member of the Zithmoloch, the Pentarchy's formidable, if rather outmatched and archaic, guild of spies. But neither the Shaggat's men nor the Zithmoloch itself suspected the deeper truth: that he was *our* man from the start. Alyash told the Five Kings what *we* wished them to believe concerning Gurishal: that the Nessarim were weak and divided, that the Shaggat's return was a fading dream. Of course quite the opposite is true. And Alyash, meanwhile, propagated a myth among those zealots, those people starving for hope.'

'Ah!' said Drellarek. 'Then it was you who spread the prophecy of the Shaggat's return!'

'I lay the tinder, and struck the match,' said Alyash. 'But the prophecy spread of its own accord, like a blaze in dry grass. And when word reaches Gurishal that the daughter of an Arquali general has wed into a Mzithrin royal family, every man, woman and child on Gurishal will know that the hour of their God-King's return is at hand.'

'To complete the story,' said Ott. 'The Mzithrinis had never seen such an effective spy – of course they hadn't; I trained Alyash myself – and they were not about to let his service end with Gurishal. So they extended his scars to the *back* of his neck, obliterating his Mzithrini tattoos, and sent him to a place they wished desperately to infiltrate: Simjalla City, where the Great Peace would begin.'

'It was a natural choice,' said Alyash. 'My father traces his family line back to the Crownless Lands. At least a part of me is Simjan.'

Ott smiled, giving his brandy an interrogatory sniff. 'You might not think so,' he said, 'but most of the best spies in history are mongrels. Transplants, half-bloods, children of vagabond fathers or women taken in war.'

'Is that so for you, Mr Ott?' said Uskins, through a mouthful of ham. 'You're His Supremacy's best, of course, so—'

'Uskins,' said Rose, 'finish your meal in silence.'

'Oppo, sir.'

'And chew your food as befits a man.'

Sandor Ott was looking at Uskins as one might a horsefly whose buzzing one has resolved to suffer no more. Under his gaze the first mate became quickly unnerved. His knife squeaked. He chewed with great concentration.

'Stukey,' muttered Alyash in disgust.

Rose shot him a dark look. 'Alyash, is it the Mzithrini in you that thinks it well to visit your captain's table with a rag knotted at your neck?'

Alyash whipped the sweaty bandanna from his throat. 'Your pardon, sir.'

'I sent ashore for a bosun, not a spy. And I do not require a bosun of divided loyalties. Tell me, whom do you serve?'

'By the will of His Supremacy, sir, you are Captain and Final Offshore Authority. That means the mission is in your hands.'

'I know exactly how far my authority extends,' said Rose, 'but do you?'

'Sir, I am a true servant of Magad the Fifth. My loyalties are as clear to me now as they have been since I boarded.'

Rose looked at the man, visibly displeased with the answer. Then Lady Oggosk cleared her throat. Scraping at a patch of flaking skin on her hand, she said, 'Nilus, you should not give them leave to walk into Bramian. The island is an eater of men, and I'm not just speaking of the savages. The Lorg has a prayer-history for the husbands of its graduates who died in unwise excursions there, and the prayer takes days to chant.' She raised her milky eyes and looked squarely at Ott. 'Dreamers fare the worst,' she said.

Ott met her gaze, unblinking. 'It might surprise you to know, Duchess, that my men have been at work inside Bramian for over a year.'

'Fifty yards inside,' said Oggosk. 'And mostly underground. Not exactly the work of heroes, is it?'

There came a knock at the door. The steward answered, and whispered with someone on the threshold. Then he walked to the captain and bent to his ear.

'Let him be brought in at once,' said Rose. 'Dr Chadfallow, you will hold your tongue, or I shall have you removed.'

The steward returned to the door and swung it wide. There stood Pazel Pathkendle, held roughly by a gargantuan Turach. The youth's hands were tied behind his back, and a gag pulled his lips back severely. Fitted around his neck was a broad leather collar with iron studs, a bit like those worn by fighting dogs, except that this collar had an odd, ratchet-like device on one side.

The Turach dragged Pazel forward, into the sunlight. It was clear now that the collar was very tight, and that the rag in the boy's mouth was dark with blood. Pazel turned wild and furious eyes from one face to another. When at last they fell on Dr Chadfallow the rage that burned in them grew even stronger.

'I didn't hit him, Sergeant Drellarek,' said the soldier defensively. 'He just bit his tongue.'

'And then bit you?'

The Turach glanced sheepishly at his own bandaged forearm. He shook his head. 'That were the Treaty Bride,' he said. 'She had a blade.'

Rose was livid. 'My orders were not clear, then?'

'Sir, they were very clear; you wanted her brought as well. It mortifies me to tell you that she slipped away. I think she was expecting us, sir – she was that wary. And the Tholjassan and the Undrabust brat got in our way, and next thing we knew she was back in her blary luxury suite. But we have the Tholjassan in chains.'

Sandor Ott looked at him with amusement. 'You captured Hercól of Tholjassa? How many Turachs did *that* require?'

The soldier glanced rather stiffly at Ott. 'We gave him a knock to remember, sir, I promise you that. Captain Rose, I—'

Rose waved a hand for silence. 'Tie Pathkendle to the stanchion. Then go.'

The man did as he was told. Pazel, bound hand and foot to the wooden post, looked again at Chadfallow. He tried to speak: just one word through the bloody cloth. It might have been *traitor*. Chadfallow was very still, but his eyes were full of thought, fear, calculation. He looked like a man resigned to being hated.

Ott dabbed at his mouth with a napkin, then stood up. 'My good Niriviel overheard a fascinating confession from this boy,' he said, approaching Pazel. 'To wit, he is not the keeper of the Shaggat's spell, although he cast it. That explains why Arunis dared try to kill him. And why we may do so, if necessary.'

He laid a hand on the back of the collar around Pazel's neck. Then he looked deliberately at Chadfallow. 'Objections, Doctor? Now would be a fine time to share them.'

Chadfallow did not even look at the spy. His eyes were locked on Pazel, and they were bright and beseeching.

Ott's hand yanked at the buckle. There was a loud *click*, and Pazel gave a strangled moan. The collar had visibly tightened.

'Another two clicks, and I crush his windpipe. Not a very good interrogation tool, as one of my men pointed out: Mr Pathkendle is already deprived of speech. But marvellous for extracting signatures and the like. Would you really shed no tears, Chadfallow, after sponsoring the lad for so long? Come, we all know you loved his mother. Surely you can't be indifferent to the fate of her son?'

Slowly the doctor raised his eyes to Ott's face. 'Entirely,' he said. Then he turned and walked back towards the window.

Click.

Chadfallow whirled about. Pazel was writhing in his bonds; a pink froth was on his lips.

Drellarek sat up, professionaly interested. Uskins gaped in horror. A faint sound escaped Pazel's throat, like the squelch of a deck-rag being twisted dry.

'For Rin's sake, Nilus, we're eating,' grumbled Oggosk.

Rose gestured at the collar. 'Remove that thing,' he said. 'Chadfallow, if you do not intend to dine I suggest you make preparations.'

Ott touched something on the buckle. The collar sprang loose, and Pazel fell forward with an agonised gasp. The spymaster returned to his meal.

'What I still cannot fathom,' said Drellarek, passing his plate, 'is the nature of the uprising you have engineered. Let us presume for a moment that the mage is mad – that he cannot grant the Shaggat the power to wield this Nilstone, however great or small a weapon it may be.'

'We presume *nothing* in this campaign,' said Ott. 'We will take the Nilstone for ourselves, and tame or kill the sorcerer, long before we arrive at Gurishal. Indeed it will be the first order of business, once the Shaggat is restored to life.'

'All the better,' said Drellarek. 'But how is the Shaggat's horde to threaten the Mzithrin? They have no navy, surely?'

Alyash shook his head. 'Fishing boats, near-shore vessels, a few brokendown brigs.'

'Why then,' said Drellarek, 'how are they even to *engage* the White Fleet – let alone threaten it? Have they any hope of a general breakout from Gurishal?'

'They have hope in their prophecy,' said Ott. 'And their faith is ferocious, while that of the Five Kings is weak. Remember that the Mzithrin nearly conquered the world, only to be defeated from within by the splintering of their own religion. The Nessarim, by contrast, have belief in a god who walked among them: a god who defied the greatest empire in Alifros, and who may yet return to rule it. Nothing will turn them from that dream.

'They have useful delusions; we have specific tactics. And tomorrow's excursion will play a part in both.'

Ott sat back, and Rose leaned his massive elbows on the table. In the silence Pazel raised his head and found all of them looking at him.

'Are you quite finished, Duchess?' Rose inquired.

Oggosk pushed away her soup bowl. *'Glah.'*

'Very well,' said Rose.

Pazel tensed. His tormentors' eyes shifted. Pazel turned his head and saw Chadfallow coming towards him with what looked like a small, swan-necked watering pail. The doctor was very quick. He grabbed Pazel's hair in his left hand and wrenched his head back, then forced the pail's spout through the boy's lips and past the bloody rag. Before Pazel knew what was happening he had swallowed a mouthful of something bitter and warm. Chadfallow removed the spout and caught Pazel's chin in his hand, making sure the rest of the liquid went down his throat. His look was fierce and dangerous, but unlike Ott he showed no sign of enjoying what he did. A moment later he released Pazel and stepped back.

'You may proceed,' he said to the spymaster.

'So soon?'

'It will have happened already, if it is going to happen at all.'

Sandor Ott moved in front of Pazel, who was coughing and shaking. 'Calm yourself,' he said. 'It is no poison. Where that's concerned I scarcely need a doctor's help. Now listen to me carefully, Pathkendle. *Urtale preda nusali ch'ulthanon.*'

The words were like a kick to the stomach. Pazel stared up into Ott's cold eyes. The spymaster nodded. And Pazel slammed his head back against the stanchion with a wail of grief that wracked his body more terribly than the pain of a few minutes before.

'Great Rin above!' said Drellarek. 'He understood!'

'Peace, boy!' laughed Ott. 'I was citing ancient literature, not telling you of my actual deeds. *Urtale preda nusali ch'ulthanon:* 'I sent your mother to an early death.' The confession of the doomed hero of the *Song of Itash*, written nineteen centuries ago by an anonymous whore in the court of the Amber Kings.'

Pazel's heart was hammering. His eyes were wide with terror and confusion.

'And yet you scarcely noticed me switching tongues,' Ott went on. 'Your Gift is working, lad. Chadfallow's drug has just induced it. And to you, Doctor, my hearty congratulations. If we can truly access his Gift whenever the need arises, Mr Pathkendle may yet prove as beneficial as once you claimed.'

Pazel twisted around to look at the doctor. Whatever mix of emotions he had felt before was gone. There was nothing in his eyes but hate.

Chadfallow did not meet his gaze. 'The drug is not perfect,' he said. 'The boy may suffer some disorientation, some loss of bearings, until the process ends in the normal manner.'

'Normal,' said Drellarek with a smirk. 'You mean with jabbering fits.'

'Just look at that face!' laughed Uskins. 'It's the *muketch* you should be afraid of, Doctor. He hates you. Give him half a chance and he'll put a knife in your belly.'

'Mr Uskins,' said Rose, 'you will escort Pathkendle to the brig. Have his dinner brought there, and his foul-weather clothes. And instruct the cobbler to make him a pair of shoes by evening. Shoes, not sandals.'

'Oppo, Captain, shoes it is.'

Oggosk squinted at Pazel. 'What are you staring at, boy?'

Pazel started. He felt as if they had beaten him with clubs. But it was true, he *had* been staring, mute and amazed – at Captain Rose. The man's sleeve had ridden up towards the elbow. Seeing it now, Rose hastily pulled the sleeve down again. But it was too late, and he knew it. Pazel had seen what Rose wished no one to see: a wolf-shaped scar above his wrist.

'Get the boy out of here,' said Rose. 'And let us conclude our business swiftly. The day is waning, and tomorrow we shall all be tested.'

'The tarboy's passed a test already,' said Drellarek, smirking again.

'Just one,' said Sandor Ott, 'the easiest.'

23

Bramian

~~~

21 Freala 941
130th day from Etherhorde

Her heart is a throbbing beast, her body a wilderness, her shores a stone wall and her few harbours held by savages who roast their foes on spits. Great teams of explorers set off for her interior; months later broken men straggle out with tales of whip scorpions and swarms of carnivorous bats, and great monsters that bask on riverbanks or blend with the trees. There are also stories of lost races of thinking beings, whole cities perhaps, in the valleys of her central range.

Whatever the truth of such tales, on this you may rely: Bramian is merciless. If you contemplate some exploitation of her riches, be warned: only the very wealthy, and very disciplined, have succeeded in turning a profit on this island twice the size of the Westfirth. 'Above all,' writes one old survivor, 'let your stay be brief. Cut a swathe of jungle, mine a little ore, take a few hundred hides – and be gone. If you do this you may live to enjoy your takings, however smaller than your appetite they prove.'

– The Merchant's Polylex, 18th Edition (959), p. 4186.

He passed a night of dark dreams in which he crept over canyons on bridges of scrapwood and straw. Every step caused the bridges to groan and bend, and yet he had no choice but to cross the dismal gorges. Now and then he would half-wake and find himself curled against the wall of the brig, intensely grateful for its solidity, for the absence of an abyss, but then the drug's haze would claim him again.

At dawn the spymaster came for him. Pazel leaped up with raised fists, light on his feet if nearly out of his mind, striking the stance Hercól had taught him at their first lesson in the stateroom. It seemed necessary to demonstrate his hatred of the spymaster, of his whole clan of murdering liars. But Ott just laughed and sidled towards him without making eye contact and felled him with three blows. Pazel never saw Ott's hands at all, until they lifted him by the shirt.

Minutes later he was on the floor of a skiff, descending the dark wall of the *Chathrand* to the rhythmic clanging of the davit-chains. Ott and Drellarek were seated near him, and ahead of them sat the tarboy brothers Swift and Saroo. Neither of the Jockeys glanced at him as the boat rattled seaward. He could hear the murmur of other men, the rasp of Turach armour. A man's voice chattered indignantly from the stern. *You should treat me as an equal, Warden. And even that is a great concession. Remove these straps! You are a mortal man. I am the son of the divine.*

They struck the waves with a smack. Pazel bolted upright, only to feel Drellarek's stone-hard hand on his shoulder. Men were fighting the chains, fending them off the *Chathrand* with oars, while the twenty-foot skiff pitched like a rocking horse. Even in his delirium Pazel knew he must keep still.

At last they were clear. The sail shot up. Elkstem held the wheel, Rose the gaff, and together they calmed the boat and took her out of the cove.

Pazel ground his teeth. Chadfallow had a drug that could force his mind open to languages, force his Gift to start performing on command. That, Pazel thought, was the missing piece of the puzzle. The doctor had not brought Pazel along as some sort of favour. He did not mean to reunite him with his family at all, because Pazel's family reunited was the *last* thing he wanted. No, he had brought Pazel along as a tool: one that could help him regain Suthinia, wherever she was; and one that could keep Chadfallow himself in the good graces of Rose and Sandor Ott. Whoever or whatever they met with on this voyage, Pazel would be there to offer his special services. *You haven't stopped the conspiracy, you've become a part of it.*

Bramian groped towards them, a giant on hands and knees. The sound of waves shattering against her cliffs grew to awesome proportions, as if Bakru's lions were indeed prowling the breakers, hurling their wrath against the land. Pazel knelt in the cold bilgewater, nauseous and dizzy. He put his fingers in his ears, but there was another kind of roaring inside.

The shore birds found them, and began to wheel and shriek. There was no shore: just the stone cliffs, and a number of titanic rocks half-submerged in the swell. Where were they to land? Elkstem kept them running straight for Bramian, while Ott stood watching at the bow. *They're all mad*, Pazel thought, shutting his eyes, *unless I am*.

When he looked again time seemed to have leaped forwards. They were in the island's shadow, right among the rocks. The sail was furled and the mast struck down, and straight ahead of them was a round black hole in the cliff.

'Pathkendle!' roared Elkstem. 'Take your blary oar!'

He stumbled to an oar-seat. The cave mouth, which all but vanished with each swell, was the width of a minor temple's doorway. On either side the waves exploded against the cliffs, vaulting skyward in spray and foam. But at the cave itself the sea raced into the dark, only to flow out again with a vast obscene slurp. 'Row!' Elkstem was screaming. Everyone but he and the Shaggat's son had taken up oars.

Twenty feet: they rose and plunged, and the sea broke over the stern. The foam atop each wave nearly brushed the roof of the cavern. Pazel saw Drellarek make a hasty sign of the Tree.

'Save me, Father!' wailed Erthalon Ness.

'Ship oars!' Rose bellowed. 'Heads down and hands inside!'

Pazel wrenched his oar into the skiff. He threw himself down, the daylight vanished, the gunnels scraped the top of the cave mouth, and then like a grape sucked through greedy lips they were through, blasting down a straight stone tunnel on the force of the wave. Pazel crouched in two feet of water, Alyash on one side and Drellarek on the other. It was impossible to guess how far the wave had borne them.

But just as it began to recede more shouts erupted – shouts from somewhere beyond the boat. A grinding noise echoed behind them, and instantly they slowed.

Pazel raised his head. The cave had widened into a circular chamber some sixty feet across. Around the perimeter stone ledges had been cut at various heights, and bright fengas lamps hung from wooden posts. Pazel looked back the way they had come, and saw men labouring on an iron platform, bolted to the rock near the tunnel mouth. They were turning a heavy wheel, connected by chains and pulleys to a half-submerged granite slab. The slab itself was mounted on rails, and it was sliding over the tunnel mouth. Even as Pazel watched it ground to a halt. The tunnel was sealed. 'Welcome to Bramian, Master,' said someone ashore.

The next thing Pazel remembered was climbing a stair. The way was steep and dark; far ahead someone carried a single bobbing lamp. '*Where* is my brother?' Erthalon Ness was whimpering. 'You killed him, didn't you? Are you going to kill me?'

It was on the stair that Pazel noticed the sharpened hearing that sometimes accompanied his Gift. He could catch every whisper and echo: Alyash's soft curse in Mzithrini, Rose's wheeze as he lurched up each step.

How is it going to end? When will the mind-fit come?

At last they reached a broad wooden door. Ott stepped to the front and gave a sharp, four-note whistle. From the far side, startling everyone but Ott himself, came a woman's laugh.

Bolts slid free. The door swung outwards, forcing them to shuffle backwards. A brighter lamplight flooded the stair. And in the doorway stood Syrarys Isiq.

She put out her hand to the spymaster. Her beauty left the men abashed. She wore a white blouse embroidered with red coral beads and a necklace of cobalt-blue pearls. Her olive skin glowed in the lamplight, and her sumptuous lips curled with mirth, as if the men crowded below her on the steps were part of some great parlour-game whose rules she knew better than anyone. 'We beat you by a full day, darling,' she said.

Ott took her hand and kissed it. 'I have been here four,' he said, 'keeping watch by sea, until the Great Ship reached her hiding place.'

Syrarys spread the fingers of the hand Ott had kissed. Along with rings of gold and silver, diamond and bloodstone, she wore a simple, tarnished ring of brass. 'A little bird gave me that one,' she said.

Ott laughed, then took the ring from her finger and slipped it on his own. 'Come, Syrarys,' he said. 'You know what this day holds.'

He swept through the door and into a great stone chamber, and the woman who had raised Thasha from a child went with him. As he stepped into the chamber Pazel recalled the creaking bridges of his dreams. He felt as if he were upon one again. They told us she died in Ormael. They told us she leaped from a tower into the sea. We know nothing, we're toys in their hands.

They bound his wrists with metal cuffs and sat him in a corner, too far from the hearth to be warmed in that chilly underground. Unlike the chamber below this was not a natural cave; the room, and several others adjoining, were carved from the living rock. They gave him water and ship's biscuit, later a handful of berries that resembled coffee beans and tasted like sweet smoked grubs.

Syrarys came to look at him, with Ott beside her. Hatred shone in her eyes.

'Thasha's little friend,' she said. 'Do you know what her father did to me, bastard? Something much worse than rape or beatings. He bought me, like a dog. He groomed and bathed me and took me out in society on a leash, so that the Etherhorde nobles could admire my tricks.'

'That's not what I heard,' said Pazel. 'I heard Isiq never asked for a slave at all. That the Emperor sent you to him, and the old man didn't think he could refuse.' He looked at Ott. 'I wonder who gave His Supremacy *that* idea.'

Syrarys slapped him, hard. Pazel raised his shackled hands to his face. 'I believe the part about doing tricks, though,' he said.

She would have struck him again if Ott hadn't drawn her away. Pazel found himself wondering what Thasha would do if Syrarys returned to the *Chathrand*.

The drug-delirium came and went. Several hours in that windowless chamber simply vanished. When his memory returned it moved in leaps, like a stone skipping on a lake. Men around a table. Captain Rose brooding over a chart. Elkstem waving his hands, shouting, *I can't blary say, Captain! You don't get that close to the Vortex and live to tell!* Drellarek sharpening a hatchet. The Shaggat's son chained to the wall, asleep.

At another moment he woke with Syrarys' voice in his ears, and flinched, expecting pain. But she was nowhere near him. He raised his head and saw her with Ott on the far side of the chamber. They were kissing, and arguing between the kisses. Pazel's strange hearing brought it all to his ears.

Want to go with you.

No, dearest. The job in Simja only you can accomplish.

You said Isiq would be the last one!

I said I hoped, Syrarys. But there was madness when the girl collapsed.

You bastard. I'll make you pay. I'll sleep with your spies. The pretty ones, the youngest.

Don't try it. They fear me even more than they desire you.

Care to bet?

Pazel's head swam. He fought to stay awake, to hear more of their argument, but the darkness closed over him again.

Later they stood him up and walked him to the table. It was by now covered with books, scrolls, loose vellum sheets. Nearly everything was old; some of the books appeared positively ancient. *Look*, they said, and spread before him something that might have been a scrap of sailcloth with old grey stains. *Look there. What is that?*

'Your finger?' he said.

Rose seized his ear and twisted savagely, as if annoyed to find it so tightly fastened to his head.

'There's writing, Pathkendle. Lean closer.'

Tears of pain in his eyes, Pazel leaned over the canvas. The faces around the table watched him breathless. Rose was pointing at a symbol in pale blue ink. Was it a character, a word? The only thing Pazel was sure of was that he'd never seen its like before.

His vision blurred; he shut his eyes, and when he opened them again he read the word as easily as though it were his own name:

'"Port of Stath Bálfyr."'

The men exclaimed: some relieved, others in doubt. 'I told you,' said Syrarys, her voice softly ardent. 'I *told* you it came from a chart.'

'What's that language, then, cub?' asked Drellarek, pointing at the canvas.

Pazel hesitated. 'N–Nemmocian,' he said at last. It was the truth, but he only discovered it by speaking the word aloud.

'Where is the tongue spoken, lad?' asked Sandor Ott.

'How in the Pits should I know?'

'The boy's Gift does not extend so far,' said Dr Chadfallow. 'He learns nothing of the culture of the languages he ... acquires. Nothing but what one may deduce from the words themselves.'

'Then we're no better off than before!' huffed Alyash. 'Why, we could spend the rest of our lives looking for a place called Stath Bálfyr, where they may or may not speak something called Nemmocian. And begging your pardon, Lady Syrarys, but we *can't* be certain this was torn from a chart.'

'I don't understand,' said Pazel.

The men looked at him uncertainly. It was Sandor Ott, of all people, who broke the silence.

'The world beyond the Ruling Sea,' he said, 'is not *entirely* forgotten. What you see before you is all that the libraries, archives and private collections of the known world have yielded to my investigators, after a decade of searching.'

He lifted an ancient book, cracked it open, blew. The page flaked and crumbled.

'Not much to show for our labours, is it?' said Ott. 'But there were a few helpful discoveries: that first canvas gives us some idea of the shape of the coastline we may reach. Another document seems to be a list of surnames – royal families, in all probability – and the lands they govern. But the jewel in this musty hoard is a page from a diary or log-book. I will not show it here, for it is so delicate that each time we remove it from its case a portion crumbles to dust. We have copied it out, however – word by word, number by number.'

Pazel's head was swimming; he was finding Ott's words very difficult to follow. 'What . . . does it tell you?' he managed to ask.

'Headings,' said the spymaster. 'Course headings, and distances, from Stath Bálfyr to lands *on this side* of the Ruling Sea. Lands we know, cities that yet exist, even though the names have changed. Eldanphul, the old name of Uturphe. Marseyl, that the Noonfirth Kings renamed for their founder, Lord Pól. And one island whose name has not changed: Gurishal. Do you see, Pathkendle? If we can but find this Stath Bálfyr, we will know the exact course to the Shaggat's kingdom, and the multitude that awaits him.'

'*If* we find it,' said Alyash, shaking his head.

'Yes,' said Ott, 'if. Unfortunately the collector of ancient manuscripts who owned this particular scrap of writing . . . died, trying to stop my men from seizing it. And his records contain no mention of the page.'

Syrarys turned impatiently from the table. 'You needn't explain things to the tarboy,' she said.

Ott looked Pazel up and down. 'I am following my instincts with this one,' he said. 'The ignorant make poor servants. For as long as he is with us, he must grasp the fundamentals. Of course, he will not be with us for ever.'

'What do you mean by *that*?' demanded Chadfallow, leaning forwards.

The spymaster ignored him. 'Pathkendle,' he said softly, 'do the words *Stath Bálfyr* mean something in themselves?'

'No,' said Pazel.

It came out too quickly, a blurted denial. Sergeant Drellarek sat back with a laugh.

Ott turned to look at Chadfallow. 'There's an answer for you, Doctor. Your tarboy has just lied, very clumsily. My boys in the School of Imperial Security tell better falsehoods after thirty minutes of training. How long will Pathkendle be with us? A short time indeed, if he fails to answer my questions. But long enough to hear one or more of his friends beg for death: a death Ramachni's spell, alas, will make it inconvenient to provide.'

Pazel swallowed. He was only too aware how easily Ott could carry out his threats. Thasha, Neeps and Marila would be forced to leave the protection of the stateroom in short order if Rose let the spymaster cut off their food.

'Look at him, he's stalling,' said Syrarys.

Fascination glimmered in Ott's eyes. 'No, he is considering his choices. He's a thoughtful lad.'

Diadrelu. Pazel closed his eyes. *Forgive me*.

'Answer the question, Pathkendle,' said Rose.

'*Sanctuary*,' said Pazel. 'Stath Bálfyr means *Sanctuary-Beyond-the-Sea*.'

Broad daylight. Somehow Pazel had slept the night away, chained once more in his corner. He shook his head fiercely. He had no memory of waking at all.

He was on horseback, clinging to the saddle horn, startled out of his trance. Birds were singing; the great black horse pranced in the mud; and around him a million leaves and fronds and flowers glittered from a recent downpour.

It was already hot; Pazel felt as though some great animal were breathing on him. Yet the noise of the sea was close and loud, and off to his left he saw a place where the trees ended, and blue sky began. He knew suddenly where he was: atop the cliffs, on the edge of Bramian's great wilderness. It felt like trespassing, like putting a toe through some forbidden doorway just to see what would happen.

Ott climbed into the saddle behind him. Pazel stiffened: it was frightful to be so close to the assassin, with his scarred and deadly hands gripping the reins on either side. Pazel had heard the phrase *Stath Bálfyr* whispered among the Ixchel. Only once or twice, when they forgot his abilities; and they spoke it with reverence, like a holy name. He had given something sacred to the most profane man he'd ever known.

Ott turned the horse in a half-circle, and Pazel caught a glimpse of the cave mouth, low like a burrow and all but invisible with greenery. There were other horses: one bore Chadfallow, another Alyash. Swift and Saroo were mounted also; their horses carried large leather purses secured to chaps before the riders' knees. The last and largest steed bore Drellarek and Erthalon Ness, the latter gazing in horror at the jungle about them.

Ott waved his men back underground. Then he turned to the other riders and raised a cautioning hand.

'The first part of this journey is likely to be the foulest,' he said softly. 'Stay close to me, and do not stop unless I do. Trust your horse's footing: these are the noblest animals His Supremacy could provide, and mountain-trained from birth. Away, now! Ride fast and silent, as you value your lives.'

With that he spurred his horse into the bush. There seemed no path at first, and they crashed (far from silently) through great sprays of palm and ferns and creepers. But very soon the underbrush thinned. Huge trees loomed over them, craggy black-barked monsters laden with vines and mosses and dangling epiphytes. The horses were indeed magnificent. They dodged roots and rocks, and somehow guarded their riders' balance at the same time.

They began a steep ascent, criss-crossing a gurgling stream. In patches of sunlight over the water Pazel saw butterflies of iridescent blue, rising in sapphire clouds at their approach.

'Where are you taking us?' he asked.

'Quiet!' said Ott. 'Or you'll find I've taken you only to your grave. We are ascending the mountain known in the Outer Isles as *Droth'ulad*. An evil corner of a vast, evil isle.'

'Evil?' said Pazel. 'But it's beautiful. Look at it.'

'I am most certainly looking,' said Ott, who was in fact peering deep into the trees ahead. 'Yes, evil: the name means Skull of Droth, the Demon-Prince. But it is not Droth who threatens us now. I am looking for the Leopard People. This has been their part of Bramian for longer than anyone from the outer world has been coming here. Fortunately for us they fear to climb Droth'ulad, but they will slip around its base sometimes, to hunt monkeys or wild dogs. They are master archers, and will kill us if they can.'

'Why do they fear the mountain?'

'Because something lives at the summit that kills *them*. Not the demon himself, I think, but perhaps something not greatly to be preferred. We would do better to avoid that place ourselves. But the ridgetop is the only swift path to our destination, and Elkstem swears we must put to sea in a matter of days or be kept from all hope of safe passage by the Vortex.'

'But what in the Nine Pits do you want on Bramian?'

'Nothing whatsoever. It is our allies' wants that concern me.'

'Allies?'

'Be silent, lad.'

The way grew steeper yet, and they were forced to slow the horses to a walk. There was a path of sorts, now: a meandering mud track, full of roots and snags and fallen trees. Weird shocks of colour met their eyes: a fleshy orange fungus that seemed to glow in the shadows, a scarlet hummingbird, a metallic-gold moth. Now and then the path left the cover of the forest to skirt clifftops, jutting like grey teeth from the blanketing green. At such moments Pazel looked down on steaming valleys, over lakes and serpentine rivers, and once he saw a ring of standing stones upon a treeless hilltop, and a thread of rising smoke.

But the sounds were a torment. Whistles, hoots and howls: the noise of countless birds and beasts, never seen except as shadows, flickers of movement, hints of wings. Worst of all were the insects. His altered hearing made their whines, drones, chirps and buzzings hideously distinct. When they bit him near his ears he heard the piercing of his skin.

Up they went, hour upon hour. Rain came and went with astonishing force. When it grew strong enough to blind them Ott would signal a halt, and the horses would stand steaming in the cold spray as the path became a river gushing about their legs. Pazel covered his ears, deafened. But the downpours were brief, and it seemed that the instant the last drops fell the sun came dappling through.

Once more Pazel's mind became clouded, and he lost all sense of time. One minute he would be clinging to the horse's mane as the animal struggled up some narrow ravine; the next he would be staring at a hairy vine as thick as his arm, only to discover that it was a monstrous centipede, scurrying up a trunk.

At still another moment he found himself listening to the half-hearted daytime hoot of an owl. No one else seemed able to hear the bird, and Pazel could not find it in the canopy overhead. But he heard its mate answer, and a soft flutter of wings. And then (Pazel caught his breath sharply) the first owl spoke in words. Its voice was black and velvety, the voice of a night hunter woken by day.

'I should like to know where they think they're going.'

'You could ask,' said the other, in a higher voice.

'They're savages, my dear fool. They speak no tongue of Bramian.'

The second owl trilled uneasily. 'I do not like this mountain. I can taste sea air, and it frightens me. The shorebirds' talk is always full of fear, warships, movements of men. Let us go inland tonight. Where the world is still whole.'

'We will go to the Court of Grethim,' said the first owl. 'The priest will *welcome us, and let us hunt in the spice gardens, and perhaps I will read another story from his book of leaves.'*

Pazel never told anyone about the woken owls. He had an awful image of Sandor Ott trying to shoot them from the branches. He stopped searching for them with his eyes, and the birds did not speak again.*

Onwards, upwards. At last Pazel's acute hearing diminished, and he began to feel more like himself. Far above them, he thought the texture of the forest changed, as though something immense stood among or behind the trees. Then Drellarek reined in his horse. He pointed up into a nearby tree. A large white monkey dangled there, its back to them, motionless, dead. It was pinned to the trunk by an arrow.

Ott cursed. 'We've startled them,' he said. 'The Leopard People don't just abandon their kills. And blood is yet leaking from that wound. Forward! It is a race now, and we must win.'

He said a soft word to his horse and it charged up the slope, abandoning the trail in favour of a straight line for the summit. Pazel heard the other horses thundering behind.

Suddenly a human voice spoke from the jungle. *'What are they, Uncle?'*

Pazel jumped, startling both Ott and the horse.

'They are men like us,' replied another, older voice. *'But they are slavers from across the sea. Don't fear them, boy. They will take no slaves today.'*

'Damn you, be still!' growled the spymaster.

'Mr Ott,' said Pazel, struggling to keep his voice low and calm. 'They've found us. They're watching.'

Suddenly Erthalon Ness gave a squeal of terror, pointing a finger at the jungle to their left. Pazel turned and saw them: scores of long-limbed figures, racing through the forest with the swiftness of cats. They wore loincloths only, and their pale yellow bodies were dabbed all over with spots of black. Some of the men carried strange iron hooks, and all had bows over their shoulders.

The riders cried out, and the horses increased their speed. But the footing was terrible now that they were running sidelong to the slope,

---

* But Greysan Fulbreech learned of them on a plundering foray into Pathkendle's footlocker. Among other thefts, Fulbreech helped himself to a few loose pages titled simply, 'In Case You Live to Remember'. After recounting the conversation of the birds, Pathkendle writes: 'Lady Oggosk must be wrong. How could the Waking Spell be a curse if it made those owls, and Felthrup, and so many other wonderful creatures?' The pages went to the Secret Fist, and so, in good time, to me. – EDITOR.

and more than once Pazel would have been thrown from the saddle if Ott had not held him fast.

'Talk to me, Pathkendle!' he roared.

'Talk?'

'Why do you think you're *here*, fool? Use your Gift! Tell me what they're saying!'

Pazel listened. But the men were only shouting things like *Fast* and *That way* and *Not the horses!*

'Just keep going!' he said to Ott. 'They're only – Wait! Damn! They're in the trees, Ott! They're going to shoot us from the trees!'

Even as he spoke Alyash howled in pain. A long black arrow quivered in his thigh. Somehow the bosun managed to spur his horse on. Above them, scores of voices cried out, like hounds on the hunt. More arrows whizzed about their ears. Looking back, Pazel saw the trees filled with the spotted men, climbing down head-first from the upper canopy, using the hooks they carried like claws. In a heartbeat they had dropped to the ground.

'Turn!' cried Ott. 'They will drive us into another trap if they can! We must gain the mountaintop!'

Once again they aimed their steeds uphill. The poor creatures were frothing with the effort now, their legs and bellies plastered with mud. But they ran on, and seconds later Ott's fears were confirmed. An even larger band of the Leopard People rose from the underbrush to their right: just where the horses would have carried them in another few strides.

The pursuit was fierce, but not even those born to the forest could run with the speed of horses. Soon only the fastest runners were still giving chase. Pazel heard them shout to one another as they fell behind:

Why do the horses obey them?
They enslave horses too.
They're going to the Ma'tathgryl.
They will die.

For ten minutes longer they charged uphill. Then at last the spymaster reined in his mount, and they walked, dazed and stumbling. Chadfallow rode up alongside Ott and Pazel.

'Your savages climbed higher on Droth'ulad than you reckoned with, Ott.'

'They hate us a great deal,' said Ott, grinning wolfishly. 'They take all outsiders for Volpeks, who set snares for their children and make

317

mercenaries out of them, or hawk them to the Flikkermen.'

'Then their hate is warranted,' said Chadfallow, 'since your operations here depend on Volpek supply ships. Let me extract that arrow, Bosun, before you faint.'

'Pah,' said Alyash. 'We should not stop here. I have lost but little blood.'

'You may before we reach the summit.'

'Look up, Doctor,' said Sandor Ott.

Pazel raised his eyes, and gasped. They stood nearly at the mountain's crest. And looming over them, all but lost in the trees crowding the summit, rose a wall.

It was a clearly a ruin – but such a ruin! Pazel had seen walls as high in the great keeps of Etherhorde and Pól, but those walls lay in the hearts of mighty cities, not lost in the wilderness. And the wall before him ran east and west along the mountain-top until it vanished in the trees. The builders, whoever they were, had not flattened the ridge but carved mammoth, sinuous yellow stones to fit its curves. The effect was of something more alive than constructed.

They drew closer; Pazel arched his neck. High overhead the wall sprouted turrets and towers and vine-laden balconies. Birds flew through gaping windows; orchids flowered in cracks. Yet for a thing so clearly ancient the wall was surprisingly intact.

When they reached the wall Ott turned them east. Chadfallow trailed a hand over the mossy stone. 'In Etherhorde we have one broken column, and a bit of an arch,' he mused.

'What's that you're saying?' asked Pazel. The doctor looked at him, startled. It was the first time Pazel had spoken to him on the island.

'I am saying that this is the work of the Amber Kings,' said Chadfallow. 'That this whole great edifice was built before the World-storm, and survived it.'

'That's a lot to swallow,' said Drellarek.

'Look at the stonework. Only the first lords of Alifros had such skill.'

'Why would the Amber Kings want to build in the middle of a jungle?' asked Erthalon Ness.

The riders stopped their horses, staring at him. Pazel had never heard half so sane an utterance come from the Shaggat's son. Chadfallow looked the man up and down, clearly fascinated. Pazel half-expected him to take the man's pulse.

'Well?' the son demanded.

'The jungle has grown back,' said Chadfallow. 'In their time – over two thousand years ago – the Amber Kings cleared many a mountain, with fire and the axe. They built great cities atop them. Fortress-cities, whole settlements in one mighty structure. No enemy could dream of taking them.'

'No enemy but Alifros herself,' said the Shaggat's son.

'Quite so,' said Chadfallow, still more amazed. 'But the Worldstorm did not strike all lands equally. Somehow this corner must have been spared – perhaps the great bulk of Bramian sheltered it from the driving winds. In any event the Amber Kings ruled from their summit cities for hundreds of years before the Storm. By day farmers descended the slopes to grow food on terraces – those flat shelvings we crossed – and by night they slept soundly in their fortress chambers. That is what the old tales tell. Do you understand me, Erthalon Ness?'

The Shaggat's son gave a nod. Then he looked back down the mountain.

'When my father returns he will cut no trees,' he said dreamily, 'for I will ask him to be kind to the white monkeys. This will be their republic. They will bear my name.'

It was almost a relief to hear him raving again. They said no more, but walked on in the shadow of the wall. Pazel found himself wondering if a sane man lay trapped somewhere inside the lunatic. The fate seemed worse than any lightless prison. *And could the reverse be true?* he wondered. *Do sane folk carry madmen locked in their minds?*

After a quarter-hour they came to the remains of a mighty gate. The ironwork had melted away with the centuries – only a few rusty spokes protruded from the stone – and no one could say what kind of sculpted beasts crouched on the pedestals to either side. A heaving of land that might once have been a road curved away from the opening and down into the trees.

Inside the gate was a portico, roofless and choked with greenery. Just beyond it a mighty staircase ascended, also open to the sky. It climbed all the way to the top of the fortress, where the sun beat down dazzling on the yellow stone.

Ott checked his horse at the threshold.

'Water the mounts,' he said, 'and dig the stones from their hooves. Give them no food, but eat a bit yourselves. Here, Pathkendle, take the reins.'

With that he slipped to the ground, adjusted his weapons belt and ran with quick, catlike movements up the stair.

'What in the Nine Pits is he up to?' said Alyash. 'He said the fortress was our destination. Now he talks as though we've another ride to look forward to.'

'I think both may be true,' said Chadfallow. 'But now I will see to that arrow, if you please.'

The tarboys picked rocks from the horses' hooves while Chadfallow tended Alyash. The bosun never made a sound, but his face creased with agony when the doctor at last twisted the arrowhead (a barbed thing made of bone) out of his thigh. After that he was quite calm. He chatted and joked as Drellarek cut slices of bacon with his dagger, and Chadfallow plucked bits of legging from the wound with tweezers.

'Mend the trousers when you're done with the leg,' said Drellarek with a laugh. 'We want him to make a good impression on our allies, don't we? Here, boys, eat.'

'Who are these allies, Mr Drellarek?' asked Swift through his first mouthful. But the Turach shook his head and made no answer.

Pazel took his slice of gristly bacon. He was famished, but all the same he felt a stab of guilt. *Eating from the Throatcutter's hand. Part of the team. Like Chadfallow, just doing a job.*

By the time they finished eating Sandor Ott was descending the stair. As he reached them Pazel saw that his face was strained.

'What's wrong, Master Ott?' asked Drellarek.

The spymaster's hands twitched at his sides. When he spoke there was a tremor in his voice. 'The stair leads onto the roof of the fortress-city,' he said, 'and from there a path runs straight and level to the place where we descend. You will ride on my left, at a walk, and you will not speak. But if I give the order you must gallop like the very wind. I have just learned who is master of this mountain. It is an eguar.'

Chadfallow's eyes snapped up. 'You saw it?' he said.

Ott nodded. 'It lies basking in the sun.'

'Fire from Rin,' whispered Drellarek.

'An eguar?' squealed Erthalon Ness. 'An eguar! What is that?'

Ott whirled and struck the man across the face. 'Something that will gladly devour you, if only you keep screaming.' To the gaping tarboys, he said, 'Never mind, lads. We shall be in the city for but half an hour, or less. And eguars cannot outrun horses any better than the Leopard People can.'

Chadfallow shook his head. 'They do not run far,' he agreed, 'but at close range they move with blinding speed.'

'Enough of your airs!' snapped Ott. 'There is no book from which to learn the truth about such a creature. And you have never walked the wild places of Alifros, as I have done all my life.'

'Yet I know this to be true,' said Chadfallow.

'How?' demanded Alyash.

The doctor closed his eyes. 'From Ramachni the mage,' he said at last, 'who makes his home in greater peaks than these, among dragons and shadowmambers and hrathmog hordes. And yes, eguar. They can catch horses, Ott. And they have means of killing even that which they do not catch.'

'But what does it *look* like?' pleaded Saroo.

'You'll see soon enough,' said Ott. 'Now pay attention: if we are separated, ride straight at the lowering sun. You'll see a little station-house, and beyond it a triple archway, the only one of its kind. Ride through those arches, and down the stairs beyond them. We will regroup at the bottom and resume our journey.'

'Master Ott,' said Drellarek, 'there is always the sea route.'

Ott glanced at the Turach with disappointment. 'We stand here because the sea route is closed. The waves are too high for smaller vessels, and we cannot wait for a calm.'

'But the *Chathrand* could easily—'

'The *Chathrand* must not be seen again by any living soul, Sergeant Drellarek! I thought you at least understood that.'

'What I should like to understand,' said Chadfallow, 'is what we're doing here at all.'

Ott took out his canteen, and watched the doctor as he drank. Then he wiped his mouth and said, 'Shorten your stirrups, and check your girth straps. We're running late.'

Alyash mounted, wincing as he swung his wounded leg over the saddle. Drellarek spat an oath, but a moment later he too was on his horse. The others reluctantly followed suit. As long as the Turach and the spies were united they had little choice. One old doctor and three tarboys could hardly fight the deadly men.

They walked the horses on the stair, trying to keep to the moss and leaf-litter, for the beasts' iron shoes echoed loudly on the stone. Ott and Pazel were in the lead. The spymaster's hand was on his sword-hilt. He whispered continually to his charger, who nickered deep in her throat despite his soothing. *That falcon of his could be useful now,* Pazel thought. *Where's he gone?*

Some dozen steps from the rooftop, Chadfallow raised a hand, and the party halted.

'Listen to me,' he whispered. 'You must not look directly at the eguar. To do so might provoke it, like a bull. And if you see some trace of the creature, some place where it has crawled, walk your horse around the spot – never through it. Above all, guard your thoughts! Stay calm! Eguar have a spellcraft all their own.'

Ott raked them with a final glance. 'No more talking,' he said.

At the top of the stair the sun met them full in the face. Pazel shielded his eyes – and saw the eguar instantly, even before his mind took in his surroundings. Fear washed over him, irrational and huge. The beast was perhaps a thousand feet away, coal black, facing them. It resembled nothing so much as a great burned crocodile with its legs tucked under its body, and a spiny fan like that of a sailfish running down its back. A vapour surrounded it – a quaking of the air, as if the creature were a living bonfire. Pazel could not see its eyes. Was it sleeping?

Ott pinched his arm savagely. Pazel wrenched his gaze from the creature and faced forwards. One by one the horses stepped onto the roof.

What he saw before him would have stolen Pazel's breath, had he any to spare. It was as if they had climbed not just onto the roof of a fortress but that of the very world, and found it hot and blinding as a desert. The courtyard was vast and severe. Towers rose at its vertices, some intact, others shattered. Clusters of rooftop halls, like minor towns unto themselves, were scattered across its expanse. There were broken domes and standing colonnades, shattered fountains, pedestals with statues of men whose features, like those of the creatures at the ruined gate, had melted over centuries of wind and rain. There was a great amphitheatre, and a bulbous cistern on stubby legs, and round shafts built straight down through the fortress-city, with staircases carved into their sides.

There were also many smooth, pondlike cavities in the stone. All were filled with black water that glistened in a way that somehow turned Pazel's stomach.

Beyond the fortress, the jungle-clad mountains swept west into the heart of Bramian; a second row of peaks marched north. The structure, Pazel saw now, stood on a bend in the range. And along both arms of the range the mighty wall raced away. It was broad as a city boulevard, and he could not see the end of it in either direction.

But from the corner of his eye he could still see the black, vapour-shrouded eguar. He felt ashamed at the extent of his fear. But the same terror shone in the others' faces, when he glimpsed them. Even Drellarek looked slightly pale.

They crept forwards. The shattered halls and pavillions dropped behind them one by one. Reason told Pazel that the triple arch was less than a mile from the stair where they had begun, yet it seemed impossibly distant. There were no leaves here, and each footfall of the horses rang out terribly distinct. Erthalon Ness appeared to be weeping.

Then the eguar opened its eyes. They were white, and burned like stars in the dark flesh. Ott stiffened. Someone's horse neighed and pranced. But still the beast did not move.

Close at hand now was the first of the water-filled cavities. Ott gave it a wide berth. Pazel saw that the gleam on the water's surface actually extended faintly to the stone on one side, as if something had been dragged from the cavity and left a trail of silvery ooze behind it. His eyes followed the trail. It meandered away from them across the rooftop, growing brighter the farther it went, until it ended (*Don't look!* he screamed inwardly, too late) with the eguar itself.

Pazel gasped aloud. He'd met its eyes – and a force like a hurricane struck him in that instant. But it was not a physical blow, for the others sat rigid as ever on their steeds, unaware of the power streaming from the eguar.

Pazel doubled over the saddlehorn, pain between his temples, bile on his tongue. Ott's hand tightened viciously on his arm but he could barely feel it. What was the creature doing to him? And then he glimpsed its moving jaws, and understood. It was speaking.

Pazel had heard many strange tongues, and learned to speak them, in the five years he had lived with the Gift. Flikkermen croaked and gurgled; nunekkam squeaked; the ixchels' tongue was full of sombre, minor-key music. The augrongs boomed out abstract metaphors, and Klyst and her murth-kin worked charms each time they spoke. But no language he had ever heard prepared him for the eguar's. It flooded his brain, violent as the waves beating into the sea-cave, and a hundred times more frightening.

'Have you gone mad?' hissed Sandor Ott. 'Be still. The creature is only yawning, or something like.'

'Run,' gasped Pazel.

'Pathkendle. Pathkendle. Compose yourself, or I swear on Magad's life I'll throw you from this horse.'

Pazel composed himself. The thing had stopped speaking, but the echoes of its words still washed about in his head. The horses were skittish now, and it grew steadily harder to keep them from breaking into a run. A terrible odour had arisen, too: a caustic smell, like acid thrown on a fire. Pazel felt his throat begin to itch.

Far across the plaza, the eguar snapped its jaws. The sound echoed from the turrets beside them. Erthalon Ness sobbed audibly, and Pazel felt Ott's body tense.

Then, miraculously, they were at the arch. Beyond it, stairs led down onto the wall, thirty feet below the level of the rooftop. In a matter of seconds they were through; it was over. Pazel released a huge breath, one he had held unconsciously since that first ticklish feeling in his throat. Swift and Saroo looked giddy with relief.

Ott beckoned them on another hundred yards or so. Then he turned and smiled.

'At your ease, and well done! Even you, Maggot Ness: I thought for a moment we would have to throttle you to stop those tears.'

'It didn't even try to harm us!' said Saroo. 'It just watched us go by.'

'Don't be too proud to learn something, Doctor,' said Ott. 'In my experience it is always better to understand a predator than to fear it.'

'I'm with you there,' said Chadfallow darkly, looking back at the archway.

Drellarek shrugged. 'The creature had a full belly, perhaps.'

'No,' said Pazel, 'it's hungry.'

They looked at him, speechless. 'Is that what your Gift made of the thing's one little bark?' asked Swift.

'*Little bark?*' said Pazel.

Saroo screwed up his face and made a brief, clipped noise, somewhere between a roar and a burp. Swift and Drellarek laughed. But Pazel was dumbfounded. 'It was talking,' he said. 'It went on and on.'

'You have something in common with the Ness family,' said Ott. 'Madness, in a word. Come, gentlemen! We have gained the highway; now we must ride like highwaymen. Thirty miles lie ahead of us, and we must cover them by nightfall, or take our chances in the dark.'

If a more spectacular thirty miles of riding were possible in Alifros, Pazel could not have imagined where. Like a great tawny serpent, the wall climbed peak after rolling peak, and they thundered over them with the steaming valleys arrayed below and a sky full of bright sun and racing clouds overhead. Flocks of bowerbirds and finches and emerald macaws swept before them; the white monkeys scattered and hid; and once they stampeded a herd of pink-snouted peccaries, rooting by the hundreds along the wall's southern flank. Twice they passed through watchtowers, where countless grey bats slept under the darkened roofs, reminding Pazel of the stowed hammocks on the *Chathrand*.

There were more furious downpours, and moments when the wind grew very fierce; at such times they walked the horses and kept far from the edges of the wall. But for the most part the wall served exactly as Ott had claimed it would: as a swift, straight road above the jungle.

Several hours passed. The sun sank low over the western mountains. Then at last came a moment when Ott said, 'Here we are,' and pointed away to the south. Pazel turned and saw the coast in the distance: a deep unquiet blue, scratched with the white lines of breakers. Gazing farther, he saw a wide delta, where rocks and sand and threads of some great river all mingled with the surf.

'The sea route is closed indeed,' Drellarek admitted. 'You'd tear a boat to pieces in all that. But surely there are calmer days?'

'Not more than one in twenty,' said Sandor Ott. 'Many weeks my men have had to wait in the Black Shoulders, with a hold full of arms or mail or medicines, listening for a break in the wind. The work is hazardous and slow – and now it will be slower still, for we must abandon the land route until—'

'Right,' Drellarek finished for him, nodding grimly.

Ott won't even consider fighting the eguar, thought Pazel, *not with all his men. He knows how deadly that creature is.*

Another mile, and Pazel could see the river itself, a dark, twisting waterway that burrowed into Bramian, and quickly vanished there. The river looked placid enough, but it had clearly proved mightier than the will of the Amber Kings, for just above the valley the wall came to its end. There was a last tower, and no more: beyond the river the jungle stretched unbroken over the rounded mountaintops.

They rode forwards into the tower. It was larger than the others, with many dark and chilly rooms. Ott announced that they were spending the night. For a few minutes they busied themselves with the horses, who were both famished and thirsty. Then Ott unbuckled one of the large saddlebags and drew out four sacks tied with rawhide.

'You will want to see this,' he told them all. Placing one of the sacks before him, he loosened the cord and tugged it open.

Green jewels blazed in the evening sun. 'Emeralds,' said Sandor Ott. He sank his hand to the wrist, raised it, let a shower of the precious stones fall back into the mound. Pazel could scarcely breathe. All the gold he had ever seen changing hands would not buy the contents of that sack.

Ott touched another. "Blue Sollochi pearls,' he said. 'And the last two hold bloodstone – choice eastern rubies, cut by nunekkam jewellers.'

'They're all for me, aren't they?' asked Erthalon Ness, rubbing his hands together in delight.

Sandor Ott laughed. 'In a sense, Maggot. Others will guard them on your behalf – and spend them, at need.'

'Spend them?' asked Saroo. 'Where? You could leave them untended for a year in this place.'

'No you couldn't,' said Ott. He glanced at the Shaggat's son, then pointed back out the door of the tower, along the wall. 'Take our friend to see the monkeys, Saroo. He overlooked them when we entered, I think.'

'I didn't see any monkeys, Mr Ott.'

'Do as I say, lad.'

Bewildered, Saroo led a happy Erthalon Ness through the eastern archway. Ott beckoned the others to follow. He walked in the opposite direction, through several dismal rooms, and at last into a chamber with a broad window facing west. Reaching it, he gazed down with satisfaction on whatever lay below.

Chadfallow reached the window next, and visibly recoiled from what he saw. 'By the gods,' he huffed, leaning heavily on the stone.

Pazel came up beside him. Far below the tower, the river made an especially sharp bend, almost an ox-bow. The teardrop of land within its curve was about the size of the city of Ormael. It was teeming with life. Men, cattle, chickens, dogs. There were barracks and stockades, wooden halls, tents of sewn hide, grain silos, mills where water-wheels slowly revolved.

'Our allies,' said Sandor Ott.

Where the river bent closest to itself, a stout wall of timber leaped from shore to shore, with a pair of mighty wooden doors at the centre. A lesser wall ran the whole length of the riverbank, broken only by the mills and some sort of massive lumber operation at the farthest point from the observers. Towers rose at intervals, each with a stout guard compliment. The fort was protected by water, wood, and men-at-arms.

'What are they building, Ott?' asked Drellarek.

'Ships,' said Pazel.

The sergeant blinked at him. 'You need glasses, if you can't see that much,' said Pazel. 'Those are framing timbers. And cutwaters. And keels.'

'Right you are, Pathkendle. Fifty ships, to be precise. There is no shortage of wood on Bramian. And we have no shortage of funds to pay for what they cannot manufacture here – sailcloth, cannon, the finer metalwork. Here they sit in the wilderness, gentlemen, unknown to anyone in the world but us, and a few dozen of my men. And yet thousands across Alifros have laboured unwittingly on their behalf. Flikkermen tracked down and kidnapped shipwrights. The slave-school on Nurth provides the wives. And Volpeks, those exquisitely useful outlaws, bring everything to the hidden anchorage at Sandplume, where my men meet them on a flagless ship. The Volpeks have no idea who their customers are, or where in Alifros their shipments go next. Bramian itself would be the last place to cross their minds! No one trades with these savages. We had the devil's own job building that wall, with their arrows raining down on us day and night.'

'But who's the wall protecting?' asked Swift. 'Who's down there, Mr Ott?'

A note of pride entered the spymaster's voice. 'They were castaways when we found them: war refugees, hiding in mangroves in the Baerrids, a few inches above sea level, surviving on gulls' eggs and rats. The Black Rags were unforgivably careless not to have killed them. Every year those men spent tortured by insect and typhoon, sleeping in burrows that filled with seawater, dying of scurvy or light wounds turned gangrenous, added to their hatred of the Mzithrin. They had spent a decade that way, since the Shaggat's rebellion was crushed at the end of the war.'

Chadfallow turned to the spymaster. His face was ashen. 'They're . . . *his* people?'

'Nessarim warriors,' said the spymaster, nodding. 'True believers, to a soul. As the Shaggat was fleeing east into our navy's gunsights, these poor bastards were running south, packed into one groaning vessel, just hours ahead of the White Fleet. Somewhere east of Serpent's Head they foundered on a reef, and half their number drowned. But that reef was good fortune, for otherwise the Sizzies would have caught them on the open sea. They were no longer taking prisoners by that point in the war.

'We took them first to a camp on Opalt, where the sick perished and the strong fought their way back to health. But on Opalt they could do little more than hide, and worship their mad king in secret. That is why, five years ago, we brought them shipload by shipload to this place. Now they number over three thousand.'

'And fifty ships under construction,' said Drellarek. 'That's impressive. But hardly a threat to the White Fleet.'

'Of course not,' said Sandor Ott. 'The contest will be as lopsided as pitting a dog against a bear, as Captain Rose put it once. You're a hunting man yourself, Sergeant.'

Drellarek smiled. 'How did you know?'

'I'd be a poor spymaster if I didn't know that much about the Turach commander. And I'm sure you'll agree that dogs have a role in any bear hunt?'

'That's a certainty,' said Drellarek. 'A good pack can corner a bear, bleed it with nips, exhaust it, until at last it can only watch as the hunter raises his spear for the kill.'

'Of course you must bring *enough* dogs,' said Ott. 'The colony below is just one in our hunting-pack.'

'And what of the dogs themselves?' asked Chadfallow quietly.

'What of them?' said Ott.

Grinning suddenly, he turned to Alyash with a gesture and a nod. The bosun hobbled forward, and Pazel saw that he too had extracted something from the saddlebags. It was a hunting-horn, stout and well-used, more powerful than lovely. Alyash faced the window, planted his feet and drew an enormous breath. Raising the horn, he sounded one long, keening blast. The high note shook the chamber, and carried far over the valley below.

When it ended, the sounds of labour from the settlement had ceased. Men were coming out of the buildings to gaze in the tower's direction. After a moment there came the sound of an answering horn.

Saroo and Erthalon Ness returned, the latter wearing an ethereal smile. He had seen his monkeys, or believed he had. Alyash passed the horn to Ott and addressed the Shaggat's son in Mzithrini.

'Forget your monkeys,' he said. 'Don't you understand where we've brought you?'

The language-switch had an immediate effect on Erthalon Ness. His glance grew sharper, his face more stern. 'No, Warden, I don't. You tell me nothing. Where are you hiding my brother?'

Alyash swept his hand over the settlement. 'Those are the Nessarim, your father's worshippers. Keepers of your holy faith.'

'Not my faith,' said Erthalon Ness. 'The common faith of all mankind, only some have yet to see it. Some are afraid to cast the demons from their hearts, to burn unto purity, become new men. They will not always be afraid, however. Is not my father a god?'

'Assuredly, sir, and these men know it better than any. They have waited long for this day. Waited for you to appear, to take your father's place as they sail forth to join him. Come, let us greet them at the river's edge.' He gestured dismissively at the others. 'These people are of no more consequence.'

Alyash put out his hand. Erthalon Ness looked at it, hesitating. A clash of emotions shone in his face: suspicion, temptation, fear – and some darker, wilder gleam.

'Men are casting off from the docks in rowing boats,' said Saroo, looking down from the window. 'And in barges, and canoes.'

Then Pazel did something that surprised them all. He ran forwards and stood between Alyash and the Shaggat's son.

'Don't go with him,' he said in Mzithrini.

'Pathkendle,' said Ott, his voice an open threat. But Alyash smiled, and raised a hand to calm the spymaster.

'They're using you,' said Pazel. 'They laugh at you *and* your faith. They're sending you down to die among those people.'

'Lies,' said Alyash. 'You've said it yourself, Erthalon. The time of your death has not yet arrived.'

'I will know the hour,' said Erthalon Ness, looking at Pazel uncertainly, 'and before it strikes I will be with my father again.'

'No you won't,' said Pazel. 'He's a blary statue in the hold of the *Chathrand*.'

Soundlessly, Ott drew his sword. Chadfallow took a step forwards, as if he would intervene. But once more Alyash waved them off.

'Whose touch was it that turned your great father to stone?' he asked. 'You were there when it happened.'

'I was there,' echoed the other, turning accusingly to Pazel. 'I had almost forgotten. It was you!'

From the river below came the sound of singing. Erthalon Ness raised his head.

'They are calling you, child of the Divine,' said Alyash. 'And have no doubt: your father will live again, and just as the old tales promise, you shall sail out to meet him as he claims his kingdom.'

'You'll sail out and be killed!' shouted Pazel.

Alyash shook his head. 'Now who is laughing at the faith?'

Pazel was desperate. With every word he spoke he grew more certain that Ott or Drellarek would kill him. But he simply had to fight. If he didn't, these men would take everything – take Alifros itself – to say nothing of the life of this broken man.

'Listen to me,' he begged, taking the other's arm. 'You must know that they hate you. Didn't they lock you up all these years?'

'I think he is referring to your palace on Licherog, Excellency,' said the bosun. 'As for your father's people, how could any sane man think we wished them harm? After all, we rescued them from starvation, and built them this place of safety and hiding, when the five false Kings were slaughtering any man pledged to your father who strayed a league from Gurishal. Enough of this nonsense, Excellency. Your people are waiting.'

The Shaggat's son looked once more at Pazel. A scowl of hatred twisted his face, and he wrenched his arm away. But as soon as he had done so the hatred vanished, and the man looked simply lost. His lips trembled, and his eyes drifted miserably over the stones.

'My people,' he said, and there was more loneliness in those two words than Pazel had ever heard a voice express.

The man permitted Alyash to take his elbow, and together they descended the stair.

24

The Editor, Being of the Opinion that Suspense is a Vulgar Commonplace, Reveals the End of the Story

One by one they died. All of them, the vicious and the virtuous, the Drellareks and the Diadrelus, their lovers, their foes. The nations they bled for, killed for: those perished too. Some in extraordinary style, a conflagration of prejudice and greed, coupled to war machinery. Others were simply buried as the vast, unsound palaces they dwelt in collapsed, those houses of quarried contradiction.

They died, you see. What else could have happened? I witnessed a number of deaths, heard others related by those who were present; I even contributed some names to the tally – your editor is a murderer; it's not as rare as you think. Until quite recently I had comrades from that time, fellow survivors, people in whose eyes a certain light kindled when I said *Chathrand* or *Nilstone* or *the honour of the clan*. Never many. Today, none at all.

It was all so long ago, an age. How many of the young scholars around me today, in my incontinent dotage, believe that the world of Pazel and Thasha ever existed – that it was ever as cruel or as blessed or as ignorant as we found it? No one in this place even *looks* like a Pazel or a Thasha. Why should they believe in them? So long as I live I am proof of a sort – but I, who sailed on *Chathrand* to her last hour, resemble myself less and less each passing year. And when I die there will be those who pause on the library stair to gaze at my portrait, wondering if the artist were mad.

What's left of those people? The ones I loved, the ones I detested? Not their faces (you must give them those yourself), nor their bones (though I keep Ott's skull on the parlour table, and talk to it sometimes; he's the only one whose looks have improved), nor their skins, shoes, teeth, voices, graves. Even the museums that collected artefacts from that time have crumbled, and the stone markers that read *Here stood the museum*. What's left? Their ideas. Still today – when the world is utterly changed, when men of learning begin to argue that human beings never had a time of glory, never built great cities, never tamed the Nelluroq or tasted the magic that moves the stars – still today, we need those ideas about the dignity of consciousness, the brotherhood of the fearless and the sceptical, the efficacy of love.

I hear your laughter. The young scholars laugh too, and whisper: *That old spook upstairs has gone sentimental, mixing up his memories and his dreams*. Laugh, then. May your mirth last longer than a thunderclap, and your ironies, and your youth. In the end you'll be left with ideas – nothing else – and one or two of you will have spent your lives working honestly to help the best ideas flourish and grow. My friends on the *Chathrand* were such people. That is why I must record their story before I go.

We are not blood and gristle and hair and spit. We are ideas, if we are anything at all. That part of us that was never truly living is the only part of us that cannot die. Now then, back to Bramian.

25

A Picnic on the Wall

—◦◦◦—

23 Freala 941
132nd day from Etherhorde

When dawn broke in the tower, Dr Chadfallow at last did Pazel a good turn: he took the youth on his own horse, getting him away from Sandor Ott. When the spymaster noticed the arrangement, he gave the doctor a long, cold appraisal, but did not speak.

It occurred to Pazel that Chadfallow might have just saved his life, but it was almost impossible for him to feel gratitude. For a long time he could think only of his last glimpse of the Shaggat's son, releasing Alyash's hand in a muddy clearing beneath the tower, and being lifted onto the shoulders of the thin, strong, wildly tattooed and altogether deadly Nessarim. He heard again the terrible war cry that had started when they lifted Erthalon Ness: a cry that swept down to the riverbank, leaped across the water, and then like a fuse that has burned its way to the firecracker, exploded from every mouth in the settlement:

> *From one spark a storm of fire, from one womb a nation!*
> *The Shaggat for us is truth entire, for others a conflagration!*
>
> *Every foe his wrath shall feel, every liar hear him!*
> *Lesser kings to him shall kneel, and fearless warriors fear him!*
>
> *So ever nearer heaven's door in prayer and blood annointed,*
> *We follow him, we follow him, unto the hour appointed!*

The chant had broken up into a high, fierce caterwauling that raised the hairs on the back of Pazel's neck. Ott had explained that the Nessarim had borrowed this last cry from the Leopard People: it was the sound they made when they attacked the colony in force.

The Nessarim actually admired the Leopard People's courage and swiftness, he said, and tried to show their respect through the mimicry. Ott's ultimate goal was conversion of the tribes themselves to the Shaggat cult: unlikely, he admitted, but not inconceivable.

Their second journey along the wall was even more spectacular than the first. A rainbow arched over the northern mountains; palms waved their emerald tresses from the ridgetops; a waterfall gleamed in the morning sun. But the beauty only made Pazel feel more sick at heart. He did not know why he had risked so much for a madman, but he knew quite well that he had failed. *The man tried to believe me. Why couldn't he face the truth?*

He clenched his fingers in the horse's mane, thoughts sliding from mystery to mystery. At last they settled on one that concerned the man behind him.

'Ignus,' he said. 'Tell me about the prisoner exchange, back in Simja. How do you know they had my mother, and Neda? Did you see them?'

Chadfallow tensed. For several minutes he said nothing at all. Then he said, 'Don't be obtuse, Pazel. When could I have seen them? My counterpart Acheleg swore that they were there, both of them, in Simjalla City.'

'When was the exchange supposed to happen?'

Chadfallow sighed. 'The morning after the wedding. Which as it turned out was also the day the *Chathrand* and the *Jistrolloq* almost came to blows. The day you translated Rose's threats.'

'Ah,' said Pazel. 'Well.'

'Yes. Well.'

Pazel was glad the doctor could not see his eyes. He was furious. Did Chadfallow think he'd had a choice? Hadn't the man noticed how he'd twisted Rose's words to make them less insulting to the Mzithrinis? Was it his fault that Arunis had dispatched some kind of demon to murder the Babqri Father?

They rode on in silence a while, watching mice and lizards at the horses' approach. Then Chadfallow began to speak again. 'I negotiated the exchange in private. I worked at it for three years – from the moment I heard of plans for a Great Peace. I obtained a writ of extradition signed by His Supremacy, to be presented to the Warden of Licherog. But all that was before I knew of the Shaggat conspiracy.'

'I don't believe a word you say,' said Pazel, his voice tight as a wire. 'You could have ended the conspiracy at the governor's table in Ormael. Instead you denied that the Shaggat was aboard. You laughed at us, said that Arunis couldn't be the *real* Arunis, called us a bunch of overexcited children. You kept us from exposing the whole festering lie.'

'I saw the Shaggat hanged!' snapped Chadfallow. 'Of course I didn't believe he'd returned! Besides, I was in shock, like you. In shock at the depth of Ott's betrayal.'

'I don't think you were shocked at all,' said Pazel. 'I think you're still a part of the conspiracy. I think your job from the start has been to make me useful to them – me and my gods-damned Gift.'

Chadfallow's knuckles were white on the reins. He was struggling with himself.

'Did you see the list of Mzithrini names, that day?'

'I saw it,' said Pazel, recalling how he and Neeps had pored over the scraps of parchment.

'How many of them did we have on board?'

Pazel hesitated 'Mzithrinis? None, as far as I—'

'None. Exactly. We never collected them – they rot on Licherog yet, if they are alive at all. Ott lied to me as he did to everyone. Three years of talks, and when the day came, I had no prisoners to give the Mzithrinis. What, then, do you imagine I planned to bargain with?'

'I don't know, Ignus. Gold?'

'The Shaggat Ness. The Shaggat, author of eighty thousand deaths in the Pentarchy. Think, Pazel: any Mzithrini old enough to recall that face would give me the keys to the five kingdoms to be allowed to put a knife in his heart! Your mother and Neda – they would have been nothing, no price at all. By now they'd be free, Suthinia would be—'

A spasm shook his body. He dropped the reins from one hand and grabbed Pazel by the jaw.

'But a *statue*? What in Rin's firebolts could I do with a *statue* of the Shaggat Ness? You ruined everything when you turned him to stone. You took away the only chance they had.'

The worst of the day's heat lay behind them. This time no rain or wind squalls slowed their progress. When five hours had passed they climbed a crooked ridge and saw the fortress-city looming ahead.

'We'll be back in your caves by nightfall, won't we, Mr Ott?' asked Saroo.

'Unless you prefer to spend the night on Droth'ulad,' said the spymaster. 'It's all downhill after the fortress: that should help us stay ahead of the savages. And with any luck the eguar will remain sated as before.'

'He *wasn't* sated,' muttered Pazel, still burning with the unfairness of the doctor's accusations.

'Hush!' whispered Swift, glancing nervously at Ott. 'Pazel, you're a hazard to your own blary health. And another thing – you ride like a sack of spuds. Why in the Pits did Ott bring you along?'

'Why'd he bring *you*?' Pazel shot back.

'Because Saroo and I are great riders, obviously. And because we're small, and that let the horses carry more gemstones. There, now what's your answer?'

Pazel looked away. His Gift was the answer, of course, but what had he done with it except overhear a few shouts from the Leopard People? Probably Ott was wishing even now that he'd left Pazel behind on the ship. Maybe, he thought bitterly, Ignus will offer to force something *really* strong down my throat, next time . . . .

Perhaps two miles from the city they came to a low saddle in the hill, and Ott called for rest. Pazel could just make out the triple arch they had passed through the day before. He shuddered at the memory of the eguar's voice.

They dismounted, and the boys watered the horses from a feedbag. Alyash tore chunks from a dark loaf of bread and handed them around. It was a gift from the Nessarim, along with two sausages and a clay flagon of wine: as if the forty-year journey of Erthalon Ness back into the fold had been reduced to a barter for foodstuffs.

'Vicious bastards, those Nessarim!' said Drellarek approvingly. 'Scrawny, but bloody-minded; I could see it plain in their faces. They'd fight like wildcats even against my Turachs, I dare say.'

'They have only their faith to live for,' said Ott. 'And if you still wish to know, Doctor, we made this journey in support of their faith. To bring them a sign, a swallow of magic to carry with them into war.'

'A war they can only lose,' said Chadfallow.

Grinning, the spymaster inclined his head.

'A diversion,' said Saroo. 'You built that whole town full of crazies as a *diversion*.'

Pazel was aghast to hear a note of admiration in the tarboy's voice. His brother Swift was more guarded, however: 'The Shaggat's son would be an old man, now,' he said, 'if he hadn't spent half his life asleep. How do they know it's really him?'

'They knew instantly,' said Alyash. 'He's the son of their god, after all. They knew the birthmark on his elbow, and his tattoos – master-pieces, they were, the artist was blinded when he finished the boys.'

'Will the Secret Fist tell those poor fools when to sail?' asked Drellarek.

Ott shook his head. 'They are their own masters. We shall merely be sure it happens before the Shaggat himself reaches Gurishal. And when they do sail we shall raise the alarm in every corner of Alifros. "The Nessarim! The Nessarim reborn, and howling that their Shaggat is coming back as well!" The world shall hear it loudly. And then we shall help the poor, ineffectual White Fleet to destroy them.'

'Destroy them!' cried Pazel, his voice cracking. '*You're* going to destroy them?'

'The Mzithrinis will do the bulk of the work,' said Ott, 'but we shall sink a ship or two – visibly, of course – and chase them into the line of fire. They'll have their moment. They'll take a bite out of the Sizzy fleet. But that will be trivial. The real wound to the Black Rags will be the humiliation. Forty years after the war, men will say, and they *still* can't eliminate the Shaggat cult! Best of all, the Five Kings will believe it themselves. As our other dogs begin to nip and bite, rumours of the Shaggat's return will spring up throughout the Crownless Lands. The Sizzies will be looking everywhere for the source of the rumour – and meanwhile they'll redouble the blockade between Gurishal and the eastern lands. But they will not be able to stamp the rumour out. And each time a dog sinks its teeth into that bear it will respond with greater desperation.'

'A diversion,' said Alyash, 'You're right, Saroo my lad. But what a diversion! The first bay, the first howl from the hunting pack. The Five Kings will hear it and tremble.'

'And those other dogs?' said Chadfallow, with quiet rage. 'Who are they, and where are they hidden? Are they to be sacrificed as coldly as the men in that settlement?'

Ott shook his head, smiling. 'Would you deprive me of all my surprises, Doctor?'

'I would deprive you of more than that.'

'Ha!' laughed Sandor Ott. 'My woman, for example? And my liberty? You have attempted both of these, and failed. And even if you had persuaded that useless Ormali governor to clap me in irons, how long do you think I would have been held?'

'Two days,' said Chadfallow. 'After that I would have seen you locked in the brig of a packet boat making for Etherhorde – with an ample guard. I paid them in advance: the guards, and the owners of that boat. I had a letter prepared for His Supremacy, with all I knew of your betrayals. Particularly how you and that—' Chadfallow bit off the word, '–*viper*, spent the last year poisoning his good friend Eberzam Isiq.'

Pazel was suddenly afraid for Chadfallow. His fury had hardly vanished – Chadfallow was one to talk of betrayals! – but in spite of everything Pazel somehow felt he would be lost without the man. *Can't you see what you're risking, fool?* he wanted to shout. *Ott's probably killed more people with his bare hands than you've saved in surgery.*

For the moment, however, Ott just looked amused. 'His Supremacy would have consigned your letter to the fire. He knows quite well the necessities of this campaign to perfect his dominion. You, for starters, are certainly expendable. As for his friendship with Isiq—' He looked at Alyash and Drellarek, and suddenly the three of them began to laugh, low and hard. Pazel watched them, recalling how Niriviel had taunted Thasha. *The Pit fiends. They* have *done something to the admiral.*

Chadfallow's face was darkening with rage. 'What of future "necessities?"' he asked. 'How many leeches will you affix to the body of the Empire? Will you have the territorial governors assassinated? The lord admiral, perhaps? Will you decide that Magad's sons are unworthy to inherit the crown, and kill them as you did Empress Maisa's?'

The men's laughter redoubled. 'Oh Doctor, stop,' said Alyash, wiping tears from his eyes.

'Yes, Ignus, stop,' said Pazel. 'They're not worth it.'

The doctor turned him a tortured look. And suddenly Pazel recalled something Chadfallow had told him years ago, about the oath Arquali doctors took before their titles were conferred: *Life in all its loveliness shall I defend, even at the cost of my own.* Did Chadfallow think he had broken that oath too many times?

'Ott kill Maisa's brats!' said Drellarek. 'That's priceless! Why don't you tell 'im the truth, Master Ott?'

Ott shook his head again. 'There are things I won't discuss with a man who'd try to brand me a traitor.'

'You are a traitor,' said Chadfallow, his control slipping further. 'You are a weak, grasping, small-minded man. You have perverted all that I lived for and held most dear. I will name your dog, Sandor Ott: it is Arqual itself. You have trained it with cruelty and fear. You have made it vicious, ready to bite anyone who crosses its path.'

The spymaster's laughter was abruptly gone. Drellarek and Alyash fell silent. Ott rose to his feet, eyes locked on Chadfallow.

'Not just anyone,' he said.

Pazel leaped up and grabbed Chadfallow by the arm. 'Please,' he hissed, 'don't say any more.'

'We're going to need him, Ott,' said Alyash, still smiling.

'There is a field surgeon here at Bramian Station,' said Sandor Ott. 'He can serve the Great Ship, in a pinch. Chadfallow, you have twice defamed me with the one insult I swore never to bear. Call me a traitor again, and you will see if I am weak.'

'You're a tr—'

Pazel struck Chadfallow as hard as he could. There was a sound like a snapped branch, and blood gushed from the doctor's nose as he stumbled to the ground. He stared at Pazel, amazed, not even trying to staunch the flow.

'Shut your damned mouth!' screamed Pazel at the doctor. 'Wait, Mr Ott, he'll take it back, please, please, I'll make him—'

Sandor Ott drew his long white knife. Pazel stood between them, arms thrown wide, pleading with the assassin. There was a dream-like quality to his voice; it sounded soft and far away, like an echo. Behind him, Chadfallow rose and tugged out his sword.

'Put it down, Doctor!' laughed Drellarek. 'That's blary suicide, and you know it. Come to your senses and apologise, if you want to live.'

'Will one of you,' said the spymaster, 'kindly take Mr Pathkendle aside?'

Alyash started to rise, but Drellarek waved him off. 'Rest that leg while you can. I'll get him.'

'Decent of you,' said Alyash.

The Turach stood and lumbered towards Pazel. He did not bother to draw a blade. When he saw Pazel's fighting stance, he pointed and grinned. 'Look at this one, Master Ott. I'm done for!'

Pazel blocked his first blow with an upraised arm, but the strength behind the Turach's fist was crushing. The second blow found his stomach; the third, to the back of his head, came close to knocking him out. As Ott sidled towards the doctor, turning the knife casually in his hand, Drellarek grabbed Pazel by the shirt and lifted him clear of the ground. Pazel lashed out with his legs and caught the man in the stomach. Drellarek winced and struck him again.

Chadfallow was backing away from Ott, sword up, body rigid, boots shuffling awkwardly on the stones. His face was frozen, like an actor's mask: the kind depicting some elemental sin, like folly or despair. Ott, however, looked like a man who had shed every worry. He was by far the older, but as he drove Chadfallow before him he was returned astonishingly to his youth. Relaxed and graceful, he took a dancing side-step, and lunged.

Something terrible and bloody occurred, but it was not what anyone foresaw. Drellarek, Ott and Chadfallow simply disappeared. Where the party had stood an instant before there was only darkness and a blast of heat. Pazel felt himself thrown backwards with terrible force. When he landed his upper body was dangling over the rimless edge of the wall, and a screaming horse lay sprawled across his legs. The animal surged to its feet, and Pazel, blind with pain and sliding towards death, flailed out with his hands and caught a stirrup. The horse spun on its hindquarters, eyes mad with terror, wrenching him back from the precipice even as the animal's own forefeet slipped over the edge. Pazel could only let go the stirrup as the horse crashed into the trees below. Then he felt heat on the back of his neck, and turned.

The eguar stood over him. Its white-hot eyes blazed in the dark crocodilian head. Pazel clawed at his throat, choking, and his eyes streamed with tears. He was inside its cocoon of vapours, and the smell was like acid thrown on hot coals; he was amazed not to have died already.

But Drellarek was dead. The Turach's body dangled from the creature's mouth, and it was shrivelling like an old squash roasted over a flame. The saliva of the eguar sizzled on Drellarek's skin, and around its teeth the man's very armour was in flames. Then the creature raised its head skywards, and swallowed the Turach with three snaps of its jaws.

Pazel felt his gorge rise. He could not turn his back on the eguar, so he dragged himself away with his arms, expecting death, that death, with every scraping inch. He saw Swift and Saroo on the wall beyond the creature, running for the fortress roof. Then he looked down. Ott and Chadfallow lay motionless beneath the eguar's feet.

Oh no. Ignus.

Pazel had crawled free of the vapours and lay retching on his side. The eguar's eyes were still fixed on him, burning his mind even as the vapours had burned his lungs. And then the creature spoke.

This time Pazel was expecting the hurricane – and the eguar, perhaps, was aware of Pazel's limits. He was not faced with the same flood of meaning as before, and yet it still seemed that the eguar put whole speeches into single words, and to hear them gave Pazel the grotesque sensation of gulping a meal in large, unmasticated chunks.

'I, Ma'tathgryl-eguar-child-of-the-south nameless-desireless-pitiless-all-these-are-prisons forward-and-backward perceive their plan, their venom, their cleverness-madness-debauchery-faith, perceive you, lidless-unarmoured-unskinned child-man, mind thrown open, with them, apart.'

That was one word, one maddeningly complicated growl. Reeling from it, Pazel managed to climb to his feet and back a few more steps away. He knew his Gift would tell him how to answer, and struggled desperately against the urge to try. Hearing the eguar's language with human ears was bad enough; thinking in it might drive him mad.

He tried something far simpler: he used the language of the Leopard People. 'Why did you help me?' he said.

'Shackles of certainty in cage of desire in dead spindrift isle of self.'

Pazel understood. He must not assume the eguar meant him well. And as if to underscore the point the creature opened its mouth wide and breathed in his direction, and Pazel felt the vapour cloud billow over him again, but now mixed with some new bile or potion from the gullet of the beast. The vapour weakened him, and his knees gave out. He fell forward, staring up at the creature, trapped by those white-hot eyes. Then the eguar spoke again, and Pazel began to scream as never before in his life.

He was not in pain, but he was horribly violated. The eguar had peeled open his mind like an orange, and was examining all it contained. Pazel did not just feel naked; he felt as though someone had cut away his skin, and shone a bright light on his muscles and veins, and told him to dance.

But he would not dance (the eguar knew this, knew it before Pazel did, knew every twitch and motive of his soul). The beast was looking for something very specific, and Pazel somehow knew he must not give it up. His rage at the intrusion was searing; he would have tried to kill any human who invaded him in this way, he was thinking like a lunatic, like an assassin, like Ott.

The eguar might have been amused. With another battering-ram of a word it told Pazel that it had already looked into Sandor Ott's mind, and that Pazel's rage bore little resemblance to the spymaster's. Then he offered to show the killer's mind to Pazel. And before Pazel could refuse the eguar gave him a foretaste.

Like floodwater released from a dam, Sandor Ott's life history washed over him. Pazel could barely stand what he saw. Dark infant years in a slum; women's hands feeding, then gouging him, twisting his limbs; other children screaming, horrible men always enraged. Slammed doors, broken windows, a barnyard stench in the crowded bedrooms, the dead wrapped in threadbare sheets. Alleys full of muttering men, victims of the talking fever; they seized at his ankles and he barely escaped. *Epidemic*, someone said. A cart heaped with paupers fleeing the city by night.

Then exile, a mud-wattle village on the side of a gritty, treeless hill. Threats from the cattlemen and gentry, the owners of that useless knob. Torched roofs, tortured parents, an elder staked and writhing on the ground. More years of road-wandering, sores on his shoeless feet, a beggar's bowl tied to a string at his waist. Cold riverbanks, hard streetcorners, kicks. The taste of spoiled meat, fermented cabbage, potato skins scraped from the cobbles with a knife.

Pazel was tearing at his own face with his fingernails. 'Make it stop! Make it stop!' he begged. The memories had spanned less than Ott's first decade of life.

The eguar took its claw from Ott's chest, and the flood ceased instantly. The spymaster began to moan and stir. The creature prepared once more to delve into Pazel's mind. And all at once Pazel knew what it wanted, and knew the weapon he could use against the thing before him. The Master-Words.

He had two of them left, Ramachni's gifts, a word to tame fire and a word that would 'blind to give new sight.' He had no idea what the latter would do, but he knew that the fire-word might save him, might even destroy this beast and its blazing power.

No sooner had he formed the thought than the eguar knew it too. With the speed of a rattlesnake it coiled its body and leaped. A great wind threw Pazel flat. Then the eguar and its cloud of dark vapours were gone, and the weakness in his limbs disappeared.

He got to his hands and knees. The wall was slick with silvery ooze. Ott and Chadfallow lay moaning a few yards away. Pazel crawled towards the doctor and shook him. Chadfallow's eyes were open but did not seem to see.

'Wake up,' said Pazel, his voice raw and burned.

From the jungle on the wall's north side came a loud crack. Pazel turned, punch-drunk. Some hundred yards away, great trees were shuddering and bending. Then he saw the eguar slide its bulk onto a huge limb. Once more the white eyes gleamed – but this time Pazel looked away before it was too late.

'Child of Ormael,' said the eguar.

'Damn you to the Pits!' cried Pazel, weeping with rage. 'You could speak like a human all this time?'

'The Pits have no place for me,' said the eguar. 'Listen, *Smythídor*: I know where you are bound, and what awaits you there, and what you will need to face it.'

Pazel covered his ears. He would not speak with the creature, not when it had just eaten—

'Your enemy,' said the eguar, as if Pazel had spoken aloud. 'A man hoping for the chance to kill you. But I do not think you should die yet, not while the Stone moves over the waters. Not while a war is struggling to be hatched – kicking, writhing in blood and fire from its shell. Not before you see the wondrous South, the world my brethren made. Rejoice, human, rejoice in your skinlessness, your immolation, the nakedness of nerves. Rejoice above all in your fellowship, ere you turn and find it a memory, a dry shell without warmth. But you must never again refuse knowledge, *Smythídor*. I would have shown you the doctor's mind next.'

'I don't want to see – and what I saw of Ott's mind was *hideous*. Stay away, stay away, or I swear I'll use that word.' He shook Chadfallow again. 'Wake up, damn you, I need your help.'

Then the eguar hissed a final word in its own language, making Pazel wince – although it was, compared to earlier utterances, remarkably brief:

'Acceptance is agony denial is death.'

With that the creature departed, thrashing and tearing through the trees. Pazel got shakily to his feet and put his hands over his ears. He could see Alyash running towards them along the wall. When he turned around Chadfallow was sitting up, filthy with slime and blood. His nose was bent sharply to the right.

'Get up,' said Pazel, smouldering. 'What happens next is your problem.'

'I have no idea what you're talking about,' said Chadfallow.

Pazel looked the doctor in the eye, and waited. One breath, two. And then he dropped to a crouch and squeezed his eyes shut as the mind-fit erupted in his skull.

26

The Taste of Treason

—⁂—

That evening on the *Chathrand*, Pazel's friends found it hard to keep up their spirits. The landing party had been two days ashore. Hercól remained locked in the brig; and Thasha, Neeps and Marila were hardly less prisoners themselves, albeit in grander quarters. Mr Uskins had painted a red line on the deck along the base of Ramachni's magic wall, and placed four soldiers there with orders to let no one in or out without his permission. Each time Thasha appeared in the doorway, they glared. They were the proudest soldiers in Alifros, and they'd bungled orders to arrest a sixteen-year-old girl.

Mr Fiffengurt came to the stateroom at eight bells, carrying a jug of drinking water and a plate of Mr Teggatz's pigsfoot-and-barley casserole. He also bore the dismal news that the skiff had not returned from Bramian, and presumably would not do so before morning.

The quartermaster did not linger, for the ship was in an uproar of last-minute preparations for the voyage out. 'Don't worry about Pathkendle,' he said as he turned to go. 'The lad's no use to them dead. They may not like him, but they'll keep him safe.'

'It's not what *they'll* do that worries me,' said Neeps. 'Pazel can get in trouble all by himself.'

Neeps wanted to pounce on the casserole, but Thasha insisted on a fighting class first, despite Hercól's absence.

'Forget your stomach for once,' she said, cutting off his objections before they began, 'and come at me hard, because if I don't think you're trying to kill me I'm blary well going to show you how it's done.'

Neeps hesitated, fuming. He wolfed one bite of the casserole, slammed down his fork and retreated to the washroom to change into his fighting-rags. Thasha whistled her dogs into her own cabin and changed as well, strapping the wooden shield to her arm and tying a leather neck-guard in place.

They unscrewed the furniture and slid it against the walls, and rolled up the bearskin rug. While Marila sat reading quietly in a corner, and Felthrup balanced on the back of her chair, muttering and swaying with exhaustion, Thasha and Neeps battled all around the stateroom with the balsa swords.

For once Neeps rose to her challenge. He had long passed the stage of angry charges, having tired of finding himself flat on the ground or symbolically beheaded. Thasha would not have told him (for Neeps' pride needed no encouragement) but she was astonished at his progress. He was the only young person she had ever known more hotheaded than herself, and yet here he was, biding his time, matching his movements to hers – fighting with his mind. And his form when attacking was better too: his jerky tarboy strength was mellowing into something more fluid, more likely to keep him alive.

It was almost a shame to have to keep winning. Still, Thasha could not approach combat with any outlook but victory: the sixth apothem reminded students that practice is never a game, but the prelude to a moment when a life may end.

'Surprise me,' she taunted him, darting from one side of a stanchion to another, bruising his left side and then his right, turning him at bay or forcing a retreat. 'Do something I haven't seen you do fifty times. Tired, are you? That's when you die, you Sollochi runt. *Come at me!*'

Neeps did not even blink. He was shutting out her insults, refusing to be drawn. To Thasha this seemed almost a miracle.

At last she raised her hand and stopped him. Neeps dropped his wooden sword and bent over, gasping, his face like a bruised tomato. He fumbled at the buckle on his shield. 'You did well,' Thasha conceded, stepping towards him. 'What made the difference, this time?'

'I just—'

He slashed at her with the edge of his shield, catching her squarely in the gut.

'—pretended—'

He had her down, pulled her against him, caught her neck in the crook of his arm.

'—that you were Raffa, Raffa—'

He spat the name, and tightened his grip uncomfortably. Thasha was furious – *surprise me* did not mean *attack when the drill is over* – and resolved to teach him a lesson. But when she thrust her elbow hard into

345

his side, none too gently, his response was not at all what she expected. Instead of doubling over as she had done upon his shield, Neeps hurled them both backwards onto the floor with amazing violence, and at the same time tightened his grip on her neck even further. *Much* further: Thasha remembered the bite of her necklace: the youth's arm was crushing her windpipe with the same deadly force. She clawed at him. She felt him buck and twist, slamming her face against the wooden floor, putting the weight of his chest against her temple. Her dogs were howling behind the cabin door; Marila was screaming, '*Stop it! Stop it!*' and then came an explosion of glass and water. But Neeps did not stop, and Thasha felt her vision dim. She had a vague impression of his sweaty, wild-eyed face above her own, still mouthing the name.

And then, thank all the gods, he let her go – and began to scream himself. Thasha fell on her side and saw Neeps throwing himself from side to side. Felthrup's teeth were locked on his ear.

'Let go! Let go! Damn you, Felthrup, you're out of your mind!'

'*He's* not!' shouted Marila, from the far side of the room.

Thasha drew a strangled breath, and Neeps whirled. A look of indescribable horror filled his eyes. '*Aya Rin,*' he whispered. 'Thasha, Thasha. What've I done?'

Ten minutes later the four of them – Thasha, Marila, Neeps and Felthrup – were all collapsed together on the divan. Thasha was massaging her neck, while Felthrup teased bits of glass (shards of the water jug Marila had hurled at Neeps) – from his fur and the fabric of her shirt. Marila, leaning back against Thasha's knees, was holding one of the Great Peace dinner napkins against Neeps' bloody ear. Neeps himself sat curled in a ball, staring at nothing. When the lamp sputtered out they were glad of it; none of them could quite stand to look the others in the face.

'I almost let the dogs out,' said Marila.

'Oh gods,' said Thasha with a violent shudder. 'He would have died. I'd lost my voice, Marila, I couldn't have called them off. They'd have torn him to pieces.'

'That occurred to me,' said Marila, 'when I heard the door starting to splinter.'

'One of you was meant to die, I think,' said Felthrup.

'Neeps,' said Thasha, touching him with her foot. 'It wasn't you.'

'Yes it was,' said Neeps quietly. 'That's just it. The ... madness. It came from inside me.'

'That still doesn't make it your fault,' said Marila.

'Then I'd like to know whose fault it is,' said Neeps.

'Now you are asking the right question,' said Felthrup.

'You were magicked, somehow,' said Marila, dabbing at his ear. 'I saw the change halfway through the practice session. Your eyes went all funny. I thought you'd had too many whacks on the head.'

'Thasha—' Neeps began.

Thasha squirmed abruptly; the divan shuddered and groaned. 'This blary thing's too small,' she said. 'Unless anyone wants dinner I suggest we all go to sleep.'

No one moved. 'I don't want to sleep,' said Felthrup.

'You've been up for days,' said Thasha.

'Neeps,' said Marila. 'You kept saying *Raffa, Raffa*. What was all that about? Raffa who?'

Neeps took the napkin from her hand and turned to face the window. After a long silence he said, 'Undrabust.'

'Ah,' said Thasha.

Neeps' voice was hollow. 'I told Pazel a bit, once. How I jumped my ship when it landed at Sollochstol, and ran home to my village. And how the Arqualis came after me, and caught me the same afternoon. But that's not . . . the worst part.'

He looked at them, angry and beseeching. 'My older brother, Raffa, asked 'em how much it would cost for them to let me go, while they were still lounging around the village, drinking. Three pounds of pearls, they said. And Raffa haggled. Right there in front of me, wheedling like, until finally they caved in. "Two pounds, since he's so small, and you're such a nuisance." Raffa told 'em he'd see what he could find. The Arqualis said they'd only wait an hour. But in fact they waited all afternoon. They wanted those pearls more than they wanted me.

'Trouble was, so did Raffa. He was the best pearl diver in the village. He had boxes of 'em hidden in the smokehouse. He was saving up for a ticket to Opalt. A cousin had come back from there years before and told Raffa our palm roof was embarrassing. He said Sollochis lived like animals. That Ballytween City was the place for a man to get ahead.'

Neeps fell silent. Thasha wanted to say something, but was afraid to; all at once she felt like a fraud. She'd grown up in a mansion on Maj Hill, in the heart of the world's greatest city. She remembered Syrarys combing her hair, telling her that they lived in the only place in Alifros that nobody could look down on. *Why don't they hate me?* she thought. *Why doesn't Pazel hate me?*

'Raffa never came back that day,' said Neeps. 'I guess the price was too high.'

Marila silently touched his arm. They stayed there, motionless, listening to the thumping and bellowing of men on other decks. Fiffengurt had said the work might go on all night, but to Thasha the noise was soothing; the warm stateroom felt like the centre of a hive. As she closed her eyes she heard a wet sound that was either kissing or one of her dogs flopping down with a contented slobber. Then she realised Marila had her arms around Neeps. *That blary vixen*, she thought, and fell asleep.

Felthrup slunk away from the divan when Neeps and Marila began to kiss. He was not quite clear why humans did such things – the written accounts varied wildly – but he knew they did not much care to be watched in the act. He crept over to Suzyt, who lay beside the washroom door.

'I won't go to sleep,' he told her.

The mastiff's tongue enveloped him like a warm, wet towel. Felthrup curled tight against her chest, looking out at the darkened stateroom. He had fought to remember the dreams until his brain ached, and had come up with almost nothing: a pair of glasses, a taste of candy and the words 'peppermint oil'. He was a nervous idiot. What could be so terrible about dreams he did not even remember? There were a million rats in Alifros who would kill for the kind of safety he enjoyed.

'Master Stargraven,' said a gently mocking voice.

Felthrup gave a start. The dog slept on beside him, but how she had shrunk! No, she was the same – but he had done it, he had fallen asleep at last, and now everyone would pay for his weakness.

He stood up and adjusted his spectacles.

The three youths slept like the dead. He walked to the divan and looked down at them. So peaceful: Neeps' head lay pillowed on Marila's lap. He saw the damage his own teeth had done to the boy's ear, and winced. But he had saved Thasha's life.

Surely it was Arunis who had called his name? There was no sign of anyone else in the room, but that would not keep him safe for long. In every dream he felt a compulsion to walk, to leave the shelter of the stateroom and wander, until the sorcerer found him and the torture began.

Tonight was no exception: his feet were already guiding him towards the stateroom door. Twice he swerved and teetered clown-like back into the centre of the room. But he could not hold still. *I will betray them again. Every time it grows worse. I will be the reason they perish, the reason Arunis comes to rule the world.*

Suddenly he knew what to do. He could end the dreams as quickly as they began. But how? A sword? A mouthful of broken glass? No, no – that was the sort of thing Arunis did to him anyway. He would be swifter. He looked at the gallery windows, gave a pitiful squeal, and ran straight for them.

He never arrived. Between one footfall and the next the ship spun about like a carousel, and instead of crashing through the window he found himself throwing open the stateroom door.

Lamplight: the Turach soldiers were still at their post. Behind them, and as invisible to humans as Felthrup himself was during their dream-walks, stood Arunis. The mage's eyes fixed him like spearpoints. He crooked a finger.

Get out here, you feeble, vacillating, sewer-pipe sniveller.

The call was terribly powerful, but Felthrup, with a last mind-cracking effort, slammed the stateroom door and leaned against it. *Help,* he thought, *help. This time I really will go mad.*

Then, very faintly, he heard the voice again. The first voice, the one by which he had woken into the dream. It was not the sorcerer's. It was coming from Admiral Isiq's sleeping cabin.

Felthrup broke away from the door and ran towards the bedchamber, crashing against a shifted chair. Anything was better than what awaited him in the passage. He kicked the bearskin rug away from the door, reached for the knob – and froze. Surely this was another trick? What if Arunis had somehow penetrated the magic wall this far? What if the very act of opening the door was all he needed to breach their last defence? Felthrup cringed. He suddenly felt very ratlike indeed.

'Turn the knob,' said the voice, almost too softly to be heard.

Felthrup turned the knob, half-expecting some horror to burst from the chamber, savage his sleeping friends, end their months of struggle in a heartbeat. Nothing of the kind occurred: the room held only dust, and the furniture Isiq had left behind. A large bed, two chests of drawers, Syrarys' jewellery table, a dressing mirror, a mannequin draped in an elaborate gown: what the vicious woman had planned to wear on Simja, perhaps.

'Over here, lad, hurry now.'

The voice was louder, and suddenly Felthrup knew it, and gave a squeal of joy. He dashed into the room, afraid now only of waking, and cried, 'Where are you, where are you?'

'The mirror, Felthrup. Dust it off.'

Felthrup looked at the mirror. It was tilted towards the ceiling, and the dust lay like a grey pelt upon the glass. He put his silk sleeve against the mirror and swept it clean.

Within the mirror there was no reflection. Instead he found himself looking into a dark and cluttered chamber of stone. He had an impression of clocks and telescopes, astrolabes and smoked-glass spheres, an icy window, lamps that threw clots of whirling colour on the floor.

But all this he saw with but a corner of his mind, for directly before him stood a tall man in a sea-green cloak. The man was perfectly bald, but he had a thick white beard and enormous bottle-brush eyebrows, and beneath them, eyes that were bottomless and dark.

'It's you, isn't it?' said Felthrup, feeling a lump rise in his throat. 'It's how you really are.'

'Right in the first count, wrong in the second,' the man replied. 'Indeed I'm surprised one as afflicted with imagination as you still clings to the notion of *real*. Now step to one side – that's it.'

The old man turned and walked away, deeper into the stone chamber. When twenty feet separated him from Felthrup he turned again, and then ran, with the ease of a much younger man, straight at the surface of the mirror. At the last instant he leaped, head first—

—and the black mink, Ramachni Fremken, sailed into the chamber as through an open door. This was the mage as Felthrup knew him: the one who had rescued him from drowning, slain fleshancs, taught Pazel the Master-Word that changed the Shaggat to stone. The one whose very name brought a look of fear into Arunis' eyes, no matter how the sorcerer tried to conceal it. He landed in a cloud of dust on Isiq's bed. Felthrup knelt beside him, sneezed, and burst into tears.

'Stop that at once,' said Ramachni. 'What on earth is the matter, Felthrup? Surely we meet in better circumstances than before?'

'Oh no, Master, not at all.'

Ramachni sprang from the bed and vanished into the stateroom. Felthrup rushed after him, still crying, though he could not have said exactly why. He found the mage on the arm of the divan, looking down at the three sleeping youths.

'How untroubled they look,' said Ramachni, echoing Felthrup's earlier thought. 'And how fortunate that your dream-life is so splendid. But look what you have done to yourself tonight, my dear rat!

Some turn themselves into warriors, angels, kings. You've become a librarian.'

'Not just tonight, m'lord. This is the form I take in every dream.'

'Every single dream?' said Ramachni, turning to him with surprise. 'That *is* something to ponder, when I have a moment. But can't you hold still, Felthrup? Why do you keep starting for the door?'

Felthrup checked himself, and dropped his head in shame. 'Arunis is calling me. He never stops. He has a terrible power over me, and he is using me against our friends.'

'We shall see about that,' said Ramachni with a hint of temper.

'My lord!' said Felthrup, rubbing his chin with both hands in a most ratlike gesture. 'Did you not say that Arunis was the stronger in this world, that when you travel here you leave a great part of your strength behind?'

'I did,' said Ramachni, 'although when next I come to Alifros it shall be with a strength you have never seen. But tonight, Felthrup, the only traveller is you. When your dream began you departed the Alifros you know and came here, to a dream-Alifros, only a small part of which was created by your mind. Arunis and I were here already, for dreams exist in a territory that the mage never entirely ceases to inhabit.'

'He is standing just outside your magic wall.'

Ramachni shook his head. 'That wall is not of my making.'

'Not of your making!' cried Felthrup. 'Then there is some other mage aboard, who wishes us well?'

'Perhaps,' said Ramachni, glancing curiously around the stateroom. 'But this I can tell you for certain: the spell that made the magic wall was cast long before the *Chathrand* left Etherhorde – years before, in fact. How cunningly hidden it must have been, to keep me from detecting it! I wonder if there are more such surprises, and if they will all prove so helpful.'

Suddenly he turned and sniffed the air. Then he bounded across the room and onto the table, where he peered suspiciously at the pigsfoot casserole.

'Do not eat this,' he said. 'Someone besides Mr Teggatz had a hand in its preparation. There is a whiff of magic about it – dark magic, you understand. It is only a distant aftertaste, nothing so obvious as a curse or a potion. But we must take no chances.'

Felthrup clenched his hands in fists, and stared at them as if he had never seen anything more impressive. Then he picked up the casserole, crossed the room to the window and flung the dish overboard.

No sooner had he closed the window, however, than doubt returned to his face. 'In my first dream Arunis flung Sniraga into the sea,' he said, 'but the cat is still aboard. My dreams change nothing, do they? When I wake that dish will again be on the table. And my waking self remembers nothing of what passes in these dreams. I shall not be able to warn them, Ramachni.'

'Do not be so certain, lad. Your dreams certainly change *you*. I hear the exhaustion in your voice: you've been fighting for your very soul. In any case, you must try. Whatever is in that food was put there with malice of the blackest sort.'

Felthrup jumped, remembering. 'Neeps took a bite!' he said. 'And a short time later he went mad and tried to kill Lady Thasha. He almost succeeded.'

Ramachni looked up from the table. Now the anger in his eyes was terrible to behold. 'It is time, Felthrup. You called out for help, and I am here to give it. Let us go and see the sorcerer.'

Felthrup swallowed, and pushed his spectacles up his nose. Ramachni jumped to the floor, crossed once more to the divan, and crawled up beside Thasha's shoulder. His pink tongue dabbed once at her forehead; then he turned and studied the chamber again. His eyes settled on the bearskin rug. A look of satisfaction crept over his face.

'How dare you keep me waiting.'

The sorcerer waited just beyond the red stripe, his mouth twisted with anger. The four Turachs leaned against the walls. Arunis watched the thin, bespectacled man leave the stateroom without closing the door.

'So you can fight my summons now? Well after tonight you'll wish you'd never tried, you mangled, three-legged misery of a rat. Get out here!'

The thin man took his time, but at last he reached the magic wall. He did not immediately step through it, however. Instead he paused with his face just inches from the sorcerer's own.

'After tonight,' he said quietly, 'you will wish you'd never invaded his dreams.'

'Whose dreams?'

'Felthrup's, you fool.'

With that the man in spectacles reached through the wall and seized Arunis by his scarf. At his touch the mage gasped aloud and tried to pull away. But the thin man held him fast, and began to chant:

Light is the purse that brimmed with deceit
Fierce are the hunters, and swift their feet
And the night so late and lonely.

Bribe them you might, but what can you offer?
A curse, and a kick, and a black barren coffer,
And the taste of treason only.

Dear have you cost us, but never so dear
That we'll tender our souls to a peddler of fear.
Pride may be costly, but pain is free:
For thee, old deceiver, it comes for thee.

On the last word he let go of the scarf, dropped to the deck, and became once more a mink. Arunis leaped back in terror. But the mink did not attack him. It fled.

'What's this?' roared Arunis. 'The great Ramachni, turning tail? Have you nothing but rhymes to fight with?'

A deafening roar filled the passage behind him.

Arunis whirled, and for one second he gaped at the bear, a huge brown boulder of an creature, looming over him, so tall its shoulder touched the roof of the passage.

'Stop, Felthrup!' he shrieked. 'I *order* you—'

Then its weight was upon him, and its claws like mallet-driven spikes, and its teeth that ripped his dream-flesh like so much tissue paper, like the wrapping on a box that held no gift, nothing but emptiness and a voice that cursed and was gone.

27

The Ambush

—◦◦◦—

24 Freala 941
133rd day from Etherhorde

By the time they reached the hill overlooking the *Chathrand*, Diadrelu was winded, and the man beside her was panting like a hound. Even at nine in the morning the heat was fierce – particularly at eight inches above the barren ground. Seabirds whirled over them, innumerable: the dry side of Sandplume was one great eyrie, where gull and plover and albatross and tern vied for every available inch of nesting space. The birds had no real stomach for fighting creatures who could take off one of their wings with the swipe of a blade, but their pecking and diving made it hard to attend to other matters. Their noises – outraged wails, honks, brays, screeches – made Diadrelu think of the torments of the damned.

'A fool's errand,' grunted the man, whose name was Steldak.

Diadrelu shaded her eyes. Three hundred feet below them, the *Chathrand* and Sandor Ott's single-masted ship lay at anchor, hidden on three sides by the horseshoe-shaped isle.

'Look there.'

She pointed. From behind the cutter the *Chathrand*'s skiff was gliding into view. Her sail was down already. Aboard the Great Ship men were running out the davit-chains to receive the little craft.

Diadrelu took a short monocular telescope from her pocket and raised it to her eye. *There was Pazel.* She heaved a great sigh of relief. The boy had survived another misadventure ashore. Rin only knew what they had done to him this time.

'Erthalon Ness is not aboard,' she said aloud.

Steldak hissed through his teeth. 'It's as I foretold, then,' he said. 'They have given him to someone on Bramian, someone who will put

354

him to evil use. How I wish you had stabbed them both!'

The rejoinder flashed through Dri's mind: *How I wish I'd stabbed you.* She closed her eyes, deeply shamed by the thought. Steldak was gaunt, despite the food and nursing lavished on him these past two months. He had spent years in a cage in Rose's desk, lifted out only at mealtimes, to test the captain's food for poison. His rescue had been a triumph of cunning on her brother's part. But Steldak's disobedience – he had tried to assassinate Rose on the spot – had cost Lord Talag his life.

He was delirious, Dri reminded herself. *He'd believed for years that he would die in that cage. And he has done his penance, and sworn an oath to the clan.*

Still she was glad she'd remembered the little scope, if only to give her something besides Steldak to focus on. The very sound of his breathing set her teeth on edge. Hate (so her people's adage went) was the place where death entered the living, the blind mote in the eye of the soul. Dri had always liked the adage, although she could not remember the last time she heard it on any tongue but her own. It was wrong to hate Steldak. But she did.

'There was a death ashore – a military death.' She pointed at a black ribbon of canvas snapping in the breeze from the masthead. 'I do not see Drellarek, the Turach commander. I wonder if it was he who fell.'

Steldak shrugged. 'It was not Rose, more's the pity. Beyond that I am not much interested.' He lunged at a gull, which sheered away with a ravenous wail. 'Let us go, Diadrelu. There is nothing more to be learned here.'

'What of the winds?' she asked. Steldak, who claimed to have been born at sea, had also declared himself a fine judge of weather.

'A storm from the north-east,' he said, glancing vaguely at the sky. 'These westerlies are not half what they were twelve hours ago. Some gale is sucking all the force from them. Soon they will turn back on themselves, and then we shall see.'

'How soon?'

Steldak's eyes travelled the horizon. 'After midday, if you force me to guess. But Bakru's lions answer to no one but Bakru, and sometimes not even to him. Lady Dri, I would return to our commander's side. He may have need of us.'

'Lord Taliktrum knows where we are.'

Nonetheless she relented, and the two ixchel started back down the hill. The footing was treacherous, and the birds, excited by movement, redoubled their attack. By the time they reached the island's highest shrubs they were winded again.

They groped beneath a stand of spiny, wind-tortured thorbal trees, their legs sinking to the knees in a powder of dead moss and lichen, and then began an easier descent, under greener growth. The Black Shoulder Ott had chosen as the Great Ship's final harbour in the northern world had two faces: the parched east, scoured by the rising sun, and the lush west, doused by the fogs that drifted almost daily from the Bramian landmass. They had crossed from one side to the other, and soon were able to slake their thirst on beads of water clinging to leaf-tips. From below the sound of pipes grew stronger.

'There they are,' said Diadrelu.

Just ahead, the land fell away in a cleft, like a jagged pie-slice cut from the island, all the way to the sea. At the edge of the precipice stood Taliktrum and two other ixchel, gazing down at the bright rock walls. The cliffs, like the hilltop, were alive with nesting birds; but here the birds were shore-swallows: cousins to the common birds that dwelled in barns and outbuildings. They screeched and bickered; you could hardly call it song. Their nests dappled the cliffs, grass-woven, mud-mortared, dried to the harness of stone. Thousands of the birds came and went on wings like dark flames, bringing grubs and insects to their fledglings.

It was, thought Dri, like a scene out of legend: the wall of sacred birds (swallows alone were sacred to her people), the crashing surf, and above them the young master of a noble House, resplendent in a swallow-suit of his own. The suit was one of but two such feathered coats in the possession of the clan. They were treasures, cared for and mended over centuries. But their value was more than ceremonial: with hands thrust into the cloak's wingbone gauntlets, any reasonably strong ixchel could fly.

Beside her nephew stood Ghali, the old Pachet seer; and his grand-daughter, Myett, a wary, wide-eyed thing of twenty, whose first glance always seemed to anticipate a threat. Sensing their approach before the others, Myett recoiled into catlike fighting stance, and relaxed but slowly as Dri and Steldak emerged from the trees.

'How do we fare, my lord?' asked Steldak, hurrying to Taliktrum's side.

The young commander of Ixphir House did not alter his gaze in the slightest, nor was his answer, when it came, directed at Steldak.

'It will not do,' he said. 'No, Pachet, it will not do at all. Where does the problem lie, can you fathom that at least? With the pipes? With the swallows? With your playing, if you'll pardon the question?'

The old man turned. He was stern and very dignified, with his combed grey beard and eyebrows thick as foxtails. In his hands was a splendid instrument: a set of black wooden pan pipes, joined with hoops of gold that sparkled in the sun.

'All three, to be sure,' said the Pachet. 'Every colony of swallows has its own music, its own signature and key. The pipes, too, have not seen use in a generation.' He lowered his eyes. 'And I, perhaps, cannot call on—'

'The skill you once were known for?'

The old man looked up sharply. 'The lungs of my youth,' he said calmly. 'That is all I meant to say.'

'Very honest of you, Pachet. But don't forget my title.'

'Your pardon, Lord Taliktrum.'

Once again Dri felt scalded by shame – this time for the conduct of her nephew. *In front of the Pachet's granddaughter! That man played at your birth-feast, you little tyrant, not to mention your father's, and my own.*

'Master Ghali,' she said, stepping forwards, 'do you have it in you to play once more?'

'It is no use,' said Taliktrum. 'The birds are deaf to him. We must think about our return to the ship.'

'You're quite right, my lord,' said Steldak. 'The weather is changing, and if thunderheads roll out of Bramian we shall not gain the ship at all.'

Dri took a step nearer, pointing. 'If we but walk a little along the southern cliff, there is an outcropping. The sound may carry better there.'

An awkward silence followed. Dri had been sprung from her house arrest and brought ashore precisely because she knew something of the old lore of the swallow-pipes. But Taliktrum did not want it forgotten for an instant that she was no longer in command. She had only made a suggestion, but to accept it – that was to play the younger nephew, not the lord.

'Come, Grandfather,' said the young woman, casting a distrustful eye on Dri. 'Let us put your instrument away.'

But Taliktrum raised a staying hand. 'We will do as my aunt recommends. Take the Pachet's arm, Myett, and guide him carefully.'

They made their way single-file along the cliff's edge. *He's learning,* thought Diadrelu. *As am I.*

When they reached the rock outcropping the plain sense of her suggestion was clear to all. The rock was nearer to the nests, and the wind did not gust back in the Pachet's face. Taliktrum grew animated. He beckoned to the old man, waved Dri and Myett impatiently away. 'You'll startle the birds, blast you, fall back!' Then he spread his hands wide, froze there for an instant, and swept them towards the old musician. He was, Dri realised with sudden heartache, mimicking her brother's gesture: that pompous double-wave that told a singer or a poet that he might proceed. She had never imagined it was something she could miss.

Pachet Ghali knelt, and filled his lungs, and played. The music was like nothing else in ixchel tradition. It was not a melody as such, and yet there was a loud and lilting refrain. It was no attempt at birdsong, and yet it was a summons to the creatures. It was spellcraft: one of the last shards of magic in the collective memory of her people. Among the ixchel, only artists retained any link to the ancient disciplines whereby (it was said) miracles had once been performed. It was part of her brother's genius and audacity that he had planned to wed ixchel magic, for the first time in centuries, to a practical use.

But her brother was dead, and the Pachet was old, and the birds did not seem to hear him.

They all stood listening, hoping. The sound contended with the wind, the surf, the noise of the swallows themselves. At last Taliktrum sliced the air with a despairing hand.

'Enough,' he said. 'Save your breath, old man.'

The Pachet did not cease playing, however. Instead he rose slowly to his feet. His eyes were wide. Taliktrum looked from the player to the cliffs and back again. And then Dri realised that the birds had fallen silent.

The others stood as tense as she, watching the cliffs. Pachet Ghali played on. Suddenly a dark shadow flitted past his shoulder. Two more followed in the wink of an eye. Then it was as if the whole colony of birds had become of one mind. They flowed over the rim of the crevasse in a dark torrent and swept among the ixchel, so close that Dri felt the caress of wingtips on her shoulders. The Pachet turned, chasing the swallows with his eyes. All at once his music changed, and from a summons it became an order, a sharp and definite command.

Only twenty or thirty birds heeded him this time, but they were enough. Peeling away from the flock, they formed a racing circle about the ixchel. The Pachet raised his song a whole octave, his face amber-red with the strain.

Then the birds fell on Taliktrum. They jostled and crowded, vying to seize some part of his shirt or leggings. Dri had coached him for this moment, from the old lore of their House, the memories passed down to her by her great-aunts and uncles. Taliktrum raised his arms as though preparing to dive, and then it seemed almost that he was diving, but *upwards*, as the swallows bore him swiftly through the tree tops.

'Gods of earth and air,' said Diadrelu.

She heard his triumphant laugh. The birds flew where he wished: up the slope of the island, out over the cauldron of waves, down in a plummeting dive from which they were scarcely able to recover.

Myett approached Diadrelu and gripped her arm. 'My grandfather tires,' she said. 'You must tell your nephew to come down.'

'Let him cease playing when he will!' Steldak laughed. 'Our commander wears the swallow-suit; if they drop him he will fly back to us himself. And he no longer answers to Diadrelu, girl: she has been sanctioned by the clan, and walks free by his mercy. *Aya Rin*, see how they obey! It is as if—'

Steldak never finished his thought. Taliktrum and his swallow-servants raced by overhead, and the young lord swept a hand over the four figures beneath him. And before they could wonder at the move the swallows were boiling around them, black eyes shining with urgency, talons seizing at their clothes.

They rose together in the grip of the birds. The flock winged after Taliktrum, who was racing out over the sea. *We'll die!* thought Dri. For the Pachet's music had ceased: he could barely hold onto his instrument, let alone play.

But the birds still held them tightly, and still flew where Taliktrum willed. He led them far from the cliff, and high into the sky. For Dri, who had flown many times by swallow-suit, it was a frightful but thrilling experience. For the others it was pure terror. Steldak wore the look of a man in free fall, watching his death rush towards him. Myett and the Pachet were reciting prayers.

Only Taliktrum was fearless: indeed he looked half-crazed with ecstasy. Roaring, he made the birds climb higher still, until they saw beneath them all five Black Shoulder Isles, and the belching cone of an active volcano, and a fantastic mountaintop ruin on Bramian with serpentine walls that vanished in the mist. *How is he doing it?* Dri wondered. *Will they obey him as long as he wears the suit?* Then the flock wheeled round and Dri saw fear enter her nephew's face at last.

Great Mother!

A human stood atop the hill she and Steldak had climbed an hour before. He was a tall man in late-middle years, head shaved, dressed in a sand-coloured cloak tied with a crimson belt. His hands were raised above his head, and in one of them he held a sceptre of gold topped with a dark and jagged crystal. The furious seabirds whirled about him, fearing for their eggs, and it was a moment before Dri saw his face. When she did at last, she knew with a certainty that it was not the first time.

The man did not glance skywards; they had not been seen. As Taliktrum brought the flock around for another pass, Dri took out the monocular and trained it on him. The man had lowered his sceptre until it pointed at the *Chathrand*, and Dri could see his lips moving in some chant or incantation. A moment later he turned and quickly left the hill.

How had he landed, and where was his boat? Dri could not imagine that such a personage had been aboard the *Chathrand* all along. But where else could he have come from? And where in the Nine Pits had she seen his face?

Taliktrum struggled to draw nearer to his aunt, but he could not control individual birds, and merely sent them all zig-zagging above the isle. 'What do we do?' he shouted in the ixchel-voice no human could hear. For a moment all his pride of lordship was forgotten.

'Land!' Dri shouted back. 'Sweep low around the isle, and land! We must get back to the ship! This magic is no use to us now!'

Taliktrum nodded, still in shock. He swept his hand in a circle, and as if reading his very thought the birds dived for Sandplume. Soon they were safely out of sight, with trees and hill between them and the stranger above.

Then Myett screamed like a child, and pointed out over the western sea.

A warship was racing towards them, around the south shore of Bramian. Dri snapped the monocular to her eye: she was a great sleek predator of a ship, seven falling stars upon her foresail and a hull painted white as snow. It was a Mzithrini *Blodmel*. No more than twelve miles off. And of course it was not making for them at all – nothing as small as an ixchel was visible at such a distance – but rather for the *Chathrand*, the unsuspecting *Chathrand*, still moored on the blind side of the isle.

Taliktrum's gestures became frantic, crude. Wary of being seen by the man above, he drove the flock so low that a few unlucky birds flew full-tilt into the crest of a wave, perishing instantly. Then the nesting-cliff came into view and he veered so sharply that Myett's birds nearly lost their grip. Their landing was rough to say the least. Dri and Steldak were flung against the sides of trees. The old Pachet landed with a grimace of pain, but he kept his instrument safe in his arms.

Taliktrum ran to Diadrelu's side. 'Get up, Aunt, we have to think! It was a *Blodmel*, wasn't it?'

Dri climbed painfully to her feet. 'Not just any *Blodmel*,' she said. 'That is the *Jistrolloq*, the White Reaper. And it cannot be here by chance.'

'But perhaps they still respect the new peace?' asked Pachet Ghali.

'Yes, and they have come all this way to invite us to a game of pass-the-sandal,' said Taliktrum acidly.

'Keep silent, old fool,' snapped Steldak, 'and let His Lordship think.'

Taliktrum pulled a large bundle from under a drift of leaves. It was the other swallow-suit, which they had hidden an hour ago. He tore it roughly from its travel sack.

Diadrelu shook her head. 'No, Pachet, they have come too far for any task but murder. They blame us for their elder's death, and indeed it was Arunis who flung the incubus at their shrine.'

'How long do we have?' demanded Taliktrum.

'If the wind does not freshen?' said Steldak. 'Perhaps forty minutes, my lord.'

'That old giant on the hilltop is in league with them, isn't he?' demanded Taliktrum. 'I know his face, somehow.'

'He is a *sfvantskor*,' said Diadrelu. 'It has come back to me at last. He was aboard the *Jistrolloq* when it came alongside us in Simja. And I would guess that the wand he holds is what Arunis called Sathek's Sceptre, which he dispatched the incubus to steal. But this is no time for guesswork. You must fly to the ship at once, Taliktrum, and take the Pachet with you.'

'And what then, Aunt? Those devils are going to sink her!'

Taliktrum's voice had come out shrill. Dri stared at him, appalled: he had the look of a cornered animal. She had any number of misgivings about her nephew's role as clan leader, but paralysis in the face of danger was something she had never imagined.

'The *Jistrolloq* is a terrible foe,' she said cautiously, 'but the *Chathrand* is not defenceless, and she is nearly twice their size. Go, Taliktrum. See the Pachet safely to Night Village, then warn the humans.'

'Of course!' laughed Taliktrum. 'What other counsel should I expect from you? Talk to the giants, trust them, embrace them! Let them decide our fate!'

'If you would not do this,' said Diadrelu, 'give me the other suit, and I will.'

'Do you believe me now, Lord?' said Myett suddenly, her eyes locked on Diadrelu. 'I warned you that she would seek to usurp your place.'

'Oh child, nonsense,' said Pachet Ghali.

'Diadrelu has no business here,' said Steldak. 'What is it she advises? To sweep into the ship, crying an alarm? That would bring doom on our clan no matter what followed. If the *Chathrand* did indeed escape, Rose's first act when out of danger would be to exterminate us all.'

'Madness,' whispered Taliktrum.

'Yes, nephew, it is,' said Diadrelu. 'While we bicker they are closing. Our people will be dead by midday if we do not act. But I never suggested that we abandon secrecy. Go to the stateroom and alert Hercól or Thasha or Neeps Undrabust, or even the woken rat. They may sound the alarm in our stead.'

Still Taliktrum demurred. Dri fell silent: the facts had all been spoken; he would face the deed before him or he would not. *And you, Diadrelu Tammariken? Will you face what must be done, if his will breaks?*

'They cannot see the *Jistrolloq*,' said Myett, 'and they will not believe the ravings of the Tholjassan or the Isiq girl, to say nothing of the rat.'

'They are still at anchor,' said Steldak. 'A light anchor, but it will take more than an hour to raise it. And if they should be caught in the cove by the *Jistrolloq* they will be utterly destroyed.'

'Then our mission fails,' said Taliktrum.

His voice was hollow with despair. While the others looked at him, speechless, Dri studied the footing between her nephew and the cliff.

'We will indeed sound an alarm,' Taliktrum continued, 'but it must be more than that. Pachet Ghali, you must play for the birds again. What my brother hoped for at Sanctuary-Beyond-the-Sea must happen now, this very minute. We must abandon the ship.'

'Lord Commander,' said the old man, turning pale, 'I do not know if my skills are equal to such a task! There are so many of us – and the birds heeded me but once out of all my attempts.'

'They will heed me, I think,' said Taliktrum, 'as soon as you cast your spell.'

'Are they to bring us … *here*?' asked Steldak, aghast. 'To this heap of an island, this birdhouse?'

'Better here than the bottom of the sea,' said Taliktrum. 'And later swallows can bear us to Bramian, a few at a time. We may rebuild our House there, and find some measure of peace, and one day our children may try again.'

'It is broad daylight,' said Diadrelu, 'and the deed on Sanctuary was to be accomplished under cover of darkness. How many will the humans kill when our people rush to the topdeck?'

'Not all,' said Taliktrum, 'that is the main thing.'

'And what of your father's dream, the one he gave his life for?'

'He gave his life to save Steldak from a cat,' said Taliktrum. 'As for dreams, it is time we woke from them. But providence does favour us in one way – had we not come ashore we would be as ignorant of the danger as the giants, and soon to perish with them. Not even you, Aunt, could prefer that fate.'

Their eyes met, lady and young lord, the old commander and her replacement. Then Dri shut her eyes, said a prayer to Mother Sky, and leaped at him.

Taliktrum had a warrior's instincts, if not a leader's. He moved into a whirling sidestep that would have kept Dri's blow from ever landing – had she tried to land one. But her nephew was not the target: she was after the other swallow-suit, gripped under the arm he raised to block her, and in that first split-second leap she snatched it from his hand.

Taliktrum's reaction was just as she hoped: the young man expected an outright attack, and sought to put distance between them lest she press her advantage. When Dri spun in the opposite direction there was suddenly a yard between them – all the room in the world for a battle-dancer.

Her second leap brought her between the Pachet and his grand-daughter. Myett was quick as a spider: she had her knife out and slashed the air before her, and Dri felt the wind of the blade as she twisted under the blow. No time to parry: she struck the Pachet as gently as she could with her elbow, seized the swallow-pipes and rolled out of range of the girl's next stab.

She came out of the roll with her feet planted, saw the flash of the descending knife and struck out with a blocking-blow almost hard enough to shatter Myett's forearm. The knife flew from the girl's hand; for an instant she seemed frozen with pain. In that instant Dri seized her by the arm and the belt and hurled her bodily at Steldak, who was sidling towards her.

A shadow. Dri threw herself sideways, and Taliktrum's sword bit the earth where she had stood a moment before. *Gods above, he's drawn his sword against his family!*

The shock of having nearly died at the hands of one she had held as an infant – and one adorned in the ancient feather-coat, like a soothsayer of old – nearly cost Dri her life. Taliktrum was in deadly earnest: he wrenched the blade from the ground straight into an upward thrust. Dri avoided the blow with room to spare, but she was off-balance now, and when the blade came down a third time it missed her chest by an inch. Her third dodge had left her so spread-eagled that Taliktrum was able to kick her right foot out from under her, throwing her backwards over his blade.

She knew as well as any fighter alive how to turn a setback into an advantage. But once more she hesitated: this time on the point of a crippling kick to her nephew's face. She knew the sound of a snapped neck, and could not live with the sound of *his* inside her, the knowledge that she had dealt the killing blow. Then Taliktrum wrenched his sword from beneath her, and as he did so the blade's edge tore a diagonal gash across her back.

What Dri did next she could not afterwards remember. She only knew (in thought too quick for words) that she must be faster than her spilling blood. She did not see her own attack, or how it felled Taliktrum in an instant; only the pain in one foot and one fist told her what she had used to bring him down. She was standing; he lay twisting in the leaves, stunned but not mortally wounded, the sword that had drawn her blood still clenched in his hand.

She turned and ran, straight out along the edge of the cliff, pulling on the swallow-suit as she went. Behind her Steldak was howling: 'Lord Taliktrum! Murder! Regicide!' And Myett was giving chase. Dri ran so close to the precipice that earth and leaves sheered off with every footfall. How her back bled! The ancient coat would be defiled for ever, and how would their descendents speak of the one whose blood stained the garment? Heroine, traitor, fool?

She stumbled. Her shoulder met the cliff's edge, and then she was falling, spinning, the boiling waves rushing towards her. She closed her eyes and extended her arms, thrust her hands into the wing-bone gauntlets—

And soared.

'What do you mean, refuses?' said Neeps.

'I mean he refuses – he flat-out won't come near her,' said Fiffengurt with a significant look at Thasha's cabin. She had retreated there well before sunrise, with Felthrup and her dogs, and had only responded to their knocking with irritated grunts. Felthrup's muffled voice went on and on, however, as if the rat were delivering an endless speech.

The quartermaster entered the stateroom and closed the door behind him. He looked worried and morose. 'As a matter of fact, Pathkendle doesn't want to see any of you. He's asked for his hammock to be brought to the midship compartment on the berth deck. He says he'll be as safe there as he would in the stateroom, because there's always hundreds of sailors around. And of course no woman may set foot there. I don't think he's in his right mind, Undrabust, if you want the truth. He says Alyash is a Mzithrini! And he says he watched Drellarek get *eaten.*'

'Did Pazel get bumped on the head, maybe?' asked Marila sensibly.

Fiffengurt shook his head. 'He *looks* like he's been wrestling snakes in the bottom of the Pits. And there's more, by Rin.' He lowered his voice, although they were quite alone. 'Pathkendle says Rose has got a wolf burned into his forearm. How d'ye like that development, lad? Rose carries the same mark as you and Pathkendle and Thasha and Mr Hercól. Does that mean what I think, now – that the captain's going to help us?'

Neeps' eyes widened in disbelief. 'Pazel must be wrong,' he said. 'He saw some other scar on Rose's arm, and got carried away.'

'I'm sure you're right, Undrabust,' said Fiffengurt uneasily.

'Hang that fool, he's impossible!' Neeps exploded. 'Gone for three days of Rin-knows-what on Bramian, and he can't even bring himself to say, "*Hello, I survived?*"'

'Obviously not,' said Marila.

Neeps glared at her. 'Anything else *obvious* to you?'

Marila nodded firmly. She began to count on her fingers.

'Pazel won't actually be safe on the berth deck, because it's full of violent men. And all that chatter from Felthrup – it's just like the night before last. He's reading to her from the *Polylex*, Neeps. And Thasha must have asked him to, because who could put up with it otherwise? And Rose hasn't imprisoned you yet because he thinks you'll be useful to him, just like Pazel must have been on Bramian.'

'Finished?' Neeps demanded.

'No,' said Marila. 'It's also obvious that you and Pazel had a fight before he left – you get angry whenever he's mentioned. And one more thing: since Ramachni left we haven't won any battles, unless you count what happened on Dhola's Rib. Mostly we've been fighting just to stay alive. We're ... lost, and our enemies are stronger than ever.'

Fiffengurt sighed and worried his beard. 'That last part's certain,' he said. 'But they did take one hit on Bramian: Sergeant Drellarek met his death, in some horrid way no one wants to explain.'

Thasha's door creaked open. There she stood, bedraggled and wild-eyed between her dogs.

'Where is Pazel?'

Awkward silence. Neeps and Fiffengurt glanced sidelong at each other, as if each was hoping the other would speak first.

Marila came to their rescue. 'He's annoyed with us – with the two of you, anyway. He and Neeps got into a fight—'

'What?' cried Thasha.

'—and Pazel's mad at you for kissing Fulbreech—'

'*What?*' shouted Neeps. 'Thasha, you kissed that snake-tongued stooge? That palace bootlick?'

Thasha looked ready to smack him. 'You don't know a thing about Greysan. He's no more a bootlick than you, he's worked for what he's got—'

'Aye,' laughed Neeps acidly. 'I've no *doubt* he earns his wages. Just didn't imagine you'd be paying 'em.'

'You *pig*!' Thasha took a step towards Neeps. 'Did you try to strangle Pazel too?'

'Are you both touched in the head?' cried Fiffengurt, stepping between them. 'I've never seen such a pair of beasts! Enough, enough, or by the Night Gods you can have done with any help from this old man!'

His rage shamed them all to silence. Fiffengurt took a deep breath. 'That's much better. Now then—'

A terrified squeal cut him off. It was Felthrup, still in Thasha's cabin. They rushed into the chamber and saw the rat upon her bed, eyes riveted on the single porthole, which stood ajar. Collapsed on the sash was what they first took for an injured bird. But then the bird rose on shaky human legs.

'It's Diadrelu!' cried Thasha, leaping to her side. 'She's been stabbed!'

She lifted the ixchel woman gently from the sill. 'The coat, don't harm the coat!' Diadrelu gasped.

'Devil take the coat!' said Felthrup. 'Where is your wound, Diadrelu?'

'Lord Rin!' said Fiffengurt. 'That thing's a crawly!'

Dri looked up at him, copper eyes sharp.

366

'Put it down, Thasha!' cried Fiffengurt. 'They're worse than scorpions! Trust me, I know!'

'Will he talk?' said Diadrelu quietly.

'Will I talk?' cried Fiffengurt. 'You can bet your ship-sinking blood I'll talk!'

'No you won't!' shouted Neeps and Thasha together.

Fiffengurt looked from one to the other, like a man being circled by strangers in an alley. 'You don't understand,' he whispered. 'That's a crawly.'

'We've no time for this,' husked Diadrelu.

'It's your back that's cut, isn't it?' said Neeps, trying to peel the coat away from the bloody spot. Dri dug her nails into his thumb.

'You're under attack,' she said.

The warning spilled from her, even as her blood soaked Thasha's arm: the old priest on the island, Sathek's Sceptre, the *Jistrolloq* tearing east with a full spread of sail. The humans stood gaping. Once more Thasha was the first to reach a decision.

'Take her, Marila.'

Gingerly she passed Diadrelu to the Tholjassan girl. 'What are you doing, Thasha?' Felthrup asked.

'Alerting Rose,' she said. 'It has to be me, don't you understand?'

Without waiting for an answer, she flew from the stateroom. They heard her shouting from the passage: 'Turachs! Rose wanted me captured, right? Here I am, take me! I surrender!'

Neeps started to run after her, but a glance at Fiffengurt's tortured expression stopped him dead.

'Listen,' Neeps said, 'we owe our lives to this *crawly*. She saved me and Pazel in the Crab Fens. And she was the one who guessed the right moment to turn the Shaggat to stone.'

'Then she's using you, Undrabust – exploiting your good nature.'

'Oh come on,' said Neeps. 'My *what*?'

Marila had put Diadrelu on the bed and was easing her out of the feather-coat. 'We'll need a doctor,' she said.

'No!' said Diadrelu. 'I told you, the wound is not deep. Give me your knife, Mr Fiffengurt.'

'You know who I am!'

Diadrelu sighed. 'I also know that the *Jistrolloq* will make short work of this vessel, if her other officers move half as slowly as you do. Come then, do it yourself – cut this shirt from me.'

No room for modesty in her manner: she was a soldier in need of aid.

'Do it!' shrilled Felthrup, pawing at the quartermaster's leg. Stunned, Fiffengurt drew his skipper's knife. He slid it under the bloodsoaked shirt, and cut it with a quick upward slash.

Like any sailor worthy of the name, Fiffengurt kept his blade very sharp. The cloth parted neatly, and Diadrelu stood bare to the waist. The quartermaster blinked and dropped his eyes. He had never seen a more beautiful woman – *not a woman, a crawly, damn it all*. She twisted to examine herself: her back was crimson. A long diagonal gash crossed her shoulder.

'*Brüch*,' she swore, 'I can't fly like this. Hear me, I beg you. We have just two swallow-suits, and my nephew is wearing the other. He and three of our people are on Sandplume. They cannot escape the isle except by relaying both suits back and forth – carrying an empty suit back to the isle after each trip, you understand? – and this must happen before the *Chathrand* escapes the harbour. We cannot fly more than a half-mile without rest. Someone from my clan *must* take this suit back to Sandplume, immediately.'

'How can we make that happen?' said Neeps.

'Leave it to me!' said Felthrup, jumping. 'I know where they are! And the Turachs will never catch this rat, even if they bother to try! Leave it to me!'

And he too was gone.

Diadrelu hissed: Marila had dipped a handkerchief in brandy and was swabbing her wound. Fiffengurt would not let himself look at her again – or just once, just to confirm a suspicion. There it was, by Rin, he hadn't dreamed it: the wolf-scar, the same shape the others carried, burned into that astonishing—

'They will need you aloft, Quartermaster,' said the crawly woman, looking at him over her shoulder.

He wrenched his eyes away, blushing. 'Never could I have dreamed that I would see such a day,' he mumbled.

The crawly woman laughed, though tears of pain streaked her face. 'Stay alive long enough and you'll see it all.'

Thasha found the captain in the chart room, checking figures in a logbook with Elkstem, a great map of the Outer Isles spooling over the table's edges and draping to the floor. His steward blocked her way, but she shouted past him. 'Captain Rose! Captain Rose! We're under attack!'

He looked up at her, threatening. Then he lumbered to the door, waving the steward aside.

'How dare you,' he snarled, leaning over her.

'It's true,' she said, meeting his wolfish eyes. 'The *Jistrolloq* is running straight for us, Captain, on the other side of Sandplume. She's probably less than ten miles off.'

Rose's eyes blazed down at her. 'The *Jistrolloq*. You are hysterical, girl. Steward, have the guard escort—'

'No!' said Thasha, seizing his coat. 'It's here, it's followed us! Captain, for Rin's sake—'

'Be silent, you little fool!'

Thasha said nothing, but a look passed between them. He had called her that before: in the Straits of Simja, when the fleshancs were storming the *Chathrand*, leaving dead men around them in heaps. Rose's face paled slightly, and she knew that he remembered which of them had been in the right.

'How do you know this?' he whispered.

'Does it matter?' she said. 'Look at me, Captain. *I know.*'

Their faces were inches apart. One moment longer Rose crouched, stock-still, only his eyes whirling here and there like bats, and Thasha had the odd impression that he was listening to voices other than her own. Then he shoved her aside and charged from the room like a marauding bull.

'BEAT TO QUARTERS! EVERY LAST MAN TO QUARTERS! THE BLACK RAGS ARE MINUTES FROM OUR BOWS!'

28

The Hunt

—◦◦◦—

For the first time in his life, Felthrup crossed a deck in broad daylight without fear of men. The only danger they posed now was trampling; rats were the last thing on their mind. After what had happened in Thasha's cabin, moreover, Felthrup felt a strange, intoxicating liberty coursing through him. When two sailors locked in an argument over battle protocol jammed the ladderway, he shrilled, 'One side, one side!' – making them leap from his path. *I scared them*, thought Felthrup. *I might have been a bear, the way they jumped! Although in fact they could kill me with one blow. Reckless, that is the word. I am a reckless woken rat!*

But also a rat with a mission. And once he had bounded down into the gloom of the mercy deck, Felthrup realised just how perilous his mission was. The normally abandoned deck was caught up in a frenzy such as he had never seen. Hurricane lamps whirled through the half-light. Sailors were running, striking at one another, bellowing for greater speed. Every voice was raised, and still they could scarcely be heard above the thunder of feet on the boards above. *Don't stop, darling Felthrup, run now or you'll never run at all.*

So Felthrup ran, straight through that frightened stampede, with men slamming and shouldering crates and hogsheads about as fast as they possibly could, securing everything that might slide or topple when the Great Ship fled. *This I do for Dri. For the lady who saw me as I truly am.*

In their cargo-crate fortress the ixchel huddled, hearing the madness of the giants spread, feeling the tremors as cargo-restraining boards were slapped down and nailed to the deck within a few yards of them. Young ixchel warriors stood armed and tensed; their elders sighed with remembered massacres; parents clutched children tight to their sides.

Not one in six hundred made a sound, not even the youngest: ixchel learn not to cry in their first month of life, and never do so again except in silence.

When they heard the rat's voice, octaves above that of the giants, they did not know what to do. It did not sound like the normal witless rat-prattle. Indeed it *could* not be: there was too much of truth about it. *You can hear me, cousins, I know you can. Your lady is wounded; the rest remain on Sandplume. Be fearless now or lose them for ever. Send me one – no more. Just one brave soul prepared to fly.*

He struggled to shout over the humans – most bellowing orders, a few exclaiming about a woken rat, and a growing number declaring that miraculous or not, they would stomp the rodent dead if it didn't shut up.

Thasha followed the captain up the No. 5 ladderway, squeezed by the men rushing headlong in both directions. It had taken Rose nearly a full minute to believe her, she mused, but the crew of the *Chathrand* had taken his word without a second thought.

They stepped out on the topdeck and she paused, overwhelmed. She thought she knew what an active ship looked like, but past emergencies paled before this whirlwind. At every hatch the watch-captains punished their kettledrums. Sailors by the hundreds were leaping for the halyards, and between them Turachs were falling in with crossbows, longbows, and *vascthas* that flung discs of sharpened steel. The rigging boiled with men, laying aloft, running out the spars, freeing the clews on sail after sail. Tarboys raced down both sides of the ship, emptying sacks of sawdust for footing. The windscoops were capped, the running lights struck down, the few passengers in sight were driven below, the tonnage hatch was sealed with oilskin, and great rolls of netting were stretched between the shrouds, to guard the men on deck from falling mastwood.

Captain Rose marched towards the waist of the ship. 'Odd mains, Mr Alyash,' he cried, with that tireless trumpet-blast voice he could keep up for hours. 'Mr Frix, cut us free. Uskins, turn out Byrd's crew to the carronades, Tanner's to portside forward, and get Drellarek's replacement to the quarterdeck as soon as his men are in hand. Mr Jonhelm, see that the galley fire's put out. Lady Oggosk, I beg you to stay indoors.'

'Soon enough, Nilus. I want a look at her first.'

The witch had an excited gleam in her eye. She meant the *Jistrolloq*,

Thasha knew, but if they caught sight of her while still trapped in the cove it would be the last thing they ever saw.

After his first explosive shout the captain had become extraordinarily calm. His voice when he raised it was deafening, but he spoke most of his orders softly to his lieutenants, who relayed them mast by mast along the ship. His face was emotionless; his eyes slid over the crew with an abstracted look. To Thasha, who had seen Rose spitting and furious over a misplaced pen, this subdued Rose was more unsettling than a thousand bellows.

'Let us have topgallants, Mr Alyash. But stand by to clew up the moment we clear the rock.'

Alyash looked at the cove's western headland. 'Oppo, sir. I can hear that wind. Not that it's doing *us* any good.'

'Full parties to the braces nonetheless,' said Rose. 'We're going to have to swing the mains about like a lady's parasol to scrape out of here.'

The anchor went by the board: Frix and Fegin, wielding a two-man hawser saw, cut through the tree-thick line in a few dozen strokes. Thasha felt the sudden kick as they floated free, and turned just in time to see the mainsail flash open, like a white castle wall suddenly raised in their midst. The forecourse and spanker-course followed: the odd-numbered mainsails, far enough apart not to fight one another for the meagre wind. Thasha raised her eyes even higher and saw men bending topsails. The upper canvas might catch a wind that the lower sails missed, but would all of them together give them speed enough to escape the cove in time? Between the stone cliffs the *Chathrand* stood nearly becalmed – even as the *Jistrolloq* raced towards them on the open fetch of the westerlies.

Suddenly a vast noise erupted to port, followed by the screams of ten thousand birds. All eyes whirled towards Sandplume. From the highest point on the island, a column of scarlet fire was rising heavenwards. Taller and taller it grew, until it resembled a great burning tree, while around it the seabirds rose in one contiguous mass of flapping terror. Many of the birds collided, or wheeled out of control into the fire itself, where they blazed for an instant and were gone.

'Silence, fore and aft,' boomed Rose over the cries of the sailors. 'Mr Coote, I want fire hoses ready at the bilge pumps.'

Even as he spoke the tree of flame blinked, trembled and was gone. But smoke still rose from the hilltop, and Thasha saw that the flame had set the brittle underbrush alight. She winced. *All those blary nests.*

Then Rose's hand closed on her shoulder. In a growl meant for her ears alone, he asked, 'What in the Nine Pits is happening, girl?'

'I don't know anything about that flame,' she said, leaning away from him. 'But there's a man on Sandplume – a priest, maybe. He has the sceptre that belonged to the old Mzithrini Father. Sathek's Sceptre, it's called. I don't know what it's for.'

'That's it?'

'That's all I know, Captain.'

Rose bent even lower, drawing her into a huddle that shut out the deck. In a throaty whisper, he asked, 'Which one of them told you?'

Thasha dared not say a word. Did he know about the ixchel after all? Then Rose glanced surreptitiously down at their feet, and Thasha's skin went cold. There were other feet beside their own, other men, pressing close as if trying to listen in. Their boots were old and battered and darkly stained. Thasha felt the same whirling disorientation that came to her when she opened the *Polylex*, the same desire to turn away.

Rose flashed her a knowing look. 'You can tell me,' he said. 'Was it Captain Mauloj, with the facial tic? Or old Levirac, with the bad teeth? Or Farsin, maybe – the one with raw meat on his breath?'

Stiff with amazement, Thasha murmured: 'N-no, sir. It was ... someone else.'

'Doesn't matter. You keep them away from me. Say whatever you like, just order them to keep their distance. Only if Kurlstaf appears, you listen to every word he says, and share it with me instantly, do you hear?'

'But which one is he?' Thasha pleaded.

'Kurlstaf, Captain Kurlstaf!' said Rose, exasperated. 'The pansy with the lipstick and painted nails!' With that he released her and bellowed for Fiffengurt – only to find the quartermaster already at his elbow.

'That flame was a signal to the *Jistrolloq*, Captain, or I'm a knave.'

'Aye, Quartermaster,' said Rose. He turned forward and boomed again: 'Tactical team to the quarterdeck. Mr Alyash, have a look at the gun decks before you join us. Mr Uskins, I want a report on the doings of the sorcerer: beat on his door until he opens it. And you—' he jabbed a finger at Thasha. '—close the shutters in that private palace of yours, then return to my side.'

I'm going mad, Thasha told herself, running for the stateroom. *My mind's coming to pieces; I've always wondered what it would feel like and now I know.*

She was seeing the dead, seeing ghosts. They had vanished when

Rose released her shoulder, without her ever catching a glimpse of their faces. But before she left the topdeck she had looked back at the captain, and there they were, milling about him like flies. They did not look monstrous – or rather, they looked monstrous in the same way Rose did: hard-bitten, brutal, weathered by years at sea. One was dressed like her great-uncle, in the old regalia of the Merchant Service. Two others wore the blue sash and high collar of the old Imperium: a uniform instantly familiar from the portraits that had adorned her father's study, portraits of naval captains of the First Sea War. A fourth was dressed in brown, like the axe-wielding men who had chased her belowdecks. Yet another wore a frock coat with outlandish tails, and grimaced with muscle spasms.

Why do they terrify us so? she couldn't help thinking. But the *Polylex* had provided one answer. She could still hear Felthrup, reading aloud two nights before: *A ghost is one thing by daylight and quite another in the dark.* At nightfall would they become the faceless people she had seen in the *blanë*-sleep? Did *that* sort of creature visit the captain night after night? It would be enough to drive anyone mad.

Rose was trying studiously to ignore the spirits, as if they were beggars ready to mob him at the least encouragement. No one else knew they were there. *Except for me*, she thought. *Why me?* Was she being punished, or warned perhaps? *Is my father dead, and calling me from the land of the dead, and giving me a way to see him? Is he searching for me right now?* The thought was like a bone in her throat.

And still she sensed them around her: a soft tug at her sleeve, a moving shadow that vanished as she turned, a voice murmuring on an empty stair. *We have him*, it seemed to say, *he's lost to you forever, he's ours—*

Clenched against the voices, she stepped out of the ladderway onto the upper gun deck and collided with Pazel, who was running in the opposite direction.

At the sight of Thasha his face lit up. He seized her arms, grinning, whirled her around – and then, just as suddenly, his eyes became guarded and evasive, and he banished the smile from his face.

'You're – different,' he said.

'Oh,' she laughed. 'Yes. And so are you.'

It was her first glimpse of him since the night of the dancing. His gaze slid to the deck. 'Made it back alive, anyway,' he said.

'So Fiffengurt told us,' she said pointedly. 'And I suppose it's good luck that we bumped into each other, since we may not be alive an hour from now.' Her anger with him was already rising to the surface. 'Excuse me, I have to close the storm-shutters.'

'Beat you to it,' he said. 'The stateroom's secured. Neeps is just finishing up.'

'How is Dri?'

'Worried. The ixchel girl Felthrup sent has never flown before.'

Thasha glanced nervously about the passage: they were still alone. 'Is it true, what Fiffengurt says?' she asked quietly. 'That you saw the scar on Rose's arm, I mean?'

He nodded. 'It's true, but that doesn't mean we can trust him. He's still the craziest man on this ship, and one of the nastiest. Thasha . . . what's happened to you?'

She knew he wasn't talking about her nicks or bruises, or anything as simple as that. But how could she explain, when she didn't understand herself? 'I stayed up late, reading the *Polylex*. What happened to *you*?'

'A giant lizard breathed on me.'

'Oh.'

'And talked. It was terrible. Thasha, are you in love with Fulbreech?'

'Maybe,' she said softly, glaring at him. Of course even *maybe* was an exaggeration; a truer reply would have been, *Not yet, but where were you?* But Pazel had no right to ask such questions. And Greysan didn't cringe when they kissed.

'I think you got older while I was gone,' he said.

'Only by three days, you blary fool.'

'They must have been Darkling Days,' said Pazel, making her laugh uncomfortably.*

---

* As well she might. 'Darkling Days' come from the myth of the Woman and the Troll, which tells of a fair young woman whose beloved ran afoul of the Elcand Firelords and was sentenced to death. The woman journeyed to the court of a great sorcerer-troll and begged him to hide her sweetheart in the valley he ruled. 'No one defies the Firelords without great cost, my child,' replied the troll. 'However, my wife leaves soon to visit her kin in the underworld, and if you will sign a contract promising to care for my sons until she returns, I will shelter you and your lover in my garden for one day, after which he must depart and answer for his offence.' The woman agreed, for she could hear the hounds of the Firelords even then, and the troll's scribe drew up the contract and gave it to her to sign. But when the scribe looked away the clever woman changed 'day' to 'darkling day,' the latter being the four-year span Rin leaves between one solar eclipse and the next. The troll signed carelessly, and as it was a magic contract it bound him to relinquish his garden to the lovers for four whole years.

But those years of joy – feasting on the sweetest of fruits, bathing in warm springs, dreaming to the pipes of fauns and the singing of the water-weird in the fountain – at last came to an end. And when they emerged from the garden the Firelords' warriors

He reached for her again. Thasha stood frozen; Pazel made as if to brush her lips with his fingers. But some kind of doubt overcame him, and he ended up idiotically pressing her nose. He snatched back his hand, gaping like one bereft of speech.

'I drank your blood,' he said at last. 'On Simja, I mean. In the milk.'

Thasha was frustrated almost to despair. 'You are absolutely the *weirdest* boy I've ever met,' she said. Turning on her heel, she raced back up the ladderway to the topdeck.

Thirty sails, and five hundred frightened men at the ropes, and terrible slow turns when the cliffs seemed close enough to touch – but they were gaining speed, and the mouth of the cove was ever nearer. Already the wind was freshening, the jibsails full and the topgallants tight and straining. Thasha looked at the headland, a black basalt cliff falling straight as a curtain into the sea, and half-expected to see the *Jistrolloq* appear from behind it, with all her guns run out, and a horde of soldiers crowding her deck. It could happen at any time: Diadrelu had not been very precise about the distance.

Rose was pulling every trick of speed a captain could in a desperate quarter-hour, backing the topsails, sheeting the jibs to windward and leeward with each tack, even firing cannon from the bow so that the recoil might aid the men's efforts at the braces. There was no hope of stealth, after all, not with that spy on the hilltop. With such a mismatch in fighting strength, moreover, the *Jistrolloq* had to know that they would run. But would they even get the chance?

Pulling herself up the quarterdeck ladder, Thasha found all the senior officers assembled, plus Ott and Chadfallow, and a huge Turach with a broad forehead and cold blue eyes: Drellarek's replacement, she presumed. She could no longer see any ghosts, although Uskins was pale enough to pass for one.

'We'll make it, surely?' he was saying. 'We'll just squeak out?'

'How d'ye expect us to answer you?' said Elkstem irritably. 'We don't know how close she is. We don't even know the windspeed out there.'

---

seized the man and bore him away to be executed. The heartless troll too had his revenge: he had divorced his wife and barred her from ever returning, and hence the woman was bound to go on caring for his malicious, sharp-toothed sons. And as trolls grow up far more slowly than humans, the woman only managed to fulfill the contract when she was very old, and weak of eye and memory, and too frail to hobble out of the valley of the troll. She stayed in his court, and served him to the end of her days, and wept for reasons no one else recalled at the time of the eclipse. – EDITOR.

'In five minutes we shall,' said Rose.

The men were all clustered around him, between the binnacle and the rail. The captain was the only man not on his feet: he had sent for a stool and his campaign desk, and had them bolted securely to the deck. The stool was finished with some tawny hide, and swivelled; the desk looked like a large wooden box on legs. Then Rose sprung two latches and raised the lid. Inside was a writing space protected by walls on three sides, and half-covered by a wooden canopy. There were small latched drawers, a stack of paper held down by battens, a plotting compass, an abacus and a knife.

Thasha found the sight of that desk alarming, and she saw that some of the officers did as well. Was Rose about to lose himself in *paperwork*? Just how crazy was he?

The captain began whittling a pencil. 'Attend me,' he said, as if the group would dream of doing anything else. 'This contest may end in minutes, or not for hours, or even days. If it ends swiftly we shall lose. The White Reaper is no idle nickname for the *Jistrolloq*. Isn't that so, Mr Uskins?'

The first mate nodded. 'Beyond a doubt, Captain. She's a killer and she wants for nothing. An armoured bow, she has, and four ship-shattering bow carronades. And a hundred and forty long guns down each flank.'

'Twice our count,' said Rose, 'and a crew drilled constantly in their use. This ship will be matchwood if the *Jistrolloq* rakes us with a broadside. And at a distance too they can best us. They'll be better shots, and aiming for a bigger target. They will also be faster, in these waters. Our size is nothing but a hazard, in short, until we find large waves and tearing wind.'

'Those may be close at hand, sir,' put in Alyash.

'Don't interrupt, Bosun!' snapped Fiffengurt. 'The captain's well aware of the conditions.'

'That I am,' said Rose. 'The storm brewing in the east will not be enough, however. Until the wind turns, Bramian herself will tame it. And there are shoals to either side of us, quelling the waves. No, we will not come into our own for two hours at the earliest. Until then we must stay alive. That means fire brigades, and chain-pumps, and any dead removed quickly to the surgical annexe, lest the sight of them demoralise the crew. Uskins, you will restrict Byrd and Tanner to strategic fire until further notice: we don't carry enough shot to waste it in a hopeless spray.

'And give no face but fury to the crew. Fury, gentlemen: not nerves, not reassurance. Let them see nothing but the mortal danger of displeasing you. That will save them from worrying overmuch about the *Jistrolloq*. Now then, Ott: will the Black Rags strike us with sorcery?'

(*Obviously, Rose*, whispered a voice from nowhere. Only Thasha and the captain raised their heads.)

'Depend on it,' said Ott. 'They have not brought Sathek's Sceptre all the way from Babqri just to send up a signal-flare.'

'What can they do with the thing? Change the winds?'

There were anxious hisses at the suggestion. But Ott shook his head. 'I haven't a clue,' he said, 'but it was for that sceptre that Arunis killed the Babqri Father.'

'And Kuminzat's daughter, as it happened,' said Rose. 'Have we any other idea of their motives?'

Alyash cleared his throat. 'Captain Rose, the Father never quite believed in the Great Peace. And he had a particular fascination with the *Chathrand*. We were already in his sights. It may be that he had already shared his suspicions with Kuminzat and the other officers assembled for Treaty Day.'

Rose pursed his lips, as though he found the remark disappointingly simple. After a moment he said, 'Their greatest advantage may be that man on the hilltop. A view to either side of Sandplume could well decide this contest. What has become of your falcon, Mr Ott?'

An expression like none Thasha had ever seen on the man came over the Spymaster's face. It took her a moment to recognise it as sorrow. 'I dispatched Niriviel the morning we landed on Bramian,' he said, 'with orders to return within a day. He flew south into the Nelluroq, looking for sign of the Vortex. I fear he met with some ... misfortune.'

Thasha felt stricken. The bird had almost hated her, but it made no difference. There was something beautiful about his loyalty to Sandor Ott. She hated to imagine him alone over the fabled whirlpool, battling the winds, dropping at last into the depths.

'Captain Rose,' she said, forcing herself back to the matter at hand.

'What is it?' he demanded.

'I don't think they can change the winds. In fact I don't think they can use the sceptre well at all, if the Father's dead. Only the most powerful mage-priests can use it safely. But the Father may have used it *before* he died, to make his *sfvantskor* stronger, or the ship itself.'

'How in precious Pitfire could you know such things, girl?' scoffed Alyash.

Thasha looked at him evenly. 'I read a lot.'

'What Thasha says stands to reason,' said Chadfallow. 'The priest cannot have meant to set the whole hill on fire, when he was standing atop it. He may even have perished in the blaze.'

Rose turned on his stool. 'First Mate, you spoke with Arunis?'

'Aye, Captain. He's prowling about the jiggermast even now.' Uskins drew a deep breath. 'He was ... of little help, sir.'

'No help, you mean?'

'He speculated that the *sfvantskors* present at the wedding ceremony had all boarded the *Jistrolloq*, Captain. And he said that the priest wielding Sathek's Sceptre could not fail to sense the presence of the Nilstone.'

Rose looked thoughtful. 'Lieutenant Khalmet,' he said.

The blue-eyed soldier nodded. 'Sir.'

'Do you command the Turachs, now that Drellarek is dead?'

'No, sir. That would be Sergeant Haddismal. The sergeant is inspecting the ranks, and begs your pardon for not attending this meeting himself.'

'He does not have it,' said Rose. 'Tell Haddismal never again to ignore a summons from the captain. And have him redouble the guard on the Shaggat Ness. I don't want the sorcerer taking advantage of our circumstances to make some attempt to reach his king.'

'Oppo, Captain. And if I might venture a thought, sir: release the Tholjassan, Hercól Stanapeth, and let him have his bow. We cannot have too many marksmen.'

'Is that your commander's advice?'

'No, sir, merely my own. Sergeant Haddismal has not ventured an opinion.'

Thasha was stunned by Khalmet's words. *Could he be on our side? A Turach, trained to throw his life away at a word from the Emperor?*

But the captain shook his head. 'Stanapeth defied my orders, and sent five of your comrades to the surgery. He is not to be freed unless the *sfvantskors* themselves come over our rails. Do I make myself clear?'

'Perfectly, Captain.'

'Mr Uskins,' said Rose, 'did Arunis have nothing else to say?'

Uskins hesitated. 'Sir, he told me we should drop sail and surrender, before the Reaper cuts us down.'

A brief silence fell. Thasha saw Rose's jaw tighten, and his gaze turn inward. He folded the knife, looked down at the blank paper before him, and suddenly began to sketch.

'Time to change tack,' he said, without looking up.

But everyone else did, and there were shouts and gasps, for they were little more than two ship's lengths from the western cliff. Fiffengurt, Uskins and Alyash flew to the rail, commands exploding from their lips. Elkstem rushed back to his mates at the wheel, and together they wrenched it to starboard, while five hundred backs strained on the deck below. The yards pivoted, the *Chathrand* heeled over, a frothy wake boiled along the starboard bow, and they cleared the point with ten yards to spare.

From the main-top a voice shouted, 'We're free, we're free!' And like a slap of reprimand the full west wind struck the foremast and carried both topgallants away.

'Clew up! Save the rest!' screamed Alyash. They were out of the cove, and the wind was four times the strength of a moment ago: too strong for the highest canvas, though the topsails could take it with ease, and the mains looked flaccid yet. Alyash cringed like a man tied and waiting for the whip: Rose had warned him about those topgallants. But the captain merely spun around and gave Elkstem the new heading, and told Chadfallow he might return to his surgery.

The next turn was effortless, for the wind shouldered them about. In seconds they were running east, skimming across the mouth of the cove that had nearly become their graveyard. Thasha looked down at the throng of sailors, snatching a moment's rest, and was not surprised to see Neeps joining the line-up on a starboard brace. *Nobody's turning down his help today,* she thought.

Then the lookout began to howl: 'Sail! Dead astern three miles! It's the enemy, Captain, I can see the red stars!'

A general groan, shouted down at once by the officers. Rose leaped from the stool and barrelled aft around the wheelhouse, extending his telescope as he went. Thasha chased after him. There was the *Jistrolloq*, tilted over like a white gravestone, slicing a neat white wake as she ran.

'Her topgallants are holding, blast her,' said Elkstem. 'By the Tree, she's a formidable ship. And closer to two miles than three.'

Rose lifted a hand for silence. A moment later he lowered the scope. 'She will have four knots on us,' he said, in a voice not meant to carry.

Thasha did not want to believe it. 'Four? That would let them catch us in – what? Less than an hour?'

'Thirty-seven minutes,' said Rose. 'Mr Elkstem, at my command we

380

shall be making a very sharp tack to the south. A very *visible* tack. But give no orders before my mark, do you hear? Don't even look at the men.'

Elkstem was clearly mystified, but Rose's face ruled out any questioning. 'Oppo, sir, she'll corner handsomely,' he said.

'You wanted to see me, Captain?' said a voice from behind them.

It was Pazel. He was looking at Rose, and quite determinedly not at Thasha.

Rose's eye did not leave the telescope. 'Aye, Pathkendle, but only to keep these grackle-mouths quiet. They have you mixed up with your father, and seem to think I need Captain Gregory's advice.'

'"They," sir?'

Rose only frowned, and Thasha, ignoring Pazel's awkwardness, took his arm and tugged him aside. 'He's seeing ghosts,' she whispered. 'But he's not crazy, they're real. I can see them too. They're the old captains of the *Chathrand*.'

Pazel was certainly looking at her now. '*You're* seeing these things?'

'Well, not this minute. Rose can scatter them, I think, but they keep coming back. Like flies. Right now I can hear them, and feel them. And this isn't the first time it's happened.'

'Are you talking about what happened the day you found Marila?'

Thasha shook her head. 'That was different. Those were real people, flesh and blood. But for weeks now I've been feeling ... strange. As if people were surrounding me, when there was no one there at all. I think it was them, Pazel. I think they've been watching me.'

Pazel stared at her, aghast, but was he concerned for her safety or her sanity? She was on the point of asking him directly when Rose gave a startled grunt.

'The priest did not die,' he said, 'but the fire has driven him from the hilltop. He's watching us right now. He'll be blind to his own ship's whereabouts, though, unless that thing in his hand lets him see through solid rock. *Ehiji*, what's this? He's got friends! *Sfvantskors*, by the gods, *sfvantskors* coming out of the bush!'

Thasha could just make them out: three tall figures in black, rushing across the smouldering slope to join a fourth, bald-headed, with a long golden object in his hand. Even as she looked another *sfvantskor* emerged running from the trees.

'That new one has a longbow,' said Rose. 'And damned if he isn't − firing! *Aloft! Take cover aloft!*'

Scarcely had the words left his lips when they heard a wail, sharp and ethereal, and then a man's scream from the rigging. Thasha looked up and saw Kiprin Pondrakeri, the muscular Simjan recruit, face down in the battle netting with an arrow in his chest. The strange wail continued for a moment, then lowered and died.

The next thing she knew Pazel had leaped on her and borne her down onto the deck. The air was suddenly full of the wailing noises, and from the spankermast came another cry of agony. Thasha struggled out of Pazel's grasp and got to her hands and knees. But even as she did so a boot kicked her flat again.

Sandor Ott had delivered the kick as he dashed to the rail with a great bow of his own. He fired in a blur, once twice thrice, and then he lowered the bow and took a breath.

'Done,' he said. 'That one will shoot no more, and the rest are running for cover. You can stand up now, lass.'

As Thasha and Pazel rose, Ott reached up and seized the dripping end of the arrow embedded in Pondrakeri's chest. He pulled, and the netting sagged, but the shaft would not let go of the corpse.

'Singing arrows,' he said admiringly. 'We still don't know how they work – must be expensive, however; they fire 'em all in the first few volleys. Marvellous way to demoralise an enemy.'

He released the arrow, having not glanced once at the dead man, and set off smiling for the topdeck.

'He's enjoying this,' said Thasha. 'I think he *lives* for fighting and killing, the beast.'

'He doesn't enjoy it,' said Pazel. 'He's ... addicted. It's not the same thing.'

Thasha gave him a sceptical look. 'How do you know so much? Did you and Sandor have a heart-to-heart chat on Bramian?'

Pazel watched the spymaster swing down the ladder. 'Sort of,' he said.

A pool of blood was forming under the dead man. Thasha looked up and saw the other victim, a mizzen topman, dangling upside-down from the rigging some seventy feet overhead.

'We're making twelve knots by the log, sir,' cried a lieutenant.

'Send for a bucket, Mr Truel,' said Rose. 'And you, Pathkendle: find a mate and get these cadavers below.'

Pazel gazed wordlessly up at the bodies. The topman was swinging perilously. Blood streamed from the arrow in his throat to his fingertips, where the wind licked it away.

Thasha took a deep breath. 'I'll help you,' she said.

Pazel looked intensely relieved. He could not, after all, order anyone to help him. 'Let me fetch a rope. I'll be right back – thank you, Thasha.'

When he returned he brought Neeps as well as a rope. The small boy was fidgeting with irritation; he and Pazel scarcely looked at one another. But he had come nonetheless. The three scaled the shrouds, and Neeps continued up to the main spankermast yard while Thasha and Pazel stepped gingerly onto the netting. It was a long crawl to where Pondrakeri dangled. They had almost reached him when Thasha saw Rose's hand sweep down like a signal flag.

'Now, Mr Elkstem!'

'Haul away starboard!' boomed Elkstem, putting his weight on the wheel. 'Look sharp, lads, we're turning on a mussel tin!'

The order raced forward, the deckhands threw their shoulders against the ropes, and with startling speed the Great Ship heeled around to the south.

Thasha and Pazel clung to the netting as the huge timbers groaned and squeaked, and blood from the topman spattered around them like rain. Thasha looked west at the *Jistrolloq*. 'What are you hoping they'll do, Captain Rose?' she called.

Rose lowered the telescope, watching the enemy with his naked eye. 'They've just done it,' he said, 'and I didn't need to hope.'

Before Thasha could ask what he meant, the lookout cried: 'Black Rags altering course, sir, due south, matching us point-for-point.'

Rose favoured Thasha with a glance. 'Admiral Kuminzat knows what he's up against,' he said. 'Unless he has the gods' own luck with weather, he has to take us soon. Every mile we can run out on the Nelluroq plays to our advantage. He's turned south to cut us off.'

'Around the far side of the island,' said Pazel. 'And you waited until he was almost on top of Sandplume, so that he'd have to make a hasty choice, didn't you?'

'A hasty choice and a bad one, Pathkendle. Maybe you do know something.'

Thasha could hear the ghosts whispering approval. In minutes Sandplume would hide the *Chathrand* from the *Jistrolloq*, and then Rose could turn as he liked without giving their course away. For the Mzithrinis, reversing direction was impossible: they would lose a good hour tacking against the wind just to get safely clear of Sandplume and back on the course she had abandoned. She could only run south now, and take up the pursuit after rounding the isle –

but Thasha doubted that the *Chathrand* would be anywhere near Sandplume by then.

High above, Neeps fed the line through a wheelblock, then tugged it through yard by yard. When it reached them, Pazel leaned out and snatched the rope, and clinging to the spar with his legs alone, tied a slipknot. Together he and Thasha eased the loop over Pondrakeri's head and arms, struggling to keep him from toppling to the deck.

As she heaved at the dead man, Thasha kept one eye on Rose. Now and then the air about him seemed to flicker, as if unseen hands were gesturing and pointing, but Rose paid no attention to the apparitions. Instead he turned from the rail and shouted:

'Hard to port, Sailmaster! East by south-east!'

'Hard to port! Haul away port!'

The frantic struggle on the deck began again, and in a matter of seconds they were back on their old eastward course.

'Brilliant,' said Pazel with grudging admiration. 'We'll gain miles on 'em this way. But there's nowhere else to hide, now that we're leaving the islands. And hours of daylight yet. Sooner or later we'll have to run south again, if Rose plans to escape into the Ruling Sea.'

'We may not escape even there,' said Thasha. 'The *Jistrolloq's* braved the Nelluroq before. She's too small to cross it, but she can handle the margins. The huge waves are mostly farther out.'

Pazel was gaping at her. 'How do you know all that, Thasha?'

She blinked at him, startled. 'The *Polylex*?' she said, uncertain.

Pazel shook his head in wonder. He tied off the extra rope around Pondrakeri's legs.

On a impulse, Thasha asked him, 'How did Drellarek die? Was it the creature who breathed on you?'

Pazel's face paled. He looked suddenly as though he was going to be sick. He nodded, breathing hard.

'I'm sorry,' she said. 'I shouldn't have asked.'

Pazel made no reply. His eyes had slid to the quarterdeck. Thasha followed his gaze and saw Lady Oggosk directly below, watching them keenly.

Pazel turned his back on Thasha. 'We've got a job to finish,' he said coldly, 'that is, if you really came to help.'

They hoisted Pondrakeri from the netting like a drowned man, and guided him, swaying and spinning, over the rail and down to the main deck. The topman was far more difficult. At seventy feet the mast pitched enormously, and at the end of each pendular swing they looked down from the ropes not on the quarterdeck but on the churning ocean. Thasha found herself mouthing prayers from the Lorg School, and was glad when the practised hands of the ex-tarboys shot out to steady her. The hands of the topman were scarlet, slippery as eels. By the time they had him down on the deck the three youths were painted with blood from face to calves. As she and Pazel wrestled the bodies down to the surgical annexe (Neeps had stayed behind to scrub the quarterdeck) Thasha had to fight the urge to vomit. The smell of blood − a rank stench of rust and wet clay − was overpowering. Flies bit her sticky arms and sweaty face.

They laid the bodies side by side. Pazel forced out a laugh − a bitter laugh, almost cruel, like nothing she'd ever heard from his lips. 'Wonder how much company they'll have before the day's done,' he said, smiling, clenching his fists.

'Let's just get out of here,' said Thasha.

They sat on the lower gun deck near Tanner's gunnery team, a tub of seawater between them, and scrubbed off the worst of the blood with rags. Thasha watched Pazel peel off his gory shirt and dunk it in the tub, where the water was already pink. *What's wrong with you?* she wanted to scream. *Why've you gone so blary hateful?* Then she saw that Pazel's eyes were moist.

'What was his name?' he said. 'The topman, I mean. Nobody on the quarterdeck even knew his name.'

They parted at the compartment door, and Thasha went to the stateroom to change. The guard outside the stateroom, curiously enough, had been withdrawn; and as she ran to the door Thasha let herself hope that Hercól had been set free as well. But her tutor was not in the stateroom − no one was, in fact, except Jorl and Suzyt, padding the bare boards in a room where everything that could not be bolted down had been stowed.

'Get off, idiots,' she said as they jumped on her. She locked the door and called out softly for Diadrelu. 'I'm alone,' she said. 'Where have you gone?'

'Here,' came a faint voice from the washroom.

Thasha opened the door. On the footstool sat Dri, washed and clothed in a new shirt of black silk. She held up her hand, stopping Thasha in the doorway, and turned to face the cast-iron bathtub.

'Ensyl,' she said, 'you have nothing to fear from Lady Thasha.'

Thasha tensed. From behind the bathtub stepped another ixchel, a thin young woman with a large forehead and wide, watchful eyes. She was heavily armed – sword, dagger, bow – and barefoot, as Dri always was. The woman's lips moved as if in speech, but Thasha could hear no sound.

'Bend your voice,' Diadrelu told her. To Thasha, she said, 'Ensyl is my *sophister* – my apprentice, if you like. She is here to be sure I behave like an invalid.'

'My lady must not make sport of me,' said the girl, who had not taken her eyes from Thasha. Her whole face clenched as she spoke; she did not appear to have much practice in pitching her voice to the human register.

'Nor shall I ever,' said Diadrelu. 'What is more, I applaud your choice. For you have made a very serious choice, you know. You are only the third ixchel on the *Chathrand* to show herself to a human. I am another; and the third is Taliktrum himself, who has since forbidden contact with humans under any circumstances, on pain of death.'

'I wanted to see you,' said Ensyl to Thasha. 'Some of my people have notions about you. They believe you will be the doom of this ship. Even today Lord Taliktrum's attendant Myett spoke of you as one bewitched. But Lady Dri is my only mistress, and if she tells me I have nothing to fear, then I fear not.'

'I said you need not fear Thasha,' corrected Dri. 'We may all have something to fear from lies and superstitions – to say nothing of cannon-fire. How goes the chase, Lady Thasha?'

'We gained a little time,' said Thasha, with a nervous glance at the window, 'but not enough to escape the *Jistrolloq*. Arunis said we should surrender before they kill us all.'

'Arunis still dreams of Sathek's Sceptre,' said Diadrelu. 'Our watch saw him looking from the gunports at the red flame on Sandplume, with a hunger so great one could all but smell it. Surrender, I think, would just be a means of bringing the sceptre within his reach. Its power is surely slight compared to that of the Nilstone – but he has no means of using the Nilstone, yet. He failed with the Shaggat, and again on Dhola's Rib. Now I begin to wonder if there might be a connection between the sceptre and the Stone.'

'What sort of connection?' asked Thasha warily.

Dri closed her eyes. 'When Arunis called up Sathek's ghost, he said, "*I must have it for my king.*" And something else: "*Imagine him when the Swarm returns. The Nilstone in one fist, your sceptre in the other. Armies*

386

shall wilt before him, like petals in the frost.' She opened her eyes. 'Arunis literally dares not touch the Nilstone. But when a poker in the fire is too hot to touch, what do we do?'

'We use a glove,' said Ensyl.

'Yes,' said Dri, 'and what if the sceptre is that glove? The Nilstone, as we learned, slays any with fear in their hearts. What if fearlessness is just what the sceptre can provide?'

Thasha drew a shaky breath. 'His precious king is still just a rock,' she said.

'That too the sceptre might reverse,' said Dri, 'once it is in the hands of a sorcerer. But enough of speculation for the moment. Thasha, where is Felthrup?'

Thasha was suddenly alarmed. 'Hasn't he come back?'

Dri shook her head. 'Felthrup completed his mission splendidly. Thanks to him, Ensyl came for the swallow-suit, and our people escaped Sandplume before the fire could overtake them. But what became of Felthrup after he delivered the message I cannot say. I hoped he had found his way to you, somehow. Marila has gone in search of him, although the odds are against one girl finding one lost rat on the largest ship in Alifros.'

'We've got to!' said Thasha. 'He isn't safe *anywhere* but the statcroom. Oh Pitfire, why did they let him go? Neeps or Marila could have gone instead!'

'And shouted at an empty corner of the mercy deck? No, Thasha, Neeps and Marila would have been stopped and questioned, and their faces would have given us all away. But you are right about the danger to Felthrup. Master Mugstur has excommunicated him, and in the rat-king's twisted ethos those who stray from Rin's path must all be killed.'

'I'm going to look for him too,' said Thasha. 'I'll take Suzyt and Jorl; they know his scent. Rose will throw a fit, though, if I don't hurry back to the quarterdeck.'

'We ixchel should do the searching,' said Diadrelu. 'We can enter the rat-spaces no human eye can pierce. Ensyl, go to Night Village. I do not have much hope that Taliktrum will listen to you, but you must try. Invoke the honour of the clan. Perhaps he will concede to a party of volunteers.

'As for me, Lady Thasha, I throw myself on your hospitality. There is no home for me among my people: indeed they are under edict to slay me, "before I further endanger the clan."'

'That edict will be lifted,' said Ensyl hotly.

Diadrelu shook her head. 'Some things cannot be undone. I have disobeyed the clan leader in a moment of crisis, and Taliktrum has drawn family blood.'

'Wait and see, mistress,' said Ensyl. 'In time they will beg you to return.'

She glanced once more at Thasha, then turned and vanished behind the bathtub.

'We have a trapdoor there,' said Diadrelu.

'I can't say I'm glad to hear it,' said Thasha. 'Oh, I'm happy that you and Ensyl can come and go. But it proves there's a gap in the magic wall. Could it be getting larger? What if it's about to fail?'

Suddenly a cry arose on the topdeck: '*Sail ho! Jistrolloq at eight miles!*'

'They've rounded Sandplume!' said Thasha. 'By the Tree, that was fast! I've got to get up there – although helping Rose is the last thing I feel like doing.'

'Help him,' said Diadrelu firmly. 'You have little hope of finding Felthrup, even with your dogs. And there will be no point in finding him if the White Reaper blasts us to pieces.'

Rose did need her help, for when she returned there were no less than seven ghost-captains upon the quarterdeck, flickering in and out of existence. Three were dogging Rose's heels, arguing over tactics in voices laced with sarcasm and antique slang. Another, an ugly, woolly-bearded giant with a naked cutlass in his hand, stood growling and threatening near the wheelhouse, his eyes on an oblivious Alyash. The others milled about the deck, hectoring the living despite the fact that only Rose had any notion of their presence.

Thasha had her orders, but it was hard to face a deck full of ghosts, every one of which had commanded the ship from this very spot. Nor did she relish talking to thin air in front of Elkstem, Alyash and the half-dozen others crowding the quarterdeck. *That's why he needs me to do it*, she thought, *to keep him from looking a perfect lunatic.*

'My heart's in the heavens,' she sang out boldly, climbing the ladder, 'my soul is the Tree, my dance is for ever, I fear not thee!'

The ghosts all turned to face her, and the cutlass-wielding giant, who was nearest, simply faded away. The others scattered about the deck, looking startled and irritated. Thasha was startled as well: the Lorg School chant had been far less effective against the wraiths in the Crab Fens.

'Very, uh, good, Missy,' said Alyash, obviously confused. 'We're not afraid of them Black Rags, are we?'

Thasha shot him a piercing look. *You're one yourself, you liar.*

Whether the chant or something else altogether had affected them, the remaining ghosts did not want to be anywhere near her. Confident now, Thasha pursued them around the mast and the wheelhouse. They dodged and scurried; it was a bit like playing tag. One by one they vanished from her sight. But as the last captain faded, he pointed at her with a long, blackened nail. 'Tonight,' he said, and was gone.

For some time afterwards she had little to do but watch the chase. It was worse than being busy, even with gruesome tasks. Rose turned them south; the *Jistrolloq* tacked instantly to a diagonal intercept, and Rose had no option but to set them east again. The wind was dying, which played into the enemy's hands. By mid-afternoon just six miles separated the ships.

Pazel, skulking behind the wheelhouse, would not look at her. *Fine,* she thought, *go boil yourself in the Pits.* But more than once she had the feeling he was watching her, though she never quite caught him in the act.

Rose spent much of this time at his campaign desk, his back to the *Jistrolloq*, sketching. When Thasha sidled close enough for a glance she saw a page covered with tiny pencilled numbers, long arrows, rough outlines of hulls.

At four bells he stood and latched the desk shut. 'Come, Thasha, Pathkendle. We shall dine in my cabin. Mr Elkstem, I will have updates by speaking-tube.'

Thasha and Pazel followed Rose down the ladder. They did not go immediately to the cabin, however, but walked the whole length of the *Chathrand*, squeezing through the busy mass of men. Thasha thought the sailors looked as frightened as any crowd she had ever been among, but as Rose passed with a smouldering gaze each man seemed to concentrate just a bit harder on his task, as if those eyes could strip away distractions like a knife stripping bark from a switch. On their return Rose paused here and there to murmur to the watch-captains, and behind their backs Thasha heard the officers shouting: 'Captain Rose is formidable proud of you, lads! Says you're the picture of an Imperial crew! His very words!'

She glanced over her shoulder, slightly awed. Rose's casual manner was doing wonders to keep the sailors calm, and the compliments, which he never gave in easy times, were bringing smiles to their faces.

Crazy or not, she thought, *he's blary good at what he does.*

Lady Oggosk joined them at table. Pazel visibly stiffened at the sight of her – and also, it appeared, at being once more in Rose's cabin. He was glancing about with a savaged expression, and Thasha reflected again that she knew almost nothing of what had been done to Pazel since the Turachs dragged him away.

'Something new in here since your last visit, Pathkendle,' said Rose, striding forwards. 'Which of you can tell me what these are?'

Ranged along the gallery windows were four stout, wide-mouthed cannon, their carriages tightly lashed to the deck. Behind them, bolted rigid as a mast, stood a long wooden rack about three feet high, and dangling from the rack were twenty or thirty canvas sacks, each one ending in a small iron disc. The sacks were about the size of hams, and bulged as if filled with giant marbles.

'They're grapeshot guns,' said Thasha.

'Not much use against an armoured hull, are they?' Pazel added.

Rose looked sternly at the two youths, and made no answer. 'Let us sit down,' he said at last.

During the meal they spoke very little. The steward poured four glasses of cloudy wine. Rose ate like a horse at a feed-bag, eyes downcast, jaw working non-stop. Lady Oggosk mashed her food with her fingers, while her red cat snored peacefully in a spot of sun.

All the while the *Jistrolloq* was plainly visible through the gallery windows. By the time they finished eating she was within three miles.

'Tell us, Pathkendle,' said Rose suddenly, 'what would your father do in these circumstances, if he were in command?'

Pazel was taken aback. 'I don't know,' he said. 'Edge his way south, maybe. Look for higher seas.'

'You misunderstand the question,' said Rose. 'I meant, what would Captain Gregory do if he commanded the *Jistrolloq*, and wanted to take us? He must have learned to think like a Black Rag, after serving with them for years. And of course your presence on *Chathrand* would present no obstacle. Gregory sailed away from Cape Córistel without a backward glance at you, didn't he? And we know he doesn't shrink from firing on his kin.'

Pazel had spent almost six years as a bonded servant, and five months under Captain Rose. He was not, Thasha knew, particularly easy to shock. But the brutality of Rose's offhand comment slipped past his defences. His eyes widened, and a spasm of anger twisted his face.

Under the table, Thasha furtively touched his hand. Pazel was on the verge of doing something drastic, something Neeps-like: over-turning the table, or cursing Rose at the top of his lungs. But at her touch he managed to check himself, bite back the words trying to detonate on his tongue.

'Well,' he said, breathing hard, 'let's see. I suppose he might think back on what he knows about the enemy – about you, in other words. He might say to himself, "Right, here's this old shifty captain who's famous for his nastiness—"'

Rose lifted an eyebrow.

'"—and his greed, and for being afraid of a shipboard cat, and for the fact that he writes letters to—"'

'Silence, bastard!' shrieked Lady Oggosk, rising from her chair and pointing at Pazel. 'Never, *never* was there a lowborn with such a reckless tongue! Walk out of here, you insolent Ormali gutter-dog, before the captain has you—'

'Peace!' Rose slammed his palm against the table. 'Lady Oggosk, your defence is unnecessary. Pathkendle remains confused, no more. Look out that window, lad, and your confusion will evaporate.'

Rose turned and gestured at the *Jistrolloq*, bright white in the sun and near enough now to count the seven falling stars on her forecourse. 'There stands a man, Kuminzat, who's crossed half the known world in our pursuit. Ott tells me that his daughter was a *sfvantskor*, or soon to be, and that she was killed by the incubus Arunis hurled at their old priest.'

'You knew.' Thasha sat up, eyes widening with anger. 'You knew about the incubus. You knew what the Sizzies accused us of was true, and denied it to their faces.'

'Very little occurs on the Great Ship that we *don't* know,' said Oggosk. 'You ought to keep that in mind, both of you.'

Thasha turned on her, bristling. 'Care to prove it?' she said. 'Can you tell me what Arunis has been doing while the *Jistrolloq* closes in? Or why he wants that sceptre almost as badly as the Nilstone? Or which of the crew might be spying on *you* for Sandor Ott?'

The old woman actually looked somewhat cowed. She dropped her eyes, as though Thasha's gaze was too sharp for her liking. 'I might if you gave me a reason,' she muttered uneasily.

'We are straying from the matter at hand,' said Rose. 'Pathkendle, what do you say to my challenge? Neither you nor I know that admiral's character. I have been substituting other men for him in my mind, and asking myself what each would do if he commanded the *Jistrolloq*. I would know what you think. Answer me, if you've a tenth the craftiness Rin gave your father. I have no more time to waste.'

Pazel's hand was tight on Thasha's own. 'Your question *is* a waste of time,' he said at last. 'I never sailed with my father. I don't know what skills he used, or what tactics.'

'Then leave tactics to me. What would Gregory have felt like? What would make him chase another vessel from Simja right down to the margins of the Ruling Sea?'

Pazel made as if to speak, then once again held his tongue. Rose smiled and shook his head.

'Not gold. If riches were his aim he could have sold his services to any number of lawless barons in the Rekere or the Crownless Lands, and become rich indeed. And not the rescue of his son. What's left? What would drive the resourceful Captain Gregory to do as Kuminzat's done, hazarding his very life and that of his crew?'

Pazel's grip on her hand was painful now, and a new fury shone in his eyes. 'Nothing, all right?' he said at last. 'Absolutely nothing would make my father go to so much trouble. He's as selfish as you.'

Rose shook his head, as if in wonder. 'From his own boy's mouth,' he said. 'Well now: that is good news. We can count on one hand the things a man will kill for. Love, lust, gold, honour, tribe: the raw ingredients of power. Ninety-nine men in a hundred will quickly show you which of these enslaves them. A ferocity lights 'em up when they're pursuing it, and there's no mistaking that look. All the trouble comes from the mystery man – that one man in a hundred who can keep his motives out of sight. Men like Gregory, you see.'

'And Admiral Kuminzat,' said Thasha.

'You have it, lass,' said Rose. 'Though my predecessors *will* keep babbling their theories. How I wish they'd shut up!'

He said the last words in a sudden fury, knocking his fists against his temples. Thasha averted her eyes. It was then that she noticed Lady Oggosk was staring at her – and also realised that she, Thasha, had shed a few silent tears. They were for Pazel, she supposed, and for herself, and the murdered topman, and the shame of so much wanting – love, lust, gold – but why did Oggosk look so enraged? The witch's eyes flickered down along Thasha's arm, extended subtly towards Pazel's lap, and Thasha knew she guessed that they were holding hands.

What's it to you, you hag?

Pazel too noticed Oggosk's look. With a start he pulled his hand away. Thasha turned and found him glaring at her. When he spoke it was against some deep resistance, as if he had to wring the words out of himself. But the words were lacerating.

'If I need pity I'll let you know,' he said. 'Meanwhile keep it to yourself. I'm – tired of this, see? Tired of being your charity case.'

'My *what?*'

'You think I'm dying for your attention. Like an Ormali should be, when a highborn Arquali girl stoops to help him, I guess. And you can spare me that wounded face. There's plenty aboard who'll be happy to tell you how special you are. Cross me off your list, that's all – leave me alone.'

He gave her a look that was almost deranged, then turned to Rose. 'As for your question, Captain Sir: you really ought to be asking Thasha, not me. She's good with *tactics*. But I'll tell you right now: ghosts or no ghosts, there's something wrong with a man who sits here tormenting people, just because he's realised that he can't outrun his enemy. That's cowardice, that is. Not that you'll ever admit it.'

No one at the table breathed. Thasha tensed herself for the fight of her life. Pazel had gone mad, Rose and Oggosk already were, and any sort of violence seemed possible. She'd lost her knife, she'd have to use things on the table, the serving fork, a shard of a plate—

Then Rose did the last thing on earth she expected. He laughed. A smile grew in the red thicket of his beard, looking like something transplanted from a merrier man. 'Outrun,' he said. 'Outrun.'

He raised his eyes to the skylight above the table, and the laugh grew until his great bulk fairly shook with mirth. And as he finished laughing the room suddenly darkened, for a heavy cloud had eclipsed the sun. At almost the same moment, on the quarterdeck, Mr Fiffengurt began to shout:

'Wind's turning! The wind's turning right about! Inform the captain, that's a north-easter blowin' in!'

A great commotion began overhead, and Rose put his hands on the table and heaved to his feet. Lumbering to his desk, wine in hand, he flipped open a speaking-tube and bellowed:

'South south-east, Mr Elkstem, and all the sail she'll bear. Full crews to their guns. I'm on my way.'

He drank the wine in a gulp and wiped his mouth.

'Back to the quarterdeck, Lady Thasha. And you, Pathkendle: stick to your schoolbooks; there's not a drop of sailor's blood in you.

Have you forgotten that we must let no one set eyes on the *Chathrand* and live? I never spoke of *escaping* the Black Rags; the only question is how best to destroy them.'

29

The Duel

—ᘒᘖᘒ—

24 Freala 941

The storm built quickly, as the new wind barrelled in from the north-east, carrying great black-hearted thunderheads and a sheet of advancing rain. By the time Pazel and Thasha reached the topdeck the topsails were all raised for the sudden turn, and the huge yards were once more being hauled into the teeth of the wind. The Black Shoulders were out of sight, and Bramian itself was a mere smudge on the western horizon, but the *Jistrolloq* looked frightfully close – under two miles, probably, and closing without a doubt.

Such sudden darkness. The clouds were sealing off the heavens like a sheet of tin; already the sun was banished to a bright streak in the south, drawing away much faster than they could advance. The waves were growing too: white-capped, they were cresting around the height of the upper gun deck. Pazel shuddered to imagine tiny Diadrelu in the stateroom, looking *up* at the grey-green water each time the *Chathrand* entered a trough. But neither waves nor wind had yet reached the awesome scale the Nelluroq was famed for, the kind that would swamp the enemy or force his retreat.

Thasha was shaking with emotion, though Pazel knew she was trying to hide it. He had never felt like such a heel. *The things he'd said in that cabin.* Oggosk had left him no choice, of course, but the fact spared him little shame. He longed with all his heart to tell her the truth, but how could he, when he needed her to hate him?

Without a word to each other they made for the quarterdeck. Rose was leaning over the rail, talking to Fiffengurt: 'Nine cannon exactly, and as soon as you may. All thirty-two pounders, all from the lower battery. Make sure they understand you.'

'Oppo, Captain, nine it is.' Fiffengurt shielded his eyes and nodded at a topdeck gun. 'And that faulty forty-eight makes ten?'

'Precisely. But before any of those the empty charge.'

'Consider it done, sir.'

Fiffengurt rushed to the hatch, shooting Pazel a furtive look of terror and anxiety. Then he was gone down the ladderway, blowing sharp notes on the whistle clamped in his teeth.

Moments later the rain caught up with them. It came with a fiercer wind, and slashed across the topdeck in rippling sheets that broke and boiled around their ankles. Everyone was running and stumbling: for deck swabs, for oilskins, for shelter.

'Batten down the Five!' boomed Uskins, seizing Pazel and thrusting him at the hatch. 'Not full-fast, but shielded, Muketch – can you manage?'

'Oppo, sir.' Pazel squatted down before the rolled oilskin and tore at its gathers. Thasha bent instinctively to help him, and for the merest instant they both froze, looking at each other. Something in Pazel's face must have told Thasha that her help was unwelcome, for she suddenly released the oilskin and dashed away through the downpour.

Neeps appeared out of the chaos, looking positively hostile as he snatched up a corner of the oilskin and helped Pazel spread it over the hatch rail. Together they stretched and tightened the canvas until it fitted tight as a drumhead, leaving a gap just wide enough for a man to squeeze up or down the stairs. 'Thanks again,' said Pazel as they finished.

'You really are a swine, you know,' said Neeps. 'Thasha's falling to pieces.'

Pazel shot him a sideways look. 'All right, mate,' he said, 'I'm going to tell you what's what.'

'Well it's about blary time.'

'But you have to *swear* to stay away from Oggosk. Can you do that?'

'Fire,' said Neeps.

'What?'

A cannon-blast drowned Pazel's question. The two boys hit the deck as men screamed warnings to each other. The *Jistrolloq* had opened up with her long guns. Pazel glanced up just in time to see the bow of the enemy ship blossom with new fire – four points this time – and then he cringed as the sound reached them, four fused explosions slamming into his chest. But none of the shots touched the *Chathrand*.

'That's all for show, lads,' Alyash bellowed, staggering aft against the wind. 'They couldn't strike us at this range on a quiet day.'

As the youths rose, there came a noise far louder than the *Jistrolloq*'s guns. It was one of their own, but something had gone wrong: the blast seemed to come from well inside the *Chathrand*. Pazel heard coughing and retching as smoke began to billow from the starboard quarter.

'Fiffengurt must have botched something terrible,' said Neeps.

Pazel watched the plume of black smoke vanish in the rain. 'Did he? I wonder.'

'What are you talking about?'

'Something Rose said. About firing off a gun with no ball, just a powder-charge, though why he— Down, down!'

The *Jistrolloq* was firing again. This time they heard the scream of the ball as it passed overhead. Pazel looked up: Thasha and Rose stood side by side on the quarterdeck. Neither one of them had taken cover.

'Damn it all!' said Neeps, also looking at Thasha. 'He may be insane, but she's not. Or wasn't, before you got to her. I think you had something you wanted to tell me?'

Pazel told him, shouting over the wind. As he listened the Sollochi boy's face grew tight with fury. 'Oggosk!' he said. 'That vulture! I'm going to shove those threats right down her scrawny old throat!'

'No you're not,' said Pazel. 'You're going to do something else for me. You're going to explain it all to Thasha.'

Neeps took a deep breath, and nodded. 'Yeah, all right.'

'And make sure she understands, Neeps: she can't so much as smile at me, even when we're alone. She should try not to *think* about me. Oggosk has ways of finding out.'

Neeps went straight to the task – and Pazel, fearing that Thasha would turn to him with some look he would have to respond to, stepped quickly behind the mizzenmast.

The rain was cold now, and the wind stronger yet. From below, Pazel caught the dim sound of Fiffengurt roaring *Fire*, and then came a series of blasts, and puffs of black smoke from the starboard gunports. On the *Jistrolloq*, nothing changed, and Pazel would have been amazed if it had. They were still too far apart, and it looked very much as though *Chathrand* was firing at a hopeless angle. What was Rose trying to prove?

More shots from the *Jistrolloq*; more wild and useless return fire from the *Chathrand*. Then Neeps returned from the quarterdeck, but his face wore no hint of satisfaction. 'You can call me a swine now, if you want,' he said. 'I – I cacked things up, Pazel. I was trying to explain that when you acted strange around her it was because you were worried about what Oggosk would think. But I was still thinking about the murth-girl, and said *Klyst* when I meant to say Oggosk. And when I realised what I'd done ... *aya, Rin*—'

'What next?' said Pazel. 'Out with it.'

Neeps closed his eyes, wincing. 'I said, "He's not in love with her."'

Pazel grabbed him by the shoulders. 'You didn't. Neeps, you *couldn't have*—'

'I thought you'd want her to know!' Neeps shouted defensively. 'It's just that the *way* I said it was all wrong! I sort of blurted it out. And it shocked her a little, I guess, because she turned her back and ran off.'

Pazel sagged against the mizzenmast rail. 'She's going to think I *do* fancy Klyst. Which I don't. Oh Pitfire—'

His collarbone gave a warning throb.

'Oggosk!' cried Neeps. 'This is all her fault, the hag! But listen, mate, don't you worry! I'll straighten things out with Thasha. I'll explain.'

'No!' said Pazel desperately. 'Don't do any more *explaining*. And don't go after Oggosk either. Just ... go stand still somewhere.'

Neither of them had the chance to stand still, however, for scarcely had Pazel spoken when they were dragged into another job, this time by the gunner, Mr Byrd. Two of the *Chathrand*'s ancient guns, crude behemoths from her early days as a warship, had stood lashed like old monuments behind the kevels since Pazel first stepped aboard. Now Byrd's men had freed the starboard gun and cranked it halfway to firing position, kicking open the gunnery door and unbolting the sliders that would let the cannon extend. Neeps and Pazel, along with eight sailors, were herded together on either side of the gun carriage. In went the powder charge, then the ram, and finally two men heaved the forty-eight-pound ball into the muzzle.

'Take hold!' shouted Byrd. 'We're going to run all-out, boys, as we slide down the next wave. Just mind you don't go overboard! Steady, now—'

Baffled, Pazel looked from sailor to sailor. Who was carrying the match?

The wave crested; Byrd cried, '*Now!*' and eleven bodies threw themselves at the big gun. It flew forwards – the sliders must have been freshly greased – and with a terrible sound of breaking wood, the cannon and carriage smashed right through the gunnery door. Men cried out, ropes snapped, ringbolts were torn from the deck. The big gun toppled forward and plunged into the sea.

Pazel gaped at the ugly wound in the *Chathrand*'s side, thinking, *Rose is going to tear off our heads.*

'That'll do nicely,' said Byrd without a hint of sarcasm. 'Carry on, tarboys – my crew, below.'

The sailors vanished. Neeps could not have looked more stunned if he'd been beaten with a shoe. '"*That'll do nicely?*" This crew's gone raving mad. And if this is how we fight they're going to slaughter us.'

'We look like a troupe of clowns,' Pazel agreed. He turned – and four men bearing lumber nearly bowled him down. They had carpentry tools as well, and immediately set about repairing the rail. As if they were expecting the job, Pazel thought.

Then he froze. *Expecting the job.*

'That sly old dog,' he said, turning to look at Neeps. 'Rose is doing it all for *them*, don't you see? The powder-charge inside the gun deck, the hopeless shots, now this big muck-up. He's making us look like clowns *on purpose*. He's setting a blary trap.'

Understanding spread across Neeps' face. 'You're right. You must be! He's reeling that Admiral Kuminzat in. But what happens if he falls for it? We're not as lame as all this, but they really can outgun us two to one.'

A shout from the quarterdeck: Rose himself was beckoning them near. When they had raced up the ladder the big man bent level with their faces.

'You both climb well,' he said. 'I need you aloft the spankermast, now, and clewing up the topgallant.'

'Captain,' said Pazel, 'we've never worked your sails. We don't know the spanker rigging.'

'Exactly,' said Rose, 'you'll look like perfect imbeciles up there. Climb!'

The boys glanced at each other. Pazel's theory was apparently proved, but they took no satisfaction from it. 'We might do some harm up there,' Neeps protested.

'See that you don't,' said Rose. 'Find a line that's bent to the topsails and foul it up, that's all – not badly, just plain to see. And keep worrying it 'til nightfall, unless I call you down.'

'Or we're shot down,' said Pazel. 'You wouldn't mind that at all.'

Rose struck at him with his massive fist. But the thousand blows Hercól and Thasha had landed on him had not been in vain. Just in time he leaped backwards, and found himself in fighting-stance, almost without conscious thought. It was the same pose that had so amused Drellarek, moments before the Turach died.

But Rose was not at all amused. 'You offal-brained Ormali layabout,' he said. 'I'm the captain of this ship! What if I'm not mad, eh, and we survive this engagement? Do you know how many ways I can make you *wish* you'd been killed? Get up that mast!'

There was no help for it: Rose was sincere in his threats, if in little else. Once more the boys took to the shrouds, bare feet on the decrepit ratlines, hands on the sturdier ropes. This time the ascent was horrifying. The topgallants rode a hundred feet above the quarterdeck, and before he'd climbed thirty Pazel began to suffer fantasies of falling, flying, letting go. The wind was like a frigid hand trying to claw them from the ship; the rain flew at them horizontally in a ceaseless, biting spray. Over and over the ratlines snapped, letting them half-drop through the shrouds, feet kicking wildly. And now the *Jistrolloq* was close enough for him to see the fire leaping from her chaser-guns.

Don't clench your hands! Captain Nestef had taught him. *If you squeeze the blood out of 'em they'll soon be too tired to hold on. That's one of the fifty ways fear can kill you.*

But Pazel was afraid – he was cold and dizzy and scared to death. Neeps' skin was pale; he looked as if the wind were trying to melt him down to bone. Up and up they went, like a pair of deranged hermits scaling a cliff in the Tsördons, going to meet the gods. At ninety feet Pazel looked down and saw Thasha pointing up at them, arguing with the captain. Then he saw Alyash grin and gesture at the stern as the largest wave yet passed like a moving hill under the vessel. *A sixty-footer*, thought Pazel, and vomited into the storm.

When they reached the topgallant yard the array of snapping ropes and heaving wheelblocks was a perfect mystery. Neeps groped to Pazel's side and shouted in his ear. Pazel could not make out a word.

Out along the yard, feet on the clew line, arms over the huge wooden beam. They flailed from rope to rope, hauling at each to see where it led. But the wind's strength so completely outmatched their own that they could barely move the thick hemp lines.

Half a mile between the ships. The *Jistrolloq* was firing selectively now. She would not have to wait long for point-blank accuracy.

Was Rose committing suicide? The *Jistrolloq* was as good a target as she would ever be, until she began to pass and rake them with her own huge array of cannon. Pazel knew for a fact that a dozen guns could fire from the *Chathrand*'s stern – thrice as many as could be wielded from the enemy's sleek bow. Yet still no guns fired from the *Chathrand* save the beleaguered nine on the starboard quarter. *He's risking everything to lure them closer. What in the Nine Pits for?*

Keep breathing. Think of something else. Strategy, tactics. What had Rose been going on about in his cabin? Motives, that was it. What had driven Kuminzat to take his vessel even this little distance onto the Ruling Sea? What did he want?

Revenge, of course, for his daughter and the Babqri Father. But Rose had clearly believed that something else was at stake for the man. Hope of glory? Love of country? Proof of Arqual's deception?

The mast shuddered. A ball from the White Reaper had punched a hole in the spanker mainsail.

What proof would the Sizzies have, though, if they sank the *Chathrand* out here in the Nelluroq? And if killing them was glorious, wasn't it ten times more so to expose a plot that could destroy the Mzithrin Empire?

They must have wanted to take us alive. Some of us, at least. But thanks to Diadrelu's warning we made it out of the Black Shoulders without a scratch. And now their settling for slaughter.

A quarter-mile. The *Jistrolloq* was pitching wildly now, and her mainsails fell limp for three or four seconds at the bottom of each trough, the wind cut off by the waves towering above her. She was slowing, she had to be: but not enough for the *Chathrand* to pull ahead.

There was a scream of fire. A blazing thing like a comet streaked from the *Jistrolloq* and exploded against the Great Ship's forcmast. *Dragon's egg!* men were howling. Everyone had heard of the weapons, but Pazel had never met a soul who had lived to describe them first-hand. Now he saw why. Deck and mast were suddenly engulfed in a dripping blue flame; and hideous to behold, so were the men, leaping from the ropes, tearing at their oilskins in a frenzy. In blind agony the fire-drenched figures scattered on the deck, as luckier men hauled desperately at the pumps and hoses.

For once the rain was their ally: the fire did not spread, not even on the tar-coated rigging. But the men at the blast's epicentre had lost control of their sails. The huge forecourse swung disastrously to leeward, tearing at the standing rigging, and the *Chathrand* heeled in the same direction, her bow diving and her stern lifting like a bucking mule. Pazel locked his elbow around a brace as his feet were torn from the clew line, and for a moment his body lifted away from the spar like a scrap of canvas. When the ship righted he crashed down painfully against the timber. He glanced over his shoulder, and a prayer of joy welled up inside him: Neeps was still there.

The *Chathrand* was yawing, rolling, and it would be minutes yet before the fore-topmen came to grips with the chaos of the sail. Pazel looked down and saw six men at the wheel, Rose among them, fighting to keep the ship from turning sidelong to the waves. And now the *Jistrolloq* was racing towards them, chaser-cannon firing one after another, and teams on her forecastle running out the hull-smashing carronades.

Another terrible crash, and the roof of the wheelhouse was blown to pieces. At nearly the same instant the mizzenmast tilted leeward with a groan: a wooden ballista-spear, dragging a kite's tail of iron barbs, had ripped through her starboard shrouds.

Pazel looked at Neeps and made a jerking motion: *The hell with this. It's over.* Neeps understood, and nodded. His lips formed one word: *Thasha.*

Pazel caught his meaning instantly. *Go to her,* Neeps was telling him, *while there's time to say goodbye.*

They were creeping back towards the mast when something inside the *Chathrand* roared. Pazel looked down and saw black smoke boiling up and over the quarterdeck, and around both sides of the hull. They had run out the stern cannon at last.

The *Jistrolloq*'s bow plating was tempered steel, but four square openings pierced it: one for each of the chaser-guns harrying her enemy. It was those four cannon, Pazel saw now, that Rose had targeted, and with devastating results. Two of the guns were utterly destroyed, splintered like bottle-stems before his eyes. The other two were blown backwards through their ports and out of sight. The *Jistrolloq* herself was all but unblemished, but she would not get another shot at the *Chathrand* until she drew up alongside.

Except for those two grim carronades on the forecastle. Such weapons were absurdly inaccurate, being roughly shaped like whiskey barrels, but they threw shot so enormous that one hit at short range could stave in a hull, dropping a ship to the sea floor in minutes. Even now the Mzithrinis were taking aim: Rose's strategy had left them wide open. Pazel thought of the gun-teams on the *Chathrand*, reloading as fast as humanly possible. It would not be fast enough.

Then, somehow, fire leaped again from the Great Ship. It was a different sort of smoke plume, ragged spokes instead of a single billowing cloud. And Pazel remembered: the grapeshot guns in Rose's cabin. They too were best at point-blank range, for they riddled a wide space with iron pellets: useless for damaging a ship, but deadly against flesh. Pazel could see the proof of that: Mzithrinis dead or squirming in their blood or crouching in fear behind the carronades. One of the guns, already loosed for firing, disgorged its knee-high iron shot onto the forecastle. The ball raced aft, catching a man by the heel and crushing him instantly; then it changed directions with the pitch of the ship and smashed through the starboard rail. Pazel could only watch, sickened and stunned. *All that with one cannon's grapeshot.*

Another of the four guns boomed, killing an officer as he stood to rally the surviving carronade gunners. A third erupted when relief gunners tried to swarm up the ladder onto the forecastle. Pazel realised with a sense of awe that the team in Rose's cabin would be able to reload the first of the four guns before the last had fired, and that such a relay could go on indefinitely. The *Jistrolloq* had given up her forecastle, and *Chathrand*'s twelve stern cannon would soon be ready to fire again.

He's going to sink them. He's going to kill them all, right before my eyes.

Whether that indeed was Rose's intention Pazel never learned, for at the height of the next swell the *Chathrand*'s foremast tore her stays, ripped free her starboard shrouds; and then the whole towering mass of spars and sail and rigging crashed down over the portside rail.

Dead! thought Pazel, as the *Chathrand* heeled terribly sidelong, and cables snapped around him. The dangling, half-submerged mast would drag their bow under as surely as a hold full of seawater; it was unthinkable that they would have enough time to cut it free. The *Chathrand* wallowed backwards down the wave; he saw the nine open gunports being wrenched shut in a panic, and a row of mailed Turachs falling like dominoes, and two sailors vanishing overboard into a cauldron of white froth. He saw Neeps struck in the chest by a flying wheelblock; they would not last another five minutes on this spar. But would the ship herself fare any better?

Even as he framed the thought, they rolled: the following sea had caught the *Chathrand* straight across her beam. The mast where they clung with locked limbs dived towards the sea, while beneath them the crown of the breaking wave swept right over the waist of the ship, making her quarterdeck and forecastle look for a moment like two rafts separated by eight hundred feet of white-water. In that torrent men clung to ropes, rails, cleats, anything that did not move, and still many were carried away.

Pazel had a blurred impression of the White Reaper at a hundred yards, as perfectly in control as they were perfectly flailing, her bowsprit pointed like a sword at *Chathrand*'s tilting flank. Dauntless, her gunners were making a third charge onto the forecastle. No grapeshot would drive them off this time, and if they managed to fire those killer carronades they could hardly miss with their eyes shut.

But then the *Chathrand* righted. Pazel could not believe what his senses were telling him. Had the foremast gone by the board? How, how had they done it? But there was no doubt, they were righting, and as he flew skywards with even more sickening speed than before, Pazel caught a sound he had only heard once before in his life – the day Rose had destroyed the whaler in a rippling broadside.

All along the starboard hull, gunports had flown open again: not just the earlier nine, but thirty, forty perhaps; and bow to stern they belched fire and smoke, straight at the *Jistrolloq*, across the trough between the passing wave and the next. Then just seconds before the wave reached them the doors were yanked shut again. Once more the Great Ship rolled.

Now at last Pazel caught a glimpse of their saviours: the augrongs, Refeg and Rer. Waist deep in foam, the creatures were even now taking axes to the last of the foremast rigging, while teams of men strained at the harnesses they wore, struggling to keep them from washing into the sea. *Bless their hides*, thought Pazel, *those brutes could part a halyard with one stroke.*

This time it took far longer to rise – who could say how much water had flooded the ship, or by how many routes? – but when they did at last Pazel knew it was over. Horrible, horrible sight! The *Jistrolloq* had lost her own foremast to the *Chathrand*'s guns, and her main was torsioned hopelessly to windward. But it was not the canvas she had lost that had doomed her; it was the canvas that survived. Like the *Chathrand*, the Mzithrini warship had slewed round, and the great power of the surviving squaresails was now pressing down on her bow, like a torturer's hand forcing his victim's head underwater, deeper, and deeper still. The next wave caught her broad on the starboard quarter, a blow the smaller ship could not absorb. Over she went on her beam-ends, masts slapping the waves, so close to the *Chathrand* they seemed almost like bridges her men might run across to safety. As the wave passed she tried to right herself, but a hundred thousand tons of water on her sails could not be shed in an instant, and the next wave buried her completely. By then the Great Ship had veered downwind just enough to ride the wave out, and Pazel felt the monstrous sidelong lurching come to an end. He and Neeps gained the shrouds, and as he began his descent at last Pazel looked for the enemy and saw nothing, nothing at all – and then a twisted length of white sailcloth, one proud red star in the corner, moving like the spectre of a whale beneath the surface, only to reach some absolute decision, and dive.

30

Sunday, 26 Freala 941. If this is what victory feels like, you may spare me the distinction for the rest of my days. We are alive (most of us) & the Grey Lady took no immediately fatal damage in the engagement, & no ship in Alifros can follow or even spot us now – yes, for all that I am thankful. And who could fail to be relieved that the storm is abating, this the 3rd night since our escape from Sandplume Cove? Two cheers for the mercy of the Nelluroq & the undeniable cunning of Captain Nilus Rose.

But never was I less inclined to celebrate. Sixteen men lost overboard & twenty more laid out dead in our surgical annexe, among them Coxilrane 'Firecracker' Frix, busybody, coward & a dedicated sailor to his entrails. Like me a product of Wasthog Strand, that unpaved, unloved corner of Etherhorde, pinched between the ironworks and the slaughterhouses. I used to see him with his pack of boys when we were young. They dressed like Burnscove thugs, a sort of fashion then, & threw rocks at us over the King's Canal. Frix always looked apologetic & out of place, a skinny dog trotting along at their heels, needing to be noticed & at the same time afraid to be. Nothing much ever changed in his life, Rin rest his soul.

Courage. One might celebrate that, I suppose, & set aside the question of whether it was given wisely or in vain. Our dead gunners had courage: with waves like cliffs bearing down on them, they kicked open their gunports, blasted the *Jistrolloq*'s rigging to pieces, slammed the ports again in the nick of time – and suffocated on their own smoke, in a deck sealed tight as a crypt. Tanner wept for his boys, though his own lungs were burned black. I sat by him three hours tonight in Chadfallow's surgery. Even his last wheezing breath smelled of gunpowder.

Pathkendle & Undrabust have courage: that spankermast would have been the next to fall, if the chaser-guns on the *Jistrolloq* had gotten off another round or two. The boys have bullwhip-scars all over their bodies, from ropes cracking in the wind. Thasha Isiq has courage, facing Rose's lunacy concerning ghosts, & fighting to get her friends brought down off that lethal spar even when the captain threatened to pitch her over the stern. Elkstem & I exchanged a look: we were with Rose in 927, when he *did* pitch a girl off the stern of the Great Ship; but that is another story.

Felthrup has courage, wherever he is. The youths are beside themselves, searching for him everywhere, sniffing about the lower decks with Thasha's dogs. All to no avail.

And tonight a woman I might once have killed without a thought told me *I* had courage. I refer of course to the crawly, Diadrelu. She was back in the stateroom when I brought Pathkendle & Co. their dinner & she walked up bold as brass & looked me in the eye. 'Quartermaster,' says she, 'I salute your wisdom and bravery.'

Now that the crisis was over it seemed even less natural to be talking to a crawly. I looked away & mumbled about how they'd picked up the pieces well. For the stateroom had been in pieces: a 24-pounder had sailed right through the big stern window, split the dining table in half, shattered the washroom door, put a whopping dent in the cast-iron tub, ricocheted back into the main cabin & blasted a stanchion to woodchips. By the grace of Rin no one was in its path; Thasha had locked her dogs in her own cabin.

I gestured at the shattered window, sealed for now with a nailed-up tarpaulin. 'We have glass stowed away for repairs,' I added. 'We can fix the casement, too, though it won't hinge no more.'

The crawly held me in her bright-metal gaze. 'History itself shall hinge on the choice you made,' she said.

'Don't know that I *have* made it,' I grumbled, 'if you're talking about the choice not to smoke you cr— you individuals, off this ship.'

'I am talking about the choice of reason over fear,' she said, 'and I'll wager my life that you have indeed decided, though Rin knows I should have no right to condemn you if you change your mind.'

'I don't want blood on my hands,' I told her. 'Nobody's blood. Not yours, even, if it ain't required.'

'You have the courage to see, Mr Fiffengurt,' she said. 'All other forms of courage spring from that well.'

I was tongue-tied with confusion. It was crawlies who sank the *Adelyne* off Rapopalni, with my uncle & his babe aboard, or so the few survivors claimed. After that my own dad started collecting crawly skulls to make a necklace, though he had just four by the time he died. Ma still keeps the gruesome things on his dresser, beside his service ribbons & his false teeth. Hating ixchel is a family tradition, you might say.

But in my fifty years no woman has ever spoken to me with more respect than this Diadrelu. Of course she's not human & so not properly a woman (though I saw evidence unforgettably to the contrary when I cut that shirt away). My kin in Etherhorde – Pitfire, *everyone* in Etherhorde – would call me a mutineer, a fool, the dupe of a shapely ship-louse; Dad would say I should be the first to drown when the crawlies strike. These past nights I've pictured their faces as I lay down to sleep & it stabs me through the heart to know how they'd condemn me. Last night they entered my dreams, bitter & scornful & hurrying off with hostile glances, & 'Shame, shame' was all I could get them to say.

But when I think of the noble bearing of that Lady Diadrelu, I feel suddenly more ashamed of my certainties about her people than the displeasure of my own. All my life I've laughed at the righteous fools who hate Mzithrinis at a personal level, who assume that whole vast land to be populated by mindless killers with bloodshot eyes. And all my life I've thought of 'crawlies' as something worse. If I'm honest (& where shall I be honest if not with you, little whelp?) my reasons make no more sense than the next man's reasons for hating the Sizzies: because someone long dead or far away set us on this path, and told us never to turn. I cannot forget the *Adelyne*. But the fact that Pazel and Thasha love this Diadrelu settles the matter: she may not be human, but she's a person all the same.

The dream ended with a rain of ash from the heavens, falling in a thin band between me & my kinfolk, & when I saw them through the ash it was like seeing figures in a painting, or on the deck of some boat heading off to the East Reach or points beyond. People who've slipped away, who you can't have back at your side under any circumstances, people gone already & for ever.

Tuesday, 28 Freala 941. Palo Elkstem, our sailmaster's nephew, succumbed to his burns this morning. He was right under the foremast when the dragon's-egg shot exploded, & the battle netting came down upon him in flames.

These last days have been bitter. Storm raging again, so that we cannot dream of shifting either of the great timbers on the lower gun

407

deck, although the carpenters have already cut & shaped one into a new foremast. Waves at 40 ft. & breaking on our port quarter: no danger to the ship provided the helm keeps us true, but lads who I've never known to be ill are heaving over the side.

Rose has called off the imprisonment of Pathkendle & Co., though he left one Turach on duty at the invisible wall, to observe who comes & goes. This presents certain difficulties for me: now that they can get their own food, what excuse do I have to visit? And if I persist, & that soldier notes it again & again, how long will it be before the captain pulls me aside & demands a report?

Friday, 1 Norn 941. I start to wonder if a gale rages perpetually on the Ruling Sea. No end is in sight; if anything the wind is somewhat fiercer with each passing hour. Gloom among the sailors, a dangerous glint in the Turachs' eyes. And this before we have even finished the fresh food we loaded at Bramian. What is to come in the months ahead I do not like to imagine.

There were at least two hints today, however – unpleasant hints, to be sure. First thing this morning came the accusation, by a Plapp's Pier man, that three members of his gang who'd died in the battle had been stripped of their rings, knives & other valuables by the lad assigned to prepare the corpses for burial at sea. The accused man belonged to neither gang, but he took the Burnscove Boys oath almost as soon as he learned of the charges, saying he feared for his life without their protection. Wish I could be certain that he was wrong.

Of course it's the worst breach imaginable of the Code to pledge oneself to anything save the ship & her captain, & Rose was in a holy fury when he heard of it. As I write the man hangs by one ankle from the main yard, slamming about like a loose wheelblock & lashed by the storm. If the Burnscovers take this as punishment for his stealing (a charge for which there is no evidence) we may yet escape a gang war.

Then at the strike of the noon bell I met Uskins near the tonnage hatch, just standing there in the rain. He caught my eye & for once there was no mockery or sneering, so I drew near & asked what ailed him. Uskins said not a word, just looked away south-east, & when I did the same I saw a purplish glaze on the underside of the furthest clouds, & a little bulge downwards.

'Humph,' said I, squinting, 'I can't account for that, Pidetor, but we've both seen stranger things.'

'You cannot account for it,' said Uskins, 'but Arunis can. He says it is the sign of the Nelluroq Vortex.'

'The Vortex! Oh, surely not. We can't be *that* far east.'

'One can see its effects for thousand of miles. It alters the weather, makes its own winds. Arunis says that they bear down through its depths and vanish from this world. That one can watch a whole sky full of clouds being sucked into its maw, with thunderheads and flocks of birds, and even cloud-murths struggling in vain against its power.'

'But why in the bubbling black Pits are you talking to Arunis?' I demanded.

Uskins looked at me sharply, & his warthog nature came back to him. 'I bring his meals,' he said, 'as you would know if you paid less attention to those youths in the stateroom, and more to our captain's directives.'

'I know Rose is trying to keep him away from the crew,' I said, trying to ignore the provocation. 'But anyone could bring a plate to his door.'

'The captain wants him *observed*, Fiffengurt, not just quarantined. He chose me for my tact, and my gift for obtaining information.'

Your slime-craft & snooping, I thought. But I left him to his vigil & said no more. Arunis may be lying through his teeth, but that purple glint on the clouds' underbellies was plain to see, & remained so through nightfall.

Tonight Dastu pressed a slip of paper into my hand. On it were these words: *Find us a safe and secret compartment. When the storm ends we're going to take some chances with trust. Pzl.*

Dastu glanced back at me over his shoulder. *There's one they've chosen to trust already*, I thought, *just as they chose me back at Simja.*

I am plotting against the captain. My mutiny is now a fact.

Tuesday, 5 Norn 941. Eight solid days of storm. Nothing to do but fight it, fight it ceaselessly. Nights by far the worst, for though we stab at the darkness with fog lamps the waves are ever breaking upon us before we rightly see them. We have been close to broaching more often than I can recall, & five or six times had water over the deck. Pumps have failed, oilskins parted, and a hand run along half the walls on the orlop comes up wet: the Nelluroq is oozing through the seams, pressed in by the battering waves. There was a ghastly morning when the water in the well rose ten feet in three hours: a wad of grime and rat-hair had clogged a bilge pipe. Dawn & dusk are blurry notions, & noon is when you stand beside one mast & can see the next.

Another three men lost, & reports of fever among the unhappy folk down in steerage. Chadfallow & Fulbreech handing out pills. The tarboy Macom Drell, of Hansprit, crushed on the mercy deck by shifting cargo. The lad was found hours after his death; he could not fill his lungs to cry for aid. Also a suicide among the Turachs. One of the guards on the Shaggat simply walked up & put his hand on the Nilstone. I saw what was left of him: bone & gristle & ash. They say he had been staring at the thing for a week.

Monday, 11 Norn 941. Wave height doubled & still we lack *[illegible]* end of our voyage & this ship's proud history unless *[illegible]* flooding the *[illegible]* down the ladderway and broke his leg *[illegible]* wind screams in the rigging with the sound of tortured animals *[illegible]* blary hand shaking too much to wr *[unfinished].*

Sunday, 17 Norn 941. Something in this universe must love the *Chathrand*, for she has looked her own death in the face every day for a week. Three days ago the waves reached 80 ft. Rose put her into the wind, for at that height the lower gallery windows were getting slapped on every swell & one rogue breaker could have smashed them in, flooding the deck & sending us to join the *Jistrolloq* in minutes flat. Once we had her about with the stormsails trimmed we were better off for a while, treading in place through the daylight hours, praying & fighting for steerage through the night.

But the day before yesterday the seas grew taller yet. Surely it has been a century or more since any man stood on the Great Ship's forecastle & looked *up* at a cresting wave, but I am that man, by Rin. Yet with Elkstem at the wheel & Rose beside him, we did all right until nightfall. Then the waves grew even larger, & the dark hours were one long frenzied struggle against obliteration, tacking up the sides of mountains, piercing the frothing crest with the bowsprit, clawing over the top & falling forwards with a hull-shaking thump, looking up again at once as the next mountain rushed us. The crew was simply breaking. No one talked anymore. No one wanted to eat, or dared to rest, or remembered the needs of their bodies. I had to order men to drink water, & watch that they did so: they were so frightened that only by working perpetually did they keep from shrieking or diving into the sea.

So passed that hideous night, & all of yesterday, & last night too. I don't think a man on this ship believed he could fight the sea as long as we did. There were lads had to be smacked to make 'em stop working the pumps, when their shifts ended. But no one had to be smacked awake. We worked like machines, like wind-up toys in the hands of a maniac, with no purpose but to see how much twisting our mechanisms could take.

Dawn seemed to have been abolished, the night stretched into weeks or months. In the worst of it I saw cloud-murths on feral steeds, galloping back & forth on the wave-crests, threatening us with their halberds & pikes. I shall never know if they were real; indeed I'm not sure I want to.

But at last the dawn did come, & with it a gentler wind & seas that rapidly diminished to a mere forty or fifty feet – waves that would have decimated any harbour in Alifros, yet we took them for our salvation. If my count is right we have been twenty days in storm (and without a foremast, by all the gods!). In that time how many hours have I slept? Ten, fifteen? We have all become like Felthrup: creatures who no longer shut our eyes, for fear of what will happen if we do.

Of Felthrup himself there is no sign.

Tuesday, 19 Norn 941. Someone must list the dead: we owe all human beings that minimum courtesy. But the bookkeeper's an oathsworn Plapp & may 'forget' to mention the losses among the Burnscove Boys; & by the Sailing Code his tabulation goes first to Uskins (Stukey), who so detests lowhorns like Uskins (Stukey) that he may abbreviate the list even further. I don't know why this strikes me as part & parcel of the wickedness being done on this voyage, but I will scribble names as I think of them & hope this book falls into the hands of some who loved these unfortunates:

[*here follows a list of 37 dead*]*
May Bakru bring them all to tearless rest, *edalage.*

Wednesday, 20 Norn 941. As fine & innocent a day as one could hope for. Swells of an easy 25 ft., wind behind us & powerful instead of crippling, very much the conditions the Great Ship was built for. We've had an easy run these past three days, though a state of nervous collapse followed the storm – men afflicted with flux, vomiting, chills & nightmares; fights breaking out between the cursed gangs; drunkenness rampant beyond anything possible on their small rations of rum.

* Names available upon request. – EDITOR.

The gods only know what sort of ship-brewed rotgut they're drinking.

Managed to raise a guide spar on the stump of the foremast: the best we can hope to do until we reach still waters. Cazencian whales, of all things, spotted a quarter-mile to windward, on a parallel run. Told Mr Latzlo & got a snarl for thanks. He does not look normal, Latzlo. He used to shave & primp & perfume himself each day for the Lapadolma girl; now he resembles something escaped from one of his cages.

Monday, 25 Norn 941. Little lad or lass, asleep yet in Annabel's womb: how I should love you to grow up knowing these four youths. If the dream of the rain of ashes should prove true somehow – if my kin disowns me for the choices I've made – still I must believe that you and your dear Mother will accept me. Lady Thasha, Pathkendle, Undrabust, Marila: we'll call them your honorary aunts & uncles, & you will scarce believe the tales they tell.

The good weather holds. Somewhere it is winter; the first frosts are surely etched on your mother's window, but here fungus is blooming in our footlockers & tar bubbles out of the deck seams at noon. The whales still with us. The Vortex gone from sight.

Last night I brought food once again to the stateroom. Undrabust & the stowaway girl, Marila, were the only ones I saw at first. Then a whirling swept across the floor at ankle-height. It was Diadrelu, of course. The crawly woman was dancing a kind of ballet with her sword in the middle of the chamber. She moved so quickly one could not tell where flesh ended & steel began. If she were human-sized she'd be a match for any Turach who ever drew a blade.

'Where are—'

Marila raised a finger to her lips. Undrabust, meanwhile, came forwards and asked loudly, 'Did you bring it, then?'

For once he meant something other than food. Undrabust had slipped me a second note, asking for the weirdest thing: my old mandoloro,* which I'd not played or even thought about since my commission began, nigh two years ago—

(Had I known then who was to be my captain, I should have left the

---

* The *mandoloro* is a small Opaltine accordion, traditionally constructed of two solid gourds and a rubbery bellows made from a shark's bladder. The instrument produces a reedy & singularly piercing yowl. It was upon first hearing a mandoloro in the Opalt back country that the explorer Jelan Gergandri doubled the number of men on night watch, declaring that 'in a country where *that* is labelled music we must be ready for anything.' – EDITOR.

mandoloro behind. How sad to recall what I imagined then: nights on the Nelu Peren with a happy ship, a crew of contented Burnscove gangsters under my command,* & one scant year before I handed the honour over to a fresh face & settled down with my own sweet 'Bel. Oh Anni, don't hate me, none of this was my choice.)

'How in the putrid Pits did you know I had a squeezebox?' I'd asked Undrabust. The tarboy replied that Felthrup had mentioned it, weeks ago. Which is odder still, as I'm sure I never discussed music with the poor little rat.

I'd no sooner taken it from its case than Undrabust snatched it up & began to play. Or rather to squeeze & mash buttons. He might have been attempting *The Lighthouse Girl*. It does not matter; I have seen men flogged for less. Undrabust himself frowned at the bleating & honking, but that did not stop him from grinding away. Marila took my hand & led me to one side.

'They may be listening,' she whispered. 'Neeps is just drowning them out.'

'Who are "they"?' I asked.

'Rose's men,' she said, 'or maybe Ott's. It was Khalmet who warned us – the Turach second in command. We *think* he's on our side.'

'A Turach, siding against the Emperor? That's impossible, missy.'

Marila shrugged.

'Skies of fire! If it's true, you must never, *never* give him away. The things they'd do to a disloyal Turach!

'That's just what Thasha said.'

'Where is the young mistress? And Pathkendle?'

Marila pointed to Thasha's cabin. 'She's in there. Reading her *Polylex*, or trying to. Since Felthrup disappeared she's acted very strange about that book. She just cracks it open anywhere, reads for a moment, and then sits still, gazing off into space. It's very strange. She looks ... old, when she's sitting there. And when she stands up she's tired.

Marila looked sourly at Thasha's door. 'She and Pazel are still fighting. Last night it got bad. Thasha mentioned Fulbreech, and Pazel just hit the roof. He said it was time she decided who her friends were, and she yelled back that he should take his own advice, and stop hating her for what her father did to Ormael. Then everyone started yelling

* The later testimony of Lady Lapadolma Yelig and others indicates that Fiffengurt was indeed to be appointed captain of the Great Ship, before His Supremacy proclaimed that the post would once again belong to Rose. – EDITOR.

at once. Pazel said he could just clear out, since she'd be wanting *Greysan* to move in any day. "Admit it," he kept saying. "You'd be happier. Admit it." Neeps said he was sure Lady Oggosk was feeling happy – I don't know what he meant by *that* – and Pazel told him to be quiet. Then Pazel asked Thasha how much Fulbreech had *got out of her*. He meant how much information, but that's not how she took it. She went into her cabin and slammed the door. And Pazel found somewhere else to sleep.'

'Horns of the hairy devil!' I exploded. 'Leave it to me! I'll straighten that fool of a tarboy out!'

But Marila had something else on her mind. 'Did you find us a room, Mr Fiffengurt?'

'I found one,' I said. 'The reserve liquor vault, in the after-hold. It's dark and small, and the stink could wilt every branch on the Blessed Tree, but it's also as remote as you can get. Just a narrow little scuttleway from the mercy deck, and there's no light-shafts or speaking-tubes to give you away. Trouble is, it's locked tight as a drum. Otherwise you'd have lads breakin' in, ye see, no matter how dire the punishment.'

Then I saw Marila's mouth twitch. Blow me broadside, I thought, the girl knows how to smile.

'Locks are nothing to worry about,' she said. And with that she produced a large brass key. It was the ship's master key – the very one Frix had used to sneak into my cabin and steal my first journal, the one he'd dropped just before I kicked him in the rump. When I babbled, 'How – how—' Marila pointed at Diadrelu, fencing with shadows on the bearskin rug.

'She found it in a crevice on the berth deck. And she brought it to us, Mr Fiffengurt, not to her clan.'

I knew what Marila was telling me: the crawly had chosen sides, turned her back on her own people, in favour of us. *But she's just one*, I thought.

'Listen,' I said to Marila, 'you must *never* be caught with that key on your person. Rose would murder you in cold blood. And that's not a figure of speech, lass. Our captain's a man of extremes, you might say – but you've not seen him angry 'till you've seen him dealing with a trespasser! Paranoia, that's what ails him. He'd think you were looking for the Imperial horde, wherever they've hidden it – or worse, spying on him, sneaking into his cabin for a look around.'

'So this *does* open his chambers,' said Marila, satisfied. 'How about the steerage compartment? And Arunis' cabin?'

I didn't much like the drift of her questions, & said so. Her response (she is a girl after all) was to ask another question. 'How many days until the dark of the moon?'

'The dark of the moon? Well now. Six, eight. Why do you ask?'

'Because that's how long we have to choose someone to bring to the council. You've got to bring someone, too. Pazel says it doesn't matter if they're strong or brave or clever – just *absolutely trustworthy*. But I don't trust anyone except the people who come to this room. Who should I bring, Mr Fiffengurt?'

Neeps' arms were slowing; the mandoloro moaned like a lynx in heat.

'Best come alone,' I said at last. 'Don't take chances. Guess wrong and Rose will have us all killed.'

Marila shook her head. 'He won't kill Pazel or Thasha. Haven't you noticed how strange he is about them? He arrests and abuses Pazel, then sets him free and invites him to lunch. He plans to sell Thasha to the Leopard People, then keeps her by his side all through the battle. Why does he put up with them, or any of us? All he'd have to do is cut off our food until we surrender.'

She might have read my mind – or this journal – so close did her wonderings mirror my own. But I'd come up with a theory & was anxious to tell someone. 'D'ye know what I think, missy? I think he doesn't *want* to beat Pazel or Thasha. He needs 'em. He wants 'em walking this ship, free and visible, and for one very good reason: *because they frighten Arunis.*'

Marila looked at me in blankly.

'Thasha defeated the mage's fleshancs,' I went on, 'and there's her friendship with Ramachni to consider. And Pazel turned his Shaggat into a lump of stone. As long as Arunis has them to worry about, he won't be so quick to try something else. Like taking over the *Chathrand*.'

'You're right,' said Marila, her face creasing with thought. 'Oh, how stupid I am! Yes, yes – and *that's* why there are Plapps and Burnscove Boys.'

'Eh – um—'

'Aboard the *Chathrand*, I mean. That's why Rose brought so many Plapps onto a Burnscove ship. Don't you understand? As long as the crew's divided he never has to worry about a mutiny, no matter what he puts us all through. It makes perfect sense.'

It did make perfect sense, & little Marila is anything but stupid. The crew is one third Burnscove Boys, one third Plapp's Pier, & one third men from neither gang. Foolproof, you might say. Their numbers were large enough to divide the crew, but too small for either gang to take over. And if the thought of mutiny ever did cross a few minds – well, the only way they could dream of taking on those deadly Turachs would be as a ship united. And we'll see the moon hatch tadpoles before that day ever comes.

These thoughts all but crushed me. 'We have no hope, do we, lass? They've been planning this for decades.'

'So has Ramachni,' she said.

'Was he planning for Arunis to whack him so hard he could barely crawl home?'

My tongue had got ahead of me; I didn't mean to speak such words of despair to this brave young thing. Marila took it calmly, however.

'I don't know,' she said, 'but I bet you'll get a chance to ask him.'

Wednesday, 27 Norn, 941. The sorcerer has murdered Peytr Bourjon. Old Gangrüne saw it happen, in the passage outside his cabin. Seems the daft tarboy never had quite left off serving Arunis. Gangrüne watched them through a crack in his cabin door: they met, talked, the boy pleaded for something on his knees. Arunis held out his hand & Peytr took it. Then the monster reached out and snapped his neck. One-handed. Gangrüne slammed his door and started howling murder murder murder. Arunis merely walked away.

No clue from any quarter as to how Bourjon had angered the mage. Perhaps he never did. Perhaps Arunis merely wanted to attract our attention, lest anyone imagine his powers or his wickedness decreased.

How sick I am of death, of walking, living, sleeping among killers. Of serving as their quartermaster, their fool. There's little I wouldn't hazard to put an end to them. Forgive me, my Anni, my heart.

31

Metamorphoses

—〜〜—

24 Freala 941

The White Reaper, pride of the Pentarchy, holy avenger of the Mzithrin, spun beneath the killing waves in a state of chaos no seafarer had ever lived to describe. Up was down, falling was rising, solid rails became splinters; the very air one tried to gulp was seawater that stabbed one to the heart with cold, and the blackness of the depths was over and under and within her. She was vanquished, and her four hundred men were perishing in the imploding coffin of her hull.

Neda Ygrael felt her body whirl in the blind cyclone, heard her people's screams extinguished chamber by chamber as the sea advanced, felt the ship's armoured bulk cleaving down into the permanent night of the Nelluroq. She was on the berth deck, somewhere; footlockers were smashing about like boulders; shreds of hammocks caught at her limbs. Her brother *sfvantskor*s had been near her when the *Jistrolloq* rolled, and she could still hear them, crying to one another, only a shade less mad than the rest. Nurin was closest, and when the lamps went out he cried her name. There was an instant when she felt his hand, a clawing thing as violent as the sea, groping at her with broken fingers before the water tore him away. Then another hand seized her, Cayer Vispek's this time, and wrenched her up (or down?) through a hatch and onto a deck where air remained, where it was possible if agonizing to thrust the debris and bodies aside and raise one's head above the flood, where a pale green glow illuminated the horrors around her. The glow came from Sathek's Sceptre, wielded in desperation by Cayerad Hael.

The elder *sfvantskor* was bleeding from the scalp. As the ship rolled over and over he was thrashed about like a rag doll. But he held on to the sceptre, and Neda groped towards him, to what purpose she could not say, and when she and Cayer Vispek were within ten feet the old man screeched one intelligible word:

'*Soglorigatre!*'

With the word came a red light, a searing light, and a blast of steam that made her plunge again beneath the water. At once the dead face of Cayerad Hael's steward rose before her, the boy's mouth open wide as a well. Then something else burst in the ship and the body was sucked instantly away. *Down, down* they were plummeting, her ears all but bleeding from the pressure, and not knowing if she were fighting to live or to hasten a merciful death, Neda thrust her head above the surface again.

Cayerad Hael had called the red flame from the sceptre, just as he had on Sandplume, but now he had used it to burn a ragged hole in the side of the ship. He himself was scalded terribly, his hand a black stump fused for ever to the magic artefact, though for ever would be brief enough. But he lived yet, and commanded them yet; and most amazing of all, four of his *sfvantskor*s remained alive to be commanded. Neda and Cayer Vispek, bobbing and thrashing towards him; and huge Jalantri close behind; and last of all, clear-eyed and furious, Malabron.

'Out, out, out!' Cayerad Hael was screaming, clinging with his good hand to the shattered planks and gesturing frantically with sceptre and stump. 'The crew's lost; they know it better than you! We must live for them, *sfvantskor*s! Begone, begone!'

They hesitated. Later Neda would think of that hesitation as a kind of miracle: the lead spike of fearlessness had been driven so deep into their souls that even this horror, this free-fall to the Nine Pits, had not yet torn it out completely. But of course the Cayerad spoke true: they could not save even a single sailor, and it was sinful to prefer one's fancies to the cold facts of the world. Arqual had beaten them, and the Father remained unavenged. Those were the facts. Neda drew a breath (the saltwater like a knife in each lung) and plunged towards the breech in the hull.

Cayer Vispek reached their leader first. He began to shout the Dying Prayer – 'I have come to the end of dreams. I bless only what *is*—' but the sea (blasting in by yet another fissure) caught him full in the face. Still he managed the essential task: he drew the sceptre to his lips and kissed the dark crystal. And for the first time outside of trance, Neda saw the Father's magic at work.

The transformation took only an instant. A white glow came over Cayer Vispek, and a blurring of his features, and then like a flag snapped open in a storm he was a man no longer but a blue-black whale, a Cazencian, forty feet of writhing muscle and fluke and fine triangular teeth, and with a single twist of his body he was through the hull breach and away.

Jalantri was next. He tried to speak to their master, the second master to face death in as many months, but Cayerad Hael shook his head and pressed the sceptre to his mouth. And then Neda understood – the old man was *not* surrendering to death. He would change too, and lead them on. All at once Neda was ashamed of her thoughts of despair. They were *sfvantskor*s unto death, but the first duty of a *sfvantskor* was to stay alive, lest the gods be deprived of a servant.

When Jalantri changed, he became so huge that his tail-fluke ripped out another dozen feet of hull. Then he too was gone. Neda looked back at Malabron. Why wasn't he coming forwards, and why did he glare in that tortured way? Could he possibly have gone rigid with fear?

Cayerad Hael was submerged to his neck. 'Come, Malabron, Mebhar's child!' he gasped. 'You know what must be done!'

'Yes!' Malabron shouted back. 'Alone of us all!'

Neda had never heard anyone snap at Cayerad before, but there was no time to wonder. She reached Cayerad Hael, and the old man lowered the sceptre. Letting go of the ship, Neda pulled the crystal to her lips and kissed it, that sacred shard of the Black Casket, by whose power they would take the fight once more to the enemy.

The change was excruciatingly painful. Always before she had undergone the metamorphosis in trance, like all her brethren. In trance, the Father had commanded her to feel no pain, and in trance she had the power to obey. Now every sinew and corpuscle screamed in protest, as if she were being injected with venom at a million points. *The burning!* There could be no recovery from such pain, neither in the body nor the mind. It was as the Father had always warned them: some changes were for ever.

But the agony vanished as quickly as it had come, leaving only a welt of memory throbbing inside her – and Neda was a whale. Limbless, free of her shreds of clothes, warm in the icy water, and utterly blind except for the green light vanishing below.

She had changed before – into a sea turtle or a shark, when the Father was still perfecting the enchantment on Simja, in the last days before the wedding – and into this same whale's body, when they began the hunt for the Great Ship. It was the sort of magic only one as mighty as the Father could work with Sathek's Sceptre. Cayerad Hael, for all his learning, had been as helpless as a toddler when he tried to use the device, but the Father's spell went on working perfectly, month after month.

Or almost perfectly. Neda's defect remained, even when her body changed. In trance she could erase her pain, but not her memory. The others could never afterwards remember taking whale-form. Neda could never forget.

The green light dwindled. How were they to proceed? Were they to follow the *Chathrand* until the weather cleared, or attempt to board her in the gale? They'd been about to discuss it when the Arquali vessel launched its attack; now they could not discuss it at all. Neda was not even certain that she would be able to hear her brethren's keening voices over the wind and waves.

Obeying a sudden impulse, she jackknifed down into the darkness, pursuing the falling ship. Perhaps the others would gather in its dim light, and together they could set off after the enemy. She swam fast into the darkness, glad she was a creature made for diving, for black depths as much as bright surface waters. The strength in her new body was intoxicating.

There was Cayerad Hael, totally submerged, seconds from drowning; and there kissing the glowing sceptre was Malabron – tortured, doubting Malabron, changing before her eyes into a Cazencian like herself. Now their master would do the same – but would his wounds follow him into whale-form? And if they did, could he possibly survive?

Cayerad Hael raised the sceptre towards his lips. And the whale that had been Malabron surged forwards and closed his predator's teeth over the sceptre, and their master's arm, and bit down, and the world went completely black.

32

The Mutineers

8 Umbrin 941
178th day from Etherhorde

The war between Plapp's Pier and Burnscove Boys took a novel twist when Kruno Burnscove awoke one morning in his bed (his gang had built him the little bed out of pilfered lumber, stuffed a mattress with hay stolen from the cows; he was too important to sleep in a hammock; besides, Darius Plapp had a bed) to find a severed hand dangling six inches above his forehead. It was black and withered and seemed to beckon him with the crook of one mortis-curled finger. On another finger the Burnscove Boys ring. Kruno let out an undignified squeal, and across the berth deck the Plapps replied with hoots and catcalls.

There was no mystery about the provenance of the hand. One of the Burnscovers killed in the storm had been mutilated in the surgical annex, before his body could be given to the sea. The crime was in retaliation for the looting of the three Plapps Pier dead. The only lingering question was where the hand had spent the previous twenty-five days.

This was the *Chathrand*'s sixth week on the Nelluroq: the longest stretch between landfalls that many sailors had ever seen, and yet by Elkstem's calculus they had more than half of the crossing yet before them. After the severed-hand incident, Rose asked for volunteers to mediate a truce. Fiffengurt and Dr Chadfallow stepped forwards, and the next morning they brought the most influential Plapps and Burns-covers together in the wardroom. Mr Teggatz provided scones.

Chadfallow came last to the wardroom, and he cut an impressive figure in the silk coat and dark purple cape of an Imperial envoy. He wore the ruby pendant of the Order of the Orb, and the bright gold fish-and-dagger medallion of a Defender of the Realm. The latter pendant, as most of them knew, was possessed by only a half-dozen living men, and was pinned to a man's chest by the Emperor alone, never a surrogate.

The adversaries sat at opposite ends of the wardroom table. Kruno Burnscove had just fired a particularly creative and personal epithet at his rival, and the doctor's appearance had made Darius Plapp lose his train of thought as he struggled to reply. He glared at Chadfallow, while the other gang members looked away in confusion, wondering what power if any remained to this friend of His Supremacy.

Chadfallow approached the furious gang leader. He rested one long-fingered hand upon the table before him, and let the silence grow.

'You are the eponymous Plapp?' he said at last.

Darius Plapp's face went rigid. He pushed back his chair and stood up. He spoke through gritted teeth.

'Who's eponymous? Yer mother's eponymous.'

The meeting went downhill from there. Rather than brokering peace, the doctor and the quartermaster were treated to comprehensive accounts of the murders, abductions, broken cease-fires, insults to virtuous gang mothers, slop buckets emptied on wedding parties, insinuations in mixed company that this or that leader's manhood was not as it should be, libellous publications and stolen pets. Fiffengurt walked out in disgust. Chadfallow laboured on straight through the afternoon and the dinner shift, but when the session finally collapsed at midnight the only agreement he had managed to wring from Plapp and Burnscove was that he himself was stubborn enough to join either gang.

Chadfallow's report to the captain noted that mental instability was a growing threat to the safety of the ship.

Two nights later, as evening fell, the now-familiar noise of the 25-foot seas was shattered by the cries of the lookout: *On the bow! Hard on the bow! Great gods, what is it?*

Men stampeded to the rail, and at once began to shout with wonder, and not a little fear. Stretched across the southern horizon, as far as the eye could see, was a ribbon of pale red light. It was not quite the colour of sunset, nor of fire; but there was something about it that reminded one of fire: a trembling, flickering quality. A volcano? No, there was no ash, and no telltale rumble. The ribbon reached as high as the lid of clouds on the horizon, so that it looked a bit like a glowing sword, held between the blue-grey tongs of sea and sky. How far away it might have been was difficult to tell. What was certain was that it lay directly across their path.

The ribbon burned on through the night. When morning broke, it swiftly faded, and by the time the sun was fully risen it was no more to be seen. But all through the night the watch-captains had observed how Arunis stood on the forecastle, gazing steadily southward, face bathed in the glow, eyes ravenous with expectation.

'I've imagined seeing you dead,' said Diadrelu. 'Or more likely, hearing that you had died, and never seeing for myself. As it was with Talag. I've imagined my own death, likelier still. But never did I think to see you locked in the brig.'

Diadrelu stepped through the iron bars. Hercól watched her from the darkness, sitting back against the wall, smiling through his seven-week beard. It was hours past midnight; except for the pair of Turachs outside the compartment door, the mercy deck was deserted. Two cells away, the captain of the whaler, Magritte, was talking in his sleep, a low, despairing babble. He had boiled over during his first interview with Rose after the sinking of the *Sanguine*, calling him murderer, pirate, Pit-fiend, devil-swine, and when he paused for breath Rose informed him that he would serve a week in the brig for each insult, plus a fortnight for his behaviour in Rose's quarters, where he had displayed 'verbal incontinence' and a tendency to gulp his food.

Hercól for his part never seemed but half asleep. The ixchel woman had come to see him with increasing frequency, not quite certain what she was looking for, and often enough forced to depart without speaking to him, if Magritte proved restless, or the Turachs left the door ajar. And though she moved silent as dust on a puff of wind, each time she reached his cell she found his eyes open, and that slight smile of expectation on his haggard face.

And yet with each visit her worry grew. Hercól's mouth was dry; he was using a good part of his water ration to clean a wound on his chest. There were bloodstains on his shirt near the collar; when he moved a cloud of flies lifted briefly from the spot. *Does he know about ixchel eyes?* she wondered. *Does he know that I can see him, better than any human could?*

'I have a little water,' she said. 'And meat. And an herb you can rub into your skin, to keep those flies away.'

'You take too great a risk with these visits,' said Hercól.

'Not especially,' said Diadrelu. 'You're a deadly fighter. Your people wouldn't dare approach this cell without lamps and noise.'

'But yours might.'

'Well, then!' she said, trying to sound lighthearted. 'If I'm not wanted—'

'Need I respond to that, my lady?'

She put down her pack, leaped in one bound to his knee, and sat, folding her long legs beneath her.

'Need I stick a pin through your lip to stop you calling me *lady*?'

Hercól laughed softly. 'Thirty years of service to the noble-born have made some habits unbreakable,' he said. 'Very well, just-plain-Dri: how goes the journey? Is there anything to see but the empty horizon?'

'I told you of the sky-ribbon.'

'That was days ago. Has it returned?'

'Yes. Men are calling it the Red Storm, a name out of some old tale of the Ruling Sea. They say Rose glimpsed it decades ago, that he sailed this far, and then turned back to safety to the north.'

'Curious,' said Hercól. 'But that is not what concerns you most, I think.'

She was surprised that her voice had given away so much. Disappointed, too: why worry him with things he could not change?

'The Vortex is in sight again,' she said. 'A little nearer, this time. The first watch saw it pull a thunderhead down from the sky and devour it, lightning and all, and this has put the fear of death in the men. Before today we were fairly flying southward. But now Rose has us beating west, away from that monster.'

Hercól's smile was gone. His eyes slid once around the cell block, professionally.

'You truly think you can break out of here?' she asked.

'It has been arranged,' he said, matter-of-fact, and glanced briefly at the ceiling. 'But the harder question is, whom can I help by escaping? When I break out, I shall have only a short time to accomplish something before I'm put back in again. I could run to the stateroom, and perhaps find refuge there, but I do not wish to do so while Rose is leaving our friends in relative peace. They would merely place ten Turachs on the doorstep, and we should all be prisoners together.'

'You would be safe, at least,' said Diadrelu.

Not a flicker of response showed on Hercól's face. 'What news of our friends?' he asked.

Diadrelu sighed. 'Neeps and Marila have become somewhat more than friends; Pazel and Thasha, somewhat less. They are cold to each other. Pazel simply will not remain in her presence, and Thasha is too proud to ask him why. In any case, they have all been busy recruiting people to our cause – and debating how much to tell them.'

'They are going ahead with the council meeting, then?' asked Hercól.

'It begins just minutes from now,' said Diadrelu. 'That's why I've woken you at such an hour, I – well, it was an impulse, I was passing near—'

'You're *not* going to show yourself to six strangers!'

'Hercól,' said Diadrelu, 'I am an outcast, not an imbecile. My *sophister*s and I will keep watch from the ceiling.'

Hercól nodded, realizing he had overstepped. 'What of your quarrel with the clan?'

'It is not a quarrel,' she said. 'It is death, if they should lay hands on me. And not because my people are hot for my blood. No, if it came to that, I think a good number would rather die defending me than obey Taliktrum's order to kill. I should have to help them do it, and swiftly.'

Hercól leaned nearer, blinking in the darkness. 'Help them? What are you saying?'

'That I would take my own life, rather than watch my clan torn to pieces by a blood feud. That is our way. Surely by now you understand?'

Suddenly Hercól cupped his hands beneath her and lifted, as though she were an injured bird that might start into flight. Diadrelu froze, her breath caught in her throat. It was all she could do to keep her mind from battle patterns, the twenty ways she had learned to slash and bite and twist out of such hands. The swordsman brought her close to his face.

'I do *not* understand,' he said. 'How can you think the clan would be well served by your death? Surely your nephew's rule will tear it apart anyway?'

'Not surely, my friend. Only probably. That is beside the point, however. Of all my people's maxims, the most sacred is *clan before self*. None of us quite live up to that maxim, but all of us aspire to. When we abandon the effort, we die. It has happened countless times in our history, as we learn when the survivors of massacred Houses share their tales. Almost always the death of a clan can be traced back to selfishness. A leader who has lost the people's love tries to stay in power through fear. An ixchel chased by humans runs *towards* the clan house instead of away. Two ixchel duel over a lover, and one dies – or two.'

'Or even three, if the lover is too heartbroken to live on,' said Hercól. 'So at least it happens in our fables.'

'I think you do understand me, Hercól,' she said. 'The sort of questions you people face only in wartime or feuds of passion, we face endlessly, throughout our lives. What deed of mine will protect the clan? What will endanger them? What will keep death at bay until tomorrow?'

Hercól's hands trembled slightly beneath her. 'I have been thinking of that day,' he said. 'The day you asked us to kill Master Mugstur.'

'I had no right to address you thus,' said Diadrelu.

'You had every right. How were you to know that we were not your equals in honesty?'

'Honesty?' Dri frowned. 'Speak plainly, man. I must go soon.'

'Of course I am a killer,' whispered Hercól. 'Did I not say that I was Ott's righthand man? That I worked his will, pursued his mad notion of Arquali "interests," until the day he went too far?'

'The day he ordered you to slay the Empress and her sons,' said Diadrelu. 'You told us.'

'I failed the sons,' said Hercól. 'They were the age of Pazel and Neeps – indeed I look at those two and am reminded of Maisa's children. Like the tarboys, they grew up with danger and loss, and yet somehow their hearts remained open. They would be grown men by now, if I had saved them. Ott keeps their bodies packed in ice, in a cave under Mol Etheg. Shall I tell you why he goes to such trouble?'

'If you wish to,' she said.

'When a spy has completed all his other training, he must pass one final test. He must go with Ott to that cave and look at Maisa's sons, lying there grey and wrinkled with their throats slit. Princes of Arqual, he tells the trainee, but also enemies of Magad the Fifth – and therefore of all the people. Ott asks for the trainee's opinion. If the young man objects, or questions the idea that blind loyalty is what Arqual needs; if he so much as *looks* troubled, then he never joins the Secret Fist. Instead he joins the host of the disappeared, one more sacrifice on the altar of the State.'

'You left that world behind,' said Diadrelu softly, 'and have atoned for it thrice over. As for her sons: you must let those memories go. You cannot save everyone, Hercól. That is another thing we ixchel learn as children.'

The warrior's hands were still trembling. A bit impatient now – did he think his burden so special? – she turned her head, so that she was looking down on the fingers encircling her.

'*Hérid aj!*'

Someone had been at his fingernails. On his left hand, one nail was torn out completely, and the finger hideously swollen. Another nail had

426

had slivers cut from it, as though by the tip of a very sharp knife, and the shards that remained dangled by their roots. On Hercól's right hand the fingertips were blue-black, the nails crushed into the flesh. It might have been done with a hammer, or the heel of a boot.

'No,' she said, breathless with fury. 'Hercól – brother – who did this to you?'

'My old master,' said Hercól, setting her carefully on the floor, 'though I swear he did not enjoy himself. Perhaps Ott still dreams that I will return to the fold, and lead the Secret Fist when he no longer can.' Hercól considered his hands. 'Something held him back, in any case. If he had enjoyed himself I would be far worse off.'

The ixchel woman drew her sword. 'All the same, he has signed his death warrant.'

'Are you mad?' said Hercól, starting upright. 'This is Sandor Ott we are speaking of. A man who has listened for the assassin's tread for fifty years. Put revenge out of your mind.'

'It is not for revenge alone that I shall strike,' she said, 'though revenge is cause enough.'

'Dri,' said Hercól, 'the man is poison. I have heard him give *lectures* on the dangers of ixchel infestations.'

'Infestations!'

Before Hercól could say more she raised her hand. A voice was calling from the passage. It was Ludunte, shouting in ixchel-speech. 'Hurry, mistress! All the giants have assembled!'

'I come,' Dri shouted back. To Hercól, she said, 'The council begins, I must go. But when it is over I will return to you. That I promise.'

'The promise I ask is that you stay away from Sandor Ott,' said Hercól.

'You do not have it,' she said. 'None of this would be happening if it were not for that man's evil inspiration. And he was not aboard when Ramachni cast his spell, so he cannot be the spell-keeper. Let us discuss it no further. I am a warrior, the same as you, and will choose my own kill.'

'No, I say! He is too deadly. Not for nothing has he lead the Secret Fist for so long.'

'Long enough, I think. *Infestations*, he actually—'

'Damn it, woman, I forbid this!'

'*Forbid?*' said Diadrelu. 'Am I your dog, then, to be sent to a corner? One man on this ship has a claim to my obedience – my nephew Taliktrum – and him too I have chosen to disobey. Forbid!

Think carefully, human, before you use that word with me again.'

Hercól dropped forwards onto an elbow, forcing her back a step. 'Hear me,' he pleaded, his voice quite changed. He held up his fingers. 'I will recover from these wounds. Don't leave me with one from which I never shall.'

She had never been so utterly lost for words. The human's breath washed over her. His eyes, rheumy and dilated and as big as her head, were close enough to touch. She could not look at both of them at once.

'Mistress!' called Ludunte again.

Now it was Dri who was trembling. What was wrong with her? She closed her eyes and reached out, burying her hand in the warm bristles of his eyebrow, which leaped at her touch like a horse's flank.

'I will never understand you people,' she said.

The space between the floor of the mercy deck and the ceiling of the hold was just four inches. Dri entered through a 'jug-stopper,' a quick improvised door, cut by Ludunte that very morning. As soon as she was inside Dri knew rats had been here before her. The smell was faint, but not old. *A terrible place to meet with rats. They would have every advantage here.*

She crawled forwards, through dust that lay like a grey snow, deeper than her wrists. She saw her hand in his eyebrow, parting the sleek black hairs. When he spoke she felt the vibration in her arm.

The planks stretched in all directions. In such crawlspaces one could usually spot the humans three compartments off, by the splinters of lamplight that pierced the cracks in floor or ceiling. Tonight not a glimmer met her eyes. But ixchel can see without the light of the sun or lamp: there ahead lay her *sophister*s, looking down through the tiny gap Ensyl had opened with the spyjack.

Dri crawled up between them. 'We must take care with this dust,' she said. 'Humans cannot hear our speech, but coughs and sneezes are another matter. The day may come when we stand with them – stand as brothers, but—'

Ensyl glanced at her in surprise; Dri was not one to lose the thread of her pronouncements. Angry with herself now, Dri wiped the dust from her clothes.

That man is not here. Banish him, face and voice.

'They're just sitting down there,' said Ludunte. 'I don't understand, mistress. For ten minutes they've just been sitting in the dark, blind as puppies, not saying a word.'

'Ten minutes was my suggestion,' said Diadrelu. 'If no one approaches, if no footfall sounds an alarm – then it will be safe to proceed.'

'There is our resistance force,' said Ensyl, shaking her head. 'Rin save us.'

Diadrelu set her eye to the crack. Ensyl was right; the scene did not inspire confidence. Ten humans perched on barrels and boxes, timid in the dark, unable to see each other's faces. Their alliance, their sea-wall against the worst storm of villainy ever to bear down on the world. 'Pazel,' she said aloud, 'if you can hear me, scratch the back of your neck.'

Pazel scratched the back of his neck. Months ago he had learned that his Gift extended his hearing to ixchel frequencies – an ability that had almost cost him his life, for Taliktrum had realised what he was hearing before Pazel himself. It was comforting, if a bit strange, to know that Dri was watching from eight feet overhead. He cleared his throat twice in the darkness. It was another sign they had agreed upon, this one for Thasha and Neeps: it meant *All present and accounted for.*

'Right, let's begin,' said Thasha nervously. 'I think we've been quiet long enough.'

'That's for damned sure,' growled Fiffengurt.

A match blazed; and Thasha's face appeared, dazzled by the sudden light she held. I miss her, Pazel thought, watching a strand of her hair singe as she tried to light the candle. The wick caught, and she raised her eyes suddenly, freezing him with the directness of her look. He felt as he did when he faced Ramachni: transparent, naked, perfectly understood. An intolerable feeling. He dropped his eyes.

'Remember,' he mumbled, 'if anyone asks, we're just here for a drink.'

The laughter was barely audible. Thasha passed the candle to Neeps, and Marila lit her candle from his. Soon half a dozen were burning around the chamber.

The reserve liquor vault was where the better drink was kept, rather than the briny rum used to mix the sailor's daily grog. It was about ten feet square. Floor to ceiling, it was jammed with casks of white Opalt rum and Hubbox sherry, tins of cider vinegar and cooking wine, vats of brandy, and here and there a case of something truly fine, like spruce gin or the cactus-orange liquor of Pól. Despite the bottled luxuries, the vault smelled putrid: they were only a few feet above the bilge well, that cesspool at the bottom of the ship, into which filth from every deck found its way. Because they were so far aft, the water slopped and churned, with a sound like cattle floundering in a pond. At least they would not easily be overheard.

So far, so good: not one person they'd approached had turned them down. Pazel's choice had been Bolutu. They'd met in the veterinarian's cabin on the orlop deck; when Bolutu had grasped what Pazel was talking about he had jumped from his chair and scribbled *As soon as possible!* on a page of his notebook. Neeps had recruited Dastu. When the older tarboy had slipped into the vault, Pazel had felt suddenly hopeful, as though only now believing that they had a chance. The other tarboys looked up to Dastu, for his decency as much as his toughness and good sense. He could bring dozens over to their side.

Marila's choice was more troubling: Dollywilliams Druffle. Neeps had urged her to choose the freebooter, reminding her that no one hated Arunis more than the one he'd magically enslaved. Pazel couldn't argue with that; Druffle grew spitting mad whenever talk turned to the sorcerer. He'd also known about the ixchel for months and not breathed a word. So for all his chatter, he could keep a secret. But did that mean they could trust him? Druffle's moods were erratic, and his way of thinking peculiar. It had never crossed his mind, for instance, to tell Pazel that his mother had had an affair with Chadfallow, until the night the doctor had insulted him. And again this morning his breath stank of rum.

Fiffengurt, for his part, had actually brought two men. His own choice was 'Big Skip' Sunderling, the new carpenter's mate. Big Skip was tall and ox-strong, a woodsman before he took to the sea. His eyes were small but very bright, often with amusement, and his hands when at rest seemed merely to be waiting for the next opportunity to wield a saw or chisel. Pazel had rarely seen him without a good-natured smile. But he was not smiling now.

The second man was Hercól's choice: Lieutenant Khalmet. Everyone in the room stole glances at the Turach soldier. Khalmet looked just as strong and twice as dangerous as Big Skip. He could not have been over thirty, but there was a hardness to his face, as if he had seen or done things that had robbed him of all merriment. Pazel wondered if any Turach escaped such a fate.

Khalmet had given only the slightest of hints that he might oppose what was happening on the Great Ship. The first had been his suggestion that Rose free Hercól, the second his warning to Marila ('someone is listening') nine days ago. Then one day he had begun to deliver Hercól's food – without stealing from the dish, like the man he replaced. Finally, yesterday, Hercól had put all their lives in the soldier's hands by telling him of this council meeting.

Once again the risk had paid off – or at least not backfired yet. For here he was, without his Turach shield and helmet, but still wearing his longsword. Pazel felt safer just looking at the man. Then he recalled that over a hundred other Turachs stood ready to cut them down.

He looked again at Thasha, and a welter of feelings – anger, worry, grief – stole over him. They'd stopped shouting at each other days ago, but they had never made up. They talked coldly of the tasks before them, and nothing else. Pazel had returned to the stateroom, but now he slept in the little reading chamber that hung like a glass shelf from the *Chathrand's* starboard flank. The room was freezing by morning, and he often woke with his face pressed to the cold glass, looking out on the slate-grey emptiness of the Ruling Sea. But Thasha's reproachful looks, and his own fear that she was going to see *Greysan* each time she left, kept him from the common room. Behind the door of the reading room he succumbed to a new temptation, and pressed his ear to her cabin wall. Often he heard her reading aloud from the *Polylex;* once, three nights ago, he caught a sob.

Last night, over a meal of rye mush and figs, Thasha had told them that she would be coming alone. Everyone was shocked, and Pazel had asked immediately if she'd misjudged someone's character. Thasha had popped a fig into her mouth and skewered him with a look.

'Maybe,' she said.

Of all strange things, she had brought a suitcase to the council. A bulky cloth-sided case, embroidered by some spinster aunt; Pazel had seen it belching shirts and sweaters onto her floor. Now it sat before her, tightly sealed, and crowding their toes.

'At last,' said Dastu suddenly. 'At last we're starting to fight back.'

Thasha was looking straight at her candle flame. 'I don't know how to start,' she said, 'so I'll start by saying thank you. For being brave enough to come here. For not doing the easy thing, which would be to turn us in. The day Arunis tried to give the Shaggat the Nilstone, some of us found out that we *had* to fight back. We're kind of stuck – me, Pazel, Neeps and Hercól, and a few others we're still looking for. But the rest of you – well, you could have just chosen to look away, and wait for some chance to escape. Or you could have decided we were crazy, that there was no hope at all. But you're here. And now I know we have a chance.'

She *is* older, Pazel thought. Where was the awkwardness, the rich-girl confusion that irritated him so? Where had that look of knowing come from, and that confidence? Was it Fulbreech or the *Polylex* that had turned her into a woman before his eyes?

Pathkendle is staring at Thasha Isiq, said a male ixchel above him.

Pazel jumped, and dropped his candle underfoot. The other two ixchel began to scold the man. *Pathkendle can hear us, you silly ass*, said Diadrelu.

Pazel scooped up his candle. 'Sorry, Thasha,' he muttered.

'Now look here, mistress,' said Druffle suddenly. 'Just by gathering we've put ourselves in danger, even in this devil's washtub in the dead of night. So I'll be blunt, shall I? This is hopeless, or nearly hopeless. Who are we to think we can take on these bastards? Ten malcontents, against eight hundred enemies. Of which one hundred are blary Imperial commandos.'

'One hundred and nine,' put in Khalmet, 'with the reinforcements from Bramian.'

'Rin's gizzard, it just gets worse!' said Druffle. 'Turachs, Ott's spies, that serpent of a mage. How are we supposed to take 'em all on? We'd have a better chance of stopping an avalanche!'

'If that's your verdict, why'd you come here?' asked Fiffengurt testily.

Druffle looked sidelong at the quartermaster. 'I owe my life to these two,' he said, looking at Pazel and Neeps, "and I'll give it for them, if the time comes. But that doesn't mean I want to hasten the day.'

'Nobody does,' said Thasha. 'But we're getting ahead of ourselves. We're not about to march on the quarterdeck, Mr Druffle. The point of this council, if you want to call it that, is to come up with a next step. One that doesn't get us killed by morning. Of course Mr Druffle's right about the odds. Whatever we do, we'll need more people to do it.'

'Then let's start with some names,' said Dastu. 'Are there others you trust?'

A moment's silence ensued. 'There have to be,' said Thasha at last, 'but choosing them may be the hardest thing we ever do. For the moment, trust me. There are more than you think.'

She's right, said Diadrelu.

'And the next step *is* to find more people, Dastu,' said Pazel. "But when we do, we're going to need to be able to tell them we have some sort of a plan.'

Big Skip shook his head slowly. 'I've been worrying over that one,' he said. 'A plan the crew might stand up and support has to do one thing. It has to keep 'em alive. You want to beat these villains? Scuttle the ship. Wreck her. Drive her onto a lee shore, if we ever see land again. Or sail her right into the Vortex. But most folk don't want to die, see? Where's the plan that gets 'em off this ship alive?'

Fiffengurt leaned forwards. In a whisper, he said, 'We could fill a crate with powder charges, and blast this ship's belly wide open. The ten of us could handle that.'

His hand shook as he drew it across his face. Pazel looked at him, aghast. Had it really come to this?

'No,' Pazel heard himself saying, 'not yet. I don't think Ramachni wants us to kill ourselves. And I think the Nilstone might be a danger to this world even at the bottom of the sea.'

'Then what *is* our plan?' said Neeps. 'What are we going to tell the next ten people we try to recruit for this mutiny?'

No one moved, no one breathed. Neeps had said it, the hangman's word, the word from which there was no turning back. Suddenly Pazel realised the terrible danger they were in. *All it would take is one of them to panic. To get up and try to leave right now. We could stop him, but not quietly enough. If anyone moves, we hang.*

The one who moved was Fiffengurt – but only to hook Neeps around the neck with his elbow, like a fond uncle. The quartermaster turned his good eye this way and that, and he smiled a mad, anxious, damn-em-all-to-the-deep-depths smile.

'Here's a plan for you, blast it. We work our backsides off for Captain Rose. We give two hundred per cent, and we're humble about it. We warm their blary hearts with our good natures, see? And we sail this Grey Lady safe across the Nelluroq.'

'All the while recruiting,' whispered Pazel.

'Bullseye,' said Fiffengurt. 'And when we've brought the *Chathrand* into whatever sheltered harbour awaits us on the far side, what'll we have? A fighting chance to turn the rest of 'em – or at least *enough* of 'em – to rush the boats. We desert, like rats. If necessary we battle our way to shore. And we refuse to come within five miles of the *Chathrand* until they hand over the Shaggat, nailed up tight in a crate where that damnable Stone can't kill anybody.'

'And drive off Arunis at the point of a spear,' said Druffle, 'or drive a spear *through* 'im. Keep talking, Quartermaster.'

'We would have to scatter across the land,' said Khalmet, 'else the Turachs could rout us with a single charge.'

'Oppo, Lieutenant, whatever you say.' Fiffengurt was growing excited.

'They can rage and spout and murder us – I'm sure they'll do a lot of all three – but they can't sail the Great Ship without a crew, now, can they? And it beats dying in gods-forsaken Gurishal.'

'We'd have to win over hundreds of men,' said Thasha doubtfully.

'Three hundred, I figure,' said Fiffengurt. 'With that many we'll have taken a big enough bite out of the crew to make handlin' the mains impossible. The Great Ship won't be going anywhere, until we say so.'

They had all leaned closer as Fiffengurt spoke. Pazel glanced from face to candlelit face, and sighed with relief. No one was backing out. The deadly moment had passed.

'Thasha,' said Marila suddenly, 'if you're going to do it—'

'Yes,' said Thasha, 'it's time.'

With all eyes upon her, she passed Marila her candle, and began to unbuckle the suitcase. *What is this?* the ixchel were muttering, *what's she doing, mistress, what's in the case?* Pazel waited just as anxiously, and just as much at a loss.

The buckles freed, Thasha looked up at the ring of faces. 'Except for Big Skip, you were all aboard when Arunis attacked,' she said. 'And except for Marila, who was still in hiding, you saw what happened.'

'Gods below, lass, we'll never forget it,' said Fiffengurt.

'You saw Ramachni. You know he's our leader, a mage as good as Arunis is evil. And maybe you've figured out that after that fight he . . . couldn't stay.'

'He was hurt,' Neeps interjected. 'Exhausted, like. He had to go back where he came from, to rest.'

'You mean he got off the boat in Simja?' said Druffle.

'No, Mr Druffle,' said Thasha. 'He's from farther away than that.'

She raised the lid of the suitcase, and there, packed carefully between folded sweaters, was the mariner's clock. The instrument was standing upright, the second hand sweeping noiselessly over the exquisite mother-of-pearl moon that was its face. Pazel started from his crate. Neeps and Marila looked at him and laughed, and Thasha's smile said *Serves you right, bastard.* Pazel didn't care. They could laugh at him for the rest of his life.

'Thasha!' he gasped, euphoric.

His self-discipline had vanished. She was looking into his eyes and knew everything – or knew at least what he felt for her, despite all the weeks he'd spent trying to deny it.

Fiffengurt too appeared light-headed with joy. 'Sweet Heaven's Tree! Does this mean—'

'Yes,' said Neeps, 'it does.'

'What they're so happy about,' said Marila, 'is that it's time for Ramachni to come back.'

'You knew!' said Pazel. 'All three of you! How?'

'I'll only know when he jumps into my arms,' said Thasha, but her eyes were shining with confidence. 'I've had this feeling for weeks. A feeling that someone was coming, someone different from any of us, and that everything would change when he got here. It's just like the feeling I got when Ramachni sent me the message in the galley. But this time instead of needing an onion, I need to open that clock.'

'What for?' said Dastu. 'It doesn't look broken to me.'

Thasha grinned at him. 'No,' she said, 'I don't think it is.'

With that she bent down and opened the clock's glass cover. Around and around she spun the minute hand, until the clock read precisely 7:09. 'Now we wait three minutes,' she said.

'What are we waiting for?' asked Big Skip.

'Deliverance,' said Fiffengurt. 'Just watch, and trust the lady!'

They all watched the second hand. As it swept through its third revolution, Thasha bent even nearer to the clock face. And just as the hand reached twelve, she whispered, 'Ramachni!'

There was a sharp pop, and the clock face sprang open on its hinge. Thasha sat back, glowing. But no whirl of black fur emerged from the clock. Nor did Ramachni step out with royal dignity, as Thasha had sometimes described to Pazel, giggling. He did not emerge at all. The only thing that emerged was a breeze – a sudden, cold breeze that extinguished Pazel's candle, and made the others quickly shield their own – and a little of the dark sand that always blew from the magic tunnel between the worlds. Thasha knelt down before the clock, and Pazel, on an impulse, dropped beside her. Thasha tugged the clock face wide.

'Sorcery,' muttered Druffle.

'Hush up, man!' snapped Fiffengurt.

The breeze became a wind, frigid and gusting. It tugged at their ankles, and blew Thasha's golden hair away from her face. 'Ramachni!' she said again, as loud as she dared. 'Ramachni, what's the matter? Where are you?'

She tried to look into the tunnel, but grains of the black sand stung her eyes. Another candle blew out. The wind began to moan from the clock face.

435

This is madness! Diadrelu cried from above. *Pazel, close that thing, before you wake the ship!*

Pazel moved to obey – but Thasha caught his hand tightly in her own.

'Wait,' she said, 'please.'

The newcomers were backing against the walls, trying to get farther from the clock – all save Bolutu, who stared at it as though at some frightful revelation. Even Fiffengurt looked anxious. Thasha's grip tightened; Pazel wondered if he would still be sitting there, holding her hand, when the Turachs kicked in the door.

If this continues your fight is over, said Dri.

Pazel turned to Thasha, but as if she guessed what he would say she shook her head fiercely. *Please*, she mouthed. The wind grew stronger, louder; the door of the vault began to shudder in its frame.

Pazel pressed his lips to Thasha ear. 'I'm sorry,' he said. He reached down and closed the clock.

Perfect silence gripped the room. The wind had vanished; the watchers uncurled their bodies, listening. No pounding feet, no bellows or cries. The immensity of the ship, or the crew's exhaustion after weeks of storm, had saved them. The *Chathrand* slept on.

Thasha put her face in her hands.

Pazel touched her shoulder, but Thasha only stiffened and leaned away. Neeps looked at him and nodded. Telling him he'd done what he had to. It didn't make Pazel feel any better.

Druffle looked at Marila, eyes blazing with accusation. 'Why'd you bring me here?' he asked.

33
The World Grows Larger

—⁓—

9 Umbrin 941
179th day from Etherhorde

If opening the clock had proved an ambiguous wonder, the fact that no one fled the room afterwards was simply a miracle. Big Skip was still staring at the suitcase, into which Pazel had quickly packed away the clock. Druffle was nipping from a flask. Bolutu, for his part, gazed fixedly at a spot in the air, bending his notebook first one way, then the other.

Thasha sat silent, face in her hands. Ramachni had not come; no help of any kind had come, and now the newcomers were terrified. Their rebellion was sinking into chaos before it had even begun. Pazel sat across from her, wishing that he could take her aside, calm her, beg her not to feel ashamed. But there was no chance of that.

Neeps and Marila, to their credit, were trying to steer the meeting back on course.

'What you've got to remember,' Neeps was saying, 'is *never* to touch Arunis of your own free will. Pazel found out the hard way: it gives him the power to look into your mind, somehow. That's why he could kill poor Peytr Bourjon. Once he knows you're not the spell-keeper, you're fair game.'

'We've been wondering what Arunis could have promised him, to make him shake hands,' Marila added.

'Safe passage off the IMS *Chathrand*,' suggested Big Skip, 'that is, if we reach the south. If there *is* a south.'

'That is the other great unknown,' said Khalmet, breaking his wary silence. 'I mean the South itself. Drellarek always spoke of resupplying quickly, making west along the southern shores, taking our bearings at some known location, and then returning north to Gurishal, behind the Mzithrini defences. But he knew nothing of the land or its people. Will we face a wilderness like Bramian, full of beasts and savages? If we fled the ship we might perish in a day, or wither slowly, while Rose and his loyalists sat at anchor, starving us out.

'But we might just as likely find a civilised country, with townships and industries, and force of arms. We must be ready to contact such people. It may be they have ships that could take on the *Chathrand*.'

'Like the *Jistrolloq* did?' said Fiffengurt. 'Don't bet on it, mister. Rose fights above his weight.'

'I'll bet there's nothing but a wasteland,' said Druffle. 'Nothing but toads and spiders, rocks and desolation, and hills all sheathed in ice.'

'Toads *and* ice?' said Marila.

Pazel saw Bolutu shaking his head, as if he had heard nearly all he could stand.

'Just a minute,' said Neeps. 'The *Chathrand* and her sister-ships used to cross the Nelluroq all the time. There has to be civilization in the south. Otherwise, why bother?'

'That was centuries ago, mate,' said Dastu.

'Aye,' said Khalmet, 'and civilizations come and go.'

Bolutu uncurled his notebook – a warped, water-stained ruin after months of abuse – scrawled two words, and held them up:

NOT THESE.

They looked back at him, puzzled. 'Whaddya mean?' said Big Skip.

The veterinarian frowned, looking from face to face. He began to write again.

'*The wa ... waking ... phenomenon*,' Druffle read over his shoulder. 'As in waking animals? What's that got to do with the Queen's Tea?'

Bolutu stopped writing and sighed. Then he dashed off a sentence and held it up.

NOTHING WILL GET DONE AT THIS MEETING.

'Well you're a right blary naysayer,' growled Fiffengurt. 'Why don't you help us get somethin' done, then? Ain't you an educated man?'

Suddenly Bolutu rose to his feet. Everyone tensed: the black man's lips were pressed tight together, and his eyes were almost closed. He raised the notebook, squeezing it as though demanding some last service from its tattered pages.

'He wants something hard to write on,' said Big Skip.

Bolutu closed his hand, crushing the notebook in his fist. 'No, he doesn't.' He tossed the notebook down with a smack. '*Jathod!* He doesn't want to write another word.'

438

There were gasps. Big Skip made the sign of the Tree. 'You can talk!' said Fiffengurt.

'And you can hear,' rasped Bolutu. His voice was dry, and his words distorted, as though he had almost forgotten how to speak. Then he opened his mouth wide, and showed them a pink and perfect tongue.

'Black spellcraft!' hissed Druffle, edging away. 'You're a conjurer! A hoojee hexman from the Griib!'

'That's ugly, Mr Druffle,' said Marila. But in fact they were all in shock. Bolutu had grown a new tongue.

Say something, Pazel! cried Diadrelu. *Khalmet has his hand on his sword!*

'Listen to me!' Pazel blurted. 'Whoever he is, he risked his life to save me from Arunis!'

'That's right, that's right,' babbled Fiffengurt. 'And if you are a hex-man, Bolutu – well, that's just fine with us. So long as you're *our* hex-man, he he.'

'I am neither *hoojee* nor *hexman*, whatever those may be,' said Bolutu quietly. 'Nor am I a Slevran, as I was forced to claim.'

'Told you!' said Neeps. 'I told you he was a Noonfirther! Didn't I?'

Bolutu shook his head. "I am not.'

A hint of panic entered the room. Neeps, trying gamely to contain the situation, forced out a laugh. 'Fine then, I got it wrong. Let's not get excited. We're all human beings.'

'I am not,' said Bolutu.

Everyone leaped up; Khalmet's sword was out in a flash; Druffle bared his cutlass, and even Fiffengurt whipped the blackjack from his pocket. Bolutu wisely raised his hands in surrender. For a moment they heard only their own breath and the slosh of the bilgewater. Then Pazel stepped in front of Bolutu, his heart pounding. *Courage, courage!* said Diadrelu from above.

Trembling, Pazel extended his hand. '*Elaya,*' he said.

'*Elaya chol!*' replied a delighted Bolutu, shaking his hand. 'And where did you learn Nemmocian, Mr Pathkendle?'

'On Bramian,' said Pathkendle. 'From a scrap of paper in Ott's hand. I've never heard it spoken before this minute. And ... it's not your native tongue, is it?'

Bolutu shook his head. 'Indeed, I barely speak Nemmocian, though I read it well. Can you guess why?'

'Not if my life depended on it,' said Pazel.

439

'What in Rin's name is happening, here?' demanded Khalmet. 'Who is this lunatic, who says he is not human?'

Suddenly Thasha gasped. 'It was you!' she said. 'It was *you* I was sensing, not Ramachni at all! But you're with him, aren't you? You're his friend!'

'Friend?' Bolutu smiled at her in turn. '*Admirer* might be a better word. I have the honour to know and revere him, but I have seen Ramachni only once in the past twenty years: at the battle of the Straits of Simja, the day he put out the coal Arunis placed in my mouth.'

He looked at the ring of startled faces. 'Don't fear me, please. I am your ally still, and will hide the truth from you no longer. My name is Belesar Bolutu Malineko Urstorch. I am a dlömu. And I must hasten to inform you that the battle we are engaged in is larger than you have ever suspected.'

No one moved. Khalmet and Druffle kept their weapons raised. Pazel realised suddenly that he and Bolutu were still holding hands. Releasing the man, he stuttered, 'A dluh. A dloh—'

'Dlömu,' said Bolutu gently. 'Just one of the million, and if you let me live a few more days you will see for yourself what we truly look like, for now I know that my disguise-enchantment is at last starting to break. My new tongue proves it. We dlömu can regrow parts of our bodies, over time. Fingers, hands, even whole limbs if we rest properly. This tongue started growing just days after the sorcerer maimed me.' He probed the tongue with his fingers. '*Gagh*. It is whole at last.'

If Bolutu meant to allay their fears, he did not succeed. Intelligent beings other than humans were not unheard of in Alifros: nearly everyone had seen the squid-eyed nunekkam, cooking on the decks of their houseboats, or playing their flutes at nightfall in some field or garden, their hairless children tumbling at their feet. A smaller number had seen ixchel sprinting for their lives along an alley, or flikkermen haggling in the flesh markets, or augrongs or bristle-backed stoors lumbering over the hills. A rare few had met with murths. But Pazel had never heard of *dlömu*, and by their faces he saw that none of the others had either. Marila stared at Bolutu like a frightened animal. Thasha's face glowed with a mix of rapture and fear. Big Skip Sunderling looked as though he had stepped into a madhouse and forgotten where the exit lay. Flinching, he whet his lips and whispered, 'A *million*?'

'Perhaps slightly more,' said Bolutu, 'spread out across the Empire.'

'The man's raving,' said Druffle with a shaky laugh. 'A million – things, running around the Empire, and no one claps eyes on you? What, do you all live buried in caves?'

'I don't think he's talking about the Empire of Arqual,' said Pazel.

'Right again,' said Bolutu. 'Arqual is but a little realm compared to Bali Adro, our vast and glorious kingdom in the South. Almost half of us are dlömu, including our Emperor and his court. Slightly less than a third are human, but their numbers are growing quickly. The remainder are a hotchpotch of other races, mostly unknown in the north. Such wonders in Bali Adro! Had we a month of council meetings I could scarcely attempt their description. And great as it is, Bali Adro comprises but a third of the mighty southern lands.'

Khalmet's look was hard and suspicious. 'You're asking us to believe... that you come from *beyond* the Nelluroq?'

'Exactly, Lieutenant. Now sheathe your sword, I pray you.'

'What do you really look like?' asked Marila.

Bolutu studied his hands, as if they might have changed in the last few minutes. 'Nothing terrible,' he said. 'We are blacker than the blackest humans. Our eyes have two lids, and shine in a way yours never can, like the eyes of night creatures. Our skin is smooth and tight; it would crack before it wrinkled. Such are the *visible* differences.

'As for this body, I am quite aware that I am too short and thick-chested to be a Noonfirther. That was to be the identity I assumed, and the metamorph-spell our wizards wrapped me in seemed perfect at first: when they finished I looked every bit the well-heeled gentleman from Pól. Scores of us agreed to such changes, trading our dlömic bodies for human ones.

'But twenty years ago, as we came north across the Nelluroq, something happened. I still do not understand it. We passed through a kind of soundless storm, a storm not of wind but of light. It blinded us, and when our eyesight returned days later we found that we had changed again. Some of my comrades had reverted completely to their dlömic bodies, and could play no part in our mission. Others still appeared human, but had reverted in one respect or another to themselves. I had regained my old height and weight. No longer able to pass for a Noonfirther, I chose to be a Slevran – the only other possible explanation for my skin colour.'

'But what in Pitfire are you *doing* here?' said Thasha. 'If you went to so much trouble to seem human and journey to the north, why are you on a boat heading south? Are you just trying to get home?'

Startled, Bolutu turned to her. 'You ... want me to tell them?' he said

'What are you talking about?' Thasha demanded. 'I want you to tell *me*.'

Bolutu's eyes darted nervously from face to face. 'Yes,' he said at last. 'I see now that I must.'

'Then be quick about it, for Rin's sake,' said Fiffengurt.

Still uneasy, Bolutu began: 'I came north over the Ruling Sea as a youth. That was two decades ago, as I told you. Oh yes, there are ships as great as *Chathrand* in the south: not many, but enough. Ours was a mission of justice, m'lady — justice and retribution. We were forty hunters: thirty humans, and ten others, mostly dlömu like myself, in magical disguise. We had sworn to each other and our monarch that we would find and slay the criminal Arunis Wytterscorm, also known as the Blood Mage. This sorcerer's meddling in the affairs of kings had left many a nation at war with its neighbours, and the whole of the mighty South was the poorer for his ravages. When I left, twenty years ago, Bali Adro was still healing, and I doubt that she is finished yet. Catastrophe is the mage's calling. And what he did to our realm, he has for the last sixty years been struggling to inflict on your own.'

Bolutu sat down once more on his crate. The others glanced at each other, and warily followed suit. 'Arunis has played this game for centuries: seeking power in one land, reaching too far, destroying what he sought to rule. And later, moving on to some place where his name and crimes are unknown. He has crossed the Nelluroq many times in his long life. He profits greatly by our forgetting.'

'You make him sound worse than all the devils in the Pits rolled together,' said Fiffengurt. 'Is he *that* strong?'

'No,' said Bolutu, 'and that is why he runs. He lacks the strength to conquer any land outright; his ruinous talent has been to set us at each others' throats. But should he find a way to use the Nilstone, he will command a power more terrible than the Worldstorm. Then I fear he will not only bleed the nations of Alifros, but begin to exterminate them.'

Bolutu sighed, and rubbed his face. 'Now to the worst part of my story.'

'It gets worse?' asked Dastu, incredulous.

'More shameful, anyway. Arunis, you see, did not simply choose to assault your northern lands. He was sent. Dispatched, as it were, by a league of criminals in my country, to steal something from yours.'

Aya Rin, hissed Diadrelu. *Now I see.*

'Of course,' said Bolutu, 'I am speaking of the Nilstone. And the league of which I speak – known as the Ravens, for they grow fat on death – has wanted it for nine hundred years. When your—'

He checked himself, as if he had almost spoken amiss. Then, taking a deep breath, he continued: 'When your great wizardess, Erithusmé, set out to rid herself of the Nilstone, she found to her horror that she was less its owner than its slave. First she tried to bury it within the hoard of Eplendrus the Glacier-Worm, but the Stone only drove the creature mad, so that he took his own life, and left the hoard unguarded. She came next to our lands, where our mages met and questioned her.'

'They wouldn't take the Stone,' said Thasha. 'I know that part of the story. They made her carry it away.'

'So they did,' said Bolutu, 'but not before the mighty of Bali Adro had seen the miracles she could work with it: a river turned backwards, a forest made to bloom in winter, a tower reduced to a termite mound. Erithusmé was, after all, the *only* being able to wield the Nilstone since the time of the Fell Princes. She knew that it would one day kill her too, if she did not relinquish it, but meanwhile it gave her powers beyond reason. She had no peer in Alifros. She was the master of the world.'

'But she never wanted to rule it,' said Thasha. 'Unless my *Polylex* has it wrong.'

Bolutu shook his head. 'I said *master,* my lady, not *tyrant.* No, she did not wish to rule the world. And she certainly did not wish to force the Stone on anyone. So she departed again, this time to a secret place, and there she laboured alone. Her goal was to pierce the very fabric of the world, and cast the Stone through the aperture, into the dark realm from whence it came. Never had she attempted anything so difficult; all her might as a wizardess she poured into the task. The effort nearly killed her – and failed, for in the end she could not use the power of the Stone against the Stone itself.

'When she returned to the northern world, she had lost the better part of her strength. The Mzithrin Kings gave her shelter, and Erithusmé was forced to plead with them for a safe place – any safe place – to leave the Stone until such time as she could recover, and try again.'

'Aha,' said Fiffengurt. 'Then it *was* the Sizzies who made the Red Wolf.'

'No, sir; that was Erithusmé's own work. The Mzithrin Kings built the Citadel around it, and more importantly, an armour of legends that wound the Nilstone up with their own fear of devils and corruption, lest anyone should be tempted to use it. They were fine guardians, until the Shaggat came.'

Pazel leaned back against the wall. 'It never stops,' he said, his voice full of weary bitterness. 'First we think we're at the start of a Great Peace. Then we find that Ott's using the treaty to bring the Shaggat back to power and start a war. Then we learn that Arunis is using Ott and his war-scheme to get the Nilstone, and make his precious Shaggat invincible. And *now* you're telling us that men from your country are using Arunis—'

'Using that damnable mage?' said Druffle. 'What for?'

'Have you heard nothing?' said Khalmet. 'To bring them back the Nilstone! They saw how powerful it was, and now they want it back!'

'Exactly,' said Bolutu. 'You have been afraid of war between Arqual and the Mzithrin, and rightly so. But another, unfinished war was simmering across the Nelluroq, and one party to that conflict, the Ravens, looked north and saw an opportunity. These Jackals included mages and men of great wealth. They were united by illusions about their own ancestry – claims that they were descended from the heroes of the ancient world – and by a certainty that they too would one day reign supreme in Alifros. No tactic was too ruthless if it increased their power.

'Fortunately they never grew strong enough to threaten the Bali Adros, our Imperial family. That is why the sorcerers among them began to dream of possessing the Nilstone. They have never forgotten it, and now they think they can master the Stone and use it as a weapon of war. Of course that is madness.'

'It's worse than madness,' said Pazel. 'It's like—'

'Being caught in a whirlpool,' said Thasha, and something in her voice made them shudder.

Bolutu turned to face her, and cleared his throat. 'Do you remember what Ramachni told Arunis, Thasha, after Pazel turned the Shaggat to stone?'

Thasha nodded slowly. 'I don't suppose I'll ever forget it. *"We are never long the masters of the violence we unleash. In the end it always masters us."* But where does it end, Mr Bolutu? Those Jackals, the men who sent Arunis to fetch the Nilstone. Are they just puppets too? Is someone using *them?*'

'I do not think so,' said Bolutu, 'and in any case, it has been nearly a century since they could truly threaten the Empire of Bali Adro. Our Empire is vast and strong – and justly governed, as you shall see. Arunis was its most vile outlaw. When it came out that the Ravens were using him, and indeed had given him a ship and helped him to flee the Crown's justice, our Emperor ordered their immediate arrest. True, some managed to flee the Empire – there is a great deal of room in the South – but most were captured and imprisoned. And we were sent north to deal with the Blood Mage.'

'Pardon me for saying so,' said Fiffengurt, 'but you've made a fishhead stew of *that* job. Arunis went north sixty years ago, you say? But you waited another *forty* to take up the chase? What took you so long?'

'Lies, first of all,' said Bolutu. 'No one knew where Arunis had gone, and the Ravens gave one false confession after another. But in a deeper sense, it's true: the fault is ours. For when at last one of the Ravens told us where Arunis had gone – and what he was sent there to find – no one believed it. We did not wish to believe. We hoped Arunis had simply fled, to harm some distant land perhaps – but not ours, never again. It was a senseless hope, but we clung to it. And so lost precious years.'

Pazel heard Diadrelu heave a sigh. *Denial is death*, he thought.

'It was only when Ramachni himself visited the north, and returned with the news that one of the Mzithrin Kings had gone mad, and seized the Red Wolf, and that a dark wizard stood at his side – only then did we face the truth. By your calendar it would have been the spring of 913. We mounted an expedition to find Arunis as quickly as possible. Too quickly, perhaps, for the ship was never heard from again, and surely perished in the crossing of the Nelluroq. My elder brother was aboard.'

Bolutu dropped his gaze a moment. Then he gave a small laugh. 'He was the ship's veterinarian. It's our family trade.'

'You're not a mage, then?' asked Thasha. 'Or ... trying to be one?'

'Trying?' Once more Bolutu looked at her in confusion. 'My dear lady, no sane person would *try* to become a mage. Would you try to drown yourself, to learn what fishes think and feel? Trying to be a mage! What one gains in power and wisdom is taken away tenfold in other ways! Do you really mean to say you don't know?'

Thasha closed her eyes, remembering. 'Felthrup read me something from the *Polylex*, about a mage from Auxlei City, who talked to his followers before he died. The only questions he refused to answer were about his childhood. He said, "My first life" – that's what he called it –

"is my own. It is the only thing that was ever mine, and it was over before I knew I could lose it.'"

'Many wizards say as much,' said Bolutu. 'if they say a word about themselves. No, I do not long to be a mage. It is hard enough being the *object* of an enchantment. Wouldn't you agree, Mr Pathkendle?'

Pazel looked at him uncomfortably. 'When it's bad, it's pretty bad,' he murmured.

'Bad or good, alteration by magic is *for ever*,' said Bolutu. 'When my disguise-spell breaks, will I look like a proper dlömu again, or will something of this face remain? Will women find me hideously human? Will children scream at me in the streets?'

'Gods below,' said Druffle, 'and you say being a mage is *worse*?'

'Different,' said Bolutu, 'more painful. But if I am called to the mystic order, I will serve. That is the way of things. It is not a matter of choice.'

'And Ramachni?' asked Thasha.

A hint of pride entered Bolutu's voice. 'Lord Ramachni saw the *potential* mage in me. He came to Bali Adro in my youth, and identified a handful of us. Some became mages, others did not. But all of us have tried to prepare ourselves for the possibility – for example, by studying Nemmocian, the language of spellcraft.'

'Listen!' said Fiffengurt suddenly.

The sound came from eighty feet overhead, but they heard it plainly: ten sharp notes from the *Chathrand*'s bell.

Time to go, Pazel, said Diadrelu.

It was time for everyone to go; men inspected the hold every morning as part of the dawn watch. The circle shifted nervously. The council had provided no answers, only frightening questions.

Once again it was Thasha who took the lead. 'All right, listen. One part of the plan hasn't changed, despite—' She gestured helplessly at Bolutu. '—what we've learned. We're still just ten people, against eight hundred. We can't wait any longer to build up our numbers. And at the same time, we can't make *any* mistakes. Remember, you only have to choose *one new person to trust*. So choose well.'

'Twenty people, crammed in here?' said Dastu, worried.

'Sure, mate,' said Neeps. 'It can't be worse than dinner shift.'

'Dinner shift is *loud*,' said Marila.

'It will be the last time we all meet here, that's for sure,' said Pazel, glancing around the vault. 'Right, Mr Fiffengurt?'

'Here or anywhere else,' said Fiffengurt. 'It'd be suicide, even on this monster of a boat, to bring *forty* mutineers together. Somebody would

446

hear us, or chance by. We'd be strung up by our heels in no time.'

'Then our first task when next we meet,' said Khalmet, 'should be to decide a means of communicating *without* coming together. A way to pass messages, and spread the word.'

Hercól is the one to ask about that, said Diadrelu.

Marila gave Thasha's arm a gentle squeeze, a reminder of the hour. 'Right,' said Thasha. 'Mr Fiffengurt, if you'll just remind us?'

'We'll leave in pairs, just as we came,' said Fiffengurt. 'Two minutes between each pair, so that we don't stumble on top of each other in the dark. Khalmet and Big Skip will go first; they're the most likely to be missed up above. Go your separate ways at the top of the scuttle – one forwards past the smoke cellar; the other off to starboard. And for Rin's sake don't use the top step – it groans like a bull with a bellyache.'

Khalmet and Big Skip rose to their feet.

'We meet in eight days,' said Thasha. 'Moon or no moon.'

'And we will stop them,' said Khalmet, with a sharp glance at Bolutu, 'help or no help, allied or alone, no matter the cost in blood.'

The words were a Turach motto; Pazel had heard it chanted by the whole battalion when their new commander was sworn in. Khalmet and Big Skip stepped out the door and were gone. Two minutes passed in silence; then Druffle and Marila followed. Neeps gave Marila's hand a squeeze as she slipped away. 'Be careful,' he said, and Marila whispered, '*Obviously*.'

Fiffengurt blew out his candle. 'We're next, Dastu,' he said. Then, with a nervous edge to his voice, he addressed Bolutu. 'You're not about to, eh, quit pretending to be – you know what I'm saying—'

'Human?'

'Tongueless, man, that's all.'

Bolutu shook his head. 'I had hoped my disguise would last across the Ruling Sea. It still may. In any case I see no reason to give it up before I must.'

'Good,' said Fiffengurt. 'Usually best to keep things simple. Let's be off, then, lad.'

They stepped out of the room. Dastu glanced back at the remaining faces. His usual strong, steady look was nowhere to be found. 'Simple?' he whispered, closing the door.

Now the three friends were alone with Bolutu. Neeps cradled a last stump of candle. Thasha caught Pazel's eye again, plainly begging for contact, for an end to his severity and distance. Miserable, raging inside, Pazel looked away.

Bolutu cleared his throat. 'One thing more. I regret I must say this now, in haste.'

In great haste, said Diadrelu sharply. *Tell him, Pazel. There are sounds of waking from the berth deck.*

Pazel felt a tightening in his stomach. 'Oh Gods,' he said. 'Be quick, Bolutu. Is it *more* bad news?'

Bolutu looked at him, and the pride gleamed again in his eyes, stronger than before. 'On the contrary, I have saved the best news for last. You can forget organizing a mutiny, forget Rose and Ott and their schemes. Arunis alone concerns us now. For I have not failed, Pazel. The good mages of Bali Adro, who sent me north two decades ago – *they are expecting us.* They see through my eyes, listen with my ears. As soon as we make landfall, and I spot a mountain or a castle or other landmark familiar to my masters, they will inform our good Emperor. His highness will dispatch a mighty force to surround and seize the *Chathrand*, and the full might of Bali Adro wizardry will fall on Arunis, and he will be crushed. And this time my masters will not allow the Nilstone, or Arunis himself, to vanish and plague them another day. They will take this burden from you, as they should have done for Erithusmé centuries ago.'

Pazel could scarcely breathe. He turned to Thasha, and she looked back at him, alarmed and uncertain. Neeps was studying Bolutu, his face blank with shock. *Wheels within wheels within wheels*, thought Pazel.

At last Thasha broke the silence. 'Why didn't you tell the whole blary council?' she said.

Bolutu gave her another glance of surprise, as if Thasha should have no need of asking such a question. But he said, 'I am under orders to confide in as few as possible. My masters' only fear is that the wrong persons aboard *Chathrand* might learn that they are watching and waiting. Of course Arunis is the most dangerous in this regard.' Bolutu's voice lowered grimly. 'He has proved it, these last twenty years. We were forty sent to slay him, but in the court of the Shaggat Ness Arunis had grown more powerful than we ever suspected. All those who had hunted him inside the Mzithrin he killed in a single week – all but one, who fled with a broken mind, and sought to warn Arqual of the Nilstone.' Bolutu looked gravely at Thasha. 'He died at your feet, m'lady.'

Thasha gasped. 'Him! That tramp who shouted at me in the garden? The one who knew about the Red Wolf?'

Bolutu nodded. 'Machal, he was called: and Ott's arrow saved Arunis the trouble of killing him. Machal was one of the last. Arunis had sought us from the Crownless lands to East Arqual. One by one he sniffed us out: he had found a way to detect the spells our masters worked through us, you see. By the time we grasped this, just two of us from Bali Adro were left alive: myself and one human being. Only his ignorance protects us. He does not know who we are, or that any of our number survive.'

'But he read your mind,' said Pazel. 'That day in the Straits of Simja – didn't he?'

'That day,' said Bolutu with a shudder, 'Ramachni shielded me, to his own great pain. The sorcerer glimpsed only what was foremost in my thoughts. Be in no doubt: if he *had* learned all I know – learned of my masters, awaiting him – he would have fled this ship before we entered the Nelluroq. And if he learns of them now, he will risk anything, kill anyone, to stop us reaching the South. That is why my masters cannot act through me, and why I cannot even speak to them, or see their faces. They look through my eyes, but hide from his. They approach me only in dreams.'

'What does Arunis expect to happen, when we reach the South?' Pazel asked. 'Does he know that the ones who sent him – the Ravens, you called 'em? – have been put in jail?'

'I don't know,' said Bolutu. 'But whether he is aware of their downfall or not, he has long since abandoned the Ravens. He has his puppet-king, through whom he hopes to wield the Nilstone. More importantly, he has ambitions all his own. The Jackals dreamed only of dominion; Arunis dreams of something darker still. And from the South he wants only what Rose and Ott desire: provisions, a course heading for Gurishal, a swift and stealthy departure.' Bolutu gave them an unsettling smile. 'They will all get more than they bargained for.'

'What happens when your masters take the Nilstone?' asked Pazel quietly.

'It will not be for me to decide,' said Bolutu, 'but I imagine that the conspirators will all be jailed, and that you will be guests of Bali Adro for as long as you like, unless you wish to take the *Chathrand* home again, under another commander.'

'But this is incredible,' said Neeps. 'Pazel, Thasha, do you hear the man? We're saved.'

Not if you don't get out of that chamber, hissed Diadrelu.

'We have but one task,' said Bolutu. 'To be sure Arunis finds no new, unforeseen way to use the Nilstone in the weeks ahead. Once we reach the south, my masters will take care of the rest. Trust me, friends: this journey began with treachery and loss, but it will end with redemption for us all.'

Neeps was staring at Bolutu as though suddenly fascinated. Pazel turned to Thasha, forgetting the need to scorn her, wanting her help. 'I don't know what to say, Mr Bolutu,' he said. 'You've changed everything, and it's wonderful, unbelievable. But—'

'I'm not sure this is how it's *supposed* to happen,' said Thasha.

'I'm sure,' said Neeps suddenly. He took a mystified Bolutu by the shoulder and made him bend, then pointed to the back of his neck. There, faint but unmistakable against the black skin, was a scar in the shape of a wolf.

34

Alliances Redrawn

—∿∿—

Pitch darkness. The candle had burned out; there was no time to light another. Neeps and Thasha had departed; in a moment Pazel and Bolutu were to follow.

Hopes and fears spun madly together in Pazel's head; it was like warming one's hands over a fire while being pelted by sleet. Bolutu carried the wolf scar. They had found their seventh and final ally; and his masters, so he claimed, were stronger than all their foes put together. Certainly they were doing as the Red Wolf had intended: bringing the Nilstone back to those Erithusmé had thought could guard it best. Surely it was all going as planned.

So why did Pazel feel such dread? Was it all too good to be true? Or were the sleepless nights, the bad food, the reek of bilge and the foul, close air just catching up with him? He tried to force himself to concentrate; it might be days before he could speak to Bolutu again.

'If you'd decided to tell us – the three of us, I mean – why did you wait so blary long? We could have started working together months ago.'

'I did as my masters advised,' said Bolutu's voice in the darkness. 'There was no way to tell you just a little, and I feared to tell you a lot. Nor did I have any idea that the scar on the back of my neck was anything special. Dlömu have excellent vision, but we're no better than humans at seeing out of the backs of our heads. You say that *Rose*, of all people, bears this mark?'

'On his forearm, yes,' said Pazel impatiently. 'Do you mean to say you weren't sure you could trust us?'

'I doubted you'd be alive long enough to trust,' said Bolutu. 'More to the point, I didn't know how well you or Thasha or Neeps could hide what you knew from Arunis. What if I had told you all this before that day on the bowsprit, when he saw into your mind?'

Pazel shuddered at the memory, knowing Bolutu had a point. He pressed on; there was so little time.

'I don't know what you've heard about Bramian,' he said.

'I heard that they asked you about a place called Stath Bálfyr,' said Bolutu.

At once the ixchel began to exclaim. *Stath Bálfyr! Who asked the boy about Stath Bálfyr? Dri, they're discussing Sanctuary! Does Taliktrum know this? He'll go mad! What if he finds out that—*

Quiet! shouted Dri.

'I also,' said Pazel, struggling for composure, 'talked to a horrible thing called an eguar. It told me something very strange: "I do not think that you should die before you see the wondrous South, the world my brethren made." Those were its exact words. Do you have any idea what they could mean?'

Bolutu said nothing at first. Pazel supposed he was thinking over the creature's words, but when his voice came again it was clear that he was in shock. 'You spoke ... to a *what*?'

'An eguar. Do you know what that is?'

'Keep your distance. You should have burned your clothes. An eguar. Gods of night, you'll have contaminated the ship!'

'We did burn our clothes,' Pazel interrupted. 'On Bramian, Dr Chadfallow insisted. And he made us scrub in a river – wash our hair, clean under our nails. We nearly froze to death.'

Bolutu gave a great sigh. 'That's all right, then. Yes, I know what an eguar is, though I have never seen one. They are ancient creatures, ancestors of dragons. The poisons in their breath and secretions are a thousand times more lethal than that of the deadliest snake, and the magic in their blood is akin to that raging fire in which the world was made. When the *maukslar*, the demon lords, reigned in Alifros, they kept eguar as palace watchdogs. Most have died out. Where they die a crater opens, as if the land itself were decaying with the corpse. Living eguar are terribly rare today. I did not know that any were to be found north of the Nelluroq.'

'And "the world my brethren made"?'

Another pause. 'I don't know,' said Bolutu at last. 'Perhaps it merely wished to frighten you.'

'Well it succeeded,' said Pazel. 'All right, it's time to go.'

'And still there is more I would say,' said Bolutu with regret. 'But I suppose it must wait.'

'You suppose right,' said Pazel firmly. 'No more talking. Follow me.'

They opened the door and stepped out of the vault, into a narrow passage formed by stacked crates. It was just as dark and stuffy here as in the vault itself, for this entire corner of the hold was cut off from the rest by a fluke arrangement of cargo and retaining walls. The crew called the area the Abandoned House, and it hadn't taken long to see why. Pazel crept along the rattling planks over the bilge well, feeling water slop against his toes, bracing himself with his hands. After a dozen steps his right hand found the ten-inch gap he was looking for, and he made Bolutu stop. Turning sideways, they slid into this crack and shuffled another ten yards. There was a second turn, and the passage widened, and then they were at the scuttle, that narrow emergency stair that was the only way in or out of the House.

Goodbye, Pazel! Diadrelu's voice came softly, from twenty or thirty feet to his left. *I will visit you this evening, if I can. Right now I must go to Hercól, who needs me. You've done well, my dear boy. You've kept your head, and followed your heart.*

He had never heard such open affection in her voice, and wondered at it, and wished he could say something in reply. He waved a hand in the darkness, hoping she had not turned away.

Up the steep stair they climbed, carefully skipping the top step, and emerging at last onto the mercy deck. The blackness was still almost perfect, but Pazel could hear distant thumps and mutterings from the decks above. *We've stayed too blary long.* He gave Bolutu a firm nudge to starboard. *That way.* A hand touched Pazel's shoulder, and then he was gone.

Pazel walked in the opposite direction, as quickly as he dared. Like every deck, the mercy had a large central compartment, surrounded by cabins, passages and storage areas. But on the lower decks, where no cannon could be placed, these central compartments were smaller, and the surrounding chambers more extensive. Pazel's escape route wound through a maze of crates and pass-throughs and dividing walls. There would not be a single soul on duty at this hour; the trouble, if it came, would be from men who were *not* on duty but there for other reasons, such as buying or selling deathsmoke. Some said that addicts would kill anyone who stumbled across them, lest their names be reported to the captain.

So easy to get lost. His fingers read the walls: old tar, bent nails, cool brass of a speaking-tube. Time and again he had to stop and feel the pitch of the ship. Several times he heard gasping exhalations in the dark: addicts tended to hold the smoke in their lungs as long as possible, wanting every last iota of pleasure from the drug that was killing them.

Then at last he caught the faint mix of smells he had been sniffing for: woodsmoke, ham, salted fish. His fingers touched a door: the smells were stronger when he pressed his nose to the crack. Pazel sighed with relief: it was the smoke cellar, where meat was cured and kept for lean times far from land. That meant the ladderway was just ahead. He could scurry up them to the orlop, slip across to the Silver Stair, and race straight to the upper decks. No one would see him, and if they did he could just say he was making for the heads, which come to think of it, wasn't a bad idea—

'Stop right there,' someone whispered.

Pazel froze. He gave a silent but very passionate curse. The voice was Jervik's.

The big tarboy stood right in front of him. Pazel could hear his breath, though he could still see only a slight perturbation in the darkness where he stood, arms spread wide across the passage.

'Don't you blary move,' said Jervik. 'I'll make a scene, I will. I know where you've been, and what you've all been doing. Your mates have been bumping around here for twenty minutes. I watched 'em all go by.'

We're dead, Pazel thought. But his new training did not fail him: before Jervik could move Pazel had sprung back two steps, and his hand, almost of its own accord, had drawn his father's knife. The knife Jervik had stolen once, and threatened to use on Pazel himself.

'What are you waiting for Jervik?' said Pazel acidly. 'Run off and tell Arunis. Get yourself another gold bead. Maybe two, if Rose actually executes one of us.'

He crouched, waiting for the attack. To his great surprise Jervik neither moved nor spoke. It occurred to Pazel that the big tarboy must actually have heard very little: they would all have known better than to talk, while still so deep in the ship. Jervik was sneaking and spying, that much was obvious. But he'd hardly be standing here, confronting Pazel in pitch blackness, if he knew what had happened in the liquor vault.

With the thought, a great rage boiled up in Pazel's chest. Always Jervik. Every time things started to go right.

'You're fishing for clues, aren't you?' Pazel said, barely able to keep his voice down. 'You didn't hear us at all, and now you're hoping I'll cough up something Arunis will pay you for. No matter what he can do with that something. No matter what he's trying to do to us all. The world can burn on a stake, can't it, Jervik? You'll still have your gold.'

'Muketch—'

'My name is *Pazel*, you useless sack of slag. Pitfire, I'm sick of you. Go on, get out of here. You want to *make a scene*, is that it? Right here?'

'Put your muckin' knife away. I want to switch.'

'I'll put it away in your god's-damned – *what?*'

'Switch,' whispered Jervik, his voice barely audible. 'I want to switch sides, is what. Rin slay me if I'm lyin' to you.'

Pazel had to steady himself against the wall. 'Jervik,' he said, 'are you ill?'

Jervik was silent, and when he found his voice again it was as tight as a backstay.

'Arunis was goin' to let me hang. He told me to watch you there on the bowsprit, but he never said you was stiff as a corpse. He wanted me to take the blame when you fell into the sea. He's unnatural bad.'

'You're just figuring this out?'

Jervik leaned closer; Pazel felt his hot sapwort breath on his face. 'He tries to get inside my head,' he whispered. 'To reach inside and take the wheel, you understand?'

'Maybe, yeah,' said Pazel, retreating a step.

'I won't let the son of a whore. He can't make me. But it hurts, Pathkendle. He *pick-picks, pick-picks*. Day and night. Sleepin', wakin', eatin'. I don't let *no one* use me that way. He's a beast from the Pits and I wish him death.'

Jervik was halfway to tears. Pazel wished he could see the older tarboy's face, although he feared what he would see there was madness. But mad or not, Jervik had never come closer to sounding sincere.

'I've been a pig,' said the older boy, wringing the words out of himself. 'A stump-stupid pig. I been tearing you down for years. Woulda knifed you back on the *Eniel*, with your daddy's own knife. No Arquali on that boat had such a fine knife, my own was rusty trash. You didn't even know how to use that knife. You shouldn't have owned it, nor been such a cleverskins. Arqualis own things, Ormalis get owned. You shoulda been a slave, not educated, not booklearned and special. I was boss of that ship until Chadfallow put you aboard.'

'I know that,' said Pazel.

'Couldn't get you to blary *respect* it,' said Jervik with a sour laugh.

'You fought like a wee girly, but you always fought. I hated you. Rin's liver, I hated you so. It got to where I thought I'd kill you, in some dark place like this, the way a coward would do it, and – you're better, Pathkendle, better than me.'

'Jervik,' said Pazel, 'I'm not special. Things just keep happening to me. Ever since I was small. It's not me, mate. It's just – what happens.'

Jervik pulled himself up straight. 'I don't know what the blary hell you're talking about.'

'Well, look,' said Pazel, 'I – Pitfire, Jervik, what do you want to do now?'

'Told you already,' said Jervik. 'Switch sides.'

'Right,' said Pazel, thinking in a desperate rush, glad the dark was hiding his panic. There was no question whatsoever of trusting Jervik with their secrets. But he had to say something, and fast.

'Right, Jervik, here's the thing. We have this – circle, that's true. But there's so few of us, and if they catch us talking, they'll just stab us dead, or lock us in the brig and torture us until we snap.'

'That's plain as piss,' said Jervik.

'Exactly,' Pazel agreed, 'so you can bet nobody wants to get caught. That's why we made this little rule, Jervik. We have to all come together and talk it through, you see, before we bring anybody else into the circle. One mistake and we're dead, after all. You understand?'

'Yeah,' said Jervik, his voice abruptly subdued, 'I'm hearing you, loud and clear.'

He'd blown it. He'd said the wrong words, talked down to him a little too much. Jervik had risked everything to trust his old enemy. He'd never be able to stomach the humiliation of not being trusted in turn. Pazel braced himself. Jervik always fell silent like this, before he went off like a bomb.

Then Pazel started. Jervik was poking him in the chest. 'Tell me when,' he demanded.

'W-when?' Pazel echoed.

'When I can help. What needs doing, who you want out of your way. That's all I need to know, see? Just what you want done – you or Undrabust, or the Isiq girl. Now tell me if *you* understand.'

Pazel was utterly stunned. 'Yes,' he said after a moment, 'yes, I do.'

'All right then.' The shadow that was Jervik straightened and turned away. Pazel listened to his footfalls. Then, on an impulse, he hissed: 'Jervik! Wait!' and rushed up to him again.

'Well?' said Jervik.

'Listen, please,' said Pazel. 'If we're going to stand a chance, there's something I have to ask you. It's important, so don't take it the wrong way. Arunis chose to come after you – why you, and not somebody else? Do you have any idea?'

Jervik nodded at once. 'That's an easy one. But I won't tell you, 'cept you swear on your mum's heart not to repeat it to nobody.'

'I swear it, Jervik. I swear on her heart.'

Jervik paused, then made a sort of grunt of acceptance. 'It's like this. Arunis thought I weren't afraid.'

'Of him?'

'Of nothin'. And it's true, I ain't afraid of that much. Spells and sorcerers, aye – those spook me, and the Vortex would scare any man who ain't plum crazy. But that's just it. He hoped I was crazy-brave, inhuman like. Maybe—' Jervik hesitated, his voice suddenly strained. '—because of how I act. Fightin', talkin' proud. But soon enough he found out I weren't crazy, and he stopped payin' me so much attention. I been wondering why that is. Do you know?'

'No, I don't,' said Pazel, 'But . . . maybe he can only have his way with crazy folks. Maybe he can't get inside your head unless it's already a little cracked.'

Jervik said nothing. Suddenly he gave a violent shudder, as if shaking off some cold and clammy touch. Then he laughed under his breath. 'You're smart, Muketch. Smart enough to beat these bastards. I knew it when I followed Dastu down here, and when I waited in the dark. I knew this one blary time I was choosin' right.'

Hercól lay on his side, his left hand tucked carefully beneath his cheek. The first pale glimmers of day were seeping down the light-shafts, distilling absolute black to nimbus gray, carving shapes out of a void.

On the muscle of his upper arm lay Diadrelu. She had fallen asleep there, just minutes ago. He was wide awake, and frightened. He could not catch his breath.

When she woke, her hand clutched for a sword that was no longer there. Remembering, she turned over and embraced his arm with her body. Trembling with wonder. How the world had changed.

'This is what was happening,' she said, still holding him. 'Why I fought with you, why I kept seeking you out. I didn't know it was possible. I didn't know it could happen to me.'

'Possible?' he said.

'You're afraid. Don't be, love. This is a victory. This is why we're here.'

Hercól was silent.

'You're warm,' she said.

He kissed her shoulders, timidly, certain he was appalling her, that his lips and beard were grotesque in their hugeness. Dri shivered, and her arms tightened around him, and for a time he was less timid. Then his eyes felt again the pinprick of light.

'Dawn is here,' he said.

She moved in a flash, sliding from his arm to the floor, gathering her things in a swift whirlwind. In a few seconds she was herself again, the sword and knife buckled in place, the pack strapped tight across the spot his lips had brushed. He struggled into a sitting position, keeping his wounded hands out of the dirt. She ran up his chest like a short slope and threw her arms about his neck.

'I will keep nothing from you, nothing.'

'Nor I you,' he said, breathless. 'But you must go, my dearest, my heart.'

'We came aboard to steal the ship, Hercól. To wreck it on Stath Bálfyr, our Sanctuary-Beyond-the-Sea.'

'Yes,' he said, 'I had begun to think so.'

'That chart in Ott's hand, that Pazel was made to read? We forged it. Do you see the sin of it now? You may have been pawns in Ott's game, once. But he remains a pawn in ours. We've depended on his machinations and his madness. We needed him to succeed.'

'Hush, lady – hush, and go now. There will be other nights.'

'No end to them,' she said, and breathed into his ear. Hercól closed his eyes, and for a moment the sound she made was enormous, larger than the envelope of wind about the *Chathrand*, stronger than the gales they had survived.

Then she fled. Hercól caught a glimpse of her, a running shadow as she passed through the bars.

'Dri!' he whispered.

The shadow stopped, and turned. Dri stepped back inside the cell and looked at him.

'I killed them,' he said. 'The princes, Judahn and Saromir, Maisa's boys. I didn't refuse Ott's command, I obeyed it. I murdered those children, for Arqual. It was me.'

'I know,' she said quietly. 'I have known for some time now. It is plain as a scar upon your face.'

458

'My great change of heart, of which I boast to other children, like Thasha who reveres me: it came only *after* those two boys lay dead at my feet. I tried to tell the Empress, before she put Ildraquin in my hand. I could not do it. I have never told anyone but you.'

Dri came forwards and touched his ankle. 'Thasha is not a child,' she said. 'And she does not revere you, Hercól. She loves you. It is a love well earned.'

Hercól looked away, as if regretting his confession.

'Hear me,' she said. 'There is a path out of the Ninth Pit, the Pit of self-torture, the bottommost. But you have only begun to seek it. This truth needs telling to other ears than mine. Will you stand before their mother, one day, and tell her all?'

At first Hercól made no answer. Then, stiffly, he replied, 'I will tell the Empress, if the chance should come.'

'Pray it does. For I fear the lie will gnaw at your good heart – gnaw like a parasite, until you tear it away.'

'Go now,' he said, 'while the darkness protects you. Let us speak of this no more.'

Still her hand remained on his ankle. 'It is you who sit in darkness. I would take it from you, if I—'

'Go!' he said, more sharply than he intended.

And with a last flash of her copper eyes, she went. Hercól sat alone with his knees drawn to his chest. The air was motionless and heavy, as though he were entombed in wax. The light grew slowly. Magritte, the whaling captain, gave a low moan in his sleep.

The ship's bell rang in the morning, his thirty-seventh in the brig. It was time for his exercises, but for once he did not move. He had finally spoken of it. Dri would not love him long.

A man's laugh floated down from the orlop. Someone hacked and spat. In the corridor, a rat crawled out of the gloom. Hercól watched its approach, indifferent. The rat's step was oddly slow.

'You're sick, aren't you?' he mumbled.

'Unquestionably,' said the rat.

Hercól jumped to his feet. 'It's you! Felthrup! Felthrup! You're alive!'

Overjoyed, he rushed to the front of his cell. But Felthrup did not even turn his head. His step was very deliberate, and clearly caused him a great deal of pain. His stump tail dragged listlessly behind him. His fur was matted with blood.

'Come in!' said Hercól. 'Come in here, I have water, I have bandages! Gods below, little brother, who hurt you? Master Mugstur, was it?'

Felthrup made no reply. He walked past the front of Hercól's cell. When he reached the next, he turned very slowly and peered inside.

'Nobody?'

'Nobody what, Felthrup? No one is in that cell, if that's what you mean. Only Magritte and I are imprisoned here. Felthrup – do you know who I am?'

Felthrup slipped through the bars of the empty cell. 'The water,' he said, 'if you can truly spare a mouthful, sir.'

Hercól fetched his water bottle and food bowl. He filled the bowl and carried it to where the two cells met, then put it down and slid it through the bars.

Instantly Felthrup blazed up, snarling. Hercól's hand jerked back.

'Never!' Felthrup hissed, lunging forwards, then turning and dashing in a circle about the cell. 'Never, never, *never* put your fingers through the bars! Don't come near, and let no one unlock that door! No matter what I say! Do you hear me? *Do you hear?*'

'I hear you, friend.'

Felthrup's strength deserted him as suddenly as it had come. He slumped immobile in the middle of the floor, and Hercól had the terrible feeling that he might have died. But a few minutes later Felthrup rose and hobbled with the same weird, mechanical stiffness to the water bowl, drank a few sips, and moved slowly to the back of the cell. He stood there, blinking out at the passage, for a very long time.

'It's starting, Hercól,' he said.

35

Unwelcome Discoveries

———⁓———

27 Norn 941
166th day from Etherhorde

Of course they could not all march into the stateroom at dawn, while the guard at the door was taking notes. By prior arrangement, Marila and Thasha went to the galley and drank tea with the groggy sailors, just off the night watch. Pazel and Neeps were to spend half an hour on the top deck, where one could linger at any hour without raising undue suspicion. They staggered up the Holy Stair, into a morning of unexpected cold. The deck was slick; a brief rain in the night had coated everything with chilly droplets, which the cold wind stripped from the rigging and flung in their faces.

The boys walked to the forecastle, where they sat down beside a sleepy Mr Fegin, who had the dawn watch. No one spoke: man and boys simply gazed at the cyclonic motions of the clouds over the Vortex, in the east; and the Red Storm, burning across the southern sky, and fading slowly with the dawn. Both the storm and the whirlpool were distinctly closer.

'Somethin' irregular goin' on,' muttered Fegin at last, in what struck Pazel as a triumph of understatement.

When the half-hour was up, the boys made their way down to their old place on the berth deck, under the copper nails. Dastu had slung their hammocks already, and Pazel fell at once into oblivion, despite the daylight and the milling hundreds of sailors and boys. He dreamed that a multitude of blacker-than-black dlömu, with shark's skin and double-lidded eyes, were surrounding his old house in Ormael, raising black spears and chanting a single word, like a war cry; but the word was *Sleep!*

Three hours later Mr Fiffengurt turned them out of their hammocks again, with many a groan and recrimination, for he had obtained Rose's leave for a short visit to Hercól. 'The girls are waiting outside,' he said. 'Come on, before these apes get too excited by their proximity.'

The girls were puffy-eyed and bedraggled. The five of them stumbled towards the ladderway together, barely speaking, and began the descent into the depths they had left a few hours before. At the mercy deck someone was waiting with a lamp.

'Step lively, there,' said Ignus Chadfallow.

What an unpleasant surprise, thought Pazel numbly, but he knew the doctor's presence was for the best. Chadfallow and Hercól had always been close, and there was no telling in what condition they'd find the swordsman.

His condition, of course, was that of a man with mangled fingernails. Five Turachs in helmets and mail were on hand as well, to supervise the doctor's access to his dangerous patient. Sergeant Haddismal, the new commander of the regiment, was among them. He was every bit as large as Drellarek, and had a belligerent, bug-eyed expression that Pazel found quite unsettling.

'You didn't mention the brats,' he accused Fiffengurt.

Chadfallow caught sight of Hercól's hands, and shoved past the commandos with a florid curse. 'Put your hands through the bars, Hercól, let me at those bandages. This is Ott's doing; I've seen his work before. Criminal! By the verdant Tree, one day I'll have his head!'

Captain Magritte was standing at the front of his cell. 'Doctor, you must attend me next! Give me something for delirium! I've seen the ghost of some old skipper, dressed like a pirate's woman. And fleas the size of kidney beans!'

'That last is no illusion,' said Hercól. 'The fleas *are* that big. And they bite like the very devil.'

Pazel thought Hercól might be close to delirium himself. Too many emotions played over his face: guilt and ecstasy, pleasure and regret. 'Hello, Thasha, boys!' he called out, beckoning with his bandages. 'Pathkendle, come here. I must tell you something.'

Pazel slipped around the watchful Turachs. 'What is it, Hercól?' he said.

The Tholjassan switched to his native tongue. 'Don't shout, lad, and don't turn your head to look when I speak. The first thing I need you to know is that I can escape at any time, and come to your aid.'

Dr Chadfallow glanced up quickly. 'Do nothing foolish, man, I pray you,' he said in the same language.

'How could you get out?' said Pazel.

'Never mind that now,' said Hercól. 'Just remember: if you're in danger, a shout down the secondary cargo hatch will bring me quickly. The other thing I must tell you is that the cell to my right is not quite empty. Our missing rat friend is crouched there at the back.'

Pazel seized the bars. 'No! Felth—'

'That's enough!' Haddismal broke in. 'Speak Arquali, if you're going to speak at all!'

Hercól continued in Tholjassan. 'He is not well at all. I'm afraid he may be rabid, or worse.'

Pazel discretely shifted his gaze. 'I see him. *Aya Rin*, he looks dead!'

'One more word in that tongue—' growled Haddismal.

Hercól switched back to Arquali. 'He is alive, I promise you.'

'Who's alive?' demanded the Turach.

'And he told me something worrisome. He said, "It's starting, Hercól." Those words, and no more.'

Thasha (who did not speak Tholjassan either) squeezed in on Chadfallow's right. 'What friend?' she said. 'And what is it that's starting?'

Hercól freed a hand from the doctor's ministrations, and gently touched her cheek. Pazel was astounded by the gesture, and the affection so suddenly visible on the warrior's face. Clearly Thasha was startled as well; she gazed at her old tutor as if afraid to speak.

'Something dreadful, I fear,' said Hercól. 'Ignus, stay close to them – and Pazel, you *must* let him help you. No matter what has passed between us before, we must stand together or die.'

'Die?' barked Haddismal, pushing Thasha aside. 'What is all this, traitor? What are you telling them?'

Hercól stood straight, looking into the Turach's bulging eyes. 'Just this,' he said quietly. 'That the ship is in danger, imminent and terrible. I do not know from what quarter it comes, but if you do not find out soon, Haddismal, I fear you will be too late.'

Bolutu was not in his cabin, nor on the topdeck, nor eating breakfast. The four youths had scattered about the ship, looking for him everywhere, but it seemed no one had lain eyes on the man since early the previous evening, well before their council meeting. They tried sickbay, the wardroom, the lounge. There was not a trace of him to be found.

But traces of Mr Fegin's 'something irregular' were plentiful. When

Marila poked her head into the first-class lounge (the luxuries of which were much reduced since Simja, along with the girths of those accustomed to them), she found Thyne and Uskins squatting in the corner, nibbling stale jelly biscuits as they examined a jagged hole in a corner of the wall. In the galley, Thasha stood where the little green door with the peeling paint had been, and saw only a wall where spoons and soup ladles dangled from hooks. Outside the forecastle, Mr Fiffengurt heard the blacksmith complaining that his assistant, Big Skip, had gone missing as well.

Neeps' discovery was the ugliest. He had gone to the live-animals compartment in search of Bolutu, and stumbled upon carnage. Something had broken into the cage where Latlzo housed his prize sapphire doves; there was nothing left but blue feathers and a great deal of blood. A number of the other animals had been terrorised as well. The pair of gold foxes from Ibithraéd were cowering at the back of their cage. The Red River hog was berserk, snorting and spinning in its wooden crate, which it had kicked half to pieces.

At noon Thasha and Pazel went to Chadfallow and begged him to do what he could for Felthrup. The doctor turned gravely from his desk, regarding them over his reading-glasses.

'I hold myself bound to aid a woken animal as I would a man,' he said. 'But you must never forget that a woken animal is *not* a man. Felthrup is a tiny creature with a volatile heart. I may only be able to end his suffering.'

'He's a tiny creature with an enormous heart,' said Pazel, 'and how can you say that, anyway, when you don't know what's wrong with him?'

'I say it *because* I don't know,' said Chadfallow.

The single Turach left outside the brig would not let the youths enter a second time, and only admitted Chadfallow under his supervision. Pazel and Thasha stood outside the door, listening, but all they could hear was Magritte's wails about his visions, and his fleas.

Sighing, Thasha leaned back against the wall. Only then did Pazel notice the redness of her eyes. He could not tell if it was the result of exhaustion or tears.

On an impulse, he said, 'You were brilliant at the council.'

She looked at him warily, as if he might be mocking her. 'I made a hash of it,' she said. 'I almost got us killed.'

'Not your fault.'

Thasha flushed. 'I was so certain he would come when I called him. Ramachni, I mean. But I was dead wrong.'

In the brig, the guard was bickering with Chadfallow. *You want to what?*

'Thasha, you and Ramachni have some sort of . . . bond,' said Pazel. 'And Bolutu says he's a follower of Ramachni. You sensed him instead of his master. Anybody could have made that mistake.'

Her eyes were unmoved; she didn't believe he meant it. 'You know I don't blame you,' she said.

'For what?'

'Giving me the cold shoulder. I'd do the same thing if I were you.'

'Would you?' The idea made him feel a little better.

'I drank before the wedding ceremony,' she said. 'I got myself trapped in the stateroom while you were being dragged off to Bramian. I'm afraid to read the *Polylex*, afraid of learning too much. And then last night, the clock . . . no, I don't blame you one bit.'

'What are you afraid of learning?'

'That I'm not . . . who I'm supposed to be. Who Ramachni was counting on me to be, from the start.' Her voice quickened nervously. 'That no matter what anyone says to make me feel better, I'm going to be the reason we fail, the reason Arunis gets the stone and learns to use it and destroys everything, and it will happen because I'm broken inside. Which is to say crazy. I'm afraid I'm going crazy.'

'Well you're not,' he said firmly. 'You're just rattled, like all of us.'

Thasha shook her head. 'You closed the clock, before it was too late. You cleaned up the mess I caused, again. Oh Pazel, the dreams, the noises. The things I keep seeing. Words painted on the anchors. Doors, where there aren't any doors. And all those ghosts – nobody sees them but Rose and me. Do you think I've caught whatever he has?'

'You're not crazy,' he said again, taking hold of her shoulders. 'You blary well ran the show down there in the liquor vault, even after things went so wrong. And Captain Magritte sees ghosts as well.'

'I see a light in your chest, Pazel.'

'*What?*'

Tears were welling in her eyes. She was looking at the spot below his collarbone, where Klyst's shell lay embedded beneath his skin. But it was not glowing; it had never glowed; there was nothing to see but flesh.

'I *am* crazy,' she said, trembling. 'I see a little shell inside you.'

'Listen,' he said, tugging down his shirt collar. 'I don't know why you can see it, but the shell is real. The murth-girl put it there.'

'Oh come on.'

'You're not crazy. You can feel it with your hand.' Pazel took a deep breath. 'Touch it. Go ahead.'

She looked at him. He nodded, and guided her hand with his own. She moved slowly, fearfully – and stopped, her fingers not an inch from his skin.

'It will hurt you,' she said, as if the knowledge had just come to her. 'Rin's teeth, Pazel, it will hurt like Pitfire. And you knew that, and you didn't mind.'

'No,' he said, breathless, 'I don't mind.'

Thasha looked at him with a warmth he knew Oggosk would never forgive. 'I mind,' she said, and dropped her hand.

They stood, holding each other's gaze for the first time in weeks. And Pazel knew it was over. The farce, the poor acting job he'd tried to make her believe in for the sake of the ixchel. He would hide what he could from Lady Oggosk, but there was no point in lying to Thasha any more. Not when she could see right through his skin.

'All right,' he whispered. 'You've got to listen to me carefully. Will you do that?'

Before Thasha could answer a noise erupted from the brig. It was an animal's screech, blood-curdling, over the shouting voices of the men. Hercól was urging someone to be careful; Magritte wanted something killed; the guard was swearing; Chadfallow was crying, '*I'll get him, stand back!*'

'He's killing Felthrup!' cried Pazel. He tried the door, but the guard had locked it behind him. '*Kill it!*' Magritte was shouting. '*Stick it with your spear!*' Thasha tried to draw Pazel away, but he ignored her, pounding the door and shouting, 'Ignus! Stop it! Leave him alone!'

Felthrup's cries ceased as suddenly as they had begun.

The door opened at last, and there stood the outraged guard – and Chadfallow, wiping blood from his hands.

'You mucking bastard!' cried Pazel, leaping at him. This time, however, Thasha caught him tightly around the chest. Chadfallow looked at him sadly. Then Pazel saw the hypodermic needle clutched in his hand.

'Felthrup was dying of thirst,' he said, as Pazel relaxed in Thasha's arms. 'He was too far gone to absorb water by drinking alone. I injected him with saline – clean water, just slightly salty, as it is in the body.'

'He bit you,' said Thasha.

'You're all blary cracked!' said the guard. 'And this doctor's a liar! He didn't want to give the Tholjassan no pills! And the Tholjassan himself's the maddest of the lot. Says that drooling rat in there's his pet – his *pet!* Out of here, all of you! The captain's goin' to hear about this!'

'Where's Felthrup?' asked Thasha.

Chadfallow examined his bites. 'I could not ... persuade him to leave,' he said.

'You'll be comin' down with whatever that rat has, now,' groaned the Turach.

'Very possibly,' said Chadfallow.

'Ignus,' said Pazel. 'I'm sorry.'

Chadfallow smiled dryly. 'Long time since anyone called me a bastard.'

'Yer a bastard,' said the Turach. 'Now get away from my post.'

Through all this the *Chathrand* was making fair speed to the south. The morning clouds had vanished, so there were no telltale disturbances to help them locate the Vortex. But there were other signs. The waves, uniform these many days, had lost their shapeliness, and were a bit collapsed on their eastern side. And the east wind, when it came, was strikingly cold, as if it had blown over some expanse of frigid water, churned up from the depths.

In mid-afternoon, one such cold gust reached in through the porthole of the chart room. Elkstem felt it, snapped his drafting pencil in two, and stormed out to the quarterdeck. 'Let go the wheel!' he said. 'Just let it go, boys, that's right.'

The baffled sailors looked at one another and obeyed. The wheel spun like a giant fishing reel, the bow of the *Chathrand* swung quickly to windward, and Elkstem shook his head in dismay. 'Catch her, catch her, gents!' he cried, then snapped his fingers for a midshipman. To the thin-lipped Sorrophrani who answered the summons, he dictated: 'A memo to the captain: my compliments, and be aware that the bow's leeward drift is approximately ten degrees. I can comfortably assume therefore that we are in the outer spiral of the Vortex, and that without intervention, our course will decay. Your servant, etc. Put the message in Rose's hand, lad, wherever he may be.'

About this time, Pazel, Thasha, Neeps and Marila found themselves together in the stateroom for the first time in days. Syrarys' dressing-table had been screwed down in place of the one destroyed. It was small, but then so were their meals, lately. Thasha had opened one of their few remaining delicacies: a jar of tiny octopuses, pickled in brine. Her father had always kept several jars of the rubbery pink creatures in the pantry at home, and Nama had seen that a dozen were laid away before they sailed from Etherhorde. Thasha had grown up hating them. But after months of galley food she ate octopuses with a will, as did the other three: spearing them with their knives, slicing off the beaks, chewing them whole. They tasted of home, and were gone in five minutes flat.

The four friends sat gazing at the empty jar. They had changed roles since yesterday, Pazel thought. He had his bare foot atop Thasha's own, enjoying the dusty warmth of it, the trust. Somewhere deep inside him a voice still protested: *take it away, take it away.* Was it fear of what Oggosk would do to the ixchel, or Klyst's jealousy? Whatever it was, he felt powerless to obey. He simply could not be cruel to Thasha any longer. *And then*, he thought, as her dry, calloused toes slid restlessly against his own, *there's this.*

Neeps and Marila, on the other hand, were barely speaking. Marila had not forgiven Neeps for pushing her to bring 'that loudmouthed, slave-trading drunk' to the council. Neeps had objected that Druffle wasn't really a slave trader, that he had only dealt in bonded servants, but his hair-splitting just made her angrier.

'Tell me what the difference is, when you get deeper in debt each time your master gives you a rag to wear, or some little piece of garbage to eat.'

Marila's anger was something to behold: icy, soft-spoken, hard as nails. She had talked Neeps into corners three times in the last two hours. They were perfect together, Pazel thought.

'Anyway,' Neeps was saying, 'I don't think Druffle specialised in buying and selling human beings. Arunis *sent* him to the Flikkermen, under his spell.'

'Which is another reason to stay away from him,' said Marila. 'For all we know he's still in Arunis' power.'

Pazel shook his head. 'Ramachni set him free. We know that.'

'But what if there's some part of him that's been weakened?' said Marila. 'What did Jervik tell you? *"He pick-pick-picks at me."* What if Arunis picked a hole in Druffle's mind, and can read it now?'

'She's right, Pazel,' said Thasha quietly. 'Arunis managed to read your mind, and control you. Or at least put ideas in your head, and make you freeze.'

'But it cost him,' said Neeps. 'I'll bet he put a lot of eggs in that basket, trying to get rid of Pazel and his two Master-Words. And he couldn't read Pazel's mind, actually – not until Pazel touched him. Druffle won't make that mistake.'

'Druffle would make *any* mistake,' said Marila. 'He's an idiot. Toads and ice.'

'Stop!' Pazel pleaded, raising his hands. 'It's done, and we can't undo it, and we can't waste any more time wishing we could. Think about what Hercól said, for Rin's sake. We stand together or we die.'

Neeps and Marila glared at one another across the table. Thasha gave Pazel a private smile.

'I still want to know something,' said Marila abruptly. 'Why isn't Arunis dead? Chadfallow says he was hanged for nine days on Licherog, chopped up and tossed into the sea. That sounds blary dead. So what happened? What's he doing here at all?'

Even Pazel found himself glancing in Thasha's direction. 'I know what you want,' she said at once. 'But I told you, I can't touch the *Polylex*. I'm sorry. Felthrup was helping me for a while; he'd turn the pages, and read aloud. That made it bearable – just. Since then I've been trying to read it on my own, but it's too awful that way. I go too fast, I learn . . . too many things.'

'Like what?' said Neeps. 'Can you tell us something, just so we understand?'

Thasha put her elbows on the table, looking down at her plate of snipped-off octopus beaks. She sighed.

'There was a barge anchored on the Ool, in Etherhorde. The spy who ran the Secret Fist before Sandor Ott had it put there to terrify the Nunekkam. It had an eight-foot wooden wall instead of a rail, and shackles all over the deck. If they didn't cooperate with his spies – tell them all about their clients, hand over their business records – he'd take their families and roll them in salt and chain them there, for days. They have soft skin, the Nunekkam, they blister in the sun, birds would come and—'

'All right!' said Neeps hastily. 'Sorry I asked.'

Thasha shuddered. 'It isn't even those stories, exactly. It's that I feel like I'm *remembering* them. As if I used to know these things, and a few lines bring it all back. It's like going into your house after it's been sealed up for years, and tugging off the dustcloths, and finding the furniture all covered in blood.'

'Just stay away from the *Polylex*, then,' said Pazel. 'Felthrup thought you should, too.'

'Ramachni said she *had* to read it,' said Marila.

'Maybe Ramachni was wrong.'

Marila gave Pazel a sceptical glance, as if she knew very well what was behind his argument. Neeps drew patterns in the brine on his plate.

Suddenly Thasha rose to her feet. Without a word she seized Pazel's hand, making him rise too, and led him into her cabin. She marched around the bed, wrenched savagely at the latch on the porthole and flung open the glass.

The sudden wind slammed shut her cabin door. Pazel rounded the bed, studying her, more worried than he liked to admit. Thasha bent to the porthole, gulping the cold breeze, and the evening sun lit her face. There were dark rings under her eyes, and the golden flag of her hair had lost much of its shine. The *blanë*, he thought: wasn't that where it started? Had she ever fully recovered from that taste of death?

He put his hands on her shoulders, and they lifted eagerly against his palms. Thasha sighed and let her head fall forwards. Pazel squeezed, then gave a nervous laugh. 'You're so blary strong,' he said.

'Syrarys used to beg me to be lazy,' murmured Thasha. 'She said with my shoulders no man would— Ouch! No, don't stop, that was a good ouch. Don't stop ever.'

He did not stop, but to his great vexation he could think of nothing to say. Thasha swayed under his hands. In the stateroom Marila and Neeps resumed their argument.

Talk to her. Tell her something clever and calm. Or just kiss her. Do something, fool, before you lose the chance!

He raised a hand to her cheek. At once the spark of pain flared up in his chest, but he didn't care. He leaned nearer, until he could see that her eyes were closed. Her breath came in little puffs against his fingertips.

'What are you thinking about?' he said.

'Greysan.'

He could not have pulled away faster if she had tried to give him a rattlesnake. What was he doing here? What kind of mucking game was this for her? But as he turned to go Thasha caught his arm.

'You don't understand,' she said.

'I don't think I want to.'

He tugged his arm free and lurched for the door. To his back, Thasha said, 'I was thinking that if you and Neeps really don't trust him, then I can't either. And I won't.'

Pazel glanced back over his shoulder. 'It didn't stop you before,' he said.

'Stop me?' said Thasha, reddening.

He shrugged. 'From, well—'

'You're a prize pig, you know that?' said Thasha. 'Tell me this: why haven't you cut that shell out of your chest?'

Pazel said nothing. He had been dreading the question for months.

'Well?' she demanded. 'Isn't that how you're supposed to tell Klyst she's wasting her time?'

Still Pazel was silent. 'I just can't,' he said at last. 'I don't know why. It isn't that I mind the blood, you know.'

In the stateroom perfect silence had resumed. Thasha gazed at him like one contemplating murder. All at once she appeared to reach a decision. She pointed imperiously at the chair at her desk. 'Sit down,' she said.

Pazel obeyed, and Thasha went to the secret wall cabinet and took out the *Polylex*. She set it down quickly before him, as though even that brief touch was something she'd rather avoid.

'We're going to find an answer to Marila's question,' she said. 'Or rather you are. One hint, though: don't look up an obvious word like "Arunis" or "Nilstone." Remember that the authors were trying to *sneak* in information, so that the Emperor would let it be published. You have to use your intuition if you want to find anything.'

Pazel took a deep breath. 'I'll try *Licherog*.'

Thasha dropped back on her bed. 'That'll do. It's probably too easy, but maybe it will lead us somewhere.'

Pazel opened the book, astonished by the thinness of the dragonfly-wing paper. The print was small and ornate, the entries infinite and strange. *Lamb's blood. Lycanthropy. Lorg Academy (Origins). Lead Tomb. Lich of Greymorrow.*

And finally, *Licherog, Prison Isle of.*

The entry ran to nine pages, and was full of horrifying detail, such as the recurrent problem of cannibalism when food shipments were delayed, and the prison guards who were held hostage for sixteen years when a rebellion broke out on an underground floor. There was quite a lot about the Shaggat Ness, his sons, and the palace vacated for him by the Warden of Licherog. Of Arunis, however, there was only a brief mention: how he was held for twenty years with his master, tried to escape, was wounded by a guard's arrow, recaptured, and hanged.

'It says he cursed the guard before he died, and the poor man had a breakdown, quit the army, moved back in with his mother on Opalt, and slowly went mad.' Pazel shook his head. 'There isn't much more.

Arunis the sorcerer died upon the gibbet, and dangled there nine days. The birds who pecked his flesh fell stone dead, as from poison; and the sharks, when he was chopped and given over to them, were found later belly-up upon the sea. That's all. Weird, but not much help.'

'Try "Death" then,' said Thasha quietly.

Pazel turned more pages. *Death* included some macabre speculations about the least and most painful ways of inflicting it, and the post-humous torments of the sinful, and Agaroth, death's shadowy Border-Kingdom in the underworld. But Pazel saw nothing about ways to cheat death, or return from it to this life.

'That's odd,' he said suddenly. 'The entry breaks off in mid-sentence. There's room for more words, but it's unfinished, listen to this—'

'Don't!' said Thasha sharply. 'I don't want to hear it!' Her voice was tight with pain, as though she were walking barefoot on glass. 'Remember what I told you the night before the wedding, about how the book adds entries on its own? That's how it happens: first a blank space, then words that grow like a vine to fill the space. But when I read those new parts I feel *horrible*. Look up something else. "Sorcery," maybe.'

Pazel tried to move faster. But *Sorcery* was no help, and neither was *Necromancy* or *Resurrection*. By the time he'd moved on to *Mage* Thasha had backed to the far side of the bed, hugging herself into a ball.

Pazel took in her vacant, frightened eyes, and slammed the book shut. 'Right, I'm putting this thing away. Matter of fact, let's put it further away from you. We can hide it in your father's cabin; that's still inside the magic wall.'

'No!' said Thasha. 'I have to keep it near me. I'm . . . responsible for it.'

Pazel was about to argue, but at that moment the door creaked, and Neeps looked into the cabin.

'I could hear all that,' he said.

'Sorry to bother you,' said Pazel sarcastically.

'Don't be an oaf, I thought of something. You read about the guard who shot Arunis with the arrow – the one he cursed. Remember where it says he went?'

'Back to Opalt, with his mum,' said Pazel.

'And who else came from Opalt?'

Thasha raised her head slowly. 'Ket,' she said. 'The soap merchant. Arunis' false identity, when he first came aboard. Neeps, you could be onto something.'

She hopped from the bed, as Pazel opened the book and began leafing through it again.

'What do you know, he's in here,' he said after a moment. 'But there's hardly anything, just two lines. *Ket, a merchant family of Opalt, specializing in salves and soaps. The m—*'

Pazel stopped in amazement, all but choking on the words. '*The most successful member of the family to date, Liripus Ket, joined the family trade after a complete recovery from madness, which befell him during military service in his youth.*'

Pazel looked up from the book, first at Thasha, then at Neeps. A chill seemed to have descended on the room.

'Ket was the guard on Licherog,' he said. 'Arunis didn't just curse him – he *became* him. That's how he escaped the island nobody ever escapes. He can do more than just get inside someone's head. He can take over. He can blary move in.'

At that moment Marila's voice called from the outer stateroom. 'Thasha! Come out here, hurry up.'

Thasha sprang from the cabin, with the boys right behind her. Marila was at the stateroom door, which was open a crack. 'It's Dastu,' she said. 'He's just outside the magic wall, with the guard. He wants to come inside.'

'Oh, I have to blary invite him, don't I?' said Thasha. She opened the door wide and beckoned, and Dastu stepped through the magic wall and hurried towards them. He looked as though he were barely able to keep from breaking into a run. Slipping into the room, he eyed the four of them with a mixture of relief and anxiety.

'You're all here,' he said, shutting the door behind him. 'That's good. Listen to me close, now. I found Bolutu.'

'You found him!' they cried.

Dastu nodded. 'He's down in the liquor vault, and he's in a bad way. That change he was expecting? Well I think it's started, mates. And he says he's got to tell you something *before* it's done, Pazel. Somethin' about Rose – about "how to get the better of Rose." He won't say more than that to me.'

'Why didn't you bring him here?' said Neeps, looking at Dastu nervously.

'*Bring* him?' Lord Rin, mate, you'll see! Pazel, you've got to come down there! It's safe, for the time being. There's nobody in the Abandoned House. And I think we can manage without a lamp.'

'We'll all go,' said Neeps.

'Come on, Undrabust!' said Dastu, more high-strung than Pazel had ever seen him. 'This ain't the dead of night. What'll our story be if we're caught? What if that guard decides to tell somebody that we all charged out of here together?'

'I *am* going,' said Thasha. 'If Bolutu's really got something to do with Ramachni, I have to be there.'

Dastu squirmed with impatience. 'Whoever's going has to come with me *now*. You don't know what's going on in there!'

Pazel turned to Neeps and Marila. 'It'll be four bells in, what, twenty minutes? Come after us then, if we're not back. Just take the long way around, and for Rin's sake, don't let anyone see you on the scuttle! All right, Dastu, let's go.'

Before Neeps could think of another objection, Pazel, Thasha and Dastu stepped out of the room. Neeps watched them until they passed the guard, then shut the door and whirled around.

'Twenty minutes!' he said to Marila. 'I'll go plum mad, worrying about them! Damn and blast, I *still* don't trust that Bolutu, even if he does have the scar. And you were a big help! Couldn't you have said *something*?'

Marila walked up to him with a scowl, as though prepared to resume their fight. But instead she placed her pale cheek against his darker one, and stood there, blinking, until he put his arms around her shoulders. 'When are you going to tell me why you really stowed away?' he said.

'Soon,' said Marila.

Five or six minutes passed. One of their stomachs growled. Jorl and Suzyt padded in circles, whining for Thasha.

Suddenly Marila tensed, and raised her head.

'How could Bolutu get inside the vault?' she said. 'Pazel locked it after the council meeting, with the master key. He said so.'

Neeps stared at her. A terrible notion seemed to be blossoming within him, broader and fouler by the second. He let go of Marila. Then he charged for the door and threw it open and ran, not caring who saw him or where they thought he was going.

'I've got matches,' whispered Dastu, 'but let's go as far as we can without 'em. The light could give us away.'

'I don't need any light,' said Thasha. 'I could find that room in my sleep.'

They were at the bottom of the Silver Stair. Voices reached them from the mercy deck, but they were far forwards, barely to be heard. They passed the spot where Jervik had accosted Pazel, then the smoke cellar, the paint room, the stacks of anonymous freight. Dastu was right: the path to the scuttle was perfectly clear.

'I wasn't expecting anything like this,' Pazel murmured. 'Bolutu didn't sound worried about changing back into himself. In fact I thought he was looking forward to it.'

'He shouldn't have been,' said Dastu grimly. 'Quiet now, we're almost there.'

Silent as thieves, they crept down the scuttle and into the Abandoned House. The smells, the slop of bilge, the maze of narrow passages were unchanged from the night before – and after the first turn, so was the blackness. The three youths linked hands, and groped slowly forwards. At last they reached the door of the liquor vault.

Pazel heard a creak. 'It's open,' whispered Dastu. But not the least glimmer of light came from the vault. Dastu whispered urgently: 'Say there, Bolutu! I've brought them. Pathkendle, and Thasha both. Where are you?'

No reply but the splash of the bilge. 'He had a lamp,' whispered Dastu, moving forwards. Then he stopped abruptly, as if he had stubbed a toe. 'Oh Pitfire,' he said. 'Come in, quick. Tell me when the blary door's shut.'

Still holding the elder tarboy's hand, Pazel stopped, making Thasha pause as well. Something was different about the room now. Was it the smell, the temperature? He couldn't be sure. But he knew he did not want to go into the room. He started to let go of Dastu – but the older boy's hand tightened sharply.

'Didn't you hear?' he said, voice sharp with anger. 'I said tell me when the door is shut!'

Dastu gave a savage tug. As Pazel crashed forwards, a knee struck him so hard in the stomach that he could not even cry out. Another blow landed on the back of his head, and he fell. When he regained his senses a moment later someone was lighting a lamp, and a heavy boot was on his chest. He began to rise, but the boot stomped with terrible violence, and at the same time a cold blade touched his throat. It was a broadsword, old, weather-stained, sharp as a razor. At the other end of it was Captain Rose.

'The door is shut,' said a second voice.

Pazel moaned with rage and frustration. The voice was Sandor Ott's. He turned his head and saw the spymaster holding Thasha from behind, one hand pulling her hair, making her arch her back and thrust her chin at the ceiling; the other holding his long white knife against her side.

36

The Cost in Blood

—◦◦◦—

Diadrelu felt like weeping, though she could not have said if it was with grief or joy. *How they commingle, those pure extremes, whenever one feels them fully.*

Two yards from her, Felthrup sat with his head on his forepaws, his throat still puffy with Dr Chadfallow's water injection, the blood from whatever battles he had survived stiff and dry in his black fur. His eyes had opened very slowly a moment ago, and were open still. But Dri knew they did not see her.

'I thought he was gone,' she said. 'I feared Mugstur had killed him at last.'

Hercól reached through the bars. She turned and leaned into his palm with a sigh. 'We are all of us exiles,' she said. 'That is what binds us: our not-belonging, our homelessness. The way our natural kin have turned on us, or turned us out, or become so strange to us that we no longer fit. But none of us are so exiled as he. Back on the Nelu Peren he begged us, begged us to accept him as a friend. My brother responded by locking him in a pipe.'

'You responded differently,' said Hercól. 'If he dies now, he at least will have known what it is to be cared for.'

Dri raised her arms in his direction. Hercól lifted her through the bars and kissed her forehead, ever so gently. When he withdrew she bent double, placed her palms flat on his open hand, and there before his worshipful eyes pressed up into a handstand, perfectly balanced and still. She smiled, crossed her legs. Hercól breathed a sigh.

'Diadrelu Tammariken,' he said, 'you're the marriage of all the dreams of women my heart has entertained.'

She laughed, gazing down at his palm. 'You yourself are not quite as

476

perfect as all that,' she said. 'Just perfect enough for me to believe that you're real, and that you might stay with me awhile.'

'Awhile?' he said. 'After I leave this cell, I hope never to know another morning when I wake and do not find you beside me.'

'And the incomprehension of your people? And mine?'

'You spoke the answer,' he said. 'We're exiles already. We're a new people. Mongrels now, later the creators of a race.'

'The warrior becomes a visionary.' Dri lowered her legs with the same perfect control, and reclined as before on his forearm, head pillowed on his hand. 'I hope your Empress Maisa has room for such a people. Giants who yearn for crawlies, crawlies whose love their touch. Magad the Fifth would lock you in a madhouse, and feed me to the snappers in his reflecting pool.'

'Maisa, on the other hand, will receive you as one queen to another, or I never knew the woman,' said Hercól. 'She is the visionary, not I. But her visions are of solid things, things that may come to be. She is not always evoking Rin or Heaven's Tree or the promise of a paradise to come, like her stepchild the usurper. "The only paradise that concerns us, Asprodel," she told me once, "is the one we can build for all people, here in this world where we live."'

'I like that,' said Diadrelu. 'We ixchel are raised on a diet of paradise, you know. Stath Bálfyr, Sanctuary-Beyond-the-Sea. A place that was stolen, a dream of an island that was ours, where perhaps our brothers dwell yet. Talag was the only one who ever thought to seek it in anything but poetry or song. But we all loved it. Sanctuary, the dream of it, made sense of our lives. It was the paradise we clung to.'

She caressed his palm. 'I don't need it anymore. Strange: two days ago I still did. Now there's something else, something closer and more real. I can let that vision go.'

A sudden noise made them both freeze: a little whimper or cough, barely audible. It seemed to come from the direction of Felthrup's cell. A moment later it came again.

'He's in pain!' said Dri, sliding to the floor. She ran towards the iron bars that separated the two cells. Hercól started to his feet.

'Keep your distance!' he said. 'Felthrup himself warned me not to reach through the bars. He gave Chadfallow a savage bite.'

'I won't get too close.'

Diadrelu slipped into Felthrup's cell. As Hercól hissed objections, she peered at the dark shape in the middle of the floor.

'He is not moving at all, Hercól.'

'Dri—!'

She took a cautious step closer, then another. 'I cannot see him breathing,' she said.

'Stay away! Lover, I beg you again! If you wish to save him, find Bolutu. Felthrup cannot even tell you what he needs.'

Diadrelu hesitated, then turned around and started back to Hercól. 'You're right,' she said, 'I will go to Bolutu at once.'

'And trust another giant not to betray us?' said Taliktrum's voice from the passage. 'How startling of you, Aunt.'

Diadrelu was airborne on his first word, springing away like a grasshopper, and drawing her sword in mid-air. But before her leap reached its zenith, something covered her, something entangling and strong. Her people had dropped a net from above. Its weights bore her crashing to the floor.

Hercól lunged forwards. Ixchel were hurling themselves from the cell bars, ten or more shaved-headed men and women, landing with spear and sword around the struggling Dri. Hercól shot his arm through to the shoulder, and ixchel blades began to stab it. The net was just beyond his reach. Within it, Dri stabbed and slashed, but a ring of spears already encircled her, and Steldak and Myett were struggling to catch hold of her weapon-hand.

'Diadrelu!' shouted Hercól.

Taliktrum himself had leaped into the fray. He spun to face Hercól. 'Shout!' he hissed, mocking. 'Shout aloud, wake the man in the next cage, bring your people running. Begin the extermination – and doom your lover with the rest of us.'

Hercól did not shout. Instead he threw himself with terrible force against the bars, stretching every muscle in his arm. Taliktrum danced out of reach just in time, but Hercól caught the nearest of his men between two fingers. He closed the ixchel within his fist, and squeezed.

'Let her go,' he growled, holding the figure up for them to see.

Steldak had taken Dri's sword. She retained her short knife, and had cut through the meshes with it in several places, freeing her head and one arm. But the spears jabbed her on all sides. There was no fighting her way out of that ring. Dri lowered her arms.

'Taliktrum,' said Hercól dangerously, 'let her come to me. This man's life is forfeit if she is harmed.'

'There's a giant talking,' said Steldak. 'We have not even drawn the woman's blood. He has no reason to think we mean to, yet he promises to kill.'

Diadrelu stood among the spear-points, gazing at Hercól. When her eyes moved to the man he held, something changed in her face.

'No,' she said. 'Ludunte.'

Her *sophister* looked down from Hercól's bandaged fist. 'You're my mistress no longer, Dri. I renounce you. I have long had misgivings, but when I heard the giants speak the name of Sanctuary, I could side with you no longer. They must be fought, not reasoned with. Their souls are not those of reasoning creatures.'

'And now she herself has spoken of Sanctuary, to her unnatural lover,' said Myett. 'Did you hear, my lord Taliktrum? She *can let that vision go* – she renounces the vision of your father the prophet.'

'Prophet?' said Diadrelu.

'Listen to the scorn,' said Steldak. 'Yes, woman, prophet! So do we of Ixphir name our lost Lord Talag, architect of his people's deliverance. Taliktrum is his living champion, born to complete his father's work, just as you were born to oppose him and test our faith.'

'You're not of Ixphir House,' said Diadrelu. 'We rescued you from a cage in Rose's desk. It was your mad attack on Rose that got my brother killed!'

'Lies, lies!' cried several of Taliktrum's shaved-headed fighters. 'You knew she would say that, Lord, you predicted it!'

'I share all that I see,' said Taliktrum. 'I am not my father, but I serve you as I may.'

There was a changed aspect to his voice, a self-conscious gravity. Dri took in the faces around her: Talag's volunteer bodyguard, plus a few newcomers like Steldak and Myett. In their smiles she saw bridled rage. In their eyes, the clarity of fanatics.

Hercól had tightened his grip, drawing a gasp from Ludunte. 'Believe what you will,' he said, 'but be certain of this: he will die unless you release her.'

'She is my father's sister,' said Taliktrum, 'do you think I wish her dead?'

'Then let her come to me,' said Hercól, blinking sweat from his eyes. 'I love her. I offer you this man, and my oath to be a friend to your people and a voice for their welfare all the days of my life. No matter in what land this voyage ends, or the circumstances of its ending.'

Dri raised her head sharply, as though he had said too much. 'He knows!' someone whispered. 'She told him our plan!'

Taliktrum raised a hand for silence. He turned and addressed a few words to Dri in ixchel-speech. Hercól could hear nothing, of course, but he saw the effect Taliktrum's words had on Diadrelu. She cried out, appalled. She shut her eyes and shook her head. Steldak and Myett pointed at her, their mouths forming curses or taunts. The others cheered them on. All eerily silent; then Taliktrum faced Hercól again.

'My aunt thinks I lack the strength to rule,' he said, 'and yet when I make strong decisions they frighten her.'

'Strength and power are not the same thing,' said Hercól.

'Who do you think to lecture?' snapped Taliktrum. 'I am the defender of this clan, and of a future race of ixchel, unless her treason prevents it. You speak of love – that is monstrous, foul. You do not know the meaning of the word.'

'I did not know,' said Hercól softly, 'before.'

Myett turned her slim body towards him and pouted, mocking. '"*I did not know.*" We saw just what you came to *know*, satyr. We watched it all.'

'Then you know that Diadrelu is the noblest among you,' said Hercól, unflinching. 'You heard her speak to me of what she holds most sacred – the good of your clan. How she would take her own life before letting you kill one another over her.'

'No one here is about to take up arms for that traitor,' said Steldak.

'They would not be here if they were,' said Diadrelu, 'and I expect few of the clan know about this ambush at all – or shall ever hear about it, afterwards. Enough! This talk wearies me. Nephew, you tried to slay me on Bramian. Were you in earnest? Do you mean to kill me now? I think you must, for I will not cease fighting for our people. And the order you just boasted of giving, which you do not wish Hercól to hear, only proves again that you do not know how such fighting is done.'

Outraged cries from the spear-bearers. But her words struck a chord in Taliktrum. His solemn demeanour vanished; he could not look his aunt in the eye. 'Don't think I lack the courage,' he warned her softly.

'I merely wonder if you have the courage *not* to be what others expect.'

A flash of annoyance crossed Taliktrum's face. 'Swear you will not reveal the order I gave.'

'Swear it, Diadrelu,' said Hercól, 'do as he wishes. Please.'

'I cannot,' she said softly. 'In fact I *will* tell the humans I trust. What you have set in motion, Taliktrum, could well destroy the ship, and the clan along with it. Have you paid *any* attention to what the humans are actually doing, where they're actually taking us? Is *vortex* a word you understand?'

There were hisses around the circle. *'She taunts him! She shames our lord! You'll pay, woman, you'll pay!'* Taliktrum gave his followers an uneasy look, as if torn between enjoying their adoration and wishing they would stop.

'My lord,' hissed Steldak, 'the time for talk is *past!* I – we, that is, we – are needed elsewhere. And quickly! Don't let her play on your family sympathies! You agreed – she is incurable. She has pledged herself to *that!*' He gestured with disgust at Hercól.

Taliktrum's face looked increasingly troubled. 'Giant,' he said at last, then, with effort, 'Hercól. You care for my aunt? That ... connects us, in a sense. We too were close; as a boy I learned at her knee. She was a good aunt, she understood a child's ... no matter. Can you make her promise to obey me *in all things*? Will she do that, for love of you?'

Hercól closed his eyes. He already knew what Dri's answer would be. When he opened them she was shaking her head.

One spearpoint was resting against Dri's throat. Steldak gripped it furiously. 'All this was *decided*,' he said.

With a trembling sigh, Hercól lowered his hand to the floor. 'Her obedience is not mine to give, Lord Taliktrum,' he said. 'I would give it, and anything else you asked of me. Here is your servant. I shall be another, if you will have me. Give me a razor; I will shave my head. Teach me your oaths and I will take them. Only spare her, spare her, my lord.'

He opened his hand, and Ludunte sprang free, astonished. But his amazement was nothing compared to Taliktrum's. The young man's lips were slightly parted; words formed on them, only to vanish unspoken. He looked suddenly at Diadrelu, standing quiet and thought-ful in his trap, neither resigned nor hopeful, merely aware.

'Aunt,' he said, and there was a plea in his voice, as if he were the one who was trapped.

Then Steldak made a furious sound, and jerked the spear. Diadrelu gave a small, clipped cry. She put her hand on her neck. The blood leaped through her fingers, a red bird escaping, a secret no one could keep. Her eyes slid upwards, searching for Hercól, but the light went out of them before they reached his face.

37

Grotesqueries of Change

—◦◦◦—

A hidden deformity,
A sore of the mind,
A wound in a world once blessed,
A chosen tumour,
A heart betrayed,
A stone whose touch is death.

The blind mote in the soul's good eye,
The slave who sells others tomorrow,
The joyless triumph,
The prayer that lies,
The lesson you learn to your sorrow.

'Hate'
Cantica of Ixphir House

9 Umbrin 941

'You're fast, girl,' said Sandor Ott. 'Almost fast enough, had you guessed that the danger lay behind as well as before you. Don't struggle, now, and for pity's sake don't try any of Hercól's tricks. Remember he learned most of them from me.'

Only now did Pazel realise what he'd sensed in the room: not a difference but a *sameness* that should have warned him. The room should have felt emptier; instead it was as crowded as before. Rose was seated; it was his boot on Pazel's chest. Dastu, holding a fengas lamp, stood to the captain's right. Sergeant Haddismal and another Turach were in the room as well. The sergeant had a thrusting dagger fitted

482

over the knuckles of his right hand. The blade was red to the hilt.

Behind the Turachs sat a row of bound men. Four had their faces concealed by leather hoods; the fifth, Lieutenant Khalmet, was slumped sideways against the wall, mouth open, blood darkening his chest.

Haddismal glared down at Pazel. 'I'll cut off your ears if you so much as sigh for that dung-eating dog! Khalmet swore to live and die for Magad the Fifth. There hasn't been such an oath-breaking in the history of the Turachs. A stab through the heart was a mercy he never deserved – and he knew it, the coward, he all but lunged on my blade. The rest of you won't be so lucky.'

Despite the hoods, Pazel recognised the others. Fiffengurt was still in the shirt he'd worn to the council meeting; he hadn't even rolled down his sleeves. Pazel spotted Druffle by his gauntness, Big Skip by his size, Bolutu by his monk's cloak and the blackness of his neck below the hood. The men's hands were tied very firmly behind their backs. All four were trembling.

'Pazel Pathkendle,' said Dastu, almost sadly, 'you never should have let old Chadfallow mix you up in all this. I hear you had a fine arrangement on the *Eniel*, and were halfway to citzenship.'

Pazel looked at him, and could not even feel the hate he expected. He was numb to any sensation but a kind of appalled disappointment. 'Why?' he said.

'You should be asking why not,' said Dastu. 'You never knew me, of course. You knew my second self – the one I'm done with *at last*, I think, Master?'

'Yes, lad, you're done with it,' said Ott. 'You've passed the exam with rare distinction.' He caught Pazel's eye, and gave a hideous grin. 'What do you say, Pathkendle? Top marks for Dastu? Certainly he had *you* believing in him. The good tarboy, the one without cunning or prejudice or vice, the one nobody could hate.' Ott looked appreciatively at Dastu, who basked in the praise. 'Six years he's been refining the part. Fiffengurt wanted to make him a midshipman; he saw *officer* material there. I think the truth hurt more than the blows.'

Rose withdrew his sword, and his boot. 'Stand up, Pathkendle. Ott, you will release the girl's hair. She knows better than to fight you.'

Ott slid his hand from Thasha's hair to her shoulder. 'There are a dozen Turachs behind me in the passage,' he said, his lips almost touching her ear.

Pazel got to his feet, still aching from the blow to his stomach.

'Dastu, how can you be with them?' he said, still incredulous in his shock. 'You were at the council. You know what they're doing is insane. You know that Arqual can't win another war – that *nobody* can, except Arunis.'

'I know you cannot face the truth,' said Dastu, 'but that doesn't surprise me. How could you be expected to embrace Arqual's coming supremacy? You lost your mother and sister in the Rescue of Chereste. You're an Ormali, with an Ormali's small, stay-at-home mind. I understand these things. But the world is large and cruel, Pazel. It needs Arqual more than ever.'

'That's not you talking,' said Pazel. 'That's just something they told you.'

'Something real,' said Dastu.

'I guess believing that is part of the exam, too,' said Thasha.

Dastu turned her a look that made the hair stand up on the back of Pazel's neck. But Sandor Ott just laughed. 'Yes, he said. 'An essential part – and the only part your tutor failed, Thasha Isiq. Hercól called it freedom of thought, but in fact his freedom began to bleed away the moment he left the Secret Fist. Was he free when he lived like a hunted thing in the Tsördons? Was he free when his lands were seized, his sister and her family beggared, his ancestral home in Tholjassa burned to the ground?'

Thasha twisted in his grasp. 'You!' she spat. 'Did you do those things to him?'

'He did them to himself, lass,' whispered Ott, pressing his lips even closer. 'And where is he now? In a cage, at the end of a wasted life. All for a withered old woman named Maisa – a cause as hopeless as petitioning the sun to rise in the west. Dastu, I'm glad to say, shows no such taste for lost causes.'

'You put it best, Master,' said Dastu. 'Arqual is the future of Alifros. In time we will need just one name, for world and Empire alike.'

'Boy,' said Rose, 'you've served your purpose well, but I don't give a damn for your Imperial platitudes. Fawn on your master elsewhere; for now concentrate on the task. Nine mutineers you spoke of; only seven have you produced.'

'Captain,' said Dastu, 'I fear I played the part too well. Undrabust and the stowaway girl meant to come, but I protested, the better to assure they'd not suspect I wanted—'

'Go and find them,' Rose interrupted. 'If they are still behind the magic wall, lure them out. Tell them their friends are in need; tell them whatever occurs to you. Haddismal, send a man along with him. I want the stateroom emptied once and for all.'

Dastu smiled. 'I have an idea already, Captain.' He looked to Ott, received a nod from the spymaster. Then he handed the fengas lamp to another Turach, and slipped out of the room with Haddismal's lieutenant.

Rose turned a stern and formal look on the captives before him, and pointed his sword at each in turn. 'Pazel Pathkendle. Thasha Isiq. As Captain and Final Offshore Authority of the IMS *Chathrand*, I hereby charge you with the crime of mutiny. The crime was both premeditated and sustained. You have held council with the aim of planning the seizure of this ship. You have recruited others to your cause. You have already assumed control of the admiralty-level stateroom, and held it by magical means, creating a space beyond the reach of shipboard justice. You have taken oaths to persevere in this crime as far as it leads – even to the destruction of this vessel, and the death of its entire crew.'

At the last words, Mr Fiffengurt began to squirm and kick, and cry out beneath his hood.

'Your quartermaster begs to differ,' said Rose. 'He would put all the blame for that last notion upon himself. But Dastu tells us that the whole council discussed the possibility – that you *hoped it wouldn't come to that*. Which means you accepted that it might.' Rose turned to the four captives seated behind him. 'Remove their hoods, Sergeant,' he said to Haddismal.

One by one the Turach unlaced the leather hoods and wrenched them free. Druffle spat at the commando, and received a blow that rang loud in the little chamber. Fiffengurt already had a gash across his forehead, straight as a chart line. Blood had trickled down one side of his nose, and left a cinnamon stain on his white whiskers.

'Pazel,' he said miserably, 'Miss Thasha. Forgive—'

'Silence!' barked Haddismal.

Big Skip was still and watchful, like a bear that has given up struggling in its chains. Bolutu, unhooded last of all, did not even glance at his captors. His eyes too went straight to Pazel and Thasha, but what was that keen glance trying to say? Help me? Save yourselves? Have faith in my plan?

A sudden glimmer of hope leaped in Pazel's mind. *Dastu left the council before Bolutu told us that his masters could see through his eyes. He can't have told Rose and Ott. They don't know that we're being observed, that Bolutu's empire is expecting us.*

485

Rose opened the chamber door, and beckoned. Turachs began to file into the room, hugely muscled men in leather armour, gauntlets, and short blades for close-quarters fighting. Two lifted the body of Khalmet and bore it from the room. The others, at a word from Haddismal, tugged the bound prisoners to their feet and made them face the captain.

'Mutiny has been a danger from this mission's inception,' said Rose. 'But despite yourselves, you have in fact helped me to prevent one.' Rose pointed at Pazel and Thasha in turn. 'I have known since Ormael that the two of you, along with Undrabust and Hercól Stanapeth, wished me harm. What I could not know was just who else might wish it also. But I did not have to find them, fortunately. I simply had to wait for you to find them for me.

Now his gaze swept all the prisoners. 'The punishment for mutiny is death. So is the attempted theft of a vessel belonging to a chartered interest of Arqual. I might have found a way to construe your crimes as falling short of these worst offences, but for the fact that you spoke of destroying this ship. For those who would hatch such a conspiracy there can be no second chances. You are all condemned men.

'The spell on the Shaggat forces me to delay most of your executions: you will be held in the brig until the matter of the Nilstone is resolved. We know Pathkendle is not the spell-keeper, but he too must wait a little longer for his punishment. That leaves us with Mr Sunderling, who joined the crew only after the spell was cast. Since you were in such haste to mutiny, sir, I see no reason to make a slow affair of your punishment.'

Big Skip's eyes went wide. 'Captain,' he said, low and serious, 'don't do it, sir. We weren't after your ship. I'm a good Arquali like you. It's a doomed voyage, sir, an evil one. You didn't want to be part of it no more than me. I've heard the talk. They sent the Flikkers after you, sir. They caught you with a ticket for an inland coach.'

'Take him aloft,' said Rose. 'Put him in stocks by the jiggermast, and nail the charges above his head.' He hesitated, studying the carpenter's mate. 'Give him some water. At midday tomorrow, he hangs.'

For an instant the room looked poised to explode. Thasha cried out; Ott had given her a warning nick below the ribcage, even as the captain spoke. Pazel whirled, and felt the captain's sword cut him through his shirt. '*Hold!*' roared the captain.

Of course there was nothing else to be done in a room full of Turachs. But as he felt his flesh torn open by the blade Pazel's wisdom simply vanished. He struck at Rose's sword-arm, the fastest and most thoughtless blow he'd ever attempted, and felt the captain's wrist buckle. Rose howled in astonishment and pain, Haddismal leaped forwards with his dagger raised, Thasha screamed *No!* Then a foot out of nowhere struck Pazel's cheek with the force of a club: Ott's foot. He had kicked the youth without taking either hand away from Thasha.

The blow turned Pazel's body like a snapped towel. Mouth agape, he crashed into Rose. The captain seized him snarling and threw him to the floor. Something – perhaps the cold, wet draught through the planks – kept him from losing consciousness. Then Rose came down on top of him and took his throat in both hands. The ferocity of his grip, the excruciating pain, left no doubt as to his intentions. Pazel smashed his knees against the captain's ribs, but Rose only grunted, lifted Pazel's head and slammed it down against the boards.

'I had plans for you,' he said. 'Plans, or hopes at least. But I can damn well make other arrangements.'

He pressed his face to his victim's chest, for Pazel was clawing desperately at his eyes. Thasha was fighting Ott, Fiffengurt was begging the captain's mercy for the youths. And Pazel was dying. He knew that, even as his eyesight dimmed. There came an instant of mental lightning, when visions of his mother and Neda, Thasha and Neeps, Ramachni and the bright eyes of the murth-girl, all became beautifully distinct, like so many gorgeous playing cards fanned across a table. Then the visions began to wink out.

'*Nilus!*'

The voice shrieked, peremptory, commanding, from the crowded passageway. The captain jumped, relaxing his grip on Pazel's neck with an almost guilty haste. The voice was Lady Oggosk's.

Her red cat preceded her, slipping among the ankles of the room's startled men. Sniraga went directly to the captain and rubbed against his leg. Then Oggosk herself appeared, elbowing a path through the Turachs, who looked twice as big beside the tiny crone. She wore a black shawl over her arms, and pointed at the captain with her walking stick.

'What are you doing, Nilus? Get up, you look a perfect fool!'

'Oggosk, how dare you interfere!' said the captain through his teeth. 'Get back to your quarters; we will speak when I am finished here.'

'Pazel! Thasha!' cried Neeps from the passage. 'I came as fast as I could! She's just so blary slow on the ladderways!'

'Quiet, you odious boy!' snapped the witch. 'Nilus, the Ormali must not be killed. Not yet, not while the girl is still – *glaya*, the way she is.'

487

She gestured vaguely at Thasha, still held fast by Sandor Ott. 'Have the girl and Pathkendle taken to your quarters. Leave the rest to Haddismal. There are more urgent problems, Rin knows, such as the apelike Mr Uskins' blunders at the helm.'

'Duchess—'

'Nilus, he is fondling her! That lascivious spy is fondling Thasha Isiq, and snuffling at her ear! He has cut her belly, too! What sort of ship are you running? Get off her, you reptile.'

She jabbed at Ott with her walking stick, but the spy only pressed his knife harder against Thasha's side. The hand on her neck had indeed slipped lower, inside her shirt. Thasha's eyes were blazing, her lips curled back in a look of consuming hate.

Oggosk made a sound of disgust. 'I'll expect you in your cabin, Nilus. Bring the doctor to bind their wounds. You can stay here, Undrabust; try not to get killed.'

She hobbled off into the passage. Sniraga, however, remained seated by the captain's knee, purring softly, the only contented being in the vault.

Rose took his hand from Pazel's throat. He did not seem to know how to carry on. Pazel lay still, breathing like a rusty spigot.

'Ott,' said Thasha quietly, 'I swear on my mother, if you touch me there again I'll kill you.'

'I swear on your *father*,' said Ott, 'that you shall never again lift a hand against me, or presume to mention where I put my own.'

'Commander Ott,' said Sergeant Haddismal, 'this is the daughter of Eberzam Isiq.'

If such were possible in a Turach's voice, Haddismal sounded afraid. Ott turned slowly to face him, astonished and cold. 'I will pretend those words never left your mouth, Haddismal. See that they never do again.'

'You are relieved, Spymaster,' said Rose suddenly. 'Unhand the girl, and be gone.'

A twitch passed over Ott's face, and his scars stood out like veins in marble. Rose had not even looked in his direction. Sergeant Haddismal glanced sharply at his fellow Turachs, whose hands went to their weapons. Still Ott remained where he was, one hand in Thasha's shirt, the other fidgeting with his knife.

'Pathkendle—' Rose began.

He never got any further, for at that moment Sniraga gave a ghastly yowl. An ixchel man had burst from between two crates, sword in hand, copper eyes alight with hatred. Sniraga pounced, but the ixchel dodged her, leaped straight at Rose, and plunged his sword into the red beard with a cry. The captain roared and swatted at him as he might a giant insect. The ixchel spun head over heels across the room, and landed on Big Skip's ankle.

The carpenter's mate kicked instinctively. Steldak flew across the room a second time, lost hold of his sword (which had drawn no blood), and bounded unsteadily to his feet. He was lithe and quick, for he was an ixchel, but he was no Diadrelu. He feinted this way and that, as if he could not decide which way to run.

It's over, thought Pazel. *Over for us, and the ixchel.*

Rose's fist smashed down. Haddismal stomped, missing Steldak by a hair. Ott gave a croaking laugh and pulled Thasha tight against him. And Steldak, quick as a spider, wriggled through a two-inch gap in the floor planks.

'That's my poison taster!' said Rose. 'Gods of death, we have to dig him out of there! We need to learn if the little bastard's alone!' He shoved Pazel to one side, clawing at the plank, which was loose already. 'Help me, Haddismal!'

'He'll be long gone by now, sir,' said Haddismal, squatting next to Rose.

'Pull, damn you! There are baffles in the floor! He's crawled right into a box!'

Sniraga growled and clawed at the gap. Rose squeezed her aside, jamming his toe under the board as it started to lift.

'Those baffles are rotted out,' said Fiffengurt from the back of the room. No one heeded him. Rose and the Turach wrenched and pried at the board. Over the slop of bilgewater, a sound of scurrying could indeed be heard from beneath it. Was that a voice, too? Pazel pulled himself up against a crate, listening. The board was starting to give way.

Steldak's voice rang out suddenly from beneath it. 'Not yet! Not yet! He isn't close enough!'

Neither Rose nor Haddismal showed the slightest reaction to the voice – *of course not*, Pazel thought, *he's using ixchel-speech.*

'Captain,' he rasped, his throat still terribly painful, 'you might want to stop that.'

Rose looked daggers at him, and gave a monstrous heave. The board lifted some ten inches, ancient nails popping from sea-rotted wood. Rose bent down to peer into the dark space beneath.

'There you are!' he cried.

The board shattered. Something wet and furious struck Rose in the face. It was a huge white rat, twice the size of Felthrup, and its head was thrust into Rose's mouth. Human and rat fell backwards, the beast clawing, Rose flailing and bucking on the floor. At last he got a grip on the squirming animal and flung it away from him with all his might. The rat's head was a hideous, hairless knob, scarlet with blood, and even before it struck the wall behind Druffle it had begun to talk.

'Glory!' it howled, from atop a crate some eight feet above the floor. 'Glory to the rats of Arqual! Glory to the Angel of Rin! Death comes to the false priest, the heretic captain who mocks the Ninety Rules and their Maker! Death to his godless crew, death to this temple defiled!'

'That's Mugstur!' gasped Pazel.

'*Kill it!*' screamed Rose, all but incoherent with blood.

Two Turachs sprang at the rat, but it squirmed away, shouting in ecstasy. 'Victory! Victory for Arqual where the Angel reigns! Victory to Magad, our Rin-given emperor! The hour is come! Rats of *Chathrand*, come forth and fight!'

And the rats came. Out of the shattered floor, the frothing bilge, they leaped and squirmed, eight, twelve, twenty, more struggling behind. Like a welling stain, they spread in all directions, and with them spread a chaos beyond anyone's control. The Turachs stabbed and stomped, killing many, but the creatures were entering the vault faster than they died, and the floorboard was in too many pieces to replace. The Turach with the lamp whirled, slamming it into Big Skip's chest and cracking the glass. The lamp sputtered, darkening.

Rose was choking, with a sound like a slaughtered bull, even as rats climbed his limbs and boiled across his back. Master Mugstur had bitten off part of his tongue, and Rose had inhaled enough of his own blood to drown a smaller man. The four bound men were screaming for their hands to be freed. Sandor Ott gazed at the bald-headed, gore-stained rat who shrieked the praises of his emperor, and for one instant appeared to forget where he was.

That instant was all Thasha needed. With a blow fuelled by rage, she drove her fist down against his knife hand, and at the same time slammed her head back against his face with all her might. Both blows connected; the knife flew from Ott's grasp, and Ott himself staggered backwards into the open doorway.

Thasha knew her only chance was to press the attack, and she did. Whirling straight into a third blow, she struck at Ott's sword-arm just as he started to draw the weapon out. It was a point-blank strike to the forearm: the spymaster snarled with pain. And then he took her. Ott's right hand, the one that had held the knife, was not too wounded to strike her bare-fisted. He smashed her chin with an upper cut. She struck back, lightning-fast but weak; she was stunned. He brought his hand slicing down against her neck. Thasha's knees buckled, and as she fell her head struck the edge of a crate. Eyes locked on her, Ott flung a fist sideways at Neeps (who was lunging in desperation) and knocked him flat on the deck. Then he drew his sword.

Pazel cried out and heaved to his feet. To his amazement, Rose also lurched at the spy. But they were both a step too far away, and too late. Thasha looked up, bloodied, disoriented. Ott grimaced and swung.

The blow was meant to kill, and would have, but for the violent collision of a body with the spymaster's own. Hercól had driven like a cannonball through the last Turachs in the passage, and the force of his leap at Ott knocked over half the men still standing in the liquor vault. Pazel was crushed once more beneath Rose, but over the captain's shoulder he saw Hercól fighting like a man possessed, his face contorted with an emotion more acute than hate. *Agony*, thought Pazel. *Agony he doesn't mean to get over.* Hercól's momentum never seemed to break, only turn into spiral energy as he rolled and whirled Ott through the room, smashing, bludgeoning him against crate and floor and soldiers and carcasses of rats. Ott's sword was gone, his blows Hercól did not seem to feel. When at last he managed a damaging blow to Hercól's jaw the Tholjassan rose with a cry and hurled him the length of the room.

Ott struck the back wall and fell senseless upon a carpet of squirming rats. When Pazel's eyes caught up with Hercól the man was pouncing, Ott's own knife in his hand, drawn back over his shoulder with the point aimed downwards at his old master's throat.

'Kill!'

Hercól froze. The voice came from just above him. It was Mugstur, perhaps the only conscious creature in the room less rational at that instant that Hercól himself. Mugstur's mad, bulging eyes glared down at him, urging him on.

'Kill, kill! It is the promised end! The Angel comes! Arqual shall be purified through blood!'

'Diadrelu,' said Hercól, and he was suddenly, obviously, a man broken by grief. He stabbed not downwards but upwards, driving the knife into the white rat's side.

Master Mugstur did not seem surprised by what had happened to him. 'The Angel comes!' he cried, gurgling. 'The Tree bleeds, the

Nilstone wakes, *and a thousand eyes are opening! Glory! Glory! War!'*

Mugstur gave a last twitch and fell limp. Hercól lifted the creature on Ott's knife, then lowered the blade and let the rat slide onto the motionless spymaster. 'No more dreams of glory,' he said. 'They are finished, for all of us.'

But it was not finished. Ott stirred, moaning, and as he did so the white rat twitched again. The next moment it was on its feet, bleeding but very much alive. And at the same moment all the surviving rats grew still, and raised their narrow faces to look at the men. They were knowing looks, looks of conscious intelligence.

'War,' said Mugstur, and the rats began to grow.

38

Holy War

——◦∿◦——

9 Umbrin 941

The humans rushed bleeding from the Abandoned House. Rose was the last one out of the liquor vault, and he personally cut the bonds on the four prisoners, screaming orders at them as he did so. Haddismal carried the half-conscious spymaster, Neeps supported Pazel, and Thasha tried her best to drag Hercól into the passage, as he swung and stabbed and bludgeoned and hacked, and a mound of twitching fur rose about him.

The rats of *Chathrand* were awake, and mad. They had swollen to the size of hunting dogs, and their voices – mewling, screeching, speaking – were so loud and hideous that the men fell back as much from the force of them as from the creature's tearing nails and bolt-cutter jaws. When Rose at last heaved himself up onto the mercy deck, he found Fiffengurt and twelve men ready to skid a carriage-sized packet of sparwood over the hatch. The captain rolled aside, shouting, 'Do it!' No sooner were the tons of wood in place than they heard the first rats slamming their thick bodies against the door.

'Angel!'

'Kill them!'

'Arqual, Arqual, just and true!'

'Pray before eating! Pray!'

Rose spat a great mouthful of blood. He did not even glance at the wounds on his legs. Seizing Bolutu by the elbow and Neeps by the scruff of the neck, he dragged them at a near run towards the mainmast, as a throng of near-hysterical sailors billowed around him, howling death and disaster. Pazel, Thasha and Hercól had no choice but to follow him.

'Report!' he thundered. 'Who's the deck officer? Bindhammer!'

'Sir, they've gone and turned themselves into Pit-vomited fiends!' cried Bindhammer, waving his short, burly arms.

'I noticed that! Damn it, man, how many rats are we talking about?'

The answer, when accounts were tallied, appeared to be *all of them*. Not a single normal rat had been spotted; the mutants were bursting from deep recesses in the hold like bees from a broken hive. Two men had perished already. The entire hold had been abandoned.

'What did you drag Neeps and Bolutu here for?' shouted Pazel, when he could get a word in edgewise.

Rose released them both with a flinging motion. 'Because I wanted to be blary sure the rest of you followed me! Shut up! Not a word! Just tell me, true and fast: do you know what's happening?'

The sailors looked at them with fear-maddened eyes. 'There are just two things it could be,' said Thasha. 'Some trick of Arunis', though why he'd turn rats into monsters I can't imagine. Or the Nilstone, working all by itself. I'd bet on the latter.'

'So would I,' said Bolutu. 'Captain Rose, since early summer I have tried to draw your attention to the *Chathrand*'s fleas. They were always large and bloodthirsty. After you brought the Nilstone aboard, however, they became positively unnatural. And there have been other deformed and aggressive pests. Wasps, moths, flies, beetles. Anything, that is, that might have touched the Nilstone. Their numbers have been greatest at the stern of the orlop, where the Shaggat stands holding his prize.'

'The Stone?' cried Rose. 'I thought the damned thing killed whoever touched it!'

'Whoever touches it with *fear in their hearts*,' said Hercól. 'Perhaps insects have no fear, at least not as we understand it.'

'The effect on insects was noted centuries ago, when Erithusmé showed the Nilstone to my people,' said Bolutu, 'but nothing came of it – the vermin lived only a day or two. We know also that the Waking Spell was cast by one who held the Nilstone. Today I fear something horribly new is occurring: the fleas must have lived long enough to infect the rats with their mutation. And as they change, the rats are also exploding into consciousness – of a sort.'

'There is worse,' said Hercól. 'Master Mugstur is still alive. He fell back, even as his servants rushed me. I did not kill him with that first blow, and I never landed another. He appeared to heal, in fact, as he grew to monstrous size.'

'He's been awake for months – or maybe years,' said Thasha.

Rose glared at her, blood running freely from his mouth. 'And is it months that you've known about him? Damn you all! I know what you think of this mission – Pitfire, I even understand it! But a rat? What could possess you to keep quiet about a blary psychotic woken rat?'

Pazel saw a struggle playing out on Hercól's face. With an inward gasp he realised the man was tempted to answer Rose's question – tempted to say *Because you would have killed the rats, and the ixchel with them*. Rose still knew nothing about the clan. What had happened to Hercól, to tempt him to betray Diadrelu's people?

The moment was shattered by a blast from Fiffengurt's whistle. They had left him behind near the scuttle; now he and eight or ten sailors came running and skidding up the passage as if demons were at their heels.

'They're on the deck! They're right behind us! Run!'

Men stampeded for the ladderways. Fiffengurt shouted at Rose as they ran: 'They're leaping up from crates, sir, through the stern cargo hatch! They must be clearing ten feet!'

Rose glanced upward: the roof of the mercy deck, where they stood, was eight feet above the floor.

'You, and you!' Rose pulled two long-legged sailors from the crowd. 'Turachs to the orlop! Twenty men at the tonnage hatch, with bows. Another twenty at the stern hatch. And a dozen at each ladderway. *Now*, d'ye hear me? *Run!*'

The sailors rushed ahead. Seconds later a many-throated howl erupted from the stern. Men turned in horror. The rats were coming: huge, twisted, loping animals, fur patchy and sparse, inflamed bites the size of walnuts on their skin. They ran shoulder to shoulder, screeching and jabbering about the Promised End. When they spotted Rose they gave another howl and redoubled their speed.

The remaining humans on the mercy deck leaped for the stair. Rose was last again, and the rats were on him as he climbed backwards, swearing and spitting blood at them, his broadsword flashing up and down like a metal wing. Hercól fought beside him, ruthless and wild. Ildraquin was scarlet to the hilt.

On the orlop there was no sign of the Turachs. Rose and Hercól and Thasha held the ladderway, as a squirming, drooling mass of the creatures tried to jam through together. The two men stood on the top steps, blocking the way with their bodies as much as with their swords. Thasha, wielding Ott's white knife (it felt good in her hand, disturbingly good) leaned over the stair from the opposite side and stabbed.

Neeps led Pazel a few yards away. 'Can you manage? I have to find out what's happened to Marila!'

'I can manage,' said Pazel, squeezing his arm in thanks. 'Go on, find her! Be careful!'

'Undrabust!' roared the captain over his shoulder. 'Send down Dr Chadfallow – or Rain, or even Fulbreech. Send the blary tailor if you see him first! Someone's got to stitch up my tongue!'

The orlop deck had a unique defensive advantage: the four great ladderways, which ran from the topdeck straight through the upper part of the ship, ended abruptly here. To descend farther, one had to cross hundreds of feet of the dark orlop, to one of the two narrow ladderways that continued down to the mercy deck. It was a point of congestion, and intentionally so. Through the centuries, pirates and other enemy boarders had often chased the crew from the upper decks, only to become lost and divided here, and ultimately overwhelmed.

But the rats were not confused. While Hercól, Rose and Thasha held one of the two ladderways against the leaping, spitting mass, forty or fifty of the creatures broke and ran for the second stair. Fiffengurt heard them moving beneath him, like a herd of wild boars, and in a flash he understood. There was no one to hold the other stair.

The quartermaster ran as he had not run in decades, to shut the compartment door. But the rats were faster. Before he was halfway to the door they were exploding up the ladderway, spinning about, and galloping back across the orlop to meet him.

One rat was ahead of the pack, a huge yellow-toothed creature, screeching the emperor's name. Fiffengurt saw that it would beat him to the door. He stopped, waiting. Squinting at the beast with his one good eye. The rat was through the doorway, and then it was on him. Leaping for his face.

With a cry of 'Anni!' Fiffengurt jerked to one side, and brought his blackjack down with a *crack*. The beast fell senseless at his feet. He kicked shut the door and rammed the bolt home.

Seconds later the rest of the creatures hurled themselves against it. The old oak shuddered, but held. Fiffengurt howled filth back at them, hoping to enrage them into thoughtlessness – for there were other ways into the compartment. 'Screw yer Angel!' he shouted, waving desperately at the men behind him, and pointing at the other doors. 'Screw the Emperor too! Magad's a worm! Rin hates you! Mugstur's a wart on the world's backside!'

Big Skip saw his gestures and understood. He flew to the other doors, slamming them one after another. Pazel and Druffle chased after him. 'We're not out of the saucepot yet,' said the freebooter, wild-eyed.

Pazel knew he was right. They had closed the doors, but the deck's central passage, which was also the widest, had no doors to shut.

'Come on, we'll block it with crates!' he said.

'Forget that – they're all bolted down,' said Big Skip. 'And who's going to hold them in place, once there's fifty rats pushing from the other side?'

Druffle looked over his shoulder, counting heads. 'Thirteen of us. And that third door looks as flimsy as the blary floorboards in the liquor vault. We're going to lose this deck, my hearts.'

Right again, Pazel thought. Armed, Hercól, Thasha and Rose were barely managing to hold a narrow staircase. The rest of them didn't have a single weapon, except for Fiffengurt's blackjack, and a crowbar Druffle had picked up somewhere. *Weapons*, he thought, *we have to put our hands on some weapons.*

He stared into the open passage, thinking furiously. The surgery lay behind them – would a doctor's blade or a bone saw be any use against such monsters? There were shepherd's hooks in racks outside the cable tiers, for guiding the great ropes into coils. Useless, useless. They wanted to kill the rats, not herd them.

Suddenly a woman's voice echoed up the passage: '*What's happening? Let us out, let us out!*' And Pazel remembered: the steerage passengers were still locked in their miserable compartment, dead ahead, in the zone that any minute would be overrun by rats.

Big Skip turned white as sailcloth. 'There's more than forty people in that room. And if the rats break through *their* door—'

Other voices joined the woman's. Hands thumped urgently at a wall or door.

'They'll draw the rats right to them!' said Pazel. 'And blast it, Marila's still got our master key!'

'Stay here,' said Big Skip. 'I'll see if Rose has a key.'

He dashed towards the melee at the stair. Druffle fidgeted and snarled. 'They're just about ready to blary *hang* us, and here we are fighting alongside 'em again! There's not a stale crumb of justice in this world. And I still say Arunis is behind it all.'

'Not likely,' said Pazel. 'The rats can't sail the ship for him. And he doesn't want men dying until he gets the Nilstone out of the Shaggat's hand. No, it's got to be the Stone itself.'

'Then why don't he come out of his damned cabin and do something useful for once?' Druffle fumed. 'Why don't he call up more demons from the Pits, to fight these carbuncular bastards? Or was all that talk back in Simja a barrel of hogwash?'

'It happened,' said Pazel, remembering Dri's account of the summoning.

Druffle looked at him sharply. 'Hogwash! That's it! Ain't there pitch-forks with the live animals, just round the corner?'

'Yes!' said Pazel, starting. 'There's two pitchforks, in a cabinet across from the cattle pens! They'd be blary useful, Mr Druffle!'

'I'll fetch 'em right now!' Druffle thrust the crowbar into Pazel's hands. 'Keep your eye on that passage, lad.'

He was gone – so quickly that Pazel couldn't help feeling suspicious. Did he really mean to come back, or were the pitchforks just a handy excuse to run away? Druffle had shown intense, almost ludicrous bravery in the past, when under Arunis' mind-control spell. But after Druffle's behaviour in the liquour vault, Pazel had begun to think Marila was right.

And yet the one who had betrayed him was Dastu. The one nobody thought twice about, the one they all adored. Pazel's feelings remained almost too painful to face. *Ramachni*, he thought, *how could you tell us to trust?*

The voices from the darkness pleaded, wailed. Pazel looked back towards the ladderway: Big Skip was still trying to get Rose's attention. *No time, no time:* surely the rats were just seconds away. There were old folks back there, and children. Whole families who'd paid dearly for the passage, believing that by now they'd be almost to Etherhorde, a great city at the start of a Great Peace, a new life for them all.

And to think Ott had wanted them aboard just to keep up appear-ances. They were about to die, for appearances. Pazel swore, and dashed headlong down the corridor.

Forty feet, past the abandoned third-class berths, the delousing chamber, the empty nursery. On his left, down a side passage, he heard the screams, howls, prayers of the rats, still crashing against Fiffengurt's door.

A ghastly smell of human waste: he was running between racks of tight-lidded chamber pots, which no one had emptied in days. Then he was at the steerage door. The men and women were thumping, screaming. 'Villains! Assassins! You can't leave us here to die!'

'Quiet!' said Pazel, as loudly as he dared. 'Listen to me! I can't open the door—'

'Can't, or won't?' they shot back. 'What in the Nine Pits is going on out there? Who's killing who?'

'Shut up and listen,' snapped Pazel, 'or you *will* be killed, and there won't be a blary thing I can do about it.'

Some of the prisoners tried to silence the rest. Pazel didn't dare tell them about the rats; it would start a panic no one could restrain. Instead he told them they had to break through the ceiling, and escape into the berth deck above. 'I don't know how,' he said, 'but you've got to do it, and fast. Believe me, nobody's going to punish you for destroying Company property! I'll try to get men to help you from up there.'

There were sounds of shoving and pushing, contending cries of 'Liar!' and 'Do as he says!' Then a fist smashed hard against the door, and a man bellowed at the top of his lungs, *'Let us out! Let us out!'*

Others took up the chant; the calmer voices were lost in the din. Pazel whirled around – just in time to see a gigantic, blood-smeared rat scurry into the corridor from the side passage. It spotted him, and screeched, and from behind it came an answering howl.

Terror and ecstasy: Pazel saw the rat charge, felt the solid weight of the crowbar in his hand, felt above all the slowing of time that Hercól said came to many before combat was joined. In that instant so much of what the swordsman or Thasha achieved in battle-dance no longer seemed unthinkable. He could not do it, maybe, but he saw that it could be done. He had time to gauge the rat's strength and its madness, the momentum of its charge. Time to consider twenty steps and stances. Time to imagine it tearing him apart.

He turned sideways, giving himself room to swing. The rat was shouting *Heretic!* Looking him in the eye, and in its own gaze was hate and torment and an intelligence unhinged. But it was not all mad: as Pazel swung it saw the danger, and spun away, so that the blow that would have cracked its skull connected instead with its shoulder – wounding instead of killing. The rat whirled completely around and came at him again. Pazel's backswing barely kept its teeth from his face. He lashed out hard with his left foot, and struck the creature full in the flank. But the rat twisted with astonishing flexibility, and sank its shovel-like teeth into his thigh. Screaming with pain, Pazel brought down the crowbar again.

Crack. The rat shuddered, but did not let go. Pazel struck again, roaring. Again. Again. On the fifth blow the rat's jaw loosened; on the sixth it fell to the floor.

Pazel turned and sprinted for the main compartment. As he raced by a second rat entered from the side passage. He swung the crowbar, never slowing, and knocked the creature from his path. But from the corner of his eye he saw scores of the beasts flooding around the corner. Another few seconds and he'd have been trapped.

'Here they come!' he shouted, racing back into the main compartment.

For the first time in his life Pazel was overjoyed by the sight of Turachs. Eight archers stood in a gauntlet, with Haddismal beside them, looking as though he was at last in his element. 'Drop, Muketch!' he commanded. Pazel saw eight longbows levelled at him, bending, and threw himself flat on the deck.

The bows sang. Yards behind him, the rats gurgled and screamed, and the deck shook as bodies crashed to the ground. Pazel dragged himself aside, not daring to raise his head. The bows twanged again, and the sounds of agony redoubled. At last Pazel realised he was out of range, and turned over just in time to see the remaining rats fleeing back down the corridor. Ten or twelve lay dying.

Haddismal beckoned to his men. 'Advance! Advance with me! Viper stance, blades and bows! Onward, in Magad's name!'

In tight formation, the soldiers ran into the darkness. Pazel hurried back towards the stair. But halfway across the main compartment he saw Hercól, no longer needed at the ladderway, cutting across his path at a run, Ildraquin still naked in his hand. Thasha ran close behind him. She gave Pazel a look of grim apprehension, a look that begged him to follow. Hercól's face was darker than ever.

Pazel rushed to catch up with them, and even before he did so, he realised where they must be bound: the surgery. It was just a few yards off the main compartment. But why were they running in such a panic? Had Hercól taken some new injury? He wasn't bleeding, except a bit around his bandaged fingers. *Someone else, then*, Pazel thought, *someone wounded before he came down to the hold.*

He and Thasha caught up with Hercól just as he reached the surgery door. There, for one breath, Hercól paused; and squeezed his eyes shut. Then he flung the door wide.

Wreckage, everywhere: the floor was strewn with broken glass, scattered surgical tools. Fluids dripped from the screwed-down tables. The single patient, Old Gangrüne the purser, was squatting atop

Chadfallow's desk in the corner. His forehead was bandaged; his lips trembled in fear. Then Pazel's eyes swept right, to the far end of the chamber, and he gasped.

Ignus Chadfallow stood backed against a cabinet. With his left hand he gripped a jagged staff, part of a broomhandle, maybe. With his right, he held a small, bloody bundle to his chest.

Ranged before him on the tables stood some fifty ixchel. All were tensed for battle. About a dozen had their backs to Chadfallow, in a protective semicircle; the rest surrounded this smaller group, menacing it with all manner of arms.

When the door flew open the ixchel scattered, like chess pieces swept from a board. At the same time Old Gangrüne scrambled off the desk and bolted for the door. 'Crawlies! Crawlies!' he howled, barrelling past them into the corridor.

The ixchel, to Pazel's amazement, simply let him go. After their first startled movements, they snapped back into positions that were almost unchanged. The larger group merely angled to one side, keeping the newcomers in view.

Hercól made straight for the doctor and his unexpected guard. 'Chadfallow, have they—'

'Stay where you are, monster!' shouted a familiar voice. It was Taliktrum.

The young lord stood among his shaved-headed guard. His swallow-suit draped on his shoulders like a holy raiment. Steldak stood just behind him, whispering something. A slim, catlike girl clutched at his arm.

Hercól took another step. Taliktrum shouted something, and ten archers fitted arrows to bows.

'We will drop you with the same poison you used on Lady Thasha,' said Taliktrum.

'I will kill half of you before I fall,' said Hercól.

'Gods below, man!' shouted Chadfallow suddenly. 'Are you out of your head? Why did you have me guard this body? What is her importance to you? I have seen them, that's enough. Rose will know what to do.'

'Hear the giant!' cried the ixchel with loathing.

'Who are you talking about? It's Dri, isn't it?' Thasha pushed past Hercól, as if daring Taliktrum to make good on his threat. Hercól gripped her shoulder.

'If I shoot you with pure *blanë* this time, you'll never wake up, stupid girl,' said Taliktrum. 'Not without the antidote. And I can promise you none will provide it.' He turned to the dozen ixchel between him and the doctor. 'Ensyl, stand aside. You know the rites must be observed.'

'I know what my mistress believes in,' said a young ixchel woman at the head of the group, 'and how you betrayed her.'

'You will quit this room, my lord,' said Hercól softly, 'or by the infernal fires, I'll end your reign here and now.'

Steldak looked up with fear at Ildraquin. 'My lord,' he said in ixchel-speech, 'this man felled Ott in seconds, alone. Do not fight him. We can come back later, when they sleep.'

Despite himself, Pazel laughed aloud. 'Sleep! When's that going to be, you mad dog? Have you seen what's going on out there? Do you *know* what's happened to your friends the rats?'

Taliktrum frowned sharply. 'Friends?' he said. 'Steldak, you know what I think of those vermin. Have you been consorting with them again?'

Steldak looked suddenly exposed, and frightened. 'My lord, the boy speaks rubbish. Like any of us, I bump into rats, they can hardly be avoided—'

'Especially,' said Pazel, 'when you're squeezed into a space the size of a shoebox with one of them, waiting to attack the captain.'

Taliktrum's face tightened. His lips curled back from his teeth in a grimace of fury. 'Again. You dare defy us *again* – defy my father's last order, when your first breaking of it put him in the jaws of that cat.'

'Don't take his word—'

'Should I take yours, rather? No: it is your head I should take. Get out of my sight before I do so.'

Steldak backed away, sputtering with indignation. From outside the room, Pazel heard screeches and cries. The rats were getting closer.

Hercól flexed his bloody fingers on Ildraquin. His face astonished Pazel. This was what he used to be, he thought. A man without kindness, a man of use to Sandor Ott and his order. A man capable of anything.

'Quit this chamber, Lord Taliktrum. Now.'

The young leader's nerves were clearly frayed. All the same he bristled at Hercól.

'What I do matters little. Steldak is right in one thing: we can come back when we please. You've lost more than her, you know. Wait a bit longer, and—'

'*Now!*' Hercól exploded.

Taliktrum fled the table, and his people fled with him, leaping, whirling, so many copper leaves in a gale. But with that uncanny ixchel coordination, they came together again a heartbeat later, schooling, sprinting as one body out the surgery door. The dozen ixchel standing guard in front of Chadfallow did not move.

Thasha rushed towards the doctor. Pazel followed, although a part of him wanted to run the other way, close his eyes, stop his ears. Anything rather than see what he was about to see.

The young ixchel woman brandished her sword at them. 'You are not to touch her, either,' she said.

'Peace, Ensyl,' said Hercól, his voice close to breaking. 'They will use only their eyes.'

'Pazel,' said Chadfallow, looking at him sternly, 'how long have you known they were aboard?'

Pazel ignored the question. He stared at the bundle the doctor held against his chest. He could not move. He felt Hercól standing close behind him, frozen like himself. At last, trembling, Thasha put out her hand – careful not to touch the bloodstained cloths – and gently tugged the doctor's sleeve. Chadfallow lowered his arm.

Diadrelu lay there, pale and beautiful and dead, her neck wrapped in a crimson bandage. Chadfallow had washed the blood from her shoulders and her hands, which were folded across her breast. She had never looked more calm, more full of vision, although her eyes were closed. Pazel didn't know just when he started to cry, but he knew he had never cried like this in his lifetime. Louder, sure, for his lost family, for Ormael, but not with this despair, this sense of something that was both part of him and too good to be part of him, and at the same time something he'd built – trust, love, language – torn away and trampled, gone. He was pathetic. Sobbing in front of Chadfallow. But so was Thasha, her head on Pazel's shoulder; and so was Hercól, leaning upon the table, his sword cast aside. The three stood there, weeping, stripped naked by their grief. Chadfallow looked at Pazel with shock. It was as if he had just realised that the boy had stepped onto some other ship, swiftly departing, leaving him behind. The ixchel too stared, as the humans cried for their queen; and one of them, Pazel never learned which, spoke under his breath.

'She knew. She insisted. They are not all the same. We used to talk as if we owned them, owned their debt to us, their sins. We were fools, because she knew them alone.'

*

It was a strange party that ascended the ladderway. Hercól held Diadrelu to his chest, where she passed for a thick bandage, hiding some wound. Ensyl and two other ixchel rode in the folds of his bloody shirt, and Thasha, Pazel and Chadfallow carried six more in similar fashion. Ensyl sent the remaining four off on foot, to contact whatever members of the clan remained loyal to Dri, and tell them who had slain her. *How many will believe it?* Pazel thought. *A giant named Hercól was the only witness.*

But another secret was out at last. Old Gangrüne had seen to that. On every deck Pazel heard the gossip flying: *It's not just the rats, it's crawlies too, they must be behind all this, they fed the rats something to make monsters of 'em all.*

The men rushing to join the battle looked at the three climbing upward with contempt. 'Running off,' Pazel heard one sailor growl, 'just as we're getting the upper hand.'

It did appear that the humans were winning. The rats had not yet been driven from the orlop deck, but all those forwards of the main compartment were slain, and the Turachs were holding both cargo hatches. There was talk of a second outbreak at the stern of the orlop: rats in great numbers erupting from the manger, where the Shaggat Ness stood clutching the Nilstone. Sailors and Turachs were dying still, but the rats were dying faster. Doors slowed them down, and for all their ferocity they could not advance through a hail of Turach arrows, or a wall of spears.

If the crew could win back the orlop, Pazel mused, they could do the same with the mercy deck beneath it. But the hold? That was where the rats had lived all along. There were few doors and endless hiding places. Cable tiers, pump shafts, wing spaces, vents. Tunnels in the sand ballast, gaps between casks and crates. Rose would surely resort to smoking them out, or using sulphur gas. And he had crawlies to kill as well now.

The middle decks were all but deserted. Outside the stateroom, even the lone Turach had been called off to join the battle. Thasha was startled to find herself momentarily stopped by the invisible wall; then she silently gave permission to the ixchel she carried (and the other six, and Dr Chadfallow) to pass through. Moments later the party was inside.

They laid Diadrelu on the bench under the windows, exactly where she had woken Thasha all those months ago. 'Taliktrum spoke the truth in one way,' said Ensyl. 'The rites must be observed. My mistress must be parcelled, and the parcels given to the sea. No peace will come to her if this is not done.'

'Is that why the nine of you are here?' said Pazel.

'To see it done, yes. But not to do it ourselves. That privilege belongs to her kin, and it is a mortal offence to deny them the same.'

'Even if they're the ones who killed her?' asked Thasha bitterly.

'Not in that case, no,' said Ensyl.

'I thank you with all my heart,' said Hercól, 'for keeping her safe. And you as well, Doctor. And I must thank Felthrup, last of all: he rose from his deathlike trance mere seconds after that beast Steldak killed my lady, as if a part of him sensed the crime. And perhaps it did at that. In any case, he flew at them in such a rage that they blundered towards my cell. It was only because of Felthrup that I was able to take her body from them.'

'Ensyl,' said Pazel, 'you realise the whole ship knows about your clan, now?'

'I do,' she said grimly.

'They'll have to come here too, won't they?' said Thasha. 'All six hundred. They won't be safe anywhere else.'

'Do not let them!' cried several ixchel at once. Ensyl agreed. 'You must not, m'lady. They do not deserve your protection.'

'Nor do they need it,' blurted a round-faced ixchel youth. Ensyl gave him a sharp look.

'No?' said Chadfallow, peering at him. 'How is that? What defences have the ixchel against giant rats and sulphur?'

'We are not permitted to speak of it,' said Ensyl quietly.

Hercól sighed. 'That phrase I have heard before. Very well, keep your secrets. It is time to return to battle.'

'You must not, Hercól,' said Ensyl with a strange urgency. 'The parcelling—'

'We will decide all that when the fighting's done,' said Chadfallow.

Ensyl shook her head. 'You don't understand, there's nothing to decide. And by the time the fighting ends it may be too late. You are her kin, Hercól Stanapeth. She chose you, and you her, and none of us who loved her dispute your right. The parcelling of her body must be done by your hand, and no other. The last one to touch her must be you.'

Thasha closed the makeshift curtain over the washroom doorway, leaving Hercól, Chadfallow and Ensyl alone with Diadrelu's body.

Pazel turned away with a shudder. Chadfallow had just handed Hercól a scalpel: probably the one blade in Alifros he didn't know how to use.

Thasha went into her cabin, and emerged a moment later wearing her sword. Then she went straight to her father's crossed blades, mounted on the wall above his reading chair, and took one of them down. She thrust the scabbard awkwardly through Pazel's belt. 'We'll fix you a proper baldric later on,' she said. 'Right now I want to get out of here.'

They left the stateroom and made for the Silver Stair. Pazel tried not to think of what was happening in the washroom. *Twenty-seven pieces.*

'It's blary cruel,' he said as they climbed the ladderway. 'To lose someone, and then have to do *that* to her. I couldn't do it.'

Thasha spoke without turning. 'You could if you had to. If your honour depended on it. And . . . the other's.'

Yours? Pazel couldn't help thinking. *If we were ixchel, and you died, would they expect me . . . ?* For a moment he thought he would be ill.

On the main deck she turned to face him suddenly. 'What is it?' he said.

'Draw,' said Thasha, and whipped out her sword.

He drew. Thasha was already lunging. He blocked her strike and another followed. She chided him – 'Faster, *faster!*' with every cut and thrust. It was a one-minute drill, his first with a real sword, and he was afraid to go on the attack. What if he actually stabbed her? He found himself driven in circles, barely able to parry her blows. I'm hopeless, he thought, as the force of their clashing blades wrenched his arm.

'Stop!' said Thasha abruptly. 'Good! You've learned something. Those were fine parries.'

'Thanks,' said Pazel, amazed.

'Fine, but useless. Blocking won't stop these rats. You stab, or they bite you. Stab them first, Pazel. Every time.'

They took to the stairs again. 'And don't let your blade swing loose in your hand,' Thasha added. 'I made that mistake once with Hercól, and broke my thumb in the knuckle guard.'

'Ouch,' he said.

'Yes. Ouch. But it sure as Pitfire taught me to— Oh!'

She caught his arm. They were emerging onto the topdeck, for the first time in many hours. And everything around them was strange.

It was past sunset; the world should have been dark. Instead it glowed a fiery orange-red. They stepped into the chilly wind. Straight ahead of the *Chathrand*, the Red Storm blazed across the sky, an unbroken wall of silent, softly boiling light. It was hard to tell just how big it was, and thus how far away – sixty miles, eighty? Whatever the distance, it was much closer than when the tarboys and Fegin had watched it at dawn.

But the storm was not the only wonder, or the worst. Roughly the same distance off the port beam, there was a lowering and twisting of clouds – and, Pazel realised with a sickening jolt, *of the sea itself.* A great, round expanse of ocean had become vaguely, but undeniably, concave, as if an invisible finger were pressing down on the dark blanket of the sea. The centre of the depression was beneath their line of sight. Above it, the clouds churned in a descending spiral.

'The Vortex,' Pazel said, 'that has to be the Nelluroq Vortex. O Bakru, Bakru! Call off your lions, save the ship.'

He had never meant the prayer more sincerely. For the last strange thing about the topdeck was how empty it was. Bow to stern, there could not have been more than thirty men at the sails. A few dozen more were flying up and down the deck, hauling the sheets, relaying orders. There should have been ten times as many hands on deck.

'Pazel,' said Thasha, her voice gone deadly cold, 'that's the whirlpool from my dream. The one I've been having since Etherhorde.'

'Of course it is,' he said. 'You've been dreaming about the Vortex.'

'But I didn't just imagine it,' said Thasha. 'I saw it, perfectly. It's *exactly* the same.'

Pazel looked at her with alarm. She had changed before his eyes. Gone was the confident *thojmelee* fighter. In its place was the haunted Thasha, the one who appeared each time she read the *Polylex*. The one who looked inexplicably older. 'What happens in this dream?' he asked her.

Thasha closed her eyes. 'I'm striking a bargain,' she said. 'Someone wants me gone from wherever I am. And I say that I'll go, as long as they agree to leave too. Whoever it is always agrees, but at the last minute they add something to the deal. Something that makes leaving much harder. Ramachni's there, looking on – guarding me, maybe, in case there's cheating. But I still have to say yes. As soon as I do, I start moving – very fast, with no effort at all. Straight towards that whirlpool. And I think, *This is how it feels, to die and remain alive.* And just as I start to fall into the Vortex I wake up.'

She opened her eyes and smiled ruefully at him. 'I'm waiting for you to say, "You're not crazy, Thasha."'

Pazel said nothing. He was trying to think of better, more comforting words. Whether or not he still fully believed in her sanity hardly mattered. Thasha stared, clearly upset by his hesitation.

Then Uskins appeared, barrelling around the starboard longboat. He was hysterical. He did not appear to be wounded, but his eyes had a wild light in them, and his face was red. He skidded to a halt before them and screamed.

'Muketch! Girl! Don't stand there, grab a line! Get forwards, to Lapwing's team on the port halyard! Run, blast you, we need everyone we've got!'

Pazel and Thasha did as they were told, if only to get away from Uskins. As they ran, Pazel became aware of a new sound, distant but immensely powerful. A sound that was neither wind nor waves. It made him think of a titanic millstone: inexorable, grinding. It was the sound of the Vortex.

'You're all right, Thasha,' he huffed as they ran, 'it's the world outside your head that's gone mad.'

Thasha burst out laughing: 'Thanks, I feel *much* better.'

'Don't mention it.'

She was so perversely amused that he couldn't help joining in her laughter. He wished he could stop right there, kiss her full on the lips.

'There's Neeps!' cried Thasha suddenly, pointing. He was halfway up the mainmast, a good hundred feet above the deck, working alongside a dozen sailors trying to reef the topsail. They were crawling out along the yard, fighting the wayward canvas, not looking down.

'They need more men for that job, don't they?' Thasha asked.

'You're damn right,' said Pazel. 'Twice as many, and hands on the halyards. Come on, let's help. Maybe together we can pull it off.'

They ran to the port rail, swung out to the great mainmast shrouds, and began the ascent. They were both sure-footed climbers: what Thasha lacked in experience she made up for in strength. But as they rose, so did the wind, quite suddenly in fact. Pazel, already exhausted by blows and blood loss, found he had to slow and catch his breath. 'I'm dizzy,' he said.

'What?' she shouted.

'DIZZY.'

How the men on the topsail yard could hear a thing he had no idea. At last Neeps saw them, and his face glowed with relief. He beckoned urgently. *Hurry up!*

Pazel resumed the climb. They passed the titanic main yard, that vast tree lashed horizontally above the ship, and for a few minutes the broad platform of the fighting top cut off their view of Neeps and the sailors. He could just hear them, though: it sounded as though Neeps was shouting his name. 'I'm coming, mate, I don't have blary wings,' he muttered testily.

They reached the fighting top, and Pazel squeezed up deftly through the climbing hole. The wind was momentarily blocked. Suddenly he could hear Neeps and all the others above him. They were screaming.

'No! No! No! Look out! Turn around!'

Pazel twisted, looking wildly everywhere for the source of their fear. Left, right, out, down—

Down.

The rats had broken out onto the topdeck. The space around the mainmast was thick with their squirming bodies. And a dozen or more were clawing straight up the wooden pillar towards them, salivating. 'Mine!' they screeched. 'Angel! Heaven! Kill!'

Pitfire, thought Pazel, *they were five decks below!*

Everything happened quickly. Pazel and Thasha could not descend, and to climb higher would have been sheer madness. The only possible choice was to make a stand on the fighting top. 'Don't slash,' Thasha shouted in his ear. 'Lunge. Thrust. If you let 'em get in close they'll tear you to bits.'

Scarcely had the words left her mouth when the first rats came boiling up from the hole. Pazel was starkly terrified. He had fought them one-on-one with the crowbar, but now there were three on him at once, and a pitching mast, and sixty feet between him and the deck. He stabbed, kicked at their faces and bellies, managing only to stay alive as Thasha killed and killed. More than once she skewered a rat through the neck or chest just as it drove its four-inch teeth past his defences. She was protecting them both, he knew, and the thought enraged him. *Focus*. He groped for an edge, for the speed required to know what those teeth and claws were doing before the creature he fought knew the same about his sword. It was possible, with fury it was possible. There, and *there*.

Neeps and the sailors climbed down to join the battle. With them, Pazel realised, was one other tarboy: Jervik. As he dropped onto the platform he caught Pazel's eye. 'Yaarh, Muketch! Now yer fightin' like a man!'

He dived into the fray, brandishing the knife he considered 'rusty trash,' throwing the rats' curses back at them. He had none of Thasha's finesse, but he did have speed and muscle, and a furious instinct for battle. Yet even with the reinforcements the fight seemed endless.

The rats kept coming, in a foul geyser of teeth and claws and fur. Everything was red: their eyes, Pazel's arms, the light from the soundless storm. What was happening below Pazel didn't dare imagine.

But a moment came at last when he killed a rat and no creature took its place. Thasha stabbed a grizzle-jawed beast on his right; Jervik kicked a third to its death. And then there were no more.

They looked down. Turachs and sailors once more held the deck, which from where he stood resembled the floor of a slaughterhouse. Big Skip was hurriedly climbing the shrouds.

'The bastards wormed their way up a light-shaft, got round behind us!' he boomed. 'Come down, lads, the fighting's nearly done. Just the hold to take back now.'

There were muttered thanks to Rin. 'We still have to set that muckin' sail,' said Jervik, glancing hastily at the Vortex.

Pazel sighed. 'Right. Let's do it, then.'

'I never found Marila,' said Neeps. 'Uskins nabbed me the minute I came outside.'

'She's dead, I reckon,' said Jervik bluntly. 'I saw what them rats— Eh! Crawly! Crawly!'

He was shouting, pointing at a spot in the topmast shrouds, about eight feet from them. There in his swallow-suit, looking very small and harried in the wind, clung Taliktrum.

They hushed Jervik with some difficulty. The ixchel man watched, clearly impatient. 'You should get down from the rigging,' he said at last, bending his voice so they all could hear.

'We've got a job to do,' said Neeps. 'What do you want?'

'Do the job later,' said Taliktrum. 'Right now you must all get down. We don't mean to kill you.'

'Kill us, is it?' growled Jervik. 'Like to see him try, the little louse!'

'Diadrelu revealed our presence to so many of you, you understand?' said Taliktrum. 'She left me no choice. I had to act before Rose killed us. And I was right, wasn't I? Even now he's getting ready to poison the hold.'

'What are you saying?' Pazel demanded. '*What* do you have to do?'

'Seize the ship,' said Taliktrum.

At that very moment a man above them gave a shrill cry. The crowd on the fighting top jumped and cried out: a body had snagged in the rigging, five feet from them. It was one of the sailors who had not helped with the fight. The arm that had caught in the rigging was wrenched at an unnatural angle.

Thasha was closest, and carefully edged nearer. 'He's still breathing,' she said. 'He's . . . *asleep!*'

Pazel looked down again. His eyes landed first on Big Skip: the carpenter's mate was dangling, arms and legs through the shrouds, head lolled to one side. On the deck, a Turach was slapping a fellow soldier hard in the face. Beside them Mr Uskins was pumping his fist, screaming at a midshipman. But even as Pazel watched, the sailor stumbled, raised a hand to his forehead, and slid languidly to the boards.

Pazel whirled on Taliktrum. 'You vicious little fool. It's *blanë*, isn't it? You shot them with *blanë.*'

'We shot no one,' said Taliktrum. 'You drank it yourselves. All of you. In your water, over the last many days. A slow-acting variety; we had to make sure everyone aboard got a taste, before you saw what was happening.'

'Abandon masts! Abandon masts, you fools! Climb down before it hits you!'

It was Fiffengurt, hobbling aft at a near-run, and leaving a bloody footprint at every other step. His voice snapped the men out of their shock; they began to swarm downwards towards the deck.

Thasha was still looking at Taliktrum. 'You blary *idiot*. We're sliding into the Vortex.'

'Get down,' said Taliktrum once again, 'we can't talk if you fall to your deaths.'

'What's there to talk about?' Neeps shouted. 'You've got to use your antidote, that's all. Otherwise we all go down together.'

'Damn you, giants! There is no more antidote! Dri stole the last of it for your little caper in Simja! But we're not butchering you, as you planned to do with us! It's a dilute formula. You'll all wake naturally, perfectly unharmed.'

'How soon?' asked Pazel.

Taliktrum was staring at the Vortex. 'Not very soon,' he said.

He let go of the rigging, teetering a moment in the wind. 'You can't judge me,' he said. 'This is war. I'm a general, and more than a general. I've been selected – yes, selected, chosen, to lead my people home. Don't deceive yourselves. If it was your family you'd have done exactly the same.'

The three friends were wide awake when they reached the topdeck, but scores of others were not so lucky. A man from Tressek Tarn had dropped from the mizzenmast and struck the rail; the fall killed him instantly. Fiffengurt was organizing men with safety lines to climb up and rescue those tangled in the rigging. Even as he did so another man vanished from the bowsprit into the sea.

Taliktrum had vanished; several Turach archers had fired arrows in his direction. What had he wanted to tell them? Pazel wondered desperately. Could it have been some clue as to how to beat the drug?

'I'm not sleepy,' said Neeps. 'Maybe they didn't manage to get it in everyone's water.'

'He sounded sure that they had,' said Pazel. 'Come to think of it, that was the *only* thing he sounded sure of.'

'They had this in mind all along, didn't they?' said Thasha. 'Ensyl and her friends knew about it – why else would they say the ixchel didn't need our protection? Which means Dri must have known too. Oh, how could she keep it from us? How *could* she?'

Pazel had no answer. All he felt certain of was that Taliktrum had unleashed forces beyond his control.

Fiffengurt came stumbling back their way, his wounded foot making a *squilch* each time it touched the deck. 'Lord Rin, children, what now?' he cried. 'Sleeping sickness?'

'Not quite,' said Pazel. They told the quartermaster about the ixchel's drug. Fiffengurt pulled miserably at his whiskers.

'It's not too late,' he said. 'We're still thirty miles from the eye of the Vortex. Elkstem worked miracles with the lads he could muster, but the best they could do was hold us steady. To break out we need hands on deck *now*. We can work the sails with safety lines, bring the lads down when they pass out, send others up in their places, but— Lo, there, midshipman! Don't lean over that blary shaft!'

A young man swayed away from the gunner's-pole hatch. The salute he tried to give Fiffengurt dissolved into a half-hearted wave. And when Pazel looked back at the quartermaster, he found to his shock that the man had sunk to his knees.

'Not too late,' he repeated, and collapsed.

Over the next quarter-hour, most of the ship's company joined him. The topdeck looked like a battlefield without victors, just a few shocked refugees wandering among the dead. Uskins snored upon a mound of dead rats. Bolutu lay curled by the No. 3 hatch, as if he had just managed to crawl into the open air before the sleep took hold. Elkstem dropped on the quarterdeck, hands clenched on a rope. He had apparently intended to lash the wheel (and hence the rudder) in a fixed position, but no one knew just what position, or what spread of sail might have accompanied it.

Neeps had begun to stumble and blink. 'Marila,' he said, again and again.

Supporting him, they ran down the No. 4 ladderway. There were bodies spread-eagled on the stairs; one man lay sleeping with a biscuit clenched in his teeth. The gun decks lay silent as a morgue. Lonely cries of *Help!* and *Wake up!* echoed from the darkness.

But farther down there were signs of life. On the orlop, men shouted and lanterns blazed. Turachs were dragging sleepers into cabins with sturdy doors. Far below, Pazel could still make out the howling of the rats.

They descended the narrow ladderway to the mercy deck, and hurried to the central compartment. Just inside the doorway they met Hercól and Chadfallow. The doctor spoke with quiet urgency. 'Get to the stateroom, you three! The fight here is lost!'

Lost? Pazel looked past the doctor. Sailors and Turachs filled the deck; the only rats in sight were dead ones. But of the hundreds of men, only a few dozen remained on their feet, and most of these were clustered about the tonnage hatch, staring into the hold, weapons in hand. The voices of the rats issued up from this darkness, cursing and insulting the men.

Even as Pazel looked, one of the men on guard began to sway. At once another sailor came forwards and and took his spear, pushing him away from the hatch.

'Rose and Haddismal are doing their best to keep up appearances,' said Hercól. 'The rats do not yet suspect what is happening. *They* are not affected: the ixchel did not bother to poison whatever slime or sludge they find to drink.'

'How many rats are left alive?' said Thasha.

'Too many,' said Hercól. 'A hundred, perhaps more. They are thick about both hatches, and both ladderways, yet hiding from our archers. We can kill no more without an assault on the hold, and there are not enough of us for that. I doubt, in fact, that we could stop the creatures, if they attack in force. Only their ignorance protects us now.'

Captain Rose walked the perimeter of the compartment, issuing calm orders as though nothing were amiss. Haddismal was peering down side passages, signalling his Turachs, pulling in every last man.

'There is another threat,' said Chadfallow. He leaned closer to the youths, and sniffed. 'Oil,' he whispered. 'Can you smell it? The ship's lamp oil is stored in the hold, and it has been spilt. Maybe the rats simply ruptured a barrel or two by accident. But we have seen them running with mouthfuls of rags and straw. And caught glimpses of firelight as well.'

'What's happening?' said Pazel. 'When they attacked in the hold they were like a pack of mad dogs. No plan, no clear thinking, except for Mugstur.'

'That has changed,' said Hercól. 'You can hear that they are screeching less. Bolutu thinks that Master Mugstur is calming them, giving them a way to understand the terror of their altered minds. If so they will become more dangerous by the hour.'

'Breathe not a word of this,' added Chadfallow. 'The men's spirits are low enough already.'

At the hatch, another man staggered away from his post. Seething, Captain Rose watched him fall. Then he turned and stumped towards the group at the doorway. His eyes were fixed on the youths.

'This is crawly work? You admit as much?'

A pause. Then Hercól said, 'Yes captain, it was done by ixchel.'

For a moment Pazel thought Rose would strike him. But just then Mr Alyash ran up to them, bearing a bright fengas lamp.

'The barricades are ready, Captain,' he said. 'They'll not be able to swarm up the ladderways again. Provided we have men left to seal them, after our retreat.'

Rose nodded. 'That is something. But not much. We must poison them, by the Night Gods, we must drop sulphur into the hold. You have found no way to seal the hatches against them?'

Alyash huffed. 'Without men to stand guard? There *is* no way, sir. They've shown us how fast they can chew through sailcloth and oil skins. We could cannibalise planks from the upper decks and nail 'em across the hatches, but that job would take half a day – even if we lost no more men.'

Pazel felt Neeps' hand squeeze his arm. The small boy was just barely awake.

'A drug,' he murmured.

'Yes, Neeps, it's a drug,' said Pazel.

Neeps gave his head a drunkard's shake. 'Find . . . another drug.'

'An antidote, you mean? No chance, didn't you hear Taliktrum? They never had very much, and it's all gone now. And even if he's lying, we'd never find—'

Neeps slapped a clumsy hand over Pazel's mouth. '*Another* drug,' he said heavily. 'Something else. Delay it. Delay.'

With that he was gone. Pazel caught him and lowered him to the deck.

Chadfallow was looking at him with wonder. 'This drug they use, this *blanë*,' he said. 'Is it magical?'

'Who knows?' said Pazel.

'I do,' said Thasha, 'and it's not. *Blanë* is just brilliant medicine. In fact the ixchel know more about human bodies than we know ourselves. They've experimented on us, over the years, just as we have on them.'

Everyone stared at her. It was another of those mystifying certainties Pazel had begun to expect from Thasha. But was she right? He shuddered, remembering the clock.

'Delay it,' said Thasha. 'Is that possible? Even if there's no antidote, couldn't we take something to hold off the sleep? Long enough to build those hatch covers, anyway?'

'A counteragent?' mused the doctor. 'Theoretically, yes. But I know nothing of this *blanë*! To find the right compound would take days of testing.' He glanced at Rose, and something in the captain's face made him add, 'Unless I got very lucky.'

Rose seized the doctor's arm and turned him bodily towards the ladderway. 'Get lucky doctor,' he said, 'that's an order.'

He needed help, Chadfallow said, and Pazel and Thasha promised to give it. Hercól, however, lifted Neeps and tossed the small boy over his shoulder. 'I will bear him to the stateroom, and meet you three at sickbay,' he said, and was gone.

It was sickbay and not the surgery that housed the Great Ship's medicines. Chadfallow and the youths raced upward again, taking three steps at a time. The middle decks were now completely silent. On the ladderway they passed just one conscious man – a Turach, stumbling on his feet, eyes half-closed. As Thasha passed he embraced her suddenly.

'Lady Thasha,' he slurred. 'Love you, love you. Goin' t'inherit a farm, see? Make you happy. Lots of kids—'

'Oh good gods.' Thasha pushed him away.

They reached the lower gun deck, and dashed along the short passage to sickbay. There to Chadfallow's delight (and Thasha's, Pazel noted) they found Greysan Fulbreech, wide awake, tending a ward full of sleeping men.

'Doctor!' he cried, 'I have lost three patients! The rats came down the Holy Stair from the main deck. They broke the latch on the door. If the Turachs had not come, everyone here would have been killed.'

'Including you,' Pazel heard himself say. Fulbreech did not even look at him. But Thasha did, reproachfully.

'Clear a table!' shouted Chadfallow, storming in. 'Listen, all of you. We are going to behave like potion-peddlars on the streets of Sorhn. I will hand you something; you will go out and find men on the verge of sleep – not uttterly lost, but failing. Make them take what I give. Tell them whatever you like. Watch them, see if they grow more alert. Then rush back and tell me. And meanwhile send anyone else you can find to me directly. Ah, sheepsgaul! Put this in some water, Greysan.'

Moments later they were out the door. Thasha had a vial of white chilli oil, Pazel a yellow pill the doctor called Moonglow. They ran straight to the topdeck; it was closer than the mercy, and the only other place they knew of where men were still awake in any numbers.

Or had been. Pazel gazed over the deck and felt his heart sink. He had hoped that he would find men still battling the sails, keeping the *Chathrand* from gliding faster towards the Vortex. But there were simply not enough of them. From where he stood, Pazel counted nineteen – make that eighteen, there went another to his knees – largely unoccupied sailors, wandering among the sleepers, shouting out prayers, making the sign of the Tree. Some kicked their shipmates in despair, begging them to wake. Pazel squeezed the pill in his hand. 'This had better work,' he said.

Not two minutes later he had convinced a blinking, frightened man to swallow the pill. 'It's from Chadfallow, it'll keep you awake,' he declared shamelessly. The man gulped it eagerly, then gave him a triumphant smile. He raised both fists above his head. "I feel it!' he said, and collapsed.

The others fared no better: Thasha's victim cried himself to sleep, having swallowed enough chilli oil to make a fire-eater beg for drink. The man Fulbreech approached vomited on the deck.

None of these fiascos dissuaded the remaining men from following the youths back to sickbay. They had lost hope. Chadfallow was offering a last straw to clutch at, and clutch they did. They waved to their shipmates, this way, this way! The doctor's workin' on a cure!

Of the fourteen men who set off for sickbay, just eight reached it. Among them were Mr Fegin, Byrd the gunner – and, Pazel saw with outrage, Dastu. The elder tarboy's feet dragged; he was fast succumbing.

But as the others shuffled into sickbay he held back, wary eyes on Pazel and Thasha.

'Come on, mate,' jeered Pazel savagely. 'Don't be shy. For you we'll find something *extra* strong.'

Dastu gave Pazel a heavy-lidded stare. 'Think you're better than me, don't you, Muketch? After all the Empire's done for peasants like you. All the doors its opened, all the helping hands.'

Something inside Pazel came apart. He crossed the floor to Dastu and with a cunning he never knew he possessed, made as if to draw Isiq's sword. But as Dastu's eyes snapped to his sword-hand, he struck the older boy's chin as hard as he could with the other. Dastu's head jerked sideways. Then he fell.

'How courageous,' said Fulbreech. 'You've just knocked out a sleepwalker. And taken someone from us who could have tried a remedy.'

Pazel shut his eyes. Bastard. Cretin. When he opened his eyes he saw Thasha watching him, shaking her head.

'Next!' shouted Chadfallow, pounding his fist on a table. 'Who's nearest to sleep? Raise your heads, look me in the eye!'

An assortment of oddities lay spread before him. Pills, potions, creams, a jar of blue seeds, a dry and blackened lungfish. The men raised weary hands. One man swallowed seeds, and dropped in mid-chew. Another bit off part of the lungfish, chewed with great concentration, and dropped to the floor. Fegin drank something from a green flask. He groaned and turned rather green himself, then lowered himself to the wall. 'I'd like to . . . apologise,' he said, as his head lolled forwards.

Chadfallow's speed increased. He popped items into waiting mouths. 'Swamp myrtle,' he said. 'Bodendel marshfly. Endolithic spore.' But the men continued to drop. In frustration Chadfallow swept all the failed substances to the floor. He tore at his hair. 'All right, damn it: Thermo-pile Red – that should keep a man working for a week! Drink it, Byrd! Drain the cup! Don't shut your blary eyes!'

When Byrd fell, unrevived by Thermopile Red, the doctor let himself sink into a chair. Only he, Thasha, Pazel and Fulbreech remained. He looked at them and sighed. But before the sigh ended it had become a yawn.

That yawn frightened Pazel immensely. At the same time he felt a cloudiness descend on his brain, and a weight in his limbs, and knew his time was close.

517

He staggered forwards and shook the doctor. 'Fight it, Ignus! Think! We're counting on you!'

'Don't,' muttered Chadfallow.

'None of these are strong enough,' said Thasha. 'What have you got that's *stronger*?'

'Nothing,' said the doctor, shaking his head. 'No use ... too late.'

'The Chadfallow I know would never talk that way, while life remained in him,' said a voice from the passage.

It was Hercól, supporting himself with a hand on the doorframe. He lurched into sickbay, jaw clenched and eyes heavy, as though staving off the *blanë* through sheer force of will. 'What's left?' he said. 'No – don't answer. What is dangerous, ludicrously dangerous? What is against your ethics to try?'

At the sight of his old friend the doctor opened his eyes a little wider. He looked sceptically at the items before him, understanding Hercól's challenge, and appalled by it. He fumbled through the items, knocking several irritably aside. Suddenly he stopped, and looked at Pazel in wonder.

'A cocktail,' he said. 'A blary three-part heathen cocktail. Fulbreech! The key, my desk, the black bottle. Hurry, run!'

Fulbreech ran across the ward. The doctor, meanwhile, lifted a tiny, round metal box, with a painting of a blue dragon on the lid. 'Break the seal,' he said, passing it to Pazel. 'My hand shakes too much; I will spill it, and there is precious little.'

'What is it?' asked Hercól.

'Thundersnuff. A stimulant, putrid, exceptional. Part of a mad Quezan cocktail, they use it as punishment for sloth. If only I can remember the third ingredient. Something very common, it was ... cloves, or horseradish ... .'

Fulbreech returned with a bottle, black and unmarked. 'There's some mistake, sir, this is grebel.'

Grebel! Pazel nearly dropped the little box. It was the nightmare liquor, the madness drink. He'd had it forced on him as punishment, by certain sadistic men on other ships. Fear, panic, hallucinations – these were all he recalled of the experiences. Except—

'I didn't sleep,' he said. 'I didn't sleep for days! But that was just because of the fear, wasn't it?'

'Salt!' said the doctor, ignoring him and surging to his feet. 'The third ingredient is salt! I have gypsum salt, it will do, we can chew it – here!'

He snatched a leather pouch from the floor, ripped at the drawstring, and took a large pinch of gravel-like salt. Without preamble he gulped it, crunched it audibly in his teeth, and grabbed the bottle from Fulbreech. He favoured the grebel with a look of loathing and respect. Then he tilted the bottle and drank.

'Glah! Horrid! Quick!'

He gestured at the little box. Pazel unscrewed the lid, breaking the seal. Inside was a teaspoon's worth of fine red dust. The doctor bent until his nose was directly over the box. He covered one nostril and sniffed. Then he began to scream.

'OH DEVILS! OH GODS OF FLAMING DEATH!'

He straightened, spasmodically, as Pazel had seen men do when stunned by a Flikkerman. He gave an incoherent roar.

'It's working!' said Fulbreech.

Looks of terror and wild mirth chased themselves across the doctor's face. He reeled, clutching at the air. Grebel sloshed from the bottle in his hand.

Hercól caught the doctor's arms. 'Hold on man! It will pass!'

Chadfallow thrust the swordsman aside and bent over the table. He put his forehead down, moaning. In his grip the table began to vibrate. Then, shaking violently, he raised his head to look at them, and spoke through chattering teeth:

'Twice ... the ... grebel ... half ... the ... snuff.'

Those were his last coherent words. Fortunately they were the right ones. When the others had chewed the salt, swallowed the grebel and inhaled the tiniest whiff of thundersnuff, they felt weird and sick, but not deranged. Chadfallow for his part sat grinning, hugging himself, occasionally letting out a strangled scream.

'Well, we're awake,' said Thasha, twitching. 'But there's no more grebel – Chadfallow spilled half of it on the floor. We're not going to be able to give this treatment to *anyone*.'

'And a hundred monsters in the hold, waiting for their chance,' said Fulbreech.

'Or more,' said Hercól. 'And there is no way to know how much time we have gained. No matter – we shall fight the fight we are given. But be careful! You are not yourselves. Above all, beware your courage. It may be heightened beyond all reason, and lead swiftly to your death. Pazel, are you quite all right?'

'Yeah,' said Pazel, sniffing. 'Just hot. I feel like I'm standing next to a fire.'

'The grebel came around to you last,' said Hercól. 'I wonder if you had enough?'

'I left him half of what came to me,' said Fulbreech quickly.

'I'm all right,' Pazel insisted. 'But listen. We can't do this alone. It's blary impossible. We're going to need—'

'Prayer,' said a voice from the doorway, 'though what mongrel god might answer you I cannot guess.'

It was Arunis. Pazel, who had not seen him since Bramian, was shocked by the change in his appearance. He had lost all the round plumpness of Mr Ket. His face was pale, almost spectral, and a deathly light shone in his eyes. He gripped his cruel iron mace in one hand, and in the other the neck of a large and bulging sack. He looked amused at the sight of the doctor.

'The Imperial Surgeon,' he jeered. 'Prince of Arquali intellectuals. Whatever you have done to him is an improvement.'

To Pazel's surprise it was Fulbreech who spoke first. 'Get away, sorcerer! You don't deserve to breathe the same air as this man! And if you have any powers at all, use them to reverse what *you* did to the rats.'

'I?' laughed Arunis. 'You witless dog! I have done nothing to the rats! You humans left the Nilstone in a compartment overrun with fleas. You humans failed to notice an ixchel clan in your midst, or a woken rat possessed by holy lunacy. Yes, I work for your destruction as a race, noble cause that that is. But how little you force me to do! My only fear is that the *Chathrand*'s crew of savages will destroy itself, before it carries us to Gurishal.'

'A noble cause was laid before you, long ago,' said Hercól. 'But you chose another path, and have cleaved to it ever since. It has made you very strong, and very empty. Will you not abandon it, Arunis? There is still time to choose a new purpose – a higher purpose, beyond your poisoned dreams.'

'Spare me the sermon,' jeered Arunis. 'Delusion is not to my taste. Was ever a life more empty than your own, Hercól Stanapeth? Where has your higher purpose led? You could have been Ott's successor – the brain behind the Ametrine Throne. You could have been the most powerful man in your Empire. But instead you chose fantasy – a mist of promises and hopes. And so did the rest of you. Where is Ramachni? Where is your father, girl? A safer place than the *Chathrand*, that is where! And the crawlies! For months you denied their true nature. You couldn't admit that they were simply beasts, born rabid, ready to kill. You wanted them to be your tiny brothers. You wished to befriend them, or—' He looked at Hercól with disgust. '—to train them to perform . . . other services.'

Hercól moved before anyone could stop him. He vaulted over the table and flew at the sorcerer, his black sword raised to strike. Arunis took a step back, lifting his mace, and shouted a word in a strange, harsh language. There was a flash of white light, and Pazel felt himself hurled backwards, as by the slap of some giant's invisible fist. Thasha and Fulbreech were thrown as well. But Hercól did not falter; he only slowed his step, as though fighting upwind in a gale. Ildraquin glowed faintly in his hand, and he shouted a challenge in his native tongue.

Six feet from Arunis he slashed suddenly at the air. Now it was Arunis who felt an unseen blow. He stumbled backwards into the passage, amazed and furious. Once more he cried out in the harsh language. There was a second flash. Again Hercól swung at nothing; again the mage fell back. As the swordsman came at him a third time, Arunis hurled the mace with all his strength, and ran.

Hercól might have dodged the mace – but not without endangering those behind him. He caught it full on his shield, which cracked in two. With a snarl of pain he cast the two pieces to the ground. Then he groped for a wall. He was badly shaken.

'After him!' he gasped. 'He is about to commit some atrocity, I felt it as we fought! Do not let him get away!'

'You're hurt!' cried Thasha.

Hercól shook his head. 'Leave me with Fulbreech! Stop the sorcerer, girl.' With sudden decision he stood and thrust Ildraquin into her hand. 'Go!' he bellowed, pushing her out.

Thasha ran, and Pazel with her. They could hear the sorcerer's feet pounding across the deck. They entered the main compartment, and there he was, fifty yards ahead, running for the Silver Stair.

He was exhausted, they were gaining on him swiftly. As he reached the stair he looked back and saw Ildraquin in Thasha's hand, and fear shone in his eyes.

Pazel and Thasha gained the stair and hurled themselves down. Pazel could feel the grebel starting to work on his mind: that bad-dream feeling, the way dark and wriggling shapes clustered at the edge of his sight, only to vanish when he looked at them directly. He would have to warn Thasha. *You're not mad, it's the drink, it's the snuff, it's every blary thing but you.*

The berth deck passed in a whirl; then they heard Arunis exit onto the orlop. 'I know where he's going!' said Thasha. 'To the Nilstone! To the Nilstone and the Shaggat Ness!'

They reached the foot of the stair – and backed away in horror, not daring to breathe.

A swarm of giant rats was crossing the orlop, port to starboard, flowing around the foot of the Silver Stair. They were eerily quiet: no more screeching, though soft cries of "Kill!" still boiled from a few bloody mouths. Their stench was alarming: not only the rat-reek the youths had suffered for hours, but a new, oily, heady smell that made them cover their mouths, lest they cough.

As they flowed by within feet of the two humans, the rats suddenly raised their twisted, nasal voices and began to sing:

> Fearless the child of Rin proclaims:
> 'Death is the promise that breaks my chains.'
> Cold is the journey, but bright the glade
> Where believers rest in the Milk Tree's shade
> Faith on fire, blood on the sea,
> Rin's fair Angel, set me free.

Eighty or ninety of the monsters passed, staring straight ahead, as Pazel and Thasha watched without moving a muscle. When the last had scurried by the youths leaned back against the wall, gasping with relief.

'Arunis must have been *barely* ahead of them,' whispered Pazel.

'That chant,' said Thasha, 'it's a hymn. The same one we used to sing at the Lorg, except for that bit about blood. And Pazel – did you see an *ixchel* walking with them?'

Pazel started. 'No, I didn't. Listen, Thasha, don't trust your eyes. That grebel—'

'I know,' she said. 'It started back in sickbay. I saw my father standing behind Fulbreech, terribly angry, reaching for his neck. And then—'

She was overtaken by a yawn. *Aya Rin*, thought Pazel, *she's not going to last.* Thasha looked at him, frightened, furious, tightening her grip on Ildraquin. 'Let's go,' she said.

They stepped onto the orlop. They could hear the rats scurrying off to starboard, and a voice – Master Mugstur's voice – berating them about their souls. Pazel was glad to find the compartment door torn asunder: it let them pass through without a sound.

They had stepped into a small chamber, a granary for the ship's livestock. The grain bins had been smashed and plundered. By the far doorway stood a pool of blood.

'The next room's the manger, where Rose put the Shaggat,' said Thasha. 'Stay behind me, Pazel, and for Rin's sake don't try anything brave.'

At another time he might have made some retort. Now he only nodded. The grebel had turned the pool of blood into a black and steaming pit; he winced as Thasha walked through it, dispelling the illusion.

He followed her into the manger. Dead ahead they could see the stone form of the Shaggat, chained tight to the stanchion. Clenched in his fist was the Nilstone, darkness made visible, nothingness given form. Bodies lay around the mad Mzithrini king: Turach bodies, and rats. Square bales of hay lay in blood-darkened mounds. But there was no sign of Arunis.

Thasha smacked herself furiously on the head. 'Wrong again! This wasn't where he was going at all!'

'But it is where you are going to die, giants,' said a voice behind them.

They whirled: alone in the doorway, bare feet in the pool of blood, stood Steldak. He had never looked more vicious or depraved. His gaunt lips were stretched wide and grinning, and his pale eyes shone with glee. Before Pazel or Thasha could move, he turned and shouted:

'Come, Mugstur! I told you it was not Arunis! It is but two humans – the last, maybe, to have escaped our vengeance.'

A great screech went up behind him, and rats began to pour through the doorway. With a decisiveness that saved both their lives, Thasha grabbed Pazel by the arm and pulled him to the back of the chamber. They clawed their way up a stack of hay bales, then turned and raised their weapons. 'Strike first!' Thasha whispered to him. 'Every gods-damned time!'

The rats were on them in seconds. Pazel fought even more desperately than he had on the mainmast, driving Isiq's sword into one set of snapping jaws after another, struggling for balance on the shifting bales. As scores of rats converged on the youths, Mugstur himself waddled into the chamber. He was astonishingly swollen and ugly. His trans- formation in the liquor vault seemed to have closed the wound Hercól had given him, leaving only a purple scar on his bone-white chest. But something had changed: Mugstur, and indeed all the rats, had become slick and slimy, as if coated with some viscous substance. *Hallucination*, thought Pazel, as a rat prepared to spring.

He killed that one, and the next, by stabbing downwards with both hands on the sword hilt. There were four scrambling to take their place, however, and eight or ten attacking Thasha. And the creatures were still shoving through the door.

He had stabbed his fifth rat when Steldak let out a piercing cry. At almost the same time a voice shouted, 'Hold! Hold, beasts, or your master dies!'

Mugstur snarled, and his servants froze where they stood. Clinging to Mugstur's shoulder was Taliktrum. The ixchel twisted the rat's loose flesh with one hand, while the other reached around the hairless neck, to the base of his jaw. There he held a long knife, point upwards. One sharp thrust would bury it to the hilt in Mugstur's brain.

Four other ixchel – Dawn Soldiers, all – were racing up Mugstur's hairy sides to stand with their leader, weapons drawn. On the floor-boards, Steldak lay with an arrow in his chest.

'Surrender, vermin,' said Taliktrum.

Master Mugstur reared suddenly on his hind legs. He had been thrice an ixchel's size before his transformation; he was thirty times it now. But the five ixchel held fast, and Taliktrum remained poised for the kill.

Mugstur flexed his claws, one by one, a weirdly human gesture. Then he laughed, deep in his throat.

'Talag's son,' he said. 'You should have brought that peppermint oil. Now you see what comes of defying a servant of the Most High. Tell us, crawly: when did you fall in love with giants?'

'I did not come for *them*,' snapped Taliktrum. 'If they had been killed months ago my clan would still be safely hidden from the giants. It is *you* I am here for.'

'Yes,' said Mugstur, 'for me. But not in the way you imagine. You have come because Rin willed it, and his Angel's power has brought it to pass. You are here because you are part of my destiny.'

'Mad creature!' said Taliktrum. 'Aren't you ashamed to peddle that pap – that watery stew of giant beliefs? Order your rats back to their warren, or my knife will decide your destiny once and for all!'

'Bring him in, my children,' said Mugstur calmly.

Noises from the granary: then a new clutch of rats entered the chamber. Two of the creatures, walking on their hind legs, carried a wooden staff between them. An ixchel man was bound to that staff, head to toe. He was gagged, and nearly as wasted and filthy as Steldak had been when Pazel first saw him in Rose's cage. All the same his look was regal. His angular face and haughty eyes resembled Diadrelu's, and Taliktrum's own. His grey beard was a wild tangle.

Taliktrum gasped. 'Father!'

'It's Talag!' whispered Thasha. 'Sniraga didn't kill him! Oggosk lied to you, Pazel!'

'Your father has been our guest since Uturphe,' said Mugstur, 'The witch gave him to Steldak, in exchange for information. And Steldak wisely brought him to me.'

'Liar!' spat Taliktrum. 'No ixchel, not even mad Steldak, could betray one of his own in this way!'

'Steldak did not wish to,' Mugstur admitted. 'He was tempted by the worship of a false prophet: you, Taliktrum. But I had hope for him always. He was a visionary like me. Weaker, of course, but as his fear left him his visions grew clearer. They gave him the strength to kill Talag's sister, when the time was right. Above all he was committed to the death of the arch-heretic Rose. It is a pity you murdered him before he could stand in triumph on Rose's corpse. But my children will not weep for him. True servants of Rin's Angel fear no death.'

'Fear no death!' howled all the rats together, as though the words were a slogan.

'Notice the ropes at Talag's wrists and ankles,' said Mugstur. 'Harm me, little lord, and my children will tear him limb from limb before your eyes.'

Pazel put a warning hand on Thasha's arm. This was going to get ugly.

'It is not I who will surrender, it is you!' roared the white rat suddenly. 'Stand aside and let us finish our kill! We are here because Steldak heard the voice of the Angel. And the last humans standing, a dark boy and a fierce pale girl, were here awaiting us – a fitting sacrifice, at the end of ends. The other humans fell before we reached them, struck down by the Angel's wrath—'

'By *us*, you fool!' said Taliktrum.

But Mugstur was no longer listening. 'Our wait is over, children! The sky has turned to blood, and a great mouth has opened in the sea! Everything is clear at last! It is the promised hour! The Angel comes!'

'The Angel! The Angel!' shrieked the rats, twitching with ecstasy.

Talag clung helplessly to Mugstur's neck. His eyes swept about the room, as if searching for an exit he might have overlooked. On the wooden staff, his father desperately shook his head. Taliktrum caught his eye, and a look of shame swept over him.

'I can't obey, Father,' he said. 'I can't let you die. Withdraw, soldiers! Your next commands will come from Lord Talag. Release him, Mugstur, and take me instead.'

'No!' shouted Thasha suddenly. 'Do not move, any of you! I forbid it!'

Rats and ixchel alike looked up in shock. Pazel gaped as well: her voice was astonishingly changed. This was Thasha speaking, and at the same time it was not: just as a fiddle becomes something utterly new when passed from a novice to a master.

There was a strange, bright light in her eye. She lowered Ildraquin until it pointed at Mugstur's heart. 'You read the signs correctly,' she said, confident and commanding. 'All but the last one, that is. Your wait *is* over. I have come.'

Such a cacophany of squeals and howls and perplexed roars followed that not even Mugstur could make himself heard. Some of the rats had dropped on their bellies, cowering. Pazel was frightened half to death. What was happening to her? Where could she take this bluff?

'Back!' Thasha shouted with a sweep of Hercól's sword. The rats who had been attacking her and Pazel leaped away. Then in one bound Thasha jumped to the floor, landing just beside the Shaggat Ness.

Mugstur dropped to all fours and backed away. His eyes shone with doubt and wonder. 'You ... *you* are the Angel? The Blessed One, the spirit who woke me, when I was a common rat?'

By way of an answer, Thasha spread her arms wide, and in that strange, powerful voice, began to sing:

> *I come as a shadow o'er the sea*
> *Swift and certain, my decree:*
> *None who would with Rin abide*
> *May from his chosen servant hide.*
> *Neither from his justice cower:*
> *For in that final earthly hour,*
> *Earth and ocean are as glass;*
> *Through them my burning gaze shall pass*
> *And scour all beasts from haunt or lair,*
> *Their souls to free upon the air.*

It was a liturgy of the Rinfaith — Pazel had heard bits of it before, chanted by devout sailors or travelling monks. But in Thasha's voice the words were frightful. Mugstur crouched low, tucking his tail and holding his head with his paws. Taliktrum and his warriors still clung to him, too shocked to do anything but watch.

'Angel,' whimpered Mugstur. 'How can I know you? How can I be sure?'

'If you do not know me, then you were never my true servant,' said Thasha.

'That girl . . . she was *always* aboard!' squeaked one of the rats. 'She's Thasha Isiq, the Treaty Bride!'

Thasha looked at the deformed rats. She was in a trance, Pazel thought. Then — before he could do more than scream a despairing *No!* — she reached out and touched the Nilstone, between the dead stone fingers of the Shaggat Ness.

Pazel thought he was seeing her die. Something like that withering flame that had consumed the Shaggat's hand raced from the Nilstone down Thasha's arm. But it did not kill her. It swept over her body like a cold flame. All colour went out of the room, but Thasha's skin took on an unearthly glow. The black radiance of the Nilstone flowed through her fingers, brighter and brighter.

'Do you believe?' Thasha demanded.

'We believe, great Angel,' said Mugstur, squirming and grovelling at her feet.

'We believe you! We believe!' squealed the rats.

Thasha frowned. 'I do not trust in words. We shall see if you stand ready to prove your faith in deeds.'

With that she wrenched her hand away from the Nilstone. She cringed, cradling the hand, as a peal of thunder rolled through the ship. Pazel slid from the hay bales and caught her before she could fall. Then the room was still.

Mugstur leaped to his feet.

'Yes!' he cried. 'I am ready! We are all ready! It is time for deeds! We will show you, Mistress of Heaven! After me, rats, the hour is come!'

He turned and flew from the chamber. Their foes forgotten, the other rats pursued him. Their cries were taken up by the horde in the outer compartment: 'The hour is come! The hour is come!'

Thasha put her arms over Pazel's shoulders. 'Well,' she said, leaning into him.

It was her old voice; he could have wept with relief. He looked her over, head to foot. She had touched the Nilstone; she should have been dead. And yet she was not even visibly wounded, although he was rather sure she would collapse if he released her. 'What ... what did you do?' he whispered.

Thasha looked up at the Nilstone in the Shaggat's hand. 'It was nothing I'd planned, believe me. I just thought it was the only chance we had.'

Beside them, Lord Talag (dropped by the rats in their haste) began to moan and twist with great urgency. Taliktrum bent and slashed at his father's bonds.

Pazel looked out through the doorway. 'Where in Pitfire did they go? What did you tell them?'

'Nothing!' Thasha protested. 'I just said *obey me*, didn't you hear? I don't know what command they think they're obeying.'

Talag retched and shouted, tearing at his gag. Taliktrum wept openly as he cut him free. 'You lived,' he managed to say. 'The rat taunted me, said he had something I wanted more than life itself. I never dreamed it could be you.'

The gag parted, and Talag spat it out. He made a raw and painful sound.

'Don't try to speak too soon, m'lord,' said one of the Dawn Soldiers.

Talag shoved him away. He bolted upright, even though his legs were still tied to the staff. 'The rats!' he croaked, his voice a husk. 'They go to die! Stop them, girl, stop them! Bring them back!'

'Father, you're ill!' cried Taliktrum. 'They're our enemies, even though they kept you alive!'

'Ill, am I?' snapped Talag. He drew his hand roughly over Taliktrum's chest, then rubbed his thumb and finger together. 'Lamp oil, you fool! Every rat aboard has *bathed* in it! They're killing themselves! They're going to *free their souls upon the air!* They're going to heaven on a plume of smoke!'

The horror of what he was saying struck Pazel like a club. Thasha gasped and sprinted from the room. Pazel chased after her, amazed that she had found yet another reserve of strength. 'Mugstur!' she shouted. 'Stop! I command you!'

But the power had left her voice, and the rats were far away. As they neared the Silver Stair Pazel realised he did not even know if they had run up or down. They skidded to a halt, listening.

'They're beneath us!' said Pazel, starting to plunge downwards. But Thasha caught his arm, and he listened again.

He cursed. '*And* above us! Mugstur could have gone either way, and— Oh, *damn it all*! Look!'

Three hundred feet away cross the central compartment, flames leaped suddenly in the gloom. They were rats, burning like living torches, and they were running this way and that, biting one another, setting each other alight. Those not yet on fire screamed at those that were: 'This way! Bless me, cleanse me, brother!' Then twenty or more rat voices rose in song:

> *Faith on fire, smoke on high,*
> *Rin's first Angel, see me die.*
> *Rise in ash to heaven's nest,*
> *Rin's Rat-Angel, love me best!*

Pazel would have found it hard to imagine things getting much worse. But they did, considerably. Thasha was still holding his arm, and when he looked at her he saw tears of frustrated rage.

'No good,' she said, nearly sobbing. 'I'm no good, I wreck everything, you're about to die, do you love me?'

'What?'

Thasha fell asleep in his arms.

He shed her father's sword, and thrust Ildraquin through his belt in its place. He caught her under the arms. What could he do, and what did it matter, now? It didn't, he thought. The fog was in his brain again; he felt stupid and slow. But he would not abandon her. He would not let her burn among the rats.

The first climb was easy. He kept her body high, and bore much of her weight against his chest. But after the berth deck he slipped in blood or oil, and fell painfully, and when he lifted her again she felt heavier, somehow. At the lower gun deck he had to put her down and clear dead rats from the ladderway. The upper gun deck was bright with flames.

When he emerged into the open air the scene was infernal. The sky throbbed red in the south; lightning crackled over the still-closer Vortex. At least fifty rats had clearly made straight for the topdeck, and set themselves aflame when they reached it. Many had not stopped there, but had pulled themselves burning up the masts and shrouds.

The tarred rigging snatched at the flame; already the mizzen topsail was alight.

Hallucination? thought Pazel hopefully. Then he gave a sobbing laugh. The stench of burned fur, the wafting heat, the swollen, blazing animals leaping crazed from the yardarms: it was all too abominably real. And so was *blanë*. He stumbled, rose with effort, dragged Thasha a few more yards. Then he sat down and propped her head on his lap, brushed her dirty hair from her eyes, and kissed her the way he'd wanted to for so long.

This is where it ends, Thasha.

The flame was widespread, fore and aft. Somewhere ixchel were shouting, cursing, muttering their ambiguous prayers. He thought, *My mind is the ship. Three hundred cabins full of smoke, full of fog. Nothing stirring much longer. No more fighting to be done.*

A rat lumbered towards them in flames, shrieking. Pazel watched it, too sleepy even to move his hand to Ildraquin. The creature stopped a few yards from their feet and bowed its head, and Pazel realised he was looking at Master Mugstur. The white rat settled on to his thick stomach and lay burning like a hideous beacon in the wind. Most of the others were already dead.

Pazel bent and kissed her once more. He closed his eyes, shutting out the world, shutting out everything but Thasha's lips, her gentle breathing. They should have done more of this. What exactly had they been waiting for?

The fog crept into the last chamber of his brain. He rested his forehead on her shoulder, and was still.

And then he raised his head, mouth agape, and blinked at the raging fire. And very much as a question he spoke the Master-Word.

39

Cold Comfort

—⟨◦⟩—

He stood alone on a blackened ship, among the sleeping and the slain. Ashes, stone cold, were blowing from tattered sails that a moment ago had been sheets of fire. The *Chathrand* pitched and wallowed on the swells, revolving, perhaps accelerating. He looked for Thasha but could not find her. The deep thunder of the Vortex was the only sound.

He staggered to portside, gazing at the Red Storm, so close now that he could make out the texture of the light within it. Somehow it was both gaseous and glass-sharp, cloud and broken mirror at once. He wondered what it would do to them, if they reached it at all.

Portside was east when he started walking, but with the spin of the ship it was west before he arrived. He turned on his heel and ran in the opposite direction, and was quick enough this time to glimpse the Vortex, hideously close, a malevolent hole too big to contemplate, inhaling everything. It was a flaw the size of Rukmast, an obscene violation of the shape of the sea.

Not out of the saucepot yet.

An ixchel raced across the quarterdeck. Pazel raised a hand in greeting, but he might as well have been a shred of flapping sailcloth for all the notice the runner took. The ash coated the deck like dirty snow. He came to where Fiffengurt lay sleeping, bent and wiped his face, and shook him gently.

'Wake up.'

Fiffengurt slept on. Ten yards or so from the quartermaster a boy he didn't recognise lay in a strange, half-seated position, bending over another figure, who looked in danger of being smothered. Pazel crossed the deck and pulled the boy upright by the shirt.

Oh.

He jerked his hand away. The boy fell back on the deck, and it was him, it was Pazel himself. Asleep like everyone else on the deck. He lay with Thasha's head in his lap, just where he'd spoken the Master-Word.

He felt a slight tingling at his shoulder, and realised that he had sensed his own touch. And yes, even as he stood here, he was dimly aware of the weight of Thasha's head upon his thigh.

He thought a walk might do him good, and descended the Silver Stair to the upper gun deck. The smells were hideous. Scorched blood and snuffed-out rat. He gagged and ducked into the stateroom.

Neeps lay where Hercól had left him, on the rug between Jorl and Suzyt. All three were snoring. There was not a trace of fire damage. Pazel felt a startling affection for the familiar chamber, where no enemy had entered yet. It was becoming home.

He continued his descent. Berth deck, orlop, mercy. There he spotted at least fifty ixchel, running towards the tonnage hatch, dragging a pair of wheelblocks and a long rope. He shouted again, but by now he didn't expect a reply.

His wandering took him at length to the brig. The outer door had been shattered by the rats, but inside he found the cells intact. A few of the iron bars had been bloodied and slightly bent, but none had given way. In the first cell Captain Magritte lay sleeping. Pazel hoped he had been one of the first affected. It didn't bear thinking about what the man had had to go through while still awake.

The next cell had a small panel missing from the ceiling, and a hole letting into some dim cabin on the orlop above. Hercól's escape route. He had used it in time to save Thasha's life, perhaps Pazel's as well. But it hadn't let him save the woman he loved.

Pazel looked into the third cell, and gave a shout of startled joy. 'Felthrup!'

There he lay: enormous, mutated, asleep. Pazel could not reach him, nor open the bars. Felthrup had drunk some of Hercól's water, he remembered. What would become of him when he woke? Was he as mad as the other rats?

When the smell became too much for him, Pazel dragged himself back to the topdeck. Frightened but powerless with fascination, he returned to the spot where he and Thasha lay sleeping. What was stranger – the sight of his own body, or the fact that he was accepting it, that he was able to contemplate it as something apart from himself, and not go mad? He *wasn't* going mad, was he?

'No, Pazel,' said a voice behind him. 'You're merely learning. Though at times the process feels like insanity, true enough.'

Pazel knew that voice. And now astonishment was a good thing, a joyful thing, and he held still a moment to savour it. 'Ramachni,' he said aloud, 'you have no idea how much I've missed you.'

He turned: the black mink was standing a few yards away, beside the sleeping Fiffengurt. The mage was even smaller than Pazel remembered, a fragile animal he might have lifted with one hand. He looked at Pazel with the deliberate stillness of a monk. Pazel walked up to him and knelt down.

'I'm not mad, and I'm not dead either. I can tell that much.'

Ramachni showed his teeth, which was how he smiled.

'Are you really back?' asked Pazel. 'Back to stay?'

'No,' said Ramachni. 'In fact you could say that I'm cheating. When I taught you the Master-Words – and how well you choose the moments of their use, lad, my compliments – I gained the power to know precisely when you speak them, and to observe you in the aftermath. Observe you: no more. But because you were literally falling asleep as you spoke, I was able to turn that observation into a travel opportunity, and to meet you here in dream. Even better, you are not bound like Felthrup by any dream-erasing spell. You should have no trouble remembering this chat.'

'Who put that spell on Felthrup? Arunis?'

Ramachni nodded. 'He attacked and tortured our friend in his sleep, for months. I put a stop to that, but I cannot remove the forgetting charm until I return in the flesh.'

'Flesh!' said Pazel, his voice suddenly altered, charged with disgust. He gave an involuntary flinch. 'I've just remembered something. I almost fell asleep on this deck, Ramachni, but I woke up when I thought of the Master-Word. And when I spoke it I saw something in the sky. It was like a black cloud, but thicker, almost solid. And it was quivering, like . . . meat, like horrible living flesh. It was the ugliest thing I've ever seen.'

Ramachni gave him a long, silent stare – a frightened stare, Pazel would have said, if such were possible for the mage. At last Ramachni drew a deep breath, and said, 'You have seen the *Agoroth Asru*, the Swarm of Night. I am sorry you had to look on it. At least your glimpse was brief.'

'What is this Swarm?' Pazel asked. 'Arunis was shouting about it on Dhola's Rib. I'd never heard of it before.'

'With any luck you never shall again. The Swarm of Night is not only the ugliest thing you will ever see, but almost certainly the most destructive. We call it a swarm because it can resemble a thick cloud of insects, and because once inside it a living creature suffers pain like ten thousand stings. It does not belong in this world but in the dark regions: the land of death and neighbouring kingdoms.'

'Then why did I see it? What was it doing here?'

'It is not in this world, Pazel – not yet. If it were I should sense it beyond any doubt. Yet the Swarm does threaten Alifros, and has done so for centuries. Every day it comes closer to breaking through, and there are those like Arunis who would hasten its arrival. I think you saw it just outside this world and pressing in, like a beast pressing its muzzle through a door we must hold shut. It was your use of the Master-Word that unlocked the door. As I told you once, such words strain the very spell-fabric of creation.'

'I don't understand,' said Pazel. 'When I spoke the first word the sun went dark for a moment. This time I saw ... *that*. But why? You and Arunis cast spells that are much bigger than putting out a fire, and the world doesn't go mad.'

'Why do you think they exhaust us so, Pazel? Only a small part of a spell's energy goes to creating the effect we wish, the fire bolt or levitation or wind where there is none. The rest goes into containing the damage that would otherwise occur. That is what makes a spell a *spell*. If magic is gunpowder, then a spell is the solid cannon that directs the explosion where we need it, and shields us from the blast. A Master-Word, on the other hand, is like a gigantic powder-charge loaded into a small cannon, and fired by someone who has never so much as struck a match.'

'This time it appears that a strand of the world's spell-weave actually gave way. Have no fear; it is a small wound in a healthy body, and will repair itself. But I am glad that you won't be speaking your last word for a while.'

'Especially since I have no idea what it does,' said Pazel. 'A word that "blinds to give new sight"? What does that mean? I'm no closer to guessing than I was the day I learned it.'

Ramachni looked at him strangely again. Was that pity in his eyes?

'There will be no guessing, if we ever reach that point,' said Ramachni. 'Which is not to say that your decision will be easy. The first two words tested your courage. Not that I had any wish to test you. I do not play such games. But in fact you had to be strong enough not to waste them, by using them too soon. The last word, I think, will require courage just to speak at all.'

'Wonderful,' said Pazel. 'Is that what you came here to tell me?'

'No,' said Ramachni. 'In fact I didn't come to tell you a thing. I came because you made it possible, and above all I came to listen. So tell me, how goes the fight? Where are the Nilstone, and Arunis? Above all, how are our friends?'

Pazel's look was incredulous. 'You don't know?'

'Pazel, you are asleep on a ship in the heart of the Nelluroq. I am asleep in a distant land, in a healing pool under a vertical mile of stone. I can see you, and a bubble of light around you the size of a woodshed, but all the rest is darkness. We are both dreaming – only when a mage shares your dream, things become possible that otherwise would not be. Choice, for instance. I hope you will choose to bring me up to date.'

Pazel looked in the direction of the Vortex. 'Is time passing?'

'Always,' said Ramachni.

He would have to be quick about it, then. But where to start? With the worst, with the part that was still misery to think of. 'Diadrelu,' he said, 'was murdered by her clan.'

Ramachni closed his eyes, letting his head sink down upon his forepaws. 'Go on,' he said.

Once Pazel began to talk it was a relief. But as he skimmed over all that had happened since Ramachni's departure he felt a growing shame. What had they managed to do, after all, besides harass the conspirators, and fight Arunis to a draw? For all the effect they'd had on the voyage they might as well have spent the past months locked up with the steerage passengers.

Ramachni shook his head. 'Things are not as dark as you believe,' he said. But his voice was low and sad.

'I'm not a fool, Ramachni,' said Pazel tightly. 'I can see how dark things are. We had a task. The Red Wolf chose seven of us to get rid of the Nilstone. You yourself said that we'd all have something vital to do, something *essential*. Didn't you?'

'Yes,' said Ramachni.

'Well Dri was one of the seven, and she's gone. That means we're failing. Why don't you tell me the blary *truth*.' Pazel rose and paced a few steps away, shaking with frustration. The low roar of the Vortex throbbed in his ears. Suddenly he stopped dead. He took a deep breath, and spoke without turning.

'I'm sorry. I can't believe I said that. I know we mustn't fail.'

'You already have,' said Ramachni.

Pazel whirled around. Ramachni was standing as still as before, watching him with those black eyes that always made him think of bottomless pits – yet never of cruelty, until this moment.

'Are you laughing at me?' said Pazel.

'No,' said the mage, 'I am telling the truth, as you demanded. And the truth is that I don't see how you can do as Erithusmé hoped you would, when she built the Red Wolf. One of the seven has died, and yes, all seven had something vital to do. I cannot tell you what, for I don't know myself: the plan was hers, not mine. But now I think it very likely that Arunis will succeed in finding a way to use the Nilstone. If he does, he will set fire to this garden called Alifros, and there will be no Master-Word mighty enough to put that fire out.'

'But we were chosen—'

'You were chosen because you had the best *chance* of success. A chance is not a destiny, Pazel. The latter was always in your hands, and yours alone.'

Pazel couldn't believe his ears. If there was one being he never thought would admit defeat, it was Ramachni. He felt abandoned, and at the same time he felt that he had let everyone down. *Everyone.* His mother and father. Old Captain Nestef, the first Arquali sailor who believed in him. The tarboy Reyast, who had died helping them uncover the conspiracy. Diadrelu. Thasha and Neeps and Hercól and Fiffengurt. Even Fiffengurt's child. He felt, irrationally, that he had betrayed them all.

It took him a moment to find his voice; when he did, it sounded lifeless and small. 'Fine, then. We've failed. You're the wise one, Ramachni. What do you propose we do?'

'At the moment I see but two options,' said the mage. 'You can take a running leap from the rail of the *Chathrand*. Or you can fight on, although that may require you to live with failure—'

'Or die with it,' said Pazel.

'—or to redefine success to fit your circumstances.'

'What does that mean? Do you think we stand a chance, or not?'

'Of course you stand a chance,' said the mage. 'Pazel, the world is not a music box, built to grind out the same song for ever. A man with your Gift ought to know that *any* song may spring from this world – and any future. If Erithusmé's plan for the Nilstone is thwarted, why, seek another way. And now I must give you a message for Arunis.'

'But I told you,' said Pazel, 'he disappeared. I'm hoping the rats ate him, personally.'

'Arunis is alive and on this ship. That much I can sense even at the distance of a dream. When he emerges from hiding, you can be sure that it will not be to talk. But I would suggest you do not wait – find him, pry him out of his den. And if you do speak to him before I have the pleasure, tell him that the bear was nothing. Can you remember that?'

'"The bear was nothing,"' said Pazel, dumbfounded.

Ramachni nodded. Suddenly he shook himself, head to tail, a movement of satisfaction and eagerness. 'My strength comes back to me,' he said. 'When you see me next you will not be dreaming. Then you shall learn what it is to have a wizard fight at your side. Unless of course you decide to take that leap.'

'Now you *are* laughing.'

'A bit, lad. But don't be angry, for I love you like a son. And that is a blessing for an ancient creature like myself, who never had children, and whose first family is so many centuries dead that even he begins to forget them. Remember: I will come when things are dark – terribly dark, darker than you thought to see.'

'Can't you tell me what that *means*?' begged Pazel.

'If I knew, don't you think I would say so? I am a prisoner to these riddles every bit as much as you, although I hear them from another source. But here in the wake of riddles is a fact: I am proud of you all. Fiercely proud, of your goodness and your strength. And now, Pazel, it is time for us both to *WAKE UP*.'

His last words exploded like a cannon shot, and with them he disappeared. Pazel had no sense of falling, but he was suddenly flat on the deck again. Thasha stirred beside him, filthy with ash and grime, and from all around them came the groans and exclamations of waking men.

40

In the Mouth of a Demon

~~~

16 (?) Ilbrin 941

The Honourable Captain Theimat Rose
Northbeck Abbey, Mereldín Isle, South Quezans

Dear Sir,

    Never were there stranger circumstances for a letter. I do not know whether to address you with pride or shame, so rather than either I shall begin with a warning: you must henceforth assume that the Lady Oggosk will read every letter you send me. She has not changed a wire hair from the days when she used to waddle into your house without wiping her shoes. She is a vulgar, conniving, calculating hag. And yet — grudgingly, and at great cost — she does perform the services of a nautical witch. I tolerate her because I cannot replace her.

    Have I failed, or triumphed? The duchess and I are prisoners of a clan of ixchel, along with our sailmaster, the Turach commander, and eleven other persons. I confess I do not know what to make of events; the disasters are so many and varied. Perhaps the worst of them all is a man by the name of Uskins. But I am getting ahead of myself.

    The Chathrand, *it appears, has been infested since Etherhorde. The crawlies have taken absolute control; they walk the decks openly, to the revulsion of the crew (except for Pathkendle and his cohorts, who knew of their presence and did nothing). Their tactics are exceedingly cunning. Besides the aforementioned prisoners they have taken Dr Chadfallow, the Plapp and Burnscove gang leaders, Sandor Ott, the stowaway girl Marila (the ship lice mistrust even their sympathizers, apparently), the tarboy brothers Swift and Saroo, two additional Turachs, and, for good measure, the thing that calls itself Belesar Bolutu. We are crammed into the anteroom of the forecastle house, that outer cabin by which one enters Oggosk's hovel, the smithy, and the henhouse.*

Our captor appears to be a young crawly messiah; he goes about in a suit of feathers, and a brooding funk, now gloating, now fearful and suspicious. A deranged but nubile crawly girl attends this figure, and chides and bullies the others into acts of devotion. Simulated acts, in many cases. They do not all beam at him with the fawning love of his pretty acolytes, or his shaved-headed guards. His father is apparently somewhere aboard, and ruled before him, but is unwilling or unable to take up the mantle again.

The doors are not locked, but we are prisoners all the same. When we woke from the drugged sleep we found ourselves alone in the forecastle house. There were rope burns on our ankles, for we had been hoisted like so many slaughtered steers. How much time had passed I do not know: many hours, to be sure, for even with wheelblocks and six hundred crawlies it is no small feat to move a man. Our weapons were gone. In a corner of the room a little fire pot was burning, filling the room with a rather agreeable, sagebrush scent. We could hear the Vortex, like the gods' own millstone, ready to grind us down to flour. From the single window I could see the clouds forming spiral-patterns above it, and the Red Storm filling half the sky.

A scrap of parchment was nailed to the topdeck door. It was a 'cordial notice,' explaining that anyone who left the cabin would die. It was signed by this selfsame messiah, whose name is absurdly unpronounceable. Below his name ran the words COMMANDER OF THE EX-IMPERIAL SHIP CHATHRAND AND HER LIBERATED CREW.

At this provocation I flung open the door, and seeing only my own startled men on the topdeck, going about the business of hacking the burned rigging down from the masts, I stormed out, shouting for Uskins. But no sound escaped my lips. I collapsed in agony, my lungs simply aflame. Nearly senseless, I dragged myself back into the forecastle house, and felt relief at my first breath of the scented air. Only the fresh breeze through the door brought back the pain; naturally I slammed it fast.

The crawly lordling soon made his appearance, through a clever bolt-hole they have carved into the ceiling, directly above the little fire. 'Ixchel keep their promises, Captain — Mr Rose,' he said. 'If we say that this or that action means death, it means death.'

The girl Marila startled us by shouting at him. 'You double-crosser! I want to see Neeps, or Pazel or Thasha. And what have you done with

539

*your aunt? Let me speak to her!' When they told Marila that the 'aunt'
she wanted had been executed, the girl wept, as though they were
speaking of a member of her own family.*

*The lordling went on to describe the trap we were caught in, with
such swaggering pride that I felt at once he was claiming another's
invention as his own. The mechanism is diabolical. If the little fire goes
out, we die. If our lungs are deprived of the vapour for even a minute,
we die. In our drugged sleep we were all made addicts, simply by
breathing the stuff for a few hours. Most staggering of all, this poison
was created (they allege) by none other than the Secret Fist, by crossing
the deathsmoke vine with a kind of desert nightshade. But unlike
deathsmoke, the poison does not weaken and wither the body, in fact it
does no harm at all until one is deprived of it. At which point it kills
faster than any rattlesnake.*

*The smoke is produced by burning the dry berries of this plant,
together with some coal to keep the fire going. The crawlies bring only
a few berries at a time, hidden in their pockets, and none of my crew
has had the slightest luck in determining where on the ship they keep
them. If we are rowdy, or the crew disobedient, they simply withhold
the berries, and we are soon screaming. But their craftiness goes even
further. They possess a little pill that, if dissolved on the tongue, effects
an immediate and total cure. This they demonstrated on the tarboy
Swift: just hours after we awoke, a crawly presented him with the pill
and told him he might go. He now walks the ship a free lad, although
his brother Saroo remains with us. In this way the crawlies buy our
submission, as much by hope as by punishment. And of course by their
choice of hostages, they have put the whole ship into a state of fear.
Everyone counts at least someone among us as too important to lose.*

*Little Lord Unpronounceable has issued no orders, yet. Kruno
Burnscove has concluded that they wish us no mortal harm: he rivals
Uskins in idiocy, and that is an achievement. One only need consider the
shifty cleverness of the trap to realise that they planned this assault years
ago. Besides, I know crawlies. How could I not, being your son?* Like
Ott, they have patience. And like Ott, or a wolverine for that matter, once
they sink their teeth into something they simply do not let go.*

---

* Receipts signed by Captain Theimat Rose indicate that he purchased ixchel for use as
poison-tasters, letter readers, and small-item (watch, compass, eyeglasses) repairmen.
To judge by the frequency of purchases, the average life expectancy for an ixchel in the
Rose household was two years. – EDITOR.

The crawly messiah does not pretend to understand the mechanics of the ship. And yet he forbids me to issue orders to the crew. The hour-by-hour decisions, therefore, have fallen to Uskins, and in this emergency the man has proven himself an irredeemable fool.

Fate [illegible] *our family* [illegible]*

By rights we should have perished shortly after waking – not by crawly poison, but in the Vortex. We were already in its grip before they drugged us, in fact. Just before the nightmare with the rats, I had to leave the topdeck for a time, in order to crush Pathkendle's mutiny. It was while I was below that Elkstem issued the warning: we had entered the whirlpool's outer spiral. I left Uskins in command (he shall never again command so much as a garbage scow), having reviewed with him exactly how one escapes such a predicament. The buffoon assured me he understood, and at the time he appeared to. But his mental frailty has worsened. I trusted him to keep watch on Arunis, and something about the task has left him distracted and easily confused, and afraid of his own shadow.

I hardly need tell you, sir, that an aggressive tack away from the eye of a whirlpool must fail, unless the wind is fierce and perfectly abeam (it was neither). But that is exactly what Uskins called for. The result was disaster: at each change of tack, the line of the ship fell hard athwart the centrifuge of the Vortex. This rolled us nearly onto our beam-ends, and built up such a force that we slingshotted _deeper_ into the spiral as we completed the turn.

The first failure was difficult to prove: we were still too far from the heart of the Vortex to be sure just how quickly we were sliding into it. But Uskins repeated the order twice, trying to make the tack sharper, and failing more spectacularly each time. All the while Elkstem and Alyash begged him to desist, and repeated the sane alternative: to run _with_ the spiral, using its strength and any cooperative wind to help the ship cut slowly, steadily outwards. Had we done that within the first few hours of Elkstem's warning, all would have been well. Uskins, however, brought us at least five miles closer to the eye.

After the third failed tack Elkstem was contemplating a mutiny of his own. But at that point the giant rats began their siege. Elkstem remained at the wheel throughout the fighting, but he could not find enough men with their wits about them to brace the mains. Working two

---

* Nearly illegible, rather. After hours of scrutiny I believe the line read: 'Fate nearly reunited our family in the depths.' Or possibly, ' . . . in death.' – EDITOR.

topsails alone, he and some thirty stout lads kept us from sliding any deeper into the Vortex, but they could not break free. And then the crawly sleeping-poison felled us, and we became a cork adrift.

By the time I awoke, imprisoned, matters had gone from bad to critical. It was midmorning. We were caught now in the lungs as well as the arms of the Vortex: the wind was cycloning towards the eye, six miles off. There were stormclouds; from the chamber's single window I saw a grey sheet of rain bend away from us as it descended, and twist into a miles-long whipcord that vanished into the maw. The port side of every object was taking on a scarlet glow. The Red Storm, whatever it was, looked set to overtake us as surely as the Vortex itself. Do you remember that mad dog on Mereldín, that ran in circles continually, all over the island, until one circle took him over a cliff? That was how we moved: around and around the Vortex, even as the Vortex itself drifted towards the storm. Which would claim us first? There was simply no way to know.

From the window I looked on as the crew struggled to replace the burned rigging, without dropping a mast into the Nelluroq, or being swept away themselves. In Etherhorde the shipwrights would take a month for such a job, in a calm port, with scaffolding and cranes. The men were trying to do it in mere hours, after bloody mayhem, at thirty knots and growing.

I will say this for Fiffengurt: the man has strength. Six hours I'd kept him tied and hooded. Then came the battle with the rats, the crawlies' poison – and immediately thereafter, the battle to save a ship without sails or rigging from the greatest calamity in all the seas. He marched first to Uskins, a broken-off Turach spear in his hand, and set the point against his chest.

'Your badges or your blood, Stukey. I'll give you five seconds to decide.' Uskins saw he meant it, and took the gold bars from his uniform. Fiffengurt took his hat too, lest there be any confusion, and sent him away to work the pumps.

The quartermaster himself summarily took charge, assigning a team to each mast, with orders to give a test-haul to every line that remained. 'If you don't like the feel of it, cut it down! Don't wait for my say-so! We can afford the rope, but not another bad tack! And no scrap over the sides, boys – toss it from the stern! If we foul the rudder we can all start singing Bakru's lullaby.'

The Chathrand was running smooth now – but only because the Vortex had churned the waves down to a swirling cream. The ship was

*settling into a glide, listing ten or fifteen degrees to port, and though
I could not see the Vortex from the window, I noted how men tried not
to look in that direction, and what came over their features when they
did. Never did a crew attack a rig so quickly, or so well. But with every
minute that passed they had to cling tighter to the ropes and rails — not
against the angle of the ship, but against the surging, screaming wind.
It had grown prodigiously in the last quarter-hour. Rain from farther
off was cracking against the deck like drumsticks. The seal on the tonnage
hatch was flapping loose. The lifeboats danced airborne in their chains.*

    *The noise, Father. No storm you or I ever braved had a tenth the
voice of that gods' monstrosity of noise. In the forecastle house, the wind
blasting under the door and through a dozen cracks and crevices began
to disperse the vapour; we felt stabbed in the chest, and plugged the gaps
with shirts and rags and straw from the henhouse. We crowded around
the little fire-pot to shield it with our bodies. Some prayed; Sandor Ott
sat brooding apart; Lady Oggosk chanted the Prayer of Last Parting,
which I have not heard her speak since I was a boy on Littlecatch, that
time we feared you and mother had died. Chadfallow folded his hands
before his face, like one preparing to accept the worst. 'Men are still
bleeding out there, still dying,' he said helplessly to Marila. Then he
added: 'My family is out there. Why am I always kept apart?'*

    *When I could stand it no longer, I gulped a chestful of poison, held
my breath, and stepped out through the door again, slamming it fast
behind me. The wind like a mule kick, the spray like a whetted lash.
I climbed the forecastle ladder, half blinded by the glow of the Red
Storm, and turned at the top rung to look at the abyss.*

    *There was no hope, none at all. I was gazing into the mouth of a
demon, and the mouth was a mile wide and deep as thought. Were I not
your son I should have released my breath then and there. But I would
not be swept from the ship, I would perish aboard her as befits her
captain. I struggled back to the forecastle house.*

    *Faint screams above the cacophony: I raised my eyes to the window
and saw two men at topgallant-height, clinging to a forestay. The rope
was straining towards the Vortex, and when it snapped an instant later
the men did not so much fall as fly, like two weird, ungainly birds, grey
on one side and glowing red on the other.*

    *'Well, Ott,' I said, catching the spymaster's eye, 'you can keep the
bonus pay we discussed. But then a third of Magad's treasury's going
into that damned hole, along with the Nilstone and the Shaggat and
the lot of us.'*

'Is that all you wish to say, at the end of a life?' said Ott, smiling acidly.

I shook my head. 'One thing more. I piss on your Emperor.'

He uncrossed his legs and stood, and would have done something painful to me had I not placed my hand on the doorknob. For once I had a way to kill faster than Ott, and more democratically.

Then, to my astonishment, the door was wrenched open from the outside, and who should fly in under my hand but Neeps Undrabust. We all reeled from the burst of fresh air, and I, closest to the door, nearly collapsed with the pain. When I recovered I saw Undrabust struggling with the stowaway girl. He was trying to embrace her; she was striking and shoving him back towards the door. 'What are you doing!' she shrieked. 'Get out of here! Don't breathe! You'll be trapped like the rest of us!'

There came a thump at the door – but this time I held the knob fast. Pathkendle and Thasha Isiq were out there, shouting much the same thing as Marila. But Undrabust stood his ground, trying to calm and hold her, telling her he had nowhere else to be. 'Stop it, Marila. There's just minutes left, you hear me? Keep still. You don't have to fight any more.'

I pressed my face to the window, and saw a gruesome sight: the watery horizon was higher than the rail. We were below the rim, descending, speeding up. We had entered the demon's mouth. Pathkendle and the girl were the only figures anywhere close to the forecastle. They must have been pursuing Undrabust, guessing what he meant to do. The lad was right, of course: it no longer mattered. I watched Pathkendle draw the girl down beside him in the biting spray. They crouched with their backs to the door, holding each other, like a pair of orphans in a picture book, and the outlandish notion came to me that perhaps these four youths were the sanest of us all, for in the midst of insanity they were caring for one another, which I might assert, Father, is an aspect of the healthy mind.

Suddenly Thasha Isiq raised her head, tensing like a deer. Pathkendle was staring at her, mouthing some question. Very firmly and quickly, she freed herself from his arms. She stood. He tried to grab hold of her again, but she fended him off with great force, her eyes still looking skyward. Then like a woman in a trance she stepped forwards, oblivious to the death she was courting, and stretched her arms high above her head. The wind surged, lifting her like a doll. Pathkendle threw himself on her legs; she did not know he was there. And then the Red Storm swept over the deck.

It was like the glow from some unthinkably colossal fire, but there was no heat. The rain and spray turned to red gold, the deck red amber; the rigging was like wire heated nearly to melting. We had completed another circuit of the Vortex, and ploughed into the red cloud at last. Cloud, I say – but it was neither cloud nor aurora, neither rainbow nor reflection. It was just what the Bolutu-thing called it: a storm of light. Liquid light, and vaporous, and edged like whirling snowflakes. It snagged on the gunnels and dripped from the spars. It burned through the outstretched fingers of Thasha Isiq.

As we plunged deeper, several things happened. The first was the cessation of all noise. The grinding of the Vortex faded swiftly, like the noise of a foundry when you walk away from it, shutting door after door behind you. That led me to a second, absolutely wondrous and blessed discovery: the Vortex itself was gone.

Not dispersed, not disrupted. Gone, as if it had been no more than a soap bubble on the waves. Men crept from the hatches, stark wonder in their eyes. We were no longer heeled over, no longer caught in a death spiral on a butter-smooth sea. There were waves again, and we were pitching on them, the wind from starboard abeam.

Then I saw that the clouds too had vanished: I mean the thunderheads beyond the Red Storm. The sky was swept clean of them, and in their place I could glimpse only shreds of cloud burning like embers in the south. The whole sky beyond the storm was new – and though I could not be sure from within that bright madness, it seemed to me that the sun itself had changed position.

Thasha Isiq was staggering towards the forecastle, red light splashing about her ankles. Pazel was still kneeling on the deck where he had held her. In the sudden quiet, he shouted: 'What in the Nine Pits is happening to you, Thasha? What did you do?'

She turned unsteadily. 'I didn't do anything. It was the storm.'

'The storm destroyed the Vortex?'

The girl shook her head. 'Nothing happened to the Vortex. The storm did something to us. Can't you feel it?'

She walked up to the window, so that we stood face to face. Light was actually dripping from her chin, from her eyelashes. She shook her head: light sprayed in droplets against the glass. 'Would you really have strangled him?' she asked me.

She was speaking of Pathkendle, naturally. But before I found words

545

to answer her the duchess gave a scream. I whirled — and beheld a creature where Bolutu had stood a moment ago. The thing wore the veterinarian's clothes, and his smile, but it was not a human being. At the same time it was more like a human than any flikker or nunekkam, or even the sedge-men one sees in the Etherhorde Natural History Museum. This thing before me had a human body and face. It was svelte, and cinder-black, with silver hair and eyelashes, and large silver eyes. Those eyes were its strangest aspect. They had catlike slits instead of pupils, and a double set of lids. The inner lids were clear as glass; I do not know what purpose they can serve.

The creature raised a hand to calm us, then thought better of it and hid the hand in his pocket. But we had all seen it, the black batskin stretched between his fingers as high as the middle joint. Then he laughed, a little nervously, and brought out his hands for all to see.

'I play the flute, you know. In the past twenty years I grew quite good at the human sort. I will have to go back to dlömic flutes now — the holes are farther apart, to accommodate our webbing.'

It was still Bolutu: his voice was unchanged, and his taste for odd little confessions. 'Dastu has already told you about me,' he went on. 'You see now that I spoke the simple truth. The truth about myself, and also, incidentally, about this blizzard of light. For it is the same manifestation that struck us twenty years ago, heading north. Clearly it has magic-cancelling properties. It nullified the flesh-disguises of some of my comrades; now it has erased my own.'

'You look a bit like a giant crawly,' said Haddismal. 'Are you in league with them?'

Bolutu stared at the Turach in disbelief. 'No,' said Dastu. 'More likely he's with the Mzithrinis. Right, Master Ott? I'll bet he signalled the Jistrolloq somehow, as we neared Bramian.'

The lad took a step towards Bolutu, as if he intended some violence, but was unsure of the creature's abilities. Bolutu backed towards the door. From his corner, Ott shook his head. 'If the Black Rags had creatures from distant countries working for them, I'd have heard about it. My guess is that we are looking at Arunis' lieutenant. Where has he gone, creature? Did he double-cross you, leave you here among your enemies when the rats attacked?'

Oggosk caught my eye and cackled, and for once I felt I understood the source of her mirth. Just minutes ago we had escaped a horrible death, and yet like performing monkeys these three had snapped back into their routines, to suspicion and intrigue and lies.

Bolutu looked from face to face. 'Incredible,' he said. 'You haven't listened to a word I've said. Why do you bother to spy on us, when your own theories are so much more attractive? For what it's worth I have but one enemy on this ship: Arunis himself. You people, you humans of the north, should have been my natural allies, but most of you have lacked the sense to see it. And now I think I shall go. I have known twenty years of interrogations by angry, frowning persons like your-selves. I find the questions as sad and stunted as the questioners. Goodbye.'

And with that he threw open the door and walked out, breathing freely. Like the others I held my breath against the outdoor air, feeling it bite at the edge of my nostrils. But Bolutu was obviously, utterly immune. A result of his transformation, I presume. He strolled away through the Red Storm, past men and crawlies alike. When he caught up with Pathkendle and Thasha Isiq (she looked spent and fragile, now, and the Ormali held her tight in his arms) the creature greeted them like old friends.

You will be wondering how I can speak of pride, when still caged by crawlies? I shall tell you briefly, and then let Oggosk do her witching best to deliver this letter. She assures me she can do so even here, locked out of her cabin, provided we wait until dark.

Like a soundless, strengthening gale, the Red Storm grew brighter and brighter. Men deserted the topdeck – I could not even see a man at the wheel, though I could not be sure: looking down the length of the glowing ship was like staring into the heart of a bonfire. The other prisoners urged me to cover the window, and there was no good reason to refuse. We tacked up another shirt, but the light crept in somehow: through the crawlies' bolt-hole, maybe, or the seams in the walls. All I know is that within a quarter-hour we were shielding our eyes from each other, and from the room itself. Another five minutes, and it was penetrating our eyelids. Sometime after that – how else can I put this? – it had filled our brains. We stood shivering, as if our eyes had been skinned and our heads surrounded by row upon row of scarlet lamps. We did not move or speak or moan. There was no pain, but there was no place to hide.

And then it was gone. Normal vision returned. And when I dared look out again, I saw the red light in pools upon the deck, running here and there as the Great Ship rolled, and pouring like rain through the scuppers. We were on a natural sea, among stout forty-foot swells. When the crawlies came to rebuild the fire they ventured to inform us that the

547

storm was visible behind us – to the north – still stretching from horizon to horizon. To this day I do no know how long we spent in that scouring light. Minutes, hours? The better part of a day?

The work that had begun in terror now resumed with sanity and calm. Or at least without panic. There was soon a new emergency: fresh water. To ensure that we all collapsed together, the damnable crawlies had poisoned every last reserve of water, from the big casks in the hold to the hogsheads used for cooking purposes in the galley. The stateroom's private supply was beyond their reach, but Uskins (I soon discovered) had stopped delivery of water to the stateroom some months ago, thinking it a smart blow against Pathkendle & Co. to force them to lug buckets from the berth deck. There were a few flagons and skins that the crawlies had missed, and some ash-polluted rainwater caught in the furled sails. The live animals compartment had a reserve, but it was smashed open at the top, and full of rat blood. Most of the animals themselves were dead: throats torn open, flesh burned black. Yet a surprising number, including Oggosk's wretched cat and the Red River hog, had simply disappeared. Those that remained (a goose, two swine, three chickens) were slaughtered at once. Mzithrinis are not the only ones capable of drinking blood.

We could, of course, still drink from the casks that had survived the fire. And quite a few men did, in days ahead, as the sun beat down mercilessly, and our thirst grew and grew. We would find them sprawled about the taps, well hydrated, asleep. We tried working in shifts, letting some men drink and sleep, while others waited their turn. No use: a pint of water would knock a man out for two days, and by the time he woke he'd be thirstier than before. And of course the work slowed with every man we lost.

So the crew lived, and in some cases died, with thirst. In the forecastle house, we prisoners sat around dry-lipped, trying not to sweat in that room where a fire always burned, and fresh air could kill us. Meanwhile Fiffengurt and his new crawly 'commander' oversaw the repairs. In just two days (the men were strongest at the beginning), they had the foremast and spankermast rigged anew, and we were able to aim the ship south once again. The augrongs (we found them by following a trail of rats torn like rag dolls to the orlop forepeak, where they had barricaded themselves) helped greatly with the larger timbers, once Pathkendle convinced them that the rodents were dead. We picked up speed. There were accidents, broken shrouds, a broken arm from a falling wheelblock. All told, however, the quartermaster proved his worth. And the crawlies? They cared not what we thought of them, so long as the ship ran south.

Eighteen days like this. It was winter in Arqual, here it was sweltering and cloudless. The men were going mad for rum, but Fiffengurt knew enough to post the Turachs about the liquor compartments with orders to kill: spirits, of course, only make one pass more water than one has swallowed. Men sucked lemons, drank up the vinegar and syrups. The crawlies began to fight among themselves. Was it their messiah, I wondered, who had ordered them to spring this trap, which had now caught them as well?

He came to see me, at last, and begged my advice. 'Your men are choosing death, Captain [suddenly I was Captain again] – drinking their fill and crawling into their hammocks, as if someone else were about to appear and sail the ship for them. Won't you tell your man to give them rum?'

'Is that what you were counting on?' I said. He did not understand the effects of alcohol, and paled when I told him that it increased thirst. 'What are they to drink, then?' he shrilled, as if I were being unreasonable.

I had him bring me Teggatz, and told the cook how he might fashion a boiler-condenser, to distil fresh water from salt. 'Use bilgewater; it will have less salt than the sea itself. Meanwhile, boil the rum in an open cauldron; the alchohol will go up in fumes.' Teggatz assembled the device, and stoked the galley stove until the whole deck felt the heat. But the machine and the flat rum together only yielded another forty gallons a day, and the men tending the stove had to drink a quarter of that just to keep from passing out in the heat.

Perhaps those forty gallons made the difference, however. For a morning came when, parched and gritty-eyed, I woke to find the little lordling's girl (Myett, she is called) standing before me with a white pill in her hand. 'Eat it, Captain, and go to the quarterdeck. Our lord wishes you to see something.'

I gulped the pill (before Ott or Haddismal chose to wrestle me for it) and staggered to my feet. Outside on the deck, I felt no pain in my lungs at all. She ran ahead of me, and I walked stiff and angry towards the bow, taking in the damage to my ship. At last I pulled myself up the quarterdeck ladder. The lordling was there, on a man's shoulder, having my own telescope held up for him. It was aimed – like six or eight others in various hands – at something two points off the port bow. Thasha Isiq saw me before the little tyrant did, and brought me Admiral Isiq's instrument to gaze through. I raised and focused it, guessing already what I would see.

'Congratulations, Captain,' she said. 'You brought us across, alive.'

I lowered the scope; was she mocking me? The choices I'd made, the alliances I'd condoned! The ship still reeked of fire, the boards beneath our feet were black. My men were lifting carcasses of rats and wondering if they dared drink from their veins.

Then I saw the ghosts clustered behind her, scores of them, the complete repertoire of former captains, six centuries strong. They were toasting me with brandy. They were shouting the name of Nilus Rose.

Only the girl and I were aware of them, of course. But as they cheered, Pathkendle came up beside her and offered me his hand. You crafty little bastard, I thought, but I shook it all the same. If they were recruiting me for something it was handsomely done.

Now I shall send this, Father, and hope that you are not ashamed to call me son.

I am, and ever shall be, your obedient
Nilus

P.S. The antidote was temporary. Within the hour, as the crawlies intended, I was back in the forecastle house. Oggosk declared that she could receive letters from you so long as we remain trapped here. We fell to arguing; and by a slip of the tongue she revealed how she has been opening and reading your letters before passing them on to me. I confess I was quite angry. I took her unlit pipe (yes, the same one; she will masticate no other) and crushed it beneath my heel.

Pray do not trouble yourself to write, therefore, until you hear that I have resumed my command. Of course I shall still write to you. But will you really see these letters? Is she truly sending them, as she feeds them page by page into the fire-pot? There is no proof one way or the other. I must trust the hag, as I have been doing (not always profitably) these many years.

Finally, I implore you not to tell Mother of my conflict with her elder sister, who is savage without her pipe. Whether she took my side or Oggosk's, the headache would be intolerable. Some things are best kept among men.

41

Thirst

———∞———

'Captain Fiffengurt,' said Mr Thyne, 'aren't you going to name it? You have that right, after all.'

'Don't call me captain,' growled Fiffengurt. 'The ixchel can't promote me, no matter what Taliktrum says.'

'The Trading Company, however, has named many a captain. And your qualifications—'

'Hang it all, man! It's not Company approval I'd go looking for, if I wanted to hold onto this job.'

Thyne sighed, gazing south over the carronades. 'Such a beautiful place. It just feels wrong to keep calling it *the island*.'

It was by general acclamation (and only because it was expected to save their lives) the most beautiful island in all the world. Not that they could see much of it: Bolutu warned of sandbars, so with five or six miles to go they had tacked westward, and were keeping a safe distance.

Even through the stronger telescopes, however, there was little to be seen. A meandering, sand-coloured smudge. No rocks, no human (or dlömic) structures. Low trees or bushes on dune-tops, possibly. That was all. The island was so flat and low to the horizon that the first men to see it confessed they had thought it a mirage.

But it was no mirage. And it was no tiny island, either, at least in length: the wall of dunes vanished west as far as any eye could discern. Bolutu had given them one name already: the Northern Sandwall, a two-thousand-mile-long barrier of offshore banks, entirely without rock or coral, torn and shaped and sifted by the Nelluroq. 'Within lies the great Gulf of Masal,' he said, 'almost a sea unto itself.'

'Gods of mercy!' Fiffengurt had exploded. 'You can't be saying we have *another* voyage to make, before we reach solid land?'

'I have no way to know that, from here,' said Bolutu. 'The coast is quite irregular. In places the Sandwall comes to within five miles of the mainland; in others it stands three hundred miles offshore. But it is solid enough, and quite broad in places. There are fishing villages, small forests, naval stations – and yes, fresh water. In other places the Sandwall is so thin one can throw a rock from the north beach into the Gulf of Masal.'

In such spots, he explained, the Nelluroq frequently punched inlets straight through the Sandwall. Entering the Gulf by one of these, a ship could make a safe landing on the Sandwall in any number of places, by following the channel-markers set by fishermen. 'Provided, of course, that we are in Bali Adro territory. That is likely, for most of the Gulf is claimed by our Empire. But I cannot know for certain without a landmark.'

'Are those inlets deep enough for a ship like the *Chathrand*?' Taliktrum had demanded, from his perch on Big Skip's shoulder.

'It depends, sir,' was Bolutu's reply.

'Depends, depends,' grumbled Fiffengurt. 'Everything blary depends.'

They had plenty of sea beneath them now: twenty fathoms, when the lead was cast. Fiffengurt called for topsails, on the masts that could take the strain. Time was against them: the men's spirits had lifted at the sight of land, but they were still half mad with thirst. And there would be no landing of any kind this side of the Sandwall. When the wind was right they could hear the breakers: a smashing, bellowing surf that would crush any vessel caught in its grip. They had no choice but to sail on.

Taliktrum ordered the release of the steerage passengers, a command Fiffengurt found it easy to obey. At first the forty pale, wasted souls had to be urged not to stand in the sun, losing moisture to sweat: Rose had kept them a long time in darkness, and some did not hide their glee to learn that he was now the one imprisoned. The sailors watched them, shamed by their filth, their long invisibility. But their hearts did not soften towards the crawly who had seized the ship.

Mid-afternoon the sea grew clearer, and they edged to within three miles of the Sandwall. Now there could be no doubt: the dunes were capped with trees. Smiles broke out on salt-crusted lips: trees meant water, fresh water; they could taste it already. But there was still no inlet, and no sign of home or village on the yellow shore.

When the sun touched the horizon, Fiffengurt cursed under his breath. 'Take us out five miles, Mr Elkstem, if you please. Mr Fegin, I want double lookouts forwards. We're going to hold this pace straight through to sunrise.'

A cold snap fell in the night, bringing down a teasing dew. Men tried to suck it from the rigging, only to end up with mouths full of salty tar. Others spent the night running their cracked fingers over sails and oilskins, then touching fingers to lips.

At daybreak the Sandwall stretched on as before. The heat grew and the wind diminished, and the *Chathrand* lost half her speed. Hope turned all at once to panic: there was almost nothing to drink. The boiled rum was gone. Captain Rose's salt-water still had twice exploded, and the repaired device produced only a trickle of fresh water. Tempers began to fray; even some of the ixchel exchanged rebellious glances; soon they would be thirsty too.

That night the wind picked up for several hours. At dawn, they found to their great dismay that the Sandwall had shrunk to a brown thread on the southern horizon: it had curved sharply away from them, and they spent the better part of the day creeping back towards it.

Outside sickbay the line grew long. Chadfallow and Fulbreech put drops of almond oil into blistered, leathery mouths. But there were serious maladies too. One man had a fever but was unable to sweat. Another had closed his eyes for a moment and found that they refused to open. A third complained of muscle spasms; they gave him linseed to rub on his arms. An hour later he lost his grip on a forestay and plummeted from the mainmast: his body sounded like a bundle of sticks when it struck the deck.

The third day along the Sandwall passed in a sort of group delirium. There were stormclouds to the north – forty or fifty miles to the north – but they failed to provide even shade, let alone moisture. There were whales to starboard, blowing froth into the air that looked like the mist over a waterfall in some forest glen.

In the evening water queue outside the galley, a Plapp's Pier sailor choked on his ration. His throat had become too dry to swallow; he coughed, and his precious quarter-cup sprayed against the wall. The Burnscove Boys laughed and hooted, and the sailor who had lost his water promptly lost his mind. He struck the nearest Burnscover hard in the jaw, and seconds later received the same treatment himself. Knives appeared, the Turachs shouted and charged the troublemakers, and the bulk of the men in line seized the chance to rush the water barrel. Mr Teggatz, swinging his ladle like a club, was knocked over; seconds later, so was the barrel. Few had even wet their lips, but four men lay bleeding underfoot. One, the unfortunate Plapp, died before his mates could carry him to sickbay.

That night Pazel went to visit his friends in the forecastle house, carrying a candle in a little glass. The window was grey with ash and salt scum. When he tapped, sullen faces glanced up through the smoky air. They had been prisoners for forty days, and had long since given up hope that a visitor might be bringing them their freedom. Even Neeps and Marila looked defeated, Pazel thought, as they tiptoed through the sprawled bodies to the window.

They expect to die, thought Pazel suddenly, and with the thought came a sharp bite of guilt. He was out here, free and relatively safe; Neeps and Marila and Chadfallow were locked in there with lunatics, nothing but a little fire between them and death. It was hard not to hate Taliktrum. The accusation still rang in his ears, however: *if it was your family you'd have done exactly the same.*

Pazel struggled not to show his anguish. His friends' eyes were red and crusty. Neeps' skin had paled to the colour of driftwood. Marila's thick black hair had lost its shine.

'No inlet yet,' Pazel managed to say. 'But it can't be far off now. Fiffengurt says we'll keep on till daybreak, just like yesterday.'

'Only slower,' said Marila.

Pazel nodded; they could not crack on at full speed in the dark. 'When . . . .when was the last time—'

'We had anything to drink?' said Neeps, completing the question. 'Depends who you're talking about. Old Plapp and Burnscove, now, they just drank their fill. *Blanë*-laced water, compliments of the ixchel. They gulped a quart apiece, and so did Saroo and Byrd and a few others. They'll sleep for ten days, and wake up drier than they started. Of course, by then—'

'Don't say it,' Marila interrupted.

She was right, Pazel thought: the situation was all too clear. Ten days from now they would either have found water or died for want of it.

'You should drink the *blanë*-water too,' said Pazel. 'Go to sleep, and wake up with a nice, safe jug at your side.'

Neeps gave a half-glance over his shoulder, then shook his head. 'Not until *they* do, mate.'

Pazel looked: Sandor Ott was lounging against the wall, arms crossed. His chisel-point eyes were fixed on Pazel.

'He's listening,' said Marila. 'One of them's always listening – Ott, or Dastu, or Rose.'

'He doesn't speak Sollochi, does he?' asked Pazel, switching to Neeps' birth tongue.

Neeps shrugged. 'With Ott you can never be sure.'

I could have been, thought Pazel, *if I'd let the eguar show me the rest of his life. I'd have known about Dastu as well, maybe – and Thasha's father, if there's anything to know. Was it trying to help me, after all?*

He looked once more into the assassin's eyes. *Would I have learned* everything *he knows? Could I have stood if I did?* He thought again of the eguar's strangest phrase of all: *the world my brethren made*. It still worried him that Bolutu had no idea what the creature could have meant.

He shook himself; this was doing his friends no good. 'We're not so bad off,' he said. 'Bolutu thinks the Red Storm may have wiped out any ugly spells Arunis was brewing. He figures it acts like "scouring powder for magic." I was afraid it might have knocked out the magic wall around the stateroom, but no fear; it's as strong as ever. And we've found all seven of our allies, all seven carrying the wolf-scar – even if it is blary strange that Rose is one of them.'

'Pazel,' said Neeps, his voice abruptly flat, 'we're not seven, anymore. Dri is dead. Whatever we were meant to do together isn't going to happen.'

'Don't talk like that,' said Pazel fiercely. 'Nothing's gone as planned for *them*, either. We'll find another way, even if we can't do what the Red Wolf had in mind when it burned us. I told you what Ramachni said.'

Neeps' eyes flashed, and Pazel feared he might be spoiling for a fight. Then the small boy took a deep breath, and nodded. 'You told me. Sorry, mate.'

'Right,' said Pazel, relieved but shaken. 'One of us will visit you every hour or so. Thasha's next, at four bells.'

'How is our Angel of Rin, anyway?'

'Back to normal,' said Pazel with a quick smile.

'You're lying,' said Marila.

Pazel blinked at her. Marila did *not* speak Sollochi; she was merely listening to his tone. Neeps' talent was rubbing off on her.

'Thasha isn't normal,' he admitted. 'In fact she has me worried sick.'

Since the Red Storm, he said, Thasha had been increasingly moody and distracted. Her hand, the one she had used to touch the Nilstone, seemed to fascinate her. Pazel had caught her staring at it, and picking at the old scar. And she was reading the *Polylex*, more and more of it, sometimes with Felthrup's assistance, sometimes alone. It still frightened her, but she couldn't seem to tear herself away. Pazel would wake in the night to the sound of her soft screams. He would sit beside her, holding her, feeling her tremble as she scanned the pages.

'Once she slammed the book and shouted at me: "What was she *thinking*, how could she do it to them? How could a mage be so cruel?" When I asked who she meant, she snapped, "Erithusmé, who else? She wasn't good at all, she was a monster." I told her that wasn't what Ramachni said, and she just snarled at me. "How would *you* like to go through a Waking, like Felthrup, like Niriviel and Mugstur? Do you think you'd still be sane, Pazel? Do you think you'd still be *you*?"'

An even worse incident had occurred two nights ago. It had been a beautiful, warm evening. The two of them had spent a quiet hour seated against the twenty-foot skiff, watching a pod of whales cross and recross a yellow ribbon of moonlight. Thasha had seemed happy and relaxed. In time they had fallen asleep, and when Pazel awoke an hour later she was gone. He did not find her in the stateroom, and alerted Hercól. Together with Big Skip and a few other volunteers they had searched for her, deck by deck, compartment by compartment. It was Pazel who had found her at last: crossing the berth deck, walking like a dreamer among hundreds of sleeping men.

He had run to her and taken her hand. 'You shouldn't be in here,' he had whispered. 'Let's go before they wake up.'

Thasha had looked at the sleepers, shaking her head. 'They can't,' she'd said.

She led him out of the compartment and down a side passage. It was a spot he'd passed a hundred times, but this time, to his great surprise, he saw that there was a little green door, only waist-high, right at the end of the passage, where he thought the hull should have been. The door looked older and shabbier than the rest of the compartment; its handle was an ancient, corroded lump of iron. Thasha had put out her hand to open the door – but slowly, as though fighting herself. When she touched the knob Pazel had reached to help her – he was curious about the door; he'd never noticed it – and Thasha had suddenly pulled him away, screaming.

'We're running out, we're running out!'

'Don't worry,' Pazel had begged. 'We'll find water, Thasha, I swear.'

'Not water!' she'd howled, clawing at him. 'Not water! Thoughts! We're running out of thoughts and we won't have any left!' And she had wept all the way back to the stateroom.

'And later on, Neeps,' Pazel concluded, 'she couldn't remember being on the berth deck at all. I'm scared, I tell you. She's just so *different*, since the storm.'

Neeps looked at him, awestruck. 'Everything is different,' he said at last. 'Don't you sense it, mate? I can't put my finger on it, but I feel as if ... I don't know, as if the whole world we come from, back there across the Nelluroq, had just—'

'Neeparvasi Undrabust!' rasped Lady Oggosk suddenly. 'Get away from the window, you atrocious boy! I can't sleep through your chatter!'

Quickly, Pazel put his hand on the glass. 'We'll free you,' he said in Arquali. 'I promise we'll free you both. You just have to hang on until we find a way.'

"Course we will,' said Neeps, raising his fingers briefly to the pane. Leaning slightly against him, Marila nodded and made herself smile.

Their courage made Pazel feel even worse. He glanced again at Ott and lowered his voice to a hoarse whisper.

'Remember what Bolutu said, after you left. The part I told you the next morning.'

'About the ones who'll be waiting for him?' Neeps whispered back. 'His masters, the ones who see through his eyes?'

'That's right,' whispered Pazel. 'But don't say another word! Just hold onto that thought, will you? They're going to find us, and help. And Ramachni's coming back as well – stronger than ever, he said. So save *your* strength. You'll see, this is all going to work out.'

He left them, feeling a fraud. Who was he to say that things would work out? What made his promises any better than those Taliktrum gave to his people – or for that matter, Mugstur to his rats? Had things worked out for Diadrelu? Would anything prevent their dying here, one by one, with three miles of the Ruling Sea left to cross?

*

He found Thasha seated on the flag locker at the back of the quarter-deck, her shoulders resting on the taffrail. 'You're seventeen,' she said, her voice flat and distant.

'By Rin,' said Pazel, for it was true: his birthday had come and gone on the Nelluroq. 'How did you know?'

Thasha made no answer. Her eyes were on Taliktrum and Elkstem, both at the wheel, arguing over safe running speeds and distances from shore. Myett stood close to Taliktrum, whispering and touching him frequently. Lord Talag, who had so far refused to discuss any return to leadership of the clan, watched his son in brooding silence from the wreckage of the wheelhouse.

On Thasha's lap lay a chipped ceramic jug from the stateroom. Pazel tipped it: bone dry.

'You'll just get thirstier, sitting out in this wind,' he said.

Thasha smiled and put out her hand. 'Come and get thirsty with me.'

He climbed onto the flag locker and settled beside her. As always when they were close, he tensed himself against the onset of pain from Klyst's shell. But it did not come – had not come, he realised, since they passed through the Red Storm. He glanced north. What had happened to the murth-girl? Was she lost in the heart of the Ruling Sea? Had she followed them (he crushed his eyes shut on the thought) into the Vortex, and perished there? Or had the Storm freed her from her own love-*ripestry* at last?

'The whales are back,' said Thasha pointing.

'I think they're watching us,' he said, trying for a joke.

Thasha's strong arm went around his waist. He smiled, remembering his childish vision of the two of them running away into the jungle, Lord and Lady of Bramian. It was time to tell her, although he'd blush, and she'd tease him, and demand to hear it all.

But before he could open his mouth Thasha hid her face against his shoulder. 'Diadrelu,' she whispered, clinging to him. And that was enough; he was engulfed in anguish and had to look away.

That night in the stateroom, while Hercól and Fiffengurt sat at table, speaking of the recent dead and the soon-to-be-born, and Bolutu sketched a drawing of his beloved Empire, pointing out its forests and castles and mountain ranges to a transported Felthrup, Pazel rummaged in his sea chest, among heaps of grimy clothes and knickknacks. When at last he found what he wanted he rose and went into Thasha's cabin without knocking. She was sprawled across the bed, reading the *Polylex* with no apparent discomfort – before his startling entrance, at least. He closed the door and went to her, and held the blue silk ribbon up for her to read.

YE DEPART FOR A WORLD UNKNOWN, AND LOVE ALONE
SHALL KEEP THEE

'I was supposed to tie this to your wrist,' he said, and did.

42

The Kindness of the King

On sunny mornings the man liked to sit by the window and watch the tailor birds repairing their nests. They never stopped or seemed to tire, these little red birds, even when the winter storms lashed the city and pulled their patchwork homes apart like old woollen hats. One of the birds came now and then to talk to him. The man had bribed him with a scrap of silk, torn from the lining of his pocket. Now with a telescope borrowed from the king he could see the silk woven into the nest. The bird had thanked him in Simjan, and when the man did not answer, tried several other tongues. The man just nodded, or tilted his head to one side. He had lost the gift of speech and the bird had gained it. The situation was awkward for them both.

Long winter nights the man would lie on the rug, staring at the firelight dancing on the ceiling and worrying about the bird. It was always good humoured but he knew it was in pain. *I'm alone in the world except for you, sir. My mate hasn't woken and I fear she never will.*

When he closed his eyes the rats came looking for him. First he would hear them scuffling below in the depths of the castle, and he would have to get up and check the lock on the door. Later he would hear them sniffing and scrabbling just outside the room. Sometimes they spoke to him in their familiar, horrid way. *Penny for a colonel's widow?* Often he heard them gnawing at the base of the door.

The man had no weapon, and no kiln in which to hide. He knew his only chance was to lie still and make no sound.

They gave him a cat, but it harassed the bird and he told the nurse with gestures to take it away. They gave him books, all the books written in Arquali that the king could readily obtain, and these were his great comfort. When they hung a mirror above the dressing table the man stood in front of it for a long time, studying himself. A bald, veined head, deepset eyes, chin held high out of habit, not feeling. Then the man turned the mirror's face to the wall.

The king's physician gave him bloodroot tea. He was not surprised that the man had lost both speech and memory. He had treated many battle survivors, and knew the caves into which the mind, like a wounded animal, withdrew in defeat.

'Traumatic semi-catatonia,' he told King Oshiram. 'He's made a pact with the gods, Your Majesty: "Torture me no further and I'll sit here quietly, you'll see, I won't make a sound."'

'Admiral Isiq is a war hero,' said the king.

'Yes, Sire. And also, unfortunately, a man.'

Daytime was pleasant enough. The room in the tower overlooked the Ancestors' Grove, a stand of gnarled beeches surrounding a rush-fringed pool where, as King Oshiram had explained, the frogs were said to sing with the voices of the royal dead. It was a small, ancient, walled-in wood. Beyond it lay the rose gardens, dormant now and dead-looking, and farther on the sprawling Cactus Gardens, where the man's last conversation with a loved one had taken place.

The king had installed a sheet of translucent glass over the whole of the window, with only a tiny aperture to look through. 'For your safety,' the king had told him, very serious and grim. 'The ones who put you in that black pit are still among us, I'd bet my mother's jewels on that. The rat creatures did not kill them all. That is why we can't let your face be seen, and why you must never, ever shout. Use the bell pull; someone will always be listening. Do you understand me, Isiq?'

The king's eyes always told him when to nod.

King Oshiram was intelligent and kind. He did not talk down to his guest or presume that what he said was forgotten. Quite the contrary, he spoke to the man seriously, as to a peer, about the intractable problems of the Isle of Simja, and darker matters in the outer world. He often called him *Ambassador* or *Admiral*. He even brought an Arquali fish-and-dagger flag and set it up on a pole in the corner, but after the king left the man had folded it sadly and left it by the door.

One day the king told him with great anxiety of the death of Pacu Lapadolma. 'An accident, they said, an allergic reaction to her food, isn't that a preposterous claim!' It was, said the king, a sign of much worse things to come. It meant the Great Peace was unravelling. Then he shrugged, and glowered, and scratched the back of his neck, and murmured almost inaudibly that perhaps it was never meant to succeed.

After that, each visit brought more awful news. The Mzithrinis were in a state of panic and suspicion. They had cancelled their goodwill missions to Arqual, and were preventing visits – *all* visits, commercial, scholarly and diplomatic – to their own country, just as in the worst years after the war. The Permanent Blockade by the White Fleet, which just that autumn they had talked of abolishing, was now tighter than ever. Ships that strayed too close to the Mzithrini line of control were met with warning shots across their bows.

The doctor advised the king to spare his guest these stories – 'if you ever want to see him recover, that is.' The king frowned, but obeyed. For almost a week. Then came a day when, after struggling through an amusing tale about his nephew's habit of putting trousers on dogs, he fell silent, until the man stopped glancing out the window and looked at the monarch with concern.

The king met his eye. 'The Shaggat Ness,' he said quietly. 'Do you remember who he was, Admiral, even if you've forgotten yourself?'

The man nodded, for he did.

'All this ferocity and paranoia, this self-quarantine they've imposed, this blasting of guns and practising for war. It's all about the Shaggat. Word's leaked out. The whole Pentarchy is ablaze with rumours that the Shaggat Ness is coming back. From the grave! From the bottom of the Gulf of Thól! His old minions on Gurishal have some daft prophecy – connected I gather with the Great Peace itself, and now they're delirious with the prospect of his return. And the Five Kings, damn them, are as superstitious as the blary Nessarim. So they're turning away every possible ship that might be trying to smuggle the madman back to Gurishal. Even though he's forty years dead and gone!'

Suddenly he laughed. 'Religious lunatics. Someone had better break it to them, that's all. "Listen, you dumb bastards, the dead don't just wake up one day and return to life."'

Then the king stopped laughing, and looked at the man uneasily. 'Of course, you did,' he said.

The tailor bird had overheard the king. 'Isiq, your name is Isiq! A splendid name! And an admiral, did I get that right?'

The man neither nodded nor shook his head. Something the king had said made him feel it would be wrong to answer.

'No matter! Isiq! We have that, and it's more than we had yesterday! Every twig in the nest, eh? Tomorrow I'll listen to His Highness again, and we shall add another twig.'

Eberzam Isiq put his fingers in the aperture. The bird for the first time let him touch its velvet throat.

But for almost a week the king did not come. Isiq heard him pass through the lower chambers, his voice high and merry as he shouted to his scribe and chamberlain. When he came at last he slipped in quietly and chattered for an hour about things that had nothing to do with war.

Isiq returned his smile, for he felt the king's new joy as his own. Something on the admiral's face must have revealed his curiosity, for the king laughed and drew his stool closer.

'I can tell you, can't I? You won't go gossiping. I've fallen in love. I'm smitten, I tell you, done for.'

Isiq sat up straight. The king went right on talking.

'Oh, she won't be queen – that'll be dreary Princess Urjan of Urnsfich, one of these years – ah, but *this* girl! Once in a lifetime, Isiq. A dancer, with a body to prove it. But she's had a hard life. Was forced to dance for piggish men in Ballytween – dance, and maybe more than dance. Now she's too timid to step in front of an audience, or even enter a crowded room. I seem to have been born to shelter— Never mind, sir, never mind. Ah, but she dances for *me*, Admiral. I wish you could see her. Beauty like that would make you recall your youth in a heartbeat.'

None of this made any great impression on Eberzam Isiq. He knew only that the king's visits would be rare henceforth, and they were. The doctor came, and the nurse brought food, and new books, and laundered clothes. The little tailor bird came and spoke sadly of his mate. The winter deepened. And Isiq grew somewhat stronger. His body at the very least was healing. He started calisthenics, though he could not recall having learned them fifty years ago as a cadet.

One day, nibbling soda bread with a blanket across his knees, staring at a page of Arquali poetry as the bird pecked crumbs from the floor, he heard the king beneath him, laughing deep in his throat. The monarch raised his voice to a shout: 'Yes, yes, darling, you win, by all the gods! Your wish is my own!' And then, very faintly, Isiq heard a woman's musical laugh.

He shot to his feet, scaring the bird back to the window. Book and blanket and cake fell to the floor. He took a step forwards, lips trembling, possessed by yearnings the very existence of which he had forgotten.

'Syrarys?' he whispered.

'Isiq!' screeched the tailor bird, beside himself. 'Isiq, best friend, only friend, you can talk!'

43

A Meeting of Empires

------~ഐ~------

20 Ilbrin 941
219th day from Etherhorde

With the lookout's cry at dawn, grown men wept with relief.

'Tower ashore! Tower ashore!'

Felthrup's eyes snapped open. Had he heard correctly?

He was in the doorway of the wedding cupboard, under Hercól's chair. Hercól was already on his feet. 'A tower!' he cried softly. 'Thank the sweet star of Rin!'

'We are saved!' said Felthrup. 'Any settlement will have water! They cannot refuse us enough to stay alive!'

'To me, little brother,' said Hercól, and lifted the rat to his shoulder. Felthrup clung tight, revelling in the strength of his three good legs. Just like Master Mugstur, he had seen his battle-wounds healed when he took monstrous shape. Then (a far greater blessing) the Red Storm had nullified the hideous change, restoring him to his true body, just as it had done to Belesar Bolutu. Even with his burning thirst, Felthrup had not felt so strong in years.

The door to Pacu Lapadolma's cabin opened, and Bolutu himself stepped out, his silver eyes shining with anticipation. The dlömic man had lately moved into Pacu's cabin, which like Hercól's cupboard stood inside the magic wall. He wore an amulet about his neck: a lovely sea-green stone, inlaid with gold likenesses of tiger and snake. It was a sacred emblem, he'd explained vaguely: and this was the first time he'd dared display it in twenty years.

He had also taken to wearing a broadsword. Felthrup didn't know where the sword had come from, but he knew why Bolutu kept it at hand, and why he had changed his quarters. The mood on the *Chathrand* was explosive; men were almost as thirsty for a scapegoat as they were for water. Felthrup himself went nowhere without a guardian. The only thing worse than being the sole dlömu aboard the Great Ship was being its last surviving rat.

Scores of men were already rushing up the Silver Stair, with ixchel flowing past them left and right.. Hercól threw open the stateroom door. 'Thasha! Pathkendle!'

Pazel and Thasha stumbled into the passage, blinking. Ensyl was there as well, riding on Pazel's shoulder. Felthrup leaped into Thasha's arms. 'Wake up, my lady!' he said, wriggling with excitement. Thasha nodded vaguely; she did not seem to know quite where she was.

Bolutu was first up the Silver Stair. As soon as he reached the topdeck a cry of joy burst from his lips.

'Narybir! *Ay dorin Alifros*, beloved home! That is the Tower of Narybir, Guardian of the East! We have reached Cape Lasung! There is a village beside the tower, and fresh water to spare! And see, there is the inlet we were hunting for!'

The others rushed up the ladderway. A joyful clamour was breaking out above: *A village! A village with water to spare!*

On the topdeck, Bolutu stood with his half-webbed hands spread wide above his head. Men crowded around him, suddenly indifferent to his strangeness, hanging on his every word. Others gazed with longing from the portside rail.

Felthrup sniffed the wind and shivered with excitement. *Forest!* He could smell wet bark and pine sap, and a boggy smell like an inland swamp. Then Thasha moved forwards, and Felthrup saw the tower.

'Rin's eyes,' said Hercól beside them.

It stood at the end of the Cape: a magnificent spire of rust-red stone. The surface was irregular and deeply grooved. The tower was broad at its foot, with curving butresses that vanished, rootlike, into the sand. As it rose the structure leaned and twisted, so that from afar it resembled some ancient, wind-guttered candle. A little wall ran along the shore at its base. Inland from the wall stood a grove of rugged pines, and then, perhaps a mile from the tower, a village of low stone houses.

Eastward, the island tapered to a sandy point. Then came a mile of open sea, and beyond it the Northern Sandwall resumed, a ribbon of dunes curving away into the distance.

'Did I not promise you?' said Bolutu, turning to Pazel and Thasha. 'Did I not say that the worst lay behind us?'

'You told us,' said Thasha uncertainly. Pazel stood hugging his coat tight about him, watchful and uneasy. Felthrup caught his eye, and felt a spark of worry ignite in his heart.

'Bolutu!' shouted Taliktrum, looking down from the quarterdeck, where he perched on Elkstem's shoulder. 'Is that a naval installation? Will they confront us with warships if we enter the Gulf?'

'There is a small detachment of Asp warriors, if I recall, sir. But it was never a great fighting base. Narybir is a watchtower; her ships are meant to carry warnings with all possible speed to the City of Masalym, thirty miles across the Gulf, where no doubt an Imperial warship or two lies at anchor. Her signal-lights also send messages to the ships themselves, and keep them from wrecking on the Sandwall.'

Another whisper of joy swept the deck. *Thirty miles to the mainland – to a city, a city, did you hear him?*

'Can we have washed up right in the heart of your blary Empire?' demanded Taliktrum.

'No indeed,' said Bolutu. 'Masalym is the easternmost of the Five Pillars of the Bali Adro Coast. Sail east another hundred miles and you leave the Empire for the Dominion of Karysk and the Ghíred Vale, and beyond that I cannot say. Our capital lies in the other direction, two thousand miles to the south-west. Farther still lies my birth city: beautiful Istolym, westernmost of all.'

'Have you ever set foot in this Masalym then?' demanded Elkstem.

The dlömu shook his head. 'Our ship set sail from Bali Adro City. I know the tower before us from paintings only, but it is unmistakable. Trust me, Sailmaster! I know *exactly* where we are.'

As he spoke these last words he glanced quickly at Pazel and Thasha, and touched the corner of one silvery eye. To the others it looked like a thoughtless gesture, but Pazel understood at once. *His masters, the mages of the South. They know where we are too, now. He's just shown them.*

'Trust me, all of you!' Bolutu went on joyfully. 'My mission was a famous one, and even if the name of Bolutu Urstorch has been forgotten after twenty years, that of my ship *Sofima Rega* never shall be. The men of Narybir will welcome us with open arms.'

'And flash a message to that city in an instant, maybe,' said Taliktrum, 'from which one or two – or twenty – gunships will be launched.'

'Aye,' grunted Alyash, who had appeared at the rail. 'A *Segral* from across the Nelluroq won't be greeted with a shrug, now, will it? They'll want to stop us cold. They'll never let us go on our merry way, traipsin' east to west through their waters. At the very least they'll board us and inspect every last corner of the ship. And what d'ye suppose they'll make of the Nilstone?'

'Better if we *had* struck land in a wilderness,' said Taliktrum, 'for your purposes, and ours.'

For a moment no one spoke. On Thasha's shoulder, Felthrup began to fidget. He sniffed the air again. 'Don't like it, don't like it,' he murmured.

'You say men live in that village by the tower,' said a sceptical voice in the crowd. 'Do you mean *real* men, or your sort of thing?'

It was Uskins, looking pale and rather sickly. He was keeping a sheepish distance from the other officers since his blunders in the Vortex. Bolutu glanced at him briefly.

'As it happens I mean both, sir,' said Bolutu. 'Let me say again: in Bali Adro the races live together in peace.'

'But you things rule, don't you?'

'Uskins!' snapped Taliktrum. 'Living creatures are not to be referred to as *things*. And you in particular must learn to keep your mouth shut. Nothing but foolishness comes out of it.'

'Mr Taliktrum,' said Elkstem nervously, 'they may have flashed that signal already.'

Taliktrum looked at him, startled. The crowd was abruptly tense.

'He's right,' said Alyash. 'What good's a watchtower if it's not quick with its warnings? And even if the mainland can't spot its signal light, there must be boats on the Gulf that can. And they'll relay the message to that city, if it's really there.'

'No,' muttered Felthrup.

'They could be weighing anchor even now!' said an ixchel at Taliktrum's side.

'And our men are in no shape for a fight,' added Uskins.

'Fight?' cried Bolutu. 'My dear sirs, you do not grasp the situation at all! We are a secure and confident people. No power in Alifros need give Bali Adro a moment's fear. We do not attack strangers who arrive on our doorstep! Why should we? Go and get your water, gentlemen! No one is going to take your ship away.'

'Listen to him!' shouted someone, and the crowd rumbled agreement.

'No, no, no,' said Felthrup, who was now practically writhing on Thasha's shoulder.

'Can't you keep that rat quiet?' Alyash snapped at Thasha.

Thasha returned his stare with loathing. 'What's the matter, Felthrup? Don't listen to him. Go ahead, speak up.'

All eyes turned to the rat. Felthrup opened his mouth to speak – but his brain was working too quickly, and his nerves got the better of him. He began to sniff hard and fast, like a monk at his breathing exercises. Then he gasped aloud.

'Grease,' he said. 'Cookfires. Last night's dinner!'

Alyash made a sound of contempt.

'I don't smell a blary thing,' said Elkstem.

'You ain't a rat, are ye?' said Fiffengurt. 'They can stand on a roof and smell a bean in the basement. It wouldn't surprise me one bit if those smells fetched across the water.'

'No!' wailed Felthrup. 'I can't smell *anything!* Wake up, wake up!'

He began to squeal pitifully and rub his snout with his paws. Thasha cradled him, whispering soothing words, but he only grew worse, convulsing with dry heaves. He spoke no more, and with a look of concern Thasha bore him away.

Myett whispered something urgently into Taliktrum's ear. He nodded, as though the thought had occurred to him already.

'Mr Elkstem,' he said, 'plot a course through the inlet. We shall go and get our water – quickly – unless there is some *coherent* objection?'

A roar of approval from the men. Pazel and Hercól exchanged a look. In the swordsman's eyes Pazel saw a reflection of his own unease. Felthrup had an extraordinary way of thinking. His nerves had betrayed him the same way in Simja, when he guessed Ott's trick with Pacu. Some deep part of him seemed to grasp things before he could explain them, even to himself.

But what choice did they have? Without water, the men would soon be more delirious than Felthrup. And then they would start to die.

Mr Fiffengurt took a tally: of the sixteen officers charged with record keeping, eleven reckoned the date to be 20 Ilbrin of the year 941.* He

---

* Of the five who disagreed: two thought the date 19 Ilbrin. Another declared with certainty that it was Ilbrin the 23rd. Mr Teggatz, charged with keeping a daily statistical log of work in the galley, confessed to having accidentally burned his log-book in the stove. Finally, Old Gangrüne the purser admitted under questioning that he considered the entire Solar Year a mirage. The sun moved faster or slower at the gods' whims, he declared: any fool who watched the sky knew that, and clocks and hourglasses changed their speeds to match the sun's. It was pointed out to Gangrüne that this belief called into question his fifty years of shipboard record-keeping. 'You've got it backwards,' he retorted. 'My logbook's our only hope of keeping track of the years. I'm an Imperial asset, if you please.' – EDITOR.

sent a request to Captain Rose to make the date official: *Without that we agree on the date, sir, I fear the men's hearts will go evermore adrift*. Rose agreed at once, and the date of the IMS *Chathrand*'s entrance into the Gulf of Masal was fixed for all time.

Fiffengurt assumed that the day would be remembered for the meeting of two worlds so long divided, and in a sense he was right. It was in any case a day no one aboard was ever able to forget.

They cleared the inlet with nine fathoms to spare. On the leeward side Cape Lasung formed a broad sandy hook, with a number of small, rocky islands clustered near the point commanded by the Tower of Narybir. Several of these inner isles had stone houses and fortifications. But no voices hailed them, from tower or village, and the channel-markers Bolutu had predicted could not be found.

'Where's the fishing fleet?' said Pazel.

'Out on the Gulf, obviously,' said Mr Uskins, as though glad to be addressing someone of lower status than himself. 'Still bringing in the night's catch.'

'Every last boat?' said Pazel dubiously.

'How many do you imagine they have?' said Uskins. 'Even by Ormali standards this hardly represents a— Look there! A ship! Ship on the starboard quarter! What did I tell you, Muketch?'

He had indeed spotted a vessel on the Gulf. But it was no fishing boat. It was a strange, slender brig, eight or ten miles off, appearing and disappearing behind the islands. Telescopes revealed three similar vessels at a greater distance.

They were not making for the Cape. All four were sailing due east – and swiftly, by their spread of sail. Those sails were tattered, however, and one of the brigs had lost its mizzenmast. Strangest of all, Mr Bolutu could make no sense of their blazing red pennants, which were not the colours of Bali Adro. 'The world is vast,' he said, shaking his head.

Perhaps, but the village at the foot of Narybir was tiny. It was hard to imagine danger of any kind lurking in that clutch of meagre cottages, listing fences, crumbling barns. Only the stonework – the mighty tower, the low wall above the water-line, a jetty protecting the fishing harbour – suggested that the outpost had any connection to an Empire.

And still there was no one to be seen. No voices answered their shouts and horns and whistles. Bolutu suggested they fire a cannon in greeting, but Taliktrum forbade it. None of the brigs had yet altered course, and he wished to keep it that way. Why announce their presence to every ship in the Gulf?

'You will get your water and return with all possible speed,' he told Mr Fiffengurt. 'But do not forget the hostages. Attempt any betrayal, and the lives of your people are forfeit.'

They lost depth rapidly. Three miles from the village Fiffengurt brought them up short. 'Furl the mains, Mr Alyash, and heave to. We've not come thousands of miles to split our keel on a blary sandbar.'

Fiffengurt pointed at the jetty. 'We'll load our water there. It's a bit outside the village, but at least it's solid stone. Mr Fegin, we shall bring the water on board with the sixty-foot yawl. See to the placement of casks in her hold, and put a cargo lift together. And for Rin's sake brace her main yard stoutly. When they're full those casks will weigh two thousand pounds apiece.'

'Oppo, Cap – Mr Fiffengurt, sir,' stammered Fegin.

'And have the carpenter get started on a wagon, for moving the casks about on shore.'

'Sir, that is pointless labour!' said Bolutu, laughing. 'There are surely wagons in the village. And these are sea-faring folk. They will come out in the hundreds to help fellow sailors in need.'

'All right,' said Fiffengurt, 'don't have him build it just yet, Fegin. But let the plans be drawn up all the same. Meanwhile we shall launch the pilot boat, and go looking for these timid folk.'

The pilot boat could carry twelve. Six of those, at Taliktrum's insistence, were Turachs. Besides Bolutu, Fiffengurt also asked Hercól, Pazel and Thasha to come ashore, for no clear reason except that he trusted them. The last member of the landing party, Alyash, he included for the opposite reason: because he didn't trust Ott's man to be left alone on the ship.

'In some ways,' added Fiffengurt quietly to Pazel as the Turachs rowed for shore, 'the ixchel made our lives easier. The most dangerous men on *Chathrand* are all locked in her forecastle.'

Except for one, thought Pazel, looking back at the gargantuan, battle-scarred ship. Taliktrum had ordered a search for Arunis, deck by deck, but somehow the mage had eluded them. *What's he hiding for? Did he find out, somehow, about Bolutu's allies? Could they be closer than we think?*

The jetty began at the foot of the tower, and was built of the same red stone. It swept in a graceful curve out into the Gulf, shattering the waves from the inlet, and leaving the water within its embrace almost becalmed. Stairs descended to the water in three places, and at one of these they moored the boat. From there, it was a short, awkward jump onto the weedy stairs.

As he climbed Pazel felt terribly dizzy. The very stillness of the jetty was to blame, he knew: after months at sea only constant motion felt natural. They'd be gone again before he got his land-legs.

His comprehension didn't stop him from slipping, however. He might have tumbled right off the wet stones if Thasha's arm hadn't shot out to catch him. Her eyes snapped to his own, and for a moment the Thasha he knew rose within them. She gave him a slight, teasing smile, her parched skin wrinkling. He felt more relief at the sight of that smile than he had to be saved from falling. But even as they stepped onto the jetty the haunted look was creeping back over her face. He clasped her hand, tightly. Stay with me, he thought.

They reached the top of the jetty. Pazel looked up at the soaring tower, its bone-like barrenness, the hundreds of narrow windows gaping darkly overhead. Then one of the soldiers cried out in surprise and pointed.

Four humans stood watching them, where the jetty met the shore. Two men, two women. All four naked. They were lean, sun-darkened, their hair long and tangled. They were motionless as deer.

For a startled instant no one said a word. Then Fiffengurt turned to Bolutu with an exasperated gesture. 'Speak, man, speak!' The dlömic man cupped his hands to his lips.

'*Waelmed!*' he shouted. '*Peace to abbrun ye, en greetigs hrom ecros ke Nelroq!*'

The four figures turned and ran. One of the women gave an odd, keening cry. Then all four vanished around one of the rootlike buttresses of the tower.

The others in the party scowled in bewilderment. What Bolutu had shouted was *almost* Arquali, and yet unlike anything they had ever heard.

'What in the tar-bottomed Pits was that gibberish?' said Fiffengurt.

'That was their language, Quartermaster,' said Bolutu promptly, 'and my own. I'm happy to tell you that our Imperial Common Tongue, which we call dlömic, is first cousin to your Arquali, for the simple reason that your empire was founded by exiles from Bali Adro, many centuries ago. Didn't I say Pazel's Gift would not be needed? Give yourselves a week or two, and you'll understand almost anyone you meet. You speak a dialect of dlömic, my friends, and have done so all your lives.'

571

'Exiles?' said Thasha faintly.

'Human exiles,' said Bolutu, 'but in Bali Adro every child – human or dlömu or otherwise – learns Imperial Common. Your histories don't reach back that far, m'lady, but ours do, and they leave little doubt. Your great Empire began as a colony of our own.'

He spoke with humility, as if he knew his words would shock. They did, of course. But no one exclaimed, or asked questions. They had gone beyond shock in recent weeks, and thirst was making it hard to think or care about anything else.

Yet in some part of his mind Pazel was still fearful and confused. 'Why did they run off, if you were speaking their language?' he asked.

'They didn't understand a word!' said Alyash vehemently. 'They're savages, obviously.'

'In these parts? Nonsense!' said Bolutu. 'I expect they were swimming, and we startled them.' His silver eyes glanced at them sidelong. 'You should see yourselves. I might run too, if you popped suddenly out of the sea.'

They headed for shore, through the cool spray of the breakers striking the jetty's seaward face. The village was out of sight behind the wall along the shore, except for a few roofs and steeples in poor repair. Little sand-coloured crabs ran before them. Grey pelicans swept by overhead.

Pazel was frowning. 'It doesn't add up,' he whispered to Thasha. 'The way they just froze, staring at us. And then ran off without a word.'

Thasha blinked, as though struggling to focus on his words. 'Their hair was still dry,' she managed finally. 'They hadn't been swimming.'

Pazel squeezed her hand tighter. The behaviour of the humans was certainly strange, but Thasha's troubled him even more. Her awareness of him, and for that matter of all that surrounded her, came and went like the sun through drifting clouds. Often her gaze turned inwards, as though her body were forgotten, and she was living in some distant country of the mind. But at other times her eyes jumped and darted, chasing things invisible to his eyes. Was it the Nilstone at work? She had touched it with the hand he held now, the one she'd maimed years ago in the garden of the Lorg. He ran a finger over the scar. It was warm to the touch.

Her hand twitched as though he'd found a ticklish spot. She gave him a look that was briefly clear, and once more that hint of a smile played over her lips.

'Oggosk can't do much to us now,' she said.

Pazel nodded, avoiding her gaze. It was true: they were free. The ixchel were no secret; Oggosk had run out of blackmail. But the witch had had a reason for her threats, something she believed absolutely. *What Thasha is to do, she must do alone. You can only get in her way.*

They reached the jetty's end. Fiffengurt stepped ashore, knelt, and kissed the sand at his feet.

'Hail Cora, proud and beautiful,' he said, and the others mumbled an affirming '*Hail.*' It was a ritual never to be skipped: the commander's greeting to Cora, Goddess of the earth, at the end of any particularly deadly voyage. Failure to do so, it was thought, could bring disasters ashore to match those just avoided at sea.

As Fiffengurt rose, something caught his eye. He chuckled, pointing. Scattered on the earth were several piles of blue-black mussel shells, still wet from the sea. A few had been cracked open. Pazel looked down, and saw the little shells clinging thickly to base of the jetty, right at the water-line.

'So that's what they were up to,' he said. 'But why didn't they bring a basket? How were they going to carry them home?'

'No clothes, no baskets, no tools,' said Alyash, frowning. 'Right free spirits, ain't they?'

'It *is* strange – I confess it,' said Bolutu sharply. 'But there are strange folk everywhere. Come, let us go and clear this matter up.'

Suddenly a cry, faint but urgent, reached them from the *Chathrand*. They turned and looked at her, but could see nothing amiss. The sound did not come again.

'We must find that water,' said Hercól. 'The crew's patience is at an end.'

The tower doors were shut; a bolt as thick as Pazel's upper arm lay across them, with locks at either end the size of dinner plates. Sand buried the foot of the ramp leading up to the doors. 'This makes no sense at all,' said Bolutu, 'unless the tower became unsafe while I was gone. But what am I saying? It has stood for a thousand years! Why should it weaken in the last twenty?'

The path to the village ran along the outside of the sea-wall, and was overgrown with trefoil and gorse. A mile ahead, near the quay with its crumbling docks and outbuildings, it passed through a stone archway. 'There should be a common well,' said Bolutu, but the confidence was gone from his voice.

They made for the village. But they had not gone twenty paces when one of the Turachs grunted, 'Look there!'

A man had stepped from the archway. He was naked like the other four, and like them strangely crouched and shuffling. He darted back through the gate before Bolutu could call to him.

Bolutu rushed along the track, no longer able to hide his concern. Fiffengurt shouted after him: 'Wait for us, damn it, don't you dare—'

Bolutu did not wait. He broke into a run, sandals slapping along the dusty track. The others followed him in some confusion, not certain whether more haste or less was called for. Hercól drew Ildraquin from its sheath.

A sudden shout came from their left, echoing off the stones. It was a man's voice, but it uttered no words. It was simply a hoot, challenging and somehow derisive.

'Where are you, blast it?' cried Fiffengurt, turning in place.

'There, sir!' said a Turach, pointing upwards. A child's face, wild of hair and eye, ducked quickly behind the sea-wall.

'We should double back,' said Alyash. 'I don't fancy walkin' alongside that wall. They could rain stones down on us, or worse.'

While the others stood undecided, Thasha pulled Pazel forwards, towards the gate. There was an urgency in the way she tugged him, as though she both needed and feared what lay ahead. Hercól came after them. Despite the others' protests the three were soon running after Bolutu, who was by now a good distance ahead.

Long before they could reach him he gained the archway. There he paused, and spread his hands as if in delight. He turned and flashed them a smile, the white teeth very bright in the black face, and then he vanished through the archway.

They were a hundred yards from the opening when they heard him scream. It was a sound of horror, or of pain. Hercól redoubled his speed, his black sword held aloft. Pazel and Thasha followed as fast as their legs would carry them.

An ambush, thought Pazel. *Aya Rin, we're probably too late.*

They reached the archway and skidded to a halt. They were not too late: there at twenty paces stood Bolutu, in a little square formed by dilapidated structures of stone. There was a round stone basin at the centre – *a basin with water*, Pazel saw with a flash of pure longing. And before Bolutu stood two of his own kind – two dlömu, blacker than black, their eyes four bright silver coins. An old man and a young. They wore tattered work clothes, wool caps pulled low over their silver hair, boots of sunbleached leather. They held no weapons, and showed no sign of threat.

Bolutu stood by the basin, gazing at them. His mouth was open, and

574

his face was clenched like that of a man told something so ghastly that he was struggling to spit it from his mind. The other two were speaking to him gently, insisting that there was nothing to fear. 'Don't worry,' they said, again and again. 'Don't worry, they obey us, they're tame.'

'Tame?' cried Bolutu, his voice almost unrecognisable.

'Of course,' said the younger dlömu. 'We knew they could be—'

He broke off with a frightened shout. He had spotted the three newcomers in the archway. 'Gods unseen!' he shouted. 'Look at them, Father, look!'

Bolutu gestured desperately: *Don't come in here, stay back.* But Hercól marched boldly through the gate and into the village, and Pazel and Thasha followed. The dlömu backed away from them.

'A miracle,' said the old man, trembling. 'A miracle. Or a curse.'

'Bolutu,' said Pazel, 'for Rin's sake tell them we're friends.'

Bolutu looked at his hands.

The father and son glanced behind them, as though tempted to run. The younger man pointed at Pazel. 'Did you hear it, Father?' he cried, his voice breaking with excitement.

'Don't . . . say *it*,' murmured the old man.

'Belesar,' said Hercól to Bolutu, 'speak to us this instant! Why are they so afraid? Why are *you*?'

Bolutu turned to face them. He clutched at the amulet around his neck. He was shaking uncontrollably. 'No,' he said, his voice little more than a whisper. 'No. Rin. No.'

Pazel felt Thasha grope for his hand. She stepped forwards, towards the three motionless figures, and Pazel walked beside her.

The younger dlömu was steadying his father, but his eyes never left the newcomers. He struggled to speak again.

'It's just that we've never – I mean, Father has, as a child, but I've never seen—'

'What?' said Pazel, 'A human? But we just saw them – we saw *six* of them.'

The young dlömu shook his head. Then he locked eyes with Thasha, who had drawn nearer still. Releasing Pazel, she put out the hand that had touched the Nilstone. Slowly, cautiously. A blind girl groping for his face.

'Say it,' she told him. 'You've never seen—'

'A woken human,' said the other, softly.

Thasha's face paled, and her eyes went wide and cold. Pazel reached for her arm, even as he grappled with the horror of what he'd just heard.

She was trying to speak but could only gasp. He thought suddenly of Felthrup's terror on the quarterdeck, and knew that something like it was stirring in his mind.

Hercól gave a warning shout: across the little square, between two crumbling structures, a small human crowd was gathering. Some were dressed, after a fashion – scraps of leggings, torn and filthy shirts – but most wore nothing at all. They stood bunched together, or bent low, staring at the newcomers, obviously afraid. One man was biting his finger. Two or three uttered wordless moans.

Thasha clutched desperately at Pazel's arm. 'I didn't mean to,' she said. 'It was never supposed to happen. You believe me, don't you?'

He pressed her head against his chest. *I love her*, he thought. And then: *Who is she? What is this thing I love?*

The older dlömu stepped towards the crowd of men. He whistled and clapped his hands. At the sound, the whole group shuffled forwards, slow and fearful and close together. When they reached the old man they pawed at him, clung to his shirt. One by one their eyes returned to Pazel and Thasha and Hercól, and there was no human light in those eyes, no consciousness but the animal sort, that fearful otherness, that measureless sea.

Here ends
The Rats and the Ruling Sea
Book Two of *The Chathrand Voyage.*

The Story is continued in
The River of Shadows
Book Three of *The Chathrand Voyage.*

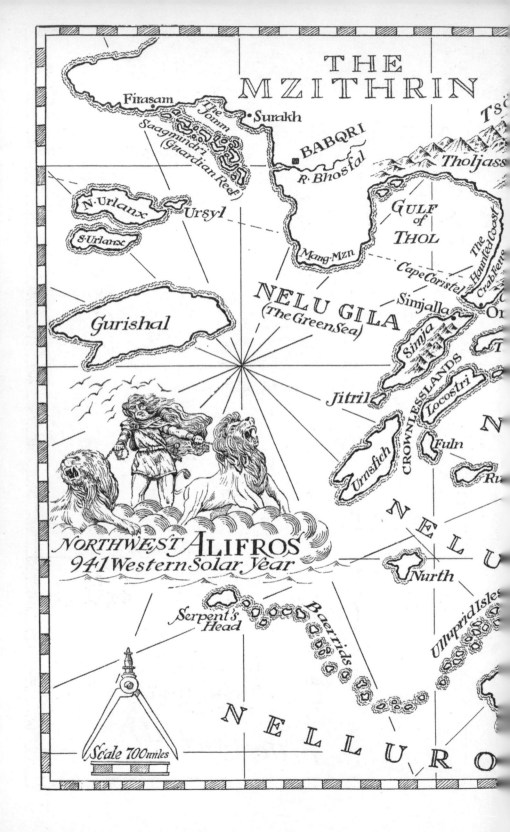

THE
MZITHRIN

Firasam
The Jomm
Surakh
Tsö
Saagmundr't
(Guardian Reef)
BABQRI
R. Bhosfal
Tholjass
N. Urlanx
Ursyl
GULF
of
THOL
The Haunted Coast
S. Urlanx
Mang·Mzn
Cape Coristel
Crab Ferns
Gurishal
NELU GILA
(The Green Sea)
Simjalla
Or
Simja
Jitril
Locostri
T
CROWNLESS LANDS
N
Urnsfich
Fuln
Ru
NORTHWEST ALIFROS
941 Western Solar Year
N E L U
Nurth
Serpent's
Head
Baerrids
Ulluprid Isles
N E L L U R O
Scale 700 miles

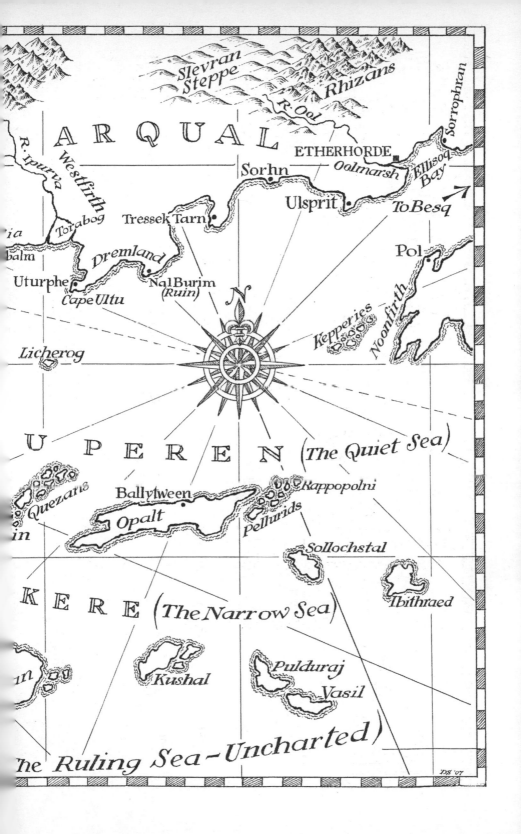

Acknowledgements

—◦◦◦—

My partner, Kiran Asher, lived with me through the arduous journey of this book. No one should be subjected to such a fate. I'm profoundly grateful for her patience and her love.

A few close friends effectively kicked the door down in their eagerness to read *The Rats and the Ruling Sea*. In addition to Kiran, Holly Hanson, Stephen Klink, Katie Pugh, Jan Redick, and Edmund Zavada all shared generous and wise responses to the rough-hewn manuscript.

As *Rats* left the home laboratory, I benefited from the insights of my wonderful editors Simon Spanton at Gollancz and Kaitlin Heller at Del Rey, as well as the indispensable guidance of my agent, John Jarrold. Additional help came from Betsy Mitchell, Gillian Redfearn, Lisa Rogers, Charlie Panayiotou, Shawn Speakman, David Moench, Jonathan Weir and teams of others whose names and heroic deeds remain trade secrets.

In addition, for encouragement and counsel, I'd like to thank Hillary Nelson, Tracy Winn, Amber Zavada, Paul Park, Bruce Hemmer, John Crowley, Corinne Demas, Gavin Grant, Nat Herold, Jedediah Berry, Karen Osborn, Julian Olf, Stefan Petrucha, Patrick Donnelly and Jim Lowry.

Many novels could end with a credits-roll surpassing those of Hollywood films, if every person who helped along the way received mention. Certainly this is such a book; and just as certainly, a few names that should not *under any circumstances* have been omitted will rise to haunt me when I see this page in print. My apologies to those deserving souls.

Before the book, there's the idea; before the idea, the habits of mind in which it gestates. Since plunging into *The Chathrand Voyage* series I've had occasion to reflect, in turn, on the origins of those habits: in this case, my addiction to tales of the wondrous and improbable. I trace part of the answer to certain cherished evenings in Iowa, over three decades ago, listening to my father, John Redick, read science fiction novels to an awestruck audience of one. Years late in all instances have been my expressions of thanks, so here's one more, Dad.